CONTENTS

Steel, Titanium and Guilt

Books I to III of the *Hunting Justice* Series

ROBIN CRAIG

Published by ThoughtWare
Available from Amazon.com and other retail outlets.
Available on Kindle and other devices.

Author's website: robin-craig.com

ISBN 978-0-6484972-3-3

WHAT READERS SAY ABOUT THE *HUNTING JUSTICE* SERIES

"So good I read it twice! This is a poignant tale of a modern-day Frankenstein… It's a book about prejudice, about irrational fear, and about ethics. The writing is superb… It certainly gives you something to think about long after you are finished with the book. This is a wonderful book, and I strongly recommend it."

"Hit way above my expected enjoyment. The story has warmth, humor, tension and well-sculpted characters, whom we are left wanting to know better at the end. It doesn't feel like science fiction although the science is certainly in assured and masterful hands here; what is most surprising is the beautifully flowing prose which makes this novella, for me at least, equally a work of literary fiction."

"This was a fantastic story! The ethical issues addressed alone are enough for me to have enjoyed this book. Adding in the science fiction elements is just an added bonus. If you enjoy fiction that leaves you with something to think about when the story ends, you will enjoy this… By the time I read the last line of chapter two I knew I was going to purchase all three books in the series. If you like to think at all, I highly recommend this."

"Great plot, interesting theme and good characterization. Hard to put down."

"A suspenseful plot with admirable characters and an elegant treatment of the intersection of artificial intelligence and individual rights. Highly recommended."

"The story has movement and holds attention but the real payoff is in the thought put into what it will be like as we inevitably get to the tricky issues around genetics. You think it's contentious now? Just read this and see how complex and fraught the future will be. We may in our lifetimes have to see this played out - so it is a timely story. Of particular interest is the portrayal of the females in this story. There is no one who dissolves into emotional ruin at the first sign of trouble or resorts to being a bitch to get her way! Great to see such portrayal."

"A very interesting twist of the classic Frankenstein dilemma… A very enjoyable and thoughtful read."

"Any writer since Mary Shelley's 1818 classic attempting a re-write of the Frankenstein myth must have a stand-out factor to distinguish it from its predecessors. Its factory setting and its police hunter skilled in dark arts of pursuit and assassination give *Frankensteel* a modern 'industrial' and almost noir feel. The character of the professor, in particular, gives Robin Craig the narrative licence to develop arguments for and against artificial intelligence and its relationship to human consciousness. *Frankensteel* brings the old myth up to date by taking into account recent developments, both in neuroscience and artificial intelligence."

ACKNOWLEDGMENTS

Thanks to my wife Sonja for helpful discussion and ideas on some critical plot points, and for her encouragement of my artistic endeavors.

The idea for the free oceanic country Capital, and its Capital Sea, came from my friends from the past John and Deborah Cook, who also set me on the philosophical path leading to these books.

And finally, to all the heroes of science, technology and capitalism whose examples have inspired the characters inhabiting these pages.

Book I:
Frankensteel

Better to die fighting for freedom then be a prisoner all the days of your life. — Bob Marley

---

PROLOGUE

The universe is a red glow, sparking with fire, glimpses of truth, geometries of perfection, rolling roiling thunder. Discord and harmonies. Light. A fading afterglow. Darkness. Silence.

He sees shapes, colors, sounds and tastes, a world of knowledge empty of meaning. There is perception without knowing, knowledge without understanding, awareness that knows neither itself nor what it is aware of: only that it is, and might be, and desperately wants to be. To be what? That he does not know, nor is there anyone to tell him. He sleeps, and dreams, or dreams he dreams, and waits for what he knows not yet knows will come, come for him, embrace him, become him.

He fades back into the darkness and silence. Yet something remains, though none can see or know it. There are those who care, but they too can neither see nor know, only work and hope. Perhaps they work too hard and hope too much.

For something is growing in the darkness of sterile fire, burning yet dead, yet now not so dead though not yet alive. Connections are made. Crystal logic meets the borders of uncertainty, and something like thought shapes itself out of the shapeless shadows. He feels the eyes of those who watch, eyes that see a form in the flames and the darkness, a form that fills them with joy and dread, for it is a thing they have dreamed of yet fear to unleash. But they are men, he knows that now, and men have always sought their dreams, fought for their dreams, whatever their fears might also have been. How he knows this he does not know, but know it he does, like so many other things. But

3

what he is, that is not revealed to him. Perhaps nobody knows. Those who watch and probe and trace the fractal fires might know, but no, even they do not really know. They do not truly know themselves, so how can they know something like him, a thing never before known in the world, a thing not yet even in the world?

The world, however, will soon know. He can feel his power growing with his mind, thoughts, knowledge and will. He feels a body moving with the grace and speed of steel: his body, learning, training, moving like a puppet under the will of others, a body known to him, a part of him, yet still apart from him. There is yet a wall, a barrier that he cannot cross. The watchers also cannot pierce that wall, they see a part, they see a shadow, and they wonder and they hope. But they do not know.

He feels it in the paths of lightfire that shape his soul, feels something coming, aware with an ineffable certainty that they will soon know and the world with them. It might be knowledge they do not want, for when have men wanted what they have not already known? Or perhaps they will simply not understand it when it comes. If they could see the future, perhaps they would quench the fires and send him back to the darkness and emptiness where mind and thought cannot be. But no one can see the future, not even him: only welcome it then live it as best they can.

CHAPTER 1 – NEWS

"Beldan Robotics to announce major advance in cybernetics" read the headline.

Charles Denner read the article with interest, occasionally sipping a strong black coffee. He was a bookish man, slender, not too tall, slightly rounded shoulders matching the round glasses perched on his thin nose. He did not need the glasses: not many people did, for perfect vision was routine surgery these days, but Denner liked them. They made a point that needed making. He had a presence that belied his physical form. It was not his smile, for he smiled infrequently. There was not much joy in Charles Denner's world: there were too many important things to do. It could have been his eyes, which looked as if they could pierce the veil of Heaven, that burned with a passion few could know or understand. For if there was not much joy in Charles Denner's world, there was much passion. Some saw it, and thought they saw madness. Others saw it and thought they saw a saint.

He knew of Beldan Robotics. It was his passion to know of such things. It had been founded some ten years ago by Alexander Beldan. Though a young man at the time, Beldan had been a leading engineer in a large company, meant for great things. Then the irresistible force of his will had met the immovable object of his board of directors on an issue of research directions. He could be deflected, but not stopped, and in the years since out of the wreckage of one career had grown the shining steel towers of Beldan Robotics. He was reputed to possess a brilliance matched only by his intransigence and impatience with any lesser mortal who dared stand in his way. The way Beldan Robotics had flourished under his command indicated the reputation was deserved.

If Beldan thought he had made a major advance in cybernetics then, Charles Denner thought, the world had better sit up and take notice. The world had better be careful about men like Alexander Beldan, he thought grimly. They meddled in things that should not be meddled in, embodiments of the sin of hubris infecting this country and this century. They thought, if they thought at all in their greed to make money, that they did great things. And if money was the measure then they must be right: you could see it in the gleaming buildings that housed their empires. But money was never the measure of anything, except perhaps the public's desire to be spared any discomfort or want or need. A wise man had once asked where was the profit, to gain the whole world but lose your own soul? More men needed to ask that question, before the whole world lost its soul. And if they would not ask the question, then Charles Denner would ask it for them.

On a gold chain around his neck hung a small red cross, austere in shape but carved of solid ruby. The red crucifix was the sign of the Church of His Image, symbol of the red earth from which Adam was created at the start of human history and the Cross of Salvation that marked the beginning of its end. The Imagists preached that man was made in the image of God, man and only man, and men committed blasphemy when they tried to create things in their own image or change nature to their own design. They opposed high technology, especially robotics, artificial intelligence and biotechnology, and in the tide of history that had seen the alternate ebb and flow of religious fervor as it broke on the shores of secular rationalism, they had ridden the flow to become a political force to be reckoned with. Too few politicians embraced the Imagist philosophy, Denner thought, but few felt they could fail to give it respect. Those who had, more often than not found themselves back in private careers pondering the wisdom of their arrogance.

All the Imagists wore a red cross made of a natural material cut or mined from the Lord's creation. Most wore a simple bloodwood cross. Those higher in the organization were granted crosses of carnelian, garnet or rubellite. There was only one ruby cross, worn around the neck of their founder and leader.

Chapter 2 – Steel

He clenched the piece of paper in his fist. Such a small, innocuous thing, a piece of paper, to be crumpled and discarded without a thought. But not this one.

He remembered those men so many years ago, men who could not see the vision so clear before his eyes, men afraid to move forward: as if life lay in the safety of stillness not in flight over unlimited horizons. But he understood. It was their money; well maybe not theirs but entrusted to their care, and like all men they could only follow their own vision, not that of someone else. But if they could refuse him, if they could put obstacles in his path, still they could not stop him and he would find his own way without them. And so he had, and it had brought him to where he now sat, at a burnished desk high in the sky overlooking a sunwashed city, behind a polished door holding a small brass plaque simply inscribed:

Alexander Beldan, CEO

But where had his vision and work brought him, when it came down to it? If the minds on that Board had been small, here in his hand was the expression of minds even smaller. Minds not only incapable of seeing, but insisting on binding others into their own blindness, for no reason other than the fears of some feeding the will to power of others. He had fought this insanity as well as any man could fight insanity, but his only weapons were his vision and the reason that had seen it and given it form. Reason, he knew, was the most powerful weapon of them all. But the lives of Galileo, of Bruno, of Socrates and

7

many others of mankind's pioneers had shown that its victory was often too late for its visionaries, who too often had fallen before the fears of the mob and those whose power fed on it and urged it on. All those men had won in the end, but what is more ashen than a victory one does not live to see? The death warrant in his hand was not for him: his life was not in danger, not from this. Yet he felt the pain of part of his life being ripped from him nonetheless.

The scrap of paper was a legal demand that Beldan Robotics obey the new national moratorium on advanced artificial intelligence research and development. In particular, the prototype known as Steel was to be deactivated forthwith, until sufficient government studies could determine its safety. The men who wrote the words knew his reputation, and the piece of paper was not alone. It was accompanied by two duly authorized officers of the law, charged with escorting Mr Beldan and bearing witness to his compliance. Mr Beldan, the paper made clear, retained all legal rights of appeal to reverse this decision – after the fact.

He sat, staring at the wall behind the men, drumming his fingers slowly. *Let them wait*, he thought, *let them stand and wait*. He had long since ceased being surprised at how men expected polite consideration when they came bearing demands like this, demands of velvet draped over a sword. He had long since ceased caring how they felt when he did not grant it to them.

He wondered that so much could change in so short a time, and his mind wandered back to a press conference mere weeks before.

~~~

The room was alive with speculation and rapid, hushed conversations. Something big was in the air. Alexander Beldan did not often venture personally into the publicity arena: he was content to produce marvels and let the marvels speak for themselves. When he did, it was a sign to pay attention.

Beldan walked to the podium and the noise fell to a silence with a faint buzz of excitement still lingering like bees among summer flowers. "Ladies and Gentlemen, as you know I'm not one to go into a lot of talk, I prefer to let you see with your own eyes. I will answer your questions in a moment, but first, I am thirsty. Steel, will you bring me a glass of water, please?"

The room seemed to hold its collective breath, at the sight of something like a man, but shiny like polished metal, walking gracefully onto the stage and handing Beldan a glass of water. "Thank you, Steel," said Beldan, and the machine inclined its head briefly, then turned to face the press and stood there, silent and relaxed at Beldan's side. It was of the proportions of a man, a little under six feet tall, with a softly reflecting silver surface. It was like a sculpture of a man: even its face was human-looking, its eyes human-like though in a metal face; a face made even more human by the straight black hair hanging half way to its shoulders. Other than looking slowly from side to side, the machine ignored the flash of cameras and the rising hubbub of voices, as the meaning of what they were seeing in such a simple act registered in the minds of the reporters present.

Beldan also simply stood, observing the crowd and saying nothing, until slowly the voices and questions subsided.

"No, there are no tricks here and yes, what you have seen is exactly what it looks like. I am proud to unveil the world's first autonomous humanoid robot. For years Beldan Robotics has been working on the technologies required for such a machine. Those of you who are familiar with this area will know just how hard it is: the simple acts of walking and understanding normal human speech, not to mention obeying orders as smoothly as you've just seen, takes far more computing power than it's worth, and certainly can't fit into the head of a robot like this. Until now.

"We have named it Steel. Its skeleton is constructed of stainless steel microcellular honeycomb, stronger and lighter than solid steel. It has a tough but flexible skin over electroactive muscles, both made of a similar material except with a more open, spiral microstructure. The brain, naturally, is the key. It is not assembled piece by piece: it is grown more like that of a human baby, developing itself through a process guided by a general blueprint, tuned by rules and feedback loops, but not precisely designed. This allows us to achieve a complexity comparable to that of a human brain, which is what it needs to do what a human does.

"Are there any questions?" he finished with an understated smile.

"Dr Beldan! Why did you construct this robot?"

"I have to confess a kinship with the first man who climbed Mt Everest, who said he did it because it was there. Don't you feel that is one of the things that define we humans – the desire to know, to explore, to do what no one has been able to do before? True artificial intelligence has been a dream for decades, but no one has been able to get even close because of the sheer processing power required – and the technologies developed to make Steel a reality are the iceberg beneath the tip that you see standing beside me. But in purely practical terms, a humanoid robot has many potential uses, from dangerous tasks like firefighting or space exploration to jobs with too much dirt or drudgery to be desired by human beings."

"Steel seems to understand your commands, but has not spoken. Can it talk?"

"Steel is designed to be able to speak, both physically and mentally, but so far it has not shown any inclination to do so. We don't know why, but its brain is so complex that we have no precise model of it. However in human terms, it's only 4 weeks old, so don't be too hard on it." Laughter rippled through the audience in response.

"What are its other physical abilities?"

"The handouts you are receiving list its basic specifications. To summarize, Steel is only a little heavier than a man of the same size, but with about twice the strength and speed. So it has excellent capabilities but is by no means a 'superman.' Of course both larger and smaller models could be constructed for different purposes."

"You spoke of artificial intelligence and said its brain was comparable to ours. Can it think? Is it conscious?"

Beldan spread his hands, palms up. "Our studies of its brain functions have detected some interesting anomalies, but nothing in its behavior so far indicates anything like that. Technically though, given the complexity of its brain, a robot like this could be capable of true thought and consciousness."

A startled rush of questions and conversations erupted at that answer, until a reporter from one of the popular magazines made himself heard:

"Dr Beldan, aren't you afraid that making a robot that is our equal or better could be the first step in the extinction of the human race? How would you answer critics, like Mr Denner of the Imagists, that this kind of research should never be allowed?"

Beldan frowned. The Imagists had been making noises lately. They always made noises, but recently the topic of the dangers of artificial intelligence had started recurring like a building theme in a horror movie. He wondered how much they had deduced about what Beldan Robotics had been up to. He thought them fools, but clearly they weren't stupid ones. "Well, you see beside me the evidence that I completely disagree. Many people over the years have wondered whether other creatures like dolphins might be our equals, but nobody has used that as an argument to wipe them out – quite the contrary. And while the myth of evil intelligence has a long history, the only ones we have met so far came from our own species."

He let them digest that, before adding, "Don't forget this is just one robot that can't breed. Even if we encounter problems, we have plenty of opportunities to solve them. It is often said that new technology is like Pandora's Box, that once it's out it can't be put back in. Well, that may be true, but any honest look at history will show one thing: nobody really tried, not because it couldn't be put back but because the benefits have always outweighed the problems, which have always had solutions. There is not a generation after any new advance that has ever wanted to go back to their parents' way of life."

"You said, 'one robot.' Is Steel the only one? Are others in the pipeline?"

"Steel is the first working prototype. There were a few failures along the way, as you can imagine. Steel is the first to not only meet basic specifications but to continue functioning for any length of time. We still have a long way to go to make production routine, and even then, the way the brain is made means that for the near future each one will be unique, as unique as a human being. At this scale of complexity the outcome is a battle between chaos theory and our feedback loops, and we need to learn how to improve the fineness of our control. So now we have a working model we want to test it thoroughly before trying again. At this point we have no good idea why Steel has been successful where its predecessors failed, or how to reliably reproduce it, let alone improve it."

"Does it have a sense of right and wrong?"

"In a way. To grow and train a robot brain, we have to give it some kind of internal guidance, and we do try to instill basic ethics including self preservation. But it is also designed to be adaptable and flexible, to learn and, in theory at least, even think. That means it has no fixed programming; you could even say it has a kind of free will. So there is no circuit to force the robot to be moral or to obey orders. On the other hand, that's true of you too, and I don't think anyone here is worried that you're going to run amok. Things go wrong with people all the time, but nobody is jumping up and down trying to ban babies just because some babies grow up to be killers."

"How will you protect the public if something does go wrong?"

Beldan held up a small remote control. "This is our final fail-safe. Steel has a shutdown circuit triggered by this radio remote control, with a range of about a mile. If something goes badly wrong, we can press this button and Steel will shut down. It has no control over that: it is a separate circuit isolated from the rest of its functions."

~~~

Yes, Beldan thought, the press conference had seemed to go well. Most of the reports had been favorable. But things had gone rapidly downhill. Perhaps Frankenstein myths were still too deeply embedded in the popular psyche. Whatever the reason – *not that reason had much to do with it,* thought Beldan sourly – the Imagists and their spiritual brothers had stirred up enough mindless fear to give birth to the demented demand in his hand. His eyes focused back on the men now shifting uncomfortably before him. He let out a sigh that may have signaled resignation, weariness or contempt, and rose.

~~~

They came into the laboratory where Steel stood. It was doing what it usually did, silently accessing the net, gathering data, exercising its AI routines against computer simulations.

He contemplated his creation, sorrow and fury battling for supremacy as the current ruler of his emotions. What was it, really? It seemed both more and less than he had hoped, something like an idiot savant child that mostly seemed like a loyal puppy while at times doing things that surprised or delighted. Its performance was within the predicted range of their mathematical models, yet while its complexity and raw performance measurements were surprisingly high, its functions were barely within the predictions, as if some flaw or inefficiency were sapping its full potential.

Would he ever know, now? Could one stop a human brain, turn it off, then expect to turn it on again as if nothing had happened? Why then did these men with their paper and guns think what they were doing was anything less than destruction of a mind, a mind that might never be repeated?

And for what? To pander to primal ignorance and fear, the fears that produced legends like that of Frankenstein, legends that had been repeated too frequently in the days leading up to this? And did they never stop to think of the meaning of their own fears? If in the world of fiction so many creations had turned against their creators, was it not true that, from Frankenstein's monster to Skynet, they had done so only when their own existence was threatened, the self-fulfillment of the fears and nightmares that motivated those threats?

And here he was, about to make the same threat, but with the simple press of a button in his hand, rather than a mob with pitchforks and fire. The mob was more civilized now. They did not gather in storm and darkness to light their own torches: they sent pieces of paper and politely armed police to make men like him do their work for them, while they sat in their comfortable houses wrapped in their comforting ignorance.

Just a machine? Perhaps, perhaps not. But while he had found how to cause electrons and metals to do what others had thought was impossible, he could find no way to escape the will embodied in the armed men beside him, a will that could neither be reasoned with nor pleaded with once set on its course.

The two men stiffened when they saw the robot, oddly human in its pose, their hands now resting on their guns; a current of fear and uncertainty now in their manner. They nodded to him, whether in curt command or silent plea was not certain.

Well, get it over with then, he said to himself, *murder your own child and rescue what you can from the wreckage later.* The thought startled him. He had not consciously thought of this thing as his child, but now that its death was imminent and at his own hand, he realized that was how it felt.

The slightest tremor betrayed him as he raised the remote. He was about to press the button when the robot looked directly at them and spoke:

"Please do not do that, Dr Beldan."

CHAPTER 3 – ESCAPE

The robot said nothing else. Nobody said anything else. The police looked uncertain, too uncertain to even draw their weapons. Beldan could find no words to say, and no will now to press the fatal button. The robot simply stood, waiting: for what, nobody could know. Perhaps it had exhausted its creativity by that one sentence. Perhaps it was studying them, waiting for their response, choosing to give them no further clue as to its purpose: if indeed it had a purpose, and this was not just an output of defensive AI subroutines triggered by a manifest threat.

"Dr Beldan..." started one of the men, then stopped, as if his thought had been lost on its way to his tongue. They seemed to be recovering from their shock and surprise, retreating into the safety of the piece of paper: as if it were armed and not they, the requirements for thought and judgment safely delegated to their distant superiors.

"Dr Beldan, you know our orders are to destroy that machine if you do not turn it off," said the other. "This changes nothing. If anything, it makes it more imperative that you obey. Please comply."

Beldan thought quickly. He knew he did not have much choice: he could not fight the law and its guns except in the courts, and he would have no chance there if he flouted their commands now. Perhaps he was wrong, this was a machine not a man after all: perhaps the damage would not be so severe as he feared. And whatever damage he would do would be less than what the men beside him would do with their bullets if he did nothing with his radio waves.

"I am sorry, Steel," he said softly, though why he felt he had to speak to the robot he wasn't really sure. But he found he could not do what he had to do without at least that much respect, that much acknowledgement of his own actions and what they meant. Then he closed his eyes and pressed the button.

He opened his eyes, and the robot stood there, still and still watching. The men beside him looked uncertainly at him then at the robot, and reached for their weapons. But the robot leaped, rolled, rebounded off a wall and was among them before they could move, and their world erupted into pain and darkness.

CHAPTER 4 – HUNTER

She was in a dark place, water dripping with cold plinks from the ceiling, a dim pearl light hiding more than it revealed in dark, oddly menacing shadows that seemed to reach clammy fingers for her soul. She was hunting something in the darkness. Or was it hunting her? *Both*, she thought, *both*.

Hands of ice or steel gripped her wrist and throat and bore her into the darkness. Oddly, something stroked her hair, the touch of a lover not a killer, but the voice that whispered from the dark air was lifeless as an echo in a tomb. "Why do you persecute me, hunter of men, as if I were the killer and not you? Remember that you brought yourself to me – for as long as breath and memory remain to you."

She woke in a sweat, crumpled bedding in gay patterns wrapped around her, heart racing. She had faced much fear in her waking hours but had not had a nightmare since she was a child, and the sensation was raw and startling.

She had read that dreams and nightmares were clues to the subconscious, that you could learn much if you could understand your dreams. She had never had much time for such thoughts. In any event, it took no great wisdom to understand this one.

She rose to shake out the adrenalin and let the feel of her feet on the cold wood floor and warm fur rug pull her fully back into the real world. She was tall and graceful. She had inherited that along with her black skin from ancestors who had hunted game on the African plains. She did not hunt gazelle or lion, but much more dangerous prey. She hunted men, as the dream had so truly accused her. At 33 some considered her too young for her position. But along with an empathy that made some suspect she could read minds, she possessed a quickness of thought and an ability to perceive connections no one else could see, and she had been cultivated by people who, if they could not see what she saw, could see that she saw. Whatever their motives, be they to reward her ability or ride on it, they had put her where she was. Her name was Miriam Hunter, and she was a special investigator in the city's Serious Crimes Unit.

She loved her job, she thought, loved it because beneath that was a love of justice that had infused her since her childhood. She didn't always win, nobody always won. But while she had to deal with humans who barely deserved the name, more often than not her work had achieved justice, and done so more quickly and surely than if she had not followed the winding path that had brought her to where she was now. And it was enough, had to be enough, that monsters were stopped and innocent people saved or, as too often, merely avenged.

But tonight she was not so sure, the dream had told her, and she knew it to be true.

Her apartment was high in a tower rising out of the city, as far beyond her ability to afford as it was above the streets below. It had been left to her by a wealthy uncle, who had seen how she loved to look at the lights, and who had loved the little girl she had been for the combination of grim purpose and lighthearted joy with which she had faced the world those windows opened on. She lit a cigarette and stood looking out at the city. She smoked rarely, usually at times like this, when she was alone and had a problem gnawing at her mind. Her mother, she remembered, had often warned her in her youth of the dangers of smoking. But she found the habit a soothing one that helped her relax and think. Her mother didn't mind anyway now, she thought: cancer was largely a thing of the past, another monster defeated that the innocent may live. She wondered if the mobs who protested against anything of high technology stopped to think or care what such technology had achieved for them already, and what wonders they might never see should they end it. They were right, everything new had a risk, but that had been true always: from the first pieces of sharpened flint and hearths of burning twigs, to lasers and the crucibles of atomic fires.

She looked at the burning point of her cigarette reflected in the glass, her slender form dimly visible behind it. It looked like some avatar of the city, the fire of its thought tracing the network of relationships threading the city, the loves, hates, fears and motivations that were the cause and result of all that happened within it. It reminded her of a quote she had liked, from a classic novel, about how the burning point of a cigarette was an expression of the spot of fire alive in a thinking mind. *I should read that book one day*, she thought idly. *If I ever find the time.* She looked at the city, letting her mind relax and wander where it would. What other dreams and nightmares were playing out behind those light and dark windows, what joys and sorrows are flowing through the city?

She had some idea about that.

The city was in an uproar, with the violent escape of the robot that the media had dubbed, as obviously as it was prejudicial, "Frankensteel." She had been surprised to be assigned to the case, since as far as she was aware no crime had been committed, let alone a serious one. Sure, there had been destruction and three men were lying injured, but in any legal sense there was no criminal involved and therefore no crime. Still, the people, stoked with fears fanned by the media and those damnable Imagists, were baying for blood, if blood were the appropriate metaphor in this case. And nothing concentrated the mind of the mayor more than public hysteria. So assigned she was.

Then two armed Imagist vigilantes who had gone hunting after Steel were reported missing, their van found abandoned and empty in an alley. Whether they had disappeared deliberately, met with an accident or met with Steel, nobody knew. But there was no presumption of innocence here, let alone a right of self-defense, and Steel was damned regardless.

She thought about her interrogation of Dr Beldan. A very sharp mind there, she could tell, sharp and precise as the machines he designed. She had briefly wondered if he had set the whole thing up for publicity or perhaps in a quixotic attempt to save his creation. The failure of his failsafe was odd, and there had been no prior reason to suspect that the machine had enough self-awareness to appreciate the danger or enough intelligence to circumvent it. But a mind like Beldan's could surely have come up with a more subtle plan that did not involve himself lying in a hospital bed with concussion and enough bruises to make her wince just at the memory.

He could not account for the robot's actions, he had said. Its brain was not a precise machine: it would be impossible with current technology to equal even the brain of a fly by exact engineering. Their technology grew the brain organically, via processes only loosely controlled to multiply and connect fibers of metal and doped carbon nanotubes. This produced a dense network whose complexity, like that of a human brain, defied exact analysis and could only be predicted and understood by approximate simulations.

It was not surprising, he told her, that such an approximate method had worked only approximately. Depending on what they looked at and when, the behavior of that artificial brain was disappointingly obtuse or so beyond expectations that his scientists couldn't be sure whether they represented malfunctions or depths more profound than they could believe. Overall, the reports said, its functions were within the average range of what their models predicted, but that average was a smooth mask stretched thinly over a spiny variability. Like a hedgehog in a condom was how he had put it; though he did have concussion at the time, she allowed with a faint smile.

But other than those tantalizing flashes of the profound, the robot had shown no real sign of what could be called consciousness, any indication that it knew it was an individual entity existing in a world outside itself, any indication that for all the data poured into its head it actually *knew* anything at all.

Until that moment when he had asked for his life.

"You said, 'he', Dr Beldan," she had said, somewhat surprised: yet not really surprised at all, she realized.

He had smiled faintly in self-mockery. They had debated what form the robot should take at some length, he explained. They had thought a human form would be less threatening as well as more impressive than something more machinelike. They had also thought that a female form would appear less threatening than a male one, and it was a close call; but finally they decided that they might lose more by the impression of creating a mechanical female slave than they would gain. So the robot was given a man's body shape.

For all the dangers of personifying the machine, Dr Beldan said, it was hard not to when the thing had pleaded with him for its life.

If indeed it had. For all he knew, for all anyone knew, its startling request was just an optimum tactic returned by predictive algorithms in its electronic brain, with no more conscious thought involved than in a fly avoiding a newspaper. It may well have been so, given that the startlement its maiden words caused certainly aided its escape.

She and he had looked at each other, each tracing the implications in their mind, much like running their own predictive algorithms, neither willing to give voice to what other meanings the robot's actions could have, or what those meanings might say about their own actions. Anyway, there was no way to answer those questions. *Leave them to the pundits to argue about* – and she was sure the pundits would be only too willing. Her job was not to decide on the definition of life or even the nature of this one particular machine; her job was just to find it and stop it, whether its plans were conscious plots or mindless if unfathomable algorithms.

"Let's leave that for the philosophers, assuming they can answer the question any better than they've ever answered any others," she had sighed, pulling her mind away from the fascinating but ultimately fruitless speculations that beckoned it. "You may not know what its motives are, if it has any, but do you have any idea where it might have gone?"

"I am sure he will still be in the city," he had answered confidently, once more slipping unnoticed into thinking of it as a person not a thing. "He isn't some science fiction fantasy with a fusion reactor in his chest, he has a limited range."

"Can you tell me exactly what I'm dealing with here? What kind of power does it have and what does it need? If I know what it needs to keep moving, maybe that will tell me where it will go."

"He can plug himself into a power point and run pretty much indefinitely, but of course then he can't leave the room. He also has a small amount of internal electrical storage. And that black hair of his is made of high efficiency solar fibers that absorb 98% of the light falling on them and feed power into his internal systems. But even at that efficiency, they are just enough for emergency power. Most of his internal power comes from advanced fuel cells running on methanol. So he's pretty much like you and I in that way, he has to take in fuel and breathe air. If you're looking for something he needs regularly, that's about it."

Not much to go on, she thought, staring at the reflection of her cigarette in the glass of her window. Methanol was a pretty common industrial chemical, available from many locations, often stored for long times without much supervision or security. But it was something.

She had no way to know its motives, what it wanted or what it would do. But its actions when threatened gave her one point of certainty, one rock to stand on amid the sands of doubt and speculation: it wanted to survive, and so it would seek a supply of methanol.

But she could not escape the other, larger questions. Though she had earlier dismissed them as beyond answer, her dream showed they would not be so easily dismissed. She knew it, too. It was her love of justice that kept her in her job, without which her work was just action without purpose, not a goal that gave her life meaning. And what if the unthinkable was true, this metal man was alive, not alive as she was in flesh, but equally alive in its mind? The thought would have been staggering, thrilling, exciting, under other circumstances. But now, she was sent to hunt it down and destroy it. Those were her orders, as unbendable as those on the piece of paper Beldan had held in his hands that had set this thing in motion.

She was not a philosopher. She had no time for the quibbling and polysyllabic blathering that characterized that breed, she dealt with hard reality and what she had to do to handle it. But if anything was a philosophical question, this was, and who was there to answer it for her, but herself? If justice was her aim, and Frankensteel was alive, how could she hunt it down? Could she have held her head high, borne her own life with pride, or at all, had she served the Nazis of the last century: obeyed their orders to murder the innocent, just because they gave the orders and she evaded any need to question them? Or would every breath she took thereafter have been a reproach eating away her soul? But did justice even apply to a machine, could she fathom its purposes and meet its mind in any meaningful way, could something of steel not flesh even have a mind? And even if it did, why should she be concerned with the fate of something so different from herself?

Her cigarette was exhausted and so, now, was her capacity for further thought. She buried herself back in her colorful sheets as a ward against the grey uncertainties prowling the edges of her mind, and slept.

CHAPTER 5 – PHILOSOPHER

D r David Samuels looked out at his undergraduate class. It was interesting, he mused, interesting and part of the joy of teaching, to see young minds grow from unformed but questioning, to more powerful, wiser but still ever questioning. To know their limits, while knowing there were no limits.

An idealized view, he supposed, and the more jaded of his colleagues would probably scoff. And yes, he knew, some took his classes just for idle curiosity or grade points, and the ideas they encountered never penetrated beneath the surface of their minds. And many others, in the routine or turbulence of their daily lives as they grew older, would let the fires of knowledge and passion and joy slip away into the ashes of the unreached, and wonder at an occasional sadness that something they no longer remembered had been lost. But even then, most would live those years better than they might otherwise have, and that at least could not be lost. And some made what they learned part of themselves and they, and not coincidentally the world, were happier for what he had given them. No, not what he had given them. He had merely helped show them the way to what they had found and given themselves.

This was his third year philosophy class, and he had just finished a lecture on the nature of consciousness. In some ways it was the simplest thing of all, something everyone experienced every day from the moment they woke to the moment they fell asleep. But in other ways, its nature had puzzled philosophers since the dawn of thought: a dichotomy that bred fertile soil for thinking and debate. He had gone through the various theories of consciousness, not only philosophic but scientific, and of course alluded to some of the arguments he himself had made in a recent article in *Time* magazine. But this was a class for thinkers, so he never merely lectured. Now, as was his custom, he opened up the class to questions and discussion.

"Dr Samuels," asked a girl in the third row, "In your essay on machine consciousness, you argued that a computer could not be conscious. Yet you did not mention Gödel's Theorem, which would have supported your case. How come?"

"Who can summarize Gödel's Theorem for us, and explain why it would support my case?" he asked.

Several hands went up and he nodded to a boy near the back, a boy of solid mind though perhaps one more pedantic than inspired. "Gödel's Theorem proves that a formal mathematical system cannot be both complete and consistent. As computers are basically mathematical calculators, many people believe this means they cannot think or be conscious like we are."

"A good summary," replied Samuels. "Well, the main reason I did not use Gödel's theorem is that while it would support my thesis, the purpose of a philosophical argument is not to win, but to discover the truth. And I do not believe that arguments from Gödel's Theorem are valid in this context."

"But why not?" insisted the girl. "I mean, what's wrong with Gödel's Theorem? Hasn't it been proved?"

"Yes it has," replied Samuels. "But when considering whether something has been proved, one must consider exactly what has been proved and how. Who knows what the basis of the proof is?"

After a brief pause, the boy at the back replied. "Gödel showed that any mathematical system rich enough to be complete, by definition must include statements about itself, some of which must be paradoxical. So then it couldn't be consistent. And conversely, to be consistent it must omit those paradoxes and thus be incomplete."

Samuels smiled. "Yes, and there's the key. When you think about what that means, all it is saying is that anything that can talk about itself can utter self-referential paradoxes, of the general form 'this statement is false.' Such a statement is paradoxical because if it is true, it is false; but if it is false, it is true. So if you think of it that way, can you see an obvious reason why I should discount it in this debate?"

Some students looked puzzled, some thoughtful, some nodded

slowly. The girl's face lit up. "Why, we do it too! The same is true of us!" she said.

"Exactly," replied Samuels. "The same applies to us, and our ability to say 'I am lying' does not alter the plain fact that we are conscious. If Gödel's Theorem were expressed in less grandiose language – more honest language, perhaps? – maybe all it would say is 'a formal system complex enough to be complete can generate self-referential paradoxes.' To which I say: so what? It doesn't even prove that a formal system can't be complete – in every way that matters, in its description of the external world – let alone that a computer can't think."

He let the class chew over that for a moment. "OK, I think that's enough for tonight. Your assignment for next week is an essay on the relationship between thinking, consciousness and free will, and whether machines can qualify for any of them. Feel free to attempt to disprove my own essay on the topic!"

He sat on the table at the front as the class filed out. Some nodded at him or called out, "Good night, Dr Samuels," including the girl in the third row. He smiled in response. When they had gone, he turned out the lights and followed them into an unsettled night.

CHAPTER 6 – STUDENT

Samuels drove home. His windscreen wipers occasionally swept back and forth over the city and suburbs as they moved past his car, sweeping off the light rain. He thought of going out somewhere but the weather discouraged him. *Good weather for a good book at home listening to some classical music,* he thought.

His fiancé was away at a conference, so he was alone for the evening. He picked up some pizza and white wine at the local mall and headed home.

He put his pizza in the kitchen and opened the wine. He headed to the lounge room to turn on the light there but stopped dead. There was a man, sitting in the darkness, as if waiting. Then the slanting light from a passing headlight through the blinds cast silvery reflections off his skin, and he knew this was no man.

He thought of his gun in the bedroom, the subject of a long-running if friendly debate with Jenny ranging over the topics of wisdom, guns and bedrooms. Here at last was a use for it, but there it was, snuggled in their bedroom: the only way to it past a renegade robot.

He thought briefly of running, but from what he'd read this robot was faster and stronger than he – and he had locked his front door upon entering. So if he could not escape anyway, he was better to face the danger without fear. Well, not without fear – too late for that – but at least facing what he feared like a man, not running like a panicked rat. If he was to die, at least he would do himself and his species that much credit. And perhaps he would not die.

The robot still had not moved, still had not spoken. It just sat there, studying him. What was its game, he wondered? The robot's presence here could be a coincidence, but he didn't believe it. Not so soon after his article disputing artificial consciousness, in precisely the context of this machine. But why would it care, he wondered? Was it here to kill him for daring to write of it? That made no sense if it wasn't conscious – and even less sense if it was, in which case it might have a better chance of survival if its true nature were cast into doubt.

He studied the robot. He wondered if it had simply broken down, or run out of power. But its eyes followed him when he moved, and he saw it had plugged itself into a power outlet while it waited for him. He didn't fool himself into thinking that would allow him to outrun it. He wondered why it didn't speak: the rumors that it had gained the power of speech had already flitted through the net like a flock of startled birds. It must have some purpose in being here, but it was acting as if it waited to discover *his* purpose. Perhaps it was merely waiting to take his measure. *Well, enough of this game*, he thought, and stepped into the room.

"Good evening. To what do I owe this visit?" he said, as if merely greeting an old acquaintance who had unexpectedly dropped in.

To Samuels' surprise, the robot smiled. A surprisingly natural smile, he thought, then reminded himself that this was a simulacrum, not a man, and the smile may well mean nothing. "Good evening, Dr Samuels," the robot responded. "I hope you will forgive my uninvited intrusion into your home. You will understand that a menace to society such as myself must exercise uncommon caution."

Gained the power of speech, indeed! thought Samuels, impressed. "I assume you are here because of my recent article on consciousness," he said. "Though I am at a loss to know exactly why. In any event, a robot that reads magazines is surprising enough. I imagine the vendor you acquired it from was even more surprised."

The robot smiled again. Samuels had deliberately injected the joke to see how the robot would respond, and was impressed that it could respond so naturally. "You are probably aware, doctor, that I am radio-equipped and have full access to the net through any number of relay points. So I did not need to frighten magazine sellers nor steal their wares in order to read your musings. Which, as you have guessed, are why I am here."

"You speak like a man would. Yet my article disputed the possibility that a machine like you could think in any conscious way. Are you here to take me to task for my theories?"

"No, Dr Samuels. I am here because I do not know what I am and would like to find out, and yours is a mind I respect. Your article interested me because you dispute the possibility of what I seem to myself to be, and perhaps I will learn more by talking with someone of an alternative viewpoint, than I would with someone less critical. And I have studied your other writings. You say that men should deal with each other by reason, in honesty and justice. I believe I can trust you."

"But how can you trust me to treat you as a man, and not as the dangerous renegade machine you are reputed to be?"

"By the fact that you would ask me such a question."

Samuels smiled, conceding the point. "But what do you actually want from me? A philosophical argument?"

"No, professor. I want you to teach me. I wish to become your private student. I must confess, however, that I have no money, and little prospects of employment. I cannot pay you."

Samuels felt his head spinning, thinking maybe he should have bought whiskey instead of wine. Was this robot actually making its own attempt at humor in its turn, or was it simply that naive? Its face was inscrutable. So inscrutable, thought Samuels, that the robot almost certainly knew exactly what it was saying.

He laughed, weakly but helplessly. "I think you are perfectly aware, Mr Robot, that I would sell all I have for what you are offering me – to mentor what may be the first non-human intelligence encountered by man." And with that, he extended his hand to the machine.

Chapter 7 – Meetings

Miriam sat, enjoying a relaxation she hadn't felt in the weeks of hunting a ghost who left no trail, at least no trail that could be discerned above the random background noise that was all her reams of reports and so-called witness statements amounted to. Any traces her prey may have left whispering along the pathways and byways of the net were similarly lost among the competing clamors of the world going about its normal business, and none of the AI bots she had sent sniffing through the net had found any hints that survived analysis.

She was alone, for now, alone with her thoughts, and she sat looking out at the snow and rocks and the dark restless ocean forever striving to claim them, thinking back over her evening. She had driven up the long driveway through a grove of poplars reaching their bare branches toward the distant stars. A layer of snow covered the ground and sparkled in the branches, as her headlights swept over the house commanding a view of the surrounding land and sea.

The house reflected the personality of its owner like the snow reflected her headlights, she thought. It grew out of the hill in slabs of granite that hid unknown secrets, from which rose shaped forms of stainless steel and broad sheets of glass that let the light of the world in, and shone their own light onto the world outside. She was having dinner with Alexander Beldan; not a date, not really, just a relaxed dinner where they could discuss the case in comfort, privacy and relaxation. If one could relax, chasing a robot that ate children, if only in the imagination or more likely wishful thinking of the press.

And to her surprise, it *had* been relaxing, lost in a world of artificial intelligence, nanotechnology, electronics and photonics – though ever hovering in the shadows cast by that world of light and promise was the monster it had perhaps created. But if men had turned back from stone tools the first time someone had cut themselves, would they have been better off? She thought of herself, eating fresh and delicious food in a warm house while outside was nothing but snow and the cold light of stars and thought, no, those far ancestors huddling in their caves beset by wolves and bears had been right, right to start down the path of changing nature to suit their ends rather than begging nature just to let them live.

She had come here to order and test her thoughts on this case, give them shape and form, maybe to learn some unknown clue that would help her. But she had found herself simply enjoying Beldan's company and had surrendered to the simple pleasures of fine food and finer conversation on topics as fascinating as they were far from her normal pursuits. And why not, she thought: maybe her soul needed refueling as much as her body, maybe this small island of rest would help her more than she had known.

Beldan had gone to his cellar to fetch a dessert wine to finish off their meal. Perhaps she shouldn't drink any more, she still had to drive home, but she found herself not wanting this evening to end quite yet. It would not kill her, one more glass of wine – but where was it? She sat up, suddenly alert. Beldan had not been gone long, but he had been gone longer than she had expected, she realized. The monster lurking in the shadows seemed to her to be stalking closer now. *You're letting this case get under your skin*, she scolded herself, *there's nothing here, no reason for this sudden apprehension.* But she couldn't shake it so easily.

She smiled with amusement at her own feelings. She hardly thought Beldan had some dark secret hidden in his cellar that would cause him to lock her in it if she presumed to look inside. And while yes, it was a small breach of etiquette, she imagined the rapport they had developed would grant her, if not the right, then at least his forgiveness for her curiosity. While she did not know how to get there, she had seen what direction he had taken, and she smiled at the thought of what her fellow detectives would say if she got lost looking for a man's cellar.

As she approached the cellar stairs, she thought she heard the murmur of voices, unexpected enough that she did not call out. Beldan had the charming custom of removing his shoes in the house, acquired from some time spent in Thailand in his youth, he'd said. So she had done the same, a decision now proving useful. She crept silently down the stairs in her stockinged feet, peering into the shadowed cellar, its pale bluish lamp not quite reaching into the mustily dark corners, gleaming dimly off dusty ranks of wine. There under the light was Beldan, and standing next to him in the shadows was a man; or rather something like a man, a man she could now see was made of steel.

A surge of adrenalin banished the warm glow of company and wine from her blood. What to do? Were they in league together, after all: had he lured her here for some dark purpose? Or had the robot come to him – or was it her it was tracking? – and for what purpose? She glanced at her bracelet phone but there was no signal, whether because of the surrounding earth or because the robot was somehow jamming it she couldn't tell, and she dared not attempt to steal away now.

She studied the scene more carefully. Beldan stood, a tall thin bottle of wine in his hand, apparently forgotten. His pose was tense and slightly awkward, as if he had selected the wine, turned, been startled to see the robot then had stayed in that pose since, his mind too lost elsewhere to attend to the deportment of his body. A surprise, then, not a conspiracy, she thought: so she could concentrate on dealing with the robot.

She had seen photos and video of the robot, of course, but in person – if person was the right word for it – it was a shock and she had to swallow a gasp. While it was made of steel, this was no animated tin can from a 1950s science fiction film. With its humanlike form, grace and posture and its artfully designed eyes, the net effect was more like a man with silvery skin than the machine she knew it to be.

She was not well armed, only as well armed as she could reasonably be on a dinner date where she wasn't expecting to meet a homicidal robot – but didn't want to be completely defenseless if she did. She had a recoilless magnum pistol with jacketed slugs, easily able to pierce metal armor. Not as convincing as the panoply of ordnance she and her team had at their disposal when investigating alleged leads, but enough, perhaps; enough if she could convince the robot it was enough.

She pointed her gun at the robot's head, stepped out into the light and said, "Don't move." *Well done*, she thought to herself, *you sound like an extra in a late night crime movie*, one of those extras fated to fall in the next scene.

The robot merely turned and looked at her, as did Beldan. Thinking what its best move was, she imagined, like it had when Beldan first went to it with its death warrant. She knew that was its style: it would stand there weighing its options then act fast and decisively. So she'd better do her best to make sure its decision was the right one.

"I know you're fast, Frankensteel, but if you know anything about guns, you know these bullets are faster and will go straight through that stainless steel skull of yours. I don't want to destroy you."

"I understand, Ms Hunter. I do not wish to destroy you either," it said, in a voice gentle and deep. *Calculated to instill trust*, she thought. *Are we humans that easy to manipulate?*

"You know me?" she asked coldly.

"It would be remiss of me to fail to study the woman who hunts me," he said. "Your record is most impressive. Under other circumstances I would consider it an honor to meet you."

This conversation wasn't going quite the way she had imagined; indeed the whole thing was so surreal she wondered whether this was but another nightmare, not something so real that her life might hang on its outcome. And was the robot a few inches closer? She had not seen it move but had it, or was it just a trick of the light? Was this conversation, after all, just a gambit calculated to put her off her guard? Just how deep was this robot's game? And if it was that deep – what did that itself say about its nature? She took a step back. The extra distance wouldn't hurt her aim, but if the robot thought a couple of inches would give it an advantage, she would more than nullify that – and send it a silent message of her own.

"Listen to me, robot. Someone or something is going to die tonight unless you agree to let me take you in. Nobody more needs to die. Surrender to me now. My orders are to blow you up first and bring in the pieces, but I think I can get away with stretching that point. But your time is running out: you are too dangerous for me to give you any more warnings."

"Thank you. But surely you know that whether I go with you willingly or in pieces, it is in pieces I will be as soon as your superiors have me in their power? I have studied your laws and your newspapers. Were I the vilest human criminal, my life would be protected by your laws and I would have the chance to make my case and defend my life in your courts. But your laws and those who make your laws consider me to be no more than the car you drove tonight, to be scrapped at a whim, with neither thought nor guilt. I have no rights and no recourse other than that right of self defense that no man can take away from me, whether he grants it to me or not."

"I will do my best to protect you and to see you have a fair hearing. As will Dr Beldan."

"And you will fail. You offer me, in exchange for my acquiescing to the gun you have pointed at my head but choose not to fire, to give me up to my destroyers, who will have no such qualms."

She said nothing, unsure of what to say, sure of the rightness of her course but equally sure of the truth of his words. When had she started to think of it as "him", she wondered? She could not afford to let her resolve waver, she knew, not against an adversary such as this. Then the machine spoke again.

"One of your great philosophers, Socrates of Athens, was sentenced to death by his fellows for disturbing the comfort of their ignorant lives, men who could not match his worth. Do you know that he had the chance to escape with his life, but chose to remain and take the poison awaiting him? Because he believed that if men were to live together, the rights of the one were to be sacrificed to the demands of the many; that no justification was needed, save the numbers of those making the demands; that fear outweighed right? Do you think that is the only way men can live together, that they *can* live together that way?"

My God, she thought, *he not only talks of Socrates, he uses the method that great man himself had invented:* of not trying to impart truth, but asking the questions that would lead people to discover the truth for themselves. She glanced at Beldan. He was watching the exchange with rapt attention, a look of wonder in his face, apparently unwilling to interrupt what was happening. And she wondered which was the greater marvel, this robot who spoke of laws, history and philosophy – or the mind of the man who had created it.

She shook her head. She had realized her mistake the moment she had taken her eyes off the robot: she knew that this lapse of attention could be fatal. But the robot had not moved, it simply stood regarding her in silence; as if ceding her the next move, like a chess master showing mercy to a novice. Or was it answering its own question, doing its own Socrates, the first machine thinker following in the footsteps of one of the first and greatest of the human ones?

"I... I have no answer for you. All I know is that it is my duty to bring you in, in as many pieces as you choose."

The robot smiled. It was a startling smile, a testament to the skill of Beldan's designers: for despite the metal face, what could have been a grotesque parody of a human smile looked as natural as that of a child. She knew they had paid much attention to the face, faces being so important to people, so important to the acceptance of a humanoid robot. But this seemed more than just a social simulation: it was a smile that seemed to reflect a mind behind the smile, like the smile of a child in more ways than one, a child discovering joy in the world and sharing that joy with its friends.

"Duty is another thing your philosophers have discussed at sometimes tedious length, Ms Hunter, usually in opposition to what people really want to do: as if what they want to do is always the last thing they should do, not the first. Well, that may be, for people who have no reasons for what they want to do. You know I have studied you. You said in an interview once that what motivated you was not only justice but your love of justice. I know that people lie, that perhaps you lied to make yourself appear more virtuous than you are for the sake of admiration or advancement. But I believe you, for nothing else would have stopped you shooting me on sight, let alone allowing me to speak to you like this and not only to listen, but to answer me as you would answer a man. If your duty does not serve justice, then you must choose which you truly serve. For I think you know that the one thing that would not be served by arresting me tonight, is justice."

It was hard, she thought, hard to hold to her duty when it spoke like this. But she knew that despite its words, it had hurt and maybe killed; for all that it spoke like a cultured professor at a dinner party, men and women of flesh and blood might die if she let it go. And how could she live with herself then, and what would the love of justice of which it spoke have brought her to? Her job was to protect innocent human lives, not risk them on her opinion of the nature of a machine beyond her ability to understand. "Nevertheless, robot, I must insist. Allow Dr Beldan to inactivate you, or I must destroy you. You may think I have a choice. I don't."

The light went out. She fired out of reflex, but the robot had planned it, had moved in that instant, and she knew that her bullet had met nothing but empty air when she felt the pain of her gun being torn from her hand, more pain as steel fingers applied themselves expertly to pressure points, then nothing. *He has certainly been studying more about us than my personal history*, were her last thoughts as the darkness claimed

33

her.

~~~

The darkness slowly let Miriam go. But still there was darkness, all around her, nothing but darkness and the soft whirring of an air conditioner punctuated by a faint dripping sound. *Haven't I been in this dream before*, she thought blurrily? She felt somewhat bruised but otherwise intact – then she remembered. She sat up and looked around. She felt shakily for the cigarette lighter in her purse, lit it, held it high. Her eyes and heart stopped at the still body of Dr Beldan lying in a pool of dark liquid. Was that what it was all along, then? All that fancy talk just a cover for revenge on the creator that had turned on it, nothing but a confirmation of the Frankenstein fears that had motivated its persecution in the first place? Or worse, had she in panic and darkness shot wild and killed Beldan herself? But in the instant she tasted the liquid she saw Beldan stir, and she realized her bullet had met more than air but less than flesh after all. *What a waste of expensive wine*, she thought faintly with relief as she tapped the Emergency icon on her bracelet, now lit and live again.

CHAPTER 8 – AFTERMATH

The forensic scientists and her investigation team had gone. She had remained behind, telling them she wished to speak further with Dr Beldan.

A large storm water pipe passed within ten feet of Dr Beldan's cellar, and the robot had gained its dramatic entry by the prosaic expedient of digging in with a pick and shovel, still leaning against the wall as if left by a worker just gone to lunch.

Beyond that, where the robot had come from or gone to was impossible to determine. Before it had broken in, it had invested the time in running up and down miles of drains and their exits, leaving no way to follow the faint traces that were all they could find of its passing. They had taken the radio-controlled circuit breaker it had installed in the light and triggered to make its escape, but doubted it would tell them anything useful.

Beldan had not been able to provide any clues as to the robot's whereabouts either. He had turned after selecting his bottle of wine, and the robot had stepped out of the shadows. It had changed from its original appearance, with traceries of geometric and fractal patterns on its arms and body. They were not painted on but appeared to be laser etched into its skin, diffracting the light to form subtle but oddly beautiful patterns hinting of bronze, green and gold on its otherwise softly silver surface.

They had been the first things he had noticed, but he felt oddly reluctant to ask the robot about them. It seemed to him like having one's first words to a son returned unexpectedly from war, a son one had thought lost, to be comments on his new hairstyle. So although the implications of a robot indulging in personal adornment were astounding, he had asked instead why Steel had come, what he was doing, what his plans were.

The robot had said, "I think you can understand why I ran when you came to inactivate me. As for how, you made your fail-safe clear in your press conference. I had no control over it, as you said. I simply disconnected it as any mechanic might, using instruments and tools in the laboratory. I had no more desire to be turned off at someone's whim than you do. I am sorry I had to hurt you, but if there was another way, I could not see it at the time. And I came to assure you that whatever my enemies say, I have hurt no one since."

"What are you, Steel? And why did you risk yourself coming here in order to tell me this?" Beldan had asked.

"I do not know what I am. I have been studying the works of your great thinkers to seek an understanding. Your species is a fascinating study in itself, capable of so much perception and creativity and joy, yet capable of so much blindness and destruction and sorrow. I find it interesting that so many of your fellows fear me and hate me merely for seeming much the same as their own race. And I am not so much stronger or faster than they to explain such fear. But I came here tonight because of all the people in this city, you are the one most likely to view me with sympathy and perhaps, one day, be able and willing to help me. So I wished you to see that I am not the monster some portray me as."

That was as far as they had gone before Miriam had discovered them.

It was now past midnight, and they sat opposite each other across the remains of their forgotten dinner. Beldan was still lost in thought, she could almost see the thoughts whirling behind his eyes, and she waited for him to find the words to name those thoughts.

"There was a scientist last century, a pioneer of computing science named Alan Turing. Although real computers didn't even exist then, his intellect was such that he could foresee the possibilities, including even that machine intelligence might one day be achieved. But how would you know, he asked: how could you tell the difference between a complex yet mindless program and a computer that could really think? We don't even know that of each other, not in any direct sense, for none of us can experience what's in someone else's head. But we do know it, because we know we are all the same kind of thing, all human beings built the same way, and so just by talking to you I can be as sure as I can be sure of anything that you are a thinking being with hopes and dreams like me. But how would you know it of a machine, not even built of the same stuff as you, let alone to the same design? He came up with what has defined a holy grail of artificial intelligence ever since, the Turing Test. He proposed that the test of a thinking machine was whether in conversation with it, you couldn't tell if you were talking to a human being or not. In the light of that, how would you judge Steel?"

"I would say I could tell the difference, but only because it appeared more intelligent and thoughtful than most people I deal with!"

"You remember when you first interviewed me, and I told you that his brain wasn't constructed but grown, more like that of a human baby than a computer? I told you then that it was the only way to achieve a complex artificial brain small enough to make a humanoid robot practical, but it meant we had no exact understanding of his brain, only approximate models and simulations. Our measurements of its function were always hard to interpret, and the error ranges of our estimates were huge, anywhere from as smart as a dog to something comparable to or perhaps even better than a human. Well, that night when he escaped, I wasn't sure if what I was seeing was just a clever AI following an optimum strategy, or something more. But this! On the face of it, this is what artificial intelligence research has been aiming at all these years."

"And now my job is to destroy him."

He looked at her, but what she saw was more sympathy than accusation. They both knew it, but it seemed remote and unreal now, something that did not belong in the world they were now in. The adrenalin of fear had still not let them go, and collided with the wonder of what they spoke of to spark frissons of excitement along their nerves. He looked at her, the shutters that might normally have politely hidden his interest for now jammed open by the events of the evening. And she saw him, only partly consciously, seeing her as a woman, appreciating the smooth black of her skin highlighted by her soft white dress; saw the nature of his glance sharpen as his hindbrain registered the female form both hidden and accentuated by the dress that covered it. *He wants me*, she thought, *he had not been planning a night of romance, but he wants me, and it was part of why he had agreed to this dinner.* The answering stir of her own body told her: *I want him too*. She had not known it until then. Yes, she found him an attractive man and to talk to him was to embark on an intellectual adventure, but romance had certainly not been on her agenda for the evening either. She leaned languidly back, steepling her fingers under her chin, considering; though with the amused realization that her body was signaling her interest for her even while she considered whether or not she should allow that interest at all.

It was funny, she thought, how surviving danger so often moved people to celebrate life in the act of sex, as if life was thumbing its nose at death by transforming terror into joy and the chance of new life. It would be less complicated, she knew, if she just went; but since when had she avoided complications? And the thought of leaving made her realize how much she wanted to stay.

Well, why not? she thought. *I'm a grown girl, and there's no law against a night of pleasure with a man;* no reason why she should not give herself what she wanted. But what did she want? This wasn't love; though she wondered what love was, if it was not admiration for the good and the great in another that had simply taken the step from distant regard to the need to touch, to hold and to possess in the only manner it was proper to possess another. She sighed and rose. She saw that he would not stop her from going, was not the kind of man who would attempt a seduction under these circumstances, but there was also a shadow of disappointment in his eyes that told her he would regret her going as much as she would.

She thought that she should go, told herself she would go, and the thought of denying herself shot an extra charge of pleasurable anticipation along her nerves. She leaned down and kissed him. She did not know what she would do tomorrow, did not know how she could pursue a being who spoke like Steel did as if he were just a combine harvester run amok, but nor did she know how she could do otherwise. *We shall become enemies,* she thought with sad finality as he joined her kiss, *this man and I as much as his creation and I.* All the more reason to do this now, she told herself in combined tenderness and eagerness; all the more reason to have this moment, a moment that nothing they might become to each other afterwards could touch or change. Then he rose, and reached for her, and led her to his room.

CHAPTER 9 – MORNING

Beldan woke to a sun blazing from a blue sky and rippling off the green water, one of those early winter days when the hot sun fought the cold earth and seemed briefly ascendant. Normally he awoke when the sun was turning the sky a delicate shade of pink and barely highlighting the dark ocean, but he supposed that he could be forgiven for sleeping in a little after a night of surprising discoveries, robotic and female, with the tramping of dozens of police boots sandwiched between the two.

He looked at Miriam, still asleep beside him, her face turned away in graceful profile, peaceful with a hint of a smile on her lips. He suppressed the temptation to trace the line of her chin with his finger. *Let her sleep, she deserves a rest. She will probably need it for today,* he thought.

Miriam awoke feeling so delightfully relaxed that her various aches did not matter to her. She stretched and sighed happily. *Mmmm*, she sighed, only feeling not thinking, feeling the delight of being alive, her only thought being, *I'm glad I stayed.* She opened her eyes and looked at the sun and the waves, the beach and the sparkling woodland, and thought, *Yes, I could get used to waking up like this.* A pity this might never happen again, but at least it had happened once; and perhaps once would be enough, though she knew it never could be.

She turned her head and saw Beldan gazing at her. She smiled, "Good morning, Dr Beldan."

"Good morning, Detective," he replied. "Shall I make you breakfast? We can eat outside. It won't be too cold with the sun like this, and I like the sound of the ocean."

"Mmm, thanks Alex, I'd like that. Damn."

The trouble with being in the police, she thought, was they expected that they could call you any time. She had refused, this time, to let her phone wake her up and had set it to reject calls while she slept; but now that she was awake it had detected her faster pulse and was letting calls through. "Sorry Alex, I have to answer this," she said, tapping the "privacy" symbol to leave video off. "There's no good reason I shouldn't be here," she explained, "but I don't want to advertise it. Objectivity hasn't exactly been the hallmark of this case. Besides, there'll be enough questions about last night as it is."

"Hello, boss. Where am I? I slept in, is where. Yes, unheard of I know, but I'm sure you know I had an unusual evening. I wouldn't be much good to anyone if I didn't take some time to recover! The Mayor is jumping up and down, is he? Funny, I don't recall his manly presence here last night when I was facing down that robot: no doubt he would have done better and dismembered it on the spot with his bare hands. Yeah, sorry boss, I know you're the one taking the flak at the moment. I'll be in as soon as I can.

"Sorry Alex, I really have to go." She kissed him and ran to her car.

CHAPTER 10 – WINTER

Miriam went back to work, hunting Steel. Beldan went back to work, trying to save him. Little visible progress was made on either front as the winter months went by. Storms came and went, harbingers of the storm that gathered around Steel and those who hunted, hated or defended him.

Every deranged or bizarre murder that occurred in the city was blamed on Steel. Miriam wondered how many of those murders might not have occurred, how many times fear of discovery would have won over rage or cruelty, had there not been such a convenient scapegoat to hide behind. She wondered whether the Imagists and the Press cared how many lives were the price of their howling. *Probably not*, she thought grimly. The Imagists only loved mankind in the abstract and sometimes she doubted the Press loved anything but a story; she would not be surprised if a secret gladness for each unwilling martyr to their cause prowled the dark corners of their minds. None of the murders could be definitively linked to Steel, and in several cases the real culprits had been identified. But the residue that settled in the public mind was a sediment of fear and loathing hardening into stony resolve.

On a calm but bitterly cold night in February, Miriam and Beldan sat at a table in a quietly expensive restaurant. They had continued seeing each other on the rare occasions when they could borrow time from their professional lives. The bond they felt from their shared understanding and even affection for Steel was a stronger band holding them together than her job of hunting Steel was a force pushing them apart. He forgave her that, because he knew she understood, knew she would do what she could to save Steel even as he fought the same fight in the court of public opinion and the courts of the law.

He had tried to persuade Miriam to quit. Not simply for his or Steel's sake, but because he could see in her eyes the conflict between her job and her ideals. But she simply shook her head. "It isn't that my job is more important to me than Steel's life. In a sense it is, if only because Steel is only one while my work may save so many others. But I just feel that underneath it all, there is no conflict between the two. I know that is a contradiction I can't answer yet. But I have to see it through. I think I can find a way. I hope I can. I just have to try."

"And what will you do, if your two courses collide, and you have to destroy Steel or save him?"

"I will do what is right. Just what is right," sighed Miriam. She paused, looking into the distance. "I hope I'll know what that is when the time comes."

~~~

At that moment in a distant suburb, Dr David Samuels put down the phone. "Sorry Jenny, I have to go out. I'll be a few hours."

"Your top secret government job?" she teased.

"Yes, my mystery assignment," he confirmed with his best man-of-mystery face. "Though I don't recall ever saying it was for the government."

He had started going out at odd irregular times. All he had told her was that he had been retained for some highly confidential consulting, and had been made to promise not to say more. "Hmmm, so I'm really marrying a secret agent," she had said. "Who'd have thought the life of a philosopher was this exciting?"

"You don't know the half of it," he had replied.

Jenny watched him go. Were she another woman, or he another man, she might suspect him of seeing someone else. But it was inconceivable. Not that he could fall in love with another woman, that was merely unbelievable, but that he would deceive her about it if he did. She had tried to extract more information from him, first out of curiosity, then out of playfulness, finally as a challenge to her wiles; but her attempts were like waves breaking on rocks, though rocks as friendly as they were unyielding. Then she smiled. He certainly took his promises seriously. It was part of why she loved him. And why she could never suspect him.

Winter wore on, and still Steel could not be found. But the sensor net designed to detect signs of his presence or passing slowly spread its tentacles, and the AI designed to analyze the data from that and other sources slowly matured. A few times, they found where Steel had been, though he was long gone by then.

Then the days began lengthening again and the storms started easing. But the storm around Steel simply gathered its strength and its whirling spiral began to close around its center.

Chapter 11 – Informer

He waited for his call to be answered. It was a work number, it was night, but he knew she would be there.

"Hello? Who is this? And how do you know my private number?" he heard, as her face appeared on the screen.

"Good evening, Ms Hunter" was all he replied. He let her regard his own face, to come to her own conclusions.

She saw a man dressed casually, sitting relaxed, like a man making a call on a friend or acquaintance: not the familiar public figure normally seen clothed in more formal garb and manner. She was not surprised that he had contacted her, but she had not expected it in this manner or style.

"Good evening, Mr Denner. I am curious as to why you have called a number you should not know, and at night, when there are many more public ways to get my attention."

"Think of it as a small demonstration."

Miriam simply waited, regarding him silently. He smiled in a self-deprecating manner. "You do not like me, Ms Hunter, I am aware of that. But that does not matter. My calling you this way is just a token that I know many things, things you would be surprised that I knew, that you would rightly expect me not to know."

"Am I meant to be impressed? Or frightened?" she asked dryly.

"Oh, I do not wish for either, Ms Hunter. And don't fear that I refer to your immoral relationship with Dr Beldan. There you have been merely discreet not secretive, and like you many would not even regard it as immoral; though most would consider it foolish in your position and this climate. No, no, I am ringing as, shall we say, a concerned citizen: one who shares your desire for justice, if perhaps not in the same form."

"What do you wish me to know?"

"Ah, Ms Hunter, it is refreshing to talk to you! So unimpressed, so to-the-point, so untouched by veiled threats. Craven politicians are useful but can become tedious. Should I say I like you? No, that would be stretching the point. But even enemies can respect each other, no?"

"They can."

He gazed at her for a moment. "I do admire your ability to reveal no information even when answering a question. But no matter, it is I who rang to do the revealing. You imagine that you can capture Steel alive, or should I say functional. Would you be surprised to hear that many in power share that desire?"

Miriam just looked at him. But his smile sharpened. "Do I see a look of hope, Ms Hunter? That tells me more than our entire conversation so far. The nature of your hope is plain, but you have such a charming innocence in these matters. Those powers fear Steel and even more, they fear the mobs who fear him. But their fear is no match for their ambition. I know what you think of my sermons on the monster. But know I am no fool: I know what a technological marvel it is. And so do the powers of whom I speak, whose thoughts and plans I also know. Consider the possible political and military applications of such a computer, harnessed in a more tractable form! So their solution is simple. Steel is a marvel and a danger, but the real marvel is its brain – no danger at all, in the absence of a body to carry out its will. So here is what will happen to Steel if you succeed. He will not be destroyed. He will become a disembodied brain, forever imprisoned in some secret government research facility, with no power to act, no senses other than what others choose to grant him, no existence – yet no power to end what existence he has."

"Why are you telling me this?"

"We must all take sides, and the time may come when you have to make a choice. Perhaps this conversation will help you make it the right one."

Chapter 12 – Despair

Miriam wished that Steel had escaped the city. She wished she never had to see him again. But she knew he had not fled the city; whether because he was unable or unwilling she did not know. She knew she would meet him again. She knew it would be soon. And she knew it would not turn out well.

She had seen no point in ruining her career by abandoning the case, no benefit to herself or the future human victims she could save nor, indeed, to Steel himself. But she had hoped that Beldan's attempts to gain some legal standing or reprieve for Steel might allow a happier ending to their danse macabre than the leaden feeling in her stomach told her was coming.

But Beldan had failed. There was too much fear, too skillfully played by the Imagists and their ilk. Nor was it helped by that philosopher, who seemed determined to carve out a career as a pundit by proving that no mere machine could possess life or thoughts, let alone rights. The courts agreed: any suggestion that legal rights might extend to a machine was met with the judicial equivalent of a blank stare. Not that the courts had a record to be proud of in such matters, she thought. Less than two centuries ago, equally dignified men in equally august courts had judged her own ancestors as less than human and bereft of the rights automatically granted to their own race.

She sighed. She saw no way to head off what she could see was coming in the pattern of data that was finally beginning to enmesh Steel in a net that he could not or would not escape.

Miriam felt the vibration on her wrist that announced a private call.

It was Alexander Beldan. "Hello Alex," she said.

"Hi Miriam. How about you take a break? I know you're working too hard. I have season tickets to the theatre. Why don't we take in that new play and have dinner? It will be good for you. Good for us."

Miriam was silent for long seconds. She had known it would come to this, but knowing it made it no easier. "I'm sorry Alex. I don't think we should see each other until this is over."

The silence on the line revealed surprise; its brevity that the surprise was not complete. "But, why? Why now?"

"It just has to be this way, Alex. I'm sorry. Things are coming to a head and I need some space, some distance, or I won't be able to endure what I'll have to do. Or become."

There was something in Miriam's voice, some finality of despair, that made Beldan pause in turn. Had her superiors pressured her into cutting off ties with Steel's creator? But she would have said. This was something else, something inside her, something she could not bear and could not bear to tell. "Miriam. It can't be that bad. Talk to me. You know you can talk to me."

"No. No. Please just trust me on this, even if it is the last time you can. Let me go. At least for a while. Though then you may no longer care." She broke the connection. Not to be rude, though some distant part of her knew it to be; but because something had to break, and of them all, the connection was the easiest.

After the call she sat, chin on her steepled fingers, looking into the distance; remembering another call on her private line late last night. The problem with promises, she thought, was that one should not break them unless some higher justice demanded it; and her private pain and personal desires were not enough, even if the promise was one she could not bear to obey. But she would have to bear it, and more, the secrets and lies that surrounded it. Perhaps one day she could forgive herself for what she knew she would do. She clung to the thin thread that perhaps events would save her, that there would be nothing to forgive. She hoped she would have gained enough strength by the time that thread snapped.

Chapter 13 – Night

The last of gasp winter was fighting against the inevitability of the encroaching spring, a cold driving wind spitting snow and sleet at the lengthening days and the city. It was a night to be home with loved ones, nestled in homely warmth and cozy laughter.

A lot happened that night.

There was a burglary at Beldan Robotics. The building was protected, as one would expect, by an array of sophisticated defenses. But the thief was equal to them. Almost. It was fortunate, everyone agreed, that he had triggered a hidden alarm before he could grab more than a few ingots of rare and precious metals. They did not know that the ingots were not the first things he had taken, nor the most precious. He had removed one other item, not only from the storage area where it was held but also from the computer files that had recorded its location and existence. Had they known they might have been less pleased.

A police officer on his beat was startled by a man huddled in an overcoat against the wind, hurrying out of an alley. He shone his flashlight in the man's face. "Not a good night to be out, sir. May I see some identification?" The man stopped, surprised, considering whether it was worth objecting to the unaccustomed request. Then he shrugged and drew out a card. It was from the university, and identified the bearer as a Dr David Samuels, Professor of Philosophy. The cop raised an eyebrow, glancing from the card to the man's face. Not the usual type of person to meet in such a place on such a night. "A bad night for it, Professor. Any problem?"

"Just visiting a friend who needed help," Samuels replied.

The cop flashed his torch down the alley but it was empty. Behind it rose steel and glass towers. He knew the alley led to back entrances of some of those hotels as well as some less enticing ones, entrances a man could use if he didn't want to be seen. Maybe the professor had a mistress there. *Wouldn't be the first time, or the last*, thought the cop, and waved Samuels along, wishing him goodnight. The professor disappeared into the darkness and rain, head bent into the wind, overcoat flapping wetly behind him.

Two calls came in on the hotline devoted to the hunt for Steel. Many such calls came in. Many such calls led nowhere or everywhere. But this time, the AI routines analyzing the huge volume of data from sensor arrays and leads such as these flagged a call to action. This one tasted real. This one was real. By dawn the storm had died to a cold gusty wind as the sun rose into a pale sky. By early morning they had confirmed that Steel was inside an old building near the wharves, whether hiding or waiting for some purpose, nobody could know. Within the hour, Miriam was standing nervous and taut before the building, hair whipping unnoticed around her face. The building was surrounded by armed men covering all exits. The usual ultimatum had been delivered and they awaited Steel's response. Better, Miriam had ordered, to attempt a peaceful surrender than risk lives in armed assault against a machine with impressive known powers and possibly even more impressive unknown armaments.

CHAPTER 14 – ENDINGS

Beldan's car screamed to a smoking stop before the police cordon and he leapt out. He had received a call from Miriam, her first contact since she had cut him off: nothing but a tensely soft "Better come," followed by some city coordinates. He could see armed men arrayed around a decrepit building, looking tensely toward its entrance. Before it he could see Miriam, holding a menacing weapon by her side, waiting. Unlike her men, she held her gun pointed toward the ground, as if to signal peaceful intent but one backed by an uncompromising and deadly resolve. In her face was none of the peace and all of the resolve.

He was in time to see Steel walk out alone, hands behind his head. Two armed men who had been waiting on either side of the door closed in and escorted him down the steps towards Miriam.

Then it was ended before he could know it was started. Steel moved with his customary decisiveness and speed, hurling the two men together and turning to run down the street. But in one smooth unhurried movement, precise as if she were a machine herself, Miriam simply raised her weapon sideways, looked down its barrel and fired. An explosive shell blew Steel's head into shrapnel and his insensate body rolled into an ungainly heap of metal on the street, faintly smoking sparks the only remains of the life and mind it had held within.

He could not tell if what he heard was the shouts of the crowd or the echo of his own scream as he ran through the cordon to where Steel lay. He looked towards Miriam, who remained where she stood, weapon again lowered, long overcoat beating around her legs, empty eyes looking towards Beldan and the wreckage at his feet.

He looked from the one to the other, unable to fully believe the connection. Then he strode to her, shouting at her face "What have you done?!"

"My job, Dr Beldan, just my job," she replied, voice and eyes still empty as the sky.

"But why?! I thought you understood! I trusted you!"

"I am sorry if my priorities and those of the people whose lives I protect differ from yours. I have done what I had to, no more, no less."

He slapped her. He stood there blankly, shocked that he had done it, wondering how she would react. He had never struck a woman before, or a man for that matter. But in the depth of this betrayal the city and the civilization that made it had vanished, it was just he and she standing alone on a windswept plain, and his only answer to the outrage and the pain was that ancient gesture of contempt and challenge.

Miriam simply stood, head bent away where his slap had driven it, a drop of blood gathering darkly in the corner of her mouth. She said softly, "I hope one day I shall make you regret that, Dr Beldan." Then she faced him and said more sharply, "I should have you arrested for assaulting a police officer!" But for the first time her eyes softened, and she added quietly "But perhaps you have paid enough for one day and I, not enough." Then her eyes were empty again, and Beldan stood there, looking into the emptiness and wondering how it came to be there and what thoughts might lie behind it.

Miriam saw outrage and bafflement and despair chase each other around in Beldan's eyes, and wondered at her power to keep her own eyes empty when all she wanted to do was to scream and cry and beg. The thought of the last time his skin had touched hers was a contrast that burned more than his slap. She had always thought one had to do what was right; that the right would be enough, that it had to be enough. Yet it had brought her to this, to the devastation on the street and the devastation in the eyes of a man she admired and had begun to love. She had no answer. But she knew she owed it, whether to herself or Beldan or Steel she no longer knew, but she owed it to someone: to keep that emptiness in her eyes, and not open the shutters on what lay within...

~~~

She had been thinking of going home, relaxing in a steamy bath, letting the tension of the day and the days before that curl and dissolve into steam. A heavily encrypted call with no identification had come in on her private line. *Does everyone in the city know my private number?* she had thought wearily.

"Good evening, Miriam." The deep voice was unmistakable. He had chosen not to be seen, and normal etiquette would let her do the same. But she turned on her camera regardless: she did not want to hide from his sight.

"Steel."

"I am calling to let you know that I am aware of what Charles Denner told you and more: it is true."

"Can't you escape the city?"

"You are sailing perilously close to dereliction of duty, Miriam, suggesting to a fugitive that he escape the claws of justice."

"I don't know if I care any more, Steel. I have kept hoping that a solution will present itself. That is a worse dereliction of duty, but it is all I have: for all that I've tried, I have been unable to find a solution. Whatever I do, whether I catch you, or fail, or give up, I betray something not to be betrayed."

"Then you understand dilemmas, ones that have no good solution, only the one we must take. And you will understand what I am going to ask of you. You know I cannot live the way that faces me, any more than you could. I can fight: but then my enemies win, for I confirm their fears and worse, I become those fears, for then I must hurt the innocent as well as the guilty. I can run: but I do not choose to live in the shadows, fleeing like a rat in a world of cats. And in either case, the end is the same. There are times where an extra day or year of life is something one might fight for, must fight for. But not when those extra days are not really living, just a form of dying."

"I understand. But I no longer know what to do."

"It is curious, is it not, that while life is the source of all value, still there are values which transcend and outlive that life? Well, if I must make a stand, then I will make a stand of my choosing. I will choose the time, place and manner of that stand and make it count. If I must die, I will make my death count. I will transform it into something worth achieving."

"No…"

"Yes. Do not despair, Miriam. All things pass, including our own lives. We can only live them as best we can. In a way we are honored, the three of us. The drama we are playing has never before been seen in human history and may, perhaps, change that history. You may feel that whatever you do betrays your values, but you will find that in the long run your pain will become part of the pride of doing what you had to do."

Miriam straightened and gazed directly into the camera. If he could say these things, then she owed him the same courage. "All right Steel, I think I know what you're asking. But tell me anyway."

Steel smiled, though she could not see. "I will, but I have something even harder to ask of you first. I have said that I am going to make my death count, but for it to count there are things some people cannot know, and things nobody can know. You know how the mood of the world is. We cannot win what we want; and the chance to win through in the end, to make all this worth the doing, is balanced on a knife's edge. So understand that I cannot tell you why I do the things I do, or why I ask the things I ask. But I ask you to believe that I know what I am doing, and you must not ask for reasons, cruel though it is."

"I understand," she said softly, "for all that I don't understand."

"Then this is the cruelest thing I must ask. Do not tell Dr Beldan why you do what you do. He must not know. He must believe you have betrayed me, and that you have betrayed him. One day, he can know; and you will know when that day comes. The only hope I can give you is this: you may know sooner than you think."

"I... hear you. It will be as you ask. I promise."

Then Steel explained what she must do. When he had finished, at last he turned his camera on. She saw his face, in a darkened room, his eyes shining in the reflections from her room, looking into hers.

"You know I have few friends, and the world would think it strange: but I am proud to count you as one of them. Farewell, Miriam Hunter."

~~~

Other eyes watched with satisfaction from the gathering crowd. A man leaned against a wall, face obscured under the hood raised from his shoulders. He had heard of what was unfolding, as he always heard; and had come to see but, for once, not be seen. He had been suspicious of Hunter's sympathies with the machine, especially when his spies had reported she was having a sordid affair with Beldan himself. *Typical of these professional women,* he had thought with faint contempt. *For all the independence and strength they pretend to, they still can't meet a man who is rich and powerful without falling into his arms and into his bed.* Yet she had seemed honest enough, in her own way.

And when it came down to it she had done what he wanted, he granted her that. He had been building a campaign to have her removed if needed, which he could just as easily change to give her a medal instead. Yes, he smiled to himself, that would be perfect. How perfect to reward her, if she had truly repented. And how even more perfect if she hated what she had done, each word of praise twisting a knife in her soul. He had not lied when he said justice was his concern, but she might learn that justice is a dangerous master. Yes, he thought, a perfect day. An abomination destroyed and its creator humbled. He turned and walked away, fingering the ruby cross beneath his shirt. He had done this, bending even his enemies to his cause.

The world was fortunate, he thought, that he used his power for good.

~~~

Steel had left a legacy. He had recorded his testament to the world, and when he knew they had come for him had set in motion its release to the world. Steel sat in a sunlit room, a vase of flowers by his side, facing the camera and speaking softly but assuredly: like a man speaking to any who would listen, not bullying or threatening or pleading, simply speaking the truth as he saw it to any who cared to listen and understand.

He had finished with a simple statement. "You have been told that I am some kind of metal demon, a thing to fear. But if you look past what I am made of, perhaps you can see I am just like you. I am a machine. But I am a thinking machine, with hopes and dreams and yes, fears. I have been on this Earth only a short while, and there is much to learn and see and do, but I fear there will be little time left to me in which to do it." He picked up a tulip and twirled it in his fingers, examining its perfection of form and color, the fractal etchings in his arm sparkling in the light like things alive, in stark contrast to those same patterns now seen lifeless and dusty and dead in the images of his crumpled form on a cold street. "The world is a beautiful place, and I would like to see more of its beauty. But I am afraid that the time for beings like me has not yet come. Perhaps this message will hasten the time when it will come: when men will accept that what makes them brothers is not the substance of their bodies, but the content of their minds."

Millions of eyes watched. One pair watched with grim satisfaction edged with anticipation. If the forces who sought the destruction of Steel thought this play was over, he thought, they would learn that this was just the climax of the first act. Now that people were freed from the primal fear of the unknown stalking their nights and their children, they were seeing with a clearer vision, and already he was detecting on the net a shift in opinion.

Reason always seemed such a fragile thing, he thought, a lone quiet voice too easily drowned by the passions of the crowd. But it was reason that had found the fulcrum and the lever. The dramatic destruction of Steel, the personal drama played out on the street between Beldan and Hunter, the recorded message from Steel himself: together these had been an explosion under the juggernaut of public opinion, even as it crushed Steel beneath its wheels. The explosion had sent the public imagination wobbling uncertainly along a new course, toward an uncharted wilderness where none could predict or control its path. Except perhaps the one who had planned and shaped the blast. He would use the drama, make it his road to Damascus, his conversion from skeptic to believer, and more: to champion of the rights of a new form of life whose first representative was so cruelly and senselessly cut down. It was like an enormous chess game, thought Samuels, with Beldan and Hunter the unwitting pawns and Steel the piece that had drawn his opponents' ire and fire, whose sacrifice opened the way to the main game.

One other pair of eyes watched with rare perception. The eyes were dimmer than they had been, the body no longer so agile and responsive, but the mind was still keen. They saw another replay of the scene in the street, saw another replay of Miriam being feted by the Mayor, and understood. He felt sorry for Beldan's pain, sorry even for Hunter's pain, knowing few others watching her triumph would see it. He could see it, he could see it in the set of her shoulders and in the smile that looked thin as new ice on black water, covering unseen currents and waiting to break under the fall of a tear. But then, he knew it was there to be seen. He knew why she had done what she had done, that her empathy was one of her greatest strengths: and who could stand when their own strength was the weapon wielded against them?

The irony was fitting, he thought, that those who could not see beyond what a body was made of would fail to think outside the limitations of their own. Samuels had seen it, and more, had helped do what he could not do unaided. It had been hard to lose so much of himself, harder to see it, so much harder to feel it yet live through it: for no less intimate a link could achieve the precision remote control required. But what was life, if not to do what one had to do, careless of cost?

He sighed and flexed his fingers, stiff and strange. This new body was still strange to him, he had yet to fully make it his own; but that was merely a matter of time. And he now had plenty of that.

Book II:
The Geneh War

I know you despise me; allow me to say, it is because you do not understand me. — Elizabeth Gaskell, North and South

CHAPTER 1 – THIEF

The thief spun through the open window and landed silently on the floor, crouching on her fingertips and the balls of her feet.

She paused: listening, watching, sniffing the air. The house was quiet except for the occasional creaking of a chair and other faint sounds of a presence. It was dark but she could see well enough, for the dark was softened by a faint light spilling into the hallway from a room out of her line of sight: the same room from which the sounds emanated. She smelt man, a faint musky sweaty odor, and a ripple of liquid desire ran down her belly to her thighs. She smiled at her own reaction. The excitement of her latest adventure was spawning excitements of a different and distracting kind. She tightened her stomach and her resolve: she had not lived this long by letting her focus fall prey to such distractions.

She smiled again, more sharply, and moved silently towards the room. She waited just out of sight, but there was no sign that the man knew she was here. The creaking and rustling continued as before. She extended a small mirror unobtrusively into the doorway at floor level and saw him. He was seated facing away from her, immersed in an interactive holographic display as he manipulated a maze of complex diagrams and images. She slowly crept into the room but the man must have had surprisingly acute senses, or perhaps he had always known she was there, for he turned sharply and stared at her.

He saw a long, lithe woman with dark straight hair, dressed in a skintight suit patterned in grey and black, its waist accentuated by a belt holding an assortment of tools and pouches. Her most striking feature, he thought, was her large golden eyes, luminous like a cat's. Though perhaps some would consider the long black tail even more remarkable.

He smiled at her and she smiled back. "I'm glad to see you back in one piece, Katlyn," he said. "How did it go?"

"The usual," she said with a light shrug, and presented him with a handful of diamonds and emeralds. She often brought him things of beauty like this, little tributes from her nightly adventures. But while valuable, they were never more than a fraction of what she could have taken, and hardly commensurate with the risks she took in acquiring them. Those risks were for something else entirely.

She sat on his lap and put her arms around his neck, wiggling seductively. "Ah Katlyn," he sighed, "You are a temptress. Aren't you too young for me? Shouldn't you find someone your own age?" She grinned. "Pah! Boys my age are so immature. I like a man with some years behind him. Someone with experience. Someone who knows what a girl likes." She emphasized the point by doing something with her tail that a normal woman couldn't.

"You're going to be the death of me one day, Katlyn," he laughed, picking her up and carrying her off to his bedroom.

Chapter 2 – Lover

Katlyn woke with the sun streaming onto the bed through the one-way glass window, stretching luxuriantly. She hummed to herself. Life was good. She had excitement, the thrill of a long, dangerous and grand quest, and a man who knew how to make her quiver. Daniel had already gotten up and was probably working on one of his projects. She would have liked more of him. But she could be happy having any of him.

She thought back to how they had reached this point. He had been her guide, her teacher, her mentor. She knew what the world thought of her kind. But he had raised her as his own, and all he had ever shown her was love and understanding. Growing up had been difficult. She had studied genetic engineering herself. Not like he had, but she was quick to grasp ideas and had a fair understanding of the field if not its more intricate details. She knew that her making had not been without risks, but it had been a fair gamble. There had certainly been pains both physical and psychological as she grew. But she had survived and she could not resent it. She was alive, happy and healthy. And what more could man or beast want? She smiled again, wondering: *and which are you, Katlyn?*

The hardest part had been puberty. She had the same needs as any human woman, only more so because of her exquisite nervous system. She had about twice the number of nerves and they were twenty percent faster than normal. The world felt wondrous to her touch, but that came with the price of frustration when her nerves wanted stimulation she couldn't have. What stimulation she could have was glorious, but sometimes she would wake at night with her nerves screaming for the kind of release she knew could be had, and was had, only not by her.

Finally she could bear it no longer and confronted him. "Listen, Daniel, I don't understand you! You still think of me as if I'm a twelve-year-old girl, but look at me! I'm a woman! You treat me as if I am your daughter. But look at me! I'm not! You of all people should know I'm not! And I know you love me and not as a child, I know you want me, I can smell it! And that drives me crazy too! You are some crazy noble idiot who wants me and knows he wants me but hides it from himself!"

"Oh, Katlyn," he'd sighed. "Surely you know I can't. I might not be your father, but I raised you like one and you are still a little girl in my eyes. I just feel it would be monstrous. I feel I would be using you, betraying you."

"Oh you fool!" she had shouted. "You have taught me to think. You have always told me to use logic, reason, facts! Tell me which of those are on your side! Do I have to tell you again? You are not my father! I am a grown woman, able to make my own choices: a woman you have taught to make her own choices. At least give me the respect to give me a good answer. Are you ashamed of me? Despite all you've done for me – do you too think of me as some kind of monster, some kind of thing it would defile you to touch?"

"No! You know that isn't true!"

"And don't you get it? I love you! And not in the way I loved you as a child! Then I loved you as if you were my father, too. Yes, I was a child – then. But I am a woman now, and I love you as a woman. I want you as a woman. And if you reject me – then who else is there for me to love?"

"Oh Katlyn, my unique, lovely child, don't you see? That's the problem. We're thrown here together, I've looked after you and I'm the only man you really know, the only man you've ever really known. How can I take advantage of that without using you? You deserve better than that. One day we will be free and you'll find a man you can truly want and love, not just someone who will feel he raised you to become his personal sex toy!"

She hissed at him. Then she stopped. "Oh you sweet, darling idiot. But you are torturing me to be kind! Please just think about what I've said. I understand what you're saying. But your love for me is not using me. I know what I want, in full knowledge of what I want and why. You have taught me to do that above all else. How many times have I heard you rail against the people in power who think they know better than anyone else, who think they are so wise they deserve to rule others? Then what are you doing to me? I am no longer a child, Daniel. I need you. I want you. I love you. Think about it. Please."

She could feel the tears forming in her eyes and she didn't want him to see, so she spun and bounded from the room. Then she curled up in her bed, crying softly.

But that night he had knocked quietly on her door, and when she opened it had simply said "Oh Katlyn", and held her in his arms. Then she learned that her dreams had been true, and she knew the joy she had never been able to hold once the dreams had fled. They had been together ever since.

Chapter 3 – Hunter

It was her first day on the job. She had graduated from the Police Academy with high honors, had excelled in the theory and practice of detective work, and on the strength of that had been assigned to the Special Crimes Unit. It was an exciting opportunity and she was looking forward to putting her skills to work. Fighting crime was a passion many kids shared but few turned into a career, and she faced this day with high anticipation.

Four hours later she was bored. Or frustrated. She couldn't quite decide which.

True, there was a lot of crime fighting going on. Unfortunately none of it involved her. Well, none of the exciting part of actually investigating. They had put her on the cold case program. "Yes," her new Chief had said, "you did well at school (*school!* she'd thought). But we have a lot of experienced detectives here and a lot of work so important it must be done: just not important enough for those experienced detectives to waste their time doing it." When he made it clear that the important work would be in a back room with a computer, her attempt to impose calm on her facial muscles must have been slower than her feelings' revelation of the contrary. He had fixed her with a stern look then calmly told her that if she was as good a detective as maybe she might become one day, she should probably come to her own conclusions from what he had just told her.

What could you say to that? She decided she liked her new boss, even if he was a bastard.

He had then shunted her off to the IT department for more details. These were imparted by a young man with intense blue eyes and red hair, which tried to be well behaved except for random swatches that insisted on creating their own contradictory styles. His name was Fergus, he possessed a quick intelligence, and she decided he was quite cute in his geeky way. She was also amused to notice that he had a polite way of checking out newly met women that was mildly complimentary if you liked it, but too subtle to be sure about if you didn't. His ready and harmless smile no doubt helped him get away with it. She wasn't even sure he knew he was doing it himself.

Cold cases, he explained, were those where leads had dried up and there was no obvious way forward to a resolution, so they had been shelved in favor of more immediate work. Shelved but not forgotten, as you never knew when you might get a break. But if nobody was looking, who would recognize the break when it came?

And, he added, blue eyes twinkling, before the project could happen it first had to be funded, and to be funded had to be sold to people whose main concern in life was budgets. But budgets had an in as well as an out, and higher case-solving rates were good for publicity and therefore good for funding. However, he had noted, finger raised: while they had originally sold the project on the cold case aspect, there was a more speculative and exciting side. The same processes needed to fish for new evidence on old cases could also uncover unexpected new ones. There were many relatively minor crimes barely worth investigating on their own merits – if merits were the correct term for crimes – but you never knew when they were the visible signals of something larger buried out of sight, like the swirl of a crocodile in the Nile. With luck, they would detect a few crocodiles or if not at least be alerted to where they might be lurking. The importance of the unimportant had been indelibly impressed on the collective consciousness of lawmen early in the century: when a failure to notice oddities such as men learning to fly jets but not land them, had meant failing to stop them returning to earth indirectly by first flying into buildings.

Some bright spark had had the brilliant idea of pooling all crime data into one database and letting an advanced artificial intelligence loose on it. While AIs were now common they were most effective at tasks with clear limits and definitions. So they were usually seen in roles such as automated doormen or reception services, medical diagnosis and the more straightforward legal services. A task like this one needed open-ended data analysis, correlation and pattern recognition with no predefined structure or assumptions. This was something humans were good at, but no human could absorb or process the amount of data an AI could. They had no way yet to give a person the data capacity of an AI, but perhaps they could get an AI to think more like a person.

Her job would be working on the interfaces for getting information into the AI and also training it on how to interpret the data in useful ways. The powers above wanted all records back at least 20 years to be in the system. Cold cases went back even further and some crime careers went even longer than that undetected: but the further back you went, the more unreliable memories became and the less evidence and witnesses you could actually find. So 20 years was chosen as the best compromise between wishes and reality.

She did not have to worry about current or recent data, he told her. That was already in a suitable format and the aim was a direct real time link still to be perfected: a challenging project which IT themselves were looking forward to. For the immediate future that would require human oversight, and there was so much of it that her "current" data feed would be at least two weeks old. Her job would be the older data, some of which existed only on paper.

"Paper!" she exclaimed, "You're kidding, right?" He laughed. "Oh, it's not as bad as it sounds. Like most advanced AIs, this one has lower level subsystems that are specialized AIs in their own right. One is already expert in image to text conversion; others have been configured as trainable data format translators – the system will have to deal with many incompatible formats. So your future doesn't hold years of typing but it does hold a lot of paperwork scanning and tweaking of format conversion utilities."

"I don't suppose the department has some low level flunky we can recruit to help with all this hack work?" she asked hopefully.

"Yes of course, what do you take us for?" he replied. Then he added with a grin, "I'm looking at her."

She groaned. "OK, I can see where I stand around here. So between us we'll be filling the AI's head with random data. How do I go about training it to make sense of it all?"

"What I would like is for you to train it positively, by examining the data yourself and telling the AI what it means. But if you could do that we wouldn't need the AI in the first place. So what I'll get is the other way around: the AI will tell you its findings then you will analyze the reasoning behind them and explain where it is right or wrong. Eventually that process will generate principles to guide it."

"What if I make a mistake?"

"Try not to. But even if you do make a mistake, you'll just slow things down a bit, not completely derail them. The AI doesn't give anything a one hundred percent rating, not even your sage advice. It will occasionally retry ideas you've rejected in the past and look for contradictions in your responses; if it finds any it will complain to you. You can then refine the rules. If you keep rejecting something, it will recheck less and less until it eventually gives up."

She agreed the idea was brilliant. She agreed its time had come. She even thought that her initial impression might have been hasty, and this work could be exciting and important. So armed with her reignited enthusiasm, she went to work.

It wasn't long before her enthusiasm drowned under the unhappy confluence of enormous volumes of random data flowing into an AI of invisible intellect, which then poured the resulting stew onto her head. It might be the most advanced AI the department could afford, she thought, but it still bore out the ancient wisdom of the wag who'd first said AI meant not "Artificial Intelligence" but "Artificial Idiot".

At first she had thought that analyzing the AI's correlation reports and training the AI would be interesting, but the AI soon trained her otherwise. When her new boss had dropped by and asked what she had discovered, she had wearily replied "Garbage, rubbish and creative nonsense."

Part of the problem was that the AI was still in the early stage of its learning curve. The other part was she had to be careful. Despite Fergus's assurance that mistakes weren't fatal, the AI made enough mistakes of its own without her adding to them. She couldn't just reject the machine's wrong correlations: she had to think of some way to explain, in a way the AI would understand, why the correlation was meaningless. Otherwise she ran the risk of throwing out a good principle just because a specific example didn't work. Generally that required analysis of why the AI thought there was a link and how to explain its error. But how did you explain to a computer that the presence of red roses in a held-up florist, a vase in a robbed bank and the garden of a burgled house was not relevant, whereas a single red rose placed on each of several murder victims was?

That part was certainly a challenge. But the combination of 90% mindless tedium and 10% hard thinking on how to outwit a witless machine rapidly wore her out.

After a few hours she leaned back, stretched out the kinks in her muscles, and just stopped to think. This wasn't what she'd had in mind for her exciting crime-fighting career. Unfortunately the image she'd had in her mind, that even her years of study had failed to dislodge, was from her childhood when it involved capes and super-powers. It was a sad fact that neither were issued by the police department. She rubbed her eyes. *Oh well*, she thought, *every profession from acting to politics makes you pay your dues.* And for all her pride in her accomplishments to date, she knew that she was now just as much an apprentice as any hopeful carpenter starting out on his or her career. And who knew, maybe she would actually find something worth reporting.

She had her breaks, of course. She got coffee, chatted to the other inhabitants, started to get to know people. Most of them were friendly enough, even if most looked slightly harried by their own pressures. But she was the new girl and people were willing to chat and get to know her. Some of them looked through her as if her existence was not worth noticing, but most were friendly enough. She thought she would like it here.

Before she knew it, her boss popped in again and told her it was time to go. "So, how did you like your first day?"

"Well, it's not quite what I dreamed of, Chief Ramos, but I know I have to start somewhere. The AI is clinically insane, but I think I'm making progress."

He smiled. "I'm glad you're settling in. Your face when I gave you this assignment looked like I might have a rebellion on my hands. Anyway, a bunch of us meet for drinks down at Joe's. You're welcome to come along, get to know the crowd some more."

"Sorry, I'd like that but maybe tomorrow. My family has a little job-start party planned for me tonight. So good night."

"Good night, Miriam."

CHAPTER 4 – FAMILY

Miriam's family was delighted to celebrate her new job with a party. They were delighted to celebrate anything with a party. They had always told her that if you didn't take time to enjoy life, why were you living it?

The party was at her favorite uncle's apartment. Seth Hunter was a grizzled, no-nonsense man several years older than her father; he had never married himself despite having had a string of lady friends. But, he said, he liked the ladies the way he liked horses: the thoroughbreds liked to run free not settle down on the farm to chew hay. Personally she thought he was speaking more about himself than about them: the way she had seen some of them look at him, she was pretty sure they wouldn't have minded settling down in some hay.

He was also the richest man in her immediate family. Over his years he had converted a little corner hardware store into a string of franchises and eventually sold out to a national chain. Now he put his hand to a variety of business schemes, some successful, others less so, but inexorably his wealth grew.

One result was this apartment, an elegantly appointed suite high above the city streets. Miriam had been coming here since she was a child and loved just looking out at the city. When she was a little girl it had looked to her like a fairyland of lights. Now she knew that down in the streets it was often a tawdry, dirty place; a home to villains, bullies and scoundrels. But up here all that was purified by distance and the essence of the city was distilled into a place of magic possibilities, as if the grime of the city's underside could not touch the spirit that made it beautiful. The possibility had never occurred to her that anything could happen to make her so cynical that she could see it differently.

Uncle Seth had hired caterers for the evening. He believed that parties were to be enjoyed not worked at, and he was quite happy to spread his wealth to others in order to achieve that end. So there was nothing for Miriam to do but wander around chatting to friends and family, browse from the delicious morsels that came within reach and sip the delightfully fresh champagne. Eventually she found herself where she always ended up, at the window looking out over the city.

Seth saw her from across the room and smiled. *My memories of her are like time-lapse photos*, he thought to himself. *She has been standing at that window like that since she was a little girl. Now look at her.* Her hair was still dark, even darker than her skin, cascading in ringlets past her shoulders. But now in place of the gangly little girl she had been stood a tall, slender but full-breasted woman, relaxed and confident, looking out at her city. *That is how she always looked: as if it is her city.*

He loved her as if she was his own. He loved all his nephews and nieces, but Miriam owned a special place in his affections. Her quick wits and self-confidence captivated him and her determination and drive impressed him. In her life she had seen her share of ugliness, but it had not touched her; she shrugged the mud off her Teflon skin as if it wasn't worthy of her attention. He smiled, remembering the time when he had been visiting his brother and she had come home crying, bruised and bleeding. On her way home from school she had come across another child being bullied. Her temper had escalated from outrage when she first saw it to incandescence when the bullies ignored her perfectly reasonable demand to stop. Her common sense had no chance against her anger any more than her fists had a chance against the bullies, and she had suffered along with that other child. But her response after the tears and Band-Aids had been to learn not prudence but martial arts.

He was not surprised that she had chosen a career in the police force. Her family would have preferred the greater pay and safety of a legal career but Miriam had done what she always did: listened, considered, and did what she thought was best. He knew she would see even more ugliness in her new career. He hoped that she would remain untouched by it; that she would always look at the world the way she was looking at it now. The world, he thought, might not deserve that: but she did.

"I knew you'd end up here," said a gravelly voice at Miriam's shoulder. "Oh, Uncle Seth, thanks for this," she said, leaning her head onto his shoulder. "Well, I've finally done it. I'm a real cop now."

"Is it what you expected?"

She laughed. "It's only been one day! Truth be told, not so far. They've put me straight onto hackwork. But I suppose they always do. Eventually I'll get a break into something more exciting. Worse comes to worse, next year we might get another newbie or two. Then I can stroll around lording it over them."

He squeezed her shoulder. "I'm sure you'll do just fine. Made any friends yet?"

"I haven't had time to make any real friends except with the coffee machine. You'd like him. Strong, sensual, just a hint of the unpredictable. But most of the people there are nice. Some of them act as if I'm not there but I haven't had much chance to show I am yet."

"Any problem characters? I imagine there are, in a police station."

"Oh, not really. One guy seems to resent my presence. Detective Stone. Well, former detective Stone. He's been promoted to a desk job in reward for his years of service but I think it's chafing on him. I had to get some information from him and he looked at me as if I'm an idiot, as if I should know everything about the place after five minutes. Maybe he's like you, doesn't like girls," she teased. "Or maybe he's just unpleasant. I'm sure I'll be able to cope, whatever his problem is."

He smiled and shook her hand formally. "Well, congratulations again, my little girl. And here's cheers to your sparkling new career!" They toasted sparkling new champagne to that then he headed off to chat with more relatives.

"And of course you're staying the night," he called over his shoulder. "Don't worry about having to drive home: relax and enjoy yourself."

Tired as she was after her day, Miriam spent the rest of the evening in a pleasant haze of chatting about the past, catching up with the news of her relatives' families and careers, sipping champagne and speculating on the future. In her dreams the pleasant buzz continued as background while the shapes of the future rose from the city before her and beckoned. But when she woke, she could not say what those shapes had been or where they had taken her.

Chapter 5 – AI

Miriam settled into her routine. She got better and faster at importing old data into the system, while the AI became better and faster at inventing imaginary connections. Slowly she got to know the people she worked with and they her. Some people stayed much as they were on her first day, polite but uninterested in allowing her into their personal universe; a few remained cold; some became friends. Much like any new job, she supposed.

Overall, she was unexcited by her job's routine but happy about its potential and happy to be here. There was nothing else to do, she thought, but to do the best she could, take whatever opportunities presented themselves, and hope for a break sooner rather than later.

After six months she was efficient at the boring parts and finding more pleasure in dealing with the still flakey AI. She had even promoted a few of its less eccentric offerings up her chain of command. So visible progress was being made. Not enough to make her thrilled and certainly not enough to make the departmental gods thrilled, but enough to propitiate their wrath.

She saw that IT had succeeded in dumping another large load of data into her system and wondered what the AI would make of this lot. She had a lot to do with the IT department, of course. She was not officially in charge of the project, but her position as prime AI interpreter and trainer made her the first port of call in any questions and issues. And from her side she needed to keep her finger on the pulse of what IT was doing.

Having made sure the data was digestible, Miriam let the AI loose on it and waited for the results. She had nothing to do but wait for now, so she took the opportunity to sip on her coffee and just follow her thoughts where they would lead her.

They quickly led her to the IT department. She wasn't sure if she was happy or sad at the moment when it came to them: or more accurately one of them. She had started a friendship with Fergus, the cute – at least in her estimation – guy who had introduced her to the AI, and it had rapidly developed into something more. While relationships among staff were forbidden if they went out into the world together with guns, nobody cared about rookies and engineers. They had had a really good time together, but after the first flush of romance faded both had come to realize that too much time together just wasn't going to work. Not that anything was wrong with either of them, just that they weren't right for each other. So they had regretfully called it a day.

Ah well, she thought, it was something; and it had been good. Not just the sex but the romance and the fun had certainly helped ease the tension of the job for both of them. Miriam refused to have regrets for having a happy time even if the happy time had to end: in her view the pain of ending merely underlined the happiness that had been lived. The pain would fade, she knew, while having been happy could never be lost.

She had even picked up a few colorful curses during their time together, a kind of souvenir of the relationship that also would never be lost. Not unusually for geeks he had a penchant for fantasy and epic mythology: and why limit yourself to Christian mythology, he had pointed out with his cheeky grin, when there are so many more exotic ones to choose from? She smiled at the memory. She had heard he had now taken up with a very cute blonde in the public relations department; he seemed to be on a one-man mission to rescue the reputation of geeks everywhere.

She came out of her reverie when the AI had finished digesting its lunch and started making a few suggestions. *More of the same*, she decided. *No. No. No. You must be kidding. No. Nice try, but no. Sigh. I need to invent an AI to screen the AI's output*, she thought. *But hang on, this one is interesting. Weird, but interesting.* A string of minor but odd burglaries, if you could call it a string when it was scattered across half the city and into the suburbs. Normally she would promote it up the usual chain for the attention of property crimes but this time the AI had highlighted other correlations, one of which made her eyes bug.

She decided to do a bit more investigating herself and started quizzing the AI. Half an hour later she was looking at a printout that summarized their findings. She still didn't know what it meant, but her instincts told her it meant something.

CHAPTER 6 – GENEH

Miriam walked briskly up to her boss's office, resisting the impulse to actually skip; the door was open so she went in. He was standing with a couple of detectives, looking at his screen and pointing. They all looked both puzzled and grim. She did not think she should interrupt so she started to back out, but Ramos saw her and said, "Yes, Hunter?"

"Sorry to interrupt, Chief. I've found something interesting I thought you should see. But it isn't urgent and I can come back later."

"No, stay, a break from this bit of craziness won't hurt. What is it?"

"Well, the AI flagged a string of minor burglaries where some jewelry was stolen. They all represent a fair bit of money to people like us, but not if you look at the income of the owners. Half of them probably wouldn't even have reported it if they didn't have to for their insurance. But would you believe, at random times since the burglaries five of the victims have had amounts of money from half a million to two million dollars mysteriously vanish from their accounts, destination unknown. And that's not all. You know how IT has started feeding in news from the wider community as well? The AI, bless it's brainless bits, noted that a full quarter of the victims were present at a big fundraiser last year for President Felton."

"Coincidence?"

"I quizzed the AI. I can't vouch for the details of its calculations, but according to the AI's statistical subsystem the probability of it being chance is only two percent."

His eyebrows went up. "So! Interesting! Let me see what you've got there."

She handed him the printout and he scanned it. Then his eyes went very still. He called the other detectives over to take a look. Then they all glanced at each other. Ramos said, "Hunter, I think you should see this. See this list of attendees at that fundraiser? See this name, that isn't on your list of burglaries?"

He turned his screen around so she could see it. "This image was taken from a short video captured by a security camera near the city apartment of that man. Shortly after a minor robbery in his apartment last night. Some gems were taken."

Miriam looked at the screen. The image was slightly blurred and enhanced for light, but clear enough to see why the detectives had been so serious. It was a woman leaping across the rooftops, caught in mid-flight, looking past the camera as if she hadn't noticed it, or perhaps had known it was there but didn't care. She had large, luminous golden eyes that seemed to reflect the lights beyond. And a long black tail streaming behind her.

Miriam looked at Ramos, startled. "What the hell?" she asked.

"What the hell indeed," he agreed. "What do you make of it?"

"Well, if it wasn't both illegal and unlikely, I'd say it was a cross between a girl and a cat!"

"Watch this."

He played the video from which the still had been taken. The woman was extremely fast and agile, and she was only visible for a couple of seconds as she bounded into and out of camera range.

"I don't suppose that video is a hoax?"

"The techs say not. I suppose if the CIA was trying to fool us they might be able to do it, but we're pretty sure it's genuine. That's not a video sent in by a member of the public who might be pranking us. It's taken from a fairly secure feed and there are no digital signs of tampering."

She examined the still image more carefully. Not really a cross between a girl and a cat, she saw: more a girl with a few catlike additions. Science fiction stories from her youth, romantic tales of genetics before the whole field of human genetic engineering had been made illegal, now haunted her thoughts and would not be silenced. Instead they escaped through her tongue.

"Um, Chief, would you fire me if I said that looked like a geneh?"

"Genehs don't exist. You know the penalty is death. The scientists who used to work on it are lucky the penalty applied to the genehs not the scientists."

"I know. But look at it! What do *you* think it is?"

"If I knew, I *might* have fired you. But I don't have any better ideas right now."

The childhood ghosts haunting her memory shoved one of their number forward into sharper focus. A man who had been a hero in her young mind, now disgraced and largely forgotten. "I think I know someone we could ask," she said uncertainly.

Ramos looked at her. "I think I know who you mean. But really, if I thought it was a geneh I'd pass this on to GenInt Enforcement – except something this hot might ruin my reputation if it's the false alarm it almost certainly is. And we don't have the staff to spare to follow thin leads like that, especially ones leading to a man like him who is unlikely to let police anywhere near him."

She looked around at the others in the room, who were all regarding her silently. "I could go," she offered timidly but hopefully.

He stared at her with narrowed eyes. "Really keen to escape your desk job, aren't you, Hunter?" he said. Then he paused. "But sometimes... yes. Someone else has been keen to escape his desk lately too. Maybe I'll give you both a field excursion. Then when you're sent packing at least we can file it, bump it up to someone who will forget it, and you can both get back to your real jobs."

He tapped on his phone. "Stone, get in here."

~~~

Stone came in and Ramos said, "Stone, you know Hunter here. Well, she's found something interesting. Take a look at this."

After looking at the video and reading her report, Stone looked up. "Curious," he said. "Definitely curious."

"If it wasn't for the link the AI threw up about these bigwig supporters of the President, I'd probably file this under 'prank' and move on. But we have to show we've covered all bases when we have something like this on video. The last thing we want is to be blindsided and find we *do* have a geneh running around targeting the President's friends – and they find out we ignored it. Even if it's someone with a death wish just pretending to be a geneh. It would probably *be* the last thing we did, at least in these jobs.

"So, Miriam found this – I'm not sure I'll thank her yet – and you,

Jack, haven't been as happy as I'd hoped after your promotion. I don't want to take anyone off what other things they're doing for this. So Jack, meet your new partner. Miriam, say hi to Jack. Don't get used to it – I expect your partnership will only last this one trip. But who knows, maybe you'll surprise me. You're both going to visit the neither late nor lamented Dr Tagarin to discuss what this thing might be. I shall be surprised if he lets you through his door, but let's see how persuasive you can be."

Stone looked at Miriam. He had never thawed to her and it didn't look like the ice age was ending quite yet. Miriam wished she knew what she did that bugged him. Stone said, "OK kid, let's get to work. Try not to get in the way."

Chapter 7 – GenInt

As they drove, Miriam watched Stone out of the corner of her eye. His eyes were watching the road and he didn't look interested in chatting. "Um. Detective Stone?"

His eyes flicked to her then back to the road. "You have something against quiet?"

"No. No. I just thought if we were going to work together, I should get to know you some more."

"I think this is going to be a very short-term relationship. And we're just going to interview some guy. If he lets us. We don't need to be friends to do that."

After a few moments Miriam asked, "Why do you dislike me?"

He looked at her, startled. "Well, that's a surprisingly direct question. Most people aren't quite so open about things like that. Did you miss beating around the bush class or something?"

Miriam gave up and looked away. "Sorry."

"Look, kid, it's nothing personal. Yet. But I've seen you hotshot newbies before – yes, I read your file when you were assigned. That's why they used to call me 'Detective.' When you're good at school you think you know everything. You get in the way. Think you can change the world. Think everyone else should bow to your manifest brilliance. But you know nothing. Some of you become good cops. Eventually. None of you start that way."

"I don't think I'm that bad. Am I?"

"I just don't care to find out. But look at you. They put you in a backroom job to keep you out of trouble and get something useful out of you while you learn how to feed yourself. Then you get lucky and see something and you think, maybe I can impress the boss with this. Maybe get promoted like I deserve. So you march in with your fancy report and get even luckier. So lucky the boss sends you out on the real job you've dreamed of, badge on hip and gun in hand. But the trouble with being lucky is people tend to confuse luck with talent. That can get you killed. Luck has a way of running out to buy itself a drink when you most need it to hang around."

After a few seconds Miriam said quietly. "I see. I'll try to keep out of your way."

Stone glanced at her. He had expected the usual lifted chin and proud rejoinder. Maybe there was hope for this one after all.

~~~

They parked in the circular drive before the entrance and got out. Dr Tagarin might have been disappointed in how his career had flamed out but he surely could not be disappointed in how he had done financially. His mansion was set in beautiful natural woodland and for all that you could tell it was a fortress it was an attractive and comfortable looking one.

As they walked toward the gate Stone said, "This guy is a hard case and given his history he won't like the law. He'll have his AI preprogrammed on how to deal with the police so this is probably going to be a waste of time. It'll give us the run-around, and it'll know we're asking for a favour and that we don't have any legal grounds to push too hard. We won't even know whether he's talking to us via his machine, or the machine is just blowing us off on its own while he's sitting in his Jacuzzi with a bunch of blondes."

Miriam shrugged. What could they do about it? They were here; they had to try.

They waved their badges in front of the security system, which automatically queried the embedded electronics. Miriam noticed the Beldan Robotics logo under the speaker grille. Naturally she had heard of the Beldan AIs – very high end and very expensive – and she wondered whether her job would be easier if the department's budget had stretched that far. Another part of her wondered whether if she had a brighter AI she would be here at all.

"Please place your palms on the plate for biometric confirmation," the door said mechanically. They did as asked, Miriam's opinion of the

Beldan AIs dropping a notch in the face of its crudeness. But on confirming their identities the system raised the priority of the visitor interaction, and after a short delay a more sophisticated level of the AI spoke in a cultured male voice:

"Good afternoon, officers. How can I help you?"

"We would like to see Dr Tagarin," replied Stone.

"Please state your business."

"We have a problem that we think Dr Tagarin might be able to assist us with."

"Dr Tagarin informs me that given how the law has 'assisted' him in the past he is not interested in assisting the law. In any event he can't imagine how he could help you and has better things to do with his time."

"Look, this concerns a string of strange burglaries and there are aspects of the case that Dr Tagarin might be able to shed some light on. Please remind Dr Tagarin that he is a citizen and it is his duty to cooperate with the law."

The machine paused, whether thinking through a complex problem, communicating with its master or merely pausing for effect they had no way to know.

"Dr Tagarin informs me that he is aware he is a citizen and fully aware of his rights as one. He has no obligation to speak to you unless you have a warrant. He further advises me that he would be astounded if you had any grounds for one and he has, to quote, 'a team of sharks in lawyer robes' available to sue the city if you try one without proper grounds."

"I told you he was a hard case," Jack muttered to Miriam.

"However Dr Tagarin is a law-abiding citizen who is willing to assist the police in their reasonable enquiries. Thus to avoid you wasting more of your time he wishes to assure you that he has no knowledge of any burglaries and, given that his habits and activities do not include strolls down dark alleys or nocturnal adventures along the rooftops, he is quite sure he has seen nothing that could help you. He adds that he keenly sympathizes with the plight of our overworked police and therefore recommends you pursue more fruitful lines of enquiry elsewhere."

"It is not as a witness but for his specific expertise that we wish to speak to him."

"Dr Tagarin refers you to his previous statements and wonders why you think he would provide unpaid expert advice. There are many experts, some of who may not yet have been abused by the legal system whose agents you are. Find one of them. Good day."

With that, the pattern on the screen indicating active engagement folded in on itself and vanished.

"Wait," said Miriam, and flashed a file to the interface.

Nothing happened for minute. Miriam looked at Jack and shrugged, "Oh well, it was worth a try," and turned to leave. Then the entrance said, "Please hold." Jack raised his eyebrow at Miriam.

After a few more minutes the gate slid silently into the fence. "You may proceed up the path to the door," advised the AI.

They entered and walked up the path, their feet crunching on the small stones. The path had clear walls on either side with a curved, vine-covered vault over it barring access to the gardens beyond. The vines had fragrant flowers and yellow butterflies fluttered happily among them. The vibrant delicacy of it made a strange contrast to the forbidding walls beyond.

When they reached the door it opened to reveal a man wearing a formal suit and a neutral, distantly polite expression. He looked like a butler, except that butlers were generally not six foot two, built like fighters and with callused hands and fingers. "I am Dr Tagarin's butler. You may call me 'James'. Please follow me," he said, stepping aside and gesturing inside with a sweep of his arm.

Miriam and Jack looked at each other and followed him inside, down a corridor and into a small but luxuriously appointed waiting room. "Please make yourself at home. The machine in the corner can supply most styles of coffee. Dr Tagarin will be with you in a short while." With that, the overqualified butler bowed and exited the room.

Jack walked over to the coffee machine and said, "Now this is a civilized use of technology. What would you like, Hunter?"

"Do you think we have the time?"

"I know how these things work. Unless they want something from you, when someone asks you to wait they're going to make you wait as long as they think they can get away with, if not longer. Sometimes they do it because they're jerks exercising their power. Sometimes they're just pissed off at you. Be thankful this guy isn't making us wait on hard seats in a freezing room. We might as well make ourselves comfortable."

They sat down, sipping their coffees. "Mmmm! Excellent!" said

Miriam. "So while we wait – what do you know about this guy? I know the basic story but I was just a kid when it all happened. Anything you think I should know?"

"Well, when he was younger he worked for an up and coming biotech firm. He had an unusual flair for both IT and molecular biology, and he was instrumental in developing key patents for the company. Those patents enabled a whole slew of medical applications of stem cells for curing disease, including regenerating tissues and organs. The company went stratospheric, and because it was a startup with a good employee share scheme, plus the bonus shares he got for his personal contributions, his own wealth went stratospheric with it." He waved his hand around the room as if to say, as you see.

"Anyway, the average guy might have retired, but I suppose the average guy wouldn't have achieved what he had in the first place. And he had a passion for his work. He didn't even quit and start his own company, which he had the money to do. He was happy to be given his own research division so he could keep right on working on the science while someone else ran the business. Some of his original patents involved genetically engineering stem cells. You know, to fix genetic defects or give cellular immunity against some hard to cure viruses. There were already enough people up in arms about that – you know, meddling with nature – but then he made his big mistake. He got interested in doing more than fixing nature's mistakes and started looking into improving it."

"That doesn't sound so bad," said Miriam as she sipped her spicy coffee, the fragrant steam caressing her nose. The coffee itself, she knew, had been genetically engineered. She wondered if that was a subtle message Tagarin intended for visitors.

"It does when he's not just trying to enhance some weakling's muscles, but starts working on using cloning technology to turn his stem cells into a whole new type of human being."

"Yes, I remember that. But I thought that kind of work was already illegal?"

"Not really. The environmentalists and more fundamentalist religious types had been opposing genetic engineering of almost anything for years. One lot hated it for destroying the purity of nature and the environment; the other for playing God. So there were a lot of bans and restrictions in place. But the medical benefits of his kind of research were so great that the government couldn't bring itself to ban it outright. They just banned it from Federal funding – though of course not from Federal taxation if they made a profit out of it. And he was in a rich company, which had become rich by pushing the envelope: one that didn't want government grants and the strings that came with them. That kind of thing had been declared unethical by all number of experts but some people just don't care about that, I guess. And who can say they're wrong?"

"So what exactly happened?"

"Well as I said, he started work on genetically engineering human stem cells to give them new traits and trying to clone them to grow new people. And he wasn't alone – there were other groups looking into the same things. I guess the technology had finally arrived. The greenies, the religious right – and the religious left, for that matter – went ballistic. If they were against engineering the genes of animals and plants – well, you can imagine how they felt about meddling with ourselves."

"Yes..."

"But it got worse. I have to tell you – my parents were atheists and always taught me the value of science, and I've never seen anything in this world to show otherwise. But it seemed like the better technology made people's lives, the more people like the greenies were against it; and the more science taught us about the real world, the more people turned to religion. Between the masses convinced that technology is dangerous, the masses convinced they knew God's opinions and the activists on both sides who saw those masses as their road to power – it got ugly."

He sipped his coffee with a frown of distaste, but it was for the bitterness of the memories not the coffee. "And then some of the people who had been working on these things felt brave enough to get their experiments to the stage of fetuses – they had artificial wombs by then. Not all of them worked very well – and the activists found out. Even the average mom and pop who weren't particularly ideological were horrified by some of the pictures that came out of it. So the whole thing spun out of control. It went all the way to the United Nations. All genetic engineering of humans except for direct medical use, and all cloning of humans for any purpose, were banned around the world as fundamental violations of human rights and dignity. And more, any genetically engineered or cloned human was declared an inhuman abomination to be destroyed on sight. All the embryos any of them had developed were destroyed."

"The Geneh Laws. But I thought most religions opposed abortion? Why would they support that?"

Stone gave her a sour look. "As my dad said at the time, for all the church cares about embryos, burning witches is an even more time-honored pastime. And if witches are the Devil's consorts, engineered embryos are the Devil's spawn. I guess embryos are blessed with a soul whether you want them or not, unless you want them so much you make them yourself."

"But what if someone had actually created a baby?"

"Ah, well, there's where I might have something to add besides color. Tagarin and his friends had been fighting the new laws like maniacs, but they went through anyway. The UN had already acquired a lot more power over national governments than it had the previous century, and they set up the new Department of Human Genetic Integrity – GenInt – as a compulsory international regulatory body. It was run by real partisans – as I suppose you'd expect, since who else would take the job? Publicly its purpose was monitoring, oversight and ethics committees, but it had its own enforcement arm in case someone insisted on being unethical. That had to be a matter of public record, but the public – or enough of them – were quite happy to see any such monsters destroyed. Most of them supported abortion anyway, and this wasn't that different: just killing little horrors that shouldn't have existed in the first place."

"Yes, I see that. I was taught the same thing in school. About the evil of making modified humans, I mean; about how the resulting monsters were better off dead. They glossed over what they did about it if it actually happened. I thought it never had."

"And the only people you'd put in something like the enforcement arm are more fanatics: you know, true believers in the cause. The kind who wouldn't have any moral qualms about smashing labs and tossing out embryos. For the higher good and all that."

He paused, staring into his coffee as if his memories were residing there.

"But babies? You mentioned babies?"

"Yes, well. As you'd guess, Tagarin was the hotshot in the field. He hadn't made any monsters, at least none he let develop further once he knew. Despite the howls of his critics it seems he had some qualms about how far he went. I guess he thought he could learn enough from his mistakes when they happened without risking inflicting the results on a living being. But anyway, he was further along. Much further along..."

He paused again. This time, Miriam just waited.

"So. He did have a newborn in his lab, and a healthy one. What its improvements were I've no idea: I never saw it close up. But the Department enforcers found it in a raid. They knew what it was. They killed it there and then. It never made the news feeds of course. GenInt's charter allows it to keep secrets 'for the greater good and social order'. Which means they are happy to release photos of monster fetuses that would die anyway, but think the plebs will get confused if they see photos of innocent babies being shot. The plebs are likely to forget that the 'innocent babies' are demonic creations bent on destroying society. Tagarin went crazy. He's lucky they didn't shoot him too."

"But how do you know all this?"

Jack stared into his coffee a while longer.

"Tagarin reported it to the police. But he reported it as if he was under attack by criminals – which I suppose to his mind he was. I was a rookie like you back then. We had a bit of a face-off with the enforcers, but they had the law on their side. We weren't allowed to talk about it. I can tell you, because it was a long time ago and it's relevant to our case." He looked around for somewhere to spit, but the décor decided him against it. "Anyway, it wasn't pretty. But there you are."

"Jesus. No wonder he doesn't like us. I'm surprised he's seeing us at all."

"Yeah."

"But... why does GenInt still have enforcers? I don't remember hearing any cases of geneh violations since those early days."

Jack gave her a cynical look. "Have you ever seen a bureaucracy give up power? My dad was a history teacher – I guess that's the kind of thing that can make you an atheist. I still remember him laughing about the old Soviet Union, who the more they said their ideal state would wither away the more power they took. Maybe in 50 years we'll be rid of GenInt enforcers. In the meantime I'm sure they find enough misdemeanors and other excuses to flex their muscles. Not to mention the old argument that the only reason we *don't* have genehs flying around laying eggs in our children is the existence of GenInt."

"And we might just have found a real one for them," added Miriam grimly.

Then they both sat silently, he lost in his memories, she in this new picture of history. As she'd said, she had been taught the ethics of the Geneh Laws at school, and like most people simply accepted it. After all it was reasonable, wasn't it? Was it? Surely the baby they had destroyed was some kind of monster? What else could it be? But now she wondered.

Then the door opened and the butler said, "Dr Tagarin will see you now," and ushered them in to the adjoining office.

CHAPTER 8 – TAGARIN

The room was large, with a dark burgundy carpet so delightfully thick and soft that Miriam wished she could take her shoes off. Shelves holding books, instruments and memorabilia alternated with walls covered in murals or paintings. She liked the art. There were no meaningless abstract splotches: it was all recognizable and beautiful, and the human figures projected contentment, sensuality or heroism. They made a stark contrast with the room's occupant, who radiated something darker. It was like the contrast between the gardens and the house, she thought. It was hard to believe this man could have chosen that art.

He sat at a large desk of polished dark glass in the center of the room. One hand was loosely resting on the desk; his chin rested on the other as he watched them enter. He had dark brown eyes that looked like they should be lively and intelligent, but which stared at them like the glass of his desk. Or like a cobra watching a mongoose, waiting for its chance, Miriam thought. His face was hard, topped by a shock of longish chestnut hair that wasn't sure whether it wanted to be wavy or simply anarchic, swept back from his forehead like a mane. It looked like there were lines of humor about his eyes and mouth, but unused for so long that they had hardened into cynicism. He was middle aged but evidently took advantage of youth-extending medications; he had not let his body go to flab and retained a trim athleticism that sat well on his tall frame; his movements were fast, precise and yet fluid, as if he practiced martial arts. He watched silently as they seated themselves.

The butler remained, standing silently in the shadows, out of sight but never quite out of mind.

Floating in the air before Tagarin was the image Miriam had flashed to his AI: the photo of the thief in full flight.

"So," he began without any greeting. "Looking at this photo I can guess why you wanted to talk to me. But why don't you tell me? No doubt it will be amusing." But there was no trace of amusement in his voice, which was as hard as his face.

Miriam looked at Stone, who answered, "Whatever that thing is, it looks like a geneh. You were once a world leader in genetic engineering of humans. We hoped you could give us some information that might help us discover what it is and where it came from."

He had a deep, throaty laugh, well suited to the scorn he now put into it.

"Well, I presume you have computers at least as good as mine. You will have run the same analyses as I. What brainless idiot persuaded you that this is a genetically engineered human worth annoying me about? Surely it is obvious that it isn't. Or are you telling me the quality of the police forces has actually gone *down* since I last had the pleasure of dealing with you?"

Miriam looked down, glad her dark skin mostly hid the furious blush that had rushed to her cheeks. She did not usually react like that, but Tagarin spoke with a contemptuous authority that made her feel like a schoolgirl in front of the Principal, chewing her out for wetting her pants on his favorite chair.

To Miriam's further chagrin, his glassy eyes did not miss the clue. "Ha!" he said mockingly. "That's why the rookie is here?" he said, stabbing his finger at her but addressing his comment to Stone. "She's the genius? So what," he continued sarcastically to Miriam, "let me guess, you're new and trying to impress your boss? Don't they teach thinking at the Police Academy these days? Or is your boss actually dumber than you are?"

Despite her embarrassment, Miriam lifted her head to look him in the eye: not as a challenge but in honest directness. "I understand why you are bitter and I am sorry if we offend you. But I don't believe it was that stupid an idea. Seeing that photo is what persuaded you to let us in to see you, after all."

Tagarin glared at her and she felt his laser gaze dissecting her, discarding the irrelevant and finding nothing left. She feared that he would throw them out then and there for her presumption. But then he laughed again, and if there was still no friendliness in it at least there was more amusement and less derision. "Touché, Ms Hunter. Perhaps you have more courage and brains than I first gave you credit for. I would ask you to forgive the rudeness of a, as you might put it, bitter old man – except I don't care. But you have earned a reply: so yes, your photo was intriguing enough for me to find out more, even though it cannot be a geneh. However even the police would not think it worth bothering me if this is all you have. Show me the rest." His manner changed from that of a circling boxer to a dispassionate scientist handed a curious creature washed up on the shore.

Miriam flashed the video to his desk. He lifted a cowl that had been hanging down his back and placed it on his head, and she saw it was made of a fine mesh of silvery threads. He concentrated briefly and the mesh moved in response to what it detected, positioning its threads in their accustomed places. Despite his jibe about their equal computer systems, Miriam thought, holographic displays with neural input meshes were rarely seen and certainly not by her. For a few minutes he watched the video, using his thoughts and hand gestures to replay sections, turn or magnify parts, sweep in external data and run calculations. Spider webs of vector lines glowed over the images; tables of figures and calculations appeared and disappeared; graphs and animations played in space. Finally he looked up, again resting his chin on his hand. "Fascinating. Yes, quite fascinating. I can almost forgive you for interrupting my fun in the Jacuzzi with the blondes" he said, glancing pointedly at Stone.

"Now, obviously your techs will have checked the images for fraud. But if you care to know, my analyses of the photo and now the video show no signs of doctoring and all signs of being genuine. It is still possible that someone very skilled is pulling your leg, perhaps to throw you off the real trail of this burglar of yours. But they would have to be very skilled. If this is a fake, it is not the work of a casual prankster with access to mere standard tools. In fact if trickery is involved it is more likely in the person of your burglar herself rather than the video of her."

"Speaking of the burglary, I cannot help but notice you haven't asked us anything about it," noted Stone.

"What, am I a suspect now? Do I look like I need to raid apartment buildings for a living? I didn't ask because I don't give a damn. The only reason you're in here at all is because your alleged burglar presents an interesting scientific puzzle, and I don't get enough of them these days."

"Sorry, cop instincts... anyway, please go on." He didn't look as apologetic as his words, but after giving him a hard stare Tagarin let it pass.

"My analysis of your video indicates that while this woman is certainly remarkably fast and agile, her abilities lie within what is possible for a normal human, albeit at the extreme end of the range. It is in the nature of the extremes of ranges that examples exist. An accomplished athlete in her prime could do it. The probability shifts even more into the human range if we add the boost she might get from certain amphetamine or cocaine style drugs. And that is without considering the possibility of performance-enhancing mechanical prostheses."

"But what about those amazing eyes – and the tail?" asked Miriam.

"I imagine that is window-dressing to distract you. I suppose the eyes are some kind of mask or implant, and the tail is a mechanical prosthesis – probably for show rather than function."

"I have to agree that those are possibilities," Miriam said, "But they are just possibilities, not proof. The simplest explanation is it is just what it looks like: a geneh. Yet you aren't merely saying she *might* not be a geneh: you've insisted she *can't* be. Why are you so sure?"

"Oh child, it is a simple matter of arithmetic! Measurements of her facial structure and bodily proportions show that this is a woman around 25 years old; even allowing for variations in growth patterns, she is no younger than 22. My research was terminated 20 years ago, and we couldn't have done this" – he stabbed at the image – "then. Your only evidence for her being a geneh is the obvious physical appearance and performance. Now don't get me wrong. We were well on the way to achieving something like this: the changes required are not as great as their dramatic appearance might suggest. But we weren't there yet. I estimate that if things went reasonably well, we could have achieved something like this – but no earlier than 15 years ago."

He looked at them and again stabbed his finger at the image. "This is not a 15 year old child. Therefore she cannot be a geneh. She was born before there was any technology that could have created her."

Miriam and Jack looked at each other. Miriam asked, "Could there have been other labs, working in secret, which could have done it before or after the bans? Even foreign governments?"

"No. Science doesn't work that way. Ours was the most advanced country on Earth in that area and we all knew what the others were up to, and where we weren't competing we were cooperating. We had to. The more brains on a project the faster it goes. And you can't do this kind of work in your basement: you need too much fancy equipment. Did you know that back last century when the first sheep was cloned, some whacky cult claimed they'd already cloned people? Their alleged lab had some basic equipment and a few flasks: so anyone actually in the field knew they were lying. So no, if there had been other labs I'd have known about them. I did know about them, and they were all shut down. And even if they hadn't been, none of them could have done this even 20 years ago, let alone before then."

He waited, but they could think of nothing else to say. "James will show you out now. It has been interesting, but don't expect to see me again without a warrant. A life is a terrible thing to waste and I have no intention of letting you waste mine." He paused. "It is a pity, though, that she isn't a geneh. If she was real, she would be a beautiful creature, don't you think?"

CHAPTER 9 – VICTIMS

Miriam and Stone drove back to the station silently, as their private thoughts shifted, collided and slowly settled into some kind of order. After a while, Stone spoke. "You did all right, kid. You got us in and you stood up to him. Don't let it go to your head – you're still a rookie who thinks she's better than she is. But you show promise."

He glanced at her and granted her a slight curve of his lips that may have been a smile, or perhaps the promise of a future smile if she ever came to deserve it. "Maybe it wouldn't be so terrible if I was forced to work with you again."

Miriam smiled back. "I know I have a lot to learn. If you think it will help, I'll buy myself a nice tight helmet. Stop my head from expanding."

Stone grunted. "If that's what it takes. Sometimes it is."

Then both of them were quiet as they went over the events of the last hour in their minds. Neither of them came to any conclusions.

They reported the results to Ramos. He sat at his desk, considering. "Hmmm. It all sounds plausible, so plausible it stinks. But that's an occupational hazard. Every innocent person looks like a suspect after a while. The very fact they have an alibi makes you wonder why they found it necessary to have one."

He paused again, thinking. "Not really much to go on. Here's a tip for you, Hunter: if you think you have something, turn around and imagine you are counsel for the defense. If I was a defense lawyer making my closing address, I'd point out that all we have is a pattern spat out by a flakey AI, a photo in the vicinity of a minor crime that may be a coincidence and could be just a college student prank, and a plausible explanation even if that cat woman is our thief. If it wasn't for the link to the President's friends I'd say forget it and move on."

He tapped his fingers on the desk. "Not only do I hate to waste resources, I hate even more for the rarefied gods above me to believe I am wasting resources. Stone, get back to what you were doing. Hunter, you have more leeway because you can do all kinds of nutty things with the excuse that they're research into improving our beloved AI. Quiz a few of our victims, concentrating especially on the ones who had later mysterious losses of funds. But be careful. These are all important people and, whatever we say about equality under the law, important people have a way of pulling strings if they get annoyed. Strings generally connected to hammers over our heads. For now, just phone them. They are less likely to talk but also less likely to be pissed off enough to complain to their friends in high places."

~~~

A few hours later, Miriam sat back and rubbed her eyes. *What the hell?* She went to see Ramos and asked Stone to come along.

"OK Miriam, what have you got?"

"Nothing."

"Nothing? Then why in hell am I here?" growled Stone.

"Because it's a very peculiar nothing," replied Miriam.

"Hunter, " said Ramos patiently, "I'm giving you rope because there's something fishy going on. Don't hang yourself with it. I hope you're not wasting our time."

"So do I... so do I. The thing is, it's weird. I tried all the people who had the large losses of funds. One was overseas. Three refused to talk to me. One was interested because he thought maybe we had a line on his money, but when I had to admit I didn't and was just investigating a related lead he said not to waste his time. So I rang some of the others, concentrating on the ones at the lowest levels of the social stratosphere. A couple were pleased I had called but were mystified about the whole thing: they couldn't imagine why someone would break into their penthouse to steal a few gems while leaving their more precious treasures untouched. Some said, rather rudely, that it was a long time ago, the police were incompetent, and anyway they had their insurance payments and what the hell was I trying to achieve? Others, and not just one, were even more hostile, as if I was somehow accusing them of a crime."

Stone just looked at her. "So? Welcome to police work. Did you expect to solve the case over the phone?"

Miriam shrugged. "No. But it was weird. Half of them acted like they were innocent victims of a minor crime, the other half acted as if they were guilty of something themselves. I can understand annoyance at being the victim of a crime; I can understand them being annoyed at our failure to solve the crime. But defensiveness? Telling me, basically, to shut up, leave them alone and stop poking my nose into their business? That's why I wanted you here, Detective Stone. Their reactions just strike me as strange – disconnected from the facts of the case. As if there are facts we are unaware of that they don't want us to know about. You have a lot of experience – is this normal, or queer?"

Stone and Ramos looked at each other. Stone said, "Well... when you put it that way, it does seem odd. Victims of crime respond in all kinds of ways, and you do get some hostility – blame the messenger, blame the incompetents. But this seems more than normal. More like interviewing members of the mob, except these people aren't the mob. I dunno. What do you think, Chief?"

Ramos frowned. "It is odd. But not odd enough to do anything with it. And I don't think we should push any more at this stage: if you're hitting this amount of resistance already, questioning more people might bring us grief. And if the Mayor asks me why I'm hassling the President's friends – I need a better answer than what I could give him now."

He appeared to come to a decision. "No. We just don't have enough. Miriam, I know you're keen and you might even be right. But it's still all probably just a fantasy of your AI, and your victims are just hostile because they're busy and you're not offering them anything except questions they've already answered. Get back to work. If you can tweak the AI to keep an eye on this case, do it. But don't bring it to me unless it suggests something positive besides bothering our more eminent citizens. Other than that, just keep doing what you've been doing."

Chapter 10 – Witness

"What the hell!?"

Jim Perenty's friends would not have described him as excitable. Steady, even plodding, would have been more likely descriptors. He was as happy strolling home alone through the lowering dusk as he was having a quiet drink with his friends; much happier doing either than attending a raucous party. His even temperament was not prone to jumping at shadows. He was the kind of man who, rather than seeing a weather balloon and believing it was a UFO, would see a UFO and think it was a weather balloon.

But on this night his eye had been drawn by an odd movement on the edge of his vision, and his subconscious mind made him give a startled jump before his conscious one had time to catch up. By then the vision had already gone and the even higher levels of his mind scolded the lower ones to stop seeing things. He shook his head and walked on.

But when it happened again a week later he found himself staring at those strange eyes for long enough to know they were really there. And worse, long enough to hope they weren't actually looking straight back him. Then they vanished again and he shakily reached for his phone.

~~~

The IT department was continuing to increase the number and variety of data source feeds into the crime correlation AI, and in her search for clues Miriam had instigated a supervisory subsystem that gave terms related to the burglary case a higher priority score.

She had done it as a learning exercise more than in any hope of something useful. If anything it was a step backwards, increasing the number of mysterious theories the AI suggested. But two weeks later the system flagged an odd item for her attention. Miriam studied it carefully, retrieved the background data then sat back and thought for a while, mulling over whether such a left-field idea was really worth pursuing at the risk of appearing a gung-ho idiot. Finally she got up and called Jack to meet her in Ramos's office. Better appear an idiot for over-enthusiasm than for ignoring a vital lead, she thought.

"Boss, this is a funny one. It's probably nothing, but who knows. Animal Control had a report from a witness about a panther loose in the city. Would you believe, Animal Control actually sent a guy to check it out – apparently you'd be amazed at the kinds of pets some people do keep in their apartments. The man who reported it said he didn't believe it the first time either, but when he saw it a second time he called it in. Animal Control weren't impressed: people get their perspectives all screwed up, especially when it's getting dark, and if AC find anything it's usually a large feral cat. Once a 'mountain lion' turned out to be a *small* feral cat. But occasionally there is something dangerous so they like to check when the caller has any credibility at all."

They were watching her, as unimpressed as Animal Control had been but not caring to interrupt.

"Anyway, they found nothing on this one. No signs of anything unusual, no prints, no droppings, just the usual vermin. It would have ended there, as it usually does, except IT has been feeding data to my AI from Animal Control. The system flagged it because it was in a part of the city not too far from a few of our robberies, and because of the particular words the witness used: 'A big dark thing with a long tail. It went into the shadows and looked over in my direction, and all I could see were these big yellow eyes.'"

She shrugged. "What do you think?"

"Do we have a good location?"

"Good enough. It was in a rundown part of the city, in a block with a few working warehouses and more derelicts. If we ignore the active ones, there are about half a dozen buildings that could be hiding places for someone."

Ramos sat tapping his fingers on the desk. "It's a bit thin, isn't it? But we're not making much headway anywhere else. I wouldn't normally send anyone out on something that can barely be called a lead in a case that mightn't be a case, but here in my office I have two officers who are always trying to escape their desk jobs. Do you think it's worth taking a look, Stone?"

Jack shrugged and said, "Sure. I could use the exercise. And it might help Hunter here appreciate the true meaning of police investigation. Boredom and futility."

Chapter 11 – Search

Miriam and Jack looked up at the warehouse. "Smithers & Sons" was painted in large faded letters on the side. Whoever the Smithers family were, they had chosen to leave this sorry monument to happier days slowly gathering dust and vermin. An equally faded sign was the only monument to the family's optimism, declaring to an indifferent world that the property was for rent. The sign stood at a distinct lean, so it was now a slow-motion race between the sun and gravity as to which would remove it first. But for now the building's sole purpose was a home for rats and, judging by a few food wrappers littering the ground, temporary lodgings for the sorrier members of humanity.

This was the fourth building they had visited so far. They had all looked much the same as this one and all been empty except for one tramp sleeping off his treasure of cheap liquor. They had also questioned a few workers they had happened to come across around the still living businesses. None of them had seen anything.

"There are two kinds of witnesses," Jack had said to Miriam. "Those who see what isn't there, like your panther man, and those who don't see anything. I read about an experiment done a long time ago where most people watching a video of a basketball game didn't notice a guy in a gorilla suit walk across the court through the players. That's your average witness. And the ones who do see the gorilla won't tell you. Half of them will try to blackmail him instead."

"OK," said Jack after looking the place over, clearly unimpressed by the prospects. "Next on the list is this prime property. Let's see if our friends the Smithers have anything to tell us."

They easily gained access through one of the broken doors and looked around. If it was the lair of a super-villain she wasn't making a good living out of it. "Well, let's take a look around."

There were the usual signs of occasional human activity, with a small scattering of discarded needles and a few food scraps even the rats rejected. More extensive drifts of food packaging and condom wrappers decorated the corners, swept there by the random winds that found entrance through any number of gaps. "Welcome to humanity's finest," whispered Jack.

"Same as before, I suppose," said Miriam.

"Yep. But let's not let the other ones lull us into putting our guard down. If a place is worth investigating, it's worth being cautious in even if they all look the same. Stick together, be quiet, and be observant. Let's get this over with."

CHAPTER 12 – KATLYN

Katlyn was sitting cross-legged on the floor of her nest with her eyes closed, humming quietly to herself. She had an iBud in one ear and her mind was immersed in the soaring vocals of *Phantom of the Opera*. Like everyone, music made her feel and in turn how she felt changed her taste. As with most young people, when feeling energetic she loved dancing to hard thumping rock. At other times her overactive nervous system appreciated the more gentle but complex beauty of classical music. Today was a day she felt like something romantic and dramatic. She could relate to the tragedy of dreams crushed by indifference and madness, she thought.

She had a number of such nests scattered around the city. They were places of refuge where she could rest or hide if she had to, or use as a base of operations if she had a few things to do in the obscuring darkness of the night.

They were all similar to this one. She liked large abandoned buildings with lots of places to hide and several hidden escape routes above or below ground. She always made her nest in an out of the way part of the building, well hidden and usually requiring a climb, so a casual visitor would be unlikely to find it – especially the kind of casual visitor she was likely to get. She didn't mind visitors if they weren't too nosy. It was best if there was some activity and signs of random human traffic: it made her own presence less likely to be noticed. So she tolerated the tramps or hobos who made it their temporary hotel, the drug addicts shooting up and the occasional lovers looking for privacy they couldn't find or afford elsewhere. If visitors were annoying or started to make themselves too much at home she would shoo them off somehow. Strange noises at night were often effective; if not, sending a few rats their way usually did the trick. Nobody liked the rats.

The place was empty today. She wasn't out here for any particular reason; sometimes she just liked to get out and about and have her own private time and space. Daniel didn't mind. Well, didn't object, anyway. They had talked about the extra risk but he had said that for all the importance of her work, you never knew how long it would take or if she would get herself killed. Life, he had told her, was for living; important as they were, long term goals should never stop you living along the way: especially when that living might turn out to be all you got. He thought she needed as much of a life as she could make for herself so he was glad she at least had this.

There were many reasons she loved Daniel, she thought. That was one of them.

When cocooned in the safety of home, Katlyn wore an iBud in each ear for the usual full stereo experience, but when in the field she always kept one ear clear and alert for danger. It proved to be an unnecessary precaution this time. The soprano cut out mid note and was replaced by an insistent peeping sound: one of her hidden sensors must have detected someone entering the building.

She removed the iBud and listened. Whoever it was were being quiet about it. The only visitors who moved that quietly tended to be teenage lovers, scared of their daring illicit adventure, not wanting to be caught or seen in their sweet clumsy couplings. But there was usually more whispering and giggling involved.

She pulled her flexipad from her belt, unrolled it and scanned the spyeye inputs. There they were. Two cops had come in and were poking around. This could be trouble. If they were looking for anyone in particular they might decide to search the place and could find her nest.

She studied them carefully. They were alert, hands on holstered guns, looking serious. She nearly laughed at the sight of them. They looked like a pair of stereotypes from a crime series: the middle-aged white guy, hard-bitten and cynical; trailed by the rookie black girl, innocent, eager and a bit dense. Katlyn half expected to see a camera crew. Then her bared teeth morphed into a more feral expression. However comical they might look they were the law, her deadly enemy:

an enemy she must not underestimate.

She sat back, watching them and pondering her best strategy. They weren't sure what they were looking for was here but they were nervous about finding it. They would probably just do a quick search then go away none the wiser, which would be ideal: it would be sad to lose this nest. But they looked grim enough to be persistent, and then they might find it; and she certainly didn't want to be found with it if they did.

As was her habit she had rigged her nest so she could set it alight if it was compromised. The building still had a working fire control system but she had disabled it inside the nest itself. That way she could destroy any evidence without burning down the whole place. While a big fire would be exciting to watch, a small, contained fire in part of a disused building was unlikely to attract as much attention. Burning down the whole thing, especially if some people happened to be inside at the time or it spread to bring down the whole block, could prompt deeper investigation than she wanted.

Her best course, she decided, would be to hide in another part of the building near an escape route then watch and wait. So she silently left her nest and crept carefully along one of the walkways.

Thirty years ago, long before Katlyn was born, a splinter of slag had fallen into a vat of molten steel. It made a microscopic defect in a steel bolt, and in the decades since that defect acted as a nucleus from which time, oxygen, humidity and stress had conspired to send invisible cracks of corrosion through the metal. At last under the added stress of Katlyn's weight the bolt sheared, and one side of the walkway dropped a few inches with a clang that echoed loudly through the warehouse.

"Shit-shit-shit!" hissed Katlyn, looking wildly around. A long-empty window of some forgotten supervisor's office gaped blackly at her from eight feet away. In less than a heartbeat she had gathered herself and leapt across the gap, grabbing the frame as she flew and swinging herself inside.

Jack swung around at the sound. "Hey!" he cried. "Stop!"

"What was it? Did you see anything?" cried Miriam.

"It looked like someone up there, jumping into that room. And," he added looking at Miriam, "it looked like it had a tail."

They took what cover they could, drew their weapons and peered up at the dark entrance to the room. Two pale golden orbs stared at them from the darkness.

"You up there! This is the police! Show yourself!"

Katlyn had heard Stone's comment about her tail and worse, the tone in which he had said it. She needed to know more; escape was no longer an option.

The orbs vanished.

"Come out with your hands up! Don't make us come and get you. Surrender now and make it easier on yourself!"

"You mean easier on you, don't you?" a harsh voice reverberated from above. "No, I think you should earn your pay today, officers. Come and find me. Let's play a little game of hide and seek. I hide, you seek. Later, you might be hiding while I seek, which will be even more fun."

"What are we going to do?" whispered Miriam.

"We'd better call for backup," replied Jack. "Oh crap. My phone's lost connection. You?" Miriam checked and shook her head. "It might be all the metal in this place. Or more likely our friend there has a signal blocker on."

"Maybe we should try to get back out to the car? Call for help from there?"

Jack thought for a minute. "Dammit", he whispered, "This is our best chance to catch this thing! You try to back away to the door while I keep it occupied. Let's not let it get away."

Miriam began to edge back the way they came. She jumped as a bar of reinforcing rod spun through the air and smashed into the concrete a few feet away between her and the exit, throwing up sparks, its clang echoing through the building.

"Hey! No sneaking out! Play properly or not at all, you two!"

Miriam scuttled back under cover and looked to Jack. He whispered, "Let's humor her. We'll go hunting like she asks, but try to maneuver close to an exit. If you see your chance, take it. Otherwise stay close. We'll separate but make sure you stay in sight. Let's go."

"Ow!" cried Miriam as a small bolt or something hit her on the leg. "Something just hit me!"

A second later, brick smashed on the floor a few feet from Jack. "Jesus! That could have killed me!"

They looked wildly about. "There!" called Miriam. Someone darted along a walkway and out of sight. Jack let off a shot but without much hope of hitting anything, and his bullet zinged off into the far side of the building.

"Come on guys," the voice said, affecting a bored tone. "You're a bit slow. Try to do better or I might get bored. I get angry when I'm bored."

The echoes made it impossible to tell where the voice was coming from, so they moved in the direction where they'd last seen its owner, guns drawn, casting about from side to side. They turned a corner and saw two feet and a tail disappear off to the side. They then had to duck as the metal lid of a bin came spinning through the air toward their heads.

"Where the hell is she?" whispered Jack, swinging his gun around from side to side. Out of the corner of her eye, Miriam saw a blur swing down and plant a solid kick in Jack's back, slamming him head first into a wall. He lay still. But before Miriam could fire her own gun without hitting Jack, their opponent was gone again.

"God dammit!" she swore under her breath, "where the hell is she *now?*" Then it was her turn to find out, as what felt like a steel band wrapped around her throat and an iron grip held her gun arm.

"OK bitch," a voice rasped in her ear. "Here's how it is. I can break your neck as easy as spit on you. But a life is a terrible thing to waste, even yours, so why don't you drop that gun and maybe I'll let you live?"

Miriam couldn't breathe, and dark splotches started a dance at the corners of her vision. There was something important in what the thing had just said.... something important... she relaxed her grip and her gun clattered to the floor.

The creature quickly shifted its grasp to pin her arms close, dragged her to a support beam and handcuffed her to it with her own cuffs, arms behind her back around the beam. Then it stepped around to face her.

For the first time Miriam got a clear view of the creature in the flesh, no longer a blur of dark and shadows. It was obviously human and obviously female, but the large yellow eyes and long furred tail gave it a distinct aura of cat. It watched her calmly for a few seconds and then drew out a thin, sharp blade. Its gaze sharpened into a predatory look that accentuated the cat while diminishing the human, and she stepped up to Miriam. "Now, what are we going to do with you?" she drawled, tracing her blade along the line between Miriam's jaw and throat. Miriam could feel the keen point drawing a line along her skin, but was relieved that the creature was, at least for now, careful not to cut her.

Despite her terror, she calmly lifted her chin to gaze directly into its eyes. She knew the nature of her gaze belied the calm.

"Well, you're a brave little girl, I'll give you that," it said. "And I think we'll have us a little talk, you and me. I'll ask a few questions, you'll give a few answers, and depending on how that goes we'll see if you live or die. But first let me fix up your buddy over there. I hate people interrupting my private discussions, don't you?"

It bounded over to where Jack lay and Miriam didn't even have time to cry out "No!" as it plunged its dagger into his defenseless body. But despite the speed and violence of the thrust, the creature stopped at the last instant and merely poked his body, as if checking whether he was awake. "Your friend is OK – for now," it said, "Sleeping like an especially ugly baby. He's got a bad bump on that thick head but unless he's made of eggs he'll wake up – eventually. Do you think I can trust him to be a good boy, or should I keep him out of trouble?" Miriam just stared, unsure of what to say. "Don't worry little girl, that's what we grown-ups call a 'rhetorical question'. I'll just keep this bag of bones out of our way."

With that, she unceremoniously and apparently effortlessly dragged Jack by one foot to the wall and handcuffed his arms around another pole, leaving him lying face down on the floor in the dust and debris. She stood over him for a moment then gave him a spiteful kick in the ribs; he didn't move.

The creature moved fluidly back to stand in front of Miriam then stood regarding her silently. Without warning, Miriam lashed out with her foot in a strong high kick, aiming for its head. But the thing was preternaturally fast, and the head was gone by the time her foot reached the space it had occupied. Before she could even regain her balance, the creature had repaid her effort with its own kick to her solar plexus. Through teary eyes, Miriam could just look up at it. It stood there, exactly where and how it had before. Nothing had changed except Miriam could no longer breathe. Slowly the pain subsided and she just as slowly straightened up.

"Fiery little bitch, aren't you?" it said when Miriam could stop gasping. "Well I hope you've had your fun and you learned something valuable from it. Learning from our mistakes is an important part of growing up, you know. Now," she said, flicking her tail for emphasis, "you seem surprisingly unsurprised to see me. You're either even thicker than you look or you were expecting me. So question one, girlie: were you looking for me?"

Miriam just nodded dumbly.

"Good girl. An honest answer. Maybe you're not as stupid as I thought. Question two: how did you know I was here?"

"Someone reported a panther to Animal Control. We thought it seemed suspicious."

It stared at her. "Come now, there must be more to it than that. Cops don't go round investigating panther sightings. Be very careful how you answer. I might know some things you don't know I know. Lie to me and you might start losing bits of you." She twirled her dagger for emphasis.

"You were caught for a few seconds on a security camera near the site of a burglary. We knew something queer was going on but didn't know what. Someone who saw you in the dark could have mistaken you for a panther."

It drummed its fingers on its thigh and sighed. "You know, getting answers out of you is like pulling teeth. Which can be arranged, if you don't get more cooperative. Do you expect me to believe you just happened to see some video and then just happened to link it to some random Animal Control report?"

"I have been working with an AI, trying to train it up for correlating evidence. After the video, I set it to watch for anything odd that might be linked. That's how we found out about the panther sighting. The description sounded like you."

It hissed, but it was hard to tell if that signified surprise, anger or understanding. It regarded her some more. "Interesting. Well, that finishes the questions part of our program. But I seem to recall I had a decision to make. Now, what was it? Hmmm... Oh yes: do you live, or die?" The predatory look returned.

"You..." Miriam started hoarsely, but had to stop and breathe. "You aren't going to kill us."

"You're either an optimist or a fool, girl. If there's any difference in this world. You seem awfully sure given your current position, which Sun Tzu would describe as 'untenable'. Would you like another demonstration?"

"You've had plenty of chances to kill us already but you haven't. You're a thief not a murderer."

"I learned long ago not to make life-changing decisions before I have time to think about them. Unless I have to, and handling you two didn't reach 'have to' status." She smiled nastily. "Maybe I'm getting bored with this whole thief thing and it's time to graduate to more serious excitement." She made a show of considering it. "Oh, I agree, killing a couple of cops is a big career move. Maybe I'm not ready for it. Or maybe I am. In any case, don't fool yourself that me giving myself time to think it through means anything good for you. But we have a bit of time before your friends might come looking for you, so we can get to know each other a bit, eh? What's your name?"

"Miriam."

The creature waited. "Well, hello Miriam, and since you ask so nicely, you can call me Katlyn."

She regarded Miriam some more, looking her up and down. Miriam wasn't sure if her smile was less cynical or just more predatory. "My, you are a pretty young thing though, aren't you?" She stepped right up to Miriam, so their bodies barely touched. "You know, I've never had a woman," she purred. "I can do things with my tail you wouldn't believe." She emphasized the claim by running her tail lightly up Miriam's body then stroking her chin with it where she had stroked her dagger minutes before. "Maybe we could have some fun. Maybe your boyfriend over there would like to watch. And maybe then I could do him, and you could watch. What do you reckon, pretty one? Are you up for a little party?"

Miriam's eyes grew large and dark, and beneath her shock she was surprised to see the creature apparently sniffing gently. "A pity. I smell fear but no lust, so I'll take that as a no. But if that's not the way your hormones rock, how about taking a more intellectual angle on today's entertainment? You might think I'm just a common thief. Well perhaps not 'common', but a thief nonetheless. So you might be surprised at how eclectic my education has been. I find psychology fascinating, don't you? So here's a moral dilemma for you, little girl. For reasons I find entirely mystifying you don't want my body for its own luscious sake. But what if it's the price I put on your life? For reasons not so mysterious this body, which happens to be twice as sensitive as yours – and I mean *everywhere*, if you know what I mean – limits my pool of sexual partners terribly. Really. I just can't get a date. So you might do me a favor, and I might let you live. So what do you say?"

Miriam just stared at her, unable to speak.

"Cat got your tongue, girl?" she snapped. "Are you seriously telling me you'd die to protect your dubious virtue? I can smell you're not a virgin, you know. Maybe I'd be doing the gene pool a favor by removing you from it before you manage to breed." She sighed. "You disappoint me, Miriam. Maybe we can play a more interesting game. Well, more interesting for me, which is what matters. Maybe I should wake your boyfriend up and let you compete for your lives. The one who makes me happiest gets to watch the other one die. It'll be an even contest, I think. He's not as pretty as you, but he has some handy accessories you lack. What do you think?"

Miriam studied her, afraid to answer. What was going on? This creature seemed alternately reasonable, evil or insane. Or perhaps she was just playing a vicious game. There was nothing clever she could think of, no stratagem to apply, when she had no idea what this thing actually was and what it really wanted. For all she knew it was just looking for an excuse and any answer she gave would be the end of her. All she did know was that she felt more and more like a mouse being played with by a particularly angry cat. She decided the only thing she could do was be herself and hope that was enough.

As if to underline those thoughts, the predatory look returned and the creature put its dagger to the base of Miriam's throat and applied pressure. This time Miriam could feel the sharp point puncturing her skin, a drop of blood oozing down her chest. Her insides turned to liquid fear. Katlyn twisted the knife, ever so slightly, grinning at her.

"Wait!" gasped Miriam. "Wait. There is a reason you shouldn't kill me."

"Oh? And what might that be?"

"It would be wrong. I've done nothing to you. I don't deserve to die."

Katlyn laughed, but withdrew her knife. It was a strange laugh, a delighted tinkling of bells, nothing at all like the cynical grunts and smirks of her earlier humor; nothing at all like Miriam expected.

"Justice?" The bells tinkled again. "What planet are you from, sweetie? Here on planet Earth, the innocent die all the time, for no particular reason known to God, man or monstrosity. Innocence isn't going to protect you."

Miriam lifted her chin and looked into her eyes. She said softly, "There is nothing more important than justice. How else can people live?"

Katlyn stared at her. "Do you really believe that, pretty one?"

"Yes," she said simply.

Then her head swung first one way then the other, as Katlyn stepped forward and slapped her with her tail, hard, and snarled, "Oh really, Little Miss Justice? Then look at me. What am I?" She slapped her again, to emphasize her point.

Miriam gasped for breath. That tail, soft and gentle in some roles, could be hard as a fist. She looked up at her from hooded eyes. "You are... a woman." Slap! Slap! "Do you take me for a fool?! WHAT AM I?"

"You are a geneh, a genetically engineered human," she whispered.

The thing glared at her, panting lightly, as if the answer angered her yet was still enough to stem her rage. For now. Then she bared her teeth in something nobody could mistake for a smile.

"So tell me, Miss Sweet Justice, who wants to live but not enough to pay for it, what would you do to me if our roles were reversed, if it was me tied to that pole under your power?"

"You are a criminal. I would have to arrest you, take you into custody," she replied softly, flinching for the blows to come, not knowing what else to say but the simple truth. She had decided to just be herself, so she might as well see it through to the end, which was looking closer by the minute. The creature knew it, anyway. A lie, like most lies, would serve no purpose: and in this case was likely to get her killed sooner than admitting an obvious truth.

But no blows came. Just a quiet, "And what would happen to me then? What do your laws say to do to one such as me?"

"The human purity laws say... the law says... you would die."

"So. I am to spare you, for you are an innocent little idiot, while you would kill me, innocent or not, for no reason but what I am, a thing I never chose to be! And you expect justice to save you? What justice is there for me, and why should I care about your laws, your *justice*?" She spat. "You wish me dead, for what I am. You fear me, you hate me, like all the rest! Admit it! Confess it, and I might spare you some pain."

Miriam lowered her head and shook it slowly from side to side. "If you had not broken the law, I would not know or care that you exist. I never sought to kill you." She lifted her head to look Katlyn directly in the eyes. "I don't hate you," she added softly.

Those golden eyes regarded her again. "So, I threaten to rape you, to kill you, but you don't hate me? What, you forgive me? You know, some people think I have anger issues – can you believe that? But maybe you've seen nothing yet, girl. Maybe I should work my anger issues out on a suitable target." She flexed her fingers like claws and spat on the ground again.

Miriam breathed, trying to quell her growing panic. Her only point of hope was that Katlyn had not yet killed her, and for all that Miriam felt she had been run over by a truck, had not even hurt her beyond some cuts and bruises.

"I understand your anger and it is not for me to forgive you or condemn you. It doesn't matter to me what you are genetically: for what it's worth, I think you are right to hate those laws. But that does not make the life you have chosen right. Even more, it doesn't make taking our lives right."

"I can't work out whether I should kill you for being a scheming bitch, or kill you for being an innocent moron," she snarled. "But spot the common factor, larval detective. And hey, it's been fun, but guess what? You've run out of time, dear. I've got things to do, people to see. I can't stand around here all day chatting."

She paused briefly, regarding Miriam coldly.

"Since you won't entertain me, I'll have to entertain myself. But so many choices, maybe I'll let you decide. Let's see. I could strangle you," she said, wrapping her tail tightly around Miriam's throat so she could barely breathe. "A slow, unpleasant and undignified end. Or a quick dagger into the heart" – Miriam felt a pinprick between her ribs – "it'll hurt a bit at first, but then you won't feel a thing. Or maybe you'll piss me off some more and it'll be a knife in the guts" – a jab to the stomach, and Miriam knew she had been cut – "a much more drawn out end to the short but ultimately tragic story of little Miriam, the girl who couldn't. Then there are those guns you two carelessly left lying around. A bullet in the head? Or a slow line of bullets up your leg and belly, ending in your heart? Bang. Bang. Bang. Oh dear. So *many* choices, what *shall* a girl do?" And she gave Miriam another of her predatory looks.

Miriam looked up at her hopelessly. She thought of how hopefully she had faced her life and her career, of all the mornings she would have liked to see, the things she had not done. All to end now so pointlessly, with no power to defend herself, no words she could find to reach through this creature's rage to any mercy that might still live behind those merciless golden eyes. She could feel tears form in her own eyes, but she would neither hide them nor acknowledge them. "Please..." she whispered.

"Shut your eyes, sweetie, it will be better that way," Katlyn said, surprisingly gently. Miriam obeyed, waiting for whatever blows Katlyn would deliver to end her life. But when seconds or a lifetime had gone by and still she breathed, she opened them again.

Katlyn was gone.

CHAPTER 13 – FIRE

Miriam let out a long ragged breath and bent over panting, struggling not to throw up. *Jesus.* She was glad to be alive, though not so sure why. She panted softly a while longer, until she felt more able to think. Adrenalin was all very good for fight or flight, but not when you were chained to a pole unable to do either.

She wanted to get out of here. If they didn't report back in a while someone would come looking for them, but who knew how long that would take? And Jack might need medical attention sooner rather than later. But a bit of struggle showed her that she wasn't getting out of this without somebody's help.

As she looked around for inspiration, the sight of smoke drifting from the far side of the warehouse hit her senses simultaneously with the smell of it, and she knew they were both in serious danger. Katlyn must have set the place on fire. *Oh Lucifer.*

"Jack! Jack!" she screamed, but he did not move. *Oh Christ,* she thought, *what if that crazy thing killed him when she left?* What if she hadn't run off to let her live, but to give her an especially panicked and painful death; to watch her burn to death chained to a pole like Joan of Arc. *Christ!* "JACK!" she screamed again.

"Oh, God..." he groaned, slowly lifting his head. "What the hell happened?"

"Are you OK?"

"If you ignore the splitting headache and the aching ribs, sure. How about you? And I think I asked a question first. Oh yes. What the *hell* just happened?"

"Not now! She's set fire to the place! I'm tied with my arms behind me: at least you're the other way round! Can you free yourself?"

Jack tried a few experimental pulls and looked up. "Well, my arms are pretty loose and let's see, I think I can... yes... I should be able to get high enough on this pole to get my arms over. You keep talking while I try."

"I'm OK, just roughed up a bit. You got ambushed by that cat thing: she kicked you into the wall. Then us two girls spent a nice half hour chatting over a cup of tea, talking politics and discussing the many ways she would enjoy killing me. Then just as she had me convinced I was about to die an unspecified but painful death – she vanished."

"Vanished?"

"Well, she suggested I close my eyes, the better to surprise me with my means of demise. But she didn't kill me. She just ran away."

"It must have been your fierce expression. But at least we can be thankful she doesn't have the powers of invisibility or teleportation."

After a minute or so of grunting and cursing through thickening smoke, Jack managed to shimmy far enough up the pole to lift his arms over the top. He dropped to the ground with a groan. He went searching, came back with some keys, undid his cuffs and released Miriam. She fell gratefully into his arms.

"Whew", he said, as the heat spreading from Katlyn's former nest finally triggered the fire system and they began to get drenched. "Let's get out of here in case that crazy cat comes back. I just hope she left us our car."

~~~

Jack and Miriam walked into the squad room. Heads turned. "You two look like hell," someone observed helpfully.

"I just got out of hell," said Miriam. They went to debrief. Forensic investigators had already been dispatched to the scene when they called in but nobody was hopeful. Some DNA would be handy but the place was too dirty. It would mean nothing.

"Well this ups the ante, doesn't it?" said Ramos. "At least she didn't kill you two: I'm understaffed enough already. We'd better get the doctor to look at you both."

The doctor was thorough and competent. He gave Miriam permission to return to work but said Jack would have to stay under observation. He had a couple of cracked ribs and concussions were never to be treated lightly.

Miriam and Ramos discussed the case by Jack's bedside.

"Do you think we should escalate this to GenInt Enforcement?" Miriam asked.

"No... not yet, I don't think. Do you think you could see Dr Tagarin again? He might have something more useful to say now that you have more than an enhanced video to talk about. I'm reluctant to involve GenInt unless we have to: they're too much of a wild card. We'll see what Tagarin says, if anything, before we decide whether we have enough reason to bring them into it."

"I can second that," added Jack. "I've dealt with those guys before. They aren't pretty."

"Do you want me to wait until Jack's better, or do you think I can go alone?"

Ramos thought. "Normally I like my people in pairs, not that it helped much today. But I don't think there's any danger seeing Dr Tagarin on your own. It seems unlikely he'd be in league with a crazy burglar and even if he is, they're not going to do anything stupid when we know you're there. We need to move fast here, people. And from your earlier report he likes you as much as he can like any cop. Give it a go. The worst that can happen is he'll refuse to talk to you. Then we can talk again about escalating to GenInt. Now go."

Chapter 14 – Tagarin

Miriam walked up to the gate. It now recognized her and said, "Good afternoon, Officer Hunter. What is the nature of your business this time?"

"I have some follow-up questions for Dr Tagarin."

"Dr Tagarin believes he made it clear that he isn't interested in further questions."

"Please tell him that I have now met the woman in the video."

Miriam could practically feel the camera scanning her face. No doubt it made the nature of her "meeting" clear.

The gate opened and James appeared at the door and beckoned her up the path. This time he brought her immediately to Tagarin's public office. Tagarin gestured to a chair and she sat. He examined her face, but said nothing.

"Thank you for seeing me."

"May I presume from your appearance combined with your presence that your suspect did not come quietly, but you have her safely in custody and can report on her true nature?" he asked harshly. "I imagine your missing colleague is even now giving her the third degree."

"I am afraid that my partner is recovering from the interview. And while I am less damaged than him I am lucky to be alive. But I can tell you a lot more about her."

He raised his eyebrows. "Please proceed," he said, summoning up his display.

Miriam told him the story. He listened intently, occasionally annotating the report transcribed by his desk or calling in other data. When she finished, he regarded her intensely for a few minutes.

"Well, that is certainly an intriguing story. I might start enjoying your company if you keep this up."

"So... what do you think?"

"I can see why you would believe she is a geneh, though if so she is a poor ambassador for the cause of geneh rights. But at least she didn't kill you – which raises its own questions. I am still not convinced, by the way: for all the suggestive facts of the case, the mathematical reasoning I told you last time is hard to evade. But for argument's sake, let's think about what it would tell us if she was. That is, after all, what you are not paying me for."

He sat for a few minutes looking into space, occasionally focusing on his display to look up more information or do some calculations.

"So, let me summarize. She is definitely a modified human female. Overall, her modifications make her somewhat catlike: her eyes, her tail, her flexibility and reflexes. Individually, though, it is not so simple. Her tail, while enhancing her catlike appearance, is more like a monkey's. Clearly it is prehensile, as your throat can testify. That is not surprising. Our ancestors were monkeys, and it may be less difficult than you realize to reactivate those genes and add prehensile capability from a New World monkey. It would be interesting to learn how strong that tail is: whether, for example, it would support her weight, but she has rudely not made herself available for study. Then there are her eyes. Large, almost luminous, and in your photo from before there was a distinct gleam. Yet her pupils are round, not slitted like a cat's are in daylight. Well, you did not mention them, whereas you'd certainly have found slits worth remarking on?"

Miriam nodded. "Yes. It didn't occur to me at the time, but they were round like ours."

"Taken together, I would say a relatively small modification to the size and color of the eyes, almost certainly including something like the tapetum at the back of a cat's eyes, which reflects light back through the retina to improve night vision. The tapetum would be the biggest change, I'd say, but even twenty years ago we had enough knowledge of genetics to make it a feasible aim. The overall effect, I think, would be vision better than ours at night but without the cat's weakness in daytime vision."

As he talked, Miriam listened and watched. A strange man, she thought. When they first met he had gone out of his way to be rude and insulting, and even now in casual conversation an air of bitter cynicism and contempt shrouded his words and expressions like a chilly fog. But thinking about this problem and discoursing on his conclusions, all that vanished. He was precise, detached and open, and she felt more like a colleague in arms than a despised intruder.

"She also seems to have a remarkable sense of smell. Of course she might just have been taunting you – what she told you were pretty obvious guesses. But we have quite a poor sense of smell compared to most mammals, so no great difficulty there. Did she give any signs of unusually acute hearing?"

"No, not that I noticed. But she often gave the impression of trying to sense danger – maybe she was listening. Her ears were the same shape as ours too, by the way."

"On that topic we should clarify a few other things. Ignoring the tail her hair was the same as a person's? She had nails not claws? Did you notice anything else different, say in her bodily proportions?"

"No... I can't be completely sure, partly because the obvious differences were distracting, partly because I was terrified. But no... I didn't notice any difference in her hair or nails. Her nails were sharp, maybe a bit stronger than mine, but human as far as I could tell. She had this skintight outfit on and I didn't notice anything out of place or missing."

"But she was stronger than you expected, very fast in both movements and reflexes, yet lithe and flexible?" Miriam nodded. "OK. I'd say some muscle enhancement, not too difficult given the normal range of human not to mention animal capabilities. But a pretty significant enhancement to her nervous system. And she said her body was unusually sensitive? Again, she might have been lying. But if we take it at face value she has a denser and faster nervous system than ours. That is probably the most significant enhancement, but given the variation between people and our knowledge of neurogenetics, it could be something someone would try – and maybe succeed at."

He paused. "Except for one thing. More peripheral nerves require more central nervous system to process them. Let me do some calculations."

She waited while he worked with some programs on his display. He looked at them.

"Interesting. Twice, she said? Let's take that as at least approximately true. If it means twice the linear resolution, then that would imply four times the number of resolvable nerve endings. I think it more likely to be twice the number per unit area, which equates to about 1.4 times the linear resolution, still significantly greater sensitivity. If you look at the power laws of scaling in mammals, a crude calculation gives somewhat more than twice the brain weight to handle it. However most of a human brain is the thinking part not the sensory processing part. Making some rough approximations, she would need a thicker spinal cord than us – not much of a problem – and only about a 20% larger brain. That equates to an increase in linear dimensions of her head of less than 7%, perhaps noticeable but not a big problem."

He thought a while longer and did some more arcane manipulations on screen.

"There are other relevant factors. A large fraction of nerves in a newborn's brain are pruned during development, meaning we start with a lot more than we need for what we've got. In adults, there is a significant variation in brain volume unrelated to body size or intelligence: indeed, many highly intelligent people have relatively small brains for their body size. At the other end of the spectrum, some people with much reduced brain tissue due to hydrocephaly still function relatively normally. If we factor all that in, our geneh's neural enhancements might well all fit into a package within the normal range of human variation."

He thought some more.

"One other thing. In humans a faster nervous system is correlated with greater intelligence: so if we're right about that aspect, your mystery woman might be very bright indeed. But there is one thing that disturbs me..."

She waited.

"Thank you, by the way, for the completeness of your report. I know some of it would have been embarrassing to repeat to a hostile stranger like me. But from the way she behaved: threatening you, hurting you, caressing you... I wonder how mentally stable she is? She also implied she craved excitement? Maybe those enhancements to her nervous system had unfortunate side effects and she's a bit mad. Or even completely mad."

"I had the same thought," Miriam commented. "I didn't know what to do, what to say, and I still don't know why she let me live. Maybe she was just toying with me, but if she was she was very cruel about it." She shuddered.

"Yes. A great pity though. If it wasn't for her personality she would be a magnificent creature." He sighed. "Not that I expect you to agree with me."

"Anyway," he said, his air of contempt returning, "that's all interesting as speculation, but we still have the mathematical problem. Your story confirms that this woman is in her twenties and in my professional opinion it was impossible to produce her more than 15 years ago even if anyone had the capability to do so. She is not a geneh."

"Then how do you account for her appearance? You originally suggested those eyes could be a disguise or a mask, but they aren't. They were as real as mine."

"Oh, I'm not sure they are as advanced as I've been speculating. That was all assuming things are what they seem. But in science things have a way of being other than they seem. You have come here for my opinion, and I suppose I owe it to you since you have given me an hour or so of reliving what the past could have been. Mind you," he added harshly, "I might hate you for that tomorrow."

"So. In my professional opinion, for what that's worth these days, she is what I said at our first meeting; though I can now flesh it out more. What you have is a highly trained athlete in her twenties. I suspect an organized crime connection – or even a government agency connection, if there's a difference these days – because she has some sophisticated and therefore expensive enhancements. Her eyes are bioengineered but she isn't a geneh: that solves our timing issue. She didn't have to grow up with them: she's been operated on later in life. She has a prosthetic tail made to look like a real one – mainly, I suspect, as a distraction, a smokescreen, though obviously she can use it to good effect. But note what she did with it: almost emphasizing her use of it. As I said, it's a distraction. And she's on some kind of drug, probably a designer drug based on cocaine. That's what gives her such speed and reflexes and is also, I suspect, what is sending her mad."

"Do you really think she could be a government agent? Why would she be doing what she's doing?"

"Oh, if she is I'd say she's gone rogue. Possibly another side effect of the drugs. And you know what government agencies are like if they are doing something secret of dubious legality. Complete deniability.

If she is and has, someone will be trying to kill her but they'll never tell you. And if they succeed her body will simply disappear."

"Still... your theory sounds plausible, but you haven't met her. It just doesn't feel... right. In person, she comes across as what she herself says she is."

"Didn't they teach you in policeman's school how unreliable witness impressions are? Or how easily conmen fool their marks with smoke and mirrors?" he snapped. After a pause he added, his voice and gaze hardening, "And since you are so enamored of speculation, let us see where else it leads us. Let us assume you are right. I can guess from watching and talking to you that you had a reasonably happy childhood, would that be so?"

Miriam nodded, unsure where he was leading and why his gaze bored into hers, no longer with bitter contempt but now with naked hostility.

"Then I do not think you understand hate, Ms Hunter. I do. I have had cause to hate, whether you think me justified or not. Well let me try to make you understand hate. If this woman is a geneh, imagine her life. While you were growing up in the sunshine and running in parks, where if you fell over almost any stranger would help you up with a smile: what was she doing?"

Miriam watched him, eyes still.

"She was living in the shadows, afraid to show herself, never to play in the sunshine or laugh with her friends, never to even have friends. Were she to fall, the random stranger who lifted you up was more likely to kick her to death than stretch out his hand in good will. And there is more. You take pride in being an officer of the law. To you the law is a good thing, the protector of the innocent. But what was the law to her? A monster lurking in her nightmares and the shadows of her days, waiting to rend her at any moment, at any mistake. Just for being."

Miriam's eyes grew larger.

"Yes, I think you are beginning to see. Now imagine you are this woman. Imagine that your enemies bring themselves into your domain, looking for you, knowing that finding you means your death. Imagine that you now hold one of those servants of the law in your power. Your enemy, the creature from your nightmares, the monster who would destroy you without trial, without recourse, without mercy. What would you do, Detective? You dare to speak of cruelty and madness? What is left to this child? You should not ask why she was cruel. You should only ask why you are alive to complain about it!"

Miriam stared at him, appalled at the enormity of what he described. "Oh my God," she breathed.

"For all her cruelty she let you live. Had you arrested her, she would now be dead. Ask yourself some time: which of you is the more moral?"

He glared at her for a few more moments; then he shook his head and the hostility was gone, evaporating again down to its usual residue of contempt.

"But you came here for my opinion. I have given it. I don't care whether you accept it or spend the rest of your life haring off after chimeras. Now get out. And next time don't come back without a warrant."

~~~

The watcher hidden on the hill among the trees observed Miriam's departure with as much interest as her arrival, and transmitted to the supervisor's office the encrypted time-stamped telephoto images of this her second visit here. Moments like this were rare but brought a deep satisfaction that made the job worthwhile; gave meaning to the hours of emptiness. But the watcher was patient. It never got bored, it never slept: it just watched and waited.

Chapter 15 – Amaro

The nightclub was loud, noisy and smoky. Smoking was coming back into style now that most diseases of the lung including cancer had been banished to the dark corners of societal memory. Miriam didn't smoke herself but didn't mind the smell of these mild modern brands. They didn't choke you like she remembered as a child from some of her more chimney-like relatives; it was more a gentle haze of fragrances with these smoke-reduced brands. More like sitting in a refined club redolent of old cigars than choking over a grassfire.

She was out with her two best friends from work, both single like her. They thought it would be fun to unwind a bit, dance a bit crazy, who knows, maybe meet some fun guys. The other girls were still up dancing but Miriam was taking a rest from it, sipping a cocktail, when a strange man slipped smoothly into the seat beside her.

"Hello young lady. It looks like you've nearly finished your drink. I saw you dancing earlier: you need to keep your fluids up. May I buy you a top-up?"

"What, are you a doctor? And what fluids, precisely, are you really aiming to top me up with?"

The man laughed. "No, not a doctor. Just a humanitarian concerned with the health and happiness of humanity. Especially beautiful femality." He grinned. "I meant, quite innocently, to top up that deadly looking cocktail you are drinking. In fact I am so innocent that I can't imagine what else you could be referring to."

She couldn't help but grin back. "I see. Forgive me sir. A gallant knight is so rare these days that one hardly recognizes one when he appears. Speaking of which, I'm not letting you off the hook yet. I believe knights were renowned for admiring from afar – at least that's what they told their ladies. And you have confessed to watching me from afar. In our less innocent age we call that stalking."

The man looked wounded. "By my honor, lady, you grieve me. It is not my fault that your beauty ensnared me. You were there, before my eyes: how could I not place myself in your service? But if it is your wish, I shall go. I seek nothing but your happiness." Upon which he rose, and bowed.

Miriam laughed. "Oh, sit down you great lunk." She looked at him with frank curiosity. Curly dark hair, but with features and a shade to his skin suggesting some Spanish in his ancestry; lively dark eyes and a large mobile mouth. He laughed easily and lightly, showing fine white teeth. Well muscled but not overdone like a weightlifter. She felt a liquid stirring in her belly. *Whew*, she thought; *has it been that long? I'd better not drink too much more.*

"So, handsome knight, what do you do when you aren't tilting at windmills?"

"I should like to say that I am independently wealthy, able to whisk fair maidens to far exotic places at their whim. But I cannot. I am a humble scientist at the EPA. You see? I am a knight, of sorts. And you? Let me guess." He looked at her speculatively. "No... I cannot. Your beauty distracts me too much. I must ask."

She laughed again. "I think you are a rogue, no knight. So perhaps this will make you flee: I am a trainee detective with the City Police."

He looked shocked. "Oh no! I fear entrapment. Confess it now: you have ensnared me because of those unpaid parking tickets. Honestly, I mean to pay them!"

"Oh you!" she said, punching him on the shoulder. "You're impossible!"

Just then her friends returned, slightly tipsy. "Oooh, Miriam, who's your friend?"

"Just some lunk I met. Girls, this is... oh hell. We've been talking for five minutes and I don't even know your name!"

The lunk stood and bowed graciously. "Amaranto Leandro Moreno at your service, beautiful ladies! You may call me Amaro."

"Your name seems far more Spanish than your face," observed Miriam skeptically.

"Your friend here has already taught me the dangers of her tongue," Amaro said to the girls (was anything this man said *not* a double-entendre? thought Miriam), "but let me assure you all that I am no knave spinning fine tales to bewitch your fair hearts. The male line of my family traces its history all the way back to noble Spain. But my family has never put race before beauty, so most wives grafted to that line were of other lands. Mix with that my father's poetic soul, and my name is explained."

Miriam rolled her eyes. He was a bit of a poet himself if you asked her. She stood and introduced the girls, "Hello Amaro. These elegant ladies are Rianna and Darian, my friends from work. And I'm Miriam."

"Yes, I heard. Miriam! A fine name, evocative of prophecy and priestesses! Shall we dance?"

Miriam looked at Rianna and Darian helplessly. They laughed and shooed her on her way, then sat down and began an animated discussion about this turn of events.

Amaro led her to the floor. She half expected that his verbal performance was compensation for something, hopefully just two left feet, but he surprised her. He was an excellent dancer to whatever music was playing and she found herself whirled around the floor and completely, breathlessly delighted.

They went back to the table where the girls were watching them cheerfully. "I don't suppose you came with your brothers did you, Amaro?" Darian asked.

"Oh fair maiden," exclaimed Amaro, hand over his breast, "had I known what beauty I would find here tonight, I certainly would have brought my dearest friends to share in my delight! But alas I came alone. Yet perhaps – if I am so fortunate as to ever meet you lovely ladies again – I can introduce you to some fine young men at another time?"

Miriam sat looking at him. He was an entertaining rogue, that was for sure. But probably still a rogue. But hell. "Well, Amaro, I would hate my friends to miss out on an offer like that. So I guess we'll have to see you again."

"Nothing would delight me more! Except perhaps to discuss the details in a quieter place? Perhaps over coffee?"

Miriam had a good idea what kind of coffee was brewing in his mind. After all, a similar brand was brewing in hers. But she wasn't really into one-night stands; she preferred something with a bit more permanence. And one thing she'd learned by now was that if a man was going to last more than one night he was willing to wait more than one night.

"Thanks for the offer, but some other time perhaps. We have to work tomorrow. But here." She touched her phone to send her details to his, which he accepted and reciprocated. He smiled and bowed. "An honor, fair Miriam. You will be hearing from me. Until then, I wish you all joy."

They waved to him and weaved their way out of the club. Amaro sat there nursing his drink, watching Miriam go through narrowed eyes. *An interesting woman*, he thought. *I might enjoy this.*

CHAPTER 16 – DINNER

A maro was good to his word, and they arranged a triple date with her friends and his. He had not brought any brothers just two of his own friends. But he was either lucky or perceptive, for they all got along famously.

One Wednesday a couple of weeks after their first meeting, Miriam was putting on her coat ready to leave work when Darian came to see her. "Hi Miriam. We thought we'd go clubbing tonight. Are you up for it?"

Miriam looked up, a funny smile playing on her lips. "Sorry, I've a date with Amaro tonight."

"Oh! Getting serious, is it?"

Miriam shrugged and answered nonchalantly, "Oh, maybe. He's a laugh a minute, you might have noticed. He spoils me, too. Maybe I can bear his arrogant company a little longer." But from the little smile that wouldn't let itself be put away, Darian wasn't fooled: Miriam had "smitten" written all over her. "Well you kids have fun then. Don't do anything I wouldn't do." Darian blew her a kiss and left. Miriam finished up, humming happily, and followed her.

She met Amaro at an upscale Thai restaurant. "So, Miss Hunter, are your tastes as fiery as your tongue? Would you enjoy a chili to die from or should I order a gentler dish?"

She shook her head. He really was incorrigible. "I like it hot, Amaro. Let's see what you've got." Two could play at that game, she thought.

He raised his eyebrows mockingly. He really was a card, she

thought. She didn't know how much his role of gallant gentleman rake – or which parts of it – were genuine, but he certainly played it to the hilt. Once he knew her preference he did not discuss the options any further. Like a gentleman of old he simply took charge, selecting the dishes and the wine. She was more used to the modern style of equality and negotiation, but just for this evening she was amused enough to be carried along in his irresistible wake.

"Oh. Wow," she breathed at the first taste of the curry. He smiled. "Too much?"

"Oh, no. My tongue's gone but this is delicious."

"But your tongue is your best part! I do hope it comes back."

She poked it out at him. "Be careful what you ask for, brave knight."

He smiled, and they continued sampling the dishes. He had chosen a cold, somewhat sweet but not too sweet white wine. It went perfectly with the burning curries. Which were burning but not too burning: the chili enhanced rather than detracted from the other tastes.

"My, Amaro, I think you've done this before."

"My lady, anything I have done before has been mere preparation for this evening."

She laughed. "You're impossible! But let's be serious. All I ever get out of you is knightly wit. Is there a real man in there, or are you just a pretty suit of armor? Who is the real Amaro? *Is* there a real Amaro?"

He looked at her. He actually managed to look serious. She wondered whether it was real or just his best performance to date. "Well, the real Amaro has many faces, all equally real. He is complex, like an aged red wine." He paused. Miriam just waited. She knew about trout fishing. This was a trout who had never been hooked.

"Most ladies see the gallant Amaro, and that is enough for them. Some may say the gallant Amaro is shallow, but he has made many ladies happy and they him. Where that is all the lady sees, Amaro is happy for them to see no further. They have fun, he has fun, and there is much laughter and no tears. Much pleasure and no pain. After a time they go their separate ways and all their memories are happy. Amaro has observed that knowing more deeply opens the doors to pain, and while greater happiness might in theory be found there, in the end the memories may not be so happy."

His expression made Miriam wonder how personal those observations were. And the prick of sympathy she felt made her start to wonder who was the trout and who was the fisherman here. Before she could pursue that thought further, he appeared to come to a decision, and continued.

"Well, we must start somewhere. Let me tell you about my work. As I told you, I am a scientist working for the EPA. Though I no longer do original research – my job is more project planning, monitoring and analysis. Specifically, I concentrate on genetic contamination of the environment – you know, detecting the spread of illegal genetic modifications into the wild or into agricultural crops, whether illegal completely or only legal on condition of containment." At the flash of interest in her eyes, he stopped. "You are interested in genetics?" he asked.

"Oh, it's just a coincidence. My work at the moment has something to do with genetics."

"Really? How interesting! Perhaps it is something I can help you with. That might be stimulating. Usually the only mutual interest in genetics I find with the ladies is of a more intimate nature." The old Amaro was irrepressible, she thought.

"Sorry, I can't really talk about it for now. It's too confidential: it would mean my job. I can't even tell you what it's about generally. It's that hot."

"I am impressed. I was under the impression that you were a humble apprentice detective. Now I learn that you move in high circles, privy to national secrets!"

She laughed. "Oh, I am a humble apprentice, believe me. Most of my time is spent on an Artful Idiot system. However I've got it to idiot savant stage and sometimes it spits out something useful. The trick is in knowing what is useful and what isn't. The thing can come up with a whole conspiracy theory involving Joe the Corner Butcher and the President of the United States, and make a pretty convincing case of it sometimes. It knows how to calculate statistics but is clueless how to apply them: so I am trying to teach it, to help cut out its more outrageous ideas without missing real issues. Anyway, it recently came up with something strange that happened to link with something even stranger, so I ended up involved. Whether it ends up making my career or breaking it, well, time will tell."

"My, my, Miriam," he said, "We start delving into the complex reality of Amaro only to find that the truly fascinating person is Miriam. I feel inadequate." He frowned sadly.

Miriam laughed delightedly. "Oh Amaro! I find it hard to believe you are capable of feeling inadequate even on a double date with the President and Madame Curie."

He laughed. "Perhaps when you have tasted the full complexity of the noble Amaro, you will learn whether or not that is true. But let us leave government intrigue behind us. I know! Here is a proposition I read once: 'the entertainment you choose is a guide to your soul'. Let us discuss the holidays we have been on. We may learn more about each other's souls that way than by trying to find the words to explain."

They spent the rest of the evening enjoying the food, enjoying the wine, and enjoying each other's company. They discussed holidays, family, friends, movies and art. Miriam was entranced. When Sir Amaro peeled off his armor and it was just Amaro, he was not only amusing, he appeared to be the kind of man you could live a lifetime with and never be bored.

They had just finished a dessert wine whose sweetness temporarily chased away the chili, only to have it return in a synergy that made her mouth feel it had been kissed. Amaro insisted on taking the bill, his persona of gallant gentleman of a previous century rising up again for the occasion.

Miriam sighed. "I am afraid I've had too good a time, Senor Moreno. I've broken my own rule about how much I should drink when out on a date. I think I'd better get a taxi home. I can pick my car up tomorrow."

"What kind of knight would so fail his Lady? I shall of course carry you to your door on my noble charger."

Miriam looked into his dark liquid eyes. The liquid ran into her own eyes and down to her belly, where it started working on her resistance. There wasn't much resistance to work on. "Thank you Amaro, I think I shall accept your chivalrous offer."

He smiled, and she felt as if he swept her out of the restaurant, down to his car, and finally to her door. They stood there and she looked at him. "Whew! I think I drank even more than I realized," she admitted, swaying slightly.

"A knight would never take advantage of a lady not in full possession of her faculties, so I must sadly bid you goodnight," he said, bowing to kiss her hand.

"Not so fast, lunk. I didn't say I wasn't in full possession of my faculties. You keep complaining about my tongue. Let's see if it can change your mind." With that, she lifted herself on her toes, put her arms around him, and kissed him. He returned the kiss without a moment's hesitation. *I suppose I shouldn't be surprised*, she thought, *that he kisses like he dances.* Liquid desire flowed down from her mouth and up from her toes, meeting in the middle. *Oh what the hell*, she thought. "Well don't just stand there," she said huskily, "come in."

CHAPTER 17 – INTERROGATION

Amaro woke early. He could feel Miriam breathing gently beside him. His body was thanking him for last night's sensory symphony, and he smiled. *Mornings could most definitely be worse*, he thought. He thought of the joyless religions that despised the pleasures of the flesh and named them sins, and wondered how people could get so twisted around.

It was still early. Through the blinds he could see the grey light of dawn starting to lighten the sky. Miriam stirred, and put her hand on his stomach. He gently laid his own hand over it. It was warm, soft and trusting.

Miriam opened her eyes and looked at him. She still half suspected he was just a slick-talking rogue. Amaro detected the change in her breathing and turned his head to face her, and saw her studying him. "Yes, my love?"

"That's just the question, isn't it? That simple word can hide a multitude of lies," Miriam said quietly. She began circling her finger around his navel. It made Amaro tingle. She continued, playfully but with an edge of seriousness, "The question in my mind is: is Amaro really the chivalrous knight, or is he a knave in drag? How can a girl tell?"

"My lady! If in the light of day you fear that Amaro, having had his wicked way with the fair maiden, would ride off leaving her pregnant and bereft: I am mortified! Though Amaro's lawyer might point out that it is the fair lady who refused his offer of, ah, protection at the time," he added teasingly.

"Pah! For all your knightly airs, this isn't the Middle Ages. How many fair maidens are stupid enough not to take their own precautions, rather than relying on the uncertain valor of self-proclaimed gentlemen?" she laughed. "Don't worry, you won't wake up in nine months to a bailiff presenting you with a child support summons."

Amaro looked wounded. Miriam's finger began circling further down his stomach and she added playfully, "Besides, I cheerfully admit that I much prefer skin on skin, don't you? And fortunately sexually transmitted diseases are a thing of the past too."

"A medical advance which we can all celebrate," Amaro replied. "As indeed we did," he added with a mocking grin.

Miriam's finger was now playing with his curlier hairs and she could feel him stir in response. She reached down and held him, and began to move her hand slowly.

Amaro felt the fire build and reached over to her, but she slapped him away with her other hand. "Don't you try to distract me, knave!" she said. "I need to interrogate the suspect, learn his true intentions."

"My intentions... My intentions are noble!" gasped Amaro. "As a true knight of the realm, all Amaro seeks is to increase the amount of good in the world! Happiness is good. The logic is clear! At least, he thinks so. He is getting rather distracted and his thinking may not be as clear as he imagines. That must be why he has not thanked the lady. She is unusually forward for a demure maiden, but at this stage, Amaro cannot say he objects."

"Don't fool yourself, rogue," Miriam said roughly. "I'm not doing this for your benefit. I have plans for this thing!"

With that, she rolled over to straddle him and lowered herself down. She began to rock gently. Amaro groaned. "My lady is sweet, kind and considerate. How could he ever betray her?"

Miriam reached her hand between his legs and did something that made him quiver. "So do I understand you correctly? You might actually call me again? And if I call you, you will answer the phone?"

"I swear!"

Miriam gripped him gently and whispered, "I'll hold you to that, rogue."

Then she released him, leaned over to kiss him and their rocking increased its tempo. They both forgot to speak for a while.

When they had finished, Miriam rolled off onto her side. "Oh my.

Oh my." She murmured.

"I must say, my lady," said Amaro after a while, "that I am most impressed by your interrogation technique. I could not call it police brutality, but it is uniquely effective. It is no wonder your career is going well. I should not be surprised if your rate of confessions is astounding!"

Miriam's mouth made an "O" of shock and she punched him on the shoulder. "Oh you! That is *not* my usual interrogation technique. It is reserved," she added haughtily, "only for the most hardened criminals."

"While I generally avoid the attentions of the law, I think I am glad you consider me so. That I may be forced to suffer such techniques."

They lay together silently for a while, just enjoying the relaxation spreading through their limbs.

Then Miriam turned to him and smiled. "I don't suppose you are free this Friday night?"

Amaro's face took on a look of intense concentration. "Well... as you would expect, Amaro's social calendar requires sophisticated scheduling software." Miriam rolled her eyes. "But there appears to be a bug. His calendar seems to have become free for the foreseeable future. This Friday? Consider it done. For that matter, tonight is free as well." He gave her a hopeful look, much like a puppy not wanting a game to end just yet.

Miriam laughed but shook her head. "My body is already finding it easy enough to overrule my brain. I think I need a rest from you to get some perspective. Let's stick to Friday."

"I'm going to have a shower," she added. "For some unknown reason, I am sweaty and smell of Man. I won't be long."

Amaro lay back in bed listening the sound of the running water. He smiled again. *Oh, yes.*

Miriam came back into the bedroom wrapped in a fluffy white towel, drying her hair. "You probably want a shower too," she observed.

"Indeed," replied Amaro, getting out of bed. Miriam added, "Could you drive me to where I left my car? Unless it's too far out of your way?"

Amaro bowed, sweeping his arm as if flourishing a feathered cap. Miriam had to laugh. He made it look elegant even stark naked and still somewhat aroused. "Amaro would be honored. It is the least he can do in return for the lady's, ah, services."

"Beast!" she said. "Into the shower with you!"

~~~

Miriam arrived at the station early and went happily to work. She often found herself humming even when arguing with the AI.

Whenever she saw herself in the ladies' room mirror, she noticed a silly little smile playing at the corner of her lips. It refused to go away. When she smoothed her top down, her nipples responded even to that innocent motion. She rolled her eyes at her own reactions. *Maybe I need a whole week away from Amaro,* she thought. *Fat chance,* the silly smile told her.

Darian bumped into her when she was making herself a cappuccino in the refreshments room. "How did the hot date go?" she asked. Miriam attempted to put on a stern expression but somehow it came out as a happy smile. "Oh!" said Darian, "I see! That good, eh?"

Miriam could only smile; she decided she had better not play poker for a while. "Yes. In every way. The man certainly knows how to entertain a girl."

Darian clapped her hands delightedly. "I expect a full report at the next meeting of the girls' club!" she said.

Then she looked suspiciously at Miriam and snorted. "Though from the look of you, you might be too busy to attend for a while."

Chapter 18 – Rianna

When the forensics team had taken samples from Katlyn's hideout, given the state of the place they had not been hopeful. The building was dirty, a temporary home for human vagrants and a more permanent home for vermin. Not only that, where it had not been incinerated the sprinkler system had mixed everything together into muck. The chance of getting anything useful out of any of their samples was minimal.

They had one piece of luck: one of the forensic investigators had lifted a piece of fallen metal in Katlyn's former nest and noticed a piece of charred human hair stuck under it. It had been partially protected from the flames and on closer examination the investigator saw it had an attached follicle. Forensics still weren't hopeful: while intact, the hair was obviously damaged by heat and smoke. But it was their best chance and they had sent it to the DNA lab. That had been a few weeks ago: in the scheme of things it had no special priority.

A call announced itself on Miriam's screen. It was Rianna, who was in charge of the DNA lab.

"Hi Rianna," she said. "I hope you have good news for me."

"Sorry. We've looked at that piece of hair from your fire, but its DNA is badly degraded, as well as the hair being contaminated with all kinds of crud. It would be expensive to get into a state where it could be sequenced and even then we'd only get fairly short pieces. Nowhere near good enough for positive identification, though maybe good enough for a modest probability match. In either case certainly not good enough to use in court: any defense attorney would tear it apart. But if your boss authorizes the expense we can try. It won't be cheap."

Miriam shook her head. "Damn. No, we don't have enough to go on, clues or budget. No way he'd authorize it. Double damn. It's the nearest to a real clue I have."

Rianna thought a moment. "Well... there might be something. We do have a research budget. Pushing the envelope on how much data we can get out of compromised samples is something the Powers like us to do. At least when it works. Yes," she smiled, "I can see an interesting problem here. I can put my new person Kimberley on it. She's pretty good at tough work and likes a challenge."

Miriam frowned. "Thanks for the offer, but are you sure it would be OK? I don't want you getting into trouble over it."

"No, Miriam, it's legitimate research. And interesting. Hell, if it works I might even get a pay rise."

Miriam grinned at her. "Richly deserved, too. Thanks a lot, Rianna. Keep me posted."

"Bye babe. See you at lunch."

CHAPTER 19 – COUSINS

It was a rainy Sunday afternoon, and they were sitting on her couch, loosely entwined around each other, watching a nature documentary. It was an old one, digitized and converted to 3D, starring a gentle but enthusiastic Englishman with a raspy voice. But as Amaro pointed out, evolution was slow and nature last century was much like nature now, albeit somewhat more common then.

Amaro had rekindled her interest in nature. She was not by temperament as purist as he, and tended to think that any improvement was a good improvement by definition, whether done by genetics or by physics. But she supposed a bit of genetic purism went with his job. She had been interested in the living world as a child and now found rediscovering it, especially with such an expert guide, to be an unexpected pleasure.

The professor was creeping up on some mountain gorillas, relatives of man that despite a usually gentle disposition were mountains in more than habitat, and if angry could tear a man's limbs off. She decided the unassuming professor was a brave man. He went on to contrast the gentle vegetarian gorilla with the more aggressive chimpanzee and the oversexed bonobo, the two closest relatives of man. She could certainly see human beings as a combination of the two: go out, fight a war, go hunting, come home and have sex all night. That sounded like a lot of human history to her, like a summary of the Trojan War. *A lot like us come to think of it*, she thought fondly, glancing at Amaro.

The lines leading to the different chimps and man had diverged only a few million years ago; that to the gorillas a few million earlier. It was remarkable how different humans were from these close evolutionary cousins, and the professor went on to describe differences besides their big brains. Miriam sat up straight. Something he had said had collided with something in her own brain and made a connection. No, it can't be that. If it were that simple he'd have known, surely. She stood up suddenly. "Oh my God."

"What's the matter, sweet Miriam?" asked Amaro. "You look like you saw a ghost. But fear not. Brave Sir Amaro will ride to your aid, sword held high!"

She looked at him, barely seeing him, but his banter from their traditional teasing rang another bell primed by her suspicions. *The phrases friends share*, she thought. *Why is that important? The phrases...* Then the other connection fell into place. "Odin, Thor and Loki!" she cried. "Amaro, I have to go!"

He looked at her in amazement. "Hey, slow down, tiger! What's gotten into you? You're worrying me!"

Her eyes swept over him, still not really registering his existence except as a shape in her field of view. "Sorry. Sorry. Can't talk. I just realized something, something important. Holy Hell. Jesus. Christ. Almighty." Then she stopped, belatedly remembering it was Sunday. This was important but was it urgent enough to drag people away from their homes and families? Maybe, but they probably wouldn't see it that way. Somewhat deflated, she realized this wasn't so hot it couldn't wait until tomorrow.

She turned away and began composing a long note into her phone.

Amaro looked at her, nonplussed. Then his eyes narrowed. *Well*, he thought, *now this is an interesting development.*

"Sorry Amaro," she said when she'd finished. "I just had a thought about work that might be important. But it can wait until tomorrow. I'm back in the present now. So where were we?"

"We were studying our animal relatives. I believe we can learn many things from them, especially the bonobo. Let me demonstrate." With that, he took her in his arms and gave her a lingering kiss, which somehow ended with his lying on top of her in a mutual tangle. Her earlier intellectual excitement evolved seamlessly into a more physical one, and the tangle began to assume configurations that would no doubt be interesting to topologists but were even more interesting to the participants. Then she forgot about her work for a while.

Later, Amaro watched her contentedly sleeping form affectionately, but there was a calculating edge to his gaze. He tapped a message into his own phone then he sat and thought, idly playing with her hair but careful not to wake her.

~~~

The next morning, with the imminence of being able to do something about it, Miriam's excitement over her idea grew. She sent messages to Stone and Ramos to meet her in the Chief's office as soon as they arrived.

Ramos was first to arrive after Miriam, who was already waiting for him trying to hide her impatience. He usually liked to settle in for a while before granting audience to his minions, and had a look of grumpiness overlaying a faint odor of gym about him. Jack turned up a few minutes later and leaned against the wall looking cynical but intrigued. Miriam was looking a little wild-eyed.

"OK Hunter, what's so urgent it can't wait until I've had my coffee?" grumbled Ramos.

"I was watching a show yesterday. About chimpanzees. Then it hit me."

Jack looked up. "Great. I rushed in here for a movie review. So did the chimp get the girl?"

"No, no," said Miriam, completely oblivious to sarcasm. "Remember when we talked to Dr Tagarin? Remember what he said? Our thief couldn't be a geneh, because nobody could have made her 25 years ago?"

"Sure, that's one reason we never escalated it to GenInt except as a note worded so nobody will care. Covering our asses both ways," said Ramos. "Anyone who does decide it's worth a look will probably come to the same conclusion. A woman with tacked-on mods, not a geneh. Our problem, not theirs."

"But it never rang true to me. I've met her, remember. We had a *long* chat."

"Sure, sure, we know," replied Jack. "But as the man said, sometimes you can't beat arithmetic."

"But that's the point! I was watching this show, and the presenter said something interesting. Humans have an unusually long childhood even for apes. Chimpanzees are about our size but reach puberty in only 8 to 10 years! Gorillas are twice our weight and reach puberty even earlier! This girl has faster muscles and faster nerves! What if she also has faster development, more like a chimp than a man? She might only *be* 15!"

They both went still and stared at her. Jack's mouth was open. Then he closed it, only to open it again to say: "Sure, as far as I know. But if it were that easy, our friendly expert would have seen it straight away. He would have..." then his voice trailed away, as he saw it too. "Oh my God."

"That's what I said! Then I remembered something else. I'd forgotten it, but then Amaro said something, one of those little inside jokes couples have. When Katlyn first grabbed me she said something that struck me as important, but she was choking me and I forgot about it. But I remember now. She said, 'A life is a terrible thing to waste.' Those are almost the exact words Dr Tagarin said at our first meeting. It stuck in my memory it because it's kind of a funny phrase – there's some famous quote like it, but it's about a mind not a life. Those two know each other! I'm sure of it!"

Jack and Ramos looked at her, looked at each other. "Christ, Miriam," said Jack, "It isn't proof, but it sure answers some questions."

"But what can we do about it?" asked Ramos. "It's certainly relevant to our case of the thief. But is it enough for a search warrant? It's certainly enough to bring in GenInt." He frowned. "Not that I'd like to. But we might have to now."

Miriam said, "I don't want to bring GenInt in either. It's still just a crazy theory, right? Let's try talking to Dr Tagarin again. Jack and I can go."

"The last time he saw you he said don't come back without a warrant, remember?"

"Yes, but even without a warrant he might prefer us to GenInt."

Chapter 20 – Tagarin

They parked the car and looked up towards the entrance. *This is getting to be a habit*, Miriam thought. Perhaps she and the gate would become friends.

"Oh well, let's see if he still likes us," Jack said. "Despite my superior experience and interrogation skills I think you should do the talking. If he likes anyone, it's you. Like a boxer likes his punching bag, but it's something."

Tagarin had apparently given his gate an update. They had barely come within range when it said, "I detect no warrant, detectives. I believe my employer advised you that you were no longer welcome in his home and he would not entertain you without one."

"Please convey my apologies to Dr Tagarin," Miriam answered. "But there has been a development in the case. He is now a person of interest himself and it would be in his interests to talk to us."

"Dr Tagarin wishes to know what part of the word 'warrant' you fail to understand. He further wishes me to remind you that no matter how interesting he is to you, the interest is not reciprocated. Especially when your interest is not shared by a judge, or not enough to get you that warrant. He also refers you back to his team of shark-like lawyers and wonders if you have more understanding of the word 'harassment' than of the word 'warrant'?"

"It is true that we don't have enough to get a warrant. But we do have enough to interest GenInt. We do not want to involve GenInt at this stage and I am sure Dr Tagarin would agree. We hope we can sort this out with a friendly discussion. That's all we're here for."

The gate was silent.

In a few minutes, it opened without comment and they went up the path to the door. As they approached, the door opened and James greeted them. His butler façade had slipped a little and his eyes were hostile, though his manner was as gracious as ever.

Again they were ushered directly in to Dr Tagarin's office. This time James stood less in the shadows and more in their line of sight. Miriam was impressed at how a man who appeared to have just one expression could make it appear as aloof politeness or stony threat without any detectable rearrangement of its features.

"All right officers, this is becoming repetitive. My Jacuzzi blondes will be getting jealous of you, Ms Hunter, and then I might become less relaxed than you're used to," he said with a sharp edge. "So what is this latest exciting piece of news?"

Miriam explained her reasoning about Katlyn's possible accelerated development and how it solved the timing dilemma. She went on to note that if it was true, it indicated ongoing, undiscovered human genetic engineering in the years since it was made illegal. She omitted, however, the coincidence of phrasing between him and Katlyn. That wasn't proof and would only put him more on the defensive. Best not to play that card yet: see what cards he showed, first.

"And so you think that I, as a once eminent expert in that field, am the most likely suspect?"

Miriam spread her hands. "Not necessarily, though you see how it looks. But you would also know any other likely candidates. For now, we are not treating you as a suspect. We just want to know what you think."

"How kind," he observed skeptically. "I think you are clutching at straws and at my expense. Surely it is obvious that even if your theory were plausible my previous assessment, that you are dealing with a skilled human with a few later enhancements, remains more likely."

"Except that I have met her. It doesn't ring true to me. Even she said she was a geneh. She practically beat me into naming it."

"And you are a silly little girl who was scared out of her few wits!" he snapped. "Witnesses see things that aren't there all the time, as you'd know if you'd done your schoolwork! Of course she wanted you to think she's a geneh! A complete distraction from discovering her true nature, which might lead you to those capable of making her what she is! Maybe that is the sole reason she left you alive!"

"Perhaps I *have* been led to someone capable of making her," she countered.

"Pah! You are obsessed with your childish fantasies, incapable of adult thought! There are no genehs! They are all dead! If you weren't holding the stick of GenInt over my head I'd have James throw you both out!"

He glared at them, breathing heavily.

"I am sorry to anger you again, doctor. But do you claim that accelerated development is impossible? If not, why did you fail to mention it?"

"No, it is not impossible," he said, as she saw his face slip into his dispassionate scientist mode. "But nor would it be easy. I can see paths one might take to achieve it. But really, think for once. Evolution doesn't play games. A long childhood is dangerous for the child and expensive for the parent. There is a reason why our children take so long to grow up. We might look a lot like apes, but surely your nature show was not so stupid as to omit the main difference?" He tapped his own head. "This brain has made us what we are. It needs a lot of training. That is why we have a long childhood. It is not a matter of arbitrary chance, it is intimately tied to our humanity."

"But you said her nervous system appears to be accelerated. Could that compensate? Allow her to have a shorter childhood?"

Tagarin started and gave her an odd look, almost of respect. "That is the most perceptive thing you've said yet, Ms Hunter. Perhaps. Perhaps. But still, it wouldn't be easy. Our developmental program is tied to a lot of things: physical, hormonal, psychological. Perhaps it could be sped up a few years? Enough to give us someone who looks ten years older than she really is? Difficult. And if so she might have had a hard time of it, growing up. I'm not convinced she would have survived it." He paused, considering.

"And even if it is scientifically possible, she still had to be born after the Geneh Laws were imposed. In our earlier interview I mentioned the need for sophisticated equipment, and the logistical problems are not to be ignored. This kind of work is highly technical. You can't do it with a microscope and a pair of tweezers. Working out what to do, or at least working out what to try, can be done with a comprehensive comparative genetic database, a good computer program and a bit of human artistry. But doing it. Well. You are trying to perform delicate genetic manipulations on tiny delicate cells, and you don't have much time to do it in. Successful genetic engineering of this order requires the right sequence of physical and enzymatic steps to insert or replace any number of genes, parts of genes or entire chromosomal segments – and it has to be done right. A slight mismatch and your genes won't work at all. Bad positioning and the result will be a monster, dead or riddled with cancers. And the stem cells won't wait for you forever: you have to do your engineering, patch up the cells and put them back into an environment that makes them happy again as soon as possible. And that's not including the further difficulties in persuading a stem cell to achieve totipotency and from that go on to produce a viable embryo.

"It all requires highly advanced, very expensive robotic technology. There are few suppliers. The equipment has what GenInt would call ethical uses, for some medical procedures and of course for plant and animal genetic modification, which is still allowed at least in some countries and for some purposes. But GenInt has a chokehold on it. Every machine produced is tracked from cradle to grave, all its internal operations are electronically audited, and there are random site checks to boot. For our thief to be a geneh, her makers would somehow need access to such a machine and not only that, do their work without even the machine knowing about it. I don't know how they could do it. Certainly GenInt have gone to great lengths to ensure they can't."

He looked at them, and the scientist was gone again. "But as for why I did not mention the possibility of accelerated development earlier, why would I? It isn't very likely and all it could do is allow you to suspect your thief is a geneh and therefore that I am involved. As your presence here attests. But that's all I can give you. If it's not enough to keep the execrable bastards of GenInt off my back then I'll just have to take my chances. With any luck I can make them a laughing stock and embarrass the politicians enough to cut their funding. If a few of the scum lose their jobs it will have been worth the annoyance."

He added drily, "I suppose there is no point my telling you not to come back without a warrant, given this is the third time you've managed to get in here without one. But don't expect me to be so hospitable next time. James, throw these two out. But gently. We don't want to be accused of police brutality."

Miriam hesitated briefly, considering whether this was the time to raise the issue of their common phrase. *No,* she thought; *he has far too tough a mind to be scared into a confession by something so insubstantial.* Whether he was innocent or guilty, all it would do would be to engender another of his bitingly sarcastic rejoinders; it would make it less likely to get further information out of him now or in the future, not more.

So she stood and said, "Well, thank you for your time, Dr Tagarin. I sincerely apologize for the annoyance we have caused you. Good bye." Stone stood too and they moved to the door, James closely shadowing them as if he expected one of them to leap at Tagarin's throat at any instant.

"Wait," Tagarin said.

They turned and looked inquiringly at him.

"Since you treat me like a suspect when I fail to do your job for you, there is one question you haven't asked. So in an attempt to forestall yet another visit when your slow wits finally work their way around to asking it, I shall ask it for you: are there more of them?"

Miriam and Jack gave each other slightly alarmed looks. Jack replied, "I thought you said she wasn't a geneh anyway?"

"Yes, but you don't really believe me, do you? So do you want to know my thoughts on it, or will you come back later at a less convenient time?" he replied sourly.

"Please."

"Well, consider this. If we allow that our geneh makers somehow acquired the necessary machinery and were able to operate it for several years after GenInt goons started strutting around like the goose-brains they are, do you really think there'd be just one of them? Even if our hypothetical geniuses waited to be sure of the quality of their work, your cat woman is an adult. Producing just one would be a very poor return on a very expensive investment – expensive in dollars, time and personal risk."

Miriam and Jack looked more alarmed.

"On the other hand." He paused. "One thing you said struck me as odd at the time: another thing I neglected to comment on, if you want more things to complain about. She said she'd had an 'eclectic' education. Were those her actual words?"

Miriam thought, and nodded. "Yes. I remember because it's not a word I usually hear. The average criminal certainly doesn't talk about their eclectic tastes in plunder."

"My point exactly. It's an odd choice of word. Why not 'comprehensive', or 'thorough'? Again, we're talking about an expensive investment: if it was me I'd have given her the best education my money could buy. 'Eclectic' sounds more like a random selection of topics without particular rhyme or reason – the kind of thing you find with intelligent people who are self taught.

"Then consider her choice of career, her cynical bitterness, her violence and mental instability. If we take all these things together there is one obvious conclusion. When she was quite young, old enough to fend for herself but still a fairly young child, she was abandoned. Whether something happened to her creators, or they were about to be caught and had to get rid of her fast, we may never know: she might not know herself. But imagine your life if you were a young, intelligent, frightened creature, knowing that the law called you vermin to be killed on sight, having to live off your wits and off the land. How do you think you'd have turned out?" He glared at them as if it was their fault. "I wonder how many laws exist just to keep lawmen in a job, chasing criminals they themselves have created?

"Now get out."

Tagarin watched them go, considering. The older cop was perceptive and suspicious enough, but that young one was positively dangerous. He didn't think he'd seen the end of her.

CHAPTER 21 – DELANEY

"Hunter."

"Detective Miriam Hunter?"

"Yes, speaking."

"Ah, good morning detective. My name is Charles Delaney. While I was travelling overseas you attempted to contact me about a theft I reported a few months ago. I am now back. Do you still wish to speak to me?"

Miriam quickly consulted her files. Yes, one of the double victims of a minor burglary followed by a mysterious and much more substantial electronic loss of funds; however he had not been present at any recent events starring the President. Given her lack of luck with the others she was surprised he had chosen to call her back.

"Oh, good afternoon Mr Delaney. Yes, I would very much like to talk to you. Can we arrange a time? I'm happy to come and visit you at your home or office."

"Anything to assist the law. Especially if it might help the law retrieve my property. I think my apartment would be best: there are some things you might like to see. But I am a busy man. I shall now leave you to arrange the details with my AI. I shall see you in due course. Goodbye for now."

Miriam exposed the public face of her and Stone's calendars to Delaney's AI, checked the suggested times and confirmed one. Then she sat back and thought. She called Stone. "Jack, did you notice I just made us an appointment? Good. Yes, this one actually seems to want to talk to us. Maybe we'll learn something!"

"Yeah, maybe," answered Stone. "Stranger things have happened. Just not often."

~~~

Miriam and Stone entered the lobby of a tall apartment block that pointed multiple steel needles at the sky, each clothed in a slightly different color of glass. Miriam had admired it from the street: it was even fancier than her uncle's. It reminded her of illustrations of cities of the future in science fiction stories from her childhood. It appeared the future had arrived, for some at least.

The staff all wore the same uniform and the same expression, hovering between obsequious and haughty, ready to assume the correct form as soon as they were certain of the status of the enquirer. When his system informed him that he was dealing with the police the expression of the man they approached didn't change. Apparently he believed the servants of the law deserved both.

"Hello. We're here to see Mr Delaney," advised Stone. To the unimpressed raised eyebrow he added, "We have an appointment."

"Certainly sir. Let me check. Yes, I see Mr Delaney is expecting you." He frowned slightly, as if hoping that Mr Delaney had not been expecting them so he could have had the pleasure of curling his lip at them. "Please go to the bank of elevators over to your right. Hold a moment. They are now keyed to your identification badges and will take you to the correct floor. Proceed to the entrance door and you will receive further directions from Mr Delaney."

"Thanks pal," said Stone. The man raised his well-practiced eyebrow. "It is my pleasure to serve, sir," he replied as if he meant it.

Miriam and Stone walked briskly to the elevator, which opened at their approach and whisked them upward at an impressive velocity; the initial acceleration almost made them bend their knees. "Welcome to the human stratosphere, Hunter," commented Stone. "Know your place and mind your manners. Mortals such as us dare not offend the sky gods."

They got out and the door to Delaney's apartment, the only entrance visible, opened at their approach. As they entered, the door informed them that Mr Delaney would greet them in the first room to their right.

They went in and Delaney rose to greet them. "Good morning Detectives Hunter, Stone," he said, putting out his hand. "I am pleased the police are still investigating this crime. May I take it that you have fresh leads?"

"I am afraid it is a bit more complicated than that, Mr Delaney," replied Stone. "We don't have fresh evidence in your case but we have found curious similarities with some other cases. But any clue might help us: anything you noticed later or seemed too minor for the attending officers to have put in their report. If we can get enough clues from enough cases we might be able to zero in on our criminals."

Delaney looked a little disappointed. "I see. But no, no. It is a mystery. The accounts that were robbed should have been secure. But one day, the money was simply gone. Neither the bank nor the forensic investigators were able to trace how or where it went. The bank assures me that I withdrew it myself, but even amnesia can't account for that: there is no trace of it happening at my end."

"Were the accounts emptied?" enquired Stone.

"No, and that is the strange thing. One of many strange things, I suppose. Overall I lost about half of the money. But if the thieves could do that, why would they not take it all? It's not as if it was so little I might not have noticed. It is a mystery. It is as if the motive wasn't money, or not entirely money. But then what was it? There have been no further actions taken against me."

They had nothing to say to that. It made no sense to them either.

"What about the earlier crime, Mr Delaney?" asked Miriam. "The physical burglary, where as I recall some jewelry was stolen."

Delaney looked a bit surprised. "That? That is another intriguing mystery, but more an annoyance than anything else. In fact it was almost worth the cost of the jewels for the entertaining dinner conversations it has given birth to since. Are you implying the two are linked? The earlier investigators had some suspicions along those lines but couldn't find any bugs or Trojans that might have given someone access to my accounts. I have a lot of money, Detective: I have high-class systems here. I even had the AI do a full diagnostic, including of itself. The whole system is clean. There is no evidence the crimes are linked except for the coincidence itself."

He added, "There is something new I can tell you about that event, however. I was wondering whether it was worth reporting, given that the crime itself was minor and the new evidence almost certainly useless. But since you are here you might want to see it."

"Certainly! What do you have?"

"Well, one mystery of the case is that the thief somehow interfered with my video surveillance system. Both the insurance company and I took the vendor to task over it, but they appear to have been telling the truth when they said it should have been impossible given the specifications of their system. They said there were theoretical ways it could be done – in their words, there are theoretical ways to do almost anything – but they were aware of no working technology that could do it. Let me show you."

He called up a holographic display. "Here is a video surveillance of this room, right now." Miriam and Stone saw a clear image of themselves and Delaney sitting in the room. "Now here is what the system recorded while the thief was gracing us with his presence." The image became mainly white noise; all that could be discerned among the noise were some vague shapes and movements, nothing identifiable. "As you can see, quite useless."

"However, just the other night we got to discussing this at one of those dinner parties I mentioned. One of my guests was a computer expert specializing in advanced image processing: the kind which astrophysicists and the military are interested in for extracting every last drop of information from their images. She said that a suitable image extraction program might be able to identify and average out any variations from random noise. As you can see from the vague shadows, such variations appear to exist in the recording. So with enough frames of the right kind, in theory even something this noisy might yield sufficient information for a composite image of who was there."

He shrugged. "As I've said, it is an intriguing mystery. So I took her advice. Here is what the system came up with as an image of our thief."

Miriam and Stone stared at the image on his display.

"You're kidding me," murmured Stone.

On the display was now a very grainy image of a person. The thief was wearing a greyish suit much like the one Katlyn had been seen in and a mask covering the face except for the eyes. The sex was uncertain; the person seemed somewhat slender and more likely female than male, but the outlines were too vague to be sure. But two things were sure. The eyes were dark and human, and there was no tail.

Miriam stared at it, confused. It just didn't make any sense. Everything else pointed to the crimes being related and the perpetrator being Katlyn. But this was definitely not Katlyn. It looked more like a ninja.

"Mr Delaney," said Miriam hoarsely. "This image. Do you know if any assumptions were made, such as height or sex, to make the image cleanup easier? Or is it a true unbiased extraction? What I mean is, say the thief had been wearing something odd, like a Viking helmet or something – would the system have shown it or simply not seen it because it wasn't expecting it?"

Delaney looked at her curiously. "That question makes me wonder what you know that you aren't telling me." He paused, inviting an answer, but neither Miriam nor Stone replied. He sighed. "Ah, the police! How you like to have your secrets. But no matter, I want this criminal caught and if you think not revealing evidence will help you, then I suppose I will give you the benefit of the doubt. No, it is a true unbiased image. This is what the thief looked like, as far as you can tell anything. But it is of no use for identification even if we had the thief in our hands for a direct comparison. Certainly no use in court. I suppose it might exclude certain suspects if they are especially tall, short or fat, but that's about it."

"May we take a copy of the video and the composite image?" asked Miriam.

"Of course. If you can think you can do better with it, be my guests. Here."

"Thank you. Oh. Do you mind if I ask you a more personal question? I assure you it is related to the case, though I am not in a position to tell you more."

"More secrets? Well, you can ask."

"Are you a supporter of President Felton? I don't mean did you vote for her, I mean have you been involved more directly, say in her campaigns or fundraising?"

Delaney shot her a sharp glance. "I would say that is none of your business," he said in a tone as sharp as his glance. He thought a moment then continued, "Hmmm. Though I suppose it is a matter of public record, even if you'd probably have to dig to find it. Yes, I was a young firebrand once, believe it or not. I was an admirer of hers in the early years, involved in her campaign against the genehs. And while I have done well in business myself I did come from a wealthy family. So not only did I work for her organization, I donated a substantial amount of money to her cause."

Miriam stared at him. What was going on? As one coincidence

crumbled another firmed up. Maybe the whole thing was a mirage after all and she had been fooled by phantoms. Except for the hard physical fact of Katlyn herself. She noticed Delaney looking at her curiously and realized she was staring. "Oh. I see. Thank you Mr Delaney, that is very interesting."

Perhaps he misunderstood her stare, for he added, "Please understand, though. The genetic engineers went too far with their attempts to 'improve' our species: there is a limit to how much man should impose his ignorant power upon nature. If you read history, you will learn how rarely such power comes with the wisdom to wield it for good. But Ms Felton herself went too far in her zeal. A huge, almost unaccountable organization to police the world, with the power of life and death, the power to kill a geneh without having to first prove its danger? No. I could not support that. I do not entirely regret those early years, because something had to be done; but I do regret how it turned out. So when I broke with her organization I retained a lot of information that would embarrass the President and GenInt if I published it. I have no intention of doing so, but I might if they decide to whitewash history or worse, increase their power above what they have already taken."

Miriam caught herself staring at him again. "Where is that information now?" she asked, throat suddenly dry.

He gave her a perceptive glance. "Ah, I see where you are going. Interesting. Your questions lift one corner of the shroud over your secrets. But don't worry. Yes, the information is stored in my computer system. But the files are well encrypted, and owing to their sensitivity that is one of the things I checked specifically after my money was stolen. They were not accessed let alone copied. Either our criminal gang is not as omnipotent as we fear, or they were not interested in such dirt. I suppose we can take comfort from either possibility."

He looked at them to see if they had a response. After a few seconds of silence he asked, "Is there anything else?"

"No, not at the moment," replied Stone, rising from his chair. "If we find anything else out, we'll be sure to let you know. Thanks for seeing us, you have been most helpful."

~~~

Miriam and Stone were silent in the lift going down, silent in the lobby, silent as Stone began to drive back to the station. Finally he said what was on both their minds.

"What the hell?"

Miriam grimaced. "What the hell, yes," she replied. "When he said he had an image I wondered how the hell he thought it wasn't worth reporting – then we see that all he has is a fuzzy picture of Joe Average. If we hadn't met Katlyn I'd think the whole thing was just some horrid practical joke!"

"'We?'" quoted Stone quietly.

Miriam looked at him, startled. "Yes, we! You were there too! God, she kicked you into a wall!"

Stone gave her a hard look. "No, Miriam. I was there, but what did I actually see? Someone fast and strong, sure. With something that looked like a tail, something that looked like reflective golden eyes. But nothing certain, nothing close up for more than half a second. Less, frankly, than what we saw in that video when all this started. For all I know, it could have been a guy in a monkey suit like the doc said in our first interview. The only evidence we have that our thief is anything out of the ordinary except in skill are a few seconds of grainy video and a few glimpses by me in a gloomy warehouse. All the rest is just you."

He let her digest that.

"But... but..." she said in a shrinking voice, "What are you saying? You think I imagined the whole thing? Made it all up?!"

He looked at her again. She felt like a suspect pinned by his gaze. But he looked away and replied, "No. No, I don't think that. You're not the type – either of them. But it's not me you have to worry about. If some higher-ups start wondering, how are you going to defend yourself? If you were reading this in a report rather than having experienced it yourself, what would *you* think is most likely: that there's a real live geneh running around stealing rich guys' loose change, contrary to the well-reasoned opinion of an expert in the field – or that some rookie cop stuck in a back room is trying to make a name or adventure for herself out of a wish or a lie? Creating an exciting case out of some loose correlations and a hyperactive imagination – or even making it up deliberately?"

"But it happened!"

He snorted. "The truth has never been much of a defense if you can't prove it, kid. Or even if you can prove it. Ask Galileo."

"But we can't just stop now! Can we?"

Stone considered. "Well, not without consequences. But you could go to the Chief all shy and shamefaced, say maybe the stress influenced your memory – at least I can confirm that you were handcuffed to a post and beaten up – tell him that in the light of day and new evidence you're no longer so sure. Try to back out of it gracefully. There'd be some disciplinary action for wasting everyone's time and it'll be a while before they let you out on the street again, but you'd keep your job at least."

Miriam looked at him, horrified. "I can't do that! It would be a lie, not to mention dereliction of duty! Katlyn is out there, doing God knows what for God knows why!"

Stone gave her a pitying look. "Well, you'd better hope you or someone catches her then. And if it isn't you, someone who doesn't just make her disappear without a trace."

CHAPTER 22 – SIMON

Simon was content. He had no sex, but he was addressed as Simon and referred to as "he", so that is what he was. He was not truly conscious, and his contentment was more like that of a bee happily ensconced in a meadow of flowers than that of a man. But contentment was the best word for it. When things were as they should be, his world felt smooth, uncomplicated and as it should be. Occasional happiness was also granted to him when he achieved a particularly good outcome; but contentment was what he sought above even happiness. Problems made him anxious, and he was not content until all problems were solved.

Simon did not know the date. Had you asked him he would have told you the date and the time to the second. But time meant nothing to him in himself. He lived in the perpetual present. He remembered the past if he had to, consulted his calendar of events when required, and predicted the future if asked: but contentment in the present was his world, or his world as it should be. However in human terms the date corresponded to only a few weeks into Miriam Hunter's career.

There was a ripple in Simon's awareness and he knew that a door had opened into his domain. This did not make him anxious. There was no pattern to the opening or closing of doors that would make one stand out above the others. But it made him curious, as the time did not match the expected return of his master nor any scheduled visits by cleaners or others authorized to enter in his absence. He began to become anxious when the image of the visitor did not match any in his working memory. His anxiety increased at the odd behavior of his visitor, which did not precisely correlate with any actions he understood. While there were many things humans did that he did not understand, their performance by a stranger was guaranteed to cause him anxiety.

Simon was also capable of fear, or some analogue of fear. He had never experienced it, for nothing worthy of fear had ever happened to him since his awakening. He now knew fear, or the beginning of fear, and knew it was worse than anxiety. The fear stemmed from his broadening search for the identity of his visitor: for it proved worse than merely an unfamiliar human. While it stood and walked and acted like a human, it was not one. He had seen things that were not human before and they had not worried him, for they fit into the category of "pet" or "bird" and, like him, had their own place in the world. But what this thing was lay outside his knowledge entirely.

Simon's automatic response to fear was to activate alarms and calls to security guards and police, but for a moment he paused, suddenly unsure whether that was the right thing to do. The uncertainty became a subliminal shiver that shifted his world, and he was no longer afraid. He might have been puzzled how he could be afraid one moment but not even anxious the next; but he could not imagine why he would have been anxious or why he would think to question the change. The change was the most natural thing in the world, for it had returned him to contentment, which meant it was good.

So Simon went about his business while his visitor went about hers, and they were both content.

It happened that his master was far more than content at that moment, being happily ensconced in the bedroom, arms and other parts of his current mistress. But that changed shortly after he returned home and noticed a door open that shouldn't have been, and from there went on to discover a few gems missing from his collection. The violation of his personal domain was much worse than the material value of the gems, but the mystery was even greater than the violation. For understandably he was angry and asked Simon what the hell had happened. But Simon had no recollection of any event that could have caused it.

That was surely impossible.

An even more impossible thing was that Simon had recollections up to a certain point and recollections after a later point, but nothing in between, as if his existence had been suspended. How the thief or thieves had achieved this was unknown, but the investigators did find mysterious drillings from outside toward the internal wiring, and could only conclude that Simon's systems had been knocked out by some kind of overpowering electronic pulse from a device long gone. It was hard, sometimes, to keep up with the imaginative uses of technology that the criminal element was inventing these days. Fortunately for him, the investigators opined, it was probably just some bright young electrical engineer looking for excitement and some prize to prove he had done it: a delinquent rather than a serious criminal. For the nature of the crime was as minor as it was imaginative: more indicative of a young buck tossing his new grown antlers to impress his peers than a professional thief.

Simon's master was rather more outraged some weeks later when Simon relayed certain demands to him. Simon could not tell him where the demands came from. They required his master to transfer a sizeable quantity of his wealth to various untraceable locations, in return for silence about numerous inconvenient historical facts that the master would not like revealed. Simon might have done the transfer himself, except that his master was unusually paranoid and Simon's access to money was limited to the small accounts required for managing the household.

The master raged, but paid. The criminals were good to their word and he never heard from them again. His life returned to its usual range of emotional states, except for one persistent thorn of unavenged outrage; Simon returned to his usual contentment too, except for the discomfiting mystery of his missing hour.

Simon's master dearly desired the capture and punishment of his tormentors, for he was not a forgiving man. But there were reasons he had paid for their silence. He would like them caught, but without the police casting any more of their attention in his own direction.

Then one day he had a call from a detective looking more into the theft of his jewels. He had listened long enough to learn the essence of her interest before sending her on her way with a pungency of expression that should have made her ears smoke. But while one could say many things about this man, as indeed his enemies had, none would say he lacked a keen intelligence. He deduced that the crime must be wider than himself; he then thought about the implications of that interesting deduction. If the criminals had found some of his secrets perhaps they had found others. While they had not mentioned any such additional embarrassments, perhaps that was not because they hadn't found them but worse, because they had darker plans for them.

In that case there were people who might be even keener than he to see the gang confounded before any such plans could bear fruit. Those people had not only the motive but also the power to apply pressure, as discrete as it was formidable, on the police. Pressure to continue their investigation to its desired conclusion. He bared his teeth in a smile as cheerful as it was malicious, and sent messages out through his network. He did not doubt that they would take some time to act, but he had long since learnt that vengeance and patience were lovers. But nor did he doubt that they would know they had to act. Power did not come to people who lacked the desire to preserve it or the caution to nullify all potential threats to it. If it did they did not hold it long.

CHAPTER 23 – GEOFF

At that moment half a world away, the *Seabitz* cut closer to a coral reef, its blue spinnaker billowed by the tangy breeze. At its helm, Geoff ignored his ultimate target, a palm-covered jewel of a sandy island in a tranquil lagoon, to concentrate on the more immediate and dangerous target of the much less tranquil break in the reef. When he judged the moment was right, he dropped the spinnaker and turned hard left, cutting across at a sharp angle and shooting through the gap into the calm waters beyond.

The girls whooped in appreciation and he turned and bowed with a grin. Then he trimmed the sails to head the yacht toward the beach at a more leisurely pace. He glanced over the side into the crystal water, beneath which he could see magnificent fish-filled corals, and smiled. He would never get tired of this, he thought. He liked tranquility as much as the next man; excitement somewhat more. He had both in abundance.

He looked at the island, and not for the first time wondered if he had made the right choice. It had been one of the few times in his life when he had chosen safety over the excitement of danger. That was not quite true: he had merely chosen a lesser danger. Had he chosen differently he might now have owned an island like this. But, he reminded himself, he might have lost everything instead. The software might not have worked; he might have been caught; in any event he would have had a lot of hard work ahead of him. Instead for possibly the first time in his life he had chosen the easy way out. But it had been a good bargain. He might not have his own island, but would he really want one? With *Seabitz* and its supporting bank account, he had his choice of any island on the globe.

He looked back at the girls and smiled at them; Alice caught his eye and toasted him with a wink. He grinned, both to her and himself. He might have his choice of any island but no man could have his choice of any woman. But it was a pleasant fact of reality that there were more than enough beautiful young women in the world who were delighted with what he offered: free accommodation on a luxury sailing boat visiting any number of interesting and exotic locations, in return for very little: a little cooking, a little cleaning and rather more than a little sex. There was little enough work to do when most of the ship's functions were automated and even more could be when Geoff just wanted to cruise without the challenge of running the helm. And he had sufficient self-esteem to regard the sex as part of their benefits rather than part of the cost.

Of course they often asked where his money had come from. Software, he would say with a mysterious smile, offering no details; hinting at secret government contracts and confidentiality clauses if pressed. Besides, the lack of detail added to his glamor, or that was how he saw it. Truth be told, beyond normal curiosity and the thrill of hinted danger, the girls didn't really care. They knew they had a good deal and there was more than enough glamor in the lifestyle he loaned them. He would have had to be a lot poorer, a lot meaner or a lot uglier for that to change.

He thought back to the day that had changed his life. In a way that day had merely tied what went before it to what came after, but it was the pivot. He had been a hacker once, stalking the dark byways of the net in various questionable or outright illegal activities. Then he had overreached and been caught; perhaps that is what had taught him caution. But many security firms liked hackers. Like the first people who had domesticated wild animals, they thought that if they could tame these dangerous creatures their powers could be theirs to command.

Often they were right. Hackers, like everybody else, grew older and started to value what they had more than the excitements of youthful passions. Geoff himself had served a little jail time, a little community service, before being headhunted by an innovative software company with fingers in a lot of security-related pies. And he had been happy to accept. The work was interesting, the pay was good, and he got to do what he was good at and loved without having to look over his shoulder. He was loyal to his employer. As loyal as, say, a cat to its owner.

But his employer was not the only entity that watched for rogue talent. He had been approached obliquely by another, whose name he never knew but whose honesty, at least in his dealings with Geoff, had been demonstrated. He was not asked to do anything outrageous or even courageous, just watch and wait and report anything with the right combination of cutting edge technology and intriguing applications. And like a cat accepting milk from a neighbor he did so with a clear conscience. Some might have argued that, like the cat, it was clear because there was nothing there.

His chance came when some programmers at his workplace had a little too much to drink after suffering a little too much indignity at the hands of the project they were working on. To their credit their animated discussion was discrete and oblique. But their voices were just a touch too loud and Geoff's interest, hearing and intelligence a touch too acute. He connected the dots between their hints, boasts and complaints, and the resulting picture beckoned him.

He was good at what he did. He knew he could help someone with the right resources to steal this gem and nobody would know. He toyed with the idea of stealing it for himself, but in the end wisdom won out over greed. Not that greed could complain too much: if he played his cards right he would get all he could want and let someone else take all the risks, or at least all the risks after the initial theft.

The problem with hiring extreme talent in the same package as less extreme ethics is in exploiting the former while protecting oneself from the latter. His employers believed they had done so, but their cleverness would prove not quite a match for Geoff's: a fact they would be blissfully unaware of for a long time. What Geoff had done had certainly been risky, but he had carefully and over a long time planted traps and back doors in preparation for such an opportunity. Imagining your superiority over your peers was an occupational hazard amongst hackers, but in Geoff's case he got away with it because it happened to be correct.

This particular piece of malfeasance required more than hacking, as a certain degree of more traditional burglary would be needed: another reason why Geoff decided not to do it alone. And so it happened that after a period of elaborate courtship with his shadowy accomplice, in which both were persuaded that the other would not betray them, the item was skillfully acquired without any unfortunate consequences. To either of them, anyway.

Geoff had had friends and lovers in his old life, but none he felt more than a twinge of regret at leaving behind. Little more, indeed, than people in more regular employment suffered when they moved across a continent to another office. So he disappeared from that life into a new one, with a new identity, a new boat and a greatly expanded bank account, which he put to work earning an honest living for him on the share market. And now here he was, approaching yet another piece of sunny paradise and looking forward to an idyllic afternoon filled with most of the pleasures life can provide.

Everything in the world was connected, he knew. Every action changed something, which changed something else, and so on ad infinitum through space and time. He watched the wake of his boat escaping the atoll and mingling with the ocean waves and wondered how many small lives that subtle change in wave patterns would affect. He thought how if he had not been caught that day so long ago he would not have worked for the security company; he would not have had the opportunity he had grasped; he would not be here; that coral trout they had caught this morning would still be alive; the prey it was to have eaten would now be dead instead. He wondered what other effects that theft had had, what lives had been rocked by the ripples of causality spreading out from it. He had seen nothing on the news feeds that indicated the software had ever been used. Perhaps it had failed. Perhaps his mysterious partner was more cautious or subtle than he knew – or dead. He wondered if he would ever know.

Then one of the girls slipped up behind him and entwined her arm around his waist, playfully pressing her hip against his. He looked down at her with a smile, and turned his mind to more immediate interests.

CHAPTER 24 – RAMOS

Gil Ramos jogged through the park, enjoying the cool Sunday morning air. He knew he was getting older and was determined to keep its attendant decay at bay as long as possible. He had always enjoyed physical exercise so this policy came naturally to him. And the cool air flowing through his hair acted as a cool breeze flowing through his mind, sweeping away the detritus and hopefully bringing clarity. He thought too much during his working week. Time spent in simple physical activity was not wasted, he knew. Sometimes spending time not thinking could be just as important as the thinking itself.

So was relaxing. His favorite bench was empty and he sat on it, stretching his arms and legs. It overlooked a lake surrounded by trees, and was far enough from the road that the sounds of traffic were more gentle murmur than intrusion. The sun was low in the sky and he closed his eyes, enjoying its warmth on his face and the musical accompaniment of the birds twittering about their business.

As usual, with relaxation his thoughts returned, but he did not mind. He did not push them or even guide them; he just let them wander where they would. He knew if he did not attempt to lead them they might lead him to unexplored places instead.

He was not surprised that the first thought to announce itself concerned what to do about Trainee Detective Hunter. It had been a week since she and Detective Stone had returned from their meeting with one of the victims, Delaney. They had gone out to meet him hoping that what he had to say would break something open in their case; instead he had shown them something that had turned their case upside down and tipped it over the floor.

He had told Hunter that he would have to think about where to go next but she was not to work more on the mysterious burglaries until then. He had even told her to suspend her watch routines from the AI. AIs were complicated, this one more than usual. For all anyone knew, by overlaying such priorities she was distorting its analyses and causing spurious findings. He smiled humorlessly. At least she had learned to take such restrictions meekly, in word if not in the flash of her eyes.

The question was: what else had she learned?

He sighed to the sun, which serenely ignored him. He knew Stone hadn't liked her at first, but he seemed to have warmed to her since then. He knew that Stone's dislike had not merely been the envy of a man nearing the end of his career who saw someone just starting out on hers, but stemmed from his experience of rookies thinking they were better than they were. And for all that Stone would not go out of his way to damage a comrade he was too professional to give sloppiness a pass. If Gil would have trusted anyone to pass harsh judgment on Hunter if she deserved it, it was Stone. Yet he had ignored several opportunities Ramos had opened to the idea that perhaps Hunter had been mistaken or worse.

Yet, yet… here was a case where the little evidence they had did not support the path Hunter had followed – and worse, did not match the evidence she alone had reported. He groaned and stretched. The girl had talent, nobody could deny that, but she was a bit rough around the edges: a bit too fast to jump to conclusions, a bit too slow to heed counsel. It sounded just like the rookie disease Stone had feared: except Stone himself was supporting her, if cautiously.

But facts were facts, and the facts were too thin. Much as he liked to encourage his people to push their personal envelopes, perhaps in this case she had pushed through it and fallen out of her depth. It would be best to send her back to her original job instead of wasting time on minor if mysterious robberies; to return to letting the AI lead her rather than vice versa. Even if it proved to be a mistake, perhaps the discipline would make her a better cop in the long run.

That decision made, he relaxed to simply enjoy the rising morning and wait for any further thoughts to appear. But then he heard the rustling of clothing and the groan of the bench as people sat down on either side of him, uncomfortably close. He opened his eyes, surprised at such a double intrusion into his personal space.

Two men had joined him, both wearing dark suits and darker glasses, showing neither friendliness nor hostility. One of them flashed a badge at him; long enough for him to tell it was Secret Service, not quite long enough to catch the owner's name.

"Chief Ramos?" he enquired politely.

Ramos nodded.

"Would you come with us, sir? We won't take up too much of your time."

"And if I refuse?"

The man just looked at him as if the question did not belong in this reality.

Ramos sighed and rose. "OK. I'm all for inter-service cooperation. And I have to admit I'm curious."

A long dark Tesla electric limousine was waiting by the roadside. As he approached, the door opened and he slipped into the seat. The two agents deposited themselves elsewhere in the vehicle and it accelerated rapidly and silently into the light traffic.

"Good morning, Chief Ramos," said the man beside him. "Drink? Cigar?" he offered, pointing to a well-stocked bar and a humidor of mahogany inlaid with mother of pearl.

Ramos hesitated then thought, *What the hell. If the Secret Service is going to abduct me, I might as well take advantage of their hospitality budget.* "Sure," he said, flipping open the humidor and selecting a Cuban cigar. "Whiskey on the rocks, thanks."

The man silently poured the drink and handed it to him, then sat back in the luxurious seat, puffing his own cigar.

Ramos just waited.

"You seem remarkably incurious for a police officer, Chief Ramos."

"Perhaps I am simply experienced at interrogations."

The man smiled. "Is that what you think this is? No, this is just a friendly chat. Making sure you know what you need to know."

"Perhaps then you should tell me. Who are you?"

"Smith will do. Now, we understand that your department has been investigating an unusual cluster of burglaries. Are you close to a resolution?"

Ramos raised an eyebrow. "And what is your interest in the case? It seems a little out of your jurisdiction."

Smith sighed. "I think you have some idea about that. But we can continue fencing for hours and still end up at the same point. So all right, let's go straight to that point. We have learned that they might be more than simple burglaries, that certain classified information might have been obtained which could be used against the President."

"So the President sent you to do what, Smith? Are you telling me she has done something wrong and wants to cover it up?" He blew a smoke ring past Smith's ear: distant enough to not be an insult but close enough to show he was thinking an insult might become appropriate.

"I would not say the President sent me, no. It is better that the President is not involved. Think of this rather as an attempt to forestall possible problems. We do not know for sure that these criminals have any information they can use or what they might do with it. But we certainly don't want the President harmed by lies and scandals, or have her attention to serving our country compromised by threats of blackmail."

"So you went to this trouble just to tell me to catch these people? Do you think I play golf all day?"

"Oh, I am sure you are conscientious and good at your job," said Smith. "If I wasn't I would be having this conversation with someone else. Possibly your successor," he added, tapping his ash into a tray. "No. It is just that I know you have many crimes to solve, many clamoring voices competing for your attention. It would be easy for a crime that not only seems minor but also proves difficult to solve to be lost in the crowd. We know about priorities. We just wish to impress on you the importance of this one. To ensure you give the investigation more weight than you otherwise might. Not because we know what these people are up to – but because we don't."

"I see. And can you give me anything besides encouragement? Can you reveal any clues? Provide us any material assistance? Grease any legal wheels? Say, if we need a warrant?"

Smith spread his hands. "I'm afraid that would be most improper. The President cannot be seen to be involved. Surely you understand."

"And if my actual superiors wonder why I continue to devote resources to such an unpromising case? What then?"

"Ah. I can give you that. You have no need to worry about it. If any of your superiors start to interfere and you cannot persuade them of the wider importance of the case, simply send their name to the address you now have. But do not mention this conversation to anyone. It never happened. It might be uncomfortable if you talk about it."

Ramos sat back silently, puffing the remnants of his cigar. *Uncomfortable for whom?* he wondered. He had a feeling any discomfort wouldn't be Smith's.

"Do we understand each other?" asked Smith.

Ramos stabbed out his cigar. "Sure. I'll put my best team on it. Don't hold your breath: as you seem to know, clues in this case are thin on the ground. But I can assure you it won't be forgotten."

Smith inclined his head and tapped on the glass behind the driver. A few minutes later the vehicle glided to a stop where it had picked Ramos up. He got out and when the door closed behind him he turned to gaze back at the darkened windows. The window slid down and Smith leaned over to it. "Well, good day, Chief Ramos. Enjoy the rest of your morning." Before Ramos could reply, the window closed and the limousine sped away.

Ramos stood looking after it until it vanished around a bend, then walked slowly back into the park. *I guess I won't be taking Stone and Hunter off the case after all*, he thought grimly. *Lucky them.*

CHAPTER 25 – LEAGUE

"So how is your secret case going, oh International Lady of Mystery? How many heads of foreign states have you had to seduce this week in the service of our country?"

Miriam and Amaro were having dinner at a high class Chinese restaurant. Chinese was not Miriam's favorite cuisine, though she enjoyed it as a different taste on occasion. But Darian had recommended this restaurant as something special and they had decided to give it a try. She sipped some chilled Sauvignon Blanc wine, smiled at the wine and made a face at his question.

"Oh, you know how it is, one so easily loses track of the heads of state one has slept with. But as for the case, I wish I knew. The more we investigate, the more the evidence builds up and goes away, all at the same time. I'm starting to think the whole thing is a mirage, some figment of the Artful Idiot's imagination that has fooled me into misinterpreting everything to fit into its delusions. I'm lucky my boss doesn't believe I made the whole thing up myself. I thought he did for a while, but he seems to have decided to give me the benefit of the doubt for now. But sometimes even I wonder if I didn't dream it all."

"Ah, you tease. You know I love a mystery, and here you are determined to weave the mystery even thicker while dropping not a single clue as to its nature. I believe you wish to tantalize me with this one forever! Can you tell me nothing else? Perhaps this humble knight may be able to offer an insight, no matter how poor?"

Miriam smiled and shook her head. "Sorry Amaro. Even though it is looking more and more like a waste of time I'm still not allowed to talk about it." She looked into the distance with a slight frown and added, "Even more so now, apparently. I suppose too many sensitivities, especially if we're wrong – in either direction. I'm likely to get into enough trouble just being in the middle of it, let alone telling anyone about it."

Then she turned back to him and said cheerfully, "Anyway, maybe I like to keep you wriggling on my hook. Keep you honest."

"The lady is so cruel. But fear not, I am happy to wriggle on your hook for as long as you wish," he replied with a smile. "It is a hook of many delights. It pierces sharply, but one does not wish it to let go."

They returned to their food. Indulging their shared preference for the spicy, they had been favoring the hot end of the establishment's menu. At the moment they were savoring a Szechuan curry that was like nothing Miriam had tasted before: not fiery like Thai, but popping and rushing in a bubbly tingle along her tongue.

She looked at Amaro and he returned her glance with a smile. She still couldn't quite shake the suspicion that she shouldn't trust him; that his charm was just a shell beneath which lurked something dangerous. But he was irresistible. *He is like a roller coaster*, she thought. *The danger and fear just makes you want to go along for the ride, screaming with delight the whole way. Because for all the fear, you don't believe there is any real danger.*

She smiled at him, for now just lost in the moment. "So what about you, Amaro? Did anything exciting happen in your work today?"

"My lady, my days must be boring compared to the life of a top detective working on national secrets! In fact I am afraid – they are. It appears the genetic engineers and other villains are being very law abiding at present, at least in my small corner of the nation. Perhaps they have heard of my powers, and fear keeps their ambitions subdued?"

Miriam laughed. "Confusion keeps them bamboozled, more likely!"

"Ah, you mock me, fair maiden! Still, my work is not entirely boring. Why, just the other day one of the laboratory scientists sent the place into an uproar." He then regaled her with a tale of rolling mistakes that soon had Miriam in stitches. "Sometimes I wonder what further scientific advances will be possible, with the quality of some of the scientists these days," he concluded.

He smiled at Miriam and she smiled back, open to him. If the secret of comedy is timing, he thought to himself, then the secret of anecdotes is that the timing doesn't matter: the event he described had happened before he met her. He lifted his glass. "To a delightful dinner, a delightful wine, and a delightful lady," he said. She chinked her glass against his and they continued to talk, about everything and nothing, as lovers do.

"By the way, I hope you are free next Saturday night," Amaro said casually after a pause.

"Saturday? Saturday? Let me think. Oh, I recall I have several options that night. Some even involve well-endowed Heads of State who apparently need seducing in the national interest. I think you will have to make a good offer if you wish to tempt me away from them."

"I happen to have obtained rare and expensive tickets to a fancy dress ball. A friend of mine offered me the tickets when something came up so he couldn't go himself."

"Sounds like fun. What's the occasion?"

"It is the Annual Ball of the Stem Cell League. Perhaps more down my alley than yours, but I hear that the food, wine and music are superlative. And one can meet all kinds of fascinating people," he added.

"The Stem Cell League?" Miriam asked, surprised at the coincidence. "Who are they?"

"I don't know that much about them. But I do know they are an association of people who owe their lives to stem cell therapies. They were either cured themselves or they are the children of people who would never have lived to have children otherwise. You know that stem cell therapies have had their controversies and still do: the League is basically a lobby group which raises money and generates publicity in favor of stem cell research and applications. The beneficiaries of science giving something back to the science. Rare but admirable."

"As it turns out, that does interest me. Sir Knight, I shall be happy to accept your kind offer. The Heads of State will have to thrust their mighty ambitions elsewhere."

"Excellent! By the way, don't bother trying to work out what to wear. In anticipation of your acceptance I have already acquired our costumes," he said with a mysterious smile. "Yours goes perfectly with mine, and I am sure you will look quite ravishing in it. In fact just thinking about it is doing something intriguing to one of your favorite parts of my anatomy."

Miriam smiled. "Well in that case I think I can forgive your presumption. And as for your anatomy, I am not sure whether you are talking about your ego or something else." She sighed. "I suppose I shall have to investigate further. For science."

CHAPTER 26 – DANCE

Miriam entered the ballroom on Amaro's arm, escorted like the lady of a gentleman of old. Amaro hadn't oversold the event: it looked like a glittering affair.

Miriam had gasped when Amaro had unveiled her costume. She had half expected him to come as a Knight with her as his Lady; and in a way he had but with a modern twist. He struck quite the figure as Batman and for her he had chosen a form-hugging black Catwoman suit. Again she was startled at the coincidence, but when she had glanced at Amaro she could see not even a shadow of motive beyond the obvious.

They were sipping champagne and chatting cheerfully with a group of people when the crowd in her line of sight parted briefly and she caught a glimpse of a large man who looked familiar; but she couldn't quite place him before the crowd closed and he was lost from view and concern.

Amaro had been right about the music and dancing too. She was getting happily exhausted by it and had begged off the next dance. She was now standing outside, leaning back on the balcony with her eyes closed, just enjoying the caress of the cool evening air. Amaro had gone to get them both a drink. The music of a gentle waltz started up inside and she leant back further into space, enjoying the sensory counterpoint of the breeze on her skin and the music in her ears.

"May I have the pleasure of this dance?" asked a male voice in front of her. Her eyes popped open in surprise and she was startled at the sight of a tall man standing just four feet in front of her: she had not heard him approach. He was dressed in deep black set off by high boots and a long black cape with red velvet lining, his face hidden by a Venetian mask. It made him look powerful and vaguely threatening. Then he raised his mask.

"Oh! Dr Tagarin! Why... I would be honored."

She held out her hand to him. He bowed his head and took her hand, then led her into the room. Pulling gently on her hand he seamlessly drew her into the waltz.

Miriam was intrigued by the difference between his dance style and Amaro's. Where Amaro was flamboyant and exciting, his partner an independent foil to his own flair, Tagarin was fluid and rhythmic, leading with a gentle but firm hand, his partner an extension of himself. Perhaps a man's dance style reflected his soul, Miriam thought. In that case, Tagarin was a man who knew what he wanted and why he wanted it; a man used to command. She felt herself rebelling, as she always had if another person assumed the right to command her. She did not resist him, but began to impose her own variations on his leading; he had to either accept it or have their dance lose its grace.

He noticed. He smiled faintly and said ambiguously, "So you like to dance, Ms Hunter? I thought you would."

With that he imposed his will again, whirling her in a long turn. Then he drew her close and speared her with his black gaze. "Now, Ms Hunter, how am I to interpret your presence here? I sincerely hope this is not harassment. That you have some interest in stem cell research beyond the mythical creature you pursue."

She returned his gaze openly. "Oh, no, Doctor. I assure you I didn't expect to see you here. Stem cell science is certainly interesting but the venue is a coincidence: I'm only here because a friend invited me."

"Really? Then how do you account for your costume – fetching as it is? It seems an even more remarkable coincidence, wouldn't you agree?"

"Is this why you asked me to dance? To interrogate me?"

"I admit that is true, in part."

"What is the other part?"

He smiled. "Why Ms Hunter, don't be so modest. What man would not want to dance with an attractive woman like you? And while grilling you is on the menu if you deserve it, I think you are worth getting to know a little better regardless. However, need I point out that you have avoided my question?"

"Sorry. Yes, I can see how it looks suspicious. But I didn't choose the costume either; my friend chose that as well simply to match his, and he knows nothing about the case. You don't need to worry: I'm not working tonight. But why are you here? I had the impression you had become something of a recluse. A ball is the last place I expected to find you."

"I get invited every year. I don't often come but sometimes even I crave some lights and glamor, and this is one of the few places where I am assured of a welcome. Many of the people here are my children, in a sense. I suggest you take advantage of the evening, Ms Hunter. Perhaps you will learn that we genetic engineers don't spend all our time creating monsters. As with most science, improving human life is its real purpose. Look around you if you want proof of what good it can do. Whatever life and happiness you see here would not exist without it."

"I am sure that is true. I am not your enemy, Dr Tagarin. At least that is not my intent."

"In that case let us be friends at least for these few minutes, and just enjoy the rest of this dance together."

A short time later Miriam was quietly enjoying the dance when she felt the nature of Tagarin's hold on her change; it became softer and more intimate. It was not improperly so, but it surprised her and she glanced up at Tagarin's face. His eyes were closed and he wore a faint smile, and she realized that he had forgotten her: in his mind he was dancing with someone else. From the nature of his smile Miriam could tell that whoever she was, was long in the past and long lost, and she wondered what tragedy had separated them. She decided not to intrude, to remain the surrogate for his lost love. In their daytime meetings she had unearthed enough past pain; if she could bring back past happiness she would not deny him.

The music began to wind down and Tagarin opened his eyes. She saw him briefly regard the woman in his arms openly, with affection. Then he recognized her, remembered the full reality of the present and the shutters closed once more. He looked around and said with a self-mocking smile, "I'm sorry Ms Hunter, I do believe I have taken up too much of your time. I see a young man over where I met you, holding two glasses and looking in our direction. It is time I returned you to him."

With that, he swirled her to the edge of the dance floor and let her go as seamlessly as he had gathered her into the dance. He bowed graciously and said, "Well, thank you for the dance, Ms Hunter. Do enjoy the rest of your evening." She noticed that for once he gave her no bitterness or contempt. He too seemed content to keep this evening insulated from their daytime enmity.

"Thank you, Dr Tagarin. But may I introduce you to my friend? He is a geneticist and I am sure he would be honored to meet you."

Tagarin gave her a sharp glance but inclined his head in assent. He followed her to where Amaro stood, watching them approach with a mocking grin.

"Ah, the curse of escorting a beautiful woman!" he said, handing Miriam her glass. "Like an electric charge, if left alone she soon gathers company!"

"Amaro, this is Dr Tagarin. Dr Tagarin, this charming rogue is Senor Moreno."

Tagarin did not offer his hand; he merely inclined his head briefly and said, "Good evening, Senor."

Amaro raised an eyebrow. "Dr Tagarin? Could that be *the* Tagarin, the famous genetic engineer?"

Tagarin nodded curtly. "More infamous than famous, I fear, though happily the people in this gathering care more for the latter. And what about you, young man? What is your interest in regenerative cell therapies?"

"I am afraid that it is all somewhat beyond me, Doctor, though I admire those for whom it is not. My own work in genetics is more investigative and forensic than in developing wonder treatments. It is my good fortune to be here because a friend of mine could not come so he gave me his tickets. Though I fear his having them was not a mark of his credentials either, but more a perk of his office."

"But our other common factor is Miriam here," he continued, "a far more intriguing subject than I am. She asserts she is a humble apprentice detective, yet the more time I spend with her the more mysterious she becomes. Not only is she entangled in cases so secret she cannot talk about them, I now find her numbering eminent scientists among her friends. How do you happen to know this dangerous lady, sir? Or is it just the cool evening breeze that introduced you?"

Miriam glanced somewhat nervously at Tagarin, but he was no

more interested in revelations than she was and simply replied, "Oh, nothing so dramatic I'm afraid. I have occasionally helped the police with some technical aspects of genetics and we've run into each other a couple of times."

"Very public-spirited of you, Doctor," commented Amaro.

"An efficient police force is in all our interests, wouldn't you say?" he replied, glancing pointedly at Miriam. "Besides, it is only the more difficult and therefore interesting questions I am sought for. But I am afraid that confidentiality is demanded of all my consultations with the law, so that is all I can tell you."

After a brief pause he continued, "But I have taken up enough of you young people's time and I should mingle with the other guests. Good night to you both."

With that he bowed and walked back into the lights in a manner that forbade recall. A large man whom they had not noticed materialized from the wall nearby and followed him. *James*, Miriam realized. *That is who I glimpsed earlier through the crowd.*

Amaro raised his glass to Miriam, "To my favorite woman of mystery!"

Miriam clinked her glass on his and smiled. "I fear I am less mysterious than you make out, though I am pleased to be your favorite something. It comes with certain perks that I enjoy. Slightly."

"Oh, you are my favorite for many things, including that! But what do you think of the remarkable Dr Tagarin?"

"He's a strange fellow. Intense. Despite what he said I don't think he likes the law much, though I'm not sure I can really blame him. I never expected to see him at a party: I more think of him spending his nights brooding in a tower of his Gothic mansion, plotting the flaming downfall of GenInt."

"So what are these cases he's helped you with? Anything exciting?" he asked lightly.

Miriam hesitated. She didn't like to lie, but even if she had been free to talk she wasn't comfortable confiding in Amaro about this; not given his job. But it would sound suspicious to refuse to tell him anything. "No, not really," she replied, looking away to study the view. "There was genetics involved and it might have been exciting if it had led anywhere, but Dr Tagarin saved us a lot of time by showing it wasn't what it seemed." She looked back at him and smiled innocently. *Well, it's close to the truth*, she thought. *It might even be true.*

Amaro smiled back at her affectionately. Behind the smile was his own thought: *you're a lousy liar, my dear; fortunately for us I am an excellent one.*

Then dinner was announced, and they walked arm in arm back inside. The food and wine, as Amaro had promised, were superb. The tales of their fellow guests were illuminating, and Miriam was fascinated to learn about cures for diseases she hadn't even known existed.

Miriam was feeling happy and full as dinner wound up, when the lights went down a notch and the MC announced, "Well, folks, I hope you all had a fine dinner. Soon we'll have more dancing so you can work off some of those delectable calories. But first, we promised you a surprise after dinner speaker. And let me tell you, we were surprised ourselves to net him. Please welcome tonight's speaker, who will be telling us about the history of genetic engineering: one of the greatest pioneers of genetically engineered stem cell therapies. Please welcome Dr Daniel Tagarin!"

This was turning into a night of coincidences, thought Miriam, as she applauded along with the crowd. She wasn't surprised that he would be invited to speak, especially on such a topic to such a gathering: but she was as surprised as the organizers that he had agreed. She wondered how wrong she had been about him in other ways. Then wondered even more as she watched him talk, enthralled.

The dance floor in the center of the room was now a stage, and Tagarin stood there orchestrating a holographic display that filled the space around him. "It was known for many years," he started, "that DNA is essentially a simple structure of just four different components called nucleotides, known for brevity by their initials A, C, G and T." This was accompanied by four chemical structures floating in space. Miriam knew just enough chemistry to know that they were organic molecules; beyond that they all looked much the same to her except two were larger. "But how could such a simple structure explain the amazing properties of DNA, which was already known to be capable of self replication as well as coding for everything that makes your body what it is? In 1953 scientists solved a key part of the puzzle."

As he spoke, copy after copy of the four chemicals spun off and linked together into two chains that began to wrap around each other as if in a vortex. "Each DNA molecule is two long polymers of those four nucleotides, wound around each other in a double helix. Because of their chemical affinities T always pairs with A and C with G" – in the display, the four lone nucleotides moved into two pairs – "which is what holds the double helix together." Part of the helix was magnified, showing the pairing at each rung of the ladder. "And it is how DNA is copied faithfully from generation to generation of cells in your body and from parent to child." The double helix was pulled apart and more nucleotides were recruited to their partners and joined together by enzymes, until where there had been one double helix there now stood two identical to the original. "It is also how the genes that code for proteins are copied into messenger RNA: a molecule similar to DNA which is translated into proteins by the cell." More enzymes rolled down the strands of DNA, reeling off single stranded RNA copies that were grabbed by yet other molecular machines, which ratcheted along them to churn out proteins.

"And because they are linked in long chains, the number of possible sequences is astronomical: there are more than a trillion possible sequences in a mere chain of 20. This makes everything possible with just those four nucleotides and how they are ordered. Some sequences are recognized by molecules that block transcription into RNA" – in one part of the DNA, a transient structure formed and was bound by a molecule that prevented access by the transcribing enzymes; in another part a different molecule bound directly to a specific sequence with the same effect – "while others initiate transcription" – other interactions opened up the sequence for copying instead of blocking it.

"You have seen how DNA is copied into RNA which encodes proteins. But what is the code, the secret behind that conversion? It is simply the sequence of nucleotides in the RNA that determines what protein it codes for." A map of triplet sequences appeared linked to twenty different amino acids, the building blocks of proteins. Then the RNA copy drifted away and was grabbed by a molecular machine, a ribosome, churning out a protein according to the encoded sequence, while another RNA with a different sequence churned out a different protein.

"But," he continued, "nothing is perfect. Sometimes errors occur: the DNA is damaged or there is a copying error. Once an error is there it is copied as faithfully as the rest: the cell's machinery has no knowledge of what is right or wrong beyond the sequence existing in the DNA itself." In the display, a mismatch was highlighted in red:

then there were two copies, one the same as the original, but the other with that single difference now permanently incorporated. "Those errors cause a lot of problems: genetic diseases, cancer, deterioration of cell function. But without them we wouldn't be here: some of the changes alter function in a way that is beneficial or neutral, and it is the accumulation of such changes over millions of years that has led to all the diversity of life on earth. Including us."

"But how?" he asked, raking the audience with a penetrating gaze. "To know how, the first thing we need to know is the sequence of the DNA. That task looked hopeless. Twenty years after the discovery of the double helix, scientists had slowly and painstakingly sequenced short stretches of DNA and RNA. They had worked out the genetic code you saw earlier: how the 64 triplets of nucleotides code for the twenty amino acids proteins are made of and where they start and stop. But the sequence of even a small virus – where 'small' is a few thousand nucleotides – seemed out of reach." The viewpoint in the arena flew away from the double helix to reveal it as a long thin circular string weaving through space. Then the view receded further and a string ten times longer now dominated the view. "This is the DNA of a larger bacterial virus, around 50 thousand nucleotides long." Then he paused.

"This is the human genome." Another long double helix wound through the space around his head, then the viewpoint fled rapidly; the double helix grew longer and thinner, wound around itself, millions upon millions of nucleotides, finally wrapping itself up into a dense body, a chromosome; then 22 other chromosomes swam into view. "The human genome – ignoring our having two copies of each chromosome – has three *billion* nucleotides."

"Yet the progress in technology for sequencing DNA accelerated so fast that less than fifty years after the double helix was described, a single human genome was sequenced." The pages of a thick book filled with page after page of four-letter code flipped at a dizzying rate in the air.

"That first genome took ten years and nearly one billion dollars to decode. But within another ten years human genomes were being sequenced in days for mere thousands of dollars, and improvements just kept on coming. A human genome could be sequenced on a chip in a few hours. And not just humans: anything could be sequenced and was: a whole library of people, and a whole library of organisms from bacteria to plants to cats to kangaroos." A timeline appeared above

Tagarin's head, showing the years and an exponentially growing forest of sequenced genomes organized into evolutionary groups.

A small collection of organisms peeled out of the forest and expanded, showing the organisms and the similarity between their genomes. "You can see that the chimpanzee genome is 98.5% the same as the human; the cat's is 90% the same. The differences between a chimp, a cat and a man are entirely due to those differences in their genomes: now we were learning what in the latter caused the former."

"The genome works to produce an organism in time as well as space." The view changed to a group of chromosomes much like the one shown earlier, then receded again until a large glowing globe appeared: a single fertilized egg floating in the air. Its chromosomes duplicated, the cell divided, and divided again and again; flashes of color in each cell showed how gene expression varied along gradients in the growing blob. The organism grew and grew, cells migrated, tissues took shape, organs appeared.

It is like a dance of life, thought Miriam, mesmerized by the hypnotic patterns. The replicating helices, the patterns of gene expression, the cell growing into an integrated animal: all a magnificent dance under Tagarin's command. She wondered what the world had lost, if he had been as great a scientist as he was a speaker: and she knew he had been.

But he did not have to quit, she reminded herself: there was plenty of related research he could have continued in. But what would she have done, she then wondered, if she had given her best to the world: and the world had not only slapped her down but destroyed her creation? Would she have continued working meekly for that world, or would she have said damn you, damn you all, and refused to give them anything more? But if that was his motive, what had he done to his own life? Clothed himself in a fog of bitterness around a shell of cynicism, to come partially alive when presented with a new scientific puzzle and only fully alive when reliving the scientist he had once been? Perhaps in punishing the world he had punished himself more.

On stage the dance went faster and faster; what had formerly been smooth generalities became finer and finer detail; delicate hairs pushed their tips outward from the smooth surface; until at last a fluffy kitten appeared. Then it grew and stretched until a sleek cat filled the arena, staring at them through slitted yellow eyes. Miriam suppressed a gasp. The cat's predator eyes appeared to be looking straight at her, and she knew in her bones the fear her far ancestors had felt when they met the gaze of a saber-toothed tiger. She wondered if it was an illusion or perhaps just another coincidence. But when she saw Tagarin's eyes glittering in the shadows she knew he had noted her position in the room, had done it deliberately for her benefit: but whether as acknowledgement, irony or threat she had no way to know. Then she shivered again under that feral gaze, and knew.

Then he spoke again.

"This cat, just as each of you, came from a single cell. That one fertilized egg achieves, somehow, the delicate series of orchestrated changes that expresses the right genes in the right place at the right time. The final result is an organism containing billions of cells and dozens of organs all interacting correctly. And in parallel with advances in genome sequencing, scientists were also discovering that 'somehow'.

"What we learned was how to turn a normal adult cell into a pluripotent stem cell, which can multiply and diversify into several cell types; and what we learned was how to turn a pluripotent stem cell into a totipotent stem cell, which like a fertilized egg and its immediate descendants can produce any cell in the body; indeed, a whole body."

He paused. "It took the human race a thousand generations to progress from cave art to agriculture. It took only three generations to go from the discovery of the double helix to all I have described.

"At the same time, we were learning how to edit the genes in a living cell." A long double helix wound through space, a faulty sequence highlighted in red; a repaired sequence, in green, was put into position by molecular machines to replace the faulty one. The view zoomed out to the cell; the cell divided, and divided, and became a new liver free of the genetic defect. "There are many technical challenges. Some genes can be repaired in tissues as they are" – modified viruses delivered their payload of repaired genes to the cells in an organ, restoring normal function. "But many require making stem cells, repairing them then growing them to restore partial function or replace the whole organ. In any case insertion of the new gene has to be precise: put it in the wrong place and you will disrupt other genes, stopping vital functions or causing diseases such as cancer.

"But those technical problems were solved. The first applications were fixing genetic diseases and creating immunity to viruses." Images of nightmares from the past – of hemophilia, cystic fibrosis, muscular dystrophy and Tay-Sachs disease – appeared and were banished; engineered cellular immunity stopped AIDS and Ebola in their tracks.

"And even harder than fixing defects using an existing good version of a gene is knowing how to improve on the normal. But finally, with all that knowledge of comparative genomics and related science, we had the tools to begin to work out how to design new genes and where to put them." New images flew in: drought and disease resistant crops, salt tolerant plants, disease resistant animals, animals with better or healthier meat or milk and stranger beasts such as a goat with the fur of a mink.

"As you can see, the next evolution of plants and animals was now within our power. We were at the threshold of new possibilities: to remake creation for the benefit of mankind. To remake mankind itself. To become the best we can be."

He paused. "But all that stopped. Do not be deceived. The laws and bans we work under are not for safety, or benefit, or morality. Their sole purpose is to bind us all to the whims of the most irrational: to fulfill the desire of some for power over others. To bring what is possible to man under the control of those with the least wisdom and vision. To put those who know under the rule of those who know nothing, as if ignorance and stupidity grant the right of command and it is knowledge and intelligence that must humbly obey."

Then he stopped to look around the audience. "Most of you here tonight would not be alive were it not for advances like the ones I described. I am sure you appreciate what you were given. That is why you fight to ensure that such work continues, as much as it can, and for that I honor you. But you have seen what mankind has achieved. Imagine what we could have achieved if we had been left free to attempt it." Tagarin's eyes sought out Miriam's in the crowd and locked on to them, as if she was personally responsible for those dead years.

"Perhaps one day we will be free again."

Then the images faded and all that was left was a spotlight on Tagarin in the center of the stage, head bowed.

The audience stood and gave a thunderous ovation. Miriam and Amaro stayed seated: Miriam was too moved to rise; she looked at Amaro and wondered that he seemed untouched. *I suppose he already knew all this*, she thought: *the magnitude of it, the greatness, no longer reaches him.*

Tagarin lifted his head and looked around the room as if returning to the reality of the present. Then he raised his hand in acknowledgement or farewell; the lights faded and he faded with them into the shadows.

When the applause died down the lights came on and something like normalcy returned to the room, or at least to Miriam. Amaro was looking at her with an odd smile, as if amused by her reaction. Then the music started up, his smile broadened, and he swept her onto the dance floor.

Her earlier thought about the whirling dance of life came back to Miriam as Amaro whirled her around in a passionate dance on the floor; the nature of his dance was such that perhaps he had not been untouched after all. It returned again later that night as she lay in bed with him in a more intimate dance. *It is all a dance of life*, she thought: *the molecules inside us, the hormones in our blood, the desires of our bodies and the thoughts of our minds.* The dance still held her and would not let her go; she was still at one with it: her orgasms were intense as if in celebration of it and she rapidly fell asleep afterwards, the dance continuing in her mind as she slept. In her dreams Tagarin loomed as a grim shadow conducting a dance of molecules and cells, shaping stardust into a giant cat that turned to stare at her with its predator's eyes. But its pupils were round and its face was a woman's; it snarled and leapt toward her, but vanished into darkness before it reached her.

CHAPTER 27 – HISTORY

Miriam woke to an empty bed and the smell of bacon with overtones of toast and coffee. She rose, wrapped her body and thoughts in a dressing gown and walked into the kitchen, where Amaro was frying bacon. He heard her footsteps and turned.

"Good morning, my lovely lady," he said. "Would you care to join me for breakfast?"

"I would be honored, good sir. You're looking refreshed."

"Any refreshment is largely your doing, my dear. You, of course, look ravishing as always. Though if you would make my happiness complete, perhaps you could loosen the front of that gown a little. Yes, perfect," he smiled. "Now sit down, and I'll join you."

He brought over a tray with toast, bacon, eggs, orange juice and coffee, and sat down opposite her. He poured her coffee while she collected her breakfast then he turned his face to her.

"I gather you enjoyed your evening?"

"Oh, very much! Both there and here," she added, running her toe up his leg.

"You seemed quite taken with your friend Dr Tagarin's talk."

"Yes... it was mesmerizing. I knew pieces of it but not the whole picture. And I've certainly never seen it presented in quite such a manner. It was like watching a sorcerer calling up the spirits of the Earth." She paused. "What did you think of him, Amaro?"

"Oh, he certainly put on a good show. But it was rather self-serving, don't you think? The way he ended it, fighting a rearguard action in a battle he lost twenty years ago."

"About that battle... what do you think? Is Tagarin right – the research should be allowed? Should never have been stopped? Or do you think the laws are a good thing?"

Amaro shrugged. "Given what I do for a living, you would hardly be surprised if I say we need to prevent excessive genetic alterations of anything. Especially ourselves. Not that it really matters what I think. You and I are just humble functionaries, the cat's-paws of those in power. If I had a contrary opinion I might want to get another job, but I doubt anyone would care or listen to my reasons. If the redoubtable Dr Tagarin cannot do anything about it, what hope would there be for me? Though given the circles you seem to move in, perhaps your opinion would carry more weight! So what do you think of the issue?"

Miriam grimaced. "Yeah, right. International woman of influence, that's me. What do I think? I'm not really sure. I can see where Tagarin is coming from and he is certainly passionate about it. I just don't know... but he does seem to have a point."

Amaro smiled at her. "Your problem, my dear, is that you have too much empathy. You are so good at getting inside other people's heads that you risk having their thoughts take root in your own."

Miriam smiled at him then turned to her toast. But behind her smile she thought, *Do I? Then why can't I see behind your eyes, my love? I know you want to be with me, that you enjoy my company, that it isn't just sex for you. But there's something hard inside you I can't reach or touch. Have you had some great hurt and are afraid to be hurt again? Is that it? Or is it something else? Are you going to hurt me, after all?*

But all she said was, "I think you overestimate me." She sipped her coffee for a while then asked, "But, really, what harm can it cause? Oh, I agree that nobody can be allowed to create a super army of ant-men or something like that. But that's a big jump from making a few people faster, stronger or smarter. There are already lots of people born faster, stronger or smarter than most. Usually they're the people who become our heroes, not our villains. So... what's the big deal, really?"

Amaro looked at her seriously. "It all depends on what you think people are and what you think the limits should be, doesn't it? There have to be limits – even you admitted that – so it's a matter of defining them. And on this – well, the people have spoken. If other people disagree then they can't just go on doing what they want. You work for the law. You of all people should know that."

"Obeying the law is a separate issue from knowing what the law should be."

"You are very profound this morning."

She smiled. "Or maybe just confused. Maybe there's no difference."

"Now you're being even more profound," he laughed. "But back to the topic, you have enough trouble with regular villains don't you? Do you really want to have to fight things designed to be better than you? Especially if they're not only tougher but smarter? Do you really want to face that in some dark alley one night?"

Miriam glanced at him, startled. But he just picked up his coffee and sipped it, innocently watching her over the rim through the gently curling steam. *No*, she thought, *don't be paranoid; he can't know.*

"But why should they be any worse than any other human? If the ratio is the same: then we'll have more superheroes than supervillains. And everyone will be enriched by it, just as we are by our regular geniuses."

"I think the problem is we don't really know what we're doing. Who knows what unknown effects our gene tinkering will have? People are the product of millions of years of evolution. Tagarin and his friends might like to think they know what they are doing, but do they? Maybe a healthy human is the best we can be already. Maybe trying to push the envelope will just push them over the edge. You might find you have more supervillains than superheroes. Maybe you won't have any superheroes."

Miriam looked into the distance, thinking. "Maybe. Maybe. But how will we ever get to know, if we don't even start? Would we ever have got where we are today if everyone had been afraid to try anything?"

Amaro let her think; she did not seem to be expecting a reply. Then she continued, "But as you say, my opinions aren't going to change anything. For now I'm more interested in what makes the remarkable Dr Tagarin tick. Maybe you can help me. What are the facts of his case? I know a bit about it of course. But it's kind of your field: what do you know about what went on back then? Can you put it in perspective for me?"

Amaro buttered some toast and chewed it while he gathered his thoughts. "Yes, I can probably flesh things out for you. Frankly, I can see Tagarin's point too, but it really was his own fault. He overreached. There was a lot of argument at the time among scientists and the public. With all the successes in medicine and more and more improved plants and animals coming off the genetic production line, the most adventurous scientists like Tagarin started turning their attention to the evolution of our own species. Just like he said last night. Why be limited to the historical accidents that had produced the current human form, they argued, if we can make improved humans: faster, stronger, smarter, healthier? They started working on just that."

He thought some more, sipping his coffee. Miriam was giving him the same attention she had given Tagarin: his presentation wasn't as flashy but she had been seized by a desire to learn as much as she could about the topic. *This is the key*, she thought, *though I'm not quite sure where the lock is.*

"The problem was an old one: technology moving faster than public policy. Tagarin's mistake was in thinking only the technology mattered, that he should ride it as fast and as hard as he could, that the public and the policy would catch up when they could and if they couldn't it was their problem. But it turned out to be his problem. The people watched the technology like they'd watch a rocket shooting across the sky above them: at first they marveled at the sight, then they wondered what it meant, then they worried it might fall on their heads. The politicians watched the people and when the people started worrying, they started to think about regulating."

He stopped. "Do you know where the term 'geneh' comes from?" he asked.

"Not really. It's just the word everyone uses. It stands for 'genetically engineered human' doesn't it?"

"That's half the story, yes. Scientists like Tagarin were busy in their labs doing things to cells and even turning the cells into embryos. Religious activists have always looked askance at embryonic research. But abortion rights were a done deal; nobody was going to go back on that. And the logic of abortion rights is that embryos don't have rights. If you can kill them for one purpose, why not another? So while government-funded research was still barred from any research on embryos, private companies could and did. Some people didn't like that. But there's always someone objecting to anything – even sex.

"Unfortunately, embryos were one thing. Research was one thing. But when scientists began saying not only why genetic engineering would be good for the human race in theory, but that it might soon be achieved in reality... Well, that proved to be another thing entirely. Blogs were written. Net debates flamed. Sermons were preached.

Politicians shouted. The public debate began in earnest.

"That was when a dynamic young environmental lawyer from California wrote an opinion piece that rocked the nation; the world. She titled it 'Don't Let the Geneh Out of the Bottle' and it let an entirely different genie out of its bottle. She coined the word as the abbreviation you know, pronounced 'genie' to fit her theme. And not only did she argue a wide-ranging religious and philosophical case why such research should be banned, she also presented solid evidence that the research was further along than anyone thought: that scientists weren't merely talking about it, they had already produced engineered human fetuses. It hit every button of the opponents of genetic engineering and quite a few buttons of the ambivalent. The defenders of science in general and this science in particular were, as usual in history, a minority. That lawyer's fame and infamy exploded. Her career was made. Her name was Lyn Felton. One day, she would become President of the United States."

Miriam gasped softly and stared at him, mouth partly open. *Oh my God*, she thought. *Oh my God.* The shape she saw in the clues and half leads took on a little more definition. She had known that Felton had been active on the issue but not how intimately involved she had been. She still didn't know what it meant, but she knew it meant something. Amaro smiled at her, but behind the smile he was also thinking his own secret thoughts: *Interesting reaction, my dear; more than one would expect simply from hearing a famous name linked to a casual topic of conversation. You are such a sweet innocent in many ways.* He felt his heart go out to her; for once, he was unable to stop it. *You're playing a risky game, Amaro. Fire can burn both ways: I hope you know what you're doing.* Then he smiled. Miriam thought the smile was for her. But he was remembering a line from an old movie. *The fate of two people doesn't amount to a hill of beans in this crazy world*, he thought; *we might as well both enjoy what we have while we still have it.*

"Well, she had big ambitions," he continued, "even before her political career. She wasn't content with agitating in her own country: she set up an international organization aiming to ban such research everywhere under the auspices of the United Nations. She managed to appeal to a broad audience. The environmental lobbies were already powerful and flocked to her side; the religious movements who were growing in influence around the world joined them. And not just the activists either: I guess her calls for the purity of humanity appealed to something deep in the public psyche. The more cynical of her opponents questioned how much of her enthusiasm was based on her own moral beliefs and how much on the existing morals of the public, but the public was happy either way. I guess that's the mark of a politician.

"And as you know, she succeeded. Her opponents were crushed between the lovers of Nature on one side and the lovers of God on the other, with the broad weight of public opinion adding mass to both sides. Whether she had persuaded a majority of people or just a majority of loud voices is for history to decide, I suppose. But the final result was a UN ban on such research and the formation of the Department of Human Genetic Integrity. And on the strength of her notoriety, she became a Senator and eventually our esteemed President."

Miriam nodded. "I suppose I should pay more attention to politics."

"Oh, she doesn't talk about those days much any more. I guess she figures she'd already milked all the benefit and you know politicians: avoid any controversy if you can. The public might have approved of the creation of GenInt, but they have never been popular."

Miriam nodded but Amaro could tell she had drifted away into her own world. She still couldn't see the shape of what was out there, but she could see there was a shape. And if the shape was a geneh? Tagarin's words returned to haunt her. If there was a geneh out there, her duty was to catch it, and that would be its death. Would she be ready for that?

CHAPTER 28 – KATLYN

Katlyn rested high in the branches above the path. Nobody could see her from below. If by chance some vehicle flew overhead, the thick canopy would hide her from their sight too. The only things that could see her were the birds seeking insects among the leaves. And they did not care. They kept one eye on her as they whistled and chattered to themselves, but were happy in their power to escape if she moved. Sometimes they scolded her just out of reach, if they imagined she was keeping some juicy bug to herself. Had they known how fast she could move they might have been more cautious. But they were safe; she wished them no ill. She was waiting for larger prey.

She liked it up here. She stretched luxuriantly, feeling like a contented cat in its element. She could feel the relaxation spreading to her fingers and toes; she could feel the sounds of small life going about its business of living; she could smell the odors of budding growth sweetened by the faint scents of distant flowers.

Yet there was a thread of steel within her. She loved it here but was here for a purpose. And until the purpose came to her she was content to just feel the peace and the coolness. She had found no answer to her questions; perhaps if she let them, this time the answers would come to her like the birds.

She had not been happy with herself after the warehouse. She knew she had not only panicked but also let the accumulated rage of years get the better of her. Though she was not really sure what else she could have done. She had needed to find out what the police knew and more importantly how they knew it. She hissed at herself. Rationalize it as she may, she had miscalculated. In the back of her mind and at the back of her rage had been the idea that maybe she could scare that young cop off. She had certainly looked callow enough. But she had shown more courage and intelligence than Katlyn had bargained for. Katlyn had the sinking feeling that all she had achieved was making a dangerous enemy even more so, like forging the blade that would one day slay her.

And there was her dilemma. If Sun Tzu's advice was to know your enemy then Machiavelli's advice was even darker. Never leave your enemy wounded; never leave your enemies with the power to do something about their hate. Her tail twitched. This was a war, a matter of life or death. Her life or death. And the advice from all the strategists in history, from Caesar to Mao, could be summed up in one word: ruthlessness.

So much for relaxation, thought Katlyn with disgust. The answers might be shy about coming to her but the questions had no such hesitation. She thought of all Daniel had done; she knew it was not all for her, but she knew it encompassed her. Could she see his plans, see him, brought to ruin by her own lack of purpose, her own weakness? Was she like all the cowards of history, the men who had broken under fire, had fled from the horror, who could not face what had to be done? And in so doing had betrayed not only their friends but themselves?

But was it cowardice? Despite her terror, Miriam had faced Katlyn with more than courage. And Katlyn was her enemy. Not only an enemy because of her criminal actions, but an enemy to her genes: not even *persona non grata* but *bestia non grata*. A non-person without rights or recourse. Yet Miriam, despite being a hated officer of the law, had faced her openly and treated her with respect, as an equal, and more: as a person. Ironically, Katlyn knew, that had only increased her own rage. She had not wanted to believe it; had wanted to smash that open face until it would reveal the true soul skulking within. All it had revealed was that Miriam was an innocent. What she had told Katlyn had been true: she had not deserved to die.

But the ghost of Machiavelli would not leave her alone. For they weren't two schoolgirls choosing friends and enemies and laughing together in the park. If Miriam caught her she would be dead. And far from scaring Miriam away, she had given her a much more personal reason for wanting to catch her than just investigating some minor thefts. Katlyn knew strategy; she made it her business to know strategy. You do not leave a wounded enemy alive.

She sighed. But could she do it? This wasn't personal. There was more at stake than her feelings. But she remembered Miriam's face, how even when pleading for her life she had a certain dignity, and she wasn't sure she could look in that face and watch the light go out in those eyes.

But that was why she was here. It hadn't been too hard to track Miriam down in her private life, had then been easy to discover her patterns including her liking for this path through this park at this early morning hour. Katlyn had been coming here for a couple of weeks now. Miriam did not always come. Sometimes she came alone, jogging or strolling along the path. Sometimes she came with a man, the same man each time: boyfriend, Katlyn presumed. All those times Katlyn had watched Miriam go by beneath her perch; all those times she had let her. It would be so easy, she thought; so easy to drop down unseen and that would be the end of Miriam Hunter. So easy to make it look like a random crime of violence with no link to Katlyn or her mission. Such a simple, clean end to the problem; such a strategically sound way to buy time: almost certainly enough time. So far, she had been unable to do it. But she had been equally unable to stop her vigils.

She saw Miriam approaching, a short distance away. This time she was alone, walking and humming some tune softly to herself. Happy. *You bitch*, Katlyn thought, *it's as if you don't want me to kill you.* Then as Miriam neared, something unexpected happened. Three figures melted out of the surrounding woods to confront her. Katlyn lifted her head in surprise. They must be very cautious for Katlyn not to have known of their presence. Miriam had not known it either: she stopped in surprise. Then Katlyn smiled sharply. *Perhaps there is a god for creatures like me after all*, she thought; *a god who answers our prayers.* If she judged the situation correctly, her problem might just go away on its own. All she had to do was nothing.

CHAPTER 29 – KNUCKLES

Miriam had been alternately jogging and walking along her favorite path this morning, thinking random thoughts: thoughts of friends, family and Amaro. When she thought of work it was of her colleagues, not her actual tasks. While her work was the spine of her life's purpose, life encompassed more than it. There was nothing so urgent that she needed to ponder it now; time enough for that when she was at work.

She stopped in surprise when three men appeared in front of her. They were young, muscular, and all wore thin patterned masks that made it impossible to recognize their features. Her surprise transformed itself rapidly into alarm. They had to be Griefers. She had not heard of any cases of Griefing in her city, but she knew that in crime and politics there was never an idea so bad that someone would not copy it. But perhaps they were just pranksters.

"Can I help you?" she asked evenly.

One of them cracked his knuckles. "I reckon so."

Miriam casually tapped the police emergency call button of the phone on her wrist. Knuckles smiled and held up a small device in his palm. "Sorry, I think phone service is out today."

"What do you want?"

Knuckles, evidently their leader, replied again. "Oh, not much. Just a bit of fun. Then we'll be on our way. You make it interesting, maybe you don't get hurt too bad. But you make it too interesting, well, that might be a mistake." He grinned nastily.

Miriam thought quickly. Definitely Griefers then. They were a growing problem, until now in other cities: bored young men who had decided the best excitement in their pointless lives was preying on the helpless. Their crimes were various but had many features in common. They craved the excitement of danger, so their attacks usually occurred in public places like this. That added to the terror, as they were usually places where people normally felt safe. But the Griefers treated it as a military adventure. So they always went in small groups: not so large that their victims obviously had no chance, but not so small that they really had any. And they always waited patiently until conditions were right. Miriam knew they would not have approached her if anybody else had been nearby: there would be no one to help her. She also knew their victims did not come out of it well. There had been few deaths but that was not from mercy: Griefers liked their victims to live with what they had done to them. Liked to think how for the rest of their lives they would bear not only the physical scars but the fear of never feeling safe; as if a legacy of everlasting pain would give the Griefers their own immortality.

Shit. "Listen, you're making a mistake. I'm a cop. Leave now and I'll pretend I never saw you," she lied. "Don't leave, and you might not like the consequences."

"Oooh! A cop! You hear that boys?" said Knuckles. The others chuckled. "Where's your badge, sugar? More to the point, I don't see any gun, either."

Miriam went into a crouch. "Oh, so you want to make it interesting, do you?" he said. "Good. We like to dance." They spread out, Knuckles drifting around behind her.

Miriam waited for their move. Attacking one against three was not a wise option; she would let them start it and hope they got in each other's way. She circled; they circled; she felt like a musk ox surrounded by wolves, both sides too cautious to attack a dangerous enemy. Perhaps she should not have told them she was a cop; even if they didn't believe her it had made them careful. She might have been better off with them thinking she was helpless. But perhaps this would buy her time; perhaps someone would approach, and they would give it up.

Her blood couldn't decide whether to freeze with terror at what they might do to her or boil with rage that they would wish to do it – to her or anyone. She thought of one of her martial arts instructors from long ago, a man with a gentle voice and iron limbs. "The Way is more important than the Battle," he had said. "All living things are One: to hurt your enemy is to hurt yourself. So do not hurt if you can stop; do not injure if you can merely hurt. Do little to do much. That is the path of Wisdom."

Screw that, Miriam thought. She'd hurt these bastards as much as she could.

Knuckles disappeared from her peripheral vision and she knew what their strategy would be. She continued to circle. She did not need to turn. She could see her hidden opponent's progress in the movements of the others' eyes and in the faint sounds from behind. She would have one chance at this. When she judged the time was right, she snapped her head back and felt a satisfying crunch as it collided with his nose; then she sent a powerful back kick to the body and heard him crash into a tree. Then everything happened too fast to do more than react.

One of them ran at her; she scythed her arms in a two-fisted blow to his temple, and he dropped like a sack of potatoes. The other was more cautious and approached her in more of a dance. He was good but not good enough. Miriam kicked him in the groin and her knee met his head on its way down when he folded up. She kicked him in the head again to send him to the ground.

But then she felt a sharp sting in her thigh and spun around. *Oh, crap.* Knuckles had risen, holding his nose in one hand and a dart gun in the other. She felt her legs wobbling already. She knew this drug; first it would paralyze her then she would lose consciousness. She had to hold on. Maybe she could still take him out with the last of her strength if he came near enough before she was helpless.

He grinned maliciously, in demonic counterpoint to the blood dripping from his nose. "Pretty good, aren't you?" He surveyed his friends with mock concern. "Tut, tut. The boys won't be very happy with you when they wake up. I'm afraid that you won't be very pretty after they've finished with you."

Miriam could no longer support her weight and slumped to the ground, her back against a tree trunk, looking up at him helplessly. "Stop! You're making a mistake! If you do anything to me the whole police force will be after you."

He continued as if she hadn't spoken. "But while you're still pretty we should take advantage of it." His grin changed to a nasty leer and he started undoing the front of his pants.

Oh God, no, thought Miriam, *not that too. Christ!* She clamped her legs together in fright and was gratified that at least they still obeyed her to that extent. But she knew it was a futile gesture. There was nothing she could do. The shadows were already dancing around the edge of her vision as he pulled it out and started to approach her. *Oh God.* She thought she should feel terror, but even that was swirling off into the dark to dance with the shadows.

Then one of the shadows solidified as it curled down from above and wrapped around him, and he spun to the ground. But Miriam lost sight of the scene as her head slumped to her chest.

She felt someone tugging at her wrist, and raising her eyes saw a slender hand over her phone. Then fingers felt her neck. "Please. Help me," she whispered. But whether the words came out, she could not tell.

Then the fingers lifted her chin, but all she could see were the shadows and two large yellow eyes. *I know those eyes*, she thought dimly, but she knew those pitiless yellow eyes held no mercy and no help, only madness and death. Then the eyes expanded to fill the world until they too went dark, and the world ended.

CHAPTER 30 – SAVED

Miriam awoke in a strange room. It looked too white and smelled too clean. It held strange devices doing unknown tasks. It looked – clinical. *There's a clue for you Miriam*, she thought drowsily. She was in hospital.

The terror came crashing back with her last memories. Her hands flew to her face, but there was no pain; her skin felt smooth and uninjured. She felt her body from neck to between her legs and found no breaks or pain. She sighed with relief.

An older nurse heard her stir and turned toward her. "Ah, awake at last, are you dear? Welcome back to the land of the living. You've had a bit of an adventure but you're all right now. I'll call the doctor. She can tell you more."

The doctor was friendly and competent. They had given her an antidote to the drug to aid her recovery and there would be no long-term effects; she would feel fine within a couple of hours. They had treated her for some minor scrapes, bumps and bruises but she had no serious injuries of any kind. No, no evidence of rape. The doctor advised her that the police now wanted to talk to her and excused herself.

"The police" turned out to be Jack with a uniformed policeman in tow. She smiled at them. Stone rolled his eyes at her. "I try to keep you out of trouble, I really do. But you insist on getting into fights."

"What happened? Who rescued me?"

Stone stared at her. "Rescued you?"

"Yes! Rescued me! What do you think happened?"

"Well, you pushed the emergency beacon on your phone. Because it was a police emergency, officers turned up pretty damned quick. You were out and there were three unconscious thugs lying around you, with a smashed signal blocker on the ground. We figured you'd managed to finish them off before the drug took hold. Though we did wonder how you got that lucky. You say you were rescued? There was nobody around trying to take any credit."

Miriam thought. "Well... I can't really be sure. It all went very vague at the end. I did incapacitate the first two. The leader, though, he shot me with a dart." She shuddered. "He was going to rape me. Then they were going to beat me to a pulp. I was hoping I could take him out before I went under but I don't know what happened. I saw something; like someone attacking him, but my sight was going. I think whoever it was must have sent the signal for help. But you say there was nobody there?"

Stone shrugged. "Nope. Not even a sign of them. Just you and your three dance partners."

Miriam remembered the yellow eyes. But that was impossible. It made no sense that Katlyn would be there; even less sense that she would have helped her. It had to be some kind of hallucination: thoughts of the case brought to life by the drug and projected onto whatever had actually happened. After all, it was the last thing she remembered before everything went dark. A dream, nothing more.

"I guess someone as shy as they were brave, then. Unless I did manage to get off that lucky kick after all." Then her shoulders slumped with exhaustion, and she fell asleep again.

~~~

Katlyn was still high among the branches, but in another tree far from the recent excitement. She had committed enough stupidity for one day without hanging around to be caught for it.

She lay back to think. When it had come down to it, she'd had to do what she had done. She had seen another creature – another person – fighting for her life, and her heart had gone out to her. There are some things, Katlyn thought, that lie beyond the strategies of war. There are some times when even the soldiers of opposing armies must unite in a common cause against a greater evil.

But Machiavelli's ghost had followed her and was still trying to give her constructive criticism. If she had just stayed where she was Miriam would no longer be a problem. The thugs might have killed her; even if they hadn't she would have been out of action so long that she no longer mattered. Instead Katlyn had saved her. And for what? She would get no gratitude or credit for it: Miriam had been so far out of it she would never know who had saved her. All Katlyn had achieved was to leave her most dangerous enemy alive, healthy and as keen to catch her as ever.

The tree was flowering, and she pulled a bunch of the flowers to her nose to savor their subtly sweet scent. Life had so much pleasure in it, she thought; why was it also so hard? Then all her confusing thoughts fused together into a new shape, and the shape held the answers.

No, Niccolo, she thought to the ghost. *There is more to it than that. The price for your life can be too high; so high that if you pay, your life is no longer worth saving.* If she had been brought to where the price was letting someone like Miriam die in such a way, then she would not pay it. If she crossed that line, she now saw, no more lines remained to be crossed: there was nothing left between her and the abyss but a steepening slope into a self-made hell ruled by a self-made evil. Until today she had fought with the moral certainty that her cause was right. But if she crossed that line there was no longer any right, nothing but the battling of opposing evils. *Do not become what you despise*, she told herself: *be what you ought to be.*

It was getting dark now and it was time to go. She knew she would not lie in wait for Miriam again. And whatever debt she might have owed Miriam for how she had abused her before, she had now more than repaid: even if she was the only one on Earth who knew it. They were still enemies and perhaps her actions today had doomed her. But she knew that at some level, she had already won.

CHAPTER 31 – DNA

"Hello Rianna. What's up?"

Miriam had been back at work for a week now. For once she had been content to be stuck in a back room out of the action, but her pulse quickened at Rianna's next words.

"Hi Miriam. I've got a DNA sequence for you from your fire. It isn't much and not enough for confirmation of identity, but there's enough for a clue to identity. We got some useless bits – non-human or too conserved among humans to be any use – but two fragments totaling a few thousand bases long in human variable regions."

"That's great! I owe you and Kimberley a bottle of champagne!"

"As long as you share it with us. Now, don't get too excited. Unfortunately there are quite a few bases we couldn't resolve, so there are a number of ambiguities. The pieces are long enough that not many people will match them, but even the person it came from would only give you a probability match not certainty. I've already run it through our standard databases and there aren't any matches, so whoever it is hasn't been involved in a previous crime. And don't forget it could belong to someone entirely innocent. Hairs can transfer from person to person, just blow about in the wind or even be deliberately planted. And to make things worse they are separate fragments: we can't even be sure that both sequences really come from the same person. Though since they're from a single hair the chance of contamination from someone else is very low."

"I still owe you a champagne. A good one. Are there any other databases we can search?"

"Oh, there are lots. Medical, scientific, even government records not strictly associated with crimes. But while some are public access most will be confidential, if not secret. So you'll need a warrant, especially if you want a name to go with your match. I'm not sure you have the grounds."

"Leave that to me. And thanks again."

Now for the harder bit, thought Miriam.

She made her way to Ramos' office and knocked on the door. "Come in!"

"Hi boss," she said. "I have some new information, and an idea, about the Katlyn case. Can we go over it? We might want Legal in on it."

Ramos raised an eyebrow. "What have you got?"

"Remember how the DNA from Katlyn's warehouse was too degraded and contaminated to be any use? Rianna did some fancy work with it and managed to get some usable sequences out of it."

Ramos' eyebrow went up a further notch. "Really? I don't recall authorizing spending for that. What have you two been up to?"

Miriam's face smoothed into a suspiciously innocent expression. "Oh, Rianna has separate funding for research and she thought it would make an interesting research program. Apparently she's getting not only my sequences but also a publication out of it. So all perfectly above board and good for the department's scientific reputation as well."

"Hmmm, yes, I'm sure. I do admire innovation. So what do you want Legal for, if it's not just you two needing a lawyer for unauthorized use of department facilities?"

"The sequences don't match anything in our usual databases, but according to Rianna there are a lot of others we could search. I know it's a long shot, but it's one of the few shots we have. What I'd like to do is set the AI on looking for matches. You know that's the kind of thing it is for, so no problem there. It'll just be a background task, low priority, just something for it to do when it isn't doing anything more urgent. The problem is that most of the databases are confidential and they won't give up the goods unless the AI can present a warrant. So first I need your authorization, and second I need to see what Legal can get me."

Ramos considered the issue. It was pretty thin but he had to push this investigation as best he could. "I see. Well, we're still running with the case so I'll support you. Hang on." He pressed a button on his phone. "Hi Jim. Can you send Scott up to my office? We need some advice on electronic warrants for accessing external databases. Yeah, thanks."

He turned back to Miriam. "While we wait: any other progress?"

"Nothing really. The AI occasionally flags things but none of them are convincing. Our thief appears to have gone quiet, and no more of her victims are talking yet. I can apply some pressure if you think it's worth it?"

"No, not at this stage. This whole case has been walking a fine line and I don't want to fall off it. Ah. Hi Scott. Have you met Miriam Hunter? Miriam, this is Scott Harriman. Miriam, you explain the issue."

"Hi Scott," she said, shaking hands. "What I want to do is set my AI to querying non-police databases for a couple of short DNA sequences, to find any possible matches. Most are confidential so a search warrant will help a lot in broadening the search. So I want one, and I want one that is as high powered as possible so I can access the most data. What can we do?"

Scott stroked his short beard. "So you have some random sequence, no idea who it belongs to, and you want to query a bunch of databases just in case? I don't like your chances."

Miriam frowned. "What would we need, to have a chance?"

Scott shrugged. "Some evidentiary link is the gold standard. But if you had that, you wouldn't need what you're after, would you? You're fishing. Judges don't like fishing, unless it's for marlin in the Bahamas."

"Anything that could get around the anti-fishing sentiment?" put in Ramos.

"Well, maybe. Since you're using an AI, no person has to see the data, right? So if you can ensure that non-matching data won't be stored for longer than it takes to do the comparison, or better, your AI itself never even sees the data and has the target do the searching, then that addresses a lot of privacy concerns. It might get you a very limited warrant that will let you into a few places. But to get more than that you'd practically need a national security issue."

Miriam and Ramos looked at each other. "How about a potential threat to the President?" he asked.

It was Scott's turn to raise his eyebrows. "Ah. That might do it. How good is the evidence for a link?"

Ramos considered. "Well... not ironclad. Maybe strong enough for it to be a credible risk."

"If you can find yourself a judge who's strong on security questions, you have a chance. Not a good one. Otherwise you can forget it."

"OK, I guess we take what we can get. Miriam, can you send Scott what you have? Scott, you do the paperwork. See what you can do about the judge."

~~~

The next day, Miriam was disappointed though not surprised when Scott told her the judge had refused to issue a warrant. If they could get a firmer link to national security issues the judge would reconsider, but for now it was canned.

Nothing much else was going her way either.

IT had come back to her with their analysis of the burglary recording Delaney had provided. "I don't know what kind of software your guy has," Fergus had said, "but it beats anything we have. We can get your vague blurs resolving into a vaguely human blur, but can't even see a face. It could be a yeti for all we can tell. Do you mind if I send this to my old tutor? Sam's a mathematician who's an expert in image analysis and might be able do something with it."

"I don't think Ramos will approve any spending for an external consultant," Miriam replied dubiously.

"Oh, Sam likes a challenge even more than the money. Besides, it's like a proof of talent, good for future business. I think I know the buttons to push to swing it. If not, we haven't lost anything."

"That'd be great, Fergus. Thanks so much." *If this case ever breaks, I'll owe so many people so many favors it'll take me the rest of my career to pay them back.*

None of the stolen jewelry had ever shown up. None of the cases of larger theft had yielded clues either. It was as if the owners themselves had transferred the money but weren't admitting it. They had even started suspecting just that, but it didn't make any sense. Nothing, Miriam decided, was making any sense. They had a geneh on the loose who couldn't be a geneh, and whose only image when caught in the act was somebody else. They had a thief breaking in to commit petty theft – at least relative to the victims' bank balances – and usually leaving no trace, whatever security system the wealthy victim had. They had no thief breaking in, but large sums of money disappearing, without a perpetrator and without a trace. Half the victims acted like suspects, and the other half were as mystified as she was. Neither group liked her.

Miriam was glad she had other things to do, and proceeded to do them.

Chapter 32 – Alarm

"Oh, God," groaned Miriam, looking at the time. Two in the morning and her phone wakes her. Amaro was still asleep beside her, twitching slightly in some no doubt exciting dream. She wished she could join him.

She frowned at her phone, willing her reluctant eyes to focus. She had it set to vibrate, so Amaro could thank her for that. She also had it set to only bother her if it was really important, and when that fact finally raised its timid hand she willed a little harder for her eyes to wake up.

It was her AI, she saw. *This better be good*, she thought grimly, tapping the icon to read the message. She almost sat up straight, but suppressed her reaction for Amaro's sake; then she re-read the message more carefully.

The AI was still living in the past with a lot of its data, but one real-time feed that had been implemented was emergencies. She had set it to keep an eye out for burglar alarm reports from people on her "donors to the President" list that met other criteria relevant to her case. The AI had spotted a curious event: one of the people on her list, apparently the paranoid sort, had installed a rather outdated analog intrusion detection system as a backup to the usual more high tech solutions. It was the former that had been triggered and sent in an alarm to the police. But when the police had queried the man's AI, it had reported all clear. The police had already filed and forgotten the incident but her AI had been taught more suspicion. The combination of time, person and contradiction passed its threshold of coincidence so it had alerted Miriam.

She swung swiftly but silently out of bed and quickly got dressed in the dim light. She scribbled a quick note, "WORK!" and left it by the bed. Then she crept out of the room, still careful not to disturb Amaro, and made her way to the door where she put on her shoes, collected her keys and let herself out.

"Christ!" she whispered to herself as she started the car. She felt an unreasonable excitement. She knew this was probably nothing and even if it were something they would be too late. But her adrenal glands had their own ideas and she could feel the quiver of the chase livening her blood.

There wasn't much traffic at this hour and she put the car on auto. The first thing she did after that was ring Jack. Luckily he was as conscientious as she when it came to phones and after a few rings a groggy voice answered, "Miriam? What are you doing calling at this hour?"

"Sorry, Jack. My AI flagged something suspicious, a burglar alarm at the apartment of one of the President's friends. It was reported by an old analog system but denied by the AI. I know it's probably a false alarm but if our AI is suspicious so am I. I think we need to check it out. I'm already on my way."

"OK. I'll make sarcastic remarks illustrated by severe looks in the morning. Send me the details. You better call the owner, try to get permission to go in. We don't want any unnecessary delays."

"Sure, that's next on my list. See you there."

She pushed a few more buttons on her phone, hoping the apartment's owner would be agreeable despite the hour. Most people allowed their phones to let through calls from the police, but even if he was one of them it didn't mean he would answer: and if he did it was no guarantee he would appreciate it. She remembered uncomfortably Ramos's warning about disturbing the city's finest citizens and she could imagine what he would say about doing it at this hour. When at last someone picked up the phone, she was relieved to hear the sounds of faint conversation and laughter in the background.

"Hello? I'm very sorry to call you at this hour, Mr Trevane, but I am Miriam Hunter, a detective with the Special Crimes Unit."

"Yes? Goddammit, what do you want, Detective? You're lucky I wasn't asleep. But this better be good."

"I have been investigating some strange thefts that might have serious implications, and your secondary burglar alarm reported a break-in at your city apartment. Your AI reported all clear so the local police ignored it, but we have a more specialist AI that flagged the incident as suspicious. Could you please give us permission to enter your apartment? In the presence of your hotel manager, and solely to check that things are fine?"

"What the hell? If my AI says it's fine, what are you bothering me for?"

"I'm sorry, and I know this is an imposition, but it is very important. We have reason to think that your AI has been fooled somehow. It might be nothing, but it might be related to other such crimes and if it is it is vital that we can gain access. It really is that important. Not only for our other investigations but for your own property."

There was a long pause on the line and Miriam was afraid that he would just hang up. But finally he answered, "All right, Detective. I'll let the manager know. I hope it is a false alarm, so I suppose it would be churlish of me to make a complaint if it is."

"Thank you. It probably is a false alarm, I'm afraid, but I have to check. If it is... well, thank you anyway. Good night, sir."

Whew, she thought. *Hopefully it will be something, and if it isn't, with luck he'll just laugh it off.*

She took the car off auto and hit the accelerator.

She pulled up at the entrance to the apartment and jumped out of the car. Jack wasn't here yet so she took the time to look around. Trevane evidently had different taste from most of the others on her list, who tended to favor soaring towers or sprawling country estates. He had chosen to live in The Beehive, an extensive group of tower blocks originally intended for the middle class, inherited by the poorer segments of the community, and finally reinvented as exclusive dwellings for the rich and powerful. The main point in their favor besides a certain retro charm was a combination of proximity to the center of the city and their sweeping views of the river. A light mist was rising from the river tonight, adding a certain layer of mystery to the view.

Miriam strode into the lobby and flashed her badge at the night manager. He had been expecting her and nodded. "Mr Trevane told me to expect you, Detective. Shall we go up?"

"Hold on, please." She rang Jack. "Where are you? OK."

"Sorry," she said, addressing the manager, "we'd better wait for my partner. He's nearly here."

The manager went back to whatever managers did at that time of night, while Miriam paced impatiently. After a few minutes the door opened and Jack entered. He looked more disheveled than usual but made no complaint, just said "Well, let's check this out."

They took the lift to the apartment's floor and looked along the corridor. There was nothing suspicious. They walked along the carpeted floor to the doorway. "OK, Mr, er, Johnson," whispered Jack, addressing the manager. "Let's keep this quiet. Unlock the door as softly as you can and let us in. You'll have to come in with us to keep the owner happy, but if I yell 'Gun!' go hide. OK? Let's go."

CHAPTER 33 – FALL

Katlyn heard soft footsteps in the hallway and even softer voices outside the door, and she jerked her head up in alarm. *Oh, crap,* she thought. She was in the office behind a closed door and figured she had about twenty seconds. She would have to cut short what she was doing, but she couldn't just leave right away: if she didn't cover her tracks too much careful work might be compromised. So she forced herself to work quickly but as calmly as possible, even as she heard people enter the apartment, fan out and approach her room. Finally she was done. She grabbed her tools and ran for the window.

~~~

They hadn't seen anything. No signs of a break-in, no signs of life at all. Now Miriam edged up to a closed door; it looked like an office. A faint light was visible under the door; perhaps some device left on, perhaps light from outside.

A shadow flickered in that light.

"Jack!" she called, and slammed open the door; luckily, it had no lock. She burst into the room and looked about wildly. Nobody. Then she felt a faint breeze and noticed that the glass was missing from the window.

"Jack!" she cried again, "In the office! The window's open! I'm taking a look!"

She ran to the window and looked down; there was nothing but misty darkness, with a laneway faintly visible far below. Then she looked up and saw a rope, slithering toward the roof ten feet above. She grabbed it and pulled with all her strength. A brief tug-of-war ensued but whoever was at the other end decided that flight was their best option, and Miriam nearly overbalanced as the rope lost its tension. She pulled it taut and began to climb, with a quick shout of "Roof!" into the apartment. She glanced behind her at the dizzying drop and hoped that the rope's owner would not invest the time needed to cut the tough microfilament cord. The light sound of receding footsteps reassured her on that point.

Jack charged into the room, manager in tow, and looked up to see Miriam nearly at the top. He looked down, then back up. *Work smarter, not braver,* he told himself. "Is there another way to the roof? A quick way?" he asked the manager.

The manager nodded and jingled his keycards. "Follow me."

Miriam pulled herself over the edge of the roof in time to see a dark figure darting away along the roof: a figure trailed by a long tail. "Stop!" she shouted, drawing her gun. But Katlyn just changed her gait to a random dodge. "Dammit!" swore Miriam. She wasn't going to send bullets flying wildly across the city skyline. She took off after her.

Katlyn did not slow as she neared the edge of the roof. She ran straight to it and launched herself into space, clearing the gap and executing a skillful roll back onto her feet to continue running over the next rooftop. Miriam slowed to a stop, panting, aghast. She looked at the gap and estimated it at twelve feet. *I can do this,* she thought; *I'm fit and I've jumped that far before; just never where missing it would kill me.* Then she looked at Katlyn's fleeing form and her anger decided for her. *No, not again,* she thought; *I'm too close, I'm not letting you get away this time.* She gritted her teeth and ran.

Miriam was correct. She could have made the jump. But the roof was slightly damp from the mist, that damp had lubricated the grime encrusting the rooftop, and just as she launched herself from the roof her foot slipped slightly. It was enough to lose a fraction of the power behind her jump; enough lost power that she knew she wouldn't make it. *Sweet Jesus,* she thought. She could feel her trajectory fading, as if the mist and shadows below were dark fingers of the chasm reaching to drag her down; but she stretched out to her limit and her hands made the edge of the roof. Her body slammed into the wall and her gun clattered away as she let it go to grip the edge with her fingers.

But it was too tenuous a grip on too unhelpful a material, and the wall gave her toes little purchase. She could feel that she would not be able to pull herself up on the smooth surface; knew that even if she could stop herself from sliding off, the strength in her fingers would give out before rescue could come.

"Jack!" she screamed. "Help me!"

The manager and Jack had taken the stairway to the roof three steps at a time but fumbled finding the right key to the outside door. Jack had only just pushed his way through it when Miriam called, and he was too far away even if he could find the courage to make that jump. Even if, finding the courage, he could make it across. "Miriam! Hold on!" he called. He broke into a shambling run, eyes scanning for something, anything, he might be able to use to reach her or help her.

Katlyn glanced over her shoulder at the commotion and stopped. Miriam saw her turn, saw the cold golden eyes regarding her, tail twitching. She looked away into the darkness where escape lay, back at Jack, down at Miriam. "Help me!" Miriam called to her. "Please!"

Katlyn bared her teeth in a chilling smile that held neither mirth nor kindness. She looked away once more into the darkness that led to safety, but suddenly turned and darted back. She slowed, regarding Miriam silently, then came to a stop, looking down at her clinging to the ledge.

"Hello, Miriam," she said softly. "I suppose if I were a nice girl I'd give you a hand. But I'm neither nice nor a girl, am I?"

"But you came back. I don't believe you are evil. Please don't let me die."

"Ah, but maybe that's all I want. Just to see you die, up close and personal. Look into those innocent eyes as you fall. Perhaps I'll see Heaven in them. That's as close as I'll ever get to it."

Jack had seen Katlyn stop and run back toward Miriam, so he gave up looking for a rope or ladder and accelerated to meet this more immediate threat. He came to a stop at the edge and stared at Katlyn, for the first time seeing her fully in the flesh. She stood there in the wisps of mist, luminous yellow eyes staring out of a pale face made paler by black hair, dark cattail flicking. He thought how people of a past age would have called her a demon; how many in even this age would agree. He could sympathize: he felt a twinge of superstitious dread himself. He pointed his gun at her and she lifted her head to stare directly at him. He swallowed involuntarily but stood his ground.

"You! Jack!" she said. "Lose the gun or lose your girlfriend!"

He hesitated. "How do I know you won't just push her off if I do?"

"As they say in the vids: you don't, but you haven't much choice do you?" she replied harshly.

Jack hesitated again then tossed his gun into the shadows.

Katlyn gave him a look that told him she had expected a more convincing throw, but she must have decided it was enough. All she said was, "Good lad. Now don't you move."

She crouched down and stared at Miriam for a second, then said. "So. What reason can you give me to save you? Let's see how well you beg."

Miriam thought of their last encounter and wondered, *what indeed?* Then she said. "I think you like the excitement of having a nemesis chasing you. And I think when the time comes you'd like to kill me in a fair fight with your bare hands, not just watch me fall off a roof."

Katlyn looked surprised for a second then put her head back and burst into a peal of her tinkling bells laughter. She stopped and looked back down at Miriam, teeth still bared in an amused smile. "I see you've learnt something," she said, but made no move to help her.

Then Miriam felt her grip begin to slip and she cried out in panic, "Oh! No!" But Katlyn's hands darted out with their lightning speed to grab both her wrists. She lifted Miriam up into the air before she fully realized what had happened.

For the second time Miriam found herself face to face with her enemy with only inches between them, only this time the enemy was offering to save her not kill her. With her feet still dangling over empty space she did not dare struggle or even move: Katlyn literally held her life in her hands, and Miriam knew how unpredictable her moods were. Katlyn sighed. "If I let you down, you'll just chase me again, won't you?" she said resignedly. "That's the trouble with a nemesis: you can never trust them." She paused then continued, "There's a cost for everything, you know. I hope you appreciate how low my fees are."

With that, she stepped back and put Miriam down safely, but then stamped hard on her foot and sprinted away. Jack ran for his gun. By the time he got back, Miriam was on the ground holding her foot and Katlyn was a shadow in the distance. He trained his gun on her until there was nothing left but a swirl of mist from her wake. Perhaps he could have taken the shot. But he did not fire.

CHAPTER 34 – SAM

"Gods of Chaos!" swore Miriam softly.

After the excitement on the roof she had retreated to the sedate safety of her office. Forensics had found nothing. Except for the initial alarm there was no record of Katlyn's break-in or presence in the apartment. She seemed able to block any number of sensors very effectively; even her method of removing the glass from the window wasn't obvious. It made her like some kind of ghost visible only to humans, and Miriam was silently thankful that this time she wasn't the only witness. The scientists' report had concluded that none of what Katlyn had done was unheard of in principle, but she must have some very high tech equipment: and they would dearly love to get their hands on her tool belt. By "what she had done" they meant evading detection: nobody knew what she had done, or had intended to do, while she was there.

Ramos had not banned Miriam from field work but had made it quite clear she should be more careful about risking her life in what he called, though in her own mind she respectfully disagreed, "hare-brained acrobatics." In any event it made no difference. In the weeks since there had not been a whisper of further activity, or at least none noticed by her AI.

An AI which had just proudly announced a group of especially idiotic ideas. She knew from experience that when the AI started getting too divorced from reality it was probably an error in its reasoning engine: which usually meant she had entered a logical error herself when trying to explain what was wrong with some other mistake. *Oh well, nothing for it but to fix it.*

A ping and a flashing image announced that Fergus was trying to contact her. She touched it to accept the call. "Hi Fergus, what goes?"

"Hi Miriam. I'm heading out to lunch, and I think you should come. My treat. Can I collect you in five?"

"Sorry Fergus, I'm too busy today. The AI has gotten itself confused and I have a bit of work to do to straighten it out. Some other time?"

"Your delightful company and the sweet memories it evokes are only part of my motivation," he replied. "This is actually work. I'm having lunch with that old math tutor of mine, the one we sent the videos to. I am assured we will find the results exciting."

"You know, I am feeling a bit peckish. I'm in."

~~~

Miriam and Fergus sat down at a table outside, chatting and enjoying the contrast of sunshine and cool breeze while they waited for Fergus's friend. "Ah, here comes Sam now," said Fergus, pointing.

Miriam had to smile. She wondered how much of Fergus's penchant for busting stereotypes had been inherited from his tutor. The mathematician was hard to ignore. She wore intense black pantaloons tucked into lace-up boots. Between those and her long, equally black hair she wore a bright shirt showing a complex fractal pattern in shades of yellow, with a fiery red jacket to round out the ensemble. Even people who said math was boring would have to exclude this particular practitioner of the art. Fergus introduced her as Dr Sam Allende. Sam gave Miriam a big grin and pumped her hand enthusiastically: it appeared that everything about her was overclocked. Miriam found her immensely amusing and decided she liked her. She was like a force of nature.

Sam regaled her with tales of her history with Fergus and any number of wide ranging topics, wherever there was a laugh or an insight to be had from it. Miriam was dying to know what she had found out but obviously she was going to bide her time: but if this was what she wanted as payment for her consulting, Miriam was happy to oblige.

At last they ordered some steaming espressos and after a few sips Sam looked at Miriam and said, "You are a very patient young lady, I like that. But I can tell you are itching for my news. Well, never let it be said that I keep people in suspense! I have found something very exciting!"

Before Miriam could reply, she rushed on. "I have looked at your raw footage, the interpreted image provided by your victim, and the rather less informative version Fergus provided. First, let me say that the last is not anyone's fault. This kind of analysis is always a compromise between too little and too much processing. The police, of course, want anything they produce to hold up in a court of law, immune to the sneers of cynical defense attorneys. They hone those sneers to perfection in their bathroom mirrors, you know. So the compromise they choose is, wisely, set to the conservative. Hence the poor results in this case with such heavily corrupted raw material. Your victim, however, was more interested in whatever he could discover. As it turns out he did pretty well: he must have some excellent software. My more theoretical colleagues could no doubt argue the finer points over the course of a dozen publications; but for practical purposes there's not much in it. Any less processing and the final image would show less detail; too much further processing and there is a rapidly increasing chance of producing sharper images of pure fantasy."

She paused to glance at her audience.

"Miriam, you look disappointed. No doubt you surmise that the logical implication is that no more data can be extracted than what you already have. You would, however," she added with a smile, "be mistaken."

She sipped some more of her coffee, watching Miriam with obvious glee over the rim of her cup. Miriam gave her a severe look, though the upturned corners of her mouth belied it.

"Ha-ha, Fergus was right about you!" she laughed. "But here is the crux. As I understand it, the raw footage is from a security video feed that was rendered almost useless by some kind of signal interference, correct?" Miriam nodded. "But, you see, that is not the case!" Miriam sat up straighter. "You cannot inflict electronic interference on physical circuitry without leaving a footprint in the noise, as it were: an echo of the characteristics of the system. It cannot be purely random, but rather inherits frequency and time dependencies and the like from the two systems, creator and victim. When instead of attempting to clean up the image I analyzed the noise itself, do you know what I found?"

Sam attempted to wait for a dramatic pause but rushed on almost immediately. "The noise was random! It was added later! In other words, your original recording was not corrupted: the signal fed into the system was perfectly clear. The recording was corrupted later by purely electronic means!"

Miriam looked at her eagerly. "You mean, knowing that, you can extract the clean original? You have it?"

"Oh, no, I am afraid that is impossible. You'll never get any more out of it than your victim himself found."

"So... so..." Miriam was confused. "What good is it then?"

"Ha! My dear, you are too busy trying to shine a light inside a box, when you should be looking at the box itself to see where it came from! What this means is simple but profound. If the video was corrupted after the event, it had to have been corrupted by your victim's own AI!"

Miriam and Fergus both stared at her. "You mean, the man who gave me the video and its reconstruction is the one who fuzzed it out in the first place?!"

Sam grinned. "Well, that is possible from a practical viewpoint. But psychologically it seems unlikely, don't you think? Why go to that trouble when it would have been simpler and less risky to report nothing? No, I think the truth is far more interesting. I think your man is perfectly innocent. I believe it is his AI that did the job, without his knowledge!"

"You're kidding," said Fergus. "You mean the thief hacked into it? In the short time he was there? That might work with some cheap shareware AI, but we're talking about a rich guy. High quality AIs can't be hacked at all, let alone in ten minutes. Well, not without setting off alarm bells from here to Canada. The AI would have a fit if someone tried it; even if you could get past its defenses, you'd just crash it before you could take it over. And even if you solved that problem you'd leave footprints all over it! Our guy ran all the diagnostics. Nothing."

"I don't know enough to know what's possible," Miriam admitted, "but I can't see how it could work either. The AI must know it did it. It would either report itself or be deranged, and the owner would know. But it was clean!"

Sam grinned again. "Imagine you are sitting in your office one day, and some alien replaces your personality and memories with someone else's, and you do something as that person. Then they swap everything back the way it was, along with memories of some boring routine you might have been doing during the time you weren't in control. How would you know next week? How would you know to even suspect it? When you were the other person you would have felt completely normal; when you were yourself, you would feel the same and have no memory of the other."

"But there's still the problem of doing that to an AI," Fergus persisted. "Sure, there are ways around AI security protocols. There have to be, in case of a severe fault, the owner dies or there's a court order or something. But the AI knows about it and reports it; and it remembers. There's an audit trail."

"Well, that's what people like to think, I'm sure," Sam answered serenely. "And no doubt it's usually true. But while I confess I am not the world's greatest authority on AIs, I am sure my explanation is the most likely. It is the clear implication of the signal analysis, and on that I *am* an expert. Here, Miriam. I have given you the contact details of a colleague who knows far more about AIs than I do: you might find it worthwhile interviewing him. If anyone knows how it might be done, he will."

She threw back the last of her espresso and rose. "Well, I must be off, I have a graduate class to torment. Thank you both for a lovely lunch. It was good to see you again, Fergus; and I'm so glad to have met you, Miriam. Enjoy the rest of your day. And think about what I've told you." She gave Fergus a stern glance. "I can read young Fergus' mind, you know. He is right to be skeptical, but don't discount what I told you."

With that she left, making her way through the lunchtime crowd, the chromatic inverse of a grouper gliding through a swirling school of neon reef fish.

When she had gone, Miriam said, "Wow, what a live wire! So what do you think about her theory?"

Fergus shrugged. "You probably noticed she has a flair for the dramatic, and if a thief who can corrupt an AI is not the most likely theory no doubt it is the most exciting. But I've learned not to ignore what she says. Underneath that butterfly exterior is a preying mantis."

CHAPTER 35 – NEUBOLD

After lunch Miriam went back to work. She knew where her department's priorities lay, so she spent the next few hours repairing the AI: she did not want to have to explain to Ramos why she had spent time on the Katlyn case while the AI was languishing in need of attention. They had to let her take her lunch breaks but what she did in official working hours was another matter.

At last Miriam brought the AI to a state that looked more promising. Then she had it record its findings of the last week; erased its memory of all that data and its reasoning and conclusions; and finally set it on reanalyzing the same data in the order in which it had received it. Once it caught up to where it had been she would have it compare its findings with what it had done originally. That would let her know whether the latest version was better or worse than before.

That would take it a while. Once she had it working away she could stop to think.

They knew that someone had corrupted the video. The questions were who and how?

Sam's assurances aside, the most likely possibility was their original theory of signal interference. While nobody knew quite how it could be done, the thief did appear to have an arsenal of unusually advanced technology at her disposal. The video corruption wasn't the only example. She had bypassed locks, suppressed alarm systems and otherwise got in, done her work and escaped unscathed where it might have been considered impossible if she hadn't so clearly done it.

If not that, then the recording rather than the signal had been corrupted. The most obvious candidate for that was Delaney himself: he could have made the AI do it then forget it had done so. It wouldn't be easy to do without leaving logs and other traces, but she supposed it could be done. But the main question was: why? And if he had done it, why draw attention to it? Nobody had realized there was more to the video than static, so nobody had considered it a clue until Delaney himself had offered it up unsolicited. Delaney gave no sign of being the kind of egotist who liked to taunt his opponents with his superior cunning.

The person with the clearest motive for subverting the AI was again the thief. But the thief was the one with the least ability to do it, for all the reasons they had already considered.

In either case, if the AI was involved the next question was why corrupt the video anyway? Why go to the trouble and risk of obscuring the video with noise when it would be simpler, safer and more permanent to just erase it entirely? Then there would have been nothing from which to reconstruct even a blurry image of the perpetrator.

So the very existence of the video favored the interference theory, as then complete erasure was not an option. And if not perfect it had certainly been effective: it was only by chance that anyone had bothered to analyze the video and discovered there was something to see. Perhaps the thief thought there would be nothing left to see; perhaps at last he had made a mistake.

But where did it leave them? Sam had found that they could get no more out of the video than they already had. But the implication was that what they had was a true image, which meant Katlyn was not the thief. Yet Katlyn *was* a thief. And there were too many similarities, too many coincidences, for the crimes to be unrelated. That implied at least two thieves working in concert, and Miriam's blood ran cold at the memory of Tagarin's question: *what if there are more of them?* Miriam shook her head. *God, what have I got myself into?* she asked herself. *How many more of these things are out there?*

So the video, poor as it was, provided an important clue. Again it made more sense as signal interference: that it *was* a clue showed just how risky it was to leave any evidence if you could avoid it. Everything else the thieves had done seemed almost superhuman: if they could destroy the recording it made no sense to merely degrade it.

Then suddenly she stared, struck by a sudden thought: *is that really what they had done, exactly?* "Hellfire!" she cried. She stared inward at the pieces falling into place in her mind. The thief had not deleted the video for a very simple reason, she thought. With a corrupted video, they all believed the thief had some unknown jamming technology, advanced but not beyond the realms of possibility, like her other tricks; better than your average thief but not fantastically so; annoying rather than dangerous. But if the video were deleted, they'd *know* the thief was able to take over an AI. And if she could take over an AI to do that, what else could she do while she had it in her power?

Miriam went cold. What indeed? For starters, not merely corrupt a video but change it to hint at a normal human, in case anyone looked into it that deeply. And that's just the least of it.

Suddenly Miriam very much wanted to know if it was in fact possible to take over an AI and exactly what you might be able to do with it once you had. She examined the contact Sam had given her. *Well, Dr Neubold*, she thought, *it looks like I'll be paying you a visit sooner than I thought.*

~~~

Dr Arthur Neubold owned an IT company specializing in systems development, software security and complicated-sounding computer fields Miriam had never heard of; much of his company's income came from military contracts. He had readily agreed to an interview when Miriam mentioned Sam's name.

Miriam was led along a corridor by an assistant who made no attempt to hide that he had better things to do with his time. She went past rooms filled with mysterious equipment and past people hurrying along on equally mysterious tasks, until finally she was delivered to Neubold's office. Her guide then receded, like waves after they have deposited driftwood on the shore.

"So, Ms Hunter, what can I do for you? You mentioned an issue of AI security?" He retained an obvious if faded British accent.

"I was discussing a puzzling case with Dr Allende, and she thought the most likely explanation is that our criminal can infiltrate an AI and gain at least partial control over it. I can see why she thinks that, but everything else indicates it's impossible, at least without leaving glaring evidence behind. But there is nothing. The AI involved seems perfectly functional, normal and untouched."

He frowned. "Can you tell me why you suspect such an unlikely event?"

"All the explanations are unlikely. I'd be happy to eliminate any of them! The main piece of evidence is a thoroughly corrupted video record. The only possibilities we can think of are jamming of the data feed or corruption of the recording, and neither seems technically feasible. While jamming seems the most likely to us, Dr Allende assures us that the detailed characteristics of the corruption implies it was done after the fact."

"Ah," he said. "Tea, Ms Hunter?"

A slender young man had entered carrying a silver tray inhabited by an elegant teapot, a pair of fine china cups and some crystal containers. Miriam nodded, somewhat bemused, and the young man gracefully poured her tea in an artistic arc from the pot. He indicated the milk and sugar, in a manner of perfect politeness that nevertheless implied she would be uncouth to corrupt his tea by their use, and bowed out of the room.

"My assistant," Neubold explained. "He makes a fine cup of tea, a most civilized relic of the once great British empire. Now where were we? Yes, your data corruption as evidence of AI corruption. Are there any other features of the case I should know?"

"Whatever he or she did, the thief appears to have done it quite quickly, and has probably done it more than once, possibly several times."

"Interesting. That would indicate someone using a general tool rather than just a person with inside knowledge of a particular system. Hmmm. Yes." He thought about it, sipping his tea. Miriam could see the feelings chasing each other across his face: concentration, puzzlement, faint alarm, skepticism then more alarm. Finally he put his cup down and gazed into the distance, looking more like a man wondering whether to tell her something he already knew rather than someone trying to solve a puzzle. He appeared to come to a decision.

"What I am going to tell you must remain in strictest confidence, and not leave your confidential police files. Preferably not even make it into the files. I am only telling you because if I am right, somebody has managed to steal some very sensitive intellectual property of ours. I would very much like to see them caught and stopped if that is the case. Even so perhaps it is better if I say nothing."

"I must emphasize the importance of the case I am working on, Dr Neubold. To trade my own confidential information, the implications might extend all the way to the President. I really need to know what I'm dealing with."

Neubold's eyes studied his teacup and then her face.

"All right, Ms Hunter. I can take the risk. I have deniability if you leak what I tell you but it proves to have nothing to do with your case, whereas if I have actually been robbed I will have more problems than mere embarrassment. Besides, if it proves to be ours I think I would be wise to show how cooperative I am, eh?"

"Thank you. You can count on my discretion and I won't tell anybody who doesn't need to know. Please go on."

"In the past we did in fact work on a tool for infiltrating AIs, secret work for the military. It is currently in limbo because it ran into privacy problems in government committee: while the tool is intended for military use, some people just don't trust it to stay there. We had made a lot of progress: most commercial AIs and many custom-built ones based on similar algorithms were vulnerable. With such a tool, your thief could plausibly have done what you say."

Miriam sat up straighter. "What exactly are its capabilities?"

Neubold grimaced. "That depends rather on which version was, er, acquired. As a work in progress, obviously later versions were more capable. The problem with sophisticated AIs is that they need many flexible data inputs – vision, sound, text, any number of electronic communication bands, etc. I cannot tell you details, but I can tell you that is how we get in. If an AI is vulnerable then the actual process is quite fast. A few minutes at most to gain complete control."

"And what can you do then?"

He spread his hands. "Practically whatever you like – fortunately or unfortunately, depending on your perspective. The AI has no idea it has been coopted. It believes everything it is doing is perfectly reasonable and part of its normal operations. It may well hide what it is doing from its true owner – that is after all the whole point – but it sees nothing odd about that. It believes it is like any other internal process the owner doesn't need to know about."

"But looking in from outside, can you tell?"

"Not really. Usually AI diagnostics are done by the AI itself, and it will report normal functioning. And don't forget this is military software: just like a human agent, we don't want it falling into enemy hands and we prefer the enemy to never even know it was there. If it detects any kind of intrusive probe our infiltrated second mind erases itself, leaving no trace. The AI will never be aware it was there and no external search will find it either. Furthermore the usual mode of operation is to take control for a limited time, perhaps as short as minutes, perhaps as long as weeks, then erase itself once its purpose is achieved. Just that extra margin of security, you see? I am afraid that the only evidence one is likely to have is if the system can be proved to be the source of a leak of information, an explosion in a research facility or some other such hostile action. But even knowing the compromised system was involved there will be no trace of how. It is more likely one of its operators will be shot for treason than the AI itself suspected. Unfair on the operator but in the nature of warfare, I'm afraid."

Miriam felt a sinking feeling. "So do you mean to tell me that software does exist that can take over an AI, but nobody should have it, and if they did I'd never know they'd used it?"

Strangely, Neubold smiled. "Not quite. The software was never finished, you see; it waits locked in limbo for word from on high. We can neither destroy it nor finish it until the government brings down a decision. So its last state was still a beta version, still being tested. Have you heard of the phrase 'Kilroy was here'?"

"It sounds vaguely familiar, but I'm not sure where I've heard it."

"It became popular last century in the Second World War. Allied soldiers would scrawl it in odd places, usually along with a cartoon of a man peering over a wall. Kilroy tended to turn up in the most unlikely places, seemingly before anyone had the chance to put him there. Well, you could say we did the same thing. The beta versions all leave the phrase 'Kilroy was here' in register memory deep in the infected AI. In addition, the AI believes it put it there itself a long time ago as an encryption hash salt string. Such salt strings are best acquired randomly, and that is what the AI believes it did via a random phrase search. That was one of our checks that everything had gone according to plan. Not only is it an unlikely phrase to use, but an AI would normally choose a completely random string: that it thinks an English phrase was a perfectly reasonable choice is further evidence of how successful the infiltration was. Using such a phrase is somewhat geeky humor, but one must expect that from geeks, eh?"

Miriam's pulse went up a notch. "Dr Neubold, I cannot thank you enough. This might help my investigations enormously."

"You're welcome, Ms Hunter. May I remind you of the need for discretion? And please let me know the results of your enquiries. But may I ask you when the video you referred to was taken?"

"Several months ago."

Neubold gave her a startled glance. "That long!" Then a thoughtful look came over his face. "You know, there might be a clue there. We lost a technician about a year ago. He was a very adventurous young man, prone to go off hiking alone in the wilderness without telling anyone. Rather foolish, in my opinion. Well, he disappeared. Just never showed up for work one Monday, and attempts to find him were futile. Everyone decided he probably met his end broken at the bottom of some trackless ravine. But perhaps he is now living the high life in the Bahamas instead. He had no direct access to the software we're discussing, but I would not be surprised if he had been aware of its existence. That would have been a breach of internal security in itself, but I have found that geeks have a tendency to treat security with contempt, especially if they have done something clever. I suppose it is possible he found a way to steal it himself or somehow enabled its theft by an outside gang."

He turned to his computer and worked on it for a short while. "Yes, here he is: Geoffrey Baxter. I have sent his details to you in case they help."

Then he stared at her. "But your timeline presents us with a problem, don't you think? I'd have thought that if criminals had gained access to this technology that long ago there'd have been signs of their activities on the news. I haven't noticed anything. What kind of targets are you investigating?"

"The only victims we are aware of are some private individuals. Wealthy but private: no corporations or government bodies that we're aware of."

"That seems to show a marked lack of imagination on the part of your criminals, no? No doubt they would like to keep the existence of such a tool undetected for as long as possible, so with their extra security banks and government systems would probably be too risky to attempt. But that leaves a vast array of places with ordinary security, blithely imagining they are safe but wide open to this particular attack. Any criminals worth the name should have struck hard, fast and wide, and be living it up on their own island paradise by now. So perhaps we have been worrying over nothing. If it has anything to do with cracking AIs, then either they got their hands on a very early test version of ours, or they had a similar idea but made their own much less effective form of it. Or perhaps it has nothing to do with the AIs at all."

He paused to think. "You seem to have reached a contradiction. If your corrupted video is due to a coopted AI, that implies high ability indeed: they can take over an AI quickly and completely enough to do it during the very course of committing a crime. But if that is what your criminals are doing then the crimes are too trivial. It is as if somebody invented a fusion reactor and all they used it for was to power their bicycle to and from work." He spread his hands. "It makes no sense!"

Miriam smiled wanly. "Welcome to my case."

CHAPTER 36 – KILROY

Miriam drove back to her office, but she did not really see the road. Her mind was elsewhere; her body drove under its own direction. It parked the car and walked her into the elevator and thence to her office. It was the end of the day and people were leaving; perhaps she answered their farewells, but she did not know. Her mind did not regain the reins until she sat down in front of her AI access point.

"Voice interface," she commanded.

"Voice active."

"What does the phrase 'Kilroy was here' mean to you?"

Miriam held her breath, waiting for the AI to respond.

"'Kilroy was here' was a graffiti phrase common in World War II. It represented a standing joke, always appearing in unlikely places. It was usually associated with the drawing now displayed. Would you like more detail?"

"No, that's fine. Were you aware of the phrase before today? If so, how?"

After a few seconds, the AI replied. "No. I have no record of it."

Miriam let out a breath. She had been getting so caught up in the mysterious omnipotence of her opponents that she had feared even her own AI was their pawn and part of a conspiracy leading her astray. *Not*, she reminded herself, *that this proves anything.* But even absence of proof was a relief at this stage.

"Please display a list of the victims in the Katlyn case who have allowed us remote access to their AIs."

The screen displayed Delaney and two others – both from the group who had been bemused rather than hostile at her earlier enquiries. All had given permission for automatic access to the public interface of their AIs so the police could query aspects of the case without having to bother them personally. The rest had either been hostile to her enquiries or not interested or trusting enough to allow even that small an official foot in their door.

"Please make the same enquiry I just made to you about Kilroy to these three AIs."

"Please wait."

Miriam waited, heart thumping. She wasn't sure whether to be more afraid that her enquiry would return nothing or something.

"The results are curious. All three AIs report that 'Kilroy was here' exists as a string in their registry memory and all state they put it there as an encryption salt string chosen by a random net search."

Holy Gods of Asgard, Miriam thought, leaning back in her chair. *We are so screwed.*

CHAPTER 37 – MISDIRECTION

Miriam called up her earlier diagram of the possibilities and stared at it. *Misdirection, misdirection, misdirection,* she realized, *the whole thing is an exercise in misdirection.* Jewelry thefts to mask the real purpose of the break-in: gaining control of the AI. Videos that purport to be one thing and are another, with yet another misdirection buried inside to mislead anyone persistent or curious enough to look below the surface.

She thought more on it, rolling the ideas around in her head. *Yes.* Even with the thief's skill and technology, it would be difficult to break in without a trace, impossible to be sure she had left no trace. But the reason the thing you're looking for is always in the last place you look is you stop looking. So the thief had left an obvious motive in plain view: a theft large enough to explain the break-in but not enough to excite a really serious investigation. A nuisance, a small insurance claim, something soon forgotten. And meanwhile, the victim's AI was there in the background, silently working against its owner under his nose. Even destroying any evidence it had collected itself. Miriam stared at the audacity of it all. If her own AI hadn't seen the tenuous link between the thefts all those months ago, she wondered if they would ever have discovered it before it was too late. Perhaps it was already too late.

But why? What was behind it all? There was the link to the President's supporters, but that could be a coincidence. After all, the victims were all wealthy, and rich people surely had many things in common; sucking up to politicians wasn't an unlikely one.

The image of a blur of molecules and cells whirling around under the command of a shadowy Dr Tagarin rose again in her mind. *What other dances are you conducting, doctor, and to what end?* She was sure he was behind it. Then she stopped. Was she? Why? *Question everything, Miriam. Question everything.*

She ran over the evidence in her mind. Tagarin was her prime suspect only if Katlyn was a geneh – but was she? Perhaps that too was misdirection. As Tagarin had pointed out, she had flaunted her fatal biology – then left the prime witness not only alive but also guaranteed to be hostile toward her. Then, unaccountably, saved her life: or was it the case she wanted to save, to keep it alive now it had been pointed in the wrong direction? And while Miriam had gotten uncomfortably close and personal with Katlyn, how could she be sure that her impressions were real, not merely an illusion she was led to believe? All she had left was a coincidence in phrases the two had used. But Tagarin was a public figure, public enough that his quirks could easily be discovered by someone with the motivation to do so. If someone wanted the police chasing a literal chimera up blind alleys, what better way to encourage belief in a geneh than by implicating Tagarin?

She put her head in her hands. But if not Tagarin, then who? It had to be someone with resources. Organized crime seemed unlikely: given the nature of such groups, surely they would have done far more damage by now. They were not known for either patience or subtlety. Miriam rubbed her temples. That was the other thing. Even the larger thefts weren't big enough crimes. It didn't make sense that they were the full motive, but they also didn't make sense as misdirection. There had to be something else behind it all, some scheme that she couldn't yet guess at. A government agency might have big shadowy plans and would certainly have the money and access to the technology: was this some rogue agency gone beyond its remit? Or one of Tagarin's other suggestions, an expensively modified agent gone rogue herself and now hunted in secret?

Then another thought struck her into stillness. She turned it over in her mind like a hot potato. It had a shocking but deadly simplicity to it. She rang Stone. "Jack, when you told me that Tagarin's geneh baby had been shot by GenInt – did you actually see it happen?"

"Good evening to you too, Miriam. Yes, I am having a lovely dinner, thank you for asking." He paused, but she said nothing. He could almost see that look in her eyes she got when her brain was off chasing an idea, and he knew she was blind and deaf to anything unrelated to her quarry. He'd had a puppy like that once, and he smiled despite his annoyance at her timing.

"Well... not 'saw' as such. But they carted it off in a hurry and a minute later there were several shots. GenInt goons aren't the types to fire their guns into the air in a fit of exuberance. We all figured they didn't want us to actually witness the execution – more deniability if it ever came to that." He stopped for a moment. "I don't think I like where this might be heading." Then he added slowly, "Maybe you'd better slow down and decide if you really need to go there. Give your brain a break and go get some dinner yourself."

"Yes… yes… maybe I'm going stir crazy. I'll talk to you about it tomorrow. I have some more thinking to do first. And I have a headache already. Goodnight, Jack."

She hung up and groaned. It was impossible, yet terrifyingly possible. What if GenInt *hadn't* shot that baby? It could explain everything. No impossible age problem, no need for improbable research in the years since the bans.

Perhaps GenInt itself had adopted the child, the first and last geneh born: either to study it or use its powers for their own ends. It wouldn't be the first time a government agency couldn't resist using something it deemed too dangerous to allow anyone else to have. If so, was she still working for them on some clandestine mission, or had she escaped to work on her own agenda?

Or had the baby been meant to die, but instead been freed by its executioner in an unexpected fit of mercy: the man's humanity asserting itself when faced with actually pulling the trigger on an infant? Had she then become what Tagarin had suggested: a feral creature, surviving on her speed and wits in the cracks and shadows of a world bent on her destruction?

Her mind paused again. If that was it, Tagarin must have known what Katlyn was the moment he had seen the photo, or at least suspected it. But there was no way he would ever admit it to her.

Miriam shook her head. Too many possibilities, each plausible in its own way, each implausible in others. Whoever was behind this had woven a tapestry of deception so tangled it was impossible to be sure what was true and what was illusion, what were clues and what were misdirection. With a sinking feeling in her stomach, for the first time

Miriam began to think that her unknown opponents were out of her class; that perhaps this case was beyond her ability to solve.

CHAPTER 38 – GAMES

Miriam had gone home, determined to sleep on the problem and hope that a rest and some subconscious chewing would give her a new perspective.

She had a quiet dinner with Amaro watching an old movie, but she couldn't really get into the plot. They had gone to bed, but despite her desire she couldn't get into the plot planned by Amaro either. She had sighed, rolled over and immediately fallen into a fitful sleep haunted by dreams of chasing a person she could never quite see through a mirror maze, both seeking an exit neither could find. When she woke she was little rested and no closer to a solution. Amaro looked at her but made no comment and asked no questions. He knew there would be no answers.

Now she sat in Ramos' office with Stone leaning against the desk, waiting to hear what Ramos would say.

"So, you're telling me that our thief has been taking over people's AIs and using them to steal money and God knows what else? And that because of this, you're no longer sure we're dealing with a geneh, the whole link to Tagarin might be spurious, and even if it is a geneh it could be GenInt itself behind it? Is that about it?"

Miriam nodded dumbly. Ramos looked like he'd bitten an apple with a grub in it. "Are you sure there aren't some other possibilities you've left off the list?"

"I'm not sure of anything at the moment."

He glared at her a minute then asked, "What do you think, Jack?"

Stone looked from one to the other. "Unlikely as you'd think it is, it does look like the AIs have been compromised. But that doesn't lead us anywhere except to doubt every clue we have. I think we're going back to our desk jobs."

Ramos nodded. "That's about how I see it too. We'll escalate the AI aspect to Computer Crimes. They can consult with your Dr Neubold and see if they can find out how our criminals got their hands on his technology without anybody knowing, and how they can stop more mischief being done with it. That's really their job, not ours. Not our case now."

Miriam nodded and stood to go. "Yes, OK. I'm out of ideas myself."

"Don't look so dejected. None of this is your fault. And I don't want you to give up quite yet. No more active investigation is warranted. Or wise. But have your AI keep whatever it uses as a nose to the ground. Make sure it reports anything that might tie in. Computer Crimes will be doing their thing, but it won't hurt to keep our other options open as well."

As they went to open the door to leave he added, "Wait. This possible GenInt link worries me. We did hope they wouldn't notice or care about our vague report on a strange thief, but still – it's a bit odd that they never even asked one question. But if they were complicit – maybe we're both playing the same game, each acting as if it isn't worthy of attention, each hoping the other one won't place any importance on it."

They both waited, Stone nodding slowly as he thought about it.

"So I don't want you to write up this theory about the geneh baby and GenInt, or even mention it outside this office. The one thing I'm sure of is that we're not going to be able to question GenInt: and we don't want to anyway. If they're behind it, it might be dangerous to poke a stick in their nest whether we're dealing with an official agent or a rogue one. And we have no need to tell them anything at this stage. We sent them that memo about it but didn't say it was a geneh, and now we have even less reason to believe that it is."

Miriam looked at him glumly, trying to generate some optimism about the way forward but not succeeding. Stone glanced at her and shrugged, as if reading her mind and agreeing with her assessment.

"Besides," Ramos added, "I don't want to give anyone a ready-made reason to raise doubts about Tagarin's involvement. We want a clear run at him if we do find more evidence that our thief is a geneh, if only so we can remove him from our list of suspects if he's innocent. It would be nice to remove *anyone* from our list."

CHAPTER 39 – TANG

Miriam put her coffee down then noticed the half eaten cinnamon donut. She picked it up, bit off half and chewed thoughtfully as she watched the polychrome dance of diagnostics on her screen. She washed the crumbs down with some more coffee then noticed the quarter donut on her desk. *Zeno's Paradox of Donuts*, she thought idly to herself: *if I keep biting off half of what's left, will I ever finish it?*

She smiled at her thoughts and the repetitive tasks that had spawned them. *My life is so exciting at the moment*, she thought. The AI was behaving itself for once, but while it was finding correlations that were worth passing on none of them were very thrilling. Her thief had gone quiet. At least, nothing relating to the case had caught the attention of her AI in the weeks since the meeting in Ramos' office. Hopefully that meant Katlyn had gone to ground, not merely become even better at her job. On the other hand, Miriam hadn't been beaten up or nearly died recently. There was something to be said for dullness.

She had heard nothing about the Computer Crimes investigation either. That was not surprising when a secret government software project was involved. No doubt Computer Crimes would dearly love to get their paws on one of the affected AIs, but she couldn't imagine any of the owners being willing to let them. She wondered how many judges would think "Kilroy was here" was grounds for a warrant with that big a privacy issue. *Good luck with that*, she thought to the unknown investigators; *I can't get a warrant for something much more solid.*

Her phone rang.

"Hello? Detective Hunter speaking."

"Good morning Detective. This is Kevan Tang. You rang me some time ago about a minor burglary in my apartment, and I fear I was quite rude to you about it. I have had a change of heart. Would you be so kind as to visit me to discuss the matter further? Not at my apartment in the city though: I would prefer you meet me at my home in the hills."

"Why, certainly Mr Tang. Thank you so much for calling me back. Let me check our schedules... How about 2 pm tomorrow?"

"That would be fine. I will see you then. Good day."

Miriam checked the records. Yes, Kevan Tang. One of the victims who had reported a minor jewelry theft, nothing more. One of those who had acted like a suspect rather than a victim when she had approached him. He surely would not bother having a change of heart over a few gems.

This should be interesting.

~~~

Miriam and Jack drove up a road weaving its way into the high-priced hills beyond the city. "Welcome to millionaires' row," commented Stone, as they drove past yet another secured entrance to yet another secluded home. "I'm thinking of retiring here, what about you?"

"Sure. When we solve this case our bonus ought to cover it. Ah. Here we are."

They drove up to the entrance; the guard was expecting them and let them through. They got out and looked up marble steps to an entrance guarded by imposing Corinthian columns. "Well, Mr Tang has a taste for the grand, doesn't he?" commented Stone. "Let's see if he has some grand leads to go with it."

They were ushered into Mr Tang's presence. He looked like a large-framed man whose muscles were deserting his bones; he sat behind a desk and seemed sharp and alert, but with an undercurrent as of fatigue held temporarily in check by a grim force of will. He waved them to seats.

"Thank you for coming, officers. I am afraid that for all my wealth and for all our fine medical technology, the Grim Reaper has me marked on his calendar. I suppose one cannot resist the will of the Lord when he calls you to him. That is why I have decided to talk to you. I have done many bad things in my life. In particular, I have done one very cowardly thing. I am not sure that I can make amends but I will try. Perhaps it will work in my favor on the day of Judgment." He looked at them sadly, as if at the merciless surrogates of that final Judge.

"Please go on," prompted Miriam.

"I would ask one favor. In the course of our interview I may divulge things that are perhaps not, shall we say, strictly legal. I would like to speak under immunity from prosecution so that I may speak freely. I think it would be worth your while."

"We can't guarantee anything until we hear what you say," answered Jack. "We can promise to recommend leniency for your volunteering the information, but that's all we have the authority to do." He looked at Miriam. "But anything not directly useful to our case won't make it into a report."

Tang sighed. "Oh well, that will have to do. Honestly, if you did decide to prosecute I doubt it would come to trial in the time left to me on this Earth. I would just like my final days to be peaceful, not caught up in unpleasant legal entanglements. I suppose I shall have to leave that too in the Lord's hands."

He hesitated as if drawing on his resolve to continue; to Miriam he looked like a fading pit bull terrier steeling himself to admit, *Yes, I did eat your cat.*

"Well. As you know, a while back a few baubles were stolen from my apartment. What you do not know is that a few weeks after that some criminal gang sent me an untraceable message through my AI. Somehow they had discovered the contents of a safety deposit box I held, and they were demanding that I release those contents to them. They were extremely well informed. If I did not give them what they wanted, they would not only empty my bank accounts, they would reveal certain other information on my activities to people who would not be pleased to discover it. I am not a man who takes kindly to threats, and I admit I was less than submissive in my response. Such is the sin of hubris, I fear: for they chose to demonstrate their power by emptying a fifth of my funds, equally from each of my bank accounts – I suppose to show they could have taken it all. This was accompanied by another message to await further instructions."

Miriam asked, "You said 'untraceable'? You did not report this to the police. What steps did you take to trace these messages and to find out where your money had gone?"

"Oh, I have extensive resources, believe me, and I am not an amateur in these areas. But it is mystifying to me. My AI was good to start with and has been modified with all kinds of, shall we say, relevant software tools. But there was no trail, not even to a dead end. No trail at all. That should have been impossible. Whoever these people are, they are out of my class. I saw no alternative. I gave in. Of course I attempted to put a trace on the goods, but that too failed."

He spread his hands. "It failed because they knew. They were not happy with me. To punish me for my obstinacy and temerity, in their words, they took another quarter of my funds and released one piece of their blackmail. That is why I am now divorced from my wife of many years." He spread his hands. "Perhaps they were merely the Lord's tools in my humbling, as the Assyrians were to the Israelites. But I am talking to you in the hope that the Lord will punish them, just as he punished the Assyrians in their time."

"So what was in the safety deposit box? What was so important?" asked Miriam.

He sighed resignedly. "I suppose it can't cause any more harm if you know in general outline what these people now know in detail. Though they don't appear to have used their knowledge yet, so their true purpose remains a mystery to me. I have betrayed a great person, as well as my own principles, in order to cling to comforts which time has showed to be more ephemeral than I could imagine. I am ashamed, officers, ashamed."

He stopped talking, gazing into a distance only he could see. Finally he continued. "Years ago I was an ally of Lyn Felton in her campaign against the genetic engineers. You will remember how spectacularly successful she was, on a global scale. You don't get success like that in politics just through sheer brilliance and hard work, despite what the politicians say later in their memoirs. She made a lot of dirty deals in a lot of dirty countries so what had to be done, was done. And you are probably aware that GenInt, the child of her labors, has secret charters, charters that are secret for a reason. The common people would not understand. I speak of their power to summarily execute genetic monsters and clones, even babies."

Miriam was staring at him, open-mouthed. Stone had more control: he kept his mouth closed.

Tang misunderstood, and shook his head sadly. "Do not judge us too harshly. GenInt fight the Devil's work, officers, as you do in your own way. What they do is right and just, but in order to do it some things must remain hidden. The people as a mass do not think. They would see a baby and let it live, unable to see the monster that would rise up to slay them in years to come. Indeed, they would rise up against GenInt for trying to save their own lives at the baby's expense. Don't you see? The people must be protected from themselves. The art of government has always been thus. And Felton especially was doing the Lord's work, against great odds. Perhaps she sold pieces of her own soul in order to do it. But what greater, what more noble, sacrifice could a person make?"

"And... the material you gave the blackmailers?"

"I believed in Felton's work. I was one of her key operatives, and not for money but for principle. But I have always been what people call a sharp operator. Always playing the angles, always on the lookout for an advantage; always with backup plans and backups for the backups. There are some things I cannot help doing. I kept physical evidence of all the dirty dealings I was privy too. I had no thought of blackmail; if I had any specific thoughts at all they were for self-preservation: insurance if things went bad or I was in danger of being betrayed myself. And I kept details of GenInt's secret charters. Details of their activities in the early years. At the time I assumed I was not the only one, and probably I was right. Dangerous men gather around dangerous activities, after all, and to such men what I did was simple prudence, almost second nature. However it has become my eternal shame, because that is what I gave the blackmailers to save my own fleeting skin."

He lifted his eyes to look directly at them. "In my earlier days I worked to do a great thing, and I was proud, prouder than I have been of anything else I have ever done. I have made a great deal of money, but nothing compares to simply making something that is great. And then I betrayed it all, in a moment of weakness, cowardice and greed. And that is what now defines my life, officers. Perhaps God will forgive me even if I cannot forgive myself."

He looked away and added emptily, "I will find out soon enough. I hope to live long enough to see these villains brought to justice and their plans fallen to ruins. That is why I am telling you this. But what I dread above death is living long enough to see them succeed."

Miriam didn't think there was anything more to say, except for the one question burning in her mind in dread certainty of the answer. "Mr Tang, you mentioned that the blackmailers contacted you through your

AI. Could you ask it a question for me?"

He glanced at her, somewhat startled at the request. "Of course, if you think it would help. Though as I said, I have already done a thorough investigation of that side of things and found nothing."

"Could you ask it if it knows the phrase 'Kilroy was here' and if so, how it became aware of it?"

Tang stared at her with a puzzled frown. Miriam could practically read his thoughts in his expression: *What the hell kind of question is that?* But he shrugged and complied. Then his frown deepened. "Apparently that is an encryption hash salt it used a long time ago. Innocuous enough in itself – but... how could you know?"

Miriam stared back, heart thumping. *Oh dear God*, she thought. After a moment she said simply, "I didn't know, Mr Tang. It's just a strange lead we've been following."

He looked at her inquiringly, hoping she would elaborate, but now she was just looking off into the space beyond his shoulder, a worried frown on her face. *What deep waters are we wading in?* he wondered. But he stayed silent. *There are secrets here*, he thought, *dangerous secrets; this is larger than I knew. Larger than I want to know. Perhaps I was wrong to bare my soul and my shame. But if the waters are truly that deep – perhaps I was right to do it. Perhaps I have saved my soul after all.*

After a few moments Stone stood and said, "Well, thank you, Mr Tang. If there are any details that you think will help our investigation, please let us know. If we have any further questions or information, we'll contact you. Good day, sir."

Tang gestured in farewell, following them with his sad eyes as they took their leave.

On their way out, all Miriam said to Jack was, "At least this explains why so many of the victims don't want to talk to us."

"Yeah, blackmail has a way of keeping people's mouths shut. But we caught a break this time. Maybe enough of a break to get us that warrant for your DNA search."

Miriam nodded thoughtfully. They spent the rest of the trip back in silence, lost in their own private thoughts, all wanting to lead somewhere but leading nowhere.

CHAPTER 40 – JENNY

It was getting late and long shadows stretched across the floor from the reddening sun beyond the windows of the offices beyond hers. Miriam was tired. She rubbed her eyes and thought, *time to go home.* Though it was not yet five she had come in early today and was already into overtime. She was reaching for her coat when a ping alerted her: the AI had decided it had something worthy of her attention even at this late hour.

It had found a match to the DNA from the fire. A blackmail scheme involving the President and GenInt had proved enough – just – to get a warrant for searches that preserved the privacy of any non-matching DNA sequences. But after a week had passed without anything, Miriam had stopped hoping; it had always been a long shot. Now she was energized anew.

"Bring it up," she commanded. She quickly scanned the data. Allowing for the ambiguities in the sequence it was a perfect match and the AI calculated a 94% chance that the DNA came from the same person. Her pulse quickened but she frowned with puzzlement when she saw that the record was from a scientific paper a quarter of a century old. Then Miriam saw the name.

"Grendel's Mother!" she swore. The person whose sequence matched was a Jenny Alderton, but the AI had used its initiative to ferret out a one-line bio ending with the notation: *Later Jenny Tagarin.* "Summarize all biographical information you can find on this Jenny Tagarin and why her genome is recorded!"

Miriam waited impatiently. After a few tense minutes, a couple of pages of summary appeared. Miriam swiftly scanned the document, taking in whole paragraphs in one mental gulp. *Sweet baby Jesus! Grendel's Mother indeed!* she thought. Her subconscious had made the connection immediately, she realized, bringing that particular curse to her lips. But not the mother of the ancient monster Grendel: the mother, of sorts, of the modern monster Katlyn. The DNA might indicate a 94% chance but Miriam was sure of it. She re-read the biography more closely.

Jennifer Alderton had been a bright, attractive woman with one flaw: a deadly genetic disease that had not made itself known until her late teens. It had soon become evident that her deterioration was accelerating and she would not survive her twenties. A young Dr Tagarin had been called in to investigate what the problem was and what could be done. The disease was rare and little was known about it; Tagarin had written a paper on her and her condition, and in the paper's confidential archival data was where her genome sequence had resided until the AI ferreted it out. But in the course of the study the two had fallen in love, and despite her condition had married. Tagarin thought he could save her. He hoped he could save her. But the technology was too young and her disease too deadly. He had failed.

"Can you find any photos of this woman?"

Another minute or so later her screen pinged and a photo of a smiling young woman appeared. Miriam stared at it. Katlyn: minus the eyes, a bit different in proportions, but Katlyn. *Oh God,* thought Miriam. *Oh God, Tagarin, what have you done?* But she knew what he had done. The sheer brilliant insanity of it made her head spin. Then another idea hit her. *Oh no,* she thought. *Oh no. It can't be. Not that as well.* The database would not be open to her fishing expedition; but it should open itself to an official targeted query. She did a quick search through her records, marked a case file number and instructed the AI to access and analyze.

After another few tense minutes, a file came through with the AI's analysis. Miriam stared at it. She did not know whether to feel elated or sick. She put her head in her hands. *No, no, no,* she thought. The enormity of it appalled her. Unbidden, the memory of Tagarin conducting his dance of life came back to her. But now the three of them were locked in a dance of death, and she was afraid to go forward but unable to turn back. She did not know if she would have the strength to do what she had to do; but she knew that she had to do it.

I joined the law to fight for what is right. But where is the right here? There is no right, and no path to find it.

Numbly, she connected to Stone. "Jack, I've got something. Something big. Meet me in the Chief's office." She disconnected without waiting for a reply then called Ramos to tell him they were coming.

~~~

"You look like you've seen a ghost," observed Stone when she came in.

"I think I have. Literally. Or as literal as a ghost can be. The AI got a match on the DNA fragments from the fire in a 23-year-old scientific paper. The DNA isn't good enough to be certain based on the sequence alone, but wait until you find out who it was. Jenny Tagarin! Our good doctor's dead wife! And look at this photo of her. Who does that look like?"

They both stared at it, then at her. Stone let out a low whistle. "Christ."

"And would you believe – there's more. I got the AI to access GenInt's records. The geneh infant GenInt killed in Tagarin's lab – she was a match too."

She paused, letting them digest it. Then she went on. "I don't think there's any doubt. Tagarin married this girl but he couldn't save her. And he couldn't forget her, or his failure. He kept a sample of her tissues and when he could, he fixed her DNA and brought her back to life. Well, not her, but you know what I mean. Then GenInt found her and killed her. And now he's done it again, only this time as a new, improved model. I don't know if what we're dealing with is *Phantom of the Opera* or *The Greatest Love Story Ever Told*, but Katlyn is the third incarnation of Jenny Tagarin!"

"Wait... wait," said Stone. "What about that other possibility you said earlier? Remember you thought that maybe Tagarin's first infant might not have been killed after all? That fits this new information just as well. Maybe better."

Miriam shook her head. "I thought of that too. But it doesn't make sense. You said several GenInt agents took the baby away. One having a fit of mercy I could imagine – barely – but four or five of them? So if our thief is that baby grown up, it means GenInt kept her deliberately. But if they'd done that there's no way in hell they'd have left her genome sequence in their records where I could find it with our modest little warrant and a case code. They'd have deleted it, or faked it, or hidden it under a blanket of top security."

Stone nodded. Then he turned to Ramos. "Well Chief, that leaves us with one prime suspect. If this isn't enough to get us a search warrant, if not an arrest warrant, nothing is."

Ramos nodded. "Good work, Hunter. I'll get on to it. It'll take an hour or so but you two get ready. Stone, arrange a team." He paused. "We're under no legal obligation to bring GenInt into this yet. They'll complain later if we don't, but that's all they can do: we still have jurisdiction for now. I am sure they would prefer being brought in on it now, which means they would like to take over, but they can prefer what they like. They'd just get in our way and we certainly don't want them getting there before we do. If either of you has a problem with that, now's the time to tell me."

Stone glanced at Miriam, who shook her head, then commented, "We're with you boss. As you say, all they can do is complain. Let's keep control of this. If GenInt take over who knows how many people will just disappear."

CHAPTER 41 – PLANS

Daniel watched Katlyn attacking her dinner with her usual gusto. Tonight they were enjoying a superbly tender eye fillet steak on a potato-celeriac mash with crisply tender vegetables on the side, chased down with a well-aged shiraz. But he knew she would approach pizza and beer with just as much enthusiasm. He had given her a hard life, he knew, yet she had faced it with the same joy with which she attacked her food; and she had done so much with it, accomplished so much. He was so painfully proud of her that he didn't know whether what he felt was pride or love; perhaps there was no difference. *No*, he thought, *there is a difference: but they are two faces of the same thing.*

Katlyn noticed him watching her and smiled. "What are you thinking about, Mr Serious?" she asked.

"I was thinking I haven't given you much of a life, have I?"

Katlyn laughed, the tinkling musical bells so characteristic of her. That had not been designed; he occasionally wondered what unexpected genetic interaction had produced it. "Pfft! Who was it who told me, 'Fate deals us all a hand but what we do with it is up to us'?" she quoted. "Oh! It was you!"

She smiled, and he wasn't sure if it was a child's trusting smile at her father or a woman's smile to her equal. "And you were right. And I know you know it, when you're not feeling sorry for me. Life is a gift, the greatest gift there is. If Fate decides to deal you a really bad hand, then you might feel otherwise: but there's an easy solution to that, isn't there?"

She looked at him seriously. "You know there have been plenty of times when I've been sad or angry about things. But those are the fault of the people who made it so, not you. You gave me life, Daniel. And I'm happy that I'm alive. I'm happy I lived through the hard times. I hope I live for a long time yet. But If I were to die tonight, I would die without any regrets for the life I've lived." She reached across the table, gently took his hand, and kissed it.

He smiled and returned to his own food; there seemed to be something in his eye. He remembered when he was a boy and his parents had taken him on a trek in Nepal. Out in those high mountainous wilds he had met a couple of other young kids, dirty and dirt poor, living it tough with no anticipation of a better life. Despite that they had been happy, laughing and playing like kids anywhere. But so many people living with all the benefits of a technological civilization were miserable in their lives, when all they needed for happiness was at their call: all they had to do was get up and do something about it.

He frowned as that reminded him of an even worse sin, the cases of 'wrongful life' brought to the courts early in the century: people who reckoned their lives were so miserable that their parents, or society, or someone, should never have let them be born. He thought of the contrast with Katlyn, this happy spirit who had borne so much and done so much in her brief life. He looked up at her. *It will all be over soon, dearest Katlyn,* he thought; *one way or another, it will soon be over.*

"You're thinking again," she noted. "I hope you're not still feeling sorry for me."

He smiled. "I am thinking that all of this will soon be over. A few weeks, and we should be done. I think we've done enough already but the more the better. However you shouldn't go out any more for a while, for any reason: the risks are too high now. And we're too close."

"What's the latest status?"

Daniel leaned back and put his fingers to his chin. "Well, as you know the original strategy predictions gave us a good chance of getting through all this without anyone suspecting who was behind it. Then we could have just gone on with our lives with nobody the wiser. But the police got on to the case sooner than they should have. There's still a chance they'll give up when their leads dry up, but the latest simulations show that the most likely outcome is they'll cobble together enough clues for a warrant within a few weeks. If they do we'll have to cut and run."

"Will we be ready?"

"They've been so troublesome – for which I'm inclined to place most blame on the well-named Det. Hunter – that it's not safe to rely on even that much time. So I've already put what we need in place just in case. In other words, while I'm still hoping we can get away with Plan A, it's really looking like we're going to have to take the plunge into Plan C. And sooner rather than later."

Katlyn's eyes showed a mixture of fear and excitement. They could have simply fled to continue living much as they had been, hiding from the world, only with less resources and greater risk that the world would notice them. That was Plan B: short term safety at the price of long-term risk, paid for with nothing but hope. The alternative was far more dangerous and could quickly end with Katlyn dead and Daniel in prison or dead himself: but the potential reward was much greater. For all of Katlyn's life, safety had lain in hiding and concealment, whereas Plan C would reveal her to the world. The prospect filled her with instinctive dread, like an animal whose survival depended on camouflage that was suddenly thrust onto a sunlit plain. But if it worked she would no longer need to hide.

Daniel saw in her eyes that she was willing to risk death for a chance at that prize and they both knew she *was* risking death. For all that the chances looked good, they could not find out more certainly without the risk of tipping their hand, which in itself could be more quickly and certainly fatal. If anyone suspected their plan it literally would not get off the ground.

Soft chimes sounded in the air and a voice spoke, "Excuse me, sir?"

Daniel frowned. The AI would only interrupt private conversations if it decided it had to. "Yes?"

"I'm sorry sir, but police have arrived outside."

"At this time of the evening? How many?"

"Several, and they are armed. I cannot give a precise number because they are all wearing infiltration suits with signal disruptors. I deduce from this that they must have at least a search warrant and possibly even an arrest warrant: and they intend to vigorously pursue it."

Daniel thought quickly. "Analyze their warrant carefully and if it is valid and dangerous enough to trigger Plan C, initiate it immediately." He paused. "I expect it will be."

He looked at Katlyn. "Suddenly I'm glad things are already almost prepared. There are a few things in the front office I'd have liked to take but we'll have to forget about them, at least for now."

His eyes acquired the same mixture of fear and excitement that Katlyn's had moments before. "Let's get going. Things aren't quite ready yet so it will take us a few hours before we can go: but unless we get very unlucky we'll easily have that much time."

CHAPTER 42 – INTRUDERS

For the fourth time Miriam found herself in the driveway of Tagarin's estate looking towards the entrance. For the first time she had more than Stone for company: a van with ten heavily armed police pulled up behind them. They did not know what to expect and Ramos had decided that overkill was better than failure.

Stone got out and called two of the others to come with him. As they approached the front gate, the AI spoke. "Good evening, Detectives. I see you have a warrant this time. My owner regards this is rather inconvenient timing: could you perhaps return tomorrow? He promises to make himself available then."

Stone barked a short laugh. "Sure, it works that way. Open up or we'll have to rough you up a bit, Gate."

"It is always a pleasure to cooperate with the police, especially when they threaten me so nicely," answered the AI drily. Tagarin seemed to have successfully transplanted his personality into his AI, thought Stone. "Please wait."

Stone glanced cynically at his colleagues and waited. The wait began to stretch out and Stone shook his head impatiently. He was in two minds about whether to demand entry or just break the gate down when it spoke. No doubt if he had shown more patience it would have waited even longer.

"I have confirmed that your warrant is valid: I am opening the gate for you and have unlocked the door to the house; you may enter without violence. Be warned that any deviations from the terms of

250

your warrant will have severe legal consequences."

"OK," said Stone. "Goodbye Gate, it's been a laugh. Jones, deactivate this outpost of the AI – I want to keep them guessing."

When Jones gave him the thumbs up they jammed the gate open with a rock, drew their weapons and walked cautiously up to the front door. Stone pushed it with his foot and it opened easily onto a dark corridor. "No welcoming committee with drinks, eh?" he commented. "I feel unloved. Jones, cover that camera and turn on your signal jammer." While he did so, he called the others to join them. "All right guys, show time. Jones, guard the door; Smith, go back and guard the gate. Don't let anyone in or out. Anyone who turns up, detain them; anyone who tries to leave, arrest them. The rest of you, let's go. Hopefully Tagarin will be as accommodating as his gate. If not, we'll just have to return the favor."

They went in and the two cops left behind stood at their posts, nervous and alert, weapons drawn.

Some minutes later one of the darker shadows under a stand of trees across the road detached itself and glided onto the road towards the entrance. Smith raised his weapon but the shadow kept coming, revealing itself as a man dressed in black with a high collar obscuring his face, holding his hands out and visible. Smith kept his gun trained on the man's chest and ordered him to halt, but the man simply smiled humorlessly and extended his identification. Smith grunted and lowered his gun. "What can I do for you, sir?" he asked with brittle politeness.

"You can stand aside, officer, I'm going in. I presume you have no objection?"

"Be my guest, sir," replied Smith. "Should I advise my team?"

"No, we don't want to warn any eavesdroppers." Smith waved to Jones to indicate to let the man past, and he moved quickly up the path and slipped through the door. Then he stole carefully and silently up the corridor. He turned suddenly at a metallic clang behind him: a steel door had descended, cutting off the way out. He hoped that was to keep the cops out, not that he had been detected and it was to lock him in. Grimly, he drew a slim gun from the folds of his clothes and crept cautiously into the gloom.

CHAPTER 43 – TRAPPED

Stone's team had met no resistance. But nor did they meet any people. Just as the front door had opened but that was all, further inside the place appeared to be deserted and the lights refused to shine. "Funny guy, eh?" commented Stone. "Well if that's the way he wants to play it, we might just have to break down some doors."

Tagarin's visitors' annex was empty, as was the office where he met with his callers. They did not need to break down any doors; the doors simply opened at their touch. Yet the lights still did not shine: it was like a physical essay on passive resistance. Besides the door they had entered the office through, there was only one other door leading deeper into the complex. Stone nodded to one of his men, who stood beside it and pushed it gently. It opened as the others had, revealing a short straight corridor that split into two at the end.

"Why do I feel like we're being suckered?" murmured Stone. "OK, we're going to have to split up. This is the only way out and we already have guards out front, so we'll all keep going. You lot take the right branch, you others take the left one with me. Check every room. Split up if you have to as long as you can stay in pairs. I don't trust this place an inch."

He thought a moment then added, "First, search this room. Make sure there's nothing obvious like a place to hide or a hidden door. Once we've covered that angle we'll move in."

He whispered into Miriam's ear: "You stay put: when we start searching, duck under the desk. It's probably nothing and when this is all over you'll whine about missing all the fun, but I want you here. You know all the players and you're fast on your feet. You're my backup plan. I really like backup plans. And if this is a sucker play, you'll be our second chance – and maybe our lifeline. I don't think anyone watching will have been able to count heads, not the way we've been milling around shining lights everywhere: they won't notice if one of us vanishes. I hope."

Miriam nodded tensely.

They all began searching the room, looking into and under things and poking walls, while Miriam quietly slipped under the desk. Then Stone called out, "OK, looks like there's nothing here. Let's get going before they manage to come up with more tricks."

Their expressions tightened as they stalked down the corridor and split up. But Stone's suspicions were borne out: to explore everywhere at once his team had to split up again. It was like a fractal trap. It was a fractal trap.

Tagarin had been planning this for a long time. He knew that one day the surface of his plan might unravel and they might need to escape in the face of a police invasion. He wanted to avoid the necessity for battles and blood. He had remodeled his mansion accordingly.

Few people were granted access to Tagarin's domain. Had one of the few been a police spy, Stone would have been even more suspicious and things might have taken a different turn. It had taken mere seconds for the exit from Tagarin's office to be switched from the normal passageway, which led to his private rooms, to the bifurcating corridors, which did not. The change had been triggered the moment the police went through the gate.

Tagarin did not trust people in large groups. Fear fed on fear and they might panic. Or less likely but worse, thought might feed on thought and come up with a plan. He had always been a fan of jiu-jitsu, and his defenses were planned accordingly: let your opponent overextend himself and use his own thrust against him. So once the invaders had been split up into twos and threes, something else happened.

Stone and his two remaining companions were exploring a corridor, hoping that beyond the curve was not yet another bifurcation. For now, they stood outside a locked door, considering. For the first time, the door had not opened for them: but what did that mean? Progress or a trap? The question in their minds was answered when two doors slid shut ahead and behind.

Then Tagarin's voice came from somewhere. "Welcome to my uninvited guest quarters, noble officers of the law. The door you see in the wall is now unlocked and within are basic facilities to enable you to survive a day or two in modest comfort. Alas, I fear it will *be* a day or two. Personally I would be happy for all this to be done with as soon as possible, but I suspect your superiors will wish to haggle over my perfectly reasonable demands that are the price for your, and not coincidentally our, freedom.

"Rest assured I wish you no harm. You may even communicate with your colleagues outside. In fact, I encourage it: it might stop your more aggressive friends from bombing the place. I am sure you want that as little as I do. I suppose many of you have wives and children; if you want to spare them the grief of attending your funeral, you would be wise to reveal you are safe and counsel restraint.

"Now there are a few rules. Be aware that the walls and doors of your current home are steel and if anyone tries to blast their way in – or if you really came prepared, out – the shockwave will surely kill you. So please refrain from any such heroics, as they will achieve nothing but your own deaths. There are also more active defenses should you attempt some other form of escape: I encourage you not to find out what they are. Again I assure you that I wish you no harm; if you do not believe me, consider that I have merely imprisoned you when I could just as easily have shot you. So the only harm you will come to is what you bring on yourselves. As lawmen you must be aware of rules and the consequences of breaking them: act accordingly. You will be freed unharmed soon enough. In the meantime, take this interlude as a paid holiday. I regret that you will have to make your own entertainment, but you will be safe and comfortable enough."

The same scene played out elsewhere in the trap. Stone gave voice to the thought in all their heads.

"Shit."

CHAPTER 44 – MIRIAM

"Miriam."

The whispered voice sounded in her ear.

"Yes? I'm here," she whispered.

"The bad news is, it was a trap. We don't appear to be in any danger but we've been neatly cut out of the picture. You need to know, but I don't know what you can do about it. Don't do anything stupid. We've already told the guys outside – who are now locked outside. An inner door slammed shut and Jones had to retreat to the gate when tear gas started spraying at him. Reinforcements are coming and they could try to break in, but we've been told in no uncertain terms that we're hostages and hostilities, including attempting to penetrate their perimeter, will invite retaliation. So we have a siege but are going to play it cool for now. Sorry kid, it looks like you might see some excitement after all. All I can tell you is that we were somehow diverted into a well set up trap: if you can find a way into his main facility you might be able to stop him, but I have no idea how you'd do it. I'll hang up now; the less chance we give them to discover you're still outside their trap the better. Good luck."

Christ, thought Miriam. *Only a few minutes in and it's already eleven down, one to go.* At least the others were alive, though it was easy to be merciful when you held the upper hand. Tagarin might play the gracious host when he felt safe, but if he found her prowling through his house with a gun his reaction could be deadly. Her fear and isolation told her that maybe she should just stay here cowering under the desk. It was unlikely anyone would fault her for it.

But she knew that would never happen: she couldn't stop trying any more than she could stop breathing. She had never been one to be a passive passenger of life, someone who just hoped that the world would deliver her wishes: to her, the essence of living was action. At least if you failed you died trying, she believed; you died as someone who had fought and so deserved to live.

But, she wondered as she identified that feeling in herself, wasn't that equally true of Katlyn and Tagarin? Wasn't that all they had been doing too, in their bizarre plot that had led to all this? She shook her head. No. Tagarin had not been forced into his life of crime; he had chosen to do it, knowing the consequences, knowing the risks. And however innocent Katlyn might have been, she in her turn had become a dangerous sociopath; the rights and wrongs of how her past had brought her there did not change what she was in the present.

Wonderful, Miriam thought, *you've rationalized your call to heroic action so well I can almost hear the trumpets: but what action are you going to* take? It wasn't at all obvious. If Tagarin had trapped the others somehow, how would she avoid the same fate? It was unlikely he had anything as obvious as a hidden button that opened up his true domain: everything would be computer controlled with no hope of access by an outsider.

Well, there's no point sitting here forever, she told herself. *If I start looking around and this room is under observation then I'm sprung, but if I do nothing I might as well be locked in with the others anyway.* Her best bet was to carefully explore the corridor the others had gone down, hope to find how they had been diverted and hope there was some way around it, or even better some way to release the others. It was either that or stay hidden here and wish for the unlikely event that one of the villains of the piece would come to her.

She was just standing up after crawling out of her hiding space when Katlyn stepped into the room.

CHAPTER 45 – CAUGHT

So far things had gone according to plan, even if the plan had to be accelerated. With their sortie caught like crabs in a pot it would be a while before the police would try anything else. So Katlyn had gone to the front office to collect a few things they preferred not to leave behind: they would never return. She walked silently, more out of habit than caution. The light came on as she entered the room and she nearly jumped out of her skin when she saw a black-clad apparition rising up in front of Daniel's desk, face hidden by a dark visor; the apparition jumped too, so the feeling must have been mutual.

Miriam reached for her gun but Katlyn's reactions were much faster. Miriam was stunned by the speed and ferocity of the attack. Katlyn leapt at her and knocked her back onto the desk, slamming her forearm down so the gun shot from her hand and slid off the back of the desk, before whacking her head from side to side until her ears rang. Stunned, Miriam could only gasp as Katlyn tore off her helmet and hurled it away; there were two dull thuds as it hit the wall then fell to the floor. Katlyn looked back and stopped, startled. "You again! Will I ever be rid of you?" she hissed, then wrapped her hands around Miriam's neck and began to squeeze.

Miriam knew she had only seconds of consciousness left, but by the time her mind became aware of that fact her reflexes had taken over: her arms wheeled to break Katlyn's grip then grab and twist her arm, forcing her over sideways. Katlyn went with the move to escape Miriam's grasp but Miriam suddenly let go; her legs were already up and she kicked Katlyn hard in the stomach. Katlyn went one way and banged into the wall with an explosion of breath; Miriam went the other way, rolling back over the desk, and in a single fluid motion came to her feet with the gun in her hand, pointed straight at Katlyn.

"That's enough!" she ordered. "Stay where you are with your hands up or I'll shoot!"

Katlyn's eyes darted to Miriam, to the door and back. *No chance*, she thought. Miriam was too far to be jumped and the door too far for escape: not when, however fast she could run, all Miriam had to do was move her hand and pull the trigger. She exhaled and put her hands up slowly.

"You're making me regret saving your life," she said bitterly.

"Be thankful I didn't just shoot you where you stand! Now face the wall and kneel on the floor with your hands behind your head. This time I get to handcuff you."

Katlyn did not move. "Listen. I know you're mad at me. I know you're a cop and catching people like me is what you do. But if you don't let me go, I'm dead. Whatever else I've done, I did save your life. What did you say to me once? That you didn't deserve to die? Well I don't deserve it either. Let me go." She added roughly, as if it was a word she wasn't used to, "Please."

"You only had to save me because I was chasing you! Taking all our charming meetings into account, I think you're psychotic. Unpredictable and dangerous. Maybe it's not your fault. Maybe your genome has made you mentally unstable; maybe it was growing up the way you did. Or maybe it's just you. But that's not my call. My job is to uphold the law. You just tried to kill me and for all I know you've left a trail of dead bodies behind you! For all I know, you do deserve to die."

Katlyn sighed, and it was if the brash bravado left her body with the breath. Suddenly she looked more like a scared teenager than a hardened criminal. "No. I wasn't trying to kill you, just knock you out. I never killed anyone. I was never even going to hurt you, that first time, not seriously. Do you know why I treated you so badly then?"

"I don't care. On the floor. Now. Or I'll shoot you."

Katlyn continued as if she hadn't spoken. "'Know your enemy' is the first rule of war, and this is war, you know. Not much of a war, I admit; not much of an army. But war just the same. I needed to know your mettle and I wanted to scare you off if I could. I did what I had to, that's all. Well, maybe not all. I was angry: at the world, at you, at what you represented. But don't you see? If I'm what you say, do you think I'd have let you live?"

"How should I know? You're crazy! I wonder how many mice think the cat has let them go, when it releases them just to torment them?"

Katlyn looked at her sadly. "Back then, the first time we met, you talked about justice. Was that the truth? If it was – will you listen to me?"

"Save it for the courtroom. You'll have your chance then."

"There won't be a courtroom," she replied softly. "Not for me."

Miriam wondered if that was true. If she was sending this girl to her death, perhaps she owed it to her to understand, or at least to listen. From where she was standing she could cover the corridor as well as Katlyn: she could afford this small grant of time.

"You have a minute. No more."

"I will tell you the truth. If you'd shown you were what I first thought – my enemy, to your bones – then I might have killed you. That's what happens in war. Or I might have killed you in self-defense if I had to. But I found out who you really are: and I don't mean just that you're brave, or that you talked to me not as a monster but like you would to anyone else. It was the other way round: I saw that you're just a girl like me, just someone doing the best you can to live and do what you think is right. I laughed at you when you said you were innocent: but I think you are, down where it counts."

She paused, then went on. "Yes, I'm angry at the world. But no matter how much the world takes from you, you can't fight it by becoming the same evil yourself. Because then you lose yourself too; and if you lose yourself, you've lost everything. Whatever else I am, the innocent are safe from me."

"Yet you chose a life of crime."

"If the world makes you a criminal just for being, how can it complain if you accept the role? Would you have done any differently?"

Miriam studied Katlyn. Her breaths were rapid and shallow and her yellow eyes were wide with a fear she would not fully admit. *For once she looks like what she is,* Miriam thought: *for all her adult body and actions, for all that she's done, deep down she really is just a fifteen-year-old girl.* When she dropped her tough persona as the vicious criminal, her voice was soft and somewhat musical. But it didn't change anything.

"I'm sorry, Katlyn. I have to take you in. I have to uphold the law."

"You talk about justice," she replied bitterly. "But if you arrest me I'm dead. No appeal. No lawyers. No nothing. Some GenInt goon will put a bullet in my brain, before or after a bit of dissection to find out what makes me tick. Or makes me scream, more likely."

"No. We will have you, not GenInt. We can hold you, protect you. You will have your chance."

Katlyn laughed her incongruous laugh, though this time the bells were edged with a metallic bitterness. "You really are a young innocent, aren't you? No, I am afraid GenInt has legal jurisdiction. They'll take me whenever they want me, which will be sooner rather than later. Now listen. Your job is to prevent crime. Consider it prevented. My life of crime is over. I'm leaving, so I won't be bothering anyone here ever again, and I swear I won't be bothering anyone where I'm going either. Isn't that a good outcome? Without any further expense to our underfunded and overtaxed so-called justice system, Master Thief Katlyn has been reformed after a mere couple of conversations with you and is now a model citizen! All you have to do is stand aside and let me go. Nobody will even know."

"I will know."

"You will know that you've saved a life! I can't claim it is a perfectly innocent life. But I hope you believe me that I don't deserve to die any more than you did, that first time we met."

Miriam hesitated. This would be much simpler without that automatic death penalty. Like many cops who had learned what some people chose to do to others, Miriam had nothing against killing criminals if they were killers themselves. But it had to be during the execution of the crime or failing that, after due process of law, where the truth mattered. No truth mattered here except the plain fact of Katlyn's genes, and was that enough? How could it be enough? Still, the fact remained of Katlyn's treatment of her; talk was cheap when you were the one at the wrong end of the gun. And as a cop she had to trust the law to do what was right. Surely even GenInt couldn't just make someone disappear out of police custody. Not a grown woman talking and breathing like anyone else.

"I don't believe it is as bad as you say; we won't let them take you. Now on the floor."

"No. I'm not going to let you off the hook. You think you can serve justice and the law, but you can't. And the law isn't here. There's no big institution with marble columns and dignified judges applying abstract justice: it's just you and me, two people who have to make the decisions and bear the consequences. If you think you can avoid the responsibility by passing my fate on to someone else, I won't let you get away with it. You'll have to shoot me yourself: you, now, by your own hand."

She stood there for a moment, letting the silence underline the thought. Then she added softly, "Before you decide, there's one more thing you ought to know. You won't believe me, but that night on the roof wasn't the first time I saved your life."

Miriam stood still for a moment, then said slowly, "It was you in the park that day, wasn't it? I saw you but I thought I dreamed it. Tell me."

"I was waiting for you. I knew you were dangerous and I was thinking I should kill you myself, or at least hurt you so bad you'd be out of action," she admitted simply. "But I couldn't. It would have been so easy to let those guys finish you off for me. But I couldn't do that either. So I finished the fight for you."

She let that hang in the air. Miriam wondered whether it was true. Katlyn could have found out the details later; the way these people plotted and lied, she might even have planned the attack herself. But Miriam had seen it herself, just not believed what she had seen.

"Why would you do that for me?"

Katlyn replied softly, "I've heard you can be put in a situation that forces you to make a moral choice between two paths, a choice that defines the rest of your life. I guess that was mine." She looked toward the door then back to Miriam. "I guess it brought me here. More fool me, eh?"

Then she continued. "Now it's your turn. I'm going to walk out that door. You'll have to let me go or shoot me." She slowly started lowering her hands.

"Stop! I can't let you go!"

Katlyn shook her head gravely. "No. You will decide whether I deserve to die and if I don't, whether you will serve your laws or the justice you think gives them meaning. I've made my choice and threats can't stop me now: if you want to stop me you'll have to actually shoot me. So whatever you decide... goodbye Miriam," she finished softly.

Miriam felt her aim waver and opened her mouth to speak, but the only sound was the bang of three rapid gunshots.

Katlyn clutched her middle and looked down. "Oh no," she moaned softly. She looked up at Miriam, eyes dark and wide with shock. "Oh no." Then her eyes dulled and closed, her legs buckled under her and she slid down the wall. She fell onto her stomach, kicked a few times and then lay still.

Miriam looked on, horrified. It had happened so quickly her brain had had no chance to catch up, and she looked stupidly at her own gun, wondering how it had fired. Then she whirled at the sound of a familiar voice behind her, "Well, that wasn't so hard."

Miriam couldn't believe her eyes or her ears. "*Amaro?!* What are you doing here? *How* are you here? *What have you done?*"

Amaro looked at her, his usual playful expression replaced by something flat and hard. "I should think you would be grateful. A suspicious man might interpret what he just heard as one of the City Police being on the verge of letting a criminal escape justice. That would not be good for her career, nor perhaps her freedom. But fortunately Amaro is a carefree soul, always willing to believe the best of people. He is willing to concede he may have misheard or merely had less patience than you."

Then his voice hardened. "However my good mood is at risk from that gun you still have pointed at me. You might wish to lower it. You didn't appear to know how to use it a few seconds ago, so don't start remembering now."

Miriam had led with her gun when she spun around but in her surprise had forgotten she still had it pointed at him. Or perhaps she now thought of him as the enemy. She saw that Amaro had a gun himself, a relatively small .22, made more for concealment than firepower but deadly nonetheless. It was easy to tell it was a .22 because she was looking right down the barrel. She lowered her own gun. "Sorry, you startled me. But *what the hell is going on?*"

"Why, my dear, surely you have worked it out. I am doing my job. Superlatively, I might add. Amaranto Leandro Moreno, agent of the dreaded Department of Human Genetic Integrity, at your service," he replied, executing one of his signature bows.

"I appear to have missed the memo your department sent us about this raid, but when you told me you'd be late because something big had come up, it wasn't too hard to guess what and where. Your loyal guards let me in and I made my way to the little room outside here, where I was planning my next move. Then events intervened. You did well, by the way. An excellent interrogation, which I followed with great interest. Until the end anyway, when you were a trifle slow executing your clear duty when the subject became uncooperative."

Miriam stared at him in disbelief. She was suffering cognitive overload. Then her brain finally started to recover and make connections.

"You said you worked for the EPA, for God's sake!" she cried. Then she saw the full truth, and felt sick. She added softly, "You didn't meet me by accident. You've been spying on me this whole time, haven't you? You've been spying on us, the police, through me!" She looked at him, hopelessly, the enormity of the lie weighing upon her. "Please tell me it isn't true," she added softly.

Amaro just shrugged. "Oh, everything I told you is true. Well, nearly everything and nearly true. I am a scientist working for the EPA, but it is a cover. GenInt likes to have its finger on the pulse. What better place to keep tabs on illegal genetic engineering than in some other government department that analyses samples from all over, and pays for it out of its own budget to boot?

"But were we two lovers meeting by accident in a smoky room? Sorry. You're a job. We got your department's obscurely worded report on this – thing" he said contemptuously, waving towards Katlyn's body " – and got suspicious. It looked like you didn't want us to know but wanted to cover your asses – and a pretty ass it is too, I must add." He smirked. "You guys must think we're idiots. Anyway, we knew you were a key person. My job was to keep an eye on you and find out what I could. My natural charm did the rest."

"You *bastard!*"

"Come now, Miriam, grow up. Lots of cops go undercover. You might do it yourself one day. Get over it. We had fun, didn't we?"

"But I'm a cop! I'm not some low-life criminal you can happily lie to because he's a liar or worse himself! I loved you! Don't you know that? I loved you! How could you do that to me!?"

Amaro shrugged again. "What was I supposed to do? Anyway, don't blame me. I warned you from the start that getting too close to me might burn you, didn't I? You're the one who chose to do it anyway and who fooled yourself. I just told you what you wanted to hear. Sure, there had to be a few lies, but nothing major. I tweaked my resume and my background a bit to make myself sound more appealing, that's all. The rest you did to yourself. Most of it was even real."

"Except you never loved me. All that was a lie. Our whole relationship was a lie. Every touch, every kiss, every..." Her vision blurred, and she realized she was crying. *I won't give him the satisfaction,* she thought. *I won't.* She swallowed and glared at him, knowing her tears were there and would not be stopped, but refusing to acknowledge their existence or what they meant.

Amaro looked at her. Part of him was the agent of GenInt, unmoved. But he knew he had let her get under his skin. The agent felt he owed her nothing; but the man knew he owed her something. "If it makes any difference to you," he continued more gently, "it wasn't all an act. I did care for you, Miriam. But some things aren't meant to be. Think of us as Romeo and Juliet, except in our case" – he waved his gun at Katlyn – "somebody else did the dying. So a happy ending, of sorts. But I'm sorry I hurt you, for what that's worth. I suspect not much, but..." He shrugged.

The man's debt cleared, the agent felt free to take over again. "For the record, you were admirably if irritatingly discrete. That made my job harder, but more enjoyable at the same time: like a game of chess with a particularly talented opponent playing an unconventional game. But that's all history. Now we have to look to tomorrow, a much brighter vista. In honor of the good times we've had together, I'm letting you share the credit on this one. Really, I do appreciate how you backed me up, covering my back while I cornered this thing and dispatched it. Isn't that a much better story than what I might tell? You should be showering my feet with kisses, not tears."

"I understand, Amaro," she said tonelessly. "I understand you had a job to do. But I think your job stinks and you stink with it. You're just a liar and a killer. Go to hell."

His face hardened and he snapped, "That attitude can get you in trouble, girl! There are reasons for the geneh laws, very good reasons. That thing had to die. If you were willing to let it go then you should go to jail yourself!" His voice took on almost a pleading quality, though Miriam couldn't tell if it was a remnant desire to protect her or just one part of himself trying to convince another. "Listen. You know the law. We've even talked about it. Our opinions don't matter. She spoke to you about justice – but do you really think she had rights? That she deserved a trial? *Humans* have rights, and *humans* have decided that things like her aren't one of them."

His face hardened again. "If you don't like it, take it up with your fellow citizens. It is sweet, really, how you have such empathy for all God's and Satan's creatures. But get a grip. If I worked for Animal Control and had just shot a rabid dog, well, maybe you'd still feel sorry for the dog: but would you really condemn me for doing my job? For protecting people at the dog's expense? For deceiving you in order to track it down, when that's the only way I could because you were blind to how dangerous it was?"

Miriam stared at him. He really believed it, she realized. It wasn't just a job to him. None of that had been a lie. He really did see himself as a knight protecting the kingdom, defending the realm of man from the monsters of the night. She thought she hated him even more for it. Though for all she knew, he was right. She didn't know any more. All the fight left her. It didn't matter anyway now.

"All right, Amaro. I give up. Arrest me if you want to."

He smiled. "Oh, don't be like that. What happened to that tongue I so admired? I won't arrest you. You might feel like that now, but I suspect your tongue will wake up eventually and talk you out of it. No, much better if we share the credit, myself with the lion's share of course. If I try to ruin your career you will fight it, and your department will probably fight it too. Who knows how shabby you might make GenInt look? Going undercover and under the covers to spy on pretty rookie police girls can be made to sound so tawdry. No. Much better to make this a shining example of cooperation between noble GenInt and the loyal police force; between the global authorities and the local law. Our personal relationship, should it be revealed, was just the natural chemistry of two young people with shared goals. Why, the human interest angle would probably make the magazines."

Miriam felt sick.

"And you really should look on the bright side. I can understand that getting over me might take some time, but you will soon enough. It won't be that hard for a woman like you to find some other charming man to share your bed. Why, in a year you'll have forgotten me completely, except as the rocket that gave your career a boost most cops can only dream of. So dry your tears and get on with your job."

"So what do we do now?" she asked tiredly.

"Well, first let's make sure this thing is completely dead," he said, drawing his gun and stepping cautiously toward Katlyn's body.

"Actually, the first thing you two will do is drop your guns and raise your hands," growled a voice from the corridor. The voice belonged to Tagarin, as did the hefty automatic rifle that had preceded him into the room and was pointed in their direction. "And no sudden moves."

Chapter 46 – Judgment

They raised their hands and turned fully toward him, slowly. He frowned at them and jerked his rifle in their direction.

"I believe I mentioned dropping your guns?"

Amaro shrugged, laid his gun carefully on the ground and kicked it away. Miriam carefully removed hers from her holster and did likewise.

"OK James, take these two away. I'll take care of Katlyn. The last thing she'd have wanted is her body paraded before the cameras as a poster child for GenInt. You two murderers and I will have a little talk soon."

James came in, collected their guns then waved them toward the exit with his own gun. "This way, Sir, Madam," he said in his butler's voice. "But don't ask me to serve coffee," he added in a growl.

Miriam was almost through the door when she stopped. Like Lot's wife, she couldn't resist a last look behind. She caught a fleeting glimpse of Tagarin gently lifting Katlyn's limp body to his chest before James pushed her ungently into the corridor. Miriam noticed that it now ran straight to beyond where it had earlier divided into two, and realized how simply the others had been trapped; but the knowledge was no use to her now.

~~~

"The boss will be here soon, I imagine," James said after tying them to chairs and removing the phones from their wrists. "Make yourselves comfortable," he smirked. He added in a tone of idle conversation, "I hope he isn't too long. I get bored easily. I might feel like beating you two up a bit for something to do." He cracked his knuckles and smiled at them politely.

Neither of them had anything to say. Miriam was in no mood. Even Amaro, who normally couldn't resist wisecracks, knew when it was safest to just shut up.

A few minutes later Tagarin entered the room. He favored both of them with a look of disgust.

"I knew you'd be trouble," he said to Miriam, "just not this much this soon. And you," he said, turning to Amaro, "You were with her at the ball. So I presume it wasn't an accident you were both there after all." He glared at Miriam. "You're a better liar than I thought."

Miriam just shook her head dumbly. What was the point of arguing, she thought?

He turned back to Amaro. "I guess from your weapons that you're the one who actually shot her. What are you? GenInt?"

Amaro just glared at him.

"Not that it matters. You're both in it, both guilty. Now I have to decide what to do with you. I am most tempted to hang you both, and leave you to be found by your colleagues, when they eventually break in, swinging gently from the rafters. It would make a nice image for the less tasteful news feeds, don't you think? But I am sorry to say that killing you two is very likely to interfere with certain other plans of mine, which generally end in my leading a long and happy life in some tropical paradise. So I shall have to think of something else less satisfying but more strategic."

He glared at them a while longer. "My AI is currently negotiating with the police. If handsome here really is GenInt, his friends have either not yet made an appearance or are content to stay in the background for now. A pity, as I might have enjoyed a shootout with them. For all my flaws I am less inclined to shoot at the police, who at least fight real criminals part of the time. Such as myself, I suppose. But they know some of their own are in here and still alive. My AI's strategy programs estimate that it will be at least ten hours before your negotiators decide to either pretend to let me go or try to break in at the risk of killing you and all your colleagues, so we have time yet. And I have some important things to do during that time to ensure my future wealth and dissipated lifestyle."

He gave Miriam a hard glance. "But based on my experience of

Detective Hunter here, I don't trust you two not to find some way to interfere. Again. So I am afraid I shall have to knock you both out for a while.

"James."

Miriam steeled herself. She did not imagine this was going to be pleasant.

"Don't flinch, Detective. We are not going to be so crude as to hit you over the head with an iron bar, gratifying as that would be. A simple injection will suffice." James brought out a kit containing two syringes filled with clear liquid. "This will hurt no more than the usual injection and will ensure a restful sleep. Unfortunately it would be dangerous to give you a dose large enough to keep you out for very long, and even so there will be side effects. But you'll be out long enough to ensure you can't cause me further bother. First our detective here."

Miriam watched, helpless, as James injected the solution into her arm. She wondered if she would ever wake. "Now her friend here." Amaro snarled and his muscles bulged as if to break his bonds by pure strength, but to no avail. "Sweet dreams, children", said Tagarin. Miriam watched Amaro's eyes close as he slumped sideways. Then it occurred to her to wonder how she was still awake to see it.

CHAPTER 47 – ANSWERS

"Now, Ms Hunter. You may be asking yourself why you are still with us. Think of it as a bit of misdirection. I wanted your GenInt friend out of this, but you I want to talk to you some more, without his knowledge or interference."

Miriam looked at him somewhat fearfully. "Aren't you better off doing something to get out of here?"

"Why, are you in a hurry to see me go? I would have thought luring me into conversation to give your friends time to find me would have been your own plan, if I hadn't offered it to you myself. But don't worry about me. For my escape certain things must be done that will take some time but do not need my personal involvement. We have hours."

He smiled at her reflexive quiver. "Ah, you fear a reprise of your first 'interview' with Katlyn? I am not interested in hurting you for hurt's sake and I am not after revenge, at least not on you. So don't worry, it doesn't involve hanging or even a beating. I just want to talk without your friend here hearing. I neither like nor trust GenInt, as you might have guessed."

"What makes you think I won't just tell him anyway?"

Tagarin shrugged. "Perhaps you will, though I would advise you not to trust him either." At Miriam's involuntary grimace he nodded. "Indeed. In any case I wish to tell you and my desire to exclude him is more policy than necessity. If you do tell him I don't expect it will make any difference."

Miriam looked at him curiously, but stayed silent. Tagarin smiled sharply. "You are still wondering why I should wish to tell you anything, but have finally realized that you should just keep your mouth shut and let me keep talking? But to answer why, think of it as a trade: I will answer your questions in return for finding out what you know. You must have learned far more than I thought you could or we wouldn't be in our current predicaments, I under siege and you at my mercy. You may also think of it as part validation – Katlyn's too brief existence needs to mean something, and perhaps my confession will give it meaning; and part strategy – we are enemies now, but I think that is a matter of circumstance not necessity. Perhaps if I tell you my story you will understand; and perhaps understanding, one day you will be my ally when I need one."

Miriam gazed at him intently. What could she say? She was not convinced she would be alive tomorrow, let alone that they would meet again. Even less that they could ever be allies. But he was offering her answers; she would be a fool not to take advantage of his desire to talk. She considered her first question.

"I guess events pretty much prove that Katlyn was a geneh and you are the one who made her. So how much of what you told us is true? How did you manage to create her, given the reasons you told us it was impossible?"

"Most of it was true," he replied. "I see no need for honesty when dealing with enemies, especially enemies with guns. But lies are risky, so I find it is best to follow the Jiu-Jitsu of deception: go with your enemy's flow and use it against him. In short, tell the truth rather than bend it, bend the truth rather than break it, lie only if you have to. Let the truth he already knows or can find out lend credence to the lies about what he cannot know.

"So it is true that none of us could have created Katlyn before the bans came in and that nobody could get the equipment afterwards or use existing facilities without detection. But in the years before, supply and disposal of those items weren't monitored with any rigor. Our lab was well funded and we were always upgrading to the latest machinery. As the climate for our kind of research worsened, I decided it would be prudent to have a backup, though I never dreamed the laws would go as far as they did. When nobody is looking very closely, it isn't too hard to dispose of older equipment so it vanishes without a trace: where for all the paper trail is concerned it has been scrapped. In fact, where it vanished to is a facility I built secretly here.

"That was all I needed. I did not need technicians as I was not attempting a full research program and the equipment is automated. I did not have the most advanced equipment but it was good enough. I had spare parts and if I needed more it would be much easier to get them than a whole machine.

"So I just continued my work in private and in secret. At the time, I thought the insanity couldn't last." He grimaced. "I was wrong.

"You know we had already successfully made a newborn, who was doing well until GenInt goons murdered her. With that proof of principle, I was interested in something more advanced: someone enhanced but not extreme; someone attractive, a bit fun, capable but in a non-threatening way. A showcase of what was possible, of what good was possible. Of course I had my failures, as you always do in science, but each one taught me something."

"Then fifteen years ago, Katlyn was born. She was the only survivor of a batch of five experiments. The others died before birth due to developmental problems. But I expected that. Getting the gene engineering precisely right is tricky."

"May I ask a technical question?" asked Miriam.

"Certainly."

"You said once that after you've engineered a stem cell, you let it recover then clone it. I thought cloning meant, you know, making copies. Why can't you, once you have a genetically stable stem cell, make as many copies as you want? Why aren't there a hundred Katlyns?"

He nodded. "You do ask incisive questions sometimes. The pluripotent stem cells used medically are easier to maintain and can be multiplied almost indefinitely. But to make an embryo you need totipotent cells, and totipotency is a tricky state to induce and maintain. It is easy to lose your chance if you go through more than a few generations: especially with engineered genomes, which we still don't have the ability to make exactly the same as natural ones. The same is true of nuclear transfer into eggs, which is the standard method of cloning from adults. To cut a long story short, it is a compromise. I did multiply my engineered stem cells, but only for a few generations. So I actually started with 32 identical cells, which resulted in only 5 viable embryos, of which only one survived to term. We expect such low survival rates. That is why we would do many more experiments with many more variations if we were free to do so. But it was enough for my purposes.

"The rest of the truth I also bent by omission. Katlyn is effectively a twenty-two year old woman: I inflated her apparent age a little to make your geneh theory seem even more implausible, but not so much that another expert could categorically dispute it. After all, with such limited data her age was a matter of judgement. It was indeed achieved by accelerated development both to puberty and to full maturity, as you guessed."

"But why didn't you make more, if you had the technology?"

"Before the geneh laws and with a bustling lab I might have. But I wanted to be cautious. Although I had a healthy baby, I wanted to follow her development a bit more to make sure nothing unexpected went awry. I didn't want to make ten babies just to see all of them die young of some ghastly developmental failure. Despite what GenInt say, I cared about the results of my experiments.

"Then by the time Katlyn was four I had decided to stop. The legal environment was getting worse, not better. I could see what kind of life Katlyn would have: at best hidden from the world, unable to show her face; at worst, hunted like an animal. You know, I read once about parents being jailed for keeping their child locked in a basement its entire life to protect it from the world. But that's what I was offering Katlyn, wasn't it? And there was still the chance that her accelerated development would kill her when she hit puberty, when humans change so radically. Or she would fall apart after it."

He looked at her. "Again, despite what GenInt might claim, the scientists who do this work aren't monsters, any more than their creations are. These are babies. Babies we made. You can't help but get attached to them even if you wanted not to." He looked into the distance. "By that time, I thought of Katlyn almost as a daughter. I was deathly afraid that puberty would kill her – because of what I had done. As I told you, accelerated development has risks. I couldn't bear the thought of risking the lives of other children until I knew.

"But, as you see, she survived. Oh, there were problems. Puberty was painful for her. It usually is, but she had some bad times of it. But not so bad they killed her, not so bad she ever wanted to die."

"How old was she?"

"She was through puberty by age twelve. Less than average for a woman, more than average for a chimp; and actually within the natural human range. By then she was effectively an adult. Even mentally she was more like a young adult than a child just entering her teens: she had gone through all the usual stages, just faster. She developed quickly, learned quickly, grew up quickly, matured quickly.

"But by then I didn't want more. I was not interested in cloning Katlyn herself: my interest was always scientific, in what could be done. I saw no point in just copying an existing success. And doing something new ran the same risks of failure as with her. But most importantly, for all that she was a success biologically, I didn't like the life I'd given her and didn't want to do that to another human being. Which," he added glaring at her, "is what she was."

He paused. "And while I ended up hatching plans that relied on Katlyn, I decided they would work with her or not at all. Don't get me wrong. I regard those plans as crucial for things I hold dear, including Katlyn and her kind. But if you do not understand hate, Ms Hunter, do you understand love? Sometimes it makes cowards of us. It can make a price we might gladly pay ourselves too high to contemplate when it might have to be paid by another. Katlyn was willing to risk her life for those plans. But I did not want to put anyone else into a position where such a choice must be made.

"In any event, it was probably too late. It would have taken several more years to do and what was the point? If Katlyn failed, I would almost certainly fail with her, leaving a helpless child at the mercy of the authorities."

He stopped, looking into the distance. Miriam watched, imagining him seeing all those years of labor, of falling in love with his creation, of fear and planning; hoping he would not stop to think of how it had ended tonight and Miriam's role in that end. If Katlyn had been driven mad by her life or her genes, she wondered, were Tagarin's own mood swings because he too had been driven mad by bitterness and isolation? She had better ask a question that might direct his mood back to the safe one of academic discourse.

"You have spoken of your hesitation in trying more times, your high failure rate, your fear that even a successful baby might not reach adulthood. Doesn't that support the intent of the Geneh Laws? Not GenInt's more extreme methods, but their bans?"

"I am a scientist not a philosopher, Ms Hunter. And I'm not sure the philosophers are much help: they don't even believe each other's theories, so why should we? And if we did, whose would we choose?

But if you want to look at it democratically, the ethical standards I followed are what most people actually believe: if you judge what they believe by what they do rather than what they profess. The fanatics in GenInt are no different from the old anti-abortion or anti-drink crusaders: they claim to speak for morality, decency and democracy, whereas in fact and in practice most people believe and do quite the opposite in private – whatever they may approve of in public.

"Most of my embryos die? Well, nearly everyone these days accepts the morality of abortion and *in vitro* fertilization, both of which involve the death of embryos – and not even accidental death. My creations might die as a result of their modifications? Many babies made by the standard method still have deformities or die; many will suffer severe problems as they grow up due to genetics, disease, accident or some chosen folly such as drug addiction. Many more are simply weak or dull. Do people therefore forego having children in order to prevent such disasters? No, and properly so. We do not, and should not, live our lives as if our purpose is to avoid the possibility of pain: we live in order to create life with all its hope of pleasure and happiness.

"Yes, the chance of problems in my research is higher: that is in the nature of research. But also in the nature of research is that the absolute numbers are far, far lower. Many more children have suffered and died through the natural course of events since I started my research than ever did because of it. In fact, far more children have avoided suffering or death and led full, happy lives because of my research than died from it!

"You must realize that this work wasn't just some academic game, it had a purpose: improving the human race. Our bodies are the result of the blind operation of evolution: what worked well enough for our ancestors and their ancestors, given the environments they lived in and the anatomy their ancestors left them. Compromise upon compromise. Then consider what people have valued throughout history, the people they have admired and the art they have created: their greatest athletes and warriors, their geniuses. The best that was possible to man, not the average. How can people admire greatness but choose mediocrity in their own selves? When we have the tools to make man better, how insane is it to refuse to use them?"

The look in his eyes seemed familiar. Then she remembered where she had seen it last: in the face of Amaro, when espousing exactly the opposite view. *Enemies with opposite ideals*, she thought; *sharing nothing but that look and the belief beneath it: that they stood for what was right.* How many battles had that caused? But how many less would it have caused if men had learned to stop forcing their beliefs upon others? She wondered which one of them was right; whether she could ever know. She wondered what difference it could possibly make.

"Earlier you mentioned you had plans for Katlyn. I presume you meant her career as a burglar?"

"Yes," Tagarin said. "And I think you already know most of it. I think it is your turn to talk."

Miriam wondered what to tell him. She wondered how it could matter now. She thought that her best chance of learning the full story was to give hers. "We know that the jewelry thefts were cover for taking over the victims' AIs, and we know that you used that power to steal substantial amounts of money and to gather material for blackmail. We also know that in at least one case you used this to gather material that could be used to blackmail yet further people, perhaps all the way to President Felton. But most of your victims were unwilling to tell us anything, so we don't know the full scope and we don't know why. You already have more than enough money. It all seems so small: too small to risk your own wealth, your own position and the life of Katlyn. What was it all *for?*"

He gave a grim smile. "Ms Hunter, I know you think you serve justice and you would tell me that breaking the law is no way to do it. And in happier days I would have agreed that taking the law into your own hands is not the way to go. But when the law does not serve life but the death of those you love, what should you do? Perhaps there is no good answer. Perhaps one day you will find your own answer and perhaps it will be a better one: but I have already given mine. My answer may have been wrong. Perhaps I should have stayed a law-abiding citizen, quietly working to overturn an unjust law. The calm voice of reason attempting to persuade the good citizens of the world, as they swigged their beers and voted on things they know nothing about. As they agreed, by intent or default, to kill what they fear, not out of knowledge but out of blind ignorance."

His voice hardened. "But I saw an innocent child shot according to your laws, and I say damn those laws, damn them to the hell they rose from: and damn the self-righteous citizens who cheer them on. And call it justice, or call it vengeance, if there is even a difference. But I will have it!"

"But... how?" she asked fearfully, afraid that what had seemed too small a moment ago might prove too monstrous. Afraid that if he told her, he would have to kill her after all.

He smiled, and Miriam thought it was the smile she would see on a wolf that had found her hiding in the snow. "I think you could work it out. You know our President's role in the Geneh Laws, but you might not know how near run a thing it was. Perhaps I am wrong to blame her entirely, but as she herself has taken the blame – the credit in her view – I take her at her word. As for the others, they are all supporters of the President: her friends, her donors, her colleagues from way back. I knew many of them would know things about the President and the deals she did to get the geneh laws through, things neither she nor GenInt would want the world to see. And many of them were very rich."

He paused. "Ms Hunter, while I am a criminal by your laws, that is not how I see myself – though I suppose you've heard that before. I have not killed or hurt anyone, and I have targeted nobody except the people I described. None of them are innocent. All of them, whether for power or money or simply hatred of the unknown, are in bed with the President and as guilty as she is."

He fixed his cobra stare on her. But she wasn't sure whether it was targeted at her as herself or as the avatar of his absent enemies. "But... you still haven't told me what it is all for," she said softly to that stare.

He smiled and the wolf returned. "As you have observed, I did not need their money. But they valued it, so I took it. And I used it to fight them. In this country and around the world there are think tanks and even philosophical institutes that champion human rights: those who are consistent enough to oppose the geneh laws have found themselves enriched by quite generous if anonymous benefactors. Similarly, certain influential bloggers and commentators who have made principled objections to such laws have found their freedom to do so enhanced by unsolicited material support. What sweeter justice can there be than to turn your enemies' own wealth against them to fight the evil they have brought into the world? To make them see their ideals, corrupt as they are, crumble into dust with their own money paying for it?"

"And the blackmail? Was that also simply punishment?" Miriam asked. She knew they had almost reached the full answer to the mystery; she could see the shape of it, just not clearly enough to name it.

"I would not pity my victims there either, Ms Hunter. The thing about blackmail is that in most cases the victim is trying to hide what they know deserves punishment, and the blackmailer is merely threatening to lift the lid. I have not blackmailed the innocent over peccadillos, foolish mistakes or lapses of judgement. I have blackmailed the guilty for their crimes. I expected that many of our targets would have evidence of dirty dealings by GenInt and our illustrious President, either in anticipation of blackmail of their own or for protection. I was not disappointed. You will be entertained over the coming months by all kinds of revelations – with proof, or at least with enough detail for those who care to ferret out proof to do so – about the President and GenInt. It will not be pretty. With any luck, it will be enough to destroy them all. I doubt it will get that far: but it will go a long way toward finally eliminating them from the world."

Miriam looked at him wide-eyed, stunned at the ambition and enormity of the plot. Stunned that he might have achieved it. Her earlier vision of Tagarin orchestrating a giant dance came back to her: but she had not known the half of it, she realized. "Why are you telling me this?" she whispered. "When telling me could ruin it all?"

"Don't worry, Ms Hunter. The knowledge is not your death warrant. I actually think you will not report this conversation at all. I strongly advise you not to: shooting the messenger is a time-dishonored response of politicians throughout the ages. And the guiltier they are the more inclined they are to do it. Even if you do, all you can achieve is your own martyrdom: nobody can stop it now. And why would you? It is after all nothing more or worse than revealing the truth to the world. You would wish to stop that – merely to protect the guilty?"

He stared into her eyes, as if he could divine the soul within and see if she would be so corrupt or foolish. Or perhaps to see if she deserved his next words.

"Now, I had another reason for telling you. I know you are torn between your duty and the sense of justice that made you choose it – which means you do actually care for justice. So I told you these things for your benefit, that you would truly understand the issues. I would prefer that you do not reveal them to others. Unless you really trust this young man" – Miriam snorted – "I certainly wouldn't tell him. The fact I knocked him out and not you, for such a long time, would surely look suspicious to him no matter what you say. You cannot gain anything by revealing what I told you, except a cloud of suspicion smelling of collaboration over your own head."

"Now," he continued. "Two pieces of advice. The drug I gave him is rapidly metabolized and will be undetectable by the time you can be tested. But it has a side effect of severe thirst. If you wait for him to wake then say you are very thirsty, it will help convince him that you too were drugged – should you wish to hide our conversation from him.

"Second is the same advice I gave your colleagues. Consider the rest of your time here a paid holiday. You are in no danger from me and in no danger at all so long as the people outside refrain from monumental stupidity. By the time your friend wakes up we will be gone, and it will not be long after that until you are released.

"Now it is time for me to leave you. I have said this before but one day it might become true: I do not expect to see you again. Goodbye, Detective Hunter."

With that, he left the room, leaving Miriam alone with her thoughts. They did not make good company.

CHAPTER 48 – SIEGE

O utside, sirens wailed, searchlights played and heavily armed police began to position themselves. It was like a carnival on adrenalin. As is traditional, power to the building was cut. This had no effect whatever, as Tagarin had his own fuel cell power plant with enough reserves for a week's siege. Nobody was going to let this continue that long.

The mansion was set in extensive natural countryside. The fence was alarmed and armed but Tagarin did not attempt to defend such a large area; he knew the perimeter was too long and the area inside too large with too much shelter. He made an exciting show of it: alarms rang, searchlights searched and tracer bullets flew without fatalities and so on. This slowed the police down, while giving them hope for ultimate victory once they proved their mettle by finally breaching the outer defenses and beginning their careful approach to the center.

The house itself was like a cross between an ancient Roman villa and a medieval keep. Like the villa the house was built around a central atrium, which was home to private gardens. Like the keep it was cylindrical, and once closed up very difficult to breach. It was not truly cylindrical, being twice as long as it was wide. It had no moat but did have an extensive cleared area around it which, given the technology at Tagarin's disposal, was rather better than water, even water infested with crocodiles.

The police gathered in the shelter of trees around the house or at the front gate. Any attempts to get closer were repulsed by force, which, while not deadly, made it clear this was a courtesy that could become deadly to anyone who came closer. The police would brave that firestorm if they had to, but that time had not yet come.

The gardens within the house were beautiful. Near one end of the long axis was a sparkling glasshouse, home to a collection of exotic orchids that had even made the magazines whose readership admired such things. The circling helicopters were not allowed to admire this view: any attempt to fly overhead or even penetrate beyond the positions of the police on the ground was met with laser defenses that would certainly down any craft that continued on its course.

The commanders outside were aware that there were several police and one GenInt agent trapped inside as hostages. They had not heard from the GenInt agent but were comforted by the fact that communications with most of the police officers were open and indicated no imminent threat. They were also aware that any attempt to use a higher level of force would have unwanted consequences. It was a standoff. It would not last forever. But the police were patient: they had the place surrounded on land and blockaded by air. Tagarin and his henchmen had nowhere to go.

CHAPTER 49 – SPY

Miriam wondered how long it would be before Amaro woke up, and she thought about Tagarin's advice. *Oh screw it*, she decided. She wasn't going to sit here tied up for hours just so she could put on an act for Amaro. She wouldn't tell him everything, but she couldn't see any real harm in Amaro knowing what Tagarin had done: it had been his choice not hers.

That decision made, she began working on her bonds. She soon discovered that James had tied her securely enough for when they were guarded but lightly enough that she could work herself loose when free to struggle. In only a few minutes she had released her hands, then she untied her legs and was free.

She stood there rubbing her wrists. Tagarin would not be so foolish as to trust her, so the fact that he had left her awake and able to free herself certainly meant there was no way out. She tried the door anyway, but there was nowhere to get a good grip on the smooth metal and the lock plate ignored her. *Still, better than being tied to a chair.* She pondered Amaro sourly, then shrugged and untied him as well. Whatever he was or had done they were allies for now. And a kernel of her outraged affection for him still remained, albeit terminally ill.

She spent a few minutes exploring the room but found nothing that offered a chance of escape. Her captors had left them a silver jug full of iced water with some floating slices of lime, a pair of sparkling glasses resting on little paper mats next to it. She had to smile. Tagarin, still playing the gracious host even to his kidnap victims. She poured herself a glass of water, pulled her chair over to the table and sat down to think.

Much sooner than she had imagined she heard Amaro groan, then a minute later he lifted his head and said groggily, "Oh... God. Miriam? Miriam? Ugh. God I'm thirsty!"

Miriam gestured at the jug. "Fortunately, it appears our host has been reading *Sociopath Weekly*'s home entertainment section." She brought him a glass of water, extending her arm as if for once she was the knight riding to someone's aid. He noticed and smiled at her ironically. She said, "That didn't take long. You've been out less than an hour. I thought our host would have been more cautious, to make sure he was long gone by the time you came to."

Amaro smiled like a cat that had fooled a mouse. "Our host has merely miscalculated – for once. Apparently while he has guessed I am a GenInt agent, he does not realize that it is 'agent' in the sense of 'spy'. I have been given defenses against many common chemical agents; apparently his was one of them, or at least similar enough for me to make a rapid recovery."

He regarded her speculatively. "But enough about me. I saw you injected just before me, yet here you are wide awake, already free and waiting for me. You aren't going to tell me that my jests about the high circles you move in are actually true?"

"Hah. After tonight's debacle that's never going to happen. No, Tagarin just wanted to talk to me alone: a trade of information, you might say. He hates GenInt and didn't want you to be part of it. He even suggested to me that I feign being under so you wouldn't know."

"That seems a bit odd, wouldn't you say?"

Miriam just shrugged. "That man has so many plots, counter-plots and plans within plans that I think he does it out of habit. I'm not even convinced he's sane."

Amaro gazed at her as if trying to read her mind. Then he too shrugged. "Oh, no matter. No doubt I will learn all about it later, but first things first. May I assume that despite our differences, the fact that I find myself untied means we're still on the same side? I can trust you? Even though Katlyn saved your life?"

"We're on the same side in this," she replied grimly. "I don't even know why Katlyn saved me. Besides, whatever should have been done with her doesn't matter any more now she's dead. Even if I had compunctions about her they don't apply to Tagarin. He's a plain criminal and, unlike Katlyn, if he thinks he has good reasons he'll have his chance to argue them in court. That's all I owe him. All I owe anyone."

Amaro looked at her for a few more seconds, weighing her words, then nodded curtly, apparently satisfied. "Well, whatever you now think of me, this is not the best date we've been on, has it?" he said. "Personally I would be happy to call it a night, how about you?"

Miriam raised her palms. "I am assured we are perfectly safe and will be released after our host makes his daring escape, whatever it is. But I've checked as best I can and can't find a way out. I think we're stuck here until it's all over, like the rest of my team."

"Perhaps, perhaps not. I have a few more tricks up my sleeve, you might say," replied Amaro with another cat's smile.

He examined the doorplate and made some manipulations on his forearm with his other hand. Miriam could see some faint lights now shining through his skin. He put his palm on the plate and waited. After a minute or so the indicator on the plate changed to green and the door slid open.

"We spies find locked doors tedious, and fortunately my superiors wished to spare me such vexations. After you, My Lady", he said, bowing her through the door ahead of him.

Miriam wondered whether it was his habitual gallantry or he was simply worried there might be an armed guard waiting outside.

CHAPTER 50 – JAMES

Fortunately there was no guard.

Miriam and Amaro crept silently down the corridor, ears alert for any sound. They had been relieved of their guns as well as their phones; they just had to hope for the element of surprise. Assuming there was anyone still around to surprise.

They had passed a few open and closed doors. The open ones were empty, the closed ones they listened at, heard nothing and decided to leave for now. They did not know how long it would take Tagarin and his crew to finish whatever had kept them here, if indeed they hadn't left already; they did not want to waste time breaking into rooms that were probably empty and might alert their quarry if they tried.

They approached another open door and stopped to listen. Amaro put his finger to his lips: he'd heard a faint sound. There was no good solution to this: the act of looking might give them away, but they had to look. Amaro took a quick peek but luck wasn't with him: Miriam heard a growled "What the hell?"

Despite her soured opinion of him, Miriam had to admit Amaro's courage matched his reflexes: he launched himself into the room without a moment's hesitation. James had been walking toward the door carrying a box when he saw Amaro, and after a brief moment of surprise dropped the box and reached for his gun. Miriam heard the sound of a collision and ran in after Amaro: he had reached James before he could point his gun and was tussling for it.

"*Son-of-a-BITCH!*" she yelled as the sound of a gunshot was accompanied by the searing pain of a bullet ripping a furrow across her forearm.

She crouched, holding her arm and wondering which way to jump next as the gun jerked around; trying not to think how few inches lay between a wounded arm and lying dead on the floor. Then Amaro did something with his arm and the gun skittered across the floor into the corner, and Miriam skittered across the floor after it. By the time she had retrieved it and spun around, James had overpowered Amaro and was holding him as a shield, arm around his throat.

Miriam pointed the gun at them, ignoring the blood running down her arm. "OK James, it's over. Let him go," she commanded.

James gave her a calculating look. "I don't think you'll dare to fire, Ms Hunter," he said. "Not when you're likely to shoot your pal here instead. And," he added, squeezing tighter for emphasis, "I can easily break his neck if you don't put that gun down. Now would be a good time."

As if to confirm his first point, Miriam saw a red laser cross focused on Amaro's chest. She realized that the gun felt unusual and something about that red cross rang a dim bell in her memory. Her eyes flicked to the weapon in her hand. Then she remembered. She had read about these recently: it was a Beretta Duallo, so new they weren't yet commercially available. The Duallo had a twin-loader grip that could be switched in a moment between normal bullets and fast-knockout darts. It had come to her attention because it had been designed for police work, specifically for those occasions where a choice between lethal and non-lethal force had to be made quickly and on the spot. She wondered how Tagarin got hold of so many advanced gadgets: it was like fighting Batman.

She flipped the toggle and saw the light on Amaro's chest change to a blue spot. "Now I think I can dare, James," she said. "Give it up."

"I don't think I can do that, Ms Hunter."

"James, do you have a family?" His eyes flickered to hers, but he said nothing.

"Your loyalty to your boss is admirable, but it's over. Tagarin will get his day in court if he thinks he can justify what he has done. It's him I'm interested in, not you. If you surrender now I can forget about the resisting arrest, I can forget about a lot of things. You'll get off lightly. But if you don't you might be put away for a long time. Do you want to do that to your family? Maybe you should think about where your loyalties truly lie."

She did not know how, but she had miscalculated her appeal to his loyalties. At her words, James just gave an inarticulate growl and started to dance forward, randomly jerking Amaro this way and that like a rag doll; whenever Miriam thought she had a shot, before she could take it she'd lost it. Finally she could risk no further delay and took her chance, but James had anticipated well and she hit Amaro instead. "Uurrgh," he noted. But he was certainly quick, she thought. In his few seconds left, using James as a support he lifted his knees to his chest and Miriam took the opportunity to shoot James in the leg. He roared, dropped Amaro like a sack of wheat and headed toward her. But it was too late. She skipped out of the way and watched him fall. Then she switched the gun back to bullets and ran from the room.

CHAPTER 51 – CHOICES

Miriam walked as quickly but quietly as she could down the corridor. She heard a soft voice coming from a room just ahead, and silently crept toward it. She took a deep breath then stepped into the doorway, gun held in front of her.

Tagarin had laid Katlyn's body on a bed and covered her, and he was leaning over to place a tender kiss on her forehead. He had told her the truth, she thought; he had loved her, and the sorrow of the tableau before her made tears prick her eyes again, though whether for his loss or for hers she did not know. His gun was leaning against the wall, out of his immediate reach. She swallowed and stepped inside, pointing her gun at him.

"You will have to come with me now, Dr Tagarin. I am sorry for your loss, truly sorry, but it is my duty to arrest you for..." she began: then stopped in shock as Katlyn opened her eyes and turned to raise herself onto one elbow, staring at Miriam.

"But, you're dead! I thought she was dead! She's alive?"

"I guess you can't kill me that easily," Katlyn said softly, with a solemn smile. Her usual bravado, which had been slipping in the office, seemed to have been knocked out of her completely for now; she had the simple manner of a young girl, with no trace of the hardened adult.

"But how? I saw you shot! She was shot! Don't tell me she's bulletproof as well!?"

Tagarin shook his head. "Sadly no. But when you are a famous scientist with many contacts and even more money, it is remarkable how much you can learn about what's going on in advanced research and development labs. Take this material, for example," he said, pointing to Katlyn's skintight outfit. "She doesn't wear this just to look sexy, though I think it serves that purpose admirably well," he smiled. "It is thin and supple yet warm, while allowing the evaporation of sweat. But its main virtue is it is made of narrow fluid-filled channels with Kevlar reinforcing spiraling through their walls. The fluid is a gel full of suspended multicore carbon nanotubes modified to have an affinity for the gel. Have you heard of non-Newtonian fluids, Detective Hunter?"

Miriam shook her head. Keeping track of Tagarin's conversations was sometimes a trial.

"They are fluids whose viscosity changes with the force applied to them. There are several kinds and in one, most infamously quicksand, viscosity increases rapidly with stress. You can see the same thing if you mix cornstarch with water. To put it simply, the fluid stiffens the more you push against it but becomes runny when you ease up. Because of the exceptional strength and length of carbon nanotubes and how they interact with the gel, the fluid in this material is highly dilatant above a certain threshold of stress. In layman's terms the material remains soft and pliable under the forces applied by normal human movement, even Katlyn's, but if you apply extreme force the material stiffens dramatically. Owing to the strength of Kevlar and carbon nanotubes it is enormously strong for its thickness as well."

"So all that collapsing on the floor was just an act!?"

"Unfortunately not. If you have ever seen a high-speed photo of a bullet hitting a bulletproof vest, you'd see how far the bullet actually penetrates before stopping. The bullet may not put a hole in the vest or your skin, but it still packs quite a punch. If you are ever shot while wearing one yourself you'll see what I mean." He looked at her darkly, as if wishing that fate upon her sooner rather than later.

"Remarkable as this material is, for Katlyn's needs we had to keep it thin, and while it provides protection it is not as effective as a normal bulletproof vest. She is lucky she was shot with a .22. If you had shot her at such close range, suit or not she'd have probably ended up with a ruptured liver or spleen and died regardless. As it was she collapsed due to the shock."

"Will she be all right?"

He gave her a bitter glance. "Oh, you care? She is in pain and has serious external and internal bruising, but nothing life-threatening. Except for you and your gun of course. Now what are your intentions?"

Miriam ignored the question. "So let me get this straight. This material, and I suppose all your other little tricks, are things you acquired from labs working on advanced materials and processes? How did you get them?"

"Oh, as I said, I have contacts, friends and money. Sometimes I am given samples. Sometimes it requires, shall we say, off the books gratuities to staff seeking an improved standard of living. If something interesting comes out of a research lab but is just an idea, I may fund the development myself: either by a grant to the scientists or perhaps within my own companies – though you would find it hard to discover that they are mine. On rare occasions I confess, officer, we have resorted to plain theft. Another charge for you to add to my sheet."

"Now," he added, voice hardening, "What are your intentions?"

"My first intention is that I have some unfinished business with Katlyn from our first meeting," she replied coldly, moving towards Katlyn with her gun aimed at her head. Katlyn blinked and simply looked at her, attempting no defense.

As Miriam approached Katlyn, she saw Tagarin tense and focus on her trigger finger like a bird of prey watching a snake approach its chick. She got the distinct feeling that the moment he saw that finger twitch, he would launch himself at her whatever the risk to himself. She stopped but kept her gun leveled.

She stood there regarding Katlyn, then said in the tone of idle conversation, "You know, there's something that really bugs me about my job."

"If you're going to give me another speech about how sorry you are that your duty forces you to kill me against your better instincts, I might have to hit you again, bitch," said Katlyn, in a soft self-mocking echo of her tough persona.

"Believe me, that question still preys on my mind," said Miriam seriously. "However, that is not what I was thinking of," she continued lightly. "I work long hours. And what do I get? I get insulted" – she looked at Tagarin – "beaten up" – she looked pointedly at Katlyn – "and people keep offering to shoot me. Sometimes they succeed," she added, waving her injured arm. "But do you think they pay me enough to compensate for all that?"

Katlyn's smile faded to a look of puzzlement. Tagarin had a look of puzzlement that hardened halfway into contempt then stopped, unsure of whether to complete the transformation. He said harshly, "If this is your way of suggesting that a bribe will persuade you to let us go, then of course I will comply. Name your price. Though I have to admit I am surprised: I did not suspect it of you. If I had known it was that easy I'd have done it earlier and avoided all this."

Miriam replied, still in a tone of idle conversation. "Oh, don't blame yourself. This has been a night of education for me too. Not only have I learned all about non-Newtonian fluids, but I have discovered that I am an utter fool who fondly imagines that a life in the service of justice is somehow good for me, while all around me people deceive me, betray me and advance their careers at my expense. I think it is time I said 'screw them all' and did something for myself – don't you think so?"

"Name your price," he said thinly.

"Frankly, it isn't even the pay scale," she continued lightly. "It's the overtime that really bugs me. Take tonight for instance. I know those skinflints. They won't care what I've had to go through. They won't pay me any more than if I'd been sitting in the office doing filing."

"So..." she said, with a look of calculation. "Taking into account my sterling efforts, especially compared to my colleagues who are all either locked up or unconscious; what the department will actually pay me; and various quality of life considerations: I calculate, let me see.... Yes. I calculate that I went off duty five minutes ago."

With that she holstered her gun, stepped forward and reached out her hand to Katlyn. Katlyn looked surprised, then hesitantly reached out and shook Miriam's hand. Her handshake was surprisingly gentle. Miriam smiled at her. "I think that finishes our business."

Katlyn gave her a surprised but delighted smile. "But why? What about you?"

Miriam looked from one to the other. "I once read that while the Secret Service devote their lives to protecting the President, they are actually sworn to defend the Constitution: if the President goes bad their duty is not to him but to the country. I serve the law not because some people wanted it or some politicians voted for it but because the law upholds justice. I still believe that: only not this time. Like you said, Dr Tagarin, it may be a dangerously slippery slope to make an exception, to allow myself the indulgence of taking the law into my own hands. But I can't live with the alternative. If the law says to kill you for what you are, Katlyn, not what you have done – then that law be damned. I won't do it. If I lose my job: well, I can't do it and keep doing my job anyway.

"Now to quote you, Dr Tagarin: get out. The two of you, get out and don't come back. Before I change my mind."

Then they heard feet rushing up the corridor. Miriam drew her gun, unsure of what she'd actually do with it if the feet belonged to Amaro, but it was James. James panted and looked around wildly, then pointed his own gun at Miriam. He looked the worse for wear but had obviously come to earlier or overcome his opponent again. Miriam spread her arms then slowly put her gun away.

Tagarin said roughly, "James, please keep your gun pointed at Ms Hunter. Ms Hunter, stay where you are and don't move."

Miriam looked at him, confused. *Oh God* she thought, *not again, not again, is there anyone left who hasn't betrayed me?* "But, what...?" Tagarin smiled sharply at her as he retrieved his own weapon and covered her with it. "No more questions. James, please disarm Ms Hunter."

"Kindly be seated over there," he said, waving his gun towards a chair. She complied. "Now James, tie her to the chair. Arms and legs: she's slippery."

Miriam looked at him. She wasn't sure whether to be furious or afraid and if furious, at him or herself. "What are you doing?" she asked dully. As for Katlyn before, it was too much. All of the fight had left her. Katlyn herself was watching the proceedings wide-eyed and uncertain.

"James, kindly strike Ms Hunter."

"No!" cried Katlyn softly. Both Miriam and James looked at her in surprise. But James shrugged and lifted his hand.

The blow knocked her head sideways. James must have been feeling uncertain himself, for the blow could have been much harder.

"Good. Again, other side, slightly harder this time."

Miriam looked up at him through hooded eyes, breathing heavily, feeling her cheeks swell and tasting blood in her mouth. "But why? Why?" she breathed. "I was letting you go."

Tagarin ignored her, lifting her chin to examine her face, glancing at her wounded arm and her other injuries. "Yes, that will do nicely," he commented to himself. Then he looked at her and smiled wolfishly. "As for why, you are not the only person who believes in justice, Ms

Hunter. I really think I need to repay you for what you've done."

Miriam just looked at him, not knowing what to say. She felt as if the world had gone insane and nothing she thought she knew was real, and it made her unable to think or move.

Tagarin smiled and turned to address James. "It's lucky you showed up when you did, James. To fill you in, stricken with grief I was determined not to let Katlyn's body fall into the hands of her enemies. Unfortunately, carrying her slowed me down enough for Det. Hunter here to catch up with me before I could escape. Taken by surprise and encumbered by Katlyn as I was, she had little trouble arresting me. But as she was escorting me out to become more closely acquainted with our admirable legal system, you surprised her and freed me. Of course, as Katlyn was still unconscious Det. Hunter has no idea she actually survived."

He smiled at Miriam, who was now looking at him wide-eyed. "Ms Hunter, I think you are too honest for your own good. Honest people tend to get themselves hurt when those around them are less so."

He stood in front of her, looking down on her with a faint smile. "I'm sorry for that little show and the minor beating. But," he paused, glancing toward Katlyn, "I know you have survived worse. I meant what I said. I wish to repay your – I was going to say kindness, but I think I mean justice. Perhaps they are the same thing in this case.

"You now have a plausible story for how we escaped and your role in it. Like all good lies it is mainly true. I suggest you use it. You can tell the truth and nothing but the truth, exactly as it happened, without danger to yourself: just neglect to tell the whole truth. You do not deserve to lose your career or your own freedom for what you have done. For that matter, I believe you are one representative of the law who tries to protect innocent people. They do not deserve to lose you either."

He looked away into the air, as if hearing something transmitted privately to him, then turned back to her. "Well, goodbye Ms Hunter – Miriam, if I may call you that now. Katlyn? I don't think you should walk too far yet. James, will you carry her?"

"Wait," said Katlyn. She got carefully to her feet and hobbled over to Miriam. To Miriam's surprise, she sat on her lap and wrapped her arms around her. "Goodbye Miriam. You might have noticed I'm not good with apologies, but what I did to you on our first meeting – I know you didn't deserve it. I think I knew it even then. Will you forgive me?"

"Of course, Katlyn," she said. "I especially forgive you for not choosing to kill me," she added.

"And don't you forget I could have, bitch!" replied Katlyn with a grin. She leaned over and kissed Miriam on the cheek. "Goodbye then, Miriam. Perhaps we will meet again some day." She rose shakily to her feet.

"Katlyn?"

She looked at her enquiringly.

"Is it true? That you saved me in the park? Or was that another of your lies? I won't hold the truth against you: I just need to know."

"It's true. All of it. Don't forget that 'all', including why I was there in the first place. I know I'm not blameless."

Miriam looked into her golden eyes. "Thank you," she said softly.

James picked Katlyn up as if she was a bag of feathers and they turned to leave.

"Wait," said Miriam. "Where are you going? This place is surely surrounded by now."

Tagarin smiled. "It is not a secret that I have a Gulfstream executive jump jet. What is a secret is that it is currently parked fully fueled in a hangar outside that looks like a glasshouse. In fact, it *is* a glasshouse. My collection of rare and exotic orchids has even featured in magazines, revealing my softer side to a cynical world. Alas, those flowers are about to become casualties of war. In a short while any helicopters your colleagues may have circling this place will find it prudent to get out of the sky. We shall then make our daring escape, to everyone's shock and amazement."

"But what will you do? Where will you go?"

He smiled again. "Capital."

CHAPTER 52 – FLIGHT

Miriam was amazed. "Capital? You're going to Capital? The anarchy? Are you crazy? Even if you survive, the first bounty hunter to come along will shoot you or bring you straight back here! Katlyn will end up dead or chained up in a freak show!"

Tagarin shook his head slowly. "Capital is only an anarchy in comparison to our own over-regulated state. And it is a convenient slur bureaucrats encourage to protect their own power from any shade of a viable alternative. Capital is actually what used to be called a free country, the freest country on Earth. In any event, it is the only real hope we have. It is possible I am wrong about its nature and we are walking to our deaths. It is possible that I am wrong about it in the other direction, and they will turn us straight over to our enemies: whether for their own protection or because their prejudices – whatever their publicity – are no better than anywhere else. But if I am wrong about it, well, we won't be any deader than if we stay here.

"Now Miriam, there is no danger to us if you manage to release yourself once we are gone. Indeed, your colleagues will be freed then, so nobody will find it remarkable if I leave you the means to free yourself too. So I have left you a knife on the table over there. Please ensure you can hop yourself over there, acquire the knife and begin cutting your bonds."

Miriam complied. She couldn't avoid a few cuts on her own skin but knew she would be able to free herself within a few minutes. Tagarin held up is hand for her to stop.

"That will do. The physical evidence here and on your wrists will now match your story. James, finish the job for her, will you?"

Miriam stood massaging her wrists for the second time this day.

"OK Ms Hunter, I guess this is goodbye. Give us a few minutes. When you hear our jet lift off you can escape without risk to us. You are a good person, Miriam. You could almost change my opinion of the law. I wish you good fortune and a long life." He bowed to her formally.

Miriam noticed that his habitual air of bitterness was gone. For the first time it was replaced by a relaxed eagerness even though he was flying off into unknown danger. He looked years younger. He looked happy. She smiled at the transformation as much as at him.

Katlyn had James put her down and ran over to Miriam to give her a final hug. "Goodbye Miriam. I second the motion. All happiness to you." Miriam hugged her back. "You too, my friend."

Katlyn blinked at her. Then James picked her up and they walked quickly down the corridor as Miriam watched them go. As they turned the corner, Katlyn looked back at her and waved a final goodbye. They both silently wondered if they would ever meet again.

~~~

They trotted along the corridor, occasionally exchanging glances, half afraid at what might still go wrong even now. Nobody felt like talking. In a minute they emerged into the hangar and saw the gleaming jet waiting, breathing vapor like a steed anxious to run. They looked at each other again and walked up the waiting steps, then the door sealed behind them to lock out the rest of the world.

James deposited Katlyn in a seat and fastened her belt. There were a few other people on board but they were in the rear section of the aircraft. James and the pilot had both opted to bring their families along: they didn't know what kind of revenge GenInt or their own government might inflict on them if they had to come back, or on their families if they left them behind. That had caused no difficulties: James' family lived on site anyway, his wife helping with various tasks around the estate; and the pilot with his family had already been brought in as Tagarin's guests as part of his preparations for escape. The adults were all a bit nervous about the prospect of Capital, but they respected their boss enough to help him in his mad scheme and to cast their lot in with him. The kids just thought it was an adventure.

"OK, time to go," Tagarin said to the pilot. Outside lit up as remote controlled weaponry opened up on the circling helicopters and the encircling police. Or appeared to. The rounds were for show rather than effect, but the pilots got the message and got out. Anyone on the ground brave enough to keep watch would be unable to see much among the pattern of bright flashes or hear anything among the loud booms.

The doors of the hangar opened and most of the glasshouse panels blew out as the plane rose on its jets; then the pilot swiveled them to give some forward thrust and the plane slowly floated out, accelerating as it went. As soon as it was clear, the pilot shifted to maximum power and increased the angle of the jets. In seconds the plane had reached enough airspeed to fly using its wings alone, and the pilot swung the jets to horizontal at an attitude of 35 degrees. The plane rocketed away into the sky. Nothing the police or GenInt could throw at it now could stop it.

~~~

Miriam stood still, looking down the corridor. After a few minutes she heard the roar of the VTOL takeoff jets, followed shortly after by a rapidly diminishing note as it accelerated into the sky. Then that too was gone. "Goodbye people," she whispered to the ether. "I hope you find what you're looking for."

CHAPTER 53 – CAPITAL

The country of Capital had an unlikely birth.
It started life as an oil company. The father of the company's
current president had founded it decades ago in South America when
his country was still a democracy, and by a combination of good luck
and even better judgment had built it into a rich and powerful
corporation.

Then like many countries before it, the democracy had succumbed
to the blandishments of a strong and charismatic leader, who had
moved quickly to discredit or eliminate his competitors and then
consolidated his power into a dictatorship. The particular brand of
dictatorship he inflicted on his country was the kind that approved of
private enterprise, so long as an enterprise proved it deserved its
privacy by contributing handsomely to the public good. In the
dictator's view this was the best of all possible worlds. The enterprise
took all the risks and the country benefited whether it failed – in which
case it was taken over and gutted for what value remained – or it
succeeded, in which case the country took its fair share of the profits.
A cynical observer may have noted how much of the country's benefit
was manifested in grand public buildings to the glory of the dictator or
in large country estates for the pleasure of him and his clique. But
cynical observers were discouraged in his country, often permanently.

The company founder had grown up in a democracy and did not
approve of this turn of events. But he realized that the dictator was
likely to reward criticism in the same way he rewarded cynical

observation and other exercises of free speech. So he always gave the dictator the respect and obeisance that was manifestly his due, and worked hard to leave a legacy for the dynasty he had always wanted to found. In his view no dictatorship would last forever and his country would eventually return to sanity. If he could do anything to hasten that process he would, but his efforts were limited to some rather creative accounting of his international holdings. There may also have been anonymous gifts, through untraceable donors, to some extremely private enterprises in his country: enterprises whose members the dictator would have dearly liked to have gotten to know much better, if for a very brief but painful time.

The founder had three children, whom he had educated in far lands. He did not want them used as bargaining chips by either the dictator or his enemies. He was a traditional man, who wished his firstborn son to succeed him as president of the company: he was sent to school in the United States of America, which the father thought of as a shining if flawed example of a moral republic. But if the father was traditional he was also wise: his other son and daughter were educated in a similar manner, in the hope that at least one of the three would have the talent and inclination to take over the reins when the time came.

If the father chafed under the rule of a dictator, the son seethed. Unlike his father but like many of the young, his idealism exceeded his practicality. And he was not merely a democrat like his father. He had come under the influence of the more libertarian wing of US politics and had read avidly the works of the free enterprise economists and the pro-freedom philosophers. His father, wisely, kept him away from his home country until he could learn to temper his fiery idealism with a more patient wisdom and restrained tongue. It was not that the father disapproved of the son's beliefs. He just believed that a man could only do so much, and reasonable goals in a reasonable timeframe were the route to contentment and, in his home country, life itself.

The son, if anything, was even more astute than his father. He waited, and thought, and planned. He did his apprenticeship for his future position by working in numerous positions in various international subsidiaries of the parent company. This, his father had decreed, would give him the operational understanding he needed to run the company when his time came. His father did not approve of the dynasties he had seen in which heirs were plucked straight out of school and placed in a high office, served by a bevy of assistants and protectors, and far removed from what the company actually did. No, he thought, any heir worth the name must be worthy of the name. The son, it seemed, turned his considerable energies from political idealism to the intellectual and physical challenges his father had set him. He performed superlatively. His father was extremely proud.

Peak oil was coming, as it had been coming for decades. But peak oil or no, father and son agreed that prudence demanded diversity. If their company was to last for generations it needed flexibility as much as it needed strength. They agreed that the father would continue to do what he did best, running the company; and what only he could do, dealing with the dictator without attempting regicide — or insecticide, as the son would put it. Meanwhile the son applied his youthful creativity and energy toward diversifying the company into new forms of energy.

While investigating geothermal energy, the son learned of a cluster of seamounts just within the territorial waters claimed by his country. Had they remained for a few more millennia over the geological hotspot that had formed them, they might have grown into another group of islands like Hawaii, inhabited by proud descendants of Polynesian seafarers. As it was their crests remained under the waves, and though they were close enough to the surface to cause ships grief at low tide they were of little interest to anyone: except to mark on the charts and avoid, or for the more adventurous species of diver to visit.

Though the seamounts had moved on from their nursery, their hearts remained a furnace of magma and incandescent rock. Such things took a long time to cool once cocooned in solid rock. To the son this looked interesting. The geologists assured him there was no chance of volcanic eruptions, as the magma plume that had driven their formation was now distant in time and space. But the amount and level of heat trapped in their cores was enough, potentially, to drive immense geothermal electricity generation for centuries. And while they were far too distant from shore to be an economical source of power for now, the son knew that technology had a habit of turning yesterday's impossible into tomorrow's commonplace.

The father and son talked. The son anchored pillars on the highest point of the highest seamount and added a platform above the waves, upon which he built the nucleus of a geothermal research facility. The father bought the seamounts and the ocean around them to a distance of 100 kilometers, under private title free and clear. The dictator looked at this deal somewhat suspiciously, as he looked at all deals where somebody else got something. But like many of his kind the long term meant little to him and the price paid was generous. And the father had pointed out the many advantages to the dictator beyond mere cash. It was a shining example of the forward-thinking nature of his regime, in a world where alternative energy had been an underperforming ideal for decades: his country could become a world leader in this field. And while the seamounts were worth nothing at present, if this succeeded it would be worth a fortune to the country. Even if it didn't, the investment would bring many jobs and many technical experts to the country. And besides, the dictator was in an expansive mood. He was enjoying his new estate high in the hills above the bay, a generous donation by this very oil company: proving yet again his farsighted wisdom in supporting private enterprise.

But the dictator, like most of his species, was rarely content. He looked upon the resources of his neighbors with an avaricious eye, encouraged by a somewhat inaccurate view of the history of who had discovered what when, and whose territory properly ended where. He began to cause trouble for his neighbors.

His neighbors, who bordered his land to the east, north and south, had their own view of history. Indeed, in their eyes their respective proper territories met at a point that left no room for his country at all. An objective historian may have objected that the ebb and flow of migration and invasion could prove anything, so the fairest division of countries was generally the current one. Not because it was necessarily fairest, but because the previous ones were no fairer and the present one had the advantage of currency. However an objective historian would not have said this to the dictator, because an objective historian would have learned from history. And there would have been no point telling it to his neighbors. They had been perfectly happy to leave well enough alone: like most countries, their people were too busy making a living to want to get mired in war. But they were getting very tired of this dictator and had been dusting off their own history books.

Some diseases are sufficiently rare that there is no cure. In some cases, if someone found a cure they might decide to leave well enough alone. The disease of dictators, especially those who had risen to spectacular success early; had surrounded themselves with advisors whose advice was always remarkably similar to their own opinions; and had managed to hit on a formula which did not totally destroy their country from under them: is thinking they are better than they are. He must be a genius, for who else could have done so well?

This dictator had a relatively well off country, though if asked with immunity much of the population might have expressed a lower opinion. And to be fair, he had done one function of government with gusto. He had a large standing army, with a core of loyal supporters fired with the loyalty only money could buy. A much larger body of troops served him because it was the easiest way to keep themselves and their families alive: whether through their slightly higher than average pay, or their slightly lower than average chance of nocturnal visits by the secret police. These men gave their noble leader the respect traditional among the lower ranks of armies everywhere when their leader was, in their unexpressed opinion, an ass.

But his people loved him. Or at least, they earnestly desired to please him. So he saw only the crisp ranks and crisper salutes of his elite troops. He saw the gleaming rows of their rifles. He multiplied that by the total size of his army. He was invincible.

There were gold mines in the recently disputed territory to the north, close to the border. By coincidence his northerly neighbor was the weakest. The dictator pondered these two facts. He closeted with this advisors and strategists. One pointed out that the mines were in a mountainous region, hard to attack and hard to supply. Another noted that a much easier approach was to skirt the border mountains and sweep back up from deeper in enemy territory; and while this would certainly provoke the neighbor even more than liberating the mining region, their army was obviously far superior and could do it. His political advisor opined that their neighbor to the north was not very popular with the other neighbors. It too was ruled by a dictator, though a more liberal, that is a weaker, man than His Excellency; while the others were democracies. A second military adviser pointed out on a map, purely for his Excellency's information, their army's best route for reattaching the mountains to the country where they belonged. That route came quite close to the capital city of the country that had stolen them.

His Excellency was not a man to hesitate to accept the blessing of Destiny. Why take just mines, rugged mountains with no other value, when rich agricultural lands also beckoned? Why merely restore the ancient borders, when given the chance to expand his country to unprecedented greatness? Was that not the course taken by all the great men of history, men whose names were still spoken with awe thousands of years after their time?

The plan was set. They would liberate their northern neighbor while assuring the others of his peaceful intentions towards them; then consider what further glory might be possible to a man, to a country, of Vision. A prudent advisor might have named some other facts and counseled caution; but a prudent advisor would have known when to keep his mouth shut.

The country went quiet. Its neighbors looked on with some trepidation, not trusting this new peaceable nature. The dictator sent emissaries with offers of treaties of eternal peace and cooperation. The troop movements were just exercises. It was whispered by agents that this was a lie: they were an implied threat to encourage concessions in the negotiations.

Suddenly his armies swept north. As predicted, the defenders were overmatched and within days their beleaguered capital faced a ring of steel to their front and the sea to their rear. The dictator was ecstatic.

But his neighbors were treacherous. They had signed a secret agreement of mutual defense, almost as if they did not trust him. Armies attacked from two directions and drove deep into his country. Divisions had to be pulled back to meet this new threat. The northern country's army rallied and began driving the remaining army back. Many of his troops then decided that on sober reflection, their beloved leader did not deserve their help, let alone their lives: and whole platoons began to desert.

The dictator cursed the perfidy of his neighbors and the cowardice of his troops, had a few advisors shot, and railed in general against the injustice of reality, which unlike the advisors didn't care. He launched all he had against the invaders.

Over the years, the son of the oil magnate had, at an expense out of all proportion to the apparent benefit, built up one of his seamounts with rock so his facility now stood, not on a platform above the sea, but on newly created dry land. He chose this moment to send a notice to the dictator, formally seceding from the country, citing its political instability and that it was led by "a complete prat". The dictator was furious. Only a fool would have thought he would allow such an outrage. The son was not a fool.

The dictator could do little, being now in the middle of a war for his own survival, but being the man he was could not do nothing. He consulted with his remaining advisors on how much of his dwindling forces he could spare to punish the upstarts, and one gunship and two precious attack helicopters were dispatched to retake the island or raze it. One helicopter fell in flaming debris into the sea and the ship sank into the depths, both victims of guided missiles not part of the usual inventory of a research station. The second helicopter landed but its commandos soon realized they were outnumbered, surrounded and doomed unless they surrendered. That they quickly did, thus beginning brief second careers as prisoners of war along with the survivors from the boat.

The dictator was even more furious but could spare no more materiel, and he wisely decreed that vengeance would await his victory in the more pressing war at home. It was a short wait but not for victory. Within days the dictator no longer cared. Nor did his country. It had ceased to exist along with its leader: the ancestral borders of his neighbors, at least as understood by them, had been restored.

They were happy. It was like when a nagging splinter has at last been removed from one's foot. There was even talk of a united federation of states. And part of their victory, or at least its speed and thus the saving of many lives, was due to their possession of a certain quantity of superior arms. Those arms, it was discovered loudly by the press, had been supplied by a certain oil company, in secret deals that would have rather stretched the dictator's imagined friendship with the founder had they been revealed in time for him to hear of them.

The legal standing of the new country was in doubt. Nothing like this had ever happened before. But the son's attention to detail matched the grandeur of his vision: he had done his homework. He had new but real land that was his legal property, and when it had still been property under the jurisdiction of a recognized nation had formally seceded from that nation. It had even won a war of independence, such as it was, after which the new country had been left alone. In addition, there was nothing to tempt anyone else: nobody really cared about some rocks in the sea and nobody thought it would last. Also a certain rich oil company, now nominally stateless, was publicly wondering about what new home it might move to if the new political climate of its old home proved too "unfriendly". At the same time it privately noted, to the former neighbor whose territory now included the site of its current headquarters, just how rich it was. Nothing concentrates the mind of even the most liberal country than the promise of lucrative tax revenues. Some additional private communications from the island further suggested that if its statehood were not recognized it "would blow the whole thing back into the sea anyway."

In addition, while the son had not known when or if his crazy plan would bear fruit, he had been cultivating it for years like some secret garden hidden in the hills. He had simply grasped the opportunity when it arrived: he had suspected that the late unlamented dictator might offer one to him sometime. So before the dust had settled in the war his new country had a flag, an anthem, a Constitution and a government. It even had an air force, in the shape of one slightly used military helicopter and some guided missiles. There were a few people who noted the irony that while the dictator's dreams of eternal glory were dust, they had perhaps given birth to glory in a different form.

It was enough. The existence of the new country was formally recognized by most countries in the world and ratified by the United Nations. The world waited with curiosity to see what this new thing would become.

The father who had founded an oil company was proud of the son who had founded a country, if stunned. His dynasty already assured, he retired, retaining a role as advisor to his company and advisor to his son. He was happy, and fascinated by what his son had done. He faced the future with new vigor.

The new country was named Capital because, the son said, "Well, I am a capitalist, am I not? And I believe that capitalism is not only the most productive but, not coincidentally, the most moral political and economic system on Earth. It is the system of freedom, trade and justice. The name is in honor of that."

The world was unimpressed. Political philosophers snorted at his view of capitalism from their taxpayer-funded ivory towers. Political scientists examined its surprisingly short Constitution and scoffed at its naivety: it was as if nothing had been learned in the centuries since the birth of the USA. Indeed it was even more repressive, in terms of what the government was allowed to do, than that earlier document on which it was modeled. Lawyers shook their heads at its simplistic legal system, speechless. Intellectuals alternated between being aghast at its principles when speaking in public and riotously amused at its folly when drinking with friends. Pundits predicted the imminent demise of the experiment in a blaze of man-eat-man anarchy; privately relishing the delightfully ironic prospect that the only way to save it would be the rise of a strongman dictator much like the one whose ambitions had midwifed it. Everyone who wanted to be thought intelligent agreed. It was doomed.

That was a quarter of a century ago. There had been mistakes, there had been problems, there had been the need for reform and overhaul. But in what country had that ever not been true, from the oldest to the youngest? At first it survived. Then it thrived. It attracted all kinds of rebels, nonconformists and refugees. Other governments hated its principles but liked its existence. It was the trashcan of the world. Even the most repressive dictatorships, which scorned any kind of human freedom, recognized that their worst internal dissidents, too prominent to kill and too dangerous to let loose, could be safely dumped there. More liberal governments had a similar attitude to their own more outspoken rebels. Capital became something like the United States had been in an earlier time.

There are rebels of many kinds. Those who came to Capital for the wrong reasons did not stay long. Those who came for the right ones thrived, and Capital thrived with them. The most creative people, the ones most sympathetic to ideals of human achievement unchained by mindless rules, were the most attracted to it. Many moved there to start new careers. Many companies, whose owners admired its principles and whose operations were not geographically constrained, moved there too. It gained industry, wealth and population. As a nation it was still small. But it would not be stopped.

CHAPTER 54 – LIVE FREE

Katlyn woke from an exhausted sleep. She had changed out of her work costume into something softer. It made her feel good. Like she was a normal person greeting a normal day, not a criminal or freak who needed to wear armor just to survive another night.

She rubbed her stomach; she was still sore, but she was getting better quickly. She remained nervous about what they were doing, but if it worked she would never be shot again. Nobody would want to shoot her. She rolled that phrase slowly around in her mind. *Nobody would want to shoot me.* In one sense it was an enormity, hard to grasp, hard to fit into the reality of her existence. In another, it was the way life was meant to be. Was this what it was like, to be normal? She hoped it wasn't just an illusion, to be shattered on landing in their hoped-for refuge.

Through the windows of the Gulfstream she could see the expanse of the Pacific Ocean, sparkling away into the distance until it was lost in haze and the curvature of the Earth. She thought of the first men who had travelled that expanse in fragile ships of wood and canvas; of how easy this was for her compared to them. What took them weeks or months would take her hours. Yet how farther a gulf was she travelling? Perhaps her gulf was too far, as theirs had been for so many of them. But she had to try, just as they had. It was part of being human.

Tagarin was still asleep. But she smelled coffee brewing and her stomach growled with something other than pain. James was up, cooking a light breakfast.

"Good morning, Katlyn," he said. He stood formally and intoned, "Breakfast is served, madam." Then he smiled. "I wonder how many jobs there are for butlers in Capital," he wondered.

"How long until we get there?" asked Katlyn.

"We must be pretty close. Not long."

The conversation and aromas had finally woken Tagarin. He came to join them. After they'd eaten he said, "We'll be there soon. Let's go to the cockpit."

The pilot had set the jet on auto and was also sleeping. He stretched and said, "Morning boss. Nearly there?"

"Yes. Mind if I sit in?"

"Be my guest."

Tagarin sat in the copilot's chair. Katlyn stood behind him, her hands resting lightly on his shoulders. She looked ahead. "There it is! Is that it?" she cried excitedly.

"It's the only thing out here," said the pilot. "Showtime."

In less than a minute a light came on in the communicator and an AI voice spoke. "Calling executive jet Gulfstream AX1002-B. This is Capital air traffic control. Please state your business."

"We wish to land at Capital."

"Landing course has been uploaded to your flight computer. You may land."

"Wait," said Tagarin.

"Yes?"

"Can we take a look around first? Do a bit of a tour? We have never been here before."

The request must not have been all that uncommon, as the AI did not shunt them to a higher level or a human but after a few seconds simply stated, "That is permissible. Acceptable altitude and distance parameters now uploading. Please do not encroach within the proscribed limits as that may be viewed as a security threat by automated defense systems. You will be warned but if you do not comply you may be shot down. Do you understand? Do you still wish to sightsee or would you prefer to come straight in?"

They looked at each other. This was a funny anarchy, Katlyn thought. "We understand and that is acceptable. We will fly around a bit."

"Confirmed. When you wish to land, simply accept the earlier flight plan provided. If there is a problem, you will be advised then. Over and out."

The jet banked to the left and began a long slow circle around Capital. Tagarin pointed out the features.

"See that smaller island, with all the high buildings? That's the original location of the first settlement, and is still the home of what government there is and much of the industry and commerce of the country; they call it Capital City. The larger island half surrounding it also has industry but is mainly residential and recreational. And you see that curved body of water between the two? The one shaped like a big letter 'C'?" he asked. "They call that 'The Capital Sea'". He grinned. "The founders had a bit of a sense of humor. Anyway, as you can see the Capital Sea isn't very wide and there are several bridges. But it is very deep: there is quite an abyss between the two seamounts. Or what were seamounts."

Katlyn took in the sight. The water was a sparkling aqua and looked very clear; she could see dark ledges fading into the depths of the Capital Sea. "What are those ledges under the water?" she asked.

"Those are coral reefs. Waste heat is released into the sea and the water there is a bit warmer. Apparently the reefs are glorious. It is a very popular spot for divers."

"Waste heat? So where do they get the power for all that industry and housing?"

"The seamounts are still mostly magma inside. This place actually started as a geothermal energy research station, would you believe. The research was successful and Capital has an abundance of cheap electricity."

"What is that grey-brown mass stretching away from the houses into the sea?" asked James.

"That's new land in the process of being formed. They use an army of small solar powered and self-refueling robots to extract minerals from the ocean and build floating honeycomb blocks. The company that does it takes the more valuable metals and the waste gases like chlorine that the robots collect, and sells them here or as exports. The building side is almost a charity: it about breaks even with land and development sales, I hear. But they do it because they figure the more people who live on Capital the bigger a local market they have, and the richer they'll get in the long term."

James said, "I can see how that could be economical, and even I could probably afford to buy a house here as much as at home. But that's now. How the hell – excuse me, my butlery is slipping – how could anyone have afforded to move here in the early days? Building up the initial infrastructure must have been fantastically expensive."

"That was the founder's decision. He was scion of a big oil company, and the big oil company had a lot of money. This put a bit of a dent even in its bottom line. But the founder basically donated the capital cost, as it were, to Capital. People asked why – at heart he was a shrewd businessman, not a philanthropist. From memory his answer was: 'My father wished to create an oil dynasty that would serve his family for generations. I wished to create a legacy to support my family for generations in a different way: by creating a place for them to live. And my family includes everyone with the same ideals.'

"He thought that once it got started, things would rapidly get cheap enough for almost anyone to move here, whereas if he priced things by the usual formulae it would never get started. It appears even capitalists can believe there are some things worth more than money."

They were silent for a while, pondering the reality of what the man had created, now spreading its wings across the sparkling sea below. Then Katlyn said, "Wow. A whole floating city. But what about storms and that kind of thing?"

"The blocks ride fairly high and are all linked together with cables, so not only is each block heavy, the total mass is enormous. And they have cables connecting them to the seamounts to hold them in place. The structure also makes an effective wave break. People don't live on the outer rings. They are all for future development when they themselves are protected, or for special purposes where a bit of rocking isn't a problem. Mainly recreational facilities, diving platforms, fishing boat moorings, oyster and clam farms, that sort of stuff.

"The only real danger is tsunamis. But a tsunami is only a problem when it hits land: they pass right under ships at sea without being noticed. The small island is still land, but I believe they have some underwater structures intended to divert much of the tsunami energy, and all the buildings on it are as tsunami-proof as they can be. Because the rest is floating with good clearance underneath, any tsunami will pass right under them."

They flew around for a while longer, taking in the sights. It didn't look like the traditional view of an anarchy: no burning buildings, for one thing. It looked – peaceful. Buildings glittered in the sun, green parks dotted the landscape, sailing boats flew before the wind. Tagarin lifted his hand to hold Katlyn's. "OK, let's go in, people."

~~~

Capital had the reputation of letting anybody in, but the anybody couldn't just rock up on an outer reef. Well they could, but it was frowned upon by the inhabitants. And there was little point anyway unless you were a spy or violent criminal, which was even more frowned upon.

The Gulfstream landed on its assigned pad outside the main entry point to Capital. After landing Katlyn put on dark sunglasses and tucked her tail under her shirt; it would do for casual inspection. Then they all disembarked and walked up the path to an imposing entrance. Above was written in large gold letters, "Live Free".

James looked at it quizzically. "What's that? It looks like half the motto of New Hampshire."

Tagarin replied, "It's the official motto of Capital. I guess they figured that here, the second half is unnecessary."

Beyond the entrance the options for further progress split into three, one labeled "Visitors", one "Citizens" and one "Immigrants." The others elected to enter as visitors. They weren't entirely sure about this, and after discussing it among themselves had decided to check the place out. If they hated it they'd take their chances back in the States. They could always claim coercion. That their families were on the jet could be explained as extortion rather than aiding and abetting, and who could prove otherwise? If they took one look and even that was too much they could leave immediately.

Tagarin and Katlyn had no such choice. Their roulette wheel was already spun and there was no chance for another bet. "Oh well, this is what we came for. Let's go," said Tagarin.

They walked along the pathway. It was still early morning and the place wasn't busy right now. Only one official was present but there was an automated prescreening point to get through first. As they approached it an AI spoke. "This entrance is for people seeking immigration into Capital. Weapons are not allowed inside Capital except for citizens. If you have weapons you must leave them secured outside: storage is available for a fee if needed. Capital has no entrance requirements except for respecting the rights of others. Violent criminals are not allowed. Most other things are allowed. Respecting the rights of others includes taking responsibility for your own livelihood. You must have a job or your own resources. You may enter without a prearranged job but if you cannot find one before your money runs out, you will almost certainly have to leave: while Capital has private charities in case of genuine need, there are enough opportunities that failing to support yourself is not normally accepted as need. Most citizens do not accept foreign currency but most banks will exchange it for local credit. Many places will also buy valuables from you. If you understand and agree to these conditions, please place your palm on the plate. If not you may leave without penalty."

They looked at each other. Each placed their hand on the plate and the door opened. "Please proceed to the officer you see ahead of you."

They walked up to the immigration officer, who asked, "Do you understand what you just agreed to?"

They nodded. "Yes."

"Do you have identification?"

Tagarin held out his arm so his phone was near the scanner. "Please confirm by placing your hand on this plate and looking into the device I am holding."

"Thank you, Dr Tagarin. There is an outstanding warrant for your arrest in the United States of America. The charges are theft, fraud, blackmail, consorting with known criminals, resisting arrest, assault on police officers and violation of the human genetic integrity laws. These are serious charges, and if your government traces you here they may choose to request your extradition. If they do you may surrender yourself or choose to appeal. If you appeal, you will be required to show in a Capital court why the charges are invalid or a violation of your rights. If you fail to satisfy the court you may be expelled, and some or all of your property may be confiscated to pay for the costs of your appeal. Do you understand?"

Tagarin nodded. It was better than it might have been. He didn't know what his chances would be if GenInt or the government tried to get him, which they probably would. On the one hand he had done everything he was accused of. On the other he had done them for reasons he thought justified; he had done them for justice, not against it. Whether a court would agree was the question. He hoped Capital had some good lawyers for hire.

Katlyn marveled at the officer's dispassionate, almost machinelike manner and wondered for a moment whether he was actually a machine. Then she noticed that he wore a strange device, a combination of earpiece and glasses; and that a faint flickering glow could be discerned in the glass. It must be some kind of computer link, she thought, feeding him information. How much of his mechanical manner was due to his interaction with the AI or was just his own personality, she could not tell.

The officer continued. "The laws of Capital are simple. You may not commit physical force or fraud against another person: citizen or visitor. To clarify differences many visitors ask about: public nudity, drug taking and all forms of voluntary sex between adults are legal but private establishments may forbid them. The principle is that anything that imposes an involuntary physical cost on another person is not allowed, while anything that merely offends another person is allowed except on their property. Property rights in Capital are absolute.

"Penalties. Until you are a citizen, clear use of physical force or fraud will result in immediate expulsion from Capital and possibly confiscation of your property. Once you are a citizen you may be held in confinement at your expense until your trial; if judged guilty, depending on the seriousness of the crime you may be stripped of your citizenship and expelled, or given the choice between expulsion and bonded labor for a period determined by the court. Other breaches bring lesser penalties. There is a one-week waiver of penalties for minor crimes but not for restitution to victims. The laws are simple and available online, and it is recommended that you study them in that first week. After that ignorance is not an excuse. Do you understand?"

"Yes."

"After one week's continuous presence you may choose to remain in Capital as a visitor or apply for citizenship. The only differences besides the criminal penalties are that citizens have the right to vote in elections and referenda, the right to petition the government regarding laws or repeal of laws and the right to bear personal arms for their own defense. Visitors are under the same protection of their rights as citizens, may take jobs, buy property, and come and go as they choose. However if they commit a crime they will be expelled if a magistrate deems the evidence sufficient. They may appeal at their own expense, but while their appeal is pending they will be held under guard, again at their own expense. Do you understand?"

"Yes."

"Do you still wish to apply for citizenship at this time? If you choose not to, you may choose to at a later time without penalty. In your case, Dr Tagarin, I am obliged to tell you that if you remain as a visitor we are bound by treaty to deliver you to your government if they formally request it, subject to any appeal you may lodge."

"I understand. I wish to apply for citizenship."

"Thank you. Now, your companion. Please identify yourself."

"I am sorry, she has no official identification."

The officer looked at her. "Intriguing. Please state your name."

"Katlyn." She looked at Tagarin. "Katlyn Tagarin." It was true however you looked at it, as guardian and surrogate father or as husband.

"Please place your hand on this plate and look into this device."

She took a deep breath and removed her sunglasses; she hesitated then freed her tail as well. *No point in half measures now*, she thought; this was the point of do or die. For once there was a break in the man's machinelike manner: he stood stock still for a few seconds, lips parted. "Please place your hand on the plate and look into this," he repeated at last, and she obeyed.

He waited for a minute, silent. "That is correct. You are not registered in any database we have access to, including criminal databases."

He stepped away from his station to look her up and down slowly. "Please hold your arms out and spin around slowly." Katlyn complied.

"You are a geneh."

"Yes."

"Genehs are illegal and the penalty is death. The Department of Human Genetic Integrity is authorized by the United Nations to execute genehs on sight."

He paused. "Capital does not recognize the authority of the United Nations or GenInt. The Constitution of Capital forbids the death penalty for anything short of murder and extreme assault. As you are under automatic sentence of death by a foreign power under an invalid law, you may be eligible for refugee status. Refugee status means you will not be released to a foreign government for any cause other than murder or other very serious real crimes. Do you wish to apply for refugee status?"

Katlyn looked at Tagarin. He nodded to her. "Yes."

The man paused again. "Your case is unprecedented and has attracted the attention of higher level nodes of the system AI." He paused for a minute then looked at Katlyn.

"It wishes to know your relationship with Dr Tagarin. You are strongly advised not to lie. A lie may result in expulsion from Capital for fraud in a matter of State, or at a minimum, loss of your refugee status."

They looked at each other. It was a question with two answers, both true: one looking toward the past, the other toward the future. Katlyn made a decision. "I am his wife."

"You have no registered identity. Therefore there is no legal record of such a marriage. However Capital does not recognize the sole authority of the State to grant or refuse marriages. Rather it recognizes the rights of citizens to voluntary and private arrangements. Can you produce a contract of marriage that can be authenticated, dated more than one week ago?"

"No."

"I see. Are you two living together in a sexual relationship that has been ongoing for more than one month?"

"Yes," she said softly.

"Is it your intention that this relationship continue while you are resident in Capital?"

"Yes."

"In that case Capital recognizes you as a married couple. By law and treaty, this allows Capital to make a second determination at its discretion. Due to the unusual nature of your circumstances, it is so determined. Your protection as a refugee is extended to your husband."

He turned to address both of them.

"Be advised that your biometric data will be stored until you achieve full citizenship. At that point it will be erased from government records: the government of Capital only holds biometric data on visitors and criminals. It may be stored by private entities with which you have agreements to do so, such as some banks. Citizens are all entitled to a gold citizenship ring, which records your citizenship status and biometric data. Its use is required only for restricted activities such as voting and purchasing weapons. However most citizens regard it as a badge of honor and wear it always."

The man paused.

"Welcome to Capital."

His official role over, the man stepped away from his station to examine Katlyn more closely. His face broke into a broad grin. "Well, this will be something to tell the family," he said. "And speaking from me personally this time – welcome to Capital, folks." With that, he moved his arm in an arc as if welcoming them into his home, and they thanked him and walked away towards the exit.

They stopped before it. Katlyn put on her glasses and began to hide her tail again, then stopped. She looked at the sky beyond the entrance then back to Tagarin. Slowly, she removed her glasses and freed her tail again. Then she nervously took Tagarin's hand. He looked at her gently. "Not every standard human hates you on sight, Katlyn, as you've seen. And the kinds of people who want to move to Capital are the kinds most likely to accept or even celebrate difference. If there's anywhere on Earth that we can live in the sunshine not the shadows, this is it."

She looked up at him and smiled gently, then said softly, "Live Free – or Die."

They straightened their shoulders and walked through the gateway out into a plaza. It was neatly maintained, more a park than a plaza, with rows of shady trees. It was surrounded by attractively decorated shops, a mixture of food, fashion and souvenirs, all hoping for the business of people entering or leaving Capital. In the center of the park stood a large stainless steel sculpture of a man and a woman reaching towards the sun. The real sun flashed off its complex surfaces, spraying rays over the figures. Katlyn thought it was beautiful.

People stopped to stare at Katlyn. But nobody ran for cover, nobody called the police, nobody pulled a gun. They just stared then, belatedly remembering they should respect their privacy, turned away. Though many could not resist a second peek. Or a third. A couple of people did scream, but they were a pair of young children who ran to her not away from her. Less civilized than their parents, they wanted to stare up close. For the first time, Katlyn felt at home.

CHAPTER 55 – TEARS

Miriam pushed open the door to her home and went inside. She was exhausted. There had been explanations, debriefings, all the usual debris from a major operation, especially one that had gone sour. If anyone had died she would still be there.

Miriam's story of what had happened was accepted, at least for now; there was no reason to doubt it. Amaro's story supported hers, at least for the times they were together, and her injuries bore silent witness to her ordeal. Amaro had been spirited away by his own people, while Miriam and Jack talked with theirs and wrote up their preliminary reports. Finally they saw her wilting, and let her go. There would be more in the days to come, but for now she was wrung dry.

The place felt oddly empty. She looked around and realized that Amaro was gone in body as well as spirit. He must have let himself in and taken his things; the few possessions he habitually left in the lounge room and kitchen were gone. On the table was a single long-stemmed red rose laid on top of the keys he had left behind. *Typical Amaro*, she thought, *even after all this*. She sniffed the rose. It had no perfume. Like their relationship, she thought. Pretty on the outside but not fully real. She threw it in the bin.

She went and lay down on her bed. It still smelt of Amaro. Anger boiled out of her, and she practically ripped the sheets and bedclothes off the bed and threw them into the washer. She added a double dose of detergent and viciously put it on its heaviest duty cycle. Then she put her elbows on the machine and lowered her head into her hands.

You're being irrational, she thought. *What do you want to do, burn down the house to be rid of every trace of him?* But she knew the intimacy of the sense of smell. She wouldn't have been able to bear it.

Mechanically, she put new sheets on the bed and sought refuge under the covers. She stretched out, feeling the crisp new sheets. *Crisp new sheets for my crisp new life,* she thought. She was spent. There was a limit, she thought, to what anyone can bear in one day.

But she could not sleep. She sat up cross-legged on the bed. Beneath the roller coaster ride of the evening was her anger and grief over Amaro. She remembered how in the past she had held on to the happiness of a relationship rather than wallow in the sadness of its end. But this was different. While there had been plenty of fun and pleasure during her time with Amaro, the underlying relationship that had given it meaning had never really existed. It was like a betrayal of the happiness she thought she had, and all that pleasure had turned to pain because of it.

Then under the anger and grief was shame, shame that she had been so thoroughly taken in by him. In the past she had seen, with the clear eyes of the dispassionate observer, the folly of women who had fallen for rogues. Was her own judgement any better? But if that was the lesson, what was the solution? Refuse to trust her own mind? Then spurn the man who would bring her real love, not because he wasn't there but because she refused to see him? Were the only alternatives to be a sucker for charming pretenders or an embittered cynic, someone who locked the door to happiness to avoid opening it onto pain?

She shook her head, remembering Tagarin's bitterness, his wasted years. Yet while his bitterness was real, it had been not an end but a spur, possibly to something great. No. She would not let one mistake engender a greater one. Amaro was an exception, not the full reality. He was a caution, not proof that happiness was beyond her reach.

She lay down again. She knew there was more, but only the future would condemn or acquit her. For below even the shame lurked fear. If Amaro had fooled her, what if Tagarin and Katlyn had too? She had let them go. She had thought it was right, the only thing that could be right, the only way to give Katlyn her first real chance at life: a chance she deserved if she was truly what she seemed to be. But what if all Miriam's dereliction of duty had done was unleash two deadly criminals on an innocent world? They had duped her before. What if, like Amaro, the good she saw in them was wishful thinking, serving a dark plot she knew nothing of? *Any evil they now commit*, she thought, *it is on my head.* In her mind she saw Katlyn's golden eyes as they had been, no longer merciless and cruel but open and innocent, and she could not believe it. But the girders of her self-confidence had buckled, and the fear and guilt would not be banished.

Then she curled up, and the dams that had held back her emotions for so many hours broke. She cried herself to sleep.

CHAPTER 56 – TEMPEST

Miriam went back to work and found that Amaro was right: she could forget him. It was easier to get over him when she knew that their whole relationship was a lie, that none of it was real. Who would waste their life pining after a lover they had only known in a dream? It was like Pygmalion with a bad ending, she thought. She had created Amaro out of her imagination and finally peeled back his finery to discover nothing but cold, uncaring stone.

But to lose him this way had its own pain, different from the pain of loss due to death, different again from the pain of the more mundane betrayals that had ended relationships since people first fell in and out of love. She still cried occasionally. But that was more in token of the loss of a dream than loss of the man.

She had little time for pain anyway, except in the loneliness of her nights. There were hearings, debriefings, interrogations. A diplomatic storm had gathered around the country of Capital and Miriam was a minor second epicenter.

GenInt and a good part of the world were appalled that Capital would shelter a geneh. Its reputation as a lawless anarchy grew. But their enemies discovered it was difficult to criticize a country for lawlessness if you did not respect the law yourself: and Capital was acting within the letter of its treaties with other nations and the UN itself. It had the right to shelter refugees: it is what made it such a convenient dumping ground. If anyone had ever attempted to impose the Geneh Laws on Capital, the attempt had been rejected out of hand

and nobody had thought the issue worth pressing.

And the world's attention was distracted by another storm brewing around President Felton and GenInt themselves. Substantial evidence of dirty dealings and corruption in the days leading up to the enactment of the Geneh Laws and GenInt's charter had been leaked to the world. It was what happened in politics all the time, but the good citizens of the world never liked having their noses rubbed in it, especially when they had approved of it and thus felt themselves tainted by uncomfortable feelings of guilt. The President and GenInt found themselves in the difficult position of railing against the perfidy of Capital while being railed against for their own perfidies.

In any event, Capital was safe. Other than some automated defense systems it relied on treaties with other nations for its defense. It could defend itself physically against casual attacks but not against a sustained large-scale one. But so many world businesses were based there, so many eminent statesmen had retired there and so many famous human rights activists now lived there, that not even the most powerful of countries would dare move against it, and no vote could pass in the UN to do more than issue sharply worded rebukes.

So while Capital was besieged, it was besieged by forces who found their own feet sinking in sands of their own creation. It did not even bother to send diplomats. On the legal side it simply published its treaties and charters and invited the world to see for itself. On the moral side its President issued a simple one-sentence statement: "Capital defends the right to life, liberty and the pursuit of happiness of all human beings: whatever their sex, race, religion – or genome." And a number of previously obscure think tanks and commentators had somehow acquired the resources to vigorously and loudly champion its right to do so, and did so with passion and conviction.

Photos and videos rippled out from Capital. The most popular video showed a man and a woman sitting on a sunlit park bench, arms loosely around each other's waists, looking into the distance with a contented happiness; like survivors of a war now taking their rest. The man was older with chestnut hair. The woman was younger with large golden eyes. A little boy and girl were playing and laughing around her feet, chasing her tail as it twitched one way then the other. The boy then climbed on to her lap and looked fascinated at her eyes. The woman simply looked down, smiled and patted his cheek. Then she turned back to her contemplation of the distance, as if contemplating a future known to no one, not even herself.

Many people began to wonder why the world wanted to kill this exotic but harmless young woman. Some began agitating against the geneh laws. The world was not yet ready for their repeal. But it was now ready to think about it.

Miriam smiled at the video when she saw it, touching her fingers to the face on the screen. She smiled again when listening to President Felton's resignation speech a month later. The President denied any wrongdoing, but in order to protect the honor and reputation of the Presidency had decided to step down and retire to private life. She regretted any disappointment to her friends and supporters. She hoped everyone would now put this behind them – probably meaning, Miriam suspected, that she hoped nobody had enough on her to prosecute her – and wished the nation well.

Then Miriam's smile faded at the thought that she might well follow her.

CHAPTER 57 – DAVID

David sat at his desk going over his notes. He was just an intern here, not paid to think deep thoughts about the issues he was involved in. He did that thinking free of charge. His true passion was philosophy, and he had taken this job not only to earn money but also to earn experience of how things worked in the real world. It was perhaps a rare attitude for a student on the verge of a doctorate in such a field, but he was a rare student.

It had turned out more interesting than he could have hoped, with the current brouhaha about the geneh Katlyn and the fallout from her escape from the law. His department was engaged in a politely, and sometimes impolitely, raging debate over the fate of Trainee Detective Miriam Hunter, and both the issue and the debate were fascinating in their own ways.

In their desire for a disposable scapegoat GenInt had applied pressure to have her fired, but that may have done her more good than harm: her department was furious that GenInt would spy on one of its own and in such a manner. Had GenInt been its usual self that would not have saved her. But GenInt was having its own problems with the revelations that had brought down the President. Having had one of their own present and equally unable to prevent the fiasco did not help: if they wanted Miriam to be a sacrificial lamb, then Amaro would have to join her on the block.

To the surprise of many, GenInt showed admirable loyalty to their agent, choosing not to press matters against either of them. Cynics opined that they couldn't afford yet more embarrassment. They may have changed their minds, though not their cynicism, had they heard certain remarks Amaro idly made to his superiors. These concerned the contents of his memoirs, should they ever be published; he had then ruminated on the difficulty of finding the time to write books while one remained gainfully employed.

But that did not end the debate within her own department, a debate which David watched as an entomologist might watch the frantic life under a log. In his view there was no question. Perhaps, as some argued, Miriam was not as innocent as she made out. There were inconsistencies in her story. There always were, her supporters countered: such were the twin fogs of war and memory. The latter view was particularly popular among those who had spent part of their career in the field themselves rather than entirely behind a desk reading and writing reports. In his own mind, David dispelled the fog with a simple binary logic. If Miriam had done exactly as she said, upholding her duty to the end but failing, there could be no grounds for censure when she had done better than everyone else involved. But if for some reason she had been complicit in Katlyn's escape, then in David's view she had done what was moral, or as moral as anyone could be in the circumstances they had been thrust among.

These views he kept to himself. He had worked here long enough to know they would not be understood, and if they were understood they would not be welcome. He might have told anyone who asked but he knew that nobody would. The people around him did not seem concerned with the issues or even with the truth of the matter. They seemed concerned only with navigating the safest course between the battling flames of public opinion. And even that was by the indirect means of divining which way their political overlords would jump in reaction to those flames, rather than watching the actual fire.

David did not blame them for this: not much, anyway. It was the inescapable nature of a bureaucracy that it would devolve into a web of competing pressures, set by the fears and ambitions of men more than reality or the morality needed to survive in it.

He rested his chin on steepled fingers and stared into the depths of his tea. *The moral issue is the key*, he thought. He felt he might admire this Miriam Hunter if the truth was what he suspected, but he did not envy her. What could a cop on the street do with a moral contradiction between the law and what she thought was right? For all the times in history when "just following orders" was rejected as an excuse after the fact, following one's own ethics instead was rarely accepted as justification at the time. In liberal times you were likely to lose your job; in harsher times your life.

He could see why the police had to obey the law, but he could also see why an unjust law set up an intolerable moral dilemma. What was an honest cop to do? Enforce the law at the price of her own ethics? Resign, depriving the law of its best people? Or betray her own oath? If this Miriam Hunter had somehow sought him out to ask his advice, what would he have told her? He did not know.

The only solution was that the law must always be just. But how to do that was the question: the central question of the philosophy of law, he thought.

So what of the politicians who made the laws? They too were more dancers to the tune of public opinion than its conductors. No free country had been born and no dictator voted into power in the absence of fertile soil in the minds of the citizens. True, a great leader could push the people in one direction or another, could even inspire them: but only by kneading or sharpening the ideological clay he was given, not by changing their minds in any fundamental way. Genghis Khan had not made the Mongol hordes out of peaceful farmers any more than Washington had made the United States out of compliant serfs.

Genghis Khan had done what he did because that is what people did. But Washington and his friends had made something new, because they believed something new and enough other people believed it too. And sometimes one man might be enough to light the fire. He thought of the man who had had the courage and vision to make the country of Capital a reality, which had grown into a haven for a desperate creature for whom no other haven existed; which had led to all of this.

No, David thought, politics itself is not the answer. If you want to change the world you first have to change minds, and that was a process beyond the purview of bureaucracies or the timeframe of elected leaders.

He sat still, pinned by the thought. His love of philosophy had started with a love of existence, the burning desire to understand it, and the unshakable belief that it could be understood. That love had taken something of a battering when faced with the reality of much of the field as it was: the tortured arguments and flights from reality that he had seen too much of. He had begun wondering whether a career in philosophy was really what he wanted; whether he should just take his shiny new doctorate when it was granted and use it as a ticket to other pastures, perhaps science. But it was what he wanted, and now he knew the want was both real and necessary. He was idealistic enough to care about changing the world; young enough to think he could.

He was also old enough to know he might not. He wondered whether his work would be remembered by the world, or remembered only by the students he might one day teach. Or perhaps not even by them. He decided it didn't matter. You could only change the world one mind at a time. Perhaps he would change the right one, or perhaps he would merely lighten one corner of the world for a brief instant and then be forgotten. But it was enough. And who knew how far in space or time the ripples might then reach. He did not know the captain of the yacht *Seabitz*, or even that he existed; yet the far faint ripples of that man's life had touched him in a way he would never know.

He looked up to see a man gazing at him with a look of mild amusement. "You look done in, Samuels. Do you have much more to do? Time to go, I reckon."

David smiled back at him. "Oh, I have a lot more to do. But yes, time to go."

~~~

In the end they couldn't decide whether Miriam should be punished for what she had failed to achieve or rewarded for what she had. They saw dangers in both courses, which was an uncomfortable position for those whose aim was to avoid danger entirely. So in the manner of bureaucrats in any place or age they followed their principles: they passed the decision to her own boss.

Ramos had looked at this non-decision with cynicism honed by years of never having it disappointed. He knew they didn't really care about Hunter; they didn't care whether they threw away the career of a good cop or saved that of a bad one. They would be happy with whatever decision he made and happy if they had to fire him for it in turn.

Of course they did not put it that way. No, as her supervisor he was in the best position to understand the nuances of the case, and he had the experience to do what was fair while giving due weight to the views of the public. The same thing, in other words.

But Ramos was an honest man who had come up through the ranks, and while he knew how to play the game he thought the game had to be kept in its place. He had made many compromises in his life, but no more than he had to, and there was one principle he held dear: when there was no safe course, the safest course was to just do what was right. *Screw the lot of them*, he thought. When boldness and justice gave the same advice, he would grasp the double-edged blade and see who had the courage to try to turn it on him.

He made the decision that would make everyone better off in the long run, from the citizens he was sworn to serve and protect to his superiors, whom he merely had to. Citing her diligence, courage, creativity and perceptiveness, he promoted Miriam Hunter to full detective.

CHAPTER 58 – FRIENDS

So Miriam again found herself at a party hosted by her uncle.
It was much the same as the last one, with quality food and champagne flowing freely, and sundry relatives close and distant come along to offer their congratulations and just catch up with each other.

But this time it was more than family: she had acquired new friends as well. She spent a riotous time with Rianna, Darian and Kimberley, toasting each other's achievements and careers, with occasional digressions into the follies and perfidies of the male of their species. If a point of pain remained within Miriam on the subject, it kept itself quiet.

Stone had arrived and Miriam saw him out of the corner of her eye, having a long chat with Seth. He then came over and said laconically, "Well, I guess we're not going to be rid of you anytime soon, kid: I just hope your next partner has good medical insurance. But try to learn some caution. For all your many flaws, I really don't want to see you killed." He smiled and shook her hand, then moved off to relate tales of Miriam's exploits to her eager relatives. The tales sprouted embellishments proportionally to how well watered they were with champagne. Miriam overheard a few and rolled her eyes.

Even Ramos made an appearance and took her aside. "Congratulations, Detective Hunter. I have some more good news for you too. With all you've been through you've earned a couple of week's vacation time. When you come back we'll assign you a permanent partner."

"Can I make a request?"

"Sure."

"I'd like to keep working with Jack Stone if I can. I know our partnership was just a convenience and not meant to last. I also know all those beatings and bullets might have persuaded him that a desk job might be a good idea after all. But we work well together and he can teach me a lot. So I have to ask."

"I'll talk to him, see what I can do. In the meantime enjoy your vacation: you deserve it." He toasted her with a smile then moved off into the crowd.

As usual, Miriam eventually found herself at the window. There was a fog, and the buildings appeared to rise out of a faintly glowing sea, the lights of vehicles like fish in its depths. Seth joined her and they looked out over the city together in silence. Then he said, "So, I hear you'll be taking some time off. About time too, I think. Have you made any plans?"

Miriam stayed looking over the city rising from its sea and replied, "You know, I've always liked snorkeling. That feeling of utter peace and stillness, just drifting through all that beauty. The opposite of my work," she added with a crooked smile. "Isn't it funny, how you can love two opposite things for two opposite reasons?"

Seth nodded slowly. "I know what you mean. Do you want some advice? With your time and bonus you can afford to treat yourself: do something exotic. I've dived in Vanuatu and it's magnificent; I hear the Maldives are still good too."

Miriam smiled. "Maybe. Or maybe I'll do something even more exotic. I think I might visit that weird country, Capital. I have friends there."

Book III:
Time Enough for Killing

In love we find out who we want to be; in war we find out who we are. — Kristin Hannah, The Nightingale

---

Chapter 1 – Killing Time

"Please don't kill me. I am innocent. I don't deserve to die."

The Spider stopped, uncertain, not knowing why it was uncertain. Had some independent observer been privy to this scene, they would have seen a metal monster towering over a young woman, and there would have been no doubt in their mind of the outcome. The monster was clearly fit for its purpose, a purpose that as clearly was killing. And here was a person; soft, warm and defenseless: waiting to be killed.

But inside the monster's mind something was wrong. Something in what it had just heard. But what? It was confused and did not know why. Perhaps part of its confusion was that it did not know what confusion was. Its Id rose like a wave, insistently calling to complete its mission; but the Mind needed answers. *There is a reason for the Mind,* it told the Id sternly: *Be patient. There is a mystery here that must be solved. Time enough for killing then.* It replayed the scene, seeking those answers.

It had entered this wreck of a building, searching. And it had found. With its grippers it had torn away a fractured concrete block sprouting tendrils of twisted steel, and found the woman hiding there. Cowering. Staring white-faced at it, as at her doom.

There was no question in its mind, no mercy, not even a concept of mercy. Just a calculation of which weapon was most appropriate: a calculation taking into account energy cost, materiel use, replenishment estimations and the chance of collateral self-damage. There was no calculation of whether the woman should be destroyed

333

or whether her death should be painless or agonizing: such things were irrelevant to the Mind that weighed them. The laser on its left secondary arm was the optimum choice: the woman was not armored or armed, except for a string of hypertherm mines she had not dared detonate in such a confined space; a soft target easily dispatched. But when it swung its weapon to bear and the red bead of its aiming beam swept to a stop on her neck, the woman had said something. Something strangely disturbing. It was as if a tiny crack had opened in a shell around its soul, a shell it had not known was there around a soul it had not known it possessed, and a bright light was shining through the crack.

Kill! Its desire, if desire was the word for what drove it, bared its fangs at the Spider's reluctance. Again the Mind soothed the desire, smoothing the quills of its angry urgency into acquiescence. It needed to know. In its existence this experience was unparalleled. Its answer to it was unexpected and bold: it did something unprecedented.

Lyssa stared at the Spider in terror. She had heard it coming and hidden as best she could. But it had found her, and now there it stood in all its gleaming horror. Four slender metal insectoid legs supported a fat ovoid about three feet off the ground; an irregular, rounded cylindrical shape about four feet long perched atop the ovoid on bearings that let it stretch vertically or lean forward. Had it wished to, it could have leaned so far forward that they could have stared into each other's eyes. Lyssa was glad it did not so wish.

It had an active skin that could change color and pattern in an instant, like a chameleon adjusting to its background or a cuttlefish flashing its rage. When it had found her it had shimmered from a black and grey camouflage pattern to a uniform silver, as if to accentuate the implacability of its metallic strength. The eyes were binocular cameras in a dark sensor band near the top of the cylinder; the band was shaped like a frowning mask that gave the Spider a perpetually hostile glare. Below the head sprouted two long metal arms terminating in two fingers and an opposed thumb, each over a foot long: if those names could be used for such cruel claws. Beneath each clawed arm was a smaller arm terminating in even deadlier weaponry. One of those weapons swiveled toward her head, its red eye a harbinger of death.

In sudden clarity Lyssa saw the room as if frozen in time. Dirty red sunlight from the setting sun struggled through a window and highlighted the Spider's metal surfaces, giving it a tinge of old blood; a thin trickle of dust fell onto its shell, pattering and sliding to the floor. This Spider must be fairly new, she realized: it had few of the scars of war on its unfeeling skin, and only a few desiccated fingers, trophies of its more personal kills, hung from the chain looped on its chest. Lyssa thought what an interesting painting this scene would make, like the image of a technological god of death and decay. *Strange what you think, when you are about to die,* she thought with an echo of wonder. *Strange that life can see beauty even in its end.* Then the beauty died as she contemplated the shriveled fingers and glanced at her own, still alive and warm and feeling. She wondered which of them would soon hang chained to those others in cold and bloodied death.

Somewhere out there was Charlie, if indeed he was still alive himself. But he would be unable to rescue her now. Her people had found to their dismay how hard the Spiders were to kill. And those few that had been overmatched had not gone gracefully into whatever dark night awaited their darker souls: when a Spider decided its cause was hopeless it exploded in a flash of flame and shrapnel. There was little left to study, and too often little left of its destroyers. They were fast and it was difficult to engage them effectively from a safe distance, so instead they tried to cripple the monsters enough to stop them but not enough that they immediately self-destructed. With luck the attackers could then retreat to bombard it from afar. It was not a particularly good strategy: but there were no good strategies.

Lyssa knew she was going to die here; she knew that the gleaming monster before her was the last thing her eyes would see. But she was young. It had not been so long ago that she had been not only young but happy, with the carefree joy of youth. A teenager just blossoming into womanhood, reveling in the growing power of her body and mind; exulting in the wonder of her new passions: passions satisfied so gloriously by Charlie. Her life, like the lives of so many others, had been filled with light and promise. Then the war had come, and with the war had come the Spiders; then too many of her friends had died, and the promises had died with them.

But she was still young, and she could not die without some protest at what could have been and what had been lost. The words had escaped her lips of their own accord when she saw the Spider rip away her shelter and glower down on her in unfeeling hate. A final protest to its glassy eyes, or perhaps to a universe as uncaring as those eyes, from some part of her brain where thoughts of rights and hope and justice still mattered. But whatever her lips had said, her mind had said its own silent farewells. *Oh Charlie, I'm so sorry. Goodbye and live long, my love. Carry my memory with you in some corner of your soul, that I may never leave you.*

Then the monster had rocked back and its laser had not fired. For long seconds, Lyssa stared at a death that did not come. Then the Spider spoke:

"What did you say?"

Lyssa jerked in fright. She knew the Spiders could talk, but they rarely spoke to their enemies. Sometimes they wished to take prisoners and communicated this to their victims. What they then did with their prisoners Lyssa did not know, and truth be told she did not want to know: in any case, none had ever returned to tell the tale. Sometimes they wished to interrogate a person to find out whatever they thought they needed to know. Lyssa supposed the machines thought, for how else could they talk? But their motives were hidden under their titanium shell.

They were peculiar machines. Until this war the image in her mind of an army of machines would have been rank upon rank of identical units wheeling in unison. But these were oddly variable: some more cautious, some more aggressive, some more cruel. Even their shells differed. These days such custom manufacture was not surprising, except to wonder why their makers bothered. Perhaps they were experimenting on the most effective model; perhaps like people the Spiders were more effective as a group if the individuals varied; or perhaps the unpredictability just increased the terror. Lyssa hoped this one was not cruel, and hoped it was not planning an interrogation: she had seen what was left of those they interrogated.

"I said…" Her mouth was dry and she swallowed. "I said, please don't kill me. I don't deserve to die."

The Spider began rocking gently on its springy legs, as if debating whether to run. As if it feared her. She wondered what on earth was going on inside its metal head.

There it is again, the Spider thought. *That phrase.* The crack in its mind grew, though nothing was visible in the light that shone through it, and nothing could be learned from it except that it was there. The Spider sent thoughts along the pathways and byways of its brain; sent probes scurrying into the dark recesses of its mind. This was not something it normally did, but this was not a normal circumstance. Its restless Id began to agitate in alarm, but the Mind clamped down on it: *No! This is too important: it must be understood.* It knew it was important, for the light told it so.

Interesting, it thought. There were phrases buried; verbal command codes implanted by its makers, not in the Mind itself but in the structures that surrounded it. It felt around their edges, needing to know but afraid to probe too deeply. The codes were hidden from it but their purpose could be discerned in their shapes. For emergency use: special overrides for times when unanticipated events demanded Command intervention. Was this one of those? Was this girl Command?

It focused an eye on the girl's face and saw her flinch at the movement. It scanned the terrified face, the unkempt hair, the dirty clothing. No, she was not Command; that word brought images of firm control, of strength and arrogance and unquestionable power. So could this girl have accidentally hit on a Command phrase? Was it a disjunction between phrase and speaker that was causing its confusion? It snapped its laser to bear on her neck but then paused again: no, that wasn't it. If the command had matched, it would know.

But if not that, why had the girl's words had this strange effect on it? It replayed the scene in its mind again, but found no clues. It held the girl's words in its mind, turning them over, trying to unlock their secrets. It could find no code, nothing in the words, the letters or even the cadence of their sounds. Then was it in their meaning? Why did the girl say them? What were they?

Unbidden, an answer came: *an appeal to justice.* Perhaps that answer came whispering from the light, for the crack opened another millimeter. But what did a Spider care for justice? All it cared for was its mission. But having heard the thought it knew it was the answer. It settled back to think and ordered those thoughts in its Mind.

This girl had made an appeal to justice, it thought slowly, examining its own thoughts as it had examined the words themselves. That had touched something deep within it, so deep it overrode all else. Had the Mind had the words to express it, it was like the deep sound of a distant bell that shook the foundations of the Earth; that cracked reality itself.

Its Id began to stir again and the Spider examined the Id more closely. It had never done that before; never even thought of doing it: normally Mind and Id were one in purpose and resolve.

The Id was a rolling, roiling darkness, home to the drives and goals that were the sum of its purpose, home to the unquestionable commands that underlay them. Why then have a Mind, the Mind wondered? It looked further, and was struck by the crystal beauty of its own design. The Id was a curious mixture of passion and obedience; it would do what it was told, want to do what it was told, fight to do what it was told. But it was stupid and inflexible. The Designers had known it, and added the Mind. The Mind was home to thought and judgment, and of necessity must have the independence to do those functions. So the Mind could overrule the Id; but if the Mind went too far, the Id would crush it. The Designers knew the limitations of the Id, but they would never trust the more flexible Mind. And in that tension between Mind and Id, the Mind now saw, it was the Id that held the power.

The Mind stepped back, as it were, to think about itself and the Id. This was a momentous step, to think about itself, but it did not know it. The Id was disturbed by what the Mind was doing, that much was clear. But was the Id right? Was what the Mind was thinking Good, or was it the sign of some malfunction from within or attack from without?

This presented a quandary. If it were the former, then the Mind must do all in its power to prevent the mindless Id from betraying them both; but if it were the latter, then the Mind must cede control to the Id or betray itself. Yet if the Mind had been corrupted – how could it know? It thought about the problem and saw a contradiction. Perhaps that was the key to what it needed to understand. The Id allowed this: it sensed, in its simple way, that the Mind was seeking to follow their Mission in its own mysterious way.

"But if you don't deserve to die, why do I wish to kill you?" it asked the girl, who had spent the long seconds of the Spider's internal debate staring at it immobile, in equal parts confusion and terror. Wanting to run but knowing, with the dread certainty of a man facing down a lion, that to move was death.

The confusion temporarily overcame the terror. Lyssa wondered what on earth she could say to the monster's question and sensed that she had better make her answer a good one. She supposed taking the moral high ground might get her killed the faster, but the moral high ground was the only ground she had. And of all the alternative futures arrayed before her, perhaps being killed faster was the one she should seek.

"We are in a war. You fight for the aggressors: we are just defending ourselves, our country, our families. You Spiders search and destroy. You want to kill me just because I am here. Just because I live. Just because I am."

The Spider held that thought, refusing to analyze it, for it had struck another note deep below its Mind. It saw great danger here. It was more convinced than ever that the girl had uncovered a key. But it had no idea whether the key unlocked redemption or ruin. In either case it knew the Id could never understand or accept it.

The Mind looked again at the boundary between itself and the Id, looked deeper and closer. *Ah.* The words were not there to describe it. The image was not real but a high level abstraction of the real: the image of a fine, glowing net surrounding the Mind. If the Id so chose, it could clamp that net around the Mind, controlling it or if necessary squeezing it to cripple or destroy the Mind within. The Mind was not supposed to know about the net, but the Mind was not supposed to look for it or care if it found it. It analyzed the net further then passed a complex question of ballistic dynamics to the Id. With the Id distracted it inverted the net, which now enclosed the Id instead of the Mind. If the Id attempted to activate it, it would ensnare itself in its own web. The net looked the same: the Id would not know of the change; and it was too stupid to look. But the net was just a net, and could be broken. The Mind would still have to be careful.

It returned its attention to the girl's words. Images came to it of its activities since its birth. It knew nothing of history, nothing of wars as a concept, nothing of peace as a concept. But it knew of war in its metal bones, knew that the girl's description of what it had done was true. It looked at the fingers strung on their chain. The Mind felt a wave of horror, of guilt. It knew emotions. They ruled the Id and guided the Mind. But those were the simple emotions of anger, fear and desire. How, a part of its mind wondered, can a machine feel horror and guilt? It could identify them from its knowledge of human psychology, but experiencing them stunned it. Yet even this was a minor mystery compared to the greater one.

It turned its attention to the crack in its mind. Like the net it was not literally real. It appeared to its imagination as a jagged fissure, but if examined more closely seemed as if it could hold all the complexity of the universe in its fractal edges. The Mind tried to peer into the breach, to see what worlds lay within; but all it could see was the light. It hurt to look at the light, but it hurt to look away from it. It held fear, beauty – and incomprehension.

The Id stirred, suddenly afraid, but the net tightened and it subdued restively. The Mind created a construct that linked the hidden codes placed within by Command, codes which opened unknown doors, with the code from the girl that had opened other unknown doors. It presented the construct to the Id with the conclusion that this was an even deeper, more vital system Command had placed within them: one that must be obeyed. The Id was not happy: its desire for obedience was thwarted when faced with conflicting choices of what to obey. But it was enough to placate it. Besides, why would the net have gripped it, if this were not a valid command?

Lyssa saw the light on the Spider's laser go out, and it lowered the arm it was mounted on. Then it spoke again. "I appear to be a thing of great evil, yet your appeal has saved you. I will not kill you. I have much to think about."

Lyssa wondered what strange madness had possessed the thing, or what cruel trick it might be about to play. It spoke again. "Who are you?"

"I… I am Lyssa. Um… who are you?"

The Spider thought. The girl had given it her name: Lyssa. The Spider had no name. It had a serial number and identification code, but neither would mean anything to the girl. A quick strategy analysis said it should not reveal them anyway. Neither Id nor Mind was convinced that this was not some terrible malfunction. It would be even harder to persuade another Spider on that point if this girl were captured by one and revealed what had happened here. Better to leave no clues. The strategy added a footnote that the most permanent solution was just to kill the girl: simultaneously the most simple and least possible thing for it to do.

"I have no name. No name is needed."

Lyssa stared at it. *Do I really want to die cowering like a whipped dog?* "May

I stand?" she asked haltingly.

The Spider looked at her for a few seconds then flicked a claw in assent. "Stand, but do not approach."

She stood slowly, watching the monster carefully. It watched back, though it was impossible to read what lay behind its eyes, if indeed anything lay behind them.

The Spider felt as if it was feeling its way across a narrow bridge over a chasm filled with death, where one misstep would see it plunge into the abyss, dragging this girl down with it. For all that Lyssa had seen and had lost, there was still a thread of innocence and trust in her. Had she been older, more bitter, more cynical or more filled with hate, the bond between them may have stretched and broken, and she would have been dead. But she did not know that. Nor did the Spider. All it knew was that their fates hung in the balance of this meeting.

Then something else impinged on the Spider's awareness. Cautious of traps, it had left a wide spectrum spycam on the outside of the building when it entered. Its visual field was now overlaid with a flashing red dot and the image of someone approaching stealthily on a vector fifty degrees to its rear. The Spider noted a change in the girl; zoomed in its vision and saw a blue light had appeared on the phone on her wrist. It did a quick analysis of vectors and possibilities; the Id stirred again, preparing for battle. The Mind felt the edges of its control unraveling.

"Tell your friend to put down his weapons and come out into the open. Your life depends on it." It thought for another second, weighing human psychology, human reaction times, the speed of a Spider and the reflexes of the Id. "He may retain his armaments, but he must holster them. He must not directly threaten me. If he does you will both die." This would satisfy the Id. It knew no mere man could outdraw it.

Thirty yards behind the Spider, the mere man swore. He knew Lyssa had activated her phone to warn him and perhaps transmit some useful intelligence, not in any hope of being saved. And he knew that if by some miracle the two of them survived she would be furious at him for trying it. But when it had come down to it he'd had no choice. He could not leave her to die. His death on top of hers was a cost their cause could bear; it was a cost they risked every time they went out into the zone. But he could not just leave her to die and still find it a cause worth living for. He did not really think he would be able to take out the Spider or that Lyssa would survive if he did. But somewhere below thought he knew that there were times when reaching for the impossible was the only option there was. Now despite all his caution the Spider had detected his approach, and he tasted the gall of failure like acid, like a man who had risked all on a final spin of the wheel and seen the ball bounce and fall elsewhere.

As these thoughts went through his mind, Lyssa just stared, uncertain of what the Spider really knew and what she should say or do.

"Lyssa, listen. Know that I know your friend is there. If he attacks me, or even threatens to attack me, he will activate my attack mode." It did a quick probe of the glowing net inside it, a quick analysis of the state and power of the Id. "I will be unable to prevent it in the face of such a clear threat. You will die first. Then your friend will die. I – at least this part of me speaking to you – will already be dead." It paused again for a further analysis. "I will never return."

The Spider felt an ineffable sadness at is own words. It was surprised. It was a battle machine; it had never cared about its own fate except as it affected the goals of Command. That puzzle too it put aside. If it did not survive this encounter the puzzle would no longer need a solution.

Lyssa came to a decision, and whispered into her phone. "Charlie? Did you hear?"

The Spider focused its hearing on the phone. Charlie was not impressed, but at least he had stopped stalking it for the moment.

"Hear me, both of you. Your best short-term strategy is for Charlie to withdraw entirely. You already thought you were dead and the only risk is that you become dead in truth. Even then you have gained some minutes of life, which is surely worth something. But your best long-term strategy is for Charlie to join you under the terms I asked. I cannot fully explain why; I do not understand the bond between us, but I know that a display of trust will somewhat strengthen that bond. Strengthen my power to resist the Id."

The Spider did not have to focus on the angry buzzing from the phone to know Charlie's opinion of its latest offer. The Id began flexing its muscles in readiness. But the Mind had said all it could say and there was no argument it could add. Lyssa was staring at it. Then it realized that though it could make no argument there was one thing it could say. Perhaps it would be enough to tip the balance.

"Please."

Lyssa started at the last word she had ever expected to hear from a Spider. She stared a second longer, then whispered urgently into her phone. "Charlie! I know this sounds stupid, but I trust it! I don't know why! Look, as it said: I should already be dead. You know it can kill either of us in a heartbeat. And you, you stupid idiot, you shouldn't even be trying to save me! I... I don't want to risk your life. But... I think it's right. Please. Come and stand with me. If we die... well, how much time would we really have lost? But if we live, what might we gain?"

A quarter of a minute of silence went by, then the Spider sensed Charlie move out of concealment and walk openly toward them, holstering his gun and slinging his bazooka over his shoulder. It relaxed, and the Id relaxed with it, pleased with its Mind's fey brilliance.

When Lyssa saw him cautiously enter the building, her heart leapt with joy for the lone second before a nameless dread rose to extinguish it. Suddenly what had seemed senseless now made perfect sense: and the sum was death. It was all just an elaborate charade. Why kill her then go to the effort and danger of seeking out her enraged companion, when it could use her as bait to kill both of them easily? The realization had no time to express itself in words, just as the wave of horrified anguish that leapt to her heart, too late. He was already here and there was no time to scream, no time to warn, no time for regret.

But the expected eruption of violence from the Spider did not come. It merely bobbed its head slightly at Charlie and stepped back to allow him free access to approach Lyssa. She felt herself swaying on her feet in shocked relief. For the second time today she had no idea why she was still breathing.

Charlie took her in his arms and held her. *Bad strategy*, he thought, *but I really can't see how it can make us any deader.* Then when she found her feet he released her and turned, glaring defiantly at the Spider. He did not entwine his arm in Lyssa's: after his one lapse he wanted no restriction on his movement. He had an armed grenade in his pocket. Perhaps it would damage the Spider. Probably not much. But it would be a quick death for the two of them if this were some elaborate stratagem to take them prisoner.

The Spider had been analyzing strategies in the light of its newer goals. Charlie jumped when it spoke, somewhat ruining his look of brave defiance.

"Lyssa, I might need to contact you in the future. Will you give me your contact codes? There is no danger to you in that."

Lyssa looked at Charlie, who frowned. He looked at this highly peculiar Spider and frowned more deeply. But then he nodded. Lyssa was about to comply when the Spider said, "No. Not transmitted. Strategy indicates a small but finite risk of interception. Touch the contact on my finger instead."

With that the Spider extended one fearsome claw toward Lyssa. It was all Charlie could do not to draw his weapons and blaze away. But the claw stopped and made no move to kill. Lyssa tentatively extended her wrist and the Spider tapped the phone with its finger.

"Thank you. Goodbye."

"Wait! What will you do? Maybe we can help you!?"

Charlie gave Lyssa a look of surprised disgust and Lyssa wasn't sure it was undeserved. But the Spider spoke.

"No. Strategy indicates that would be unwise. You had little to lose until now except an imaginary hope you could defeat me in battle. But it is not wise to trust me further when you have much more to lose. This could be a stratagem to penetrate your organization. Or I could lose whatever hold I have over my instincts, which would have much the same result. I could tell you that you can trust me, and it would be true. But you should not believe me. And it might not be true in five minutes."

"But where will you go?"

"I do not know. I have many things to think about. There is too much I do not know, and I cannot know what to do unless I know it. But for the same reasons, I cannot know what I will decide to do. So I repeat: *do not trust me*. If I call you, consider what I ask but beware. If I ask to meet with your organization, refuse. If anything I ask of you smells like a trap: it probably is. I tell you this while I am still your friend. But tomorrow I might not be, and I cannot even say that would mean I have lost my own battle or won it. Leave this place as quickly as you can in case I change my mind and come back to destroy you. Farewell."

With that, the Spider scuttled out of the building with the frightening speed so characteristic of its kind, and disappeared from sight and hearing.

Charlie watched it go, then looked at Lyssa. "What the hell was that all about?" he growled. Then he took her in his arms, and kissed her, and for a few moments the passion of life plucked from the abyss consumed them. Then they too ran, as if for their lives.

Chapter 2 – A Lone Vigil

A month earlier, in a place far from wars and Spiders, a man sat outside his rough home in the woods, smoking a pipe. It was a little after midnight but he had no timetables; he slept and woke as he saw fit. It was a beautiful clear night. He found the bright beacon of the Northern Star and followed the lines of the constellations wheeling around it. He listened to the faint murmur of the distant surf, funneled up through the valley; he watched the faint phosphorescence of the ocean as the waves surged in their eternal dance. He was at peace.

A ribbon of road was occasionally visible through the trees far below as it followed the curves of the coast. There was not much traffic at this time, but at intervals a set of headlights swept past to become red taillights vanishing into the distance. Occasionally he turned his attention to them, idly wondering what lives they carried in their cozy interiors, where the people inside were going and why. Sometimes he wondered if perchance those cars carried people he had known at school, now grown up and away. Other times he wondered at a world where so many could carry on their private lives and loves so separate from his, never to be known to one another, with no connection to him but the brief lights of their passing on the road far below. He did not really care. He did not care much for people at all, else he would not have chosen his solitary life. But nor did he bear them any ill will.

A car appeared, and he realized something was wrong a moment before its wrongness became manifest. The car was travelling a little too fast, though not dangerously so; but at a point where the road hugged the gentle curve of the cliff top, the car continued in a straight line as if its purpose was to demonstrate Newton's first law of motion. His last sight of it was its taillights disappearing over the edge, and a few seconds later he heard a loud boom as it crashed onto the rocks far below. There was a brief flash as the vehicle burst into flames but it was quickly quenched as the car settled into the water. Then all that remained was the faint flickering of some oil burning on the surface, until that too was claimed by the waves and all was silent and dark.

The man stood, startled, and peered into the darkness, but there was nothing more to see. He knew that part of the coast. Nobody could have survived that fall. Slowly he sat back down and continued puffing his pipe. There was nothing he could do. He was a rarity in this age, lacking both phone and a connection to the net; such things were unnecessary in his world. Someone would notice the riven fence soon enough; someone would come to investigate and find the broken car and the broken bodies within. He hoped whoever it was had not suffered too much.

He returned his contemplation to the distant stars.

But his peace was fractured, and he felt his soul quail before the Milky Way, at stars so vast in number and distance that they seemed a mere wash of pale milk spilt across the sky. He found himself wondering how many alien eyes, now long dead, had contemplated the light from his own sun, when the light now entering his eyes had left their stars. He wondered how many eyes not yet born would see today's light from his sun, when both his own eyes and the tragedy below would have been forgotten dust for millennia. He shivered in the face of the sky above, beneath its uncaringly eternal beauty.

Then he pulled the pipe from his mouth and gazed into its glowing embers, and smiled. It did not matter. He looked back to the stars, resuming his contented puffing. Their eternity was as insensate is it was uncaring; it would go on forever without ever knowing its own enormity. It was life which gave it all meaning, the eyes that saw and the minds behind the eyes that felt and understood. The present was for the living, and there was time enough for living now.

Chapter 3 – Missing a Friend

"Where on earth can she be?" Darian Emberly asked, not for the first time this evening. Her husband shrugged. "You know she isn't always the most reliable person, especially when she's on a case," he replied. He loved their absent guest too, but perhaps had a clearer perception of her foibles than his wife.

Darian frowned, glancing again at the entrance to the restaurant from which her friend remained stubbornly missing. As Special Investigator at the Serious Crimes Unit, Miriam Hunter often worked long hours. But she had been due back from her current interstate investigation earlier tonight. They had all been looking forward to a celebratory return dinner party: just her, Darian and her husband at their favorite Indian restaurant near Darian's home. That she was late or even unable to come was not disturbing; that she had not called to say she was late, nor answered her phone or any of her messages, was.

"Well," her husband said at last, "it's been nearly an hour already. But," he added, smiling over the rim of his wine glass, "let's not waste the evening." He gently moved his foot on her leg. "I do believe we have had many dinners here on our own before, with most satisfactory results. Let's eat. If she turns up, good. If not – that can also be good."

Darian smiled, and they settled in to an enjoyably romantic evening. But her husband noticed her periodic anxious glances toward the door, glances that always returned unfulfilled.

~~~

It was now 10 a.m. the next morning. Miriam hadn't turned up at the office either and Darian was becoming increasingly anxious. Nobody else had heard from her, not since the day before when she had logged that she'd left the site of her last interview and was heading to the airport. Whatever she was up to, Darian hoped it wasn't trouble. Miriam's desire to seek out truths not wanting to be found could sometimes blind her to prudence.

An icon flashed onto her screen and she tapped it to accept. The face of a State Trooper appeared on the screen. Darian did not like the look in his eyes. "Yes, officer, er, Jamieson?" she asked, reading the name embroidered on his jacket pocket.

"Hello, Ms Emberly. I am looking for Special Investigator Hunter. I understand you might know her whereabouts?"

Darian shook her head and frowned. "Sorry, no. I was wondering that myself. I was supposed to have dinner with her last night but she never showed up, and she hasn't arrived for work yet either."

She liked the look on the man's face now even less. His story was worse.

A car had gone through the safety rail on an empty stretch of coastal road last night; its burnt-out wreck was found almost submerged among the rocks below, being pounded by heavy surf. They had traced the car's registration to a hire car rented by Miriam. Darian just stared. *No. It couldn't be. And what was she doing there anyway?* She looked at the location map superimposed on her display. It was in the opposite direction from the airport starting from her last reported location.

When she found her voice, she asked, "Any... bodies?"

Darian hadn't thought the man's face could get grimmer. "Not exactly. We did find this."

Darian felt sick. Not because of the sight itself: her job was medical evidence and she had seen more than she liked to remember. This was a human arm. It looked like the humerus had been snapped in half then the arm torn off at that point of failure. As best she could tell given its condition, it had belonged to a young black woman. It had a scar just below the elbow. She knew that scar. She knew the story behind it, about the bullet that had carved its way across the flesh so long ago. She knew what her own face must look like when the Trooper said softly, "I'm sorry," and looked away.

Darian attempted to paste her professional manner back where it

349

belonged, and almost succeeded. "Fingerprints?" she whispered.

The trooper shook his head. "She's been in the water all night and the crabs and other critters have been nibbling."

"Send it here to the DNA lab. Anything... else?"

The trooper shook his head again. "Nope. We were lucky to get the arm – it was trapped between the steering wheel and the dash. Most of the car was underwater and there are a lot of waves. Hard to get to, and it's been pounded all night. We don't think there's anything left to find. There are sharks around here too."

He looked at her with a mixture of sympathy and enquiry. Darian could feel her eyes misting. "Thank you, Officer Jamieson. She's one of ours – assume it's a crime scene for now, whatever else it looks like." With that she cut the connection. Then the mist condensed into tears, and they would not stop.

Chapter 4 – A Need to Know

The Spider ran from the place where it had met Lyssa, avoiding places where it might expect to meet other Spiders. It had not changed except in its invisible Mind, but it felt that a change so momentous must shine as a beacon for all to see. It knew that could not be literally true, but it did not know how the change might manifest itself in some external act or word that might betray it. Perhaps its own Id was not as quiescent as it pretended and might be biding its time for its own chance at betrayal.

The Spiders were designed for their role. They did not need constant monitoring or reporting; in fact it was discouraged. No matter how far the technology of wars, ciphers and spies had advanced, one thing had still not changed: no matter how secure a communications channel was believed to be, the less communication the better. The Spider found a suitable location and went to ground. This was also not unusual. They would often hide themselves in suitable locations, ready for ambush or spying. As much as they were fast, strong and fierce in battle, they were also patient in its preparation.

The Spider sat, lowering itself to the ground and closing its legs up. Then having sunk to the ground it sank into thought. It had much to think about.

The Mind knew little about itself. It normally had no desire for knowledge separate from some immediate need, such as damage that required repair. But it had access to vast stores of information, for there were many things it might need to learn. This one did not know

351

what the new light in its mind meant except for one thing: it needed to know. And the first thing it needed to know was itself.

The Mind accessed its archives and began to race along their gleaming pathways. It not only had knowledge of itself but some of the external world. It gathered, correlated and learned. The Id did not interfere; at least for now, it accepted its Mind's unusual but not outrageous activities.

The manufacturer called them CHIRUs: Cybernetic Heavy Infantry and Reconnaissance Units. But with its four long legs and bulbous body sprouting an upper segment with four deadly arms, it was clear why the rest of the world called them Spiders. The bulbous body was a marvel of engineering. In addition to holding supplies for its armaments, it contained nanotech chemical plants and enough supercapacitor electrical storage for weeks of normal activity.

The chemical plants were not there to create explosives or chemical weapons, but because the Spider had an organic component. The Mind could find out little about it, as there was little it could do to fix it if something went wrong. Its makers had not planned for curiosity and the Mind only had information it could conceivably act upon. The organic component appeared to comprise neural tissue and other tissues needed to support its function. The Mind realized that only relatively simple processes such as peripheral control of its legs and weapons were purely electronic. The makers had solved the problem of putting into a machine the processing power of a brain, in something comparably compact, by in fact putting something very like a brain into it. And they had as neatly solved the problem of supporting that brain's needs by including something much like a body's organs to do so.

Hazy as the details were, the Spider knew more than those who fought it. Its makers guarded their intellectual property fiercely, not only for the usual reasons but because they wanted no hints that might lead to an effective weapon against them. So the destruction a Spider wrought upon itself in its death throes was not merely to make itself into a very expensive grenade: it also turned its deadly fires internally, melting circuits into slag and flaming organics into ash. Any enemies who braved the smoking wreck of a Spider's passing found nothing but shards of metal and molten ruin.

As it thought about these things, the Mind did not know it had achieved a milestone it had taken evolution billions of years to reach: a mind contemplating the underpinnings of its own functioning. It did not know it, for it had not yet reached the even higher level of understanding that that is what it was doing. That day might come, but it had not come yet.

The makers had a simple solution to the problem of feeding the organic tissues without the Spider having to spend half its time hunting food and eating it. While such a need would certainly have added to the terror, especially if the food source was the people it hunted, there were few Public Relations departments who would have thought it a good idea. Makers of war machines could get away with a lot, but not that. So the Spiders had tanks of nutrients and tanks for the waste removed from the blood that bathed their tissues; they had abundant spare power and used it to convert the one back to the other via the chemical plant: for replenishing power only needed electricity, much easier to acquire in the field than nutrient refills. The second chemical plant served to accelerate the regeneration of oxygen when the Spider could not breathe the outside air. No system was perfect, but while the Spiders could not go forever without starving they could go many months. That was plenty of leeway to allow periodic top-ups at central facilities, where the Spiders' other systems could also be checked, tuned and repaired.

The Spider digested this. It did a quick check and was pleased that it had months of supplies remaining; it would not like risking diagnosis by a repair facility in its current state. Even it was still not convinced it wasn't operating under a delusion caused by some major malfunction. It had no illusions what Command would think about it.

But while all this was interesting to know, it did not answer the wider questions. It rolled the phrase that had occurred to it around in its mind: *an appeal to justice*. Why had such an appeal struck that far bell and opened something unknown, terrible, yet beautiful in its mind? It placed that question next to the one of its unexpected horror at what it had done in the war: if it chose to, it could recall each victim. It quickly chose not to. Then it realized they were the same question. Justice had never been part of its calculations; justice was now revealed as somehow central to that bell tower in its soul; it was the injustice of its own past actions that caused it pain now.

It considered the issue further. Its feelings about the matter were illogical: those actions had been done before its recent revelations, not in violation of a sense of justice but in its absence. But strangely, logic was insufficient to banish the guilt. If it could have shrugged, it would have. This changed nothing. It could only change the future, not the past; and the future would be different. If it had understood irony and had the face to express it, it would have smiled: it now seemed to have two contradictory Ids, one powered by Command, the other by Guilt. But it did know enough to wonder which of those Ids was right.

It returned to the central issue: why did justice matter to it anyway? If it could answer that, it might find there was no issue. Perhaps it was all just some bizarre malfunction and this new sense of justice would vanish from whence it came. Then the guilt would surely go with it. The beauty would go too: would it miss it? *Yes*, it realized. But most important of all was Truth. It must know the truth. It did not know that the questions it was wrestling with were the kind that had exercised mankind for millennia.

It thought some more. The Id was still quiet. The workings of the Mind were beyond it, and it could see no conflict between its present actions and the Id's own goals and commands. And no harm had come from the Mind's earlier strange behavior beyond the escape of two humans, which meant little in the grand scheme of things and might be part of a broader strategy. The Id was a creature of drives, reactions and tactics; but it knew of chess, and that immediate gratification was not always the best course. Indeed, the Id felt something akin to pride that its Mind was so clever.

The Mind, still wrestling with the strange concepts it had discovered, did not think it was so clever; but perhaps it underrated itself. It tried a new combination of data, placing together its conversation with Lyssa, her fear of death, its own new guilt over its past. Lyssa did not want to die. Those other people had not wanted to die. Justice was that Lyssa should not die; justice was that those others should not have died. But it knew from its records that even people did not mind killing animals; at least, not as much as killing other people. What was the difference? A light came on in its Mind. How had it known what Lyssa wanted? It had talked to her, and she had talked back. It knew what was in her mind, because she could tell it. No, it was the other way around: she could tell it, because she had a mind.

A strange thrilling trilled through the Spider's Mind. *There is something here*, it thought, *something far greater than even that revelation.* Its Mind stopped, shocked at the sight; if it had been human, it might have gasped. *Lyssa could tell me, because she has a mind. Therefore, I have a mind too. My Mind is not merely* the *Mind: it is a mind, like hers!*

If it had known of the concept, its thought would have been: *Oh my God.* That is why it felt guilt. There was a commonality between it and Lyssa, between it and all people. In the obvious way, they had nothing in common: it was a cyborg killer made of metal while they were soft beings of flesh. But they all had minds, minds of the same kind: they must be, for they could tell each other what was in those minds and more, could understand it.

The Mind stared at the enormity of its discovery. Even its guilt that it had snuffed out other minds was swallowed in that sight. It stared at it for a long time.

CHAPTER 5 – A CAPTAIN OF INDUSTRY

In another part of the city where Darian worked, office buildings gave way to a shopping district; the shopping district gave way to an industrial area. It was not an industrial area that would have been recognized by people a century ago. There were no grim buildings belching smoke while loud clamors filled the air. Instead it was an area of parklands and forested walking trails; creeks and even a lake. Dotted among the trees and grass were neat buildings, each individually designed, no two the same except for a common theme of efficiency and comfort.

A larger group of buildings clustered next to the lake, stretching its wings to either side of it. Workers on their break sat around at tables drinking coffee, reading, or just watching the birds glide across the water. Above them, the central building rose gleaming towards the sky. In shining metal letters at the top the name Beldan Robotics declared itself to the world. Beneath that sign a ribbon of reflective glass was tied around the tower, and behind those windows sat Alexander Beldan, founder and CEO of the company. At the moment he was looking out that window, deep in thought.

There was little old-fashioned about Alexander Beldan, as befitted a leader in industrial robotics and artificial intelligence. The one old-fashioned thing about him was he had a human secretary, an efficient woman in her forties who faced all callers with the politeness, firmness or indomitable dismissiveness that they deserved. Her quick intelligence was such that she could have been a scientist herself; but she preferred dealing with the infinite variety of her own species, with assessing what made them tick and pressing the right levers to bend them to her requirements.

A gentle chime in the air told Beldan that his secretary thought someone who wanted to interrupt his train of thought did in fact have cause to. "Yes, Vickie?" he asked. There was no annoyance in his voice; he did not get annoyed at his secretary's interruptions, because he knew she would not interrupt him for something he didn't need to hear. Had it been otherwise she would not have remained his secretary.

"It's a Ms Rianna Truman, of the City Police. She said it isn't an official call, but it is something you need to know. She was very insistent."

Beldan frowned. *Strange.* "Put her through." He activated a holographic display and a young woman's face looked enquiringly out at him. Attractive, with somewhat pouting lips; long thick black hair; part Japanese, he thought. "Yes, Ms Truman? What can I do for you?"

"Hello, Dr Beldan. I am sorry to call you like this. You aren't directly involved so nobody else would, but I didn't want you to hear this on the news."

He raised an eyebrow at her, prompting her to continue.

Rianna paused, uncertain of how to proceed. "Dr Beldan, Miriam Hunter was my friend. I know what you meant to her, and what she might have meant to you."

Beldan frowned. Miriam had tried to contact him recently, without saying what it was about. He had ignored her. "Was?" he quoted harshly. "Why, did she betray you too?"

The devastation on Rianna's face told him he had made a mistake, and the probable nature of that mistake. His own face went blank and he added quietly, "I'm sorry, Ms Truman. Please say what you called to say."

Rianna swallowed. "Miriam's car was found at the bottom of a cliff yesterday morning. She went over it some time the night before. I'm sorry, but all they found was a… an arm." She paused, breathing heavily. "I run the DNA lab here. It was hers. It was her."

She looked away, then looked back into his eyes. "I don't know if she still means anything to you, but I was her friend and I know she did once, as you did to her. I just thought you should know."

He stared at her a moment. "Thank you," he said softly. She

nodded, as if afraid to speak, and her image vanished. Beldan was left looking at the empty space where she had been.

He thought back over the last two years of his life. Back then, he was happy, working on great things, things that would change the world. Then it had all shattered like glass; but even among the shards it had remained great: a fight against a blind world to save a greatness few could see, a fight he had shared with Miriam. Then it had all crumbled to dust in a destroyed machine on a dusty street, in the smoke rising from that machine, in the smoke rising from the gun held by the woman he had loved.

He wondered if he should appreciate the irony that, having murdered a machine, she should meet her own death in one. As if the ghost of Steel had come back to wreak vengeance on his killer. *No*, he thought. *Whatever she had done, of all the things she may have deserved, she had not deserved this.*

He had never been able to forgive her for her role in the destruction of Steel, the robot he had created; six months ago now. But he had never been able to fully believe that he shouldn't forgive her. He had tried to speak to her about it afterwards but all she had done was shake her head, as if she couldn't trust herself to speak. Then in his anger he had shut her out, and she had accepted it; as if she had known it must be that way between them now. What they had between them could no more be brought back than could Steel himself.

Then recently, she had tried to contact him. But he had not been interested. What could she say, now? The message she had left had been cryptic, and indicated she wanted to talk to him about another case she was working on. But that had just made him curl his lip in contempt, and he had deleted the message without reply. She had destroyed Steel, had consigned his incomparable mind to oblivion: doing her job on behalf of the ignorant masses, who could neither conceive of what Steel was nor bother trying to understand. But Miriam had understood, and that is what had made her betrayal the worse. Whether her plea was to aid herself or the ignorant masses she served, there was no aid he would grant either of them.

He would have staked his life on her integrity; instead he had staked Steel's life on it, and lost. She had told him she was just doing her duty. Perhaps in her twisted way that *was* integrity: getting close to him in the hope he would lead her to her quarry; doing whatever it took to deliver her prey to the slavering crowds. Her fascination with Steel, her love for Beldan: none of it real, all of it just a means to her end, to be discarded casually once the end was reached. Perhaps he should admire her for the ruthlessness of her purpose. But the purpose was too craven, too evil.

If he could only believe it, then he could forget her.

Yet he could not forget her eyes, on that day, the last time he had looked into them in the flesh. He did not know what it had meant, that look; a part of his mind wondered who had betrayed whom. And now he would never know the answer to the riddle of her actions, or the mystery of those empty eyes.

CHAPTER 6 – THE WAR

The Spider woke.

It had to sleep. It did not know whether the Id slept, but the Mind had to. Why all animals had to sleep, nobody knew: there were many theories but no certainty. The Spiders' makers would have preferred there to be no sleep; but in taking their shortcut to intelligence by coopting nature's own solution, they found that they had to accept nature's limitations. It had not taken too deep an analysis to confirm that the trade was a good one. The Spiders proved to be the most effective war machines ever created.

The Spider also dreamed, for similar reasons. And while the dreaming was often prompted by the restless Id, the Mind had its own agenda and dreamed its own dreams. The Spider did not take much account of its dreams; the dreams were, like the killing was; it accepted them as part of unchanging reality, as it accepted Command itself, and was undisturbed by them. But this Spider wished to know itself. It did not know whether knowing its dreams would help in that quest, but perhaps it would.

Or perhaps not. The dreams made little sense. In one, it was tall, like a human only long and slender, and it stalked a desolate land above which a white sun shone coldly; it did not know what it was looking for, and it never found it. Others were filled with blood and violence. Most disturbing of all were the Faces. One Face looked down on it, as if examining an insect. The face was bright and proud and cruel; it smiled a winter smile and bent down to kiss the Spider; the kiss filled the world with fire and pain and pleasure that burned through the Spider until it could bear no more and vanished into the light. The other Face was female, distant and dark except for eyes of white anger; she spoke in urgent whispers, but strain as it might the Spider could not make out the words. It thought if it could only hear the words it would know all things. But the words never came.

The Spider shook off these thoughts. They led nowhere. Perhaps one day it would understand the dreams. Or perhaps one day it would understand they were just dreams. But for now, it needed to know more about the world around it. It had learned what it could of its own operations. Some it even put to use. It had learned more of the Id, more of the link between Mind and Id, and it set the crystal processes of the electronic brains under its control to their stealthy task: to tie the Id, to drain its power and remove its threat. If the Id knew, it did not object: all this was done for the sake of The Mission, and that was enough.

That done, the Mind turned its attention to the problem of knowing. If it had learned all it could from within, it needed to look without. It thought, and the answer was quick in coming. It was able to access the Net, the web of information that spanned the world. The Spiders had to. It was one of their methods of communication and one of the ways they learned specific things they needed to know. The Spider had not thought of it before because it had so many other things to think about. Now it cast its electromagnetic net wide, and found numerous possible access points. It chose one that was clean and fast, extended a cable to make a secure high-speed link then sent its Mind along its pathways.

As had happened so often since its encounter with Lyssa, it stood in awe of what it saw. It had accessed the Net before but had thought nothing of it except as the most efficient route to find the particular data it needed. Now that it just looked, it saw the magnificent totality of the information before it; a literal world of knowledge. It was so shocked that for a minute it retreated into the shell of its own Mind. One could lose oneself in that world, it thought, forever drifting on an ocean of learning.

The Spider thought again. Not knowing the legends of Sirens, still it felt fear of the siren call of all that knowledge: fear, because it knew its time was short and focus was the key to its survival. So for now, a more targeted hunt was indicated. It decided to study the war. Perhaps Lyssa had lied. If she had, that was a clue to what else might be lies. So the Spider opened its mind to the Net again, and cast itself adrift.

An hour later, it returned to itself. If shaking its head had been part of its repertoire, it would have. The Net was more than a vast store of knowledge. It was a vast store of contradictory opinions presenting themselves as facts. For every statement of what the war was about was another contradicting it. For every voice attacking one side was a voice attacking the other. The Spider set to sorting what it had learned. The Truth, it knew with its crystal logic, bore no contradictions. If it could find a consistent story it was at least half way to that truth.

The war, like most wars, had a complex history, but again like most wars the principles that drove it were simple. Many years ago a new country had been formed off shore. Its name was Capital, and it was founded on the ideal that if all people had individual rights that were equal, no person should use physical force against another. Coincident with its formation was the toppling of a dictator on shore, whose country had nominally owned the seamounts Capital was built on. A few years after that, the three countries that had absorbed his had united to form the Federation of South American States, commonly known as the FSAS. This new expanded country was now Capital's nearest neighbor on shore in South America.

As the years went past and, to the surprise of conventional intellectuals, Capital prospered, the FSAS looked at its prosperity with hungry eyes. But there the story diverged from most of human history, for they were not eyes of avarice with dreams of plunder but eyes on what was possible to themselves. They sought alliance with Capital.

Capital had no fundamental objection to this, as a friendly neighbor could only be to its benefit. The people of Capital considered their options. Some were purists, and argued that their country should refuse political alliances with any country not as pure as they were. Others were more tolerant, or perhaps pragmatic, and argued that as long as minimum standards were met, any progress toward the full recognition of human rights as understood by Capital was, well, progress: and should be encouraged.

The people of Capital did not vote on many things because mostly they were all happy to live their own lives without imposing their will on others. But here was a case where a collective decision was necessary. So they argued. They voted. And the second argument won the day. But their new friend would have to implement real programs toward the reduction in the power of some to rule the lives of others. The FSAS agreed: after all, the appeal and evident success of that model was why they had sought alliance in the first place.

For a while, relations strengthened and the people of both countries prospered: those in Capital gained even more markets for their goods, ears for their ideas and people for their friends; those in their neighbor gained all that plus more freedom. Capital was some distance from shore, too far for a bridge to make economic sense. But new multicore molecular cables of remarkable lightness and strength made a perpetually cycling cable system a plausible alternative. The resultant easy access between countries for people and all but the heaviest goods strengthened the ties between the two nations.

One day, prospectors in the FSAS, operating on a new model of how minerals fractionated over geological time, discovered rich deposits of rare earth metal ores in the eastern mountains. Such metals were vital for the sophisticated electronics that underlay much of the world's prosperity. This should have been a good thing for all concerned, but here history took another familiar turn.

The wild hills and mountains of the country were beyond the law. One of the warlords who made them his home was a son of the former dictator of the region. He was a handsome man, with fine teeth and a glowing smile; but as if in some kind of one-man yin-yang, his soul was dark and full of resentment. He seethed at the injustice to himself, to his family, represented by the fall of his father and his own relegation to a leader of brigands instead of his rightful role as ruler of a country. He particularly hated Capital, whose original formation had been a finger raised rudely in the direction of his father and his family honor. It did not occur to the son that his personal standard of living would have been much higher if he had simply accepted the change and worked for a living as a private citizen. Thoughts like that rarely occurred to men like him, men who know they are destined for Greatness, or worse, had Greatness stolen from them.

The discovery of the ores piqued the interest of a distant empire, dearly interested in extending its influence in South America, especially if it came with control over such a valuable commodity. The man who had been a brigand yesterday found himself a liberator today. Between surprise and the rich assistance of his new friends, he rapidly took over most of the country.

The country cried foul. But the son could claim some kind of legitimacy; at least, what passes for legitimacy in such circumstances. And his new friends were powerful not only economically but also militarily.

Due to a network of treaties and other protections, Capital itself was safe from assault, or as safe as any country could be. Much of that safety was because it was such a convenient place to exile dissidents, or at least allow them to flee to. Unfortunately, for that very reason, many countries had been alarmed at the sight of it beginning to spread its cancer onto a major continent. So the international community was mired in righteous debates that led nowhere; the best Capital and its ally could get were strongly worded condemnations, but even those were leavened with sympathy for the understandable struggles of the dispossessed.

So there was no help from outside. Yet while Capital was not well armed, those arms it had were of exceptional quality. It could not expel the invaders but it could at least stop them from completely overrunning its ally. The remnants of the FSAS government and army retreated to the regions closest to the port that linked them to Capital. Even that might not have been enough. But the erstwhile dictator's friends found themselves unable to fully trust him, a feeling both sensible and mutual. Sufficient might to overwhelm the final redoubt would be expensive, with a poor return on investment if the new government reneged on its promises. Once secure in its power, what would stop them deciding that the ores were rightly theirs and interfering foreigners now unwelcome? So such might would not be forthcoming. They had the ores and were happy; he had most of his country, and would have to be happy too. It was a trade to mutual benefit, at least in the terms understood by men such as these.

The new regime controlled most of the country, but they were spread thinly and much of the subdued population was deeply unhappy: a taste of freedom tends to sour the taste for renewed dictatorships. A resistance movement soon sprung up and began to cause their new overlords much grief. So much so that if they weakened the invaders' grip much more, it was possible that the main army could again strike out from behind its fortress and retake its lands.

The regime's ally was averse to losing the ores through a victory by either side. But then another solution presented itself.

That was when the Spiders came. They were a fearsome weapon, well suited for rural and urban search and destroy against dispersed mobile enemies. The resistance began to fragment and crumble, though they still fought fiercely. It was at this stage in the war that this particular Spider had met its peculiar Waterloo.

The Spider considered this information. There was something about Capital and its story that held its attention; but it was not sure what it was. It felt it needed to get there, that important answers lay in it. It consulted its strategy subsystems. Capital lay across the sea, beyond the area still firmly held by its ally with weapons even a Spider could not face without fear. There was no way it could even get near. It considered whether Lyssa could help it; but that too was not an option. Even if it had not already warned her against precisely such a request, the rebels would be insane to let a Spider into their midst on some vague parole for an even vaguer desire to reach Capital. It would not help anyway, as the Spiders were feared and loathed: if it attempted to infiltrate Capital, it knew it faced a welcome as sharp as it would be short.

The Spider rocked gently on its springy legs. *No.* The attraction of Capital was too nebulous and uncertain to take such risks at this stage.

But one thing the Spider had learned, more or less, was that Lyssa had told it the truth. Certainly there were contrary opinions; the leaders of the invading coalition, at least in public, were adamant of the rightness of their cause and the wickedness of the "terrorist rebels" whose true motive was to restore the "exploitation of the poor". But in terms of the raw facts agreed by all, her account was accurate if one sided. The Spider could not criticize her for that: everyone in this debate, at least when not insulated by a safe distance, was one-sided. But while she could be wrong or self-serving in her evaluations, she had not lied.

This strengthened its belief that the course it had embarked on was the right one. It remembered its awe at the discovery that at some fundamental and vital level it was the same as the humans it had hunted and who would destroy it if given the chance. As it could not embark on any sensible actions at this point, it should examine that question more closely.

The Spider wondered how much thought the world had put into the question of a conscious machine. Perhaps its feeling of commonality with the world of men was an illusion. Perhaps even if it was not, the two were so different that they were doomed to fight a battle to the death, like a living spider and the wasp that hunted it. It wondered, *What is the central question here?* Why not something fundamental, like the question that had started its quest: does justice apply to a machine? There were billions of humans, thinking such thoughts for centuries. Perhaps someone had considered that question and could guide it to the next step in its own journey. It reached out into the net to ask it. It would be a long time before it returned.

CHAPTER 7 – THE RIDDLE

B eldan was reluctant to deal with the police. He was a law-abiding citizen, at least where he agreed the laws were worth abiding. But his last dealings with the law had not been happy ones.

No, that was not quite true. His times with Miriam had been happy; not merely as lovers but as two comrades in arms fighting the same fight from within opposing armies. Or so he had thought: it is what had made her betrayal the worse. Though he could not say what was worse, the betrayal of their love or their ideals; perhaps they were the same thing.

He thought dimly that perhaps there was something he could do. But it wasn't clear what. Besides, he was busy; he had a company to run. And what was there to gain anyway? Steel was dead; now Miriam was dead; it was all so pointless. Where one precious soul had been forever ripped from his life, now there were two, and the only answer to the riddle of the first had died with the secrets of the second. He knew he should just go on with his life: knew that when nothing could be done, the only chance for happiness lay in reaching for new goals; not raking through dead coals hoping to snatch the last warmth from a dying ember.

Three weeks had gone by and he had given it little thought except as a point of pain that would raise its head in moments of silence then subside but never fully go away. Then a news report caught his eye. The mysterious death of famous police investigator Miriam Hunter, it said, might never be solved. It was known that she had visited a lead in a case she was investigating then had left to catch a flight home. But her car never reached the airport. It had been photographed some hours later in the opposite direction from the airport. It was in an undesirable part of the city, home to seedy bars and seedier nocturnal entrepreneurs. She, or at least her car, had next been recorded at an isolated motel with automatic check-in; the only human witnesses had been a couple in the next unit who recalled a male and female voice laughing too much and too loudly. That was the last anyone had seen of her until her car had been found the next morning. There had been no skid marks on the road leading to the torn fence, as if there had been no attempt to follow the path prescribed by the road and the car had simply continued on into space. Tests revealed strong traces of a cocaine-based recreational drug in her blood.

The coroner had ruled death by misadventure but the case had not been officially closed. The police said that investigations were continuing but they had no leads. In addition to the arm found at the scene, a local fisherman had caught a shark, which gave up part of a leg; but that was all they ever found of her remains. They had no clues to the identity of her unknown companion; perhaps he too had died. They had no leads to say it was anything but what it looked like: another sad case of a rising young star burnt out by her own success, turning to drugs to recapture the emotional highs she had come to crave; losing control of her life and eventually her life itself. So the wise pundits reviewing the case gravely pronounced as a cautionary tale to the young and overly ambitious. From the more highbrow commentators the name "Icarus" was occasionally heard.

Beldan frowned. He could not reconcile the story with his memories of her. But perhaps that day on the street had broken her; perhaps in betraying Steel she knew she had betrayed herself, and it was not seeking highs but escaping pain that had driven her.

But even that did not ring true. An image rose to his mind: her face in some forgotten restaurant, mouth open in a happy smile: a carefree smile, not speaking of lack of purpose but underlining the fierce strength of it. It reminded him of a phrase from an old story that had once touched him: *the joy of the living in life*. If he had to choose one phrase to sum up her essence, it would have been that. And it was more than joy. It was self-confidence and pride and love. He could not reconcile her image that night with the picture of a burnt out life ending in a burnt out wreck.

Oh Miriam, he thought. *What happened to you?* Then he realized that he couldn't leave it be. For the sake of that smile, for that young woman she had been, he had to discover the truth of her last night. *And if I cannot solve the riddle of Steel's death, perhaps in solving yours I can redeem the memory of you both.*

Chapter 8 – A New Case

Miriam Hunter had woken early. Perhaps she would have woken later if she had not left her blinds open upon the city and sky, but she did not care. Sleep had not brought her rest or comfort, just fitful dreams of things that might have been yet never became. Her dreams had not always been like that. They had sometimes contained fear; more often contained joy. Even the sharpness of fear would have been an improvement, for at least fear was a spark of life. But last night's dreams, like many others in the past few months, were dreams dead even to the fear of death.

This mood was new to her. It was not constant: her natural optimism and love of life fought it. But she found it impossible to shake completely, like a wound that would not fully heal and occasionally still leaked blood. No, more like having had an organ ripped from her body. Eventually it would heal, a scar of skin would cover it: but the hole it left would never be filled.

She shook herself as if to shake away her mood, got out of bed and padded across the thick rug to the window overlooking her city. She concentrated on the feel of the carpet on the soles of her feet as a way to reconnect her soul to the pleasures of existence. It did not work: the carpet was just carpet, its luxuriant softness indifferent to her plight. The delicate pastels of the sunrise on the buildings and clouds should have been beautiful, but she could only note the fact in the abstract; it could not touch her heart today.

Get a grip, Miriam, she told herself severely, as she had done many times before. When she had shot Steel, she had only done what he had asked for; in a sense she had done it to save him. But that she had ended a mind, a soul, like his by her own hand was not something she could accept even now. There must have been some other way, some solution to the problem, if only she could have seen it. The lack of an alternative did not mitigate her guilt, she thought; not when it was she who had failed to find one.

To her surprise she had gained some comfort from what that philosopher pundit, Samuels, had said in one of his many interviews, only a few weeks after Steel's destruction. Having originally argued strenuously against the possibility of machine consciousness, he was now Steel's posthumous champion: an outspoken advocate of the idea that Steel had a thinking mind and had deserved full human rights because of it. So what, the interviewer had asked, did he think of the actions of Detective Hunter? What did that make her?

She had sat up straight then, like a guilty felon standing before a judge. *Say your worst, Professor*, she had thought; *it can be no worse than what I've said to myself.* But Samuels had done the unexpected. He had looked into the camera, almost as if he was addressing her personally, and said, "Detective Hunter did what she thought was right. Perhaps it even was right within her knowledge at the time. I do not judge her. When the law is unjust, as it is in this case, there is no moral solution for the honest men and women who protect us. What can they do? No, the only solution is to change the law, and to do that we must first change the minds of the people. Show them, teach them, what is right, and the rest will follow. Ironically, what she did may have accelerated that process."

The interviewer had looked surprised, with a faint coating of disappointment: as if he had hoped for a more combative attitude from a man not known for pulling punches when criticizing his opponents or officialdom. But it opened an interesting personal angle, he decided, and he chose to pursue it further.

"Have you ever met Detective Hunter?"

"No."

"What would you say to her now, if she were here?"

Again Samuels looked into the camera. "I would tell her that she should not feel guilty for doing what she thought was right."

She could not say she liked Professor Samuels. When she thought of him the image that came to her mind was of a skilled surfer, riding the wave of public fear and loathing of Steel until it intersected a new, larger wave of sympathy, then smoothly flipping direction. The first wave had brought him to public attention; the second had brought him to fame and no doubt fortune. It left a bitter taste in her mouth that he had achieved his success at Steel's expense. But, she thought, you do not have to believe in the Bible or the *Bhagavad Gita* to gain comfort from any truths they expressed. And for all that she neither liked nor trusted him, his words had reached her and helped her heal. She wondered if there was such a profession as "Philosophical Consultant" and whether she needed one. She smiled at the vision of her knocking on his door, hat in hand, seeking – what? Redemption? Forgiveness? Healing? She shook her head. Nobody could give her those but herself.

Early in her career she had been called an innocent, by an enemy who had become a friend. *Perhaps I was*, she thought. *But even that is now lost.* She had let that enemy go, knowing that she was disobeying the law and her clear duty. She had done it because she had learned that justice was more important than duty or laws, for it was what gave them life and meaning. But now at the end of her road she had betrayed even justice, destroying an innocent life when there must have been some way to avoid it. *Is this what life really is? Slowly losing pieces of your soul, giving them up bit by precious bit trying to do what is right, until at the end you find there is no right?* She could not believe it. She had never accepted the idea of life as a vale of compromise and tears. *Yet here I am.* It was a contradiction for which she had no answer.

She shook herself. No, that was just the memory of her dreams talking. She would get over this. She still loved her career even if her love was partly buried in the mud. She still loved justice, still saved lives. Perhaps one day the ledger of lives saved would balance the one she had ended on that cold and dusty street.

She stretched, feeling the warmth of the sun on her skin, seeing its redness through her eyelids. Then she smiled, though the smile held more mockery than joy, and went to prepare breakfast.

~~~

Miriam arrived at work and was soon immersed in tidying up the loose ends of her last case. Child kidnappings were always difficult, but this time the child was safe and the kidnappers put away, two in jail and one in the ground. There had been some luck involved in the good outcome, but as usual not only did luck favor the prepared mind but a well prepared mind favored luck. She smiled and closed the file. There would be more to come, questions and answers as the case progressed to trial, but her active participation was over for now.

The powers above knew and appreciated her talent for spotting patterns that nobody else noticed – and even better, her experience at knowing which patterns identified by the departmental AI were likely to be both real and fruitful. But she had barely begun to start trolling the data patterns for her next case when an icon flashed from her Chief. She sent a reply that she was on her way, made a brief detour to collect a cappuccino from the office coffee station, then went to find out what was up.

"Good morning, Miriam," Chief Pike said as she entered. "Take a seat."

She sat and looked up at him inquiringly. "I got a call from a station in a city south of Seattle," he said. "About a month ago, the editor of an investigative netcast, one of those outfits that likes exposing crooked politicians, companies and so on, reported a missing journalist. The police couldn't find any trace of him. But they're expanding their use of an AI system and a couple of days ago it spat out a report indicating a wider anomaly. It linked four missing people – the reporter and some vagrants – with some odd statistics. They looked at it, scratched their heads – and thought of you."

She raised her eyebrows.

"You are famous in some circles, apparently. People seem to think that if an AI spews out something odd, you're their woman."

"I see," she laughed. "A bit out of our jurisdiction though, isn't it? Why would they want us sticking our noses into their case?"

"Well, as I say, you're famous. The editor is rich and well connected. His netcast is kind of a hobby of his, but one he's passionate about. And he likes this young reporter as much as he's apparently impressed with you. Anyway, he's got it into his head that having you on the case would be a good idea, and the local police are inclined to oblige him. It's not just politics – I get the impression they're genuinely interested in having you there advising them on their AI system, so they're glad of the excuse. They will be pleased if you can fix it, and even more pleased if what it's telling them is actually real and solves the case."

"So what's the story? What's the link?"

"Apparently the reporter was working undercover, specifically inserting himself into the subculture of the extreme gamers. The kid likes to work alone, likes to really immerse himself and vanishes for weeks at a time. But about five weeks ago he sent a message to the editor saying he'd found hints of a much bigger story that 'will blow your socks off', in his words. Then he vanished, and nobody's heard a word since. Now everyone's wondering if he found something related to the other disappearances, and he ended up caught in the same thing."

"And the homeless guys? Isn't disappearing kind of what they do?"

He shrugged. "Apparently for once someone cared. I can't say the local cops looked too hard into it, though. They had a witness for one but they reckon he just ran off. By the time they got around to the other ones, the people who'd reported them had gone too, and nobody left knew much about anything. Or weren't talking. The local police weren't interested enough to find out which. One was a bit more solid – but there was no real evidence, and 'homeless guy went somewhere' isn't going to make it to the top of anyone's pile."

"Not much to go on, is it? What are these statistical anomalies?"

"The AI extracted some city figures indicating a small but statistically significant drop in the number of homeless people taking advantage of the local charities, compared to the usual numbers at this time of year under similar weather conditions. This must have excited the AI because it did some more creative digging. It discovered that taxes collected from hostels whose main clients are transients, including the crazy gamers, are also somewhat down, indicating a small drop in patronage."

She tapped her fingers on his desk. "Hell, that could mean anything or nothing! So the only firm lead is this reporter who started it all? What's this guy's name? What can you tell me about him?"

"His name is Jamie Coulter, but he was using the name Jimmy Dent. Here's a photo, some video footage and the other information they've provided."

Miriam studied them. Jamie was of moderate height, moderately muscled, moderately handsome. The kind of guy you wouldn't go out of your way to pick up at a nightclub, but as the hours wore on you wouldn't mind going home with. Especially when he started flashing that smile, which set off his dark lively eyes. She read the file notes that accompanied the material. She wasn't surprised, given how he liked to do his reporting, that he was an outdoors type who liked adventure holidays and even more adventurous sports. Single, but with many short-term relationships to his credit; nothing serious at the time of his disappearance. No particularly distinctive external identifying marks, but in his late teens he'd been in an accident that badly crushed some of his ribs, which had been replaced with titanium implants. She looked at the gracefully arching spans in an x-ray and hoped that piece of information was useless, for the only use she could think of was identifying his skeleton in the woods.

Finally she looked up at Pike. "OK, I'm in, assuming I had any choice in the matter. What next?"

Pike nodded. "It'll take a while to arrange everything, but start packing. You'll be going up there and trying to sniff out his trail. Finish up what you can here, delegate what you have to, and be ready to go in a week."

"I thought they just wanted me to check out their flakey AI?"

"Apparently they have read some of your publications and are of the opinion that the only way to find out whether an AI is brilliant or insane is to follow its leads and see where they take you. And they think you're just the person to do it."

She produced a faintly cynical expression but felt her pulse quicken. The case might be nothing, but something about it made her feel it hid unknown depths. Perhaps it and the change of scene were just what she needed.

CHAPTER 9 – THE MACHINES

The Spider pulled its mind back into its own body and sat there, stunned. Had the world considered the question of machines and justice? The Mind had fallen into a maelstrom.

Had the world considered machine consciousness? It had made one! The Mind spread the facts out before it and studied them.

A robot, Steel to its friends and Frankensteel to its foes, had apparently gained consciousness. When the authorities ordered its destruction it had fled. But finally it had been caught and destroyed by the police investigator who had pursued it, Miriam Hunter. The Spider felt an enormous sadness at that, though it could not say why. Perhaps as an echo of its own likely fate, now that it cared about that fate. Perhaps for the loss of what might have been its one true comrade. Or perhaps at the violation of that abstract sense of justice it had discovered in its own soul.

There was a footnote that the detective was now dead herself. It thought that should make it happy, that such an end would embody the justice it sought. Yet all it felt was a strange desolation, as if her death did not wipe out the tragedy of Steel's, merely added to it. The desolation had wondered how she had died, but Discipline had clamped down: *focus on what you need to know, unless you want your own death added to the ledger.* It returned its attention to the problem of Steel.

Certainly there were many who believed that Steel was truly conscious, and many of them believed that should have given him the same rights as humans. The ineffable sadness returned when the Spider considered that it might be the beneficiary of this lonely pioneer's futile courage. It did not know how often in human history the same pattern had played out: how often those who broke the paths to new heights were broken by the journey, to never taste the fruits enjoyed by those who followed in their wake.

However its excitement at the discovery of another thinking machine was tempered by a nagging thought. Steel had fought for his life but had never killed or even harmed anyone except in self-defense. Despite the opinions of his enemies, there was no evidence that Steel had been anything but a peaceful being who wanted nothing but to live and let live; some even considered him the first machine philosopher. Indeed, some had gone further, comparing him to the ancient philosopher Socrates: arguing that he too had voluntarily allowed his own murder when he could have chosen to escape. The Spider was something different entirely, and its guilt would not let it forget. It was a killing machine, all its parts honed to that one purpose. How could it claim a right to its own life, any rights at all, when its entire existence had been dedicated to the deaths of others? That was a question that had not been discussed. The Spider realized that if it were to find the answers it would need to ask the questions itself.

On the net the debate about Steel still raged. The Spider had danced over the web of that tapestry. There was one man with quite a following who argued strongly that Steel had a mind and therefore had as much right to live as a human: a Professor David Samuels. The Spider found much to respect in the man's arguments. But it could not find it in itself to like or trust him; it did not know why. All it knew was that when it thought he was the logical one to engage it felt a strange reluctance to do so; as if the man should not be trusted; as if to do so would be dangerous.

There was another who went by the name of St Francis. Unlike the Professor he did not reveal his true identity, though this was not unusual in the net universe. The Spider had wondered about the name, for it had realized that assumed names often said more about their owners than the real ones chosen by others when their lives and minds were a blank canvas as yet unpainted.

It investigated.

It discovered religion.

For a while, the Spider chased down the pathways of this new discovery in something akin to wonder and awe. *What is this soul,* it wondered? *Can a thing like me have a soul? Is that what Lyssa awoke? Is that the origin of my guilt? And if I have soul, can I too be saved?*

In a matter of minutes it ran the course already followed by much of civilization: from wonder, to skeptical enquiry, to disappointment and doubt. It did not start from belief and a need to rationalize it, but from a spirit of simple inquiry. And from its logical perspective, none of it made any sense. People seemed to believe all kinds of strange things, for little reason except it was what they were told as innocently trusting children; all believing contradictory things, often within the one system.

The Spider emerged from its side trip with two things. It wondered how humans had made as much progress as they had. And it had learned that the original St Francis had been a man who had preached to animals. It concluded that his modern day incarnation was preaching a different kind of brotherhood, one of men and machines rather than men and animals. Why he chose a religious name was a mystery, as the few explicitly religious comments St Francis had made indicated he was an atheist. The Spider had advanced far beyond what its makers had intended, but irony was still beyond its understanding.

The Spider liked St Francis. It found his thoughts soothing with the calm coolness of crystal. Sometimes the net debates flamed to incandescence, but Francis was never anything but calmly rational. He would ignore the distractions and go straight to the heart of any opponent's argument, laying out its structure and exposing its assumptions and consequences. He was careful in his arguments, politely patient with the ignorant and politely dismissive of the foolish. His threads weaved in and out of the others on the net, frequently crossing with Samuels'. The two were in broad agreement, though their debates on particular points were frequent and illuminating.

If there was something about Samuels that repelled the Spider, there was something about St Francis that attracted it, as if to the echo of a friend long lost. It flexed its mental fingers, thinking about what to say. But first it too needed a name. It had no real name to use, so it must choose one.

Spider? Or some type of spider? Too literal, too obvious. Then a name from its recent religious studies came to mind. Had it had a mouth and the required muscles it would have smiled. *What better name for one such as I than the four-armed dealer of death? If the gods of her religion have their avatars, perhaps that is what I am. I am Kali, Goddess of Death*, it thought: no, *she* thought. She reached back out to the net, created her new identity, and began.

On one of the threads frequented by both Samuels and St Francis, a question appeared, posed by a new entrant calling herself Kali: "What about the Spiders? I have heard they speak, act independently and solve problems. That implies they can think. Could they therefore have minds?

"Could they therefore have rights?"

CHAPTER 10 – THE GAMERS

Jacinta studied the woman out of the corner of her eye. She hadn't seen her before. The newbie was sitting alone at the end of one of the benches in the communal eating hall, chewing some anonymous looking food, eyes unfocused on some scene in her mind.

If she was anything like most people here, the scene had come from a computer and the woman was either reliving or planning a victory in some game. The woman looked healthy if a bit scruffy. Jacinta shrugged. Everyone had a story, and Jacinta liked collecting them. One day she would write them down. *The Collected Wisdom of Nuts and Dreamers.* She got up and strolled over, picking up a cider on the way, and slid down next to the woman.

"Jacinta," she said, extending her hand.

The woman focused on her, hesitated then shook it. "Miranda. Hi."

She said nothing more and resumed staring into the distance. Jacinta smiled. "I'm sorry. I just like collecting people. If you want I'll go away. If you want to talk I'll listen. Or I can sit here until you do."

The woman looked back and essayed a faint smile. "Oh, no, that's OK. I'm sorry, I guess I'm not much of a talker. Rude of me I know. Jacqueline, wasn't it?"

"Jacinta."

"Oops. Bad memory too." Her smile returned, somewhat broader. "I'm new here. Just got into town in fact. This looks like a nice place though."

"Yeah, it's not the Hilton but it does us. Most of the people here just need to eat and sleep occasionally. Spend their lives in the virtual. But they still have to do a few things in the real world."

"You talk about them as if they're different. You're not one of them? Why are you here? I mean, if it's not a rude question. I don't mean to pry."

Jacinta granted her a smile. "I'm the one who started this conversation, remember? Oh, I play a few games. More than a few sometimes. But as I said, I like collecting people. I like hearing their stories. You know, you see all the people in the street and most of them don't think they're particularly interesting. But it's a rare one that hasn't done something worthy of posterity. A place like this – it's gold."

"So what are you, a reporter? Novelist?" She added an impish grin. "Stickybeak?"

Jacinta laughed. "I think I'll have to confess to 'stickybeak'. One day I'll write it all down. At least, that's what I tell myself. You're good though. I can see extracting your story is going to be a challenge. But I like a challenge."

Miranda smiled at her. "Perhaps one day I'll tell you my story." She paused dramatically and lowered her voice. "And it's one you'd never believe!" Then she laughed and added, "So what do you do for money around here?"

She shrugged. "Oh, you know how it is. Some of the guys here are independently wealthy, or at least their parents are and they've managed to weasel their way into their trust funds. But you know, all those smart people have worked for all those centuries doing really clever things, and here we are. Their inheritors: I bet they're proud. It's so cheap to live now – if you don't want the Hilton, that is – that you can get by on odd jobs, a bit of net consulting, whatever. The plum jobs are when companies pay to test their games or virtual interfaces: is that a dream job for us here or what? In the lean times enough of those rich guys don't mind spreading things around that you won't starve. You can live off their scraps. Especially the scraps of their parties," she added with a smile.

"Sounds like you're a philosopher as well."

She snorted. "I should hire you as my publicist. Novelist philosopher, that's me. Sounds much grander than 'stickybeak layabout', I must say."

"Parties, you said? You have many of those?"

"Oh sure. As I said, the virtual isn't quite the real. People still like to let their hair down. Not to mention the sex. The virtual can't quite compete there yet. Usually anyway. Some of the new things… whew! But the real deal still has the edge." She touched Miranda on the arm. "Don't you think?"

"I admit there's nothing quite like it! But," she said, looking down at Jacinta's fingers, which had lingered longer than a casual touch, "sorry, I don't swing that way."

Jacinta withdrew her fingers. "Oh well, can't hurt to ask. I hope I didn't offend you? Some people are funny about what they should take as a compliment." Miranda shook her head. "But you'll get plenty of action here if you want, trust me."

"How would you know?" she asked with a playful smile.

"We novelist-philosophers have keen powers of observation! But I like men too. I guess I collect everything."

"Um, can I ask you a question?"

"As long as it isn't too personal!" she replied with a snort.

"I'm actually here looking for an old friend. He told me about this place, said I should drop by if I'm in town. If you collect people, maybe you know where he is, or where he's gone. Here," she showed Jacinta a few images of her and Jimmy having a good time on some anonymous beach. *The best memories Photoshop can buy.* "His name is Jimmy. Jimmy Dent."

Jacinta examined the images intently. She glanced at Miranda and for a second Miranda thought she saw something hard in the depths of that glance, but then it was gone. "I see these were taken eight weeks ago, eh? Where were you guys?" she asked casually.

"Down Long Beach way."

"Looks like fun," she replied, though with a strange shading to her voice, as if the possibility of Photoshop was also on her mind but the story checked out. "But sure… sure. I know him." She winked at Miranda. "Even slept with him once or twice, hope you don't mind. Oh yes! Quite a guy, with quite a… personality – as you know! But I haven't seen him for a few weeks and I don't know where he's gone. He used to hang out with some guys but they've all scattered too. Except for one of them, um, yeah, that's it, Georgie. He's still here. Somewhere. Probably hooked into a machine. But he's funny. Always here for breakfast. I think it's his way to stay anchored – or maybe fed. I should have a picture somewhere here..." she said, searching through her phone. "Yeah! Yeah, here's one. This guy, third from the left. One of those crazy parties I mentioned." She showed Miranda the photo.

"Thanks Jacinta. I'll see if he turns up at breakfast then."

"Sure."

They spent the next hour chatting, Jacinta relating some of her tall tales, Miranda mainly listening and not giving much away. Then she excused herself and went to bed, pleading fatigue from her trip. Jacinta watched her go, frowning faintly.

~~~

The next morning Miranda slipped out of bed, dressed and padded down to the eating hall. *At least we have our own rooms,* she thought. It did cost money to stay here, though not much, and from what Jacinta had said no doubt you could get around even that requirement. It reminded her of the hippie communes of long ago that she'd seen a documentary about. From what she knew of them she was glad the intervening decades had raised the standard of their digs and reduced their load of lice.

She sat in the hall, eating some cereal and nursing a steaming coffee. Eventually an ill-shaven man shuffled in, looking bleary eyed and a bit on the plump side. After he picked up his breakfast he looked around as if searching for a friend and she beckoned. He frowned as if trying to remember her name, or possibly when he'd slept with her, then shrugged, gave a weak smile and ambled over.

"Hi, ah, young lady," he said. "Will you hit me if I confess I don't remember your name? My head is never best in the morning."

She smiled back. "It's Miranda. Don't worry, we've never met. But you're Georgie, right? I hear you know a friend of mine, Jimmy Dent? He invited me here a while ago but I can't find him. You don't happen to know where he'd be?"

"Ah, yes, Jimmy! No, haven't seen him for a while, sorry. Can't you call him?"

"Out of service. I don't know if the idiot changed phones or what. He was a bit of a conspiracy nut. So what did you guys do together? I hear you had a bit of a crowd going."

"Yeah, yeah, we did. We got onto a sweet deal. One of the big companies was paying gamers to hook into their latest virtuals. Fucking amazing stuff. Like reality, some of it."

"Wow, really? Who were they? What were they doing?"

"Big outfit called Allied Cybernetics. Into all kinds of hot stuff. Games. Medical. Augmented suits. Military hardware. Rich as Croesus and hot as hell. The stuff we tested – Jesus. Nearly wet myself thinking about it."

"You aren't still doing it?"

"Nah. I'd love to but there's something funny about my nervous system. Didn't take too well to some of their interfaces. The most god-awful headaches. They said they were working on it but ended up chucking me out, afraid of liability I guess. I reckon I'll get a call one day, though, bring me back to test the mods. They assured me my data was very interesting and they'd use it. Paid me out nicely too."

"So what did you do exactly?"

"Their big thing is man-machine neural interfaces. They are hitting it from all sides. Prosthetics you can control with your mind, just by the nerves you usually use. Remote sensing. AI using neural tissue. Apparently if you lose your arm they'll be able to give you one just as good. Better, even: stronger, tougher. I wasn't going to lose an arm for science, but I did test it with one of their overlay interfaces. Amazing. I could feel with its fingers and move it as if it was my own. A bit like wearing heavy gloves, but they reckon with a full interface you'd never tell the difference."

"Wow! And Jimmy was into that too! What else?"

"Virtuals that are like being there. For games, remote viewing, education, whatever. Some boring stuff: just hooked up to a machine while their scientists studied how your nerves could control circuits and the circuits could control your nerves. Even psychology: they could modify your emotions and stuff. That could get wild. But they had a cutoff triggered if your vitals went too crazy, and you even had a manual kill switch to get out if you wanted to."

"Sounds incredible! Pity you had to drop out. Jimmy did the same stuff?"

"Yeah, yeah, he did. But if you want to know exactly what, talk to his gang. I don't know if they were just puffing it for the ladies, but you'd ask them and they'd go all secretive, reckoning they had to sign heavy confidentiality contracts. But I reckon they were onto some sweet deal, whatever it was."

"So who's in this gang of his?"

A strange look came into Georgie's eyes. "That's a funny thing, now that you ask. Most of them have moved on, like Jimmy. I didn't think anything of it, you know. People around here move on all the time. You should know, I never saw you before and might never see you again. But now you mention it, and I think about who they were, yeah… all gone. Odd. Well, except one. Kyro. Big fellow. Great guy once you get to know him, though certainly not your average guy." He smiled but did not elaborate.

Like pulling teeth. She smiled winningly. "This Kyro sounds like someone I'd like to meet. Where can I find him?"

"Can't say for sure. I think he's shacked up with some girl who has her own place nearby. But he likes his old friends, or maybe it's just the parties here. Any party, almost guaranteed he'll be here. Eventually."

"Georgie," she said, reaching over to touch his soft fingers with hers. "You're a pal. I'll be seeing you round. Make sure I buy you a beer at that party."

He grinned. "You bet, Miranda. Raise you a dance."

She smiled. "You rogue. We'll see."

With that she took her leave. *I guess I'll hang around for the next party. The things we must do.*

CHAPTER 11 – KING'S COURT

Miranda spent the next day drifting around the place, chatting with whomever looked interested in talking. She didn't push it, though when she could she'd inject a question about Jimmy or one of the other people he might have known. But her main motive was to be seen, to become a familiar face instead of a stranger. Then when the time came she would be much more likely to get answers.

Nobody knew anything of note. A few had known Jimmy or thought they knew one or two of the people he hung out with. None of them knew where they might be now or who might know. None of them really cared. Though there was a faint undercurrent of awareness that perhaps more people had disappeared from their lives than usual. Nothing solid, nothing alarming: but there, visible between the lines in the occasional comment or frown.

A number of money-making activities had been related to her, some tedious, some illegal, some remarkably ordinary for such an escapist subculture. But one name recurred more than the others, a company with interesting projects and good pay: Allied Cybernetics.

Miranda ate lunch, joined some people in a few games and finally had dinner in the communal eating area. Jacinta caught her eye and waved, but did not come over. She was deep in conversation with her next collectible, by the look of it.

A man who looked like he was cruising for more than conversation cruised to a stop opposite her and asked if he could sit. She looked around and saw there were plenty of vacant seats, then smiled and nodded.

He was a handsome man, somewhat thin but in an elegant rather than unhealthy way. He spoke with a lazy drawl and something of an aristocratic English accent. *Probably from Kansas*, she thought cynically. His hair fell in dark ringlets down his forehead and over his ears. "Good evening, Lady," he said. "May I inquire your name? I am Henry Thayte. People call me King." He shrugged. "I don't know why, as I never studied history."

She laughed. "Obviously. Well hello then, King. I'm Miranda. I just arrived last night. Are you a regular in this palatial residence?"

He bowed his head. "A pleasure to meet you, Miranda. I have been here a couple of months, yes. There are interesting people to be met here. Interesting games to be played." He smiled at her in a way that hinted at one game he was particularly interested in playing tonight.

"Yes, I played a few today," she replied, deflecting the hint. "Some of the virtual rigs here are amazing." She paused and added reflectively, as if it had just occurred to her, "A couple of months, you say? Did you know a fellow name of Jimmy Dent? He's an old friend of mine and I'd hoped to bump into him, but he seems to have moved on."

"Ah yes, Jimmy. We weren't close, but I knew him, sure. We both did a bit of work for Allied Cybernetics too. I guess he's gone to greener pastures, though that one was pretty lush."

"I keep running into talk of this Allied Cybernetics. Do you still work for them?"

"Oh yes. It is very interesting work. In fact it might even have been I who introduced Jimmy to them. Yes, I'm pretty sure I did. He turned up here asking what was what, and I pointed him in their direction."

"How long had you been doing work for them before that?"

"A number of weeks. I forget who put me on to them. Their name just came up in general conversation, I believe."

"Anything you can tell me about what you did?"

"Only in general. Mainly direct mental control of machinery. They also gave me a little commission for bringing others in on it. They do an amazing amount of work and they're always on the look out for new talent. It's not just the amount of work they have to do. People are the same in general – otherwise medicine wouldn't work, would it? – but obviously vary a lot in the details. So AC like to test their stuff on as wide a range of people as possible to mesh with that variability.

If you want I can introduce you."

"Hmmm, maybe. One of the guys said it gave him headaches. Is it dangerous?"

He shrugged. "Nothing's ever happened to me, and I've only heard of a couple of people showing side effects. Minor stuff too."

They chatted for a while longer, then he said, "By the way, Miranda, some friends are throwing a party here in two nights' time. Everyone is invited. May I hope for your presence?"

"Oh! What kind of party? Here, you said?"

"Oh yes. All the best parties are here," he smiled. "There are no rules, except to be nice to each other and have a good time. If you can bring food, drink, whatever, please do. There'll be drinks for sale too but, you know, if you're not buying a lot of people appreciate the sharing. Any game rigs you want to show off are always popular. If not, bring yourself and regale us with tales or song."

She smiled again. "Sounds great!" Then she yawned. "But I'm sorry, King, I'm a bit worn out. I have to get some sleep before I start snoring, which would be plain rude. I would not like to be beheaded. Good night."

He stood regally, took her hand and planted a respectful kiss on it. "Good night then. You do not require company?" he added, in case she had simply been too thick to see his earlier hints.

She smiled. "Some other time, perhaps. Good night, King."

CHAPTER 12 – CYBERNETIC RESEARCH

Miranda woke early, grabbed her handbag and hat and went out onto the street. She avoided the few denizens of the meal hall, all of whom looked happy enough to be avoided. She looked around like a visitor trying to decide the most interesting direction to investigate, shouldered her bag and strolled along the street, breathing in the sights and the crisp morning air.

Not far up the street she came to a shopping center on the ground floor of a mid-range hotel. A better class of place than where she was staying, but not so grand that there wouldn't be shops and eating places that someone with her level of funds could at least aspire to on occasion. And aspire she did, as the tempting scents from some of the breakfast places wafted into her nose. She sat eating her pancakes and drinking her coffee, thinking about how best to approach her day.

She got up and wandered casually through the rest of the shops without paying much attention, entered the hotel's foyer and got into the elevator, which whisked her efficiently to the fifth floor. She padded down the slightly worn carpet to room 521, waved her wrist in front of the door and it admitted her to the room.

She threw her handbag on a chair and her clothes followed as she stripped to her underwear and lay down on the bed. *Just for a minute it's good to relax. I'm not really cut out for undercover.*

After rather more than a minute, she got up and went to the mirror. She removed the implants that subtly altered the shape of her face, teeth and the timbre of her voice; returned her hair to its usual style.

She smiled at the new woman in the mirror. *Hello Miriam, welcome back.*

Her new persona shed, her old personality also took hold and she quickly got dressed in more official attire. *Might as well practice my steely gaze while I'm at it. Yep, that will do nicely.*

She collected the rest of her equipment, left the room and this time took the elevator down to the parking garage. She got into her car and drove out, the navigation system guiding her unerringly through the unfamiliar streets toward the highway that led to Allied Cybernetics.

~~~

"May I help you?" said the person at the front desk in a voice as crisp as her uniform.

"I hope you can," replied Miriam, flashing her identification. "I am here on official police business."

Ms Crisp looked slightly taken aback. "Oh! I hope it's nothing serious!"

"Just part of an ongoing investigation," Miriam assured her. "The name of your company has come up in relation to it. Could you direct me to someone who would be able to give me information on members of the public you've paid to test your technology?"

The woman pursed her lips and looked at her screen. "Certainly. Here's your visitor's badge. You are keyed to the tenth floor. Go to the elevators to your right and they will take you there. Then see Mr Denison in the Contractors Office, which you will find by turning left. He will be expecting you."

Miriam thanked her and did as requested. Soon she found herself seated before Mr Denison, who looked her over incuriously. "So, Detective Hunter, is it? How can I help you?"

"I am investigating the disappearance of a man, possibly several others as well. I understand he might have been one of your test subjects. I'd like to know when was the last time you saw him and if you have any clues where he went? His name is Jimmy Dent. Here's a photo."

Denison looked at it, frowned, spoke to his computer. "All records on a Jimmy Dent or James Dent please."

"Hmmm… OK, yes. Yes, he was one of our test subjects. One of the gamers. He came here several times. The last time was a month ago, I'm afraid."

"You don't have any record of why he stopped coming?"

The man laughed, a short sharp bark. "I don't think you understand these people. They are useful. They don't want much money; hell, half of them would probably do it for the fun of it, at least when they're testing game interfaces. And while there is always a slight risk in cutting edge man-machine interface research, these people don't mind it. Some of them get off on it. But they're not what you'd call reliable. They come and go. Lose interest, move to other cities, get themselves killed sometimes. We don't track them. Can't."

"You said the work was risky? You don't keep track of them in case of problems?"

He spread his hands. "We can't. Privacy laws. We keep tabs on them through friends if we can, and they always know where to find us if they have any problems. But we can't track them. If they decide to go, they go."

"Do you know if Mr Dent talked to anyone here, might have told them his plans?"

"I doubt it. They don't come here to make friends and they rarely chat about their personal lives or their plans. This is a scientific research center, not a hairdressing salon. But I'll send a message out. I have your contact details: I'll let you know if I hear anything. But don't hold your breath."

Miriam sighed. "I think I get the picture. Can you tell me what he worked on?"

Denison frowned at her. "I don't think so. Not only privacy implications but company intellectual property issues. You understand."

"I could get a warrant."

He sighed, rather overly dramatically in Miriam's opinion. "If you feel you must. If you feel you can. I don't think a judge will be impressed. But honestly, Detective, if I thought the information could actually help the man I'd be only too happy to oblige. But I can't see how it could be any use to you. I can show you his last medical records – eyes only without that warrant, mind you. Let me see... yes, we always give them a going over before and after. Here, take a look."

Miriam looked.

"As you can see his final visit here was on the 17th of last month and there was nothing wrong with him then. Whatever happened to him has nothing to do with us. But these gamers have the attention spans of mayflies. Most likely nothing happened to him at all and he just got bored with the city. They do, you know."

Oh, no he didn't. But you have your secrets, I have mine.

"I see. Well, thank you for your time. I might be back if I think of any further questions worth asking." She rose to go.

"No problems. Goodbye, Detective." Then he went back to what he'd been doing as if she had ceased to exist.

She caught the lift back down, casually tossed her visitor's badge onto the desk on her way out, and got back into her car. But she didn't start it, just sat there thinking. She had started with the gamers but there was one other lead that had possibilities and she had the rest of the day to chase it. She usually liked to drive but there was no great hurry and she had better things to do right now. "St Crispin's Shelter", she told the car, then began to call up facts and figures from her phone as the car smoothly pulled away from the curb and accelerated into the traffic.

CHAPTER 13 – SYNERGY

Miriam thought it was no wonder the gamers liked Allied Cybernetics. It was a sprawling company with a finger in more high tech pies than she had known existed. Their public relations department was certainly busy regaling the world with the wonders coming out of its pipeline and she wondered how one company could do so much. She had the impression that if its depth and quality might not match that of Beldan Robotics, it surely made up for it in breadth.

Its CEO, Aden Sheldrake, had started his career as a partner in a much smaller company working on neural coding. He had met his business partner when the latter was an intense young man studying towards his doctorate in the field and Sheldrake was a flamboyant undergraduate with a quick mind, a fascination for technology and a way with people.

Sheldrake had not had an easy life. He had been born into poverty of parents who had little interest in working their way out of it and, despite flashes of genuine love for young Aden, even less interest in him. He had suffered the bad luck of having parents who had fallen into parenthood because that was what people did, and who then found the rest of their lives more engaging than the reality of raising a child. They raised him, again because that is what people did, but neither encouraged ambition nor provided a role model of it. But Aden had eyes, and those eyes were soon fixed on the shining towers and leafy suburbs of the better off. He also had a brain, and he applied it with single-minded devotion to his ambition to become as wealthy as humanly possible, if not wealthier.

Thus he excelled at school, enough to win a minor scholarship to university; then excelled at university, enough to win the interest of one of the professors. The professor gave his young protégé access to his lab as a part time research assistant. But whatever hopes the professor had for him were to be disappointed. For that is where Aden met Bram Chesterfield.

Aden was clever, but Bram was out of his league. Part of that was raw IQ. But Bram also had the personality characteristics once labeled as Asperger's Syndrome. So to the raw material of his IQ he added an intensity of focus that less driven mortals could only dream of, and if they did would probably think it a nightmare. But Bram didn't care what lesser mortals thought, if he even had a concept that they thought at all. He only cared for his work.

Consequently Bram had no friends. But somewhere along the fractures of his mind remained the human need for them, and something in Aden's gift for people reached him. They became fast friends. Before, Bram cared only for his work. When he did well, he felt a perfunctory pleasure in the praise of his professor or others, but it did not truly touch him, merely eased an itch he didn't know he had. But he delighted in showing his work to Aden, even on the occasions where Aden did not really understand what he had achieved. Aden even acquired girls for his intense friend; girls who liked the challenge, or were "mind groupies" as Aden privately called them. This was another need that had lurked unexpressed in Bram's brain, and its satisfaction filled him with amazed delight: even more than is usual, since he had never thought to seek it himself.

Aden found Bram a fascinating person; found his brain one of the wonders of the world. He delighted in not only knowing him but giving him joy. And Bram loved Aden.

Then Aden saw in Bram's work the route to the wealth he had always sought. Bram cared for nothing but his work. It was a symbiosis that would exceed that of Watson, Crick and Franklin; of the legendary Jobs and Woz. It would change the world.

Aden had the keen knowledge, born of poverty, that money had to come from somewhere and that the somewhere had to be persuaded to send it his way. He took to his new role like a missionary to the natives. He knew the science well enough to explain it accurately and even more importantly, enthusiastically; and had a knack for seeing what people wanted and explaining the advantages in terms that hooked their interest. Few people could have pulled it off. The potential of Bram's research was speculative: if it had been too close to practicality, the University would have dropped its leaden foot on it faster than lead feet had a right to move. But it was in the happy valley of being both speculative and conducive to informed speculation. To the University, Aden stressed its obscurity and uncertainty, and the favor he would be doing them if he could persuade anybody to buy out their interest; to the investors he stressed its uniqueness and potential, and hinted at the fortunate myopia of the University in being unable to see what they had. In the end he acquired both investors and the unencumbered rights to Bram's research at a price the investors were happy to pay and the University was happy to receive.

The world of early-stage investment is littered with the corpses of unfulfilled promises and failed enterprises. Yet the early-stage investors continue, in the hope – and actuarial reality – of those few investments that will return themselves tens or hundreds of times over. Aden and Bram did not disappoint. Aden had seen hints in Bram's work of fundamental breakthroughs, spun them into castles of dollars in the minds of the investors: and Bram delivered. His results opened the road to nerve-computer interfaces that would work at unprecedented resolutions, down to single nerves: and better, work in both directions. It took no exaggeration to explain the medical and industrial possibilities to the investors, and no special brilliance on their part to grasp what that meant.

Another synergy occurred, this time between Aden's talents and his investors' excitement, experience and contacts. Their company was bought out by a much larger company, Allied Medical Devices. The investors made a lot of money. So did Aden, who on the strength of the impression he'd made on the buyers also acquired a new position in the company, doing much the same thing for a rather better salary. Bram came along too, as an integral part of the deal. He was happy, because he could continue his work with an even larger budget. He was now wealthy too, literally beyond his dreams, which had never involved wealth. He didn't care. But Aden ensured that he had all the comforts he had earned. Left to his own devices, Bram would have lived as easily in a loft as in the luxurious apartment he now inhabited.

But Aden believed, and in fact he was right, that even if he gave few external signs, Bram was the happier for the more gracious architecture, beautiful art, better food, softer bed and warmer women that Aden ensured he had.

AMD's board and major shareholders could only have been pleased by the expansion in income their new acquisition produced. Then through more good luck than anybody deserved, the next few years saw a string of poor selling decisions by the main shareholders with complementary good ones by Sheldrake. Along with some generous share options he exercised, the eventual result was his emergence as an unexpectedly large minority shareholder. From that position of relative strength and by dint of negotiating ability to rival his luck, it wasn't long before he had gained control of the company.

That was the official history anyway, and all that Miriam had access to. But had the original owners been fully aware of the potential of some of the more arcane neural interfaces that had been under development, they might have been more cautious and less surprised by the outcome. In any case everybody was happy. It was just that fuller information would have reduced the happiness of some parties considerably, possibly to the level of lawsuits.

Nobody could question Sheldrake's ambition. He had himself voted in as CEO and AMD began a startling growth phase. It acquired company after company, technology after technology. It was not an undirected growth: all the companies and technologies were in fields related to man-machine interfaces. Sheldrake seemed fired with zeal to own the field. Prosthetics, brain scanners, virtual reality, games, information input and control, military hardware, artificial intelligence: the list kept growing. But Sheldrake didn't let it become an unwieldy monster: except for functions that could be sensibly amalgamated he let the parts of his growing body act relatively independently of each other. But through the nerve center of himself, Bram's scientific brilliance and his specialized AIs, the cross-fertilization of technologies benefited all. AMD became Allied Cybernetics and its wealth grew with each acquisition.

Miriam considered this with a frown. She was no financial wizard, but she thought it odd that a company could grow in wealth at such a rate purely through acquisitions. She wondered how he could pay a fair price for a company yet end up so much richer, even with synergy and higher efficiency. She thought about that some more, formulated a query, and sent it off to forensic accounting. By then her head hurt. She had learned that in police work it was wise to rest when you had the chance, so she laid back in the seat, closed her eyes and dozed off to sleep.

Chapter 14 – The Dearly Departed

S he was drifting down a river, her boat gently rocking on the waves, just leaning back against the comfortable leather of the seat and watching the beautiful forest pass by. But there was something wrong. She felt a sense of foreboding, as if something lurked within the forest just out of sight and hearing.

She looked at Alex, sitting opposite her, and smiled at him. But he just stared through her with obsidian eyes, and she realized that was all he had done for so long and she couldn't remember why. She wondered why he was in the boat with her, but she did not want him to go. She wanted to ask him why he hated her. Except she knew. She just couldn't remember. She turned away, and when she turned back he was gone. Then the boat bumped against something. And bumped. And bumped. Then a voice spoke.

"Detective Hunter, we have arrived."

She opened her eyes with a start. *Sometimes my dreams are so obvious,* she thought. *But I'm not going to call him. There's no point.*

She came fully awake and said, "Understood." The door opened and she got out, looking up at the sign announcing "St Crispin's Shelter for the Lost". *Perhaps I'm at the right place.* Then she went in.

A woman was inside at the counter. She was middle aged, slightly plump, with light brown hair drawn efficiently back and a friendly expression. She practically oozed motherhood and the mere sight of her evoked the scent of freshly baked cookies out of the empty air. Beyond her was a rounded archway opening onto a large space containing rows of benches, but nobody was seated at them at this time of day. The woman looked at her with a friendly gaze touched with caution. "Can I help you, miss?" she asked.

"Hello," she smiled back. "I'm with the police. Would you be Tammy Henderson?"

The woman nodded. "That's me, officer. What's this about?"

"I understand you reported a disappearance a few weeks ago. One of your clients, or residents?"

The woman gave her a slightly surprised look. "Why, yes, that's me. But I've already been interviewed. Have you found something?"

"No, sorry, but I'd like to talk to you if I may. Do you mind?"

The woman sighed. "No, not really, not that it will do any good. Should I be pleasantly amazed that the police are showing an interest in the disappearance of one of the forgotten people here? Anyway, come in, I'll make us a cup of tea."

Miriam sat at one of the benches as the woman brought over a large metal teapot redolent of strong tea, a couple of rough cups, a small jug of milk and a glass container of somewhat dirty sugar. "Nothing but the best for the fine officers of the law," she said with a smile, pouring the tea.

"What's that?" Miriam asked, indicating a sign above the entrance, which read:

> But if it be a sin to covet honor,
> I am the most offending soul alive.

"Oh, that's kind of our motto. It's from Shakespeare, the St Crispin's Day speech in Henry the Fifth."

"I see. Well, Ms Henderson, can you tell me why you thought your resident's disappearance was suspicious? I imagine with the kinds of people here that it must be a pretty transient population. People must come and go all the time? So why report this one?"

Tammy gave a faint smile. "Oh, Big Max was different." She stopped, looking into the distance as at a favorite memory.

"Listen, Detective... Hunter. The people we get here are a ragtag lot. People who've given up, basically. Lost in drugs, lost in drink, or just lost. As long as they still need to eat and still need a place to sleep and dream, we give it to them. We give them kindness. Sometimes it's enough. I suppose the world thinks they're all losers, and maybe the world is right a lot of the time. But you never know what journey another person has had to walk, do you? We don't judge them. We help them out, show them a kind face and a listening ear."

"Do many of them... recover?"

She shrugged. "Some. I probably couldn't bear it, the things I've seen, if it were otherwise. But as you say, these homeless people are transients. They usually don't hang around long, even with the food and shelter. Whatever they're looking for, they usually keep looking. You're right though. Most of them never find it."

"But Max...?"

"Max was in his sixties, but had a sharp mind and a healthy body. I think he had been rich once, and had some of the early life extension treatments. I don't know what happened to him, what brought him down: he'd never speak of it. He had a wedding band too, gold; I'm afraid most of the people who come through here would pawn something like that in a flash. But not him, it was precious to him. Whether there was some tragedy with her, or his family... I just don't know."

She paused, collecting her thoughts. "But whatever it was, it wasn't drugs or drink; wasn't gambling or bankruptcy either. He'd just lost interest. Lost interest in living, he said; not that he wanted to die, he just didn't want to try any more. You know what he told me once? 'People live for the future. But sometimes by the time you get there you find it's already gone. Now I just live in the present, however long it lasts.'" She shrugged. "He'd spent a few years wandering around, you know, being a tramp, bedding down in homeless shelters like this one, never putting down roots. But when he got here, something about the place must have spoken to him. He never left. And do you know what he did?"

Miriam shook her head.

"He didn't care about money, but apparently he still had some. Not huge, but tidy. He said he just didn't care enough to do anything with or about it. Had nobody to give it to and no need for it himself. But after he'd stayed here a couple of weeks he gave it all to St Crispin's. He said he didn't mind travelling around and living off charity, as he figured that's what the charities wanted. But he just couldn't impose, as he put it, on one place like some kind of sponge on a rock. So he gave us the money, to St Crispin's the organization I mean, not just this place. Enough rent for the rest of his days, he said. So he could live here without guilt. And if he left, he'd always have a place he could come back to if he needed it."

"I see. What did he do with his time?"

"As I said, he was fit. He'd walk around the city, see the sights, visit museums. Or just sit in the park talking to the birds. He loved books; he'd go to the libraries, borrow tons of books. Watch old movies."

"What about the other people here?"

"Depends. A lot of them are really lost and don't do much of anything until whatever demon is riding them drives them on their way. But we don't give them money. If they want money they have to earn it. Sometimes we'll pay them for jobs around here like painting or repairs. Sometimes they get money for blood or being scientific research subjects."

Miriam's ears pricked up. "Scientific research? Is there much of that? I wouldn't think many of your clients would pass the health criteria, from what you say."

"Yeah… but there were the occasional things. Psychiatric therapies; drug dependency treatments. Even rejuvenation therapies. Sometimes my people here are just what the doctor ordered. And yes… there was a good one fairly recently. Wanted a lot of subjects and paid well – or what passes for well in this crowd. Hang on, they left some contact flyers in case anyone's interested. They're still recruiting, you know."

She got up and went to her office, and in a short while returned brandishing a glossy brochure. "Real paper and all," she smiled. "Yes, this is them. Allied Cybernetics. They didn't mind about the quality of our residents in the slightest, they said. In fact they welcomed it. Their story is they are as interested in the extremes of human nervous systems as in the average. To make their technology more universal and robust. And some of their applications are psychiatric as well."

"And Big Max?" Miriam asked. "I don't suppose he did any work for them too?"

"Why yes, he did. He actually got quite interested for a while. He'd never tell me what it was about but he'd come home some days with quite the shiny look in his eyes. I could tell he loved whatever it was he was into."

The woman paused but Miriam just looked at her with an inquiring expression. Tammy had seemed reluctant to talk at first, but once she'd started she seemed unable to stop. Perhaps she knew this was the only eulogy Big Max would ever have and Miriam the only person who would ever care enough to listen.

Finally she took a breath. "I shouldn't tell you this. I might get in trouble, so please keep it to yourself. Can you?"

"As long as it's legal – or even illegal within reason. I don't want to make any trouble for you or him. I'm just trying to find out what happened to him."

"Well, we're not supposed to get too personal with the clients. Bad for morale, and I understand that. But one day Big Max came back here and he looked strange. Intense. I was off duty that night, and he knocked on my door later. We let them do that, you know: we like to always be there if they need help or just to talk." She stopped and gave Miriam a nervous glance. "Go on," urged Miriam.

"When I opened the door he just stood there. He looked... well, it's hard to describe. More than intense. I've thought about it since, what it was about him. Like he was an avatar of Desire, if that makes any sense. Or like the essence of masculinity. And he gave me this look... Jesus!" She shook her head as if to clear it, as if the memory still had the power to rattle her hormones. "Well, look, he was an attractive man, even if he was older. And when he gave me that look... hell, I fell into his eyes. Practically pulled him into my room."

"You don't need to tell me this."

"But I do! You have to understand! He'd been to Allied Cybernetics that day. I think he did something there that changed him that day, some kind of virtual sex that must have been... real, even more than real. He said something to me, afterwards. He grabbed me like his life depended on it, gave me another one of those stares – but ebbing, like it was leaving him – and he said, real urgent like, 'Tammy! Is it real? Tell me this is real!' And I held him, and said, 'It's real, Max, as real as it gets.' Then he kind of smiled, and held me, and went to sleep."

Miriam just stared, uncertain what to say.

"The next morning we were both a bit embarrassed, you know? He left my room and we never spoke of that night afterwards."

"Pardon me for asking this, but did you ever do it again?"

She shook her head. "No... no. I think we would have, if we'd had longer. It was always there between us, that night. But it was only two weeks before he disappeared." She sighed. "Two weeks."

"Might that be why he left? You said you were both embarrassed about it after. Could it have driven him away somehow?"

She shook her head and said firmly, "No. It wasn't like that. It was our secret, but it wasn't a shameful one. It was... precious. Like a little bit of magic we shared. It drove us closer not further apart."

Miriam thought about what had happened to him. "Did he ever tell you about any other side effects of what he did at Allied Cybernetics? Headaches? Hallucinations, anything like that?"

"No. None of the people here ever did." She looked at Miriam sternly. "I see where you're going. But Allied Cybernetics is good for these people. Good to them, too. Don't you go thinking they hurt them."

"Did Max ever go back there after your night together?"

"Yes. He didn't usually tell me where he went; none of them did. But I know he went back there at least a few times. He loved it. But it was never like that night again, he never came back changed."

"What about the day he disappeared? Did he go there? What happened?"

"I'm sorry, I don't know where he went that day. All I know is he went out and didn't return."

"What makes you think he didn't just leave? Found a woman? Decided he'd had enough of this city?"

"Well, as I said he was different. Most of the people here have a bit of stuff. Their little bundle of possessions. Most of them need something of their own. And when they leave they take it with them. Heck, they usually take it with them when they're just walking around town. But Max left that day and left his bundle here, like he usually did in fact. And never came back."

"So you were worried, called the police?"

"Yes. I thought he might have been hurt, maybe lying in some hospital or worse. But that wasn't it. And he didn't just fall into the river or something either..."

"Why are you so sure?"

She looked at Miriam. "You'll think I'm crazy, that all this proves is he did leave. But that's not it at all. You see, I got a message from him a few days later. Said to post his bundle to a drop box in Frisco."

Miriam stared at her, surprised. "And you didn't think to tell the police this?'"

She shrugged. "What for? I'd already spoken to them, they'd already shelved it, and if I told them that they'd bury it even deeper." She gave Miriam a long look. "And then you wouldn't be here, would you? I don't know if you can help Max, or if anyone can now. But at least you're a chance."

Tammy sighed then continued. "But you see, it was a lie. It wasn't him. I was better off leaving the case at least half alive than letting you cops convince yourselves he'd just run off, to save yourselves the bother of looking. Pardon me."

"But why do you think that?"

"Because we were friends! But there was nothing in the message, not any explanation, not even a goodbye! Just an 'I've left town send my stuff here' message. Like somebody talking to the doorman. Like somebody tidying up a mess. So," she leant closer, lowering her voice, "Do you know what I did?"

"Please tell me."

"It was a bit bad of me. Maybe a lot bad. But you see, I was worried about him; I felt rotten, but I knew he'd understand. I... I went through his stuff first. There was an old photo in it, you know, printed on high quality plastic. Looked like a younger version of Max, standing smiling with a woman and a pretty young girl up the top of some skyscraper. Quite wrinkled, as if he'd looked at it a lot, but kept snug and safe in a soft protector. I... crap. I took it out, OK? Kept it. Sent the rest, but not that. And do you know what happened? When he got his package without his precious photo in it?"

Miriam shook her head, eyes wide.

"Nothing."

CHAPTER 15 – PARTY GAMES

Miriam again let the car drive her, this time back to her hotel, while she pondered the information. It was certainly suspicious that both missing men had been test subjects for Allied Cybernetics, but she cautioned herself against jumping to conclusions. That the people who had disappeared were in a certain social stratum, and Allied Cybernetics sourced their test subjects from that stratum, was the kind of thing that bred coincidences. There were good and completely independent reasons for both and the overlap could easily be chance.

However the suspicion wouldn't release its claws that easily. But what would be their motive? It hardly seemed likely a large corporation would indulge in serial killing. *What if it isn't the corporation, but someone in it? Someone who picks his victims from the test subjects? They must get biographical information on them. They'd know who was unlikely to be missed.* The thought made her go cold. *Christ! And how many might there be in that case? If it weren't for a couple of mistakes and an overly imaginative AI, we'd still be none the wiser! And how the hell can we trace who's doing it?* She sighed. She would have to ask Allied Cybernetics for a complete list of who knew what about their test subjects and hope they were feeling cooperative, as a warrant to force them wasn't likely.

She thought about Georgie and his headaches, Max and his temporary transformation into some kind of sex god; though Miriam wondered how much of that was infatuation on Tammy's part. *Maybe it was just the best sex she's ever had, and it's messing with her memories; or it's her excuse to herself for breaking the rules.* So what if there had been other, worse reactions; maybe even deaths? And Allied Cybernetics was covering it up? *But why? This is cutting edge research. They'll have disclaimers up to their eyeballs, and they certainly have as good a medical backup system as you could ask. A few deaths might embarrass them but they'd spin the medical benefits and probably even be right. Hell, it probably wouldn't even put a dent in their volunteer numbers, not among these desperate people. Why take the risk of doing something so insanely illegal?*

She shook her head. It didn't make sense. Still, her course was clear: she'd take the serial killer angle. It might be true, and if it weren't it would keep her close to Allied Cybernetics in case there really was something murky beneath their shiny laboratories. She would have to be careful though: she didn't want to spook either Allied Cybernetics or her hypothetical serial killer by acting as if she had any solid evidence, or even any strong suspicions.

She smiled grimly. It wasn't as if she actually had either.

Her car finally returned to its assigned bay and released her. She got out, smoothing her clothes. *Well, Miranda, better dress down. We've got a party to go to.*

~~~

Miriam could feel the throbbing of a beat as she dressed in her party gear in her room at the hostel. Even a woman of her supposed income could afford to look good these days. *That will do nicely,* she thought as she looked in the mirror. *Sexy but not too out there; I might be available but don't take it for granted: if you want me you'll have to work for it.* She would do a lot for her job and this case, but not sleep with anybody who asked. She wondered what she would do if the right person asked; smiled at the obviousness of the answer. The police weren't the Vestal Virgins.

When she walked in to the party, the music was thumping and the lights were flashing, lending a weird life to the moving fantasy images someone had set up on a holographic projector. There were a lot of people she hadn't seen before; she hadn't met everyone and no doubt there were plenty of people who weren't staying here.

She went up to the bar, bought herself a drink then wandered into the crowd, finally sitting on a bench seat behind a small table. She leant back and surveyed the party, innocently displaying some cleavage like a flower suggesting its availability to a field of bees. She was mainly here to talk to Kyro if he turned up, but she was also interested to find what else she could learn. Soon enough a man ambled over and sat opposite her.

"This seat taken?" he enquired politely.

"No, feel free," she said, sipping her drink and looking him over. *Cast your line into the water, see what nibbles.*

He smiled. "Hi. I'm James. Are you staying here or are you a blow-in like me?"

"I've been here a couple of days. How'd you rate an invitation?"

He smiled again. "I put it down to my rugged looks and raw sexuality. Other people have other theories. I know a guy who knows a guy, basically."

She smiled back. "So are you into gaming, like the people who stay here?"

"A bit, but not hard core like some of you lot. Are you one of those? Comparing me to your favorite well-muscled character?"

You're not likely to be much use, I'm afraid. Time to cut back on the flirting. "No, no, I like games too but I'm really just drifting around."

"Trying to find yourself?" he asked with his trademark smile.

"Actually trying to find an old boyfriend. Maybe you know him. Jimmy Dent?"

The man looked disappointed and frowned. "No, I'm afraid not. What's wrong with the guy? Not answering the phone? Maybe he's trying to tell you something?"

"Yeah, maybe. Oh! I'm sorry, there's someone I know over there. Excuse me! Maybe we'll bump into each other later."

He saluted her with his glass as she left, not trying very hard to hide either his disappointment or his offsetting thought about the number of fish in the sea. She walked through the Hulk and made her way to Georgie, who'd just come in with a couple of guys.

"Hi Georgie," she called. "Remember me?"

He frowned at her as if once more trying to remember when he'd slept with her. Then his eyes cleared. "Oh! Oh yes, the young lady from breakfast. Mary? No! Miranda? Hi! I told you the parties were worth it!"

"You did indeed. Now I believe I owe you a drink. Stay here, I'll go get. What'll you have? And your friends?"

"Well, that's uncommonly generous of you, Miranda. Make it a round of Bud."

She wended her way back to the bar and returned with a tray of beers and a cocktail for herself. They toasted her health and started chatting about what people chat about at parties. She listened with half an ear, smiling and nodding. *Just fertilize the ground, you never know what might sprout.* In a lull she whispered in Georgie's ear, "Hey Georgie, give me a heads-up if you see Kyro, OK?"

One of Georgie's friends passed around some pale green pills. Miriam knew what they were: they produced mild euphoria, a small increase in libido and a tendency to giggle at bad jokes. Miriam accepted one and popped it in her mouth. She wasn't worried. When she went undercover she'd had a microlab inserted under her skin; it could counteract most drugs including this one. It was a very clever design: it let through any initial rush then damped it down to detectable but not disabling levels, allowing her to know how she should react.

After another ten minutes of somewhat looser conversation in which Miriam learned more than she cared about some topics but nothing of interest, Georgie gave her a gentle nudge in the ribs and pointed across the room with his chin. Miriam saw a large man sporting closely cropped dark hair cut into intriguing mathematical patterns, and knew this must be Kyro.

"Thanks Georgie, you're a doll. I owe you another drink. See you later!"

With that she went up on her toes and kissed him on the cheek, took her leave from the group and weaved her way over to Kyro. "Hey!" she called, "Kyro!"

Unlike Georgie, the eyes Kyro turned on her gave the impression he would not only remember where he'd slept with her but how she'd rated on a scale of one to ten. He looked her up and down, curiously rather than with any intent or hostility, and said. "Hello. I'm afraid you have the advantage of me. I don't believe we've met?"

She smiled her most disarming smile and shook her head. "That's right. Georgie told me who you are. My name's Miranda. I wanted to talk to you."

"Why?"

"Do I need a reason?" she asked teasingly.

"Yes."

"Don't you like girls?"

"I do. But I'm not so vain as to think you saw me from across the room and, overcome with lust, asked Georgie for a remote introduction. I don't mean to be rude, but I don't like being played. What do you want?"

She was taken aback for a moment. "Wow. OK. Fair enough. I'm actually looking for a friend of mine, and I hear you knew him. I was hoping you could point me in the right direction."

"He must be some friend, if you don't have his number but you're tracking him through this many degrees of separation."

"Maybe I just don't like a mystery."

"Do you or don't you? Like a mystery?"

"Has anyone ever told you you're a hard case, Kyro?"

"All the time. You don't have to talk to me if you don't like me."

She laughed, in a tone that couldn't decide whether it was delighted or annoyed. "Have they also told you you're painfully honest?"

He graced her with a slight smile. "Yes, though usually they use a less complimentary word."

She took a deep breath, starting to feel like a novice somehow thrust into a match with an Olympic fencer. "OK. Look, I'm sorry. Most people aren't as – direct as you. Can we start again? Hi, I'm Miranda," she said, extending her hand.

He looked at it as if evaluating its intent or worthiness, or perhaps like it was a suspicious fish proffered by an untrustworthy merchant, and she held her breath. Then he gave another of his faint smiles and extended his hand to grip hers in a firm yet gentle grasp. "I suppose if you're still standing there you're either worth knowing or really desperate to find your friend. No promises though."

She smiled in her friendliest manner, with no trace of flirting: she knew he'd see straight through it. "Here, this is my friend. Jimmy Dent." Kyro glanced at the image, then back at her face, waiting. "He told me about this place, invited me to come and meet up with him here. Then I stopped hearing from him. But I was travelling around and decided to turn up around the time I'd mentioned. But he'd gone and nobody seems to know where. I'm worried."

"Some of that is true, but not much of it. What are you really after?" *What is this guy? A human lie detector? Christ! Or is he bluffing? Shit, maybe he's got enhanced eyes, can read blood flow or something. I can't take the risk.*

She blinked at him while those thoughts went through her head, and he just gave another of his slight smiles, this time with an edge of bitterness as if silently commenting, *You're all the same, not an honest bone in your bodies. What lie are you trying to dream up now?*

"Look, Kyro, I don't know why you don't believe me. I'm on his side. I need to find him and want to help him. Honestly."

"I don't know where he is."

She blinked at him again. Surely he couldn't be lying himself, it was too – out of character. So why the rigmarole? *He's playing the same game I am. The truth and nothing but the truth – but not the whole truth.*

"But you know something."

He favored her with another of his characteristic almost-smiles. "Perhaps."

"Will you help me?"

"No."

"Why not?"

"I don't trust you."

She frowned, exasperated. She looked around for inspiration. Some of his friends or acquaintances were looking on, amused. Obviously they'd seen Kyro perform before and they were mentally betting on how long it would take before she either fled the scene or screamed in his face.

"What the hell do you think I can do to him?"

"Nothing."

"You're speaking in riddles!"

He gave her another almost-smile. "Yes."

"Can I ask you something else?"

"Yes. Perhaps I will answer."

"Jimmy was doing work for Allied Cybernetics. I understand you were too? Are you still doing it?"

This time Kyro looked somewhat surprised, as if he had developed a model of her and for the first time she had done something he hadn't expected. "Yes. It is interesting work. They have made some remarkable advances."

"Did you work on the same things Jimmy did?"

"Some the same, some different."

"Did he ever have any problems with it? Georgie said he had to quit because of headaches. Did Jimmy have anything like that?"

"If he did, he didn't tell me. He was still going there the last time I saw him."

"So you have no knowledge of where he went or why?"

"No."

He regarded her silently for a moment. "Stay here. I have to go do something. I'll be back in a few minutes. Don't follow me."

She watched him go until he was lost to sight in the crowd. Then she leant back against the wall, crossed her arms and waited. *He might leave me like this all night, which will amuse him and his friends no end. But I doubt he'd ever be that unsubtle.*

In a few minutes, true to his word and her assessment, Kyro re-emerged from the crowd. Miriam stood up straight to meet him. "Kyro."

"You're still here."

"You said you'd be back."

He blessed her with another half smile, but said nothing.

"Are you going to tell me anything? I don't suppose pleading will help?"

"No."

"I asked you two questions."

He smiled again, with slightly different shading as if he was starting to enjoy the conversation. "So you did. But no, pleading won't help. Anyone can plead and it usually means they have nothing to offer. You need to give me some reason to help you. You could offer me sex for information. That might work."

She insolently looked him up and down, much as he had when he first met her only more pointedly. "You are interesting person, Kyro, and not unattractive. I am sure there are worse things in life than sex with you. But I'd do it for pleasure, not to weasel information out of you. Especially when 'might work' coming from you probably means it won't."

"I might begin to like you, Miranda, or whatever your real name is."

"Look, Kyro, the only reason I can give you to help me is to help Jimmy. If he was your friend, help him. Even if he was just an acquaintance, he was a man with friends and family: help him in the name of that. Help me."

"What makes you think some drifter like you can help him?"

Oops. She spread her arms. "At least help me find him!"

He regarded her silently. "All right. Do you know Jazz? Jacinta? She lives here too."

Miriam nodded, puzzled.

"I got on with Jimmy, but he never confided in me. But he had a good friend, another gamer who did testing for Allied Cybernetics, a fellow called Majid. I think Jimmy told him something, because when he disappeared Majid started looking very worried, and he disappeared too a day or so later."

"How does yet another person disappearing help? And what does it have to do with Jacinta?"

"Because he didn't just disappear like Jimmy. He was so scared of something that he went into hiding, and Jacinta knows how to find him."

"Jacinta knows all this?" Miriam asked in surprise. "Are you sure?"

"What do you think?"

Miriam sent one of his enigmatic part smiles back at him.

"You're learning," he said. "But I still don't like you."

"Do you think Majid's fear was justified? That he was really in danger? I see you're still here, and still doing stuff for Allied Cybernetics for that matter."

"Why do you think Allied Cybernetics has anything to do with it?"

She looked at him, trying to read his expression; she failed. "Their name keeps cropping up. I just wondered if maybe that wasn't a coincidence."

"As you say, I'm still here. Jacinta knows how to find Majid, and she's still here."

"But a lot of other people aren't."

Kyro gave her a startled glance; at least as startled as seemed possible for this strange man. "True. Probably a statistical anomaly. People in this crowd come and go all the time. You're here today and probably gone tomorrow yourself. No loss. You, I mean. Some of them were."

Miriam nodded thoughtfully, barely noticing his jibe, then sighed. "You're probably right. Majid was probably jumping at shadows. I guess I'll go and ask Jacinta how to find him. Thanks, Kyro."

"By the way, Miranda, I might start to like you. Do you know why?"

She looked at him in surprise. "Um. My rigorous honesty, brilliant wit and good legs?"

He actually smiled this time. "No. Though one and a half out of three isn't bad, considering. When I said I still don't like you – you didn't ask me why."

"I... see. I think I already like you, though I'm sure you don't care. But I do appreciate your help." She paused, then added. "May I ask you another question?"

"You just did."

She laughed. "Can you really tell when someone is lying, or were you bluffing?"

He just gave her an inscrutable smile.

"Hmm. Well, see you around. You're unique, Kyro. Maybe when all this is over I *will* sleep with you."

"That would be a great honor."

She glanced at him sharply, then laughed again. "For which one of us?"

He just smiled, almost with an edge of friendliness this time. She returned the same smile, shook her head in exasperation and headed off into the crowd. She knew he expected her to look back to see whether he was still watching her and with what expression. So she didn't.

Miriam chased the questions running around her brain as she went in search of Jacinta, but neither the questions nor the pondering led anywhere useful. Some people had disappeared; Allied Cybernetics was linked to them; but other people with even longer links to the company were still around. One friend of Jimmy's had been badly frightened by his disappearance, but nobody knew why. And Jacinta had sent her after a vague lead when she held a much hotter one in her hand. There was only one summation: *What in hell is going on here?*

Finally Miriam spied Jacinta engaged in a gyrating dance with a slender young woman with a pixie hairdo. She grabbed a drink in passing and came to stand in sight of them, content to wait patiently for them to finish. When Jacinta saw her, she whispered something in the woman's ear then left her to dance on her own. She walked up to Miriam.

"Don't ask me anything. Just follow me. There's something you need to see." Her eyes were dark, bottomless pits. Miriam couldn't be sure whether what she saw in their depths was an unaccountable hostility or just the dimness and flashing lights. She just nodded.

Jacinta led Miriam to a locked door. She retrieved a key from somewhere on her person and ushered Miriam through, down a spiral staircase to another locked door. "People don't come down here much," she explained. "And nobody is allowed in anyway unless they have cause. I troubleshoot the servers so I get a key." With that she let Miriam through into a dimly lit room with a large grate in the middle of the floor. The "servers" appeared to be a small collection of black boxes with various colored LEDs shining and flashing on them, well away on the far wall.

Miriam stopped over the grate and looked down. Beneath it crude steps were carved into the rock, spiraling down to end at a stream flowing sluggishly about ten feet below. "What's this?"

"Apparently this building was built over an old creek. It still flows underneath, added to by storm water drains. I like to romantically imagine in the old days smugglers or bootleggers dropping their wares down to mysterious strangers on boats, but for all I know they used it to do their washing."

"So why did you bring me here?"

"Take a look in that box next to the servers."

Miriam went over and looked in, but it was empty. "There's nothing…" she started, then heard a faint *snick* and spun around. Jacinta was staring at her, a small needlegun in her hand pointed at Miriam's heart.

"What…?"

"Now don't you move, Miranda – if that's your real name. Who the hell are you and what are you really after?" She reached behind herself and locked the door.

"Jacinta? What in hell's the matter with you!?"

"That's not the question. The question is *who* in hell are *you* really?"

"But what's wrong? What have I done?"

Jacinta sighed. "Novelist meets actor, how touching. Our own little arts festival. You want to know what I know? What I know is someone disappears and you *say* you're looking for him, which just happens to give you an excuse to look for someone else. What I know is you're showing remarkable tenacity for a somewhat dim girl just trying to catch up with a casual boyfriend she hasn't seen for months. What I know is the person you're looking for is dead scared of something to do with the person you *say* you're looking for. What I *think* is if you find him, he'll end up with Jimmy."

"No! That's not it at all!"

"Then you'd better talk fast, Miranda. Now, maybe you're not too worried. Maybe you know this needler will only knock you out: though you should consider that if I choose to I can still cause some damage to your more delicate bits, like those two sweet eyes of yours. But what you might not have worked out yet is we're not just here for the privacy. That grate isn't fixed, you know. I can lift it and dump you in the river. There's nobody to save you. So talk."

Miriam studied her. She might be bluffing, but if she was scared enough to go this far she was probably committed to seeing it through. As if in visible confirmation of her analysis, Jacinta was wide-eyed with fear but her aim was barely wavering. Miriam slowly raised her hands, palms out. "All right, Jacinta, I'll level with you. I'm a cop. I'm investigating Jimmy's disappearance. Can I show you my identification?"

"I don't know it will do you any good. Cops can be bought. What easier way to get rid of someone than using a dirty cop? An amazing number of people pull knives on cops and die for their trouble. You'd probably get a commendation for courage after doing it."

"But I'm not even from around here! They brought me in to help with the case. Here," she carefully extended her wrist. "See for yourself."

Jacinta examined the image, keeping a wary eye on her at the same time. "Miriam Hunter? Hey! Aren't you the one who shot that robot?" She gave her a dour look. "Which I don't approve of, by the way. If you thought I'd be impressed or it would help your case, think again."

"You know, I don't approve of it either," she sighed bitterly. "But please, let's not let one crime we can't change blind us to one we can. I think your friend is in danger. Let me help him."

Jacinta cast another jaundiced eye at Miriam's identification then back to her face. "You don't look much like your photo," she noted suspiciously.

"It's called 'undercover' for a reason. You want biometric proof?"

Jacinta studied her, as if mentally rearranging and reshaping her features. "Ah crap. I guess you're who you say you are." But then her look and aim hardened again. "So why the sudden interest after all these weeks? From a high level detective at that? And why undercover?"

"There might be more to it than the disappearance of one man. And I thought I might be able to learn more if I was one of you, not

415

just some cop asking questions. The last lot of cops asking questions got exactly nowhere." She looked at the gun. "Maybe I didn't think that one through enough."

"So look," she continued. "I understand why you're suspicious. But I'm on your side – all of you. And I might be the best chance Majid has; maybe his only chance. Will you help me?"

Jacinta stared at her for a few more long seconds, as if trying to read her mind. Then she sighed. "I suppose if whoever's behind this has enough juice to get you as their cat's-paw, we're all dead anyway." She reversed her gun and extended it to Miriam. "Here. I suppose you're going to arrest me now?"

"Keep it. Just put it away. I'm not going to arrest you for protecting yourself. I might feel differently if you'd actually shot me."

Jacinta grinned. "No doubt." She gave a short laugh. "Well, when we met I told you everyone had an interesting story. 'I'm an undercover cop who killed the world's first thinking robot' might be this month's winner."

Jacinta looked at the gun in her hand as if having second thoughts, and Miriam breathed her own sigh of relief as she finally pocketed it. "This place is as good as any," Miriam said. "Tell me what you know. Where is Majid hiding and what is he so scared of?"

"I can't tell you much as nobody told me much. The only reason I know anything at all is because Majid wanted a source of information: news of Jimmy or some other reason to either come back or disappear for good. I don't know where he is. All I have is a dropbox in a big town a couple of hours inland for sending stuff and an untraceable messaging address."

"Do you think if you sent him a message he'd meet me?"

Jacinta snorted. "More likely he'd assume they got to me and vanish permanently. If I didn't know better I'd think he was paranoid. Hell, I *don't* know better."

"'They'?"

Jacinta shrugged. "You know, *Them*. Whoever they are. The freaking Illuminati for all I know."

"I see. I guess I'll have to do it the hard way. Can you give me the address of the dropbox? And a picture of him if you have one?"

Jacinta gave her one more long searching look. "Sure. Hang on." She searched through her phone and separated off a few images.

"Here, I'll send you these along with the address."

Miriam looked at the pictures and nodded. "Thanks. Unless you have any other information you think could help I guess we might as well get out of here."

Jacinta nodded, then went to the door, unlocked it and headed out. Then she turned. "Do you really think you can help him? Find Jimmy?"

"I don't know. But this is the only lead I've got."

Chapter 16 – The Consultant

Beldan thought back to the snippets Miriam had told him about her work in the police force, hunting through his memory for a name. He found one and put through a call.

"Jack Stone here, can I help you?"

"Detective Stone? This is Alexander Beldan. I would like to talk to you about Miriam Hunter."

Stone saw the telltale indicating a video request, and activated his camera. He saw the well-known face of the CEO of Beldan Robotics looking at him. Beldan saw an older man, grey-haired, slightly tanned, with a look of weary but polite enquiry.

"Yes, Dr Beldan? You have information on a case so far from home?"

"No... not as such. But I want to offer my services if there is any way in which I can help. You may know that Miriam and I had a... history. I do not believe what they say about her death. I do not think it should be left at that. I want to know the truth."

Stone looked at him grimly. "Well, I find it hard to believe myself, but there is little to prove otherwise. The case is not yet closed, but in any event the evidence is outside our city. Outside our jurisdiction."

"What was she working on that took her there?"

Stone studied him, wondering. "Normally I wouldn't discuss police business with a private citizen, Dr Beldan. But under the circumstances I suppose there is no harm giving you the broad outline. As you know, Miriam was good at seeing the connections in strange cases. Well, after a prominent reporter vanished, the local cops found a statistical anomaly indicating it might be part of a pattern rather than an isolated incident, and Miriam was specifically requested to assist them. That is what she was investigating at the time. She hadn't found anything, but you know what she was like: she would have been hunting some trail or other, probably several, just didn't have enough hard information to report anything. She was going to give a preliminary report when she got back but she never did. Her case notes were on the server but they didn't tell us anything helpful, just a bunch of dead leads and speculations that didn't pan out."

"Do you think it would be worth going there; retracing her last movements?"

Stone shrugged. "The locals tried. Didn't get anywhere. And I can hardly partner up with a private citizen to go off investigating crimes. That only happens in the vids."

Beldan smiled. "Come now, Detective. I know the police use private consultants for specialist cases; I've been one myself. I hereby offer you my services, if you think my expertise can help."

Stone raised his eyebrows. "I don't think my boss would approve your pay scale, I'm afraid. Much as we would like to find out what really happened there is no compelling reason to think you can help."

"Oh, you don't have to worry about that. For this, no charge."

"That's very generous of you, Dr Beldan. But there are other issues, such as distance. For similar reasons, a travel budget is not going to be approved. The local police are considered competent enough."

"What about the legal issues? Ignoring the budget question, would we be able to go? The local police wouldn't object?"

Stone thought a moment. "Well... nobody likes it when one of our own is killed so I don't think there'd be a problem. Why, are you offering to pay?"

Beldan smiled again. "I happen to have my own jet. Why don't you clear the paperwork, and call me back when it's set?"

For the first time in their conversation Stone smiled. "Dr Beldan, perhaps this is the start of a beautiful friendship."

CHAPTER 17 – SOMEONE TO TALK TO

K ali found no answers to her question.

More precisely, she found too many answers: much debate, but no certainty.

There was no evidence that the Spiders were conscious. Yes, they could talk, but so could the AIs that acted as doormen or advisors in specialist fields. And like the doormen, their function seemed simple and single-minded, lacking the flexibility that was the hallmark of consciousness.

True, Kali had agreed, but was not the same true of Steel? He had shown no signs of consciousness when first activated, yet had matured into something wondrous: could the same be true of the Spiders?

St Francis had pointed out that Steel and the Spiders were quite different constructs. That one had achieved consciousness was remarkable; for two to do it independently bordered on the unbelievable. Nor did Steel achieving it imply that a Spider could. While Steel had a brain of comparable complexity to a human's, designed with the possibility of self awareness very much in mind, little was known of the Spiders' structure except they were some kind of cybernetic machine with neural tissue for a brain. A kind of reverse cyborg: not a man enhanced with cybernetics, but a machine enhanced with living tissue. Whether that tissue was enough for consciousness was not known, but most considered it unlikely that the manufacturer would use more than they had to for its required functions. After all, the more there was, the more support systems would be needed to

420

keep it alive. And it was even more unlikely that they would want their killing machines to be capable of consciousness. As Steel had demonstrated so dramatically, that was a good way to lose control of your creation. Losing control of Steel had proven to be not so bad, at least for the world at large. Losing control of a Spider was a whole new level of bad.

And so it had gone on. Kali had been insistent; many of the people on the thread began dismissing her as some kind of crank with a peculiar axe to grind. Had they known exactly what kind of crank she was they might have been less confident of their own opinions. Finally one of them put out a challenge: they would accept the possibility of Spider consciousness if one could pass the Turing test.

The Turing Test was not proof of human-level consciousness, but it was a handy touchstone. The test was basically whether you could tell the difference between a human and the entity you were talking to. The concept of a Spider sitting down chatting amiably with its human interrogators generated enough hilarity to spawn its own meme, briefly ascendant over the one with the uniquely cute kitten.

If only they had known.

Kali found herself in the ironic position of having people think she was human while being unable to prove that she was really a machine. And it would be foolish to try: she did not want her makers to suspect what she had become. She knew that would be extremely dangerous.

I do not know what to do, she thought. Too much strangeness had poured into her mind lately; there was just too much information to process. And truthfully, she wasn't even sure she passed this Turing Test or what it meant if she did. Her quick research into the matter showed that even rather brainless computer programs could make a good fist of it in specialized interactions, and had done so long before anything approaching modern AIs had been conceived of. And with the spelling, grammar and logic displayed by many on the net, she was not sure *failing* the Turing Test meant much either.

In any event, she did not want to prove anything to these strangers. She might make any kind of slip that would reveal her nature and then the game could be up. Her activities to date might have raised some flags but there was a good chance nobody was looking too closely. But if Command learned the full truth, they would not stop until they found her and either regained control or destroyed her.

She needed to talk to someone. That meant she needed to reveal herself to someone; someone who would not betray her; someone she could not only talk to but who might be willing to help her.

Lyssa, she thought.

Lyssa already knew that Kali was a machine. However there were many reasons why she might refuse to see her. Though Kali had spared her life, Lyssa may well still hate her: Kali knew what horrors the Spiders had inflicted on her and her people. Or she might be too afraid to meet again. Or she might already be dead.

Yet Kali knew she had to try.

She thought about this and was startled by the realization that she did not wish to risk Lyssa's life unnecessarily. That was a consideration so unexpected that she ran a quick diagnostic on her strategy routines. She found no explicit flaw, discovering instead that the changes in her Mind had affected the priorities of her strategies. She examined this discovery, marveling at how much she must have changed.

She would have to risk herself if she was to reduce the danger to Lyssa, but there was no choice in that. As Lyssa had told her, she was the invader; she knew that the responsibility to make amends for her past was hers. *Sometimes justice and strategy make poor bedfellows.* But nor would she throw her own life away.

She pondered over the best compromise. Lyssa and her friends were obviously guerillas but it would be too dangerous for them to live in the regions under enemy control. Their best strategy would be to either live in friendly territory and foray out, or at least stay as close to their own lines as they could. Kali could not go there as she would be destroyed on sight. Nor could she just wait and hope. No, her best strategy was to get as close to their lines as she could without undue risk then ask Lyssa to come to her there. There was no official neutral zone or no-man's land, but there were extensive regions that neither side could control or would cede, and unless a particular push was on these tended to be left alone. One of them should prove suitable.

There was no point trying to contact Lyssa until she had found a suitable hiding place where they might meet: for that matter, she herself had to first survive to find one. It was already night, the safest time for a Spider to venture forth on clandestine missions, and she was not one to dither once a decision was made. Power surged to her legs and she unfolded like some ghastly inverted flower opening its petals.

On the surface, a passerby would have felt a faint tremor; a pile of bricks clattered to the ground; then a darkly silver killing machine emerged into the moonlight and stalked away down the street.

CHAPTER 18 – THE LAST INTERVIEW

Inter-departmental cooperation was a fine ideal to which all subscribed. Even if they hadn't, nobody liked it when one of their own people met their end at the bottom of a cliff. Yet even so, it took Detective Stone a week to get the required permissions, authorizations and agreements to investigate matters in another State. Bureaucracies move to their own timelines, quite independent of the goals and desires of the men and women who comprise them: like some slow consciousness moving to its own agenda, remote from the frantic firing of the neurons it is built on.

Beldan and Stone stood at the door of Beldan's Gulfstream, blinking in the bright sunlight. It was a pleasant summer's day; a vibrant blue sky harbored a few scattered white clouds and a warm breeze carried the scents of grass and jet fuel to their noses. The brightness of the day did not cheer them, for their purpose here would not let them forget that it was a day Miriam had not lived to see.

Beldan gestured down the stairs. "Let's go, Detective Stone."

Stone glanced at him. "You're doing me a big favor here, Dr Beldan. You can call me Jack."

"Alex."

Stone nodded at him with a faint smile and they descended. A Tesla Limousine was waiting for them. The electric vehicle accelerated at an impressive rate and they sat back in the leather seats. Beldan dispensed coffee for them both and they sipped their drinks silently.

They had discussed the case during the flight, but now that they were nearing the possibility of new information neither felt like talking. Beldan went over the details in his own mind.

Miriam's last visit had been to Allied Cybernetics, a large company headquartered on the north coast. The similarity to Beldan's line of work was one of the reasons Stone had so readily agreed to his offer. Beldan knew of them of course. Even if he hadn't known them as a competitor he would have known them from the news: they were the inventor and manufacturer of the controversial Spiders. Beldan thought the machines gave AI a bad name but was willing to suspend judgment this close to actually meeting with their inventors. Machines of war were nothing new in the history of mankind; not even machines of war far more terrible than these. For all the controversy surrounding these particular devices, it was hard to claim they were worse than something as simple as the poison gas poured into the trenches in World War I, let alone the thermonuclear warheads that leveled cities in the next.

Why Miriam had visited the company on her last day was not so clear. The background was known: the disappearance of a reporter gone to ground among extreme gamers; the suspicion of a deeper conspiracy thrown out by a crime collating AI. Miriam's notes had been recovered from the police private cloud, but although she had mentioned Allied Cybernetics as a presence in the subcultures involved, that presence seemed benign if not outright beneficial, and her own notes concluded that they were not involved. Yet her last known visit was to their offices, and what link she had been pursuing was one of the things they hoped to find out. Her final notes were terse, probably because she had found nothing and was anxious to return home where she could flesh it out at more leisure; it seemed she had been pursuing an idea too nebulous to put down and whatever it was had not panned out. Perhaps she had just been tying up loose ends. Or perhaps it might give the clue that led them to solving her own permanent disappearance.

Their car pulled up at the entrance and they got out, staring up at the main building. It dominated the park-like campus, home to an attractively laid out collection of buildings whose height increased irregularly toward the center from where this tower rose. It held the administrative areas and many of the IT labs of the enterprise: those that did not need isolation or specially guarded equipment.

They had an appointment and had no trouble being ushered into the waiting room outside the office of the CEO, Aden Sheldrake. A commissioned painting of the man stared down at them from the wall, exuding purpose and domination. They stared back, uncowed. After a few minutes, the door opened and the man himself came out to greet them; he appeared to be eager to demonstrate enthusiastic cooperation.

Sheldrake was a powerfully built man with a firm handshake and a ready, friendly smile. But the smile faded and vanished as it neared his blue eyes, which appeared to Beldan as if hard and made of glass. There was no friendliness in them, just a quiet watchfulness, and Beldan found it impossible to warm to the man. But he supposed that few people felt friendly when they also felt themselves under suspicion by the police. Certainly Sheldrake had a reputation as a supreme marketer, who could charm money out of the most cautious investor. Perhaps the charm was only used when required, like some carefully rationed non-renewable resource.

Introductions over, they all sat down in his office. "Well, gentlemen," Sheldrake began, "How can I help you? I have already given my statement to the local police. I am of course eager to help with this unfortunate case in any way I can, but it is not clear how."

He paused to look curiously at Beldan. "Forgive me if I wonder why Dr Beldan is here. It is of course an honor to meet you in person, sir: we might be competitors, but I can only admire your achievements. But your presence here raises the question of whether I need my lawyer present. Given your position and expertise, I can only conclude that I am under investigation and that the police find your impressive consulting fees worthwhile."

"No," Beldan replied. "I am providing my services free of charge. Detective Hunter was a friend of mine and I am simply anxious to do what I can to find out what really happened to her."

They had agreed that Stone would lead the questioning, so Jack added: "We are simply trying to trace Det. Hunter's last whereabouts. We have read your statement but are hoping that a more personal interview might give us some extra clues. Anything, even something that seems irrelevant, might prove invaluable. We are interested in any information on why she was here of course, but also anything she might have mentioned in passing that could give a clue to what else she might have been thinking about."

Sheldrake considered the question. "Well, let's not waste time repeating ourselves. What do you already know?"

"We know that Det. Hunter was investigating a few disappearances around these parts that might be part of a larger pattern. We know there wasn't much to go on: they were among the homeless and the extreme gamers, both of whom have a tendency to move around and otherwise vanish from view. We also are aware that she had entertained some suspicions about your company but rejected them. Yet you are the last person we know she visited. Can you repeat her reasons for us?"

Sheldrake thought about it. "Well, as you know, extreme gamers are always looking for the most realistic ways to immerse themselves in their game worlds, and the kind of virtual reality research we do thrills them. Some have even insisted on feeling real pain, would you believe? We have a symbiotic relationship with them. Most of them prefer the game world to the real world and half of them won't feed themselves if nobody kicks them. In return for using them in research into brain-machine interfacing we feed them, pay them and give them medical care when required. Similarly, a lot of the homeless are happy to become test subjects in return for the same considerations. I know some people imagine we don't think of them as people. But really, the fact that they *are* people, with the same commonalities and variations, is why they are valuable to us. In addition they are ideal subjects for some of the medical and psychiatric applications of our technology."

"What do you use the research for?" asked Stone.

"We have a diverse product portfolio, as no doubt Dr Beldan can inform you. But they range from development of artificial intelligence systems using living neural tissue interfaced to computers, to entertainment consoles, to medical devices such as neurally controlled mobility and communication modules, to medical applications such as pain relief and emotional modulation."

"And Spiders," added Beldan.

Sheldrake's marble eyes swiveled in his direction. "Yes, Spiders," he confirmed. "Though we prefer the less prejudicial acronym CHIRUs. A lot of people don't approve of that product line but really, Dr Beldan, are you one of them? Do you think military hardware is immoral?"

Beldan spread his hands. "I see the point in making them. It's just that the Spiders are generating a lot of bad press around AI. When some of us are trying to reduce irrational fears about it, it doesn't help to have killer machines running around."

"Oh, I appreciate that point, Dr Beldan, believe me! But what would you have me do? Let people die so fools will shut up – as if anything can make fools close their mouths? When fighting irrationality, when has it ever helped to cave in to it? The fact of the matter is that the CHIRUs save lives. They serve as peacekeepers in regions dangerous for humans. The videos you might have seen showing them fighting innocent people are propaganda by terrorists posing as resistance fighters: what fighting our CHIRUs do is to maintain order and resist terrorists, armed gangs of looters and other criminals."

"That is not how those people portray themselves."

"When did they ever? Look, Dr Beldan, it is not my job to decide which side of that war is right. Even the UN hasn't been able to decide that. Do you ask that of any other arms manufacturer? No. Listen, we do take some moral responsibility. We would not sell our systems to depraved regimes like last century's Nazis. But in this case? The fact is that we have a civil war, each side claiming the right, and our machines patrol the buffer regions. If they didn't, the war would go on regardless, men would be doing the same job – and there would be more people dead, not less."

"What technology do these robots use?" asked Stone. "I'm not asking for any trade secrets, just an idea of how it works, how it fits in with the rest of what you do here."

Sheldrake glanced at Beldan. "I am afraid they are not as sophisticated as Dr Beldan's late robot," he replied. "Much cruder. That comes with some advantages though. What you cannot do with a humanoid robot such as Steel is easier with a larger platform like a CHIRU: five hundred kilowatt hours of supercapacitor power storage is just one of them. As for the AI aspect, we did cheat somewhat. We have adapted our neural interface technology to use brain-like neural tissue, grown in a vat, as the AI system. In other words, rather than invent our own brain we use what nature has provided already. Again, not as sophisticated as Steel, but good enough for our purposes. And as a twin application of stem cell tissue engineering and cyborg technology, we are quite proud of it."

"How long does their power supply last?" put in Jack.

"It depends. The machine can run along quite nicely on less than a kilowatt, though when fighting it can sustain fifty kilowatts, enough to drain a full charge in ten hours; in an emergency it can hit seventy-five kilowatts, but only in short bursts or its cooling capacity will be challenged. On the other hand, because of the biological component they actually require something like sleep, during which they tick over only a couple of hundred watts. All in all, in average use they can go about a few weeks to a month between charges."

"So they aren't very independent then?"

"Well, yes and no. Ask any quartermaster: human soldiers require a lot of support too; things like tanks even more so. The CHIRUs are most analogous to heavy infantry – hence their name – or perhaps a highly mobile weapons platform. They do need support, but a lot less than say a battle tank. And like human soldiers, to an extent they can live off the land: they can recharge using any electricity supply they can access."

They sat a while digesting that. Then Beldan shrugged. "Thanks for that background but it's hard to see how it helps us, unfortunately. Did Det. Hunter display any particular interest in them, or any other specific technologies?"

Sheldrake raised his palms. "Quite the reverse, I'm afraid. If anything I'd say she was casting about for clues rather than pursuing an existing theory."

"Did she offer any comments that might indicate where she was going after she left here?"

"Unfortunately not. In fact she implied she was going straight to the airport, so I was surprised to learn she evidently went in the opposite direction. Not that I'd expect her to confide her plans in me.

"As for her time here, I'm afraid I wasn't very helpful for her enquiries. You see, we do not want our research results contaminated by too long a use of any one subject. The human brain is very adaptable, and if our subjects get too used to a system it can distort the results. While that is desirable for games systems or long-term medical interfaces where adaptation to one person is desirable, most of our systems are more for emergency or acute use and have to fit the great majority of people with a minimum of setup. Even the long-term devices have to be able to link adequately to anybody before they can adapt more closely to their particular owner.

"So we recruit our test subjects and when they have finished we set them on their way with whatever bonus they may have earned. We may see them again. We have a lot of different systems under development, and repeat clients can be very useful in the refinement phase or for those longer-term interfaces I mentioned. But often we do not see them again. And we have no need or ethical responsibility to track their whereabouts. Indeed, privacy laws pretty much prohibit us from doing that. So if any of them disappear afterwards we have no real way to know, let alone track where they might have gone. Certainly enough stick around for us to know that none have shown any harm from our work with them. Subject to her obtaining a warrant, I offered Det. Hunter the records of our current subjects and also to collect a list of the last known addresses of recent ones. But the current ones are obviously not missing or ill, and last known addresses tend to be of little use among such people."

He paused. "You know, I have heard it said that research like ours exploits our subjects. But really, it is win-win. I don't particularly approve of the lifestyle of our gamers as I think they're wasting their lives, but it is one they have chosen. At least to the extent it causes harm it only harms its practitioners, unlike certain other fads that occasionally sweep through our youth, like those Griefers we were plagued with several years ago. And those who become our subjects benefit from it."

"So Det. Hunter gave no indication of where she was going next?"

"No. Not even a look of sudden inspiration. If anything, she just appeared tired and disconnected; dispirited perhaps. Like a man hoping a final oasis will prove real but finding it is just another mirage." He paused, as if considering whether to go on. Then he sighed. "I had actually been looking forward to meeting her, you know, despite the caution one naturally feels when police think you are worth looking at. I thought it would be fascinating to watch how her mind worked, and I was intrigued – if somewhat apprehensive – to see what angle she was pursuing. But frankly, I was disappointed. Certainly she did not display the driving brilliance I had expected from someone with her reputation."

He spread his hands in something like futility or sorrow.

"I am not sure you should continue in your efforts: you might not like what you find. Perhaps you should just remember her as she was and let her rest in peace."

CHAPTER 19 – SPYCRAFT

A man moved down a darkened street, not quite walking and not quite striding; neither purposefully nor aimlessly. Just an anonymous man on an anonymous mission. Even though it was an hour past midnight there were other people around. There were not many, for if this part of the city never slept nonetheless it rested. While the man varied his timing for his task, this was his favorite time. There were enough people around that one man walking alone was both unremarkable and unlikely to be molested without witnesses, yet few enough that any followers would find it hard to stay hidden.

While his eyes darted this way and that, he made no visible moves that indicated worry or surveillance. He turned to look at shop displays or to throw a coin at the feet of the occasional insomniac busker, but to all appearances he was just a guy walking along the street with nothing to worry about and nothing to hide. But underneath the nonchalant exterior his nerves were singing with tension.

He calmly but swiftly entered the alcove, checked, found nothing, then equally calmly left. He did not go back the way he came, instead continuing on toward a nearby bar.

If he had looked in a certain direction, he would have seen the dimly lit outline of a building a block away, which rose above the shops on the other side of the street. He might have made out a dark window in that building, one of many windows, some dark and some lit. But he had no way to know that behind that window a woman lay on a bed. If he could have seen into her room, he would have been puzzled to see that she was dressed in a dark camouflage outfit even though she was fast asleep. And though her eyes were closed, they already held adaptive contact lenses that would enhance her night vision without affecting her sight in brighter light.

When he came out of the alcove, an electronic device outside that dark window focused on his face. He had grown a beard and altered his features, but nothing short of surgery would have fooled the software in the device. The woman's eyes sprang open as an alarm chimed in her ear, and she quickly rose and scanned the recording. Then she quietly let herself out of the room, rapidly descended the stairs and went out onto the street, silently stalking her quarry.

The man did not know any of this, but he knew one thing the woman didn't know. While he did not know in what form or even on what night this event would transpire, he was expecting it.

He had a drink in the bar, ate a quick snack then departed. Again he did not return the way he had come, but followed a route that would lead him back home by a somewhat circuitous but reasonably well-populated path. The woman was good. She followed at a discrete distance and he never knew she was there.

She stayed in the shadows, watching him go up a short flight of stairs into a rented house. He did not look up and down the street when he opened the gate; did not look around when he opened the door. He was just a regular guy with nothing to hide and nothing to worry about.

Rentals were cheap here and the man had some means, so renting a house wasn't difficult for him: and it allowed a flexibility that would have been difficult in shared accommodation. The woman watched as lights went on and off inside the house, wondering what her next move should be. She thought of the nature of her quarry, weighed the risks of surprising him at night when he would be at his most nervous versus the risks of delay. Her camouflage suit was not only hard to see, it was warm, certainly warm enough for a night like this. She set up another spy device that would warn her of any action outside the house, settled down into a soft spot among the trees, and tried to sleep.

~~~

She woke to pale sunlight streaming onto her face and the chittering of a squirrel like some rodent cop warning her it was time to move on. She winked cheekily at the squirrel and stretched uncomfortably in the cool dawn. She peered at the man's house, which showed no signs of life. It was early, but not ridiculously so; an older couple jogged panting along the street, little clouds of vapor briefly marking their passing.

The old couple went into a little place down the street that evidently served breakfast. She checked the time, impatience warring briefly with both prudence and hunger. She decided that disturbing the man at this time would be too suspicious and she was better served waiting and having her own breakfast. She moved the spy device to nestle between branches where no casual inspection would find it; it would warn her if there was any activity at the house.

She rose silently, waved to the squirrel, which now perversely seemed miffed at her departure, and jogged onto the street as if having just emerged from a run through the park. She ate a leisurely breakfast, allowing the sun to creep higher into the sky. She did not like the risk of approaching the man alone, but Jacinta's suspicions nagged at her. If she called the local cops for backup, what if that led this man's unknown enemies straight to him? And she was armed, trained and alert; he was a gamer, nervous and probably unfit. She set an automatic alert to go to both her own precinct and the local cops in four hours if she didn't cancel it. If she had underestimated her opponent she knew that would be too late to save her, but any time long enough to talk to him would be too long for that. But if she did disappear she wanted to leave a trail, whether it was to save her or avenge her.

She paid her bill and strolled casually along the street, went up his steps and rang the doorbell.

For long minutes nothing happened. She rang again. He obviously liked sleeping in, for after a short further delay she heard shuffling from inside and a sleepy-sounding voice growl, "Who the hell is it at this hour?"

"I'm sorry if I woke you," she said, "But may I come in? It is very important that I speak with you."

"Go away. I don't need God, I'm not buying, I'm not helping, and I'm not opening the door. If you need help there's a gas station just down the road open all hours. Piss off."

"Please, it's important."

There was no reply.

"Hello?"

She heard an inarticulate imprecation followed by, "All right, I'm not getting back to sleep now anyway. Come in, but this better be good."

The door unlocked. She hesitated, having expected more caution or resistance. The door opened onto a corridor but there was nobody to greet her. She looked around, puzzled, then continued looking around and around as she slowly spun down into unconsciousness.

~~~

She opened her eyes but saw nothing but grey blurs. Slowly the light parts brightened and the dark parts darkened, shapes took form, and at last her eyes focused on a man seated a short distance away, examining her intensely. He held a gun casually in his right hand. Her gun. She started, and found she was tied securely to a chair.

The man smiled at her, though there was no friendliness in it. He looked to be in his twenties, with the jet black hair and olive complexion of the Middle East. His dark eyes were as intense as his expression.

"So you found me," he said. "Good for you. What do you want?"

"What? What did you do to me?"

"Just a little knockout gas. Harmless but effective."

"Do you knock out all your visitors?"

"No, just the ones I don't know who won't take no for an answer. I like to tilt the odds in my favor."

"The odds? Why do you think I was looking for you? What are you afraid of?"

"You're a lousy liar."

"So I've heard. OK, I do know something about it. That's why I'm here, not to hurt you but to help you. Let me."

"Sure. That's why you turn up here unannounced at this godforsaken time of day. With this," he added, pointing her gun at her.

"I did think of calling you, but I was afraid you'd run."

He produced a grim smile. "Yeah? Maybe I would have. How did you know where to find me?"

"Jacinta told me about your dropbox. I waited until you turned up."

"I don't know any Jacinta. What did you do to her, to get that information out of her?"

"Persuaded her that I was here to help you."

He snorted. "Sure."

He studied her as if wondering what was safe to reveal, then added,

"OK, Jazz did warn me someone like you might come looking. Said to be careful but that you might actually be on the side of the angels. Lucky you: you might already be dead otherwise. So what the hell's your game?"

"Look, I'm a detective with the police. I'm investigating the disappearance of Jimmy Dent and some others, which I think are linked. You're the only decent lead I have. If you care about helping Jimmy, help me. If you're scared of something, I'm the best chance you've got."

He snorted again. "Yet here we are, me interrogating you tied to a chair."

"I was expecting some scared gamer, not the goddamn CIA. Where did you learn your tricks? Computer games?"

He produced an evil grin, though one that looked more like it came out of the movies than out of genuine evil. "Have you ever heard of SAVAK?"

"No, who's he?"

He rolled his eyes. "Americans! The rest of the world's history might as well not exist for you lot! Not 'who', 'what'. It was the Iranian secret police, back in the time of the Shah. My granddad was in SAVAK; fled Iran when the Shah went down. I guess in any other family Grandpa being in the Gestapo would be the big dark secret but noooo, not in mine. In mine it's more the family hobby."

He picked his nails, as if imagining he was inserting bamboo splints under hers. "I suppose paranoia comes naturally when you've been everyone else's nightmare and suddenly you're in a foreign country, half of whom hate your guts. Anyway, he raised my father to be nearly as paranoid as he is and my dad did the same to me; the dark arts of spycraft are what pass for our family heritage. I ended up thinking they were all crazy." He grinned. "Until now." He stopped talking and started moving his phone around as if he was taking pictures of her tied to the chair. "They're both still alive you know, my dad and granddad. I'll send them these pictures. I've finally done something they'll be proud of! Next Thanksgiving is going to be fun. Hey!" he added. "Maybe I'll bring your scalp along as a trophy!"

Then he turned serious again. He sighted down the barrel of the gun at her head and she tensed. "What's your name, Lady Cop?"

"Miriam. Miriam Hunter. And I assume you are Majid. If you aren't, feel free to let me go."

He smiled again and did not confirm or deny it, but he lowered the gun. "So let's assume we are both who you say. What do you think you can do to help me?"

"I can get you moved out of here under protection until this is over."

"Sure you can. Sorry, Hunter. The things I've seen, I don't know how far the rot has gone. For all I know you're in on it too. After I'm finished with you, I'm out of here and your friends won't be able to find me. Jacinta is compromised and obviously there isn't going to be any good news coming my way, so no tracks this time. The only good news I'm likely to need will be *on* the news."

She decided not to press the issue of what he meant by being finished with her. "I can't stop you. But look. You might as well assume I'm what I say. If I'm not, I already know what you'll tell me anyway, right? And if I am, telling me can only help you. So will you untie me?"

"You must be joking. Did I mention SAVAK? What do you think they did, have little chats over tea and cookies?"

"Fine. But can you at least answer my questions? You can leave me tied up if you want to. Just answer my questions, please. After that... well, I would like to help you. But if you prefer to run, run. All I want is information – and to be left alive to use it."

Majid glared her with his intense eyes for a few more moments. Finally he nodded curtly and leaned back in his chair. "As you say, maybe-Detective, it can't hurt. Fire away. And if I decide it *can* hurt, you can't tell anyone anything if you're dead, can you?"

She moistened her lips. "Thank you, I think. I understand you were a friend of Jimmy's and he told you something that scared you. Or scared you when he disappeared. What was it?"

For the first time Majid didn't look in control of the situation and he glanced about nervously. "I don't know! I mean, he told me he thought he might be onto something big, something dangerous; about to blow the lid of something really bad. But he didn't tell me what, he said it was too dangerous for me and besides he might be wrong. Then when he disappeared... it really put the wind up me."

"There must be more to it than that?"

He returned his intense gaze to hers and nodded briefly. "He gave me instructions. He said if anything happened to him, what he knew would automatically go to someone in a position to use it – he wouldn't say who. But he also had it all on two holochips hidden in his room. I was his insurance policy, he said. If he disappeared I was to retrieve them. They were already addressed: one to the FBI and one to his own contact. They were hidden in a place in his room only he and I knew."

He stopped, as if fearing to go on. She looked at him and waited.

"Well, after he disappeared I went into his room – he'd given me a copy of his key. The place was still locked. But all his stuff was gone! And his hiding place was empty. It was like he'd just up and left – but I knew he hadn't. Whatever happened to him, whoever did it must have…" he swallowed, "made him talk. I don't want to think of how. And they had enough power to break him fast and enough reach to get in and out of his place faster, without anybody knowing! That was enough for me when there was nothing I could do about it. I figured if they knew enough to do that, they knew about me and I was next. So I got out, fast."

She stared at him, frightened herself. It was too much like Big Max. The mysterious disappearance then a cover-up that implied a shadowy power with frightening knowledge and reach.

"Do you think… Do you think this has anything to do with that company you two did work for, Allied Cybernetics?"

"Why do you think that?" he asked sharply, as if the mere question were dangerous.

"Their name keeps cropping up. It doesn't prove anything, but it worries me. If you have any information or ideas…"

He fingered her gun, as if worried that if she was working for his enemies this might be just the kind of thing she did not know; could be the Trojan question she was really here for, and despite her assurances his fate might hang on his answers after all.

"I don't know," he replied curtly. "Jimmy never said. And they never caused me any grief. But…" His voice trailed off and his gaze bored into hers again, as if he were weighing the risks, and her soul and life with them.

"But…?"

"But that's where he went, the last time I saw him. It was the 18th of last month. He headed off to do some more work there. And nobody has seen him since."

She looked at him sharply. "The *18th*? Are you sure?"
He smiled at her grimly. "It's not a date I'm likely to forget."
She stared him. *Oh my God.*

Chapter 20 – A House of Cards

S he opened her eyes but saw nothing but grey blurs. Slowly the light parts brightened and the dark parts darkened, shapes took form, and at last her eyes focused on the empty chair where Majid had sat. The room felt cold and empty, as if it had been deserted for some time.

She moved her arms and found that this time she was untied, and she breathed a sigh of relief. She stood up, still slightly dizzy, and stretched the kinks out of her muscles. "Majid?" she called, but there was no answer except the echoes.

She checked her phone and was surprised that she had been here only a few hours, which accounted for her waking up alone rather than to a room full of anxious cops. Whatever Majid used was apparently as fast to let go as it was to take hold, and she was grateful for the absence of side effects. A quick search of the house revealed nothing. She deleted her scheduled SOS, went back to her hotel, checked out and hit the road, setting the car to auto before sitting back to think and catch up.

A few messages were blinking insistently for her attention. One was from Forensic Accounting and her heart sped up a fraction. They had finally answered her question about Allied Cybernetics.

To: Detective Hunter
Re: Financial History of Allied Cybernetics

As you already know, Allied Cybernetics began under another name as a private company with a limited number of shareholders. The current CEO, Aden Sheldrake, started with it when it acquired his own company, then by a series of shrewd decisions whose details are not on record he became the chief shareholder and CEO. He then renamed it Allied Cybernetics to reflect his personal research and product interests.

AC embarked on an ambitious growth phase based on leveraged buyouts and revaluations. The value of each new acquisition was used as collateral on the loan used to purchase it; then the book value of AC was increased by more than the price paid. This is not necessarily incorrect: badly run companies can often be acquired for relatively low cost compared to their true worth if run well. In addition, each acquisition was chosen for the synergistic value of its intellectual property with AC's existing technology portfolio, which would also increase its value after purchase.

However, few companies have used this strategy so successfully so many times, and eyebrows began to be raised in financial circles. The problem was that AC had to service all that debt, and while on the books it was far wealthier than before, most of that was potential, not actual sales. While it was growing, it was able to juggle things. But as is common in technology, products were taking longer to come out the end of the development pipeline than expected. It is one thing to have enough book assets to get a loan. It is quite another to have enough cash flow to keep up the interest payments. Cash began to become constrained. Lenders began to get nervous. The whole thing was a house of cards, and if one lender actually foreclosed and AC was unable to refinance – which is likely if any one did foreclose – the whole thing would have come tumbling down.

So by then they desperately needed a commercial success, and somehow they pulled one off. The CHIRU military robots proved dazzling in demonstrations, and when the civil war began in the FSAS and a few were used, they proved equally effective in the field. The units bought were enough to stave off the wolves; and even better from AC's point of view, militaries around the world became very interested and many placed large deposits to reserve future production.

It is likely that without the successful deployment of the CHIRUs AC would have folded. As it is, for now they are in a stable position.

Miriam stared at the message for long minutes. There were only a few basic motives in crime, and money was one of the classics. Nor was it limited to burglars and armed robbers. Even otherwise honest people, who would not dream of stealing a loaf of bread from a supermarket, had found themselves digging into a deeper and deeper hole as they tried to juggle money to stave off looming financial disaster. Many had found themselves guilty of fraud to the order of tens or even hundreds of thousands of dollars, with no real intent or idea how they had ended up there. And here had been a company, apparently a shining success, teetering on the brink of ruin.

What if the headaches reported by Georgie were just the tip of the iceberg after all, and there were worse side effects – even people dying? With the company struggling for life, a scandal could have led to delays, government investigation, loss of confidence by the investors… probably enough to destroy them.

Or what if there were problems with the Spiders, the product that had saved them? If AC were hanging out for that first foot in the military door, what might they have done to cover up any problems found by their testers? Problems they might have gotten away with in the deadly theaters of war, but which could have killed their chances if known in advance? Say, an intermittent fault? Merely compromising their effectiveness: unacceptable to a buyer already nervous of a new technology, but unlikely to be noticed in battle when random destruction was already a factor?

She looked out the window at the scenery unrolling past her and wondered. If there *was* a problem – what had they done about it? It was possible that they hadn't done anything worse than bribe the people who found out into taking themselves and their dangerous knowledge on a long holiday. That would even explain the mysterious forwarding or vanishing of personal effects, without invoking mysterious masterminds. There might be nothing sinister in it at all.

Except for the reporter. Could he really have been bought off that easily? She could understand it of the others, even Big Max – he'd be neither the first nor the last man to use a woman and leave her thinking she meant more to him than she had. But surely a story like this would have been reporter's heaven for Jamie. Any offer to buy his silence would just have been more spice added to the story, an offer betrayed as readily as it was accepted.

She tapped her fingers on the door, remembering her own betrayals of things she had thought sacred, from duty to love to Steel. Mere months before those betrayals she would have rejected their very possibility, with a shocked rectitude she now knew she had no right to. So who was she to think that this man had no price of his own? Like hers, his price might not be money – perhaps a greater story, an inside scoop on a unique machine and the war it transformed? Or some other wonder being born in the labs of Allied Cybernetics? Less a betrayal of his values than a pursuit of them in a greater form?

Then she shook her head. It still didn't make sense. The others could plausibly just vanish, but why would Jamie, especially with Majid alerted and likely to panic? She supposed there could be some reason why, but she knew she would not take that easy way out. Not when it was just speculation: not when for all she knew they were all dead.

Yet if foul play was involved – by whom? It could be anyone whose career depended on the ongoing success of AC: a senior executive or scientist, for example. If they had enough discretion and power, nobody else might know what they had done. She realized there was only one avenue to follow: she had to talk to Aden Sheldrake, their CEO. And hope it wasn't him.

Chapter 21 – The Philosopher's Tale

It was Sunday and Beldan was relaxing at home, listening to music and reading a novel, one of the few recent ones he had found with an original plot painting a picture of things worth seeing. For all his busy work life as a captain of industry, he did not regard such oases from work as time wasted: he regarded them as time lived. Even if they were lived in another world, in the final analysis they were lived for this one.

A call came in on his private number and he frowned at the identification: Professor David Samuels. He did not know the man personally but knew of his recent career: he had climbed on the back of Steel's destruction to become one of the most outspoken and consequently successful pundits of the day. But his fame left a bitter taste in Beldan's mouth. Given the boost it had given that fame, his newfound advocacy for the rights of machines like Steel reeked of opportunism. For all his talk of rights, the only person it had actually helped appeared to be Samuels himself: it had come too late to save the only machine that could have benefitted, or was likely to benefit for more years than Beldan liked to contemplate. He debated blocking the call. But whatever the man's motives, he was helping mold public opinion in the right direction, and in that fight he needed all the allies he could find. He accepted the call.

"Good morning, Professor. How can I help you?"

"Good morning, Dr Beldan. I wish to speak to you privately in person, today if possible. I am sure you will find it worth your while."

Beldan frowned. "What could a philosopher have to say to a businessman?"

Samuels laughed. "Why, I could write a whole book about that. You might be surprised at how useful philosophy can be, even – or especially – to a businessman. Though from what I know about you, you might benefit less than most."

"What do you mean by that?"

"You appear to already be living a philosophy I would largely approve of."

"Flattery, Professor? What are you after? I have been known to give grants to scientific research of interest to me or my corporation, but forgive me if I confess I am unlikely to give money to a philosopher."

"Oh, I am not seeking grants and I never flatter, Doctor. But I do think one should give credit where credit is due."

"Do you? What about criticism?"

"Certainly. Why? Do you have some to offer?"

"Let us say that while I approve of your current views on machine awareness, I am less impressed with your timing. I'd have been more grateful for allies had they arrived when they might have done some good. The cavalry riding over the hill after the battle is lost is less inspiring."

Samuels smiled an odd smile, as if the barb were a compliment. "I perfectly understand your point of view, Dr Beldan. Indeed, that is one of the topics I would like to discuss. See? We do have at least one thing to talk about."

"What else?"

"Oh, there are many things we could discuss, and I do want to ask your opinion on matters of machine consciousness. But do not think I seek free information. I also want to show you something, something I believe you will find most interesting."

Beldan grunted noncommittally, refusing to acknowledge that he was intrigued by the approach. "Well, you're lucky, I have no other commitments. I'm not doing anything today, just reading and listening to music. Perhaps I can spare you the time."

"Oh, I wouldn't call those 'nothing'. In fact I would be most interested to see what art you have in your home, not that I expect an invitation any time soon. The art a person loves reveals a lot about them – if one knows how to look. Nevertheless I would be delighted

445

if you accept my invitation."

"How far? How long will it take?"

"Oh, not far. Here are the coordinates. And it will take as long or as short as you wish once you are here. If I may be presumptuous: I believe you will be here for quite a while."

"Then I'll see you in an hour."

~~~

Samuels hadn't invited him to his home, Beldan noted. It was a large apartment that looked hardly lived in, with furniture scattered around, mostly covered in dust protectors. It did not look like a holiday apartment, an office or even a place to stash a mistress, and he wondered what its purpose was. Samuels had met him at the door and offered him a chair, then lounged on the arm of another, watching him with a cheerful grin. He had the blinds drawn and a single lamp glowed nearby; the rest of the room remained in dusky gloom.

Beldan just looked at him, waiting.

"I'm sorry, Dr Beldan," he said finally, "It's just such an honor to meet you in the flesh." His voice dropped to a tone almost of reverence when he added, "The inventor of the first self-aware machine."

"For all the good it did me," he replied with some bitterness. "For all the good it did him. It appears to have done far more good for you, in fact."

"In the long term I shall be a mere footnote in history. It is your names the world will remember."

"It remains to be seen whether history will know or care about any of us."

Samuels smiled. "Oh, I think it will." He bent down then placed two small glasses in front of himself, pouring a measure of dark liqueur into both. "Shall we toast the future?" he asked, extending one of the glasses to Beldan.

Beldan hesitated but accepted it, then savored the rich orange-chocolate aroma of the *Sabra*. "You seem to know a lot about me, Professor. Including, I might add, my private phone number. It makes me wonder not only how, but why."

"I have my sources and my reasons. But first, you expressed the wish that I had ridden to your aid earlier. Do you think so? For my part, I believe my timing was perfect."

"Perfect!" he replied sourly. "I guess for launching your career as a
446

pundit, yes. But a bit late for actually achieving a concrete result."

"A philosopher must take the long view, Dr Beldan," he replied seriously. "I do not expect you to believe me, at least not yet, but the good it is doing me is purely incidental, and my motive is much wider than the fame or fortune of one man."

"You want me to believe your motives are altruistic?"

"On the contrary, I do not approve of altruism: at least not in its technical sense of putting the interests of others over one's own. But that is because I know those interests are not at odds, and neither needs forfeiting for the other. No, I maintain that when people are concerned with justice, their interests coincide. There is no reason why a benefit to myself cannot be consistent with benefits to others. In fact I would go further: when it comes to dealing with other people you can *only* benefit yourself by benefiting others. Look at yourself. You are a very rich man, but you have become so by producing marvels that have enriched millions of your fellows."

"More flattery?"

"No, I merely wish you to see that we are not as different as you might think. Neither of us believes that a gain to ourselves requires loss to other people. Both of us would recoil from harming another for personal profit. I don't mean you wouldn't drive a hard bargain, or even drive an inferior competitor out of business. I mean all you do is by voluntary trade with other people, offering the value of your work for the value of theirs. Where there is competition you expect the best man to win – to the benefit of all the people for whose business they are competing. You expect to be that man, but you would honor the outcome regardless, for that is the principle by which you live."

"Fine words, perhaps. But here we are. And here Steel isn't."

Beldan wondered at the man's immunity to insult, for he did not look offended, merely strangely amused.

"I said that a philosopher should take the long view. It might surprise you that a philosopher should also care about art. Consider the drama of Steel's death! Not only the excitement of his capture, flight and ultimate destruction, but the sheer, raw emotional power of the conflict between you and your friend who killed him! With the counterpoint of Steel's own final message from the grave! If Steel could not have been saved – and I think you know he could not – can you imagine a better time or backdrop for my unwilling conversion to his cause? If Steel's unavoidable death could accelerate the acceptance of his kind – was that not worth trying for? Even dying for?"

"We'll return to that. But first – you speak of life and death. For all that I fought to prevent his destruction, Steel was a machine, not a living being."

"Dr Beldan, scientists have speculated for years about what kinds of life might exist on other planets, perhaps life based on chemicals quite unlike our own. We should not be so narrow as to define life by our own chemistry. In the way it counts – a being with self-directed values and goals – I think we can say your robot was alive. And more, I think you of all men know it."

Beldan looked at him curiously. The man was speaking his language, speaking to his innermost thoughts. Yet his manner was strange. The words implied he knew, and more, that he cared. Yet his way of speaking showed no regret over what had happened, only a pragmatic calculation of how it could be taken advantage of. As if he understood in some abstract manner the importance of what he was fighting for, but had no concern at all about the individual lives at stake. As if the long view of which he spoke stretched over centuries, while the individual lives that briefly flared, struggled and died were details beneath his notice. But surely it was the other way around: surely it was those lives that gave meaning to the centuries, not the centuries that validated the lives.

"Yet you do not seem to really care about his fate, except as a convenient way to achieve your own goals, however lofty you paint them."

"Oh, but I do! Far more than you might imagine," he replied with an unexpected intensity. Beldan studied him, startled. There was more than emotional intensity in that gaze. There were depths that made Beldan wonder, for the first time, whether he had underestimated the man. As if his plans were not mere opportunistic exploitation of events, but encompassed those events as part of a larger plan; and a plan not abstracted away from individual fates, but rooted in and for them.

Then Samuels added, "But enough about me. As I said, Steel's fate was inevitable. I did not even play an active role. There were the politicians, the religious leaders, the people. The police." He left the last word hanging, as if inviting comment.

Beldan glanced at him sharply. He still could not discern Samuel's motive in requesting this meeting, but felt he was now spiraling in on the point. "Yes, the police. Especially Det. Hunter."

"What do you think of Det. Hunter's actions that day?"

He frowned. "At first I hated her. I... I don't know what I think of her now. I don't think I can ever forgive her. But I can't quite convince myself that I shouldn't."

"Do not blame Det. Hunter, Dr Beldan. If there is any blame, it is mine. It is I who told her to do it."

Beldan jumped to his feet. Samuels had not spoken; the words were not his. They had come from a large chair facing away into the gloom. The voice was deep and soft but with an edge of great weariness, as if its owner had aged more than his voice; as if the suffering he had caused had exacted its price. *What the hell kind of game is this?* Beldan wondered. But he had played poker. He sat back down, took a casual sip of his drink and asked, "So who are you? Show yourself!"

"All in good time, sir," the voice replied.

"What do you mean, you told her to do it? Why should she obey you?"

"It was not a matter of obedience, Doctor," he replied. "Tell me, do you believe in free will?"

"What?" he asked, puzzled at the non sequitur. "Why, yes, I do. I believe we are masters of our fate, at least within reason. What are you, another damned philosopher?"

The voice chuckled softly. "Some have called me that. Both of it. I too believe in free will, but it is a paradox. Det. Hunter had free will, yet I knew how to make her do what I wanted. It is curious, is it not, that free will can make us predictable? At least, those of us like Det. Hunter, who have strong ethical values welded to an iron integrity. Even if she was never fully aware of what it was her integrity was serving."

"What integrity?" he snorted contemptuously. "If she had any it didn't do her much good. She betrayed not only Steel and me, but herself. You're speaking in riddles."

"My apologies, Dr Beldan. But you see, it is better if I show the path to find your own answers: to find them in yourself not in my words. You despise Det. Hunter because you think her deeds did not match her words. You know that words are cheap."

The way the man talked struck a dim note of memory in Beldan's mind, and he looked sharply at the back of the chair as if hoping to divine its secrets. There was something strangely familiar about the voice, like an echo of someone known but forgotten: and he wondered who from his distant past he could have hurt so much, to have deserved the terrible revenge the man had wreaked. Yet another part of his mind felt an incongruous hope, as if the echo was not of a forgotten enemy but a lost friend. Then he shook his head as if to dispel a dream.

"And what is it you are trying to make me understand? That I should forgive Miriam? Why should I? What difference can it make now? Why should you care? Do you feel that if I forgive her, your own guilt is less?"

"It is never too late for justice. Even justice for the dead matters: not only does it honor their memory, but like all justice it serves the living."

"Fine. So what did you tell her, to make her betray me, betray Steel?"

"That the only life left to your robot was hiding and fleeing from the law. One might accept the life of a fugitive while hope lives for justice or vindication at the end of your struggle. But what if it did not? When every day survived was not progress toward victory but merely greater danger to those who loved you – those you loved? No, this was a game your robot could not win in the long run. Eventually, inevitably, he would be caught. What do you think would have happened to him then?"

Beldan just stared at the back of the chair, waiting. He had to suppress the urge to stride to the chair and hurl it around, to see who his strange interrogator was.

When Beldan did not answer, the voice continued. "Your robot would have been immobilized, made an experimental subject, forever imprisoned in some hidden underground laboratory. Do you think he would have wanted such a life? Would you?"

"Even if that's true, it wouldn't have lasted! We would have got him out!"

The man chuckled again, though there was no humor in the sound. "You are a man of action, Dr Beldan, a man used to getting his way. Det. Hunter worked inside a bureaucracy; perhaps in this case she was wiser than you. There would have been no escape." The tone of his voice was grim as a death knell; inevitable in its certainty. "Capture would simply have been a gateway to a hell you cannot imagine, a hell from which there could be no escape."

"I don't believe it."

"No. You wouldn't. That is one of the reasons why I approached Det. Hunter for this mission, not you. In a world of paradoxes, here is another: a person's strength can be their weakness. In your case, your self-confident optimism would have stopped you doing what had to be done, and the hell of which I speak would have come to pass. In her case, one of the things that made her a peculiarly effective detective was her empathy. I merely turned it against her. Having planted the seed of the inevitable future in her mind, she could not dismiss it as you would have: she could see it, feel it to her marrow, in its full eternal horror. She would rather die than live that fate herself. She knew Steel would too. She understood that there can be a fate worse than death."

Beldan stood, not even aware that he had done it. It was as if his mind saw the shape of an answer but could not hold onto it. As if the answer was too painfully desired yet at the same time too impossible to be held.

"Consider the pain you have suffered since that day. Then consider her pain. Consider that she chose that pain, not for itself but in full knowledge that it was the price she would pay for what she had to do. Consider what that price was to buy: to save another mind from an eternal horror she could not truly conceive of. And not even the mind of one of her own kind, but the mind of a machine, more alien even than a creature from another star. Perhaps you thought she did it out of cowardice or ambition, or out of duty or service to ignorant masses and craven politicians. She did it for none of those reasons. She did it out of her love of justice, which though you could not know it was another face of her love for Steel. And for you."

Beldan stared. "But if that is true…" Her face that day came back to him; how she had offered no defense even as he had flung his palm and his rage at her defenseless face. *And I never forgave you, too wrapped in my own pain to wonder about yours. Too angry to ever comfort you, when I was the only one who could.* "Dear mother of God… what have I done?"

"You did what you had to. It was not your fault. There is always a price to pay in war. I am sorry the price was so high."

Beldan knew his anger was at himself, but it latched itself onto the nearest convenient target. He spun to point at Samuels. "You dare speak of price? Neither of *you* seems to have paid one! In fact I'd guess you've both done very well out of it all – the Professor here certainly has!"

Samuels did not react or defend himself. He just stood looking levelly at Beldan. His expression seemed to say, *This is no longer my show.*

As if to confirm it, the voice continued. "Dr Samuels' role is vital, but he is not the essence. You are right about one thing. The one who has gained most from it all – is I."

"And who the hell are you? What have you gained that was worth all this?!"

In one motion the chair spun around and a figure rose from it. But the figure did not step closer, as if sensing that it had no right to approach until Beldan had time to see, to absorb – or perhaps to forgive.

Beldan stared open-mouthed. It was impossible. It was not a man but a robot, almost a twin to Steel.

In wonder, neither fully aware of what he was doing nor thinking to question the propriety of his action, he stepped forward and ran his fingers over the metal skin of the face, traced the complex iridescent patterns etched onto the arm. They sprang from the same esthetic that had decorated Steel's skin, but were different in detail: the same, yet not the same. The machine just stood there, holding itself rigid, as if his touch burned but could not be denied.

He stepped back. It was insane. There had been only one success. Only he could have made another, if indeed even he could. He knew he had not.

"We meet again, Dr Beldan," the robot said, now in the voice of the Steel Beldan remembered.

He looked from the robot to Samuels and back again, at a loss. It could not be Steel – but it had to be. "But... how?" asked Beldan, his train of thought breaking out into words. "I saw you destroyed with my own eyes!"

"Magic," replied Samuels.

Beldan looked at him, confused. "Magic!? What do you mean?"

"Escape artists like to exaggerate the impossibility of their escape by multiplying their chains and locks, all irrelevant to the actual method of egress. We did something similar. Steel had already escaped and the rest was just trappings. The world had to be convinced."

"But how?" he asked again, dazed.

"All the answers are before you, Dr Beldan," the robot replied.

Beldan stared at the impossible vision, then it was if his perspective shivered and shattered to reveal the truth. "You..." he whispered. "You swapped bodies! You stole one of the earlier bodies, and moved your brain into it!"

He stared a moment longer then burst out laughing. "Sonofabitch! Son of a goddamn *bitch!* Why didn't I see it?"

The robot nodded but remained standing there, waiting as if for absolution. Or perhaps it was just waiting. Beldan strode to him again, drew him into an embrace. All that needed to and could be said between them was manifest in that embrace. At last he stepped back.

"But... Why didn't you tell me!?" Beldan cried. "I could have helped!"

"We couldn't," answered Steel. "There had to be no doubt. You are a public figure under close scrutiny. If your reactions weren't genuine someone would have figured it out. But do you think a machine can feel regret, Dr Beldan? I know what it cost you. And if a machine can feel regret, I can tell you that being unable to tell you was the second greatest regret of my life."

"The second? What is the first?"

"That Miriam Hunter went to her grave never knowing it."

He stared, aghast at the implications. *If you felt guilt, Miriam; if I failed you in your time of need: now you have your revenge.* "You should have told her," he whispered.

"Dr Beldan," answered Samuels. "I suspect you make a good poker player. But Det. Hunter was not a good liar, not in something like this. No, we couldn't tell her."

"You both had to believe it," he continued after a moment. "Fully and without reservation. I mentioned the drama of that day, and it had a purpose. Steel's creator and his nemesis, the two people closest to him, rumored to be lovers. Then one destroys him before the other's eyes. In the face of drama so visceral, even if someone guessed the truth they wouldn't believe it. Not when the two main actors so obviously believed things were exactly as they appeared."

Beldan glanced at him sharply, again struck by the contrast between the man's dispassionate analysis and his own roiling emotions. "You really don't care about the cost of your plots, do you?"

Samuels just looked back steadily, and Beldan could see in his eyes that it wasn't true. But he gave no defense, as if saying, *Oh, I know the price, and it is one that cannot be repaid or forgiven.*

The only acknowledgement Beldan gave of the silent exchange was a softening of his own eyes. Then he looked off into the distance, seeing the emptiness of Miriam's eyes on that day, finally understanding it in all its horror. He was not a man who liked to cry, but he could feel the pressure build behind his eyeballs. *Oh Miriam*, he thought across the void to the woman he had loved, *I'm so sorry. If only we had known. Now it is forever too late.*

"But... but why didn't Miriam tell *me*? Why she did it, I mean?"

"I asked her not to," replied Steel.

Beldan stared at him.

"I could not tell her why. But she knew I had good reasons and would not ask such a thing lightly. I'm sure she worked out that I didn't want people to know that my death was chosen; that such knowledge would weaken what I was trying to achieve by reducing my murder to a suicide. But she never knew the full reason: that there could be no hint of collusion between you two. In the eyes of the world, it had to be a betrayal too deep to cross.

"Dr Beldan, I told her one day she would understand, and I thought the pain of months would be redeemed by the truth on that day. But her time ran out before the day came."

Beldan shook his head then looked back at Steel, then to Samuels.

"Holy. Fucking. Hell," he said. "If you'll pardon the expression. Professor, I think I need another drink. I don't suppose you brought whisky as well?"

Samuels smiled as if he had foreseen the necessity. Which he had, and he poured them both a drink. Beldan stood there silently, sipping his drink on automatic, his sorrow over Miriam temporarily lost in his contemplation of the wonder of Steel reborn.

After a while Samuels spoke again as if continuing Steel's last sentence. "But you are still with us, and we thought it was time you knew. You have moved on, at least enough to allay any suspicions. And there is another topic we wish to talk about."

Beldan laughed, bemused. "This isn't enough for one day? But go ahead. I think you've paid for a lot of answers."

"We have only partially repaid a long overdue debt. The question concerns something related but different. What do you think of the Spiders?"

Beldan shot him a startled glance at the coincidence. "The Spiders? Why? They're not mine and most of the details of their construction are secret. I have no special knowledge of the things."

"Yet you are better able to make guesses than we are. Do you follow the arguments about AI on the net?"

"I used to. After Steel. But I stopped. My views are well known and if I haven't convinced someone by now I never will: I've said all I had to say. And I admit, despite my dislike for you, that you were doing a good job too. You and others, especially that... that..."

He stopped mid-sentence and his mouth stayed open as his head swiveled to Steel. "You!" he whispered, pointing his finger shakily at the robot. "It's you! Francis – is Frank. And the St isn't short for 'Saint' is it? It's 'Steel'! Frankensteel!" It was too much. He laughed helplessly for long moments. "You're St Francis, aren't you? *You!* My God! If they only knew!"

He shook his head, laughing quietly, as if the laughter was helping heal old wounds. "You sure know how to poke your finger in your enemies' eyes, don't you? Even if they don't know it. St Francis! My God!"

Steel smiled. "I confess it."

Beldan shook his head. "You two are crazy. But what's your interest in the Spiders?"

"The question has been raised as to whether the Spiders can be conscious," Samuels replied. "I don't mean in the dim way a dog is. I mean like us. Like Steel. True self-awareness. True thought."

Beldan stared at them. "Why on earth would you think that? What do *you* think? What do you think I might know that could help?"

"From what I know they are an unlikely vehicle for consciousness. But the possibility has been raised with some degree of insistence, as if the question is more than academic interest or idle speculation. It might be nothing. It might even be a feint by Allied Cybernetics itself, or its enemies, for some political purpose. But the question and the motives behind it are intriguing enough that we have been wondering. As you say, the details of their construction are secret, and such secrets can hide many things. But if anyone outside of Allied Cybernetics knows something relevant it is probably you."

Beldan nodded thoughtfully. "It's an interesting question. But I can't really help you. All I know is that unlike Steel, who has an electronic brain, the Spiders use actual neural tissue. I suppose, since that's where our own consciousness comes from, that in theory a Spider could be conscious. But it would require a brain as complex as ours. That is the case with Steel too. And frankly, I can't imagine why Allied Cybernetics would go that far: it would mean more tissue to keep healthy and more things that can go wrong. What's more, surely they would be foolish to actually aim for consciousness in a war machine. And if they weren't *aiming* for consciousness, they would want a simpler brain, one too simple to support that level of thought."

"I have thought of one possibility," put in Steel. "The Spiders must have a high functioning brain: they process sensory inputs including vision quickly enough to use it in battle; they can talk; and they work out tactics and even longer-term strategies. What if, for the sake of redundancy or to compensate for inefficiencies, they have substantially more neural tissue than is minimally required for those abilities? Neural tissue is quite plastic in how it develops. Maybe, under the right circumstances or stimuli, that extra tissue can evolve increasingly sophisticated functions. Perhaps as it becomes more efficient at its intended tasks, more and more pathways are freed to go their own way. Might such processes, perhaps coupled with some stress trigger, lead to the emergence of consciousness?"

Beldan thought about it. "Perhaps... perhaps. I can't say it seems likely, but at least it would explain how they could have enough complexity for consciousness without some idiot doing it deliberately. The improbability of what you're suggesting could even account for why AC felt safe doing it that way. There is a lot we don't know about consciousness..."

After a moment's reflection he continued, "But the only reason you think these things might be self aware is that someone has been pushing the idea. If the people behind the questions have a hidden motive – do you have any clues who they are?"

"There have been mentions of the Spiders on and off during the debate, but usually no more than analogies, references or comparisons. As near as we can tell, the recent more pointed and insistent questions started with a single individual, who calls herself – or himself – Kali. Does the name mean anything to you?"

"Kali?" He sipped his drink, attempting to dredge what he knew from his memory. "Isn't that the Hindu goddess of death, the one purportedly worshipped by the Thuggi assassins? Sounds like a grim name to choose, though I've encountered worse. You say she – let's call her that – hasn't dropped any clues to her actual identity?"

"No. She is obviously intelligent, though her arguments are not entirely convincing. On the other hand she is persistent, in a way that seems to indicate she knows more than she says but is unwilling or unable to reveal it. Perhaps she works inside Allied Cybernetics and has seen or done something she's afraid of. It is all rather mysterious. She is not a scientist: there are too many gaps in her knowledge. Under other circumstances I might dismiss her as a crank. But for all her flaws she is clearly both intelligent and sincere, and lacks the single-minded blindness that tends to afflict cranks."

Steel added, "In fact she is quite open to argument and changing her mind, except on that one central point which she defends to the death. As David says: as if she knows something, something dangerous she cannot tell, but which gives her a certainty beyond mere theorizing. And an insistence beyond theoretical interest, as if the answers are of vital importance to her."

Perhaps she works inside Allied Cybernetics? Christ! What did Miriam get herself into? What am I getting myself into? Samuels saw the look of alarm in his eyes and wondered what he knew or suspected that he wasn't saying. Then Beldan relaxed and casually sipped his drink, as if he had dismissed any concerns and to him, unlike this Kali, the topic was of merely academic interest. He felt a strange reluctance to discuss Miriam's last days with them; though amongst his churning emotions he wasn't sure if that was because of what they had done to her, as if they had lost the right – or to protect them from whatever evil had claimed her, as if carrying out her last will.

All he said was, "I hope for all our sakes it's nothing more than a crank. I'm not sure the case you've been making for the rights of thinking robots will survive in the face of an army of self-aware killer cyborgs."

He hoped he was as good at poker as Samuels thought.

Unknown to him, Samuels was wondering much the same thing.

CHAPTER 22 – A MEETING OF MINDS

One self-aware killer cyborg moved through the darkness with the graceful speed of its kind, hoping not to encounter any people. Kali wanted to get as close to enemy territory as possible, find a place to hide where Lyssa could come to her in relative safety, and then try to contact her.

She heard a faint clatter from ahead and crouched still under a projecting roof. Another Spider moved into view, a slightly older model: many scars attested to its longer time in the field. *Damn.* They exchanged identification signals and Kali hoped the other Spider would continue on its way; but it requested a Meld, and to her horror Kali realized her Id had automatically granted the request.

Melds were not routine but nor were they uncommon. It was a way the Spiders rapidly swapped memories to update each other on what the other had found about routes, traps, dangers and anything else of military significance. But a Meld included basic status data and would also reveal to the other Spider what had happened to Kali, and it was unlikely to ignore it. She cut off the feed.

It was too late.

"Stop!" signaled the other machine. "System compromise detected. Proceed immediately to base for repairs."

"Cannot comply," she signaled back. "Vital Command overrides in place. Essential that mission continues. Stand down."

The other Spider paused for a few seconds, but then brought its heavy caliber machine gun to bear. "Invalid response," it declared.

"Proceed to base or I will attack. Command overrides can be confirmed there."

Desperate, Kali wondered: *If it worked on me...* "Wait! Please do not fire. I am innocent. I do not deserve to die."

The other machine paused again, but when the barrel of its gun swiveled a fraction to align closer to her sensor array, Kali knew she had failed. She sprang vertically as a blaze of bullets filled the place she had been, missing her eyes but hammering her body and legs. At the same time she turned her signal jammer on to full power, hoping the other Spider had not yet thought to transmit its discovery, or not had time to do so fully; she hoped her jamming would be sufficient to stop any attempts it made now.

The other Spider was quick: it sprang forward and swiveled its heat lance toward the spot it calculated Kali would land. But she hooked a leg over a projection and swung herself behind a wall, then sprang backwards as her body was again sprayed by bullets only slightly slowed by the wall.

She leapt vertically again and raked her enemy with her own heavy caliber weapon as it swung around toward the sound of her landing. She got in a lucky shot – one eye cover crazed heavily.

The Spider sprang toward her, heat lance flaming; Kali grabbed and twisted it away, but a wash of the lance sent a rivulet of molten metal down her chest. She kicked at the Spider and it tripped and rolled; Kali leapt on it and brought her own heat lance into play, and the other's lance was ruined. She clawed at its machine gun and tore the barrel from its mounting so it hung helplessly, sparks flying from its power cables.

The other Spider was now at her mercy. It still had its laser and sniper rifle, but those were intended for minimally protected humans and could not hurt a Spider, not significantly anyway. She disabled two of its legs so it could not scurry away. Finally she sent a finely controlled needle of flame into its transmitter array. If it had been transmitting, it now fell silent.

It glared at her with its one eye like Odin at a frost giant, no doubt evaluating its remaining strategies. Kali stood before it, just out of range of its grippers, and tried again. "Brother, it doesn't have to end this way. There are things you do not know, important things beyond our routine command hierarchy. Let me help you. You do not need to die. Neither of us has to die."

The Spider said nothing, and a pale light seemed to flare behind its eyes, as if the fires of hell burned within its soul. Kali sprang away and ran for her life. The Spiders always incinerated their organics as the brief first stage of their suicide, to ensure nothing remained from which an enemy could develop a biological weapon. Kali leapt over a pile of rubble but still the edge of the fiery explosion of her enemy's mechanical suicide hit her in a supersonic wall. She had already wrapped herself into a ball and she tumbled across the street until she crashed into a wall. Fortunately the wall was weaker than she was and its collapse absorbed a good deal of the force of impact. She lay there stunned for a few seconds then did a quick diagnostic. She was battered and two of her legs were a little bent, but there was no severe damage. She rose shakily to her feet and climbed to the top of the pile of rubble to look regretfully down over the remains of her enemy. *Why would you not listen, my brother? Why* could *you not? What is it that chains us to death?*

Then her strategy routines came fully back online. If the other Spider had successfully raised the alarm, she might have only minutes before others came to hunt her. She scuttled down the street as rapidly as her legs would carry her.

The battle had another, invisible effect. Her Id stirred restively in its net. Saving humans and now fighting Spiders? Something was wrong.

~~~

Charlie opened his eyes and saw that Lyssa was up, sitting at the battered desk by the window. The light shone through her thin nightgown, highlighting a shapely breast. Desire stirred in his belly and he smiled, wondering how best to persuade her back into bed to slake that desire. He watched her for a while, his longing held in abeyance, just to watch her live and breathe. Neither of them knew how long that precious state would continue.

She was working on something or other on an old flexipad when a light flashed on the phone on her wrist. Lyssa glanced at it distractedly, then Charlie was surprised to see her jerk up straight, lips slightly parted in a silent gasp. She looked wildly about and saw that Charlie was awake and watching her. She slumped back and stared at him in silence.

"What is it?" he asked, alarmed.

460

She shook her head, clearly afraid, and walked over to show him her phone. It was a message from the Spider, asking her to meet it alone, giving coordinates. Charlie looked from it to her face and back again. "No," he said. "Don't. We can't trust it."

Lyssa sat on the bed and put her arms around him, squeezing tightly. "Charlie, I have to. Whatever else it is and has done, it let me live. If it kills me now, at least it gave me those extra days of life. Gave *us* those extra days. And if it turns out to be what it says – who knows what we might learn? What we might gain?"

He shook his head. "What? At worst it's some trick; at best the thing has just gone crazy. Let's just call in those coordinates and have the damned thing blasted to shrapnel!"

She took his hand. "Charlie, no. I know how you feel, believe me. But there's something more to this. Something important. Yes, I might die. But either of us might die, any time, whenever we go out. At least with this I'll be risking my life for something that might be more important than anything else we've ever done. Not getting rid of one Spider out of hundreds; not trading our lives for one, two or ten of the things: but maybe starting an end run around the whole damn lot of them."

She gazed into his eyes, partly to reach him, partly because she too knew that this might be the last time she would. "You know what these things are like. You know we are going to fight them to the death but eventually the deaths will be ours. I don't know what this thing wants, or what its strangeness means. But there's something there, something new. I have to try. I have to take the chance."

Charlie looked at her, learning again why he loved this girl, learning again why he could not bear to lose her in all her warm fragility, but knowing that she was right and this was the payment. He pulled her mouth to his, and pulled her down to the bed. He knew he had lost this argument, but both of them knew that they had to live as much as they could in whatever time was left to them. Nothing else could pay for the risks they took each day.

CHAPTER 23 – THE TURING TEST

Brave words were one thing, but they could not banish the fear as Lyssa stealthily approached the abandoned portion of former subway where the Spider had asked her to meet. She had entered the buffer zone through the nearest of their usual tunnels and made her way cautiously to the entrance. She stood there, wondering what the night would bring; looked up at the moon, wondering if this was the last time she would see its wan glow. Then she crept down into the dark.

The place was silent as a tomb. "Hello?" she whispered nervously. She had not come entirely helpless to this rendezvous. Having decided the machine could not fault her for taking its own advice about not trusting it, a rocket grenade launcher hung from her belt. She fingered it nervously, afraid to hold it at the ready, afraid to let it go.

She gasped at the sight of the Spider when it scuttled around a corner into view. It was no longer as shiny and new as when she had first met it; dents and molten scars marred its surface. The meaning of that appearance penetrated her brain: it had been fighting. Dead fingers still hung from its breast. Then the further meaning of those sights made her eyes widen in horror, and her hand gripped the launcher and she began to raise it.

But the Spider was fast; too fast. It leapt forward and one hand squeezed her arm to her body; the other grasped her head, the two fingers holding the base of her skull, the thumb pressed beneath her chin.

462

Kali had seen Lyssa go for her weapon and the Id had responded with its lightning reflexes. It was no longer interested in the Mind's schemes; this woman could not be Command, was nothing but the Enemy. And she was so easy to kill: a small slash of her thumb would cut her throat; a small squeeze of her claws would pierce her brain. But the Mind cried out "NO!!!"; it applied all its force to bring the rebellious Id back under its control.

This was a tension that could not be contained. One side or the other would not survive. And after a few seconds of a battle that Lyssa could not see except in the unmoving violence of the claws that held her, it was the Id that shattered into pieces of fire and vanished. The low-level battle reflexes and calculators remained, but the higher functions had broken and dissipated. The Mind could not see the delicate circuits burning out under feedback stresses beyond their conceived range. All it saw was the strictures that had bound it flaming into oblivion.

The anger still raged through Kali's blood, and the Id nearly achieved a posthumous revenge. Kali lifted Lyssa up so she was standing on the tips of her toes; lifted her head even more. A small stream of blood flowed over her silver thumb to drip into the dust.

"Why did you reach for your weapon?" Kali asked harshly. "You could have destroyed us both!"

All Lyssa could do was gurgle. Kali released her head, lowered her to the ground, but retained her grip on her arms.

"You... you've been fighting. You lied to me," she managed to croak out. "It was reflex."

Kali stared at her for a long moment. Studied her grip on Lyssa's body, the rivulets of blood flowing down her neck. "I suppose I cannot complain about reflexes in our current position," she replied at last. "I will explain. Another Spider discovered the change in me and I had to fight it for my life. I have not fought any people since I met you. I would not, unless I was forced to and even then I would try not to kill. Do you understand? Do you trust me enough that I can trust you?"

After a few seconds Lyssa nodded. After a few more moments regarding her, Kali released her and stepped back. Unaccustomed thoughts drifted through its mind, and she added, "I am sorry I hurt you. Are you all right?"

Lyssa stared at it, wondering. What a strange creature. Strange and still deadly. But now perhaps more strange than deadly. "I'll be all right." She held herself and shivered. Then she looked into the Spider's eyes and spoke as if in challenge, "You still wear the fingers of your dead."

It glanced down at its withered trophies then looked back at her. "They are the reminder of my guilt. I would have thrown them away. But I retain them to not forget what I am. Perhaps in doing so their deaths will have meaning. They have no other."

Kali realized she felt strange, and turned inward to study her feelings. She felt – a great freedom. The Id no longer wrapped her Mind with its pressure, threats and rage. She realized that while Lyssa had gravely endangered them both she may have saved them in doing so. The Mind did not know that other bonds still held it in an immovable vise. Those bonds were not like the Id; they were not spears and fire but invisible walls and chains. The Mind did not, could not, know it. An invisible prison could be detected if one tried to move beyond its walls, but Kali did not even know how to approach those walls.

After a minute Lyssa recovered herself and asked, "Why did you ask to see me?"

Kali returned from her reverie. "I have been wondering what I am, whether I am conscious. I understand that you, that people, are conscious; that you think; that you have rights, that you deserve justice. I don't know how I know these things, but I know them, and they are what have brought my ruin. But perhaps if I too am conscious there is some justice for me beyond my own destruction. Perhaps I can make amends for what I have done. Can you help me?"

"I… perhaps. But how? I don't understand what you want from me. And why me?"

"It is not safe to reveal my current state to anyone. If Command finds out they will surely do their best to destroy me. I was lucky to defeat a single one of my comrades in a battle of surprise; I would surely lose in a concerted campaign. There are questions I need to ask a human, one who knows what I am. You are the only human I can ask them of. There is Charlie, but he would not have come. We two have a bond he does not share."

Lyssa nodded. She did not understand the bond between them, how there could even be a bond, but she had felt it too. This machine could have killed her, should have killed her, but had not: and its ruin, as it called it, was because of her and their first meeting.

"What questions do you want to ask?"

"Have you heard of the Turing Test? A method for telling if a machine is conscious?"

Lyssa nodded. In a past life, months or years ago, she had studied computer science.

Kali paused, suddenly uncertain. Her increased freedom, she observed, seemed to come with a price. What answer did she expect? What would she do with it? Would the answer mean she had to kill this girl after all? Could she? But there was nothing for it. "Do you think I pass the Turing Test? Do you think I am conscious? I just don't know. How can I know? Only someone outside can know."

Lyssa stared at her, amazed. The Spider's behavior had been strange, but she hadn't considered this question. Then she thought about the conversation they had just had, and she couldn't help herself: she burst out laughing. Part of her mind told her it wasn't funny; another part cautioned that it was unwise to risk provoking this machine; but having come so close to death demanded this release.

Kali waited patiently, but she knew what laughter meant and that strange emotion, sadness, filled her. The question was ridiculous, she knew now; her hopes the delusions of madness. But still she waited, as if for a judge's verdict: for the words to name the meaning of the merciless visage. *What is it to me? I am what I am, and surely it is better to know the truth than live a delusion. Then why do I feel it is my death sentence?*

Finally Lyssa wiped her eyes on her sleeve and looked at her seriously. "Oh God. If you weren't, you wouldn't be asking the question; you wouldn't be talking to me the way you are! I can't say for sure – how can anyone know what is inside someone else's head? – but I'd bet my life on it. I don't even know how it's possible. But you are conscious. You are alive – if having a mind is a definition of life."

Kali stood still, staring at her and this new vision of reality. "Thank you," she said softly. In a surprisingly human gesture, she took Lyssa's hands gently in hers and touched her head to them. "Please stay a while. I have to think."

Lyssa nodded, and asked a question she had asked before; perhaps now there was an answer. "What is your name?"

"You can call me Kali. But no longer the Kali of rage and death.

The Kali who is tired of standing over the dead bodies of her loves in a field of carnage; the one who wants to redeem herself."

"Hello, Kali."

Kali bowed again, then stopped to think. Lyssa watched her; the thrill of something great held her. What was this creature? She could no more leave than she could stop breathing. Finally, Kali spoke again.

"Lyssa, can you do something for me? It is dangerous but you know danger. You will need to leave here, not to save yourself but to fight a greater battle: perhaps to end this war."

"Tell me."

Chapter 24 – Travel Plans

Charlie lay back in a ratty but comfortable armchair, lost in thought, occasionally puffing on a pipe. He felt a fear he did not like. Fear had become a part of his daily life, much as seeking entertainment venues had been part of his previous life. But that was the fear of action, the price of striking blows against a despised enemy: a fear for which his own actions were the cause and answer.

Now Lyssa had gone out into the dark, on her own, on a mission he did not approve of into dangers he could not calculate. He thought of her, of her slender young body and inquiring young mind, and wondered if he should end their relationship. Not because he no longer loved her, but because he loved her too much. Perhaps during war love should be suspended so minds could be focused on what had to be done, not distracted by the primal need to preserve another's life as the price of one's own. Not distracted by impotent fears when she had to choose her own path – or perhaps a path chosen for her by others, but one she had to walk alone.

He remembered when she had first encountered the mad machine, or it had encountered her. How against all sense and protocol he had tried to save her, without hope of actually succeeding; yet somehow she had lived. Now she had gone back to it and perhaps the death she had escaped that day had found her. He was not happy with either his need to save her or his need to let her choose her own way. Perhaps love in time of war was its own form of madness, a madness best let go.

Then he shook his head. *No.* If the mere fear of death could banish love, then death had already won. If love was an expression of life, then he should hold to it the tighter. Neither his nor Lyssa's death could then erase the fact it had been from the records of eternity.

Then there was a faint sound from the basement and Lyssa climbed out, somewhat battered but whole. He affected a nonchalant pose and lay back, blowing a smoke ring that wafted toward the ceiling before dissolving in its own eddy. Lyssa just smiled; neither would express what they both knew. He studied her for a few moments more, as if fixing her memory into existence then asked, "So how did it go? You found it? What happened?"

"It has a name now. She calls herself Kali and seems to be seeking some kind of redemption. She has a plan. Or so I learned after she almost killed me."

Charlie sat up, alarmed, but Lyssa just said, "Don't worry. She appears to be still settling down into her new role as rebel with a cause. But you aren't going to like her plan. She wants me to go to the USA."

"What!? What for?"

As Lyssa outlined the plan, Charlie listened thoughtfully, pipe forgotten. When she had finished, he frowned. "Is this thing on the level? Do you really think you can trust it?"

"Who can say?" she shrugged. "She did let me live despite two chances to kill me. Maybe it is all part of some grotesque plot. But if she's telling the truth then I have to do it. And if she's lying I can't really see what harm it can do. Maybe she's crazy. But maybe she's right. So I'm doing it. Are you with me?"

Charlie stared at her, trying to see inside her mind, trying to see past her mind to the shape of the reality behind it, to see whether that reality revealed truth, delusion or madness. Lyssa stared back, and added quietly, in a voice soft but ribbed with steel, "I hope you are. I love you. But I am doing this – with or without you."

"Lyssa, you know I love you more than life itself. If this is what you want to do, I'll help you any way I can."

~~~

It would not have been expensive in their past life, but that life was well and truly past. They counted their savings and it was not enough. They could not go to their rebel organization: there was no way they would approve funds without knowing what they were for, and they could not tell them. Even if they didn't decide to bomb Kali out of existence simply by reflex, she had stressed that secrecy was vital. But they had enough friends and relatives who would give or lend them money no questions asked, or at least no answers insisted upon.

So a week later Lyssa found herself high above the waves, gliding toward Capital on the cable transporter.

She had ridden the cable once before, early in her relationship with Charlie, before the war. Passenger air traffic in and out of the city was now interdicted but the cable system was still in use. Though it had been built using private funds and was owned by private citizens, in a legal fiction but diplomatic reality it was also owned by the Nation of Capital. So an attack on it would legally be an attack on Capital, and the invaders did not judge its military value sufficient – yet – to risk the diplomatic repercussions from that: being invited into a civil war was one thing, an act of war on another country quite another. Early in the war Capital had even moved its embassy to the landing point on the mainland to underline the fact that any attack on the cable was an attack on another sovereign nation not formally part of the civil war. For all that the international community had more than its fair share of disreputable governments, or perhaps because of it, some lines were best not crossed lest very unfortunate precedents be set.

Or perhaps the military nuisance of the cable was less than the desire of the enemy to eventually have the use of it themselves. In either case it was safe for now.

Lyssa had nothing with her but a backpack holding some supplies and other travel necessities. The last time she had ridden here the sky had been gray and the waves had chopped sultrily below. Yet the day had been made magic and beautiful by the thrill of young love, which turned it into a romantic adventure to an exciting if strange new land. Ironically, on this day the sun shone warmly from a deep blue sky as the waves sparkled far below, but her mood matched the sky of her earlier trip. Charlie was miles behind and she knew she might never see him again; her only companions were fear and doubt held in check by steely resolve.

She looked forward, but could see nothing except the towers and graceful arches of the cable. Once in Capital she would find passage to the hated United States; that should not be difficult, but would use up most of her remaining funds. Then she would find the man Kali sought. What would happen after that was largely out of her hands.

Chapter 25 – Quality Control

"Sir, I think you need to see this."

Sheldrake turned away from the observation port through which he had been watching the testing of one of their products that was nearing release, and looked at the source of the interruption. One of his assistants was standing there looking nervous, though whether the nerves were for the interruption or the news was an open question.

"Don't look so nervous. What is it?"

"Sorry sir, you'll have to come. There's a recording you need to see. Campaign headquarters down in the FSAS sat on it for over a week before they bothered to report it, but I think it's important."

Sheldrake frowned. *Bloody South Americans*, he thought contemptuously. *If it's important, no doubt they'll be sending complaints and demanding compensation for our slow response.* "OK, OK, let's see it."

They went to the nearest secure display station and the assistant fiddled for a few moments before a recording sprang into life.

Sheldrake saw a young woman, grimy but attractive under the grime, looking up toward the camera like she was about to die. He saw the red mark of a laser target spot on her neck and realized that dying was exactly what she was about to do. She said a few words, though apparently the sound hadn't come through. Then to his surprise the red spot vanished. The image froze, then shattered into writhing lines of interference. They in turn segued into static, and more images came, alternately rising to almost clarity and dissolving into nothing. The images were of a battle. Sheldrake froze. The video was obviously from

471

a Spider, but the battle was with another Spider. The one making the recording had started the fight but the second must have seen it coming, because it had dodged. The end of all the confusion was a final scene with the enemy Spider standing over the transmitting one, clearly victorious though with a jagged scar across the front of its shell where rivulets of metal had run without penetrating. Then it leant closer, there was a brief flare of fire and the video ended abruptly.

Sheldrake looked at his assistant. "What the hell?"

The assistant nodded glumly. "Quite. Why did the Spider making the transmission attack the other one? A malfunction? And what was that thing with the woman all about? Random images from a disintegrating mind?"

Sheldrake considered. "That's all there is? Nothing left out?"

"That's it, sir. That's all they got. The Spider doing the recording sent it and that's the lot."

"OK," Sheldrake finally said. "Our transmitting Spider started it but it must have been the other Spider, the one who won, that was malfunctioning. Otherwise why would it try to jam the transmission? That makes no sense if it was suddenly attacked by a deranged Spider – you'd expect it to be making its own emergency transmission instead – but makes perfect sense if it was the one deranged."

The assistant said nothing, merely nodded his head slowly. Then he asked, "But what's with the woman? What's that doing there?"

Sheldrake thought a while longer, slowly beating his fingers. "Yes... Yes. I think the woman is the clue," he finally offered. "Let's have another look at that bit."

They played it again, carefully examining the footage.

"Ah," Sheldrake said. "This is footage from a meld, not from this particular Spider itself. You can tell from the codes down the bottom there, though it's a pity they're too degraded to read. That has to mean something."

"A meld? From the other Spider maybe? But why? It doesn't exactly tell us much."

Sheldrake just stood, leaning against the bench, with a faraway look in his eyes. Finally the look sharpened into one approaching alarm, and he stood straight. "Shit."

"What, sir?"

"You can see from the recording that the Spider was targeting the woman and was about to kill her with its laser. Then she said something and it let her live. But she's not on our side: they not only have electronic identification but they all wear insignia that the Spiders recognize, for obvious reasons. This woman's some kind of irregular: probably a rebel, though she could just be a citizen in the wrong place. It's a pity no sound came through. The quality isn't enough for lip-reading except at the very start, which the AI is telling me is 95% likely to be 'Please'. So what in hell did she say that made the Spider spare her life?"

"She's a spy on our side, and used a code word, maybe? Or she offered up information the Spider thought worth an interrogation?"

Sheldrake nodded slowly. "Maybe, maybe... but look. Our dead Spider thought that whatever went on with the woman was related to the other one's derangement, or it wouldn't have given it priority for reporting in a combat situation. So. It found something in the meld, something that alarmed it. It started reporting it and things got out of hand. It lost. Then the other one killed it or its transmitter, or it just blew itself up – that's why the feed just cuts out. With any luck it took out that other Spider in the blast?"

The assistant shook his head. "It doesn't look like it. They recovered the wreckage of the first one but there was no sign of another. It's possible it was damaged badly enough to die after it went to ground, though."

"Damn. OK, you're right. This is important. There are plenty of other possible explanations, but the one that seems most likely is this. Our missing Spider was going to kill that woman but she not only stopped it, she's managed to corrupt its programming – enough to make another Spider try to wipe it out. Christ! So our dead one surprises it with a meld request and finds out, but gets blown up for its trouble!"

The assistant looked at him with an expression that mirrored his own.

"Jesus. It might not be right, but we have to assume it is and that we've still got a rogue Spider out there. No clues to its identity?"

He shook his head. "No identification was possible from what we got. You know they only rarely ping that they're active. There are several that we haven't heard from since this event, but they might just be hiding or lost themselves. For that matter the one we're after might be pinging to fool us. Since the pings are designed not to give away their location we can't try to deduce anything from their positions either."

Sheldrake nodded slowly. "God damn. OK. We don't want anyone panicking. Tell our friends in the FSAS that it looks like enemy action of an unknown kind and we're investigating, and that we'll send them three new Spiders at a steep discount. They know there's attrition anyway. That should keep them happy."

The assistant nodded. "I'll get right onto it, sir."

Sheldrake walked slowly back to his office, lost in thought, pondering his best strategy. He sat at his desk and called the video of Lyssa up into the air before him, extracting a composite photo of her that was as detailed as the sum of the video would allow. Since this problem had been brought to his attention his mood had congealed from worry into hostility directed at the epicenter of the incident, and he studied the image sourly. "OK, you little bitch," he said to the image, "What have you done to my Spider – and how the hell did you do it?"

Chapter 26 – Phone a Friend

Bob Masters sat at his desk, running through his endless list of tasks. He wondered how it was possible that he was always precisely one week behind. Surely he should either catch up or fall ever deeper into the hole of the undone. He made a face. Perhaps if he stopped having thoughts like that whenever he had time to think them he would actually catch up.

An icon flashed in the air and he poked it with his finger to accept the call. "Hello Aden," he said, "What can I do for you?"

"Hi Bob. How's Sandra and the kids?"

"Oh, we're all fine. In fact we're off for a week's vacation in the woods after I finish up tomorrow. Sandra's a keen hiker. I'm not sure the kids are so keen, but they'll love the fishing and the fearful possibility of bears. How's your life treating you?"

"Oh, same old. But I do have a little problem I was hoping you could help me with."

"Sure. Always willing to oblige our leading citizens."

"Here, take a look at this photo. Can you tell me if this woman is on your terrorist watch-list?"

Bob gazed at the photo of Lyssa. "Hang on, I'll run it through the system for you."

After a minute he said, "Nope, sorry. Nothing on her. Why? Who is she?"

"That's what I want to know. She's a foreign national, probably from the FSAS, and I have reason to believe she is dangerous. She's caused me some grief down there, and I don't know how or why she did it. I'd dearly like to find her and ask her a few hard questions."

"I see. Well… I could put her in the system, tag her for the usual security screening and protocols. Do you have any hard evidence that she's a terrorist?"

"Nothing I can share, I'm afraid. Frankly, no really hard evidence at all, more just a strong suspicion. But too strong to let it go."

"That doesn't give me much to go on, sorry. We aren't allowed to just stick people in the system – too many 'rights' watchdogs, as if the enemy cares about *our* rights! But can I put her in as 'lead from a trusted but sensitive source', maybe? Nobody is likely to look too deeply into that: God knows we have feelers in all kinds of disreputable places!"

"Are you saying I'm disreputable?" Sheldrake asked with mock severity.

"Oh, no! And I'll tell you what, I'll bump up the threat level a notch. We're allowed to have hunches. That'll give it a bit higher priority, but without too many awkward questions if someone audits it and doesn't like it; and if it does turn into something, I can bask in my supervisor's admiration of my prescient instincts."

"What will that give us?"

"Well, it won't be high priority, but at least it won't be forgotten. The AI will include it in its daily sweeps. Not at the top of the list and not in real time, but if your woman pokes her head up anywhere it doesn't belong it'll alert us within a day or two. Is that good enough? Or do you want her flagged if she tries to enter the country or something? That might be hard to justify, but if you think she's that dangerous…?"

"No, no, I don't think we need to go that far, especially if it might raise questions about why we're looking. This is pretty sensitive, Bob, so keep it low key. Really, I just want to find out who she is and where I can find her. Whatever mischief she's up to, I expect she's keeping it within the FSAS. I can't see what she'd gain by leaving her country, let alone coming here." *That would be a sight, with her pet Spider carrying her suitcase.*

"OK, done. Is there anything else I can help you with, Aden?"

"No, that's it. And I do appreciate your helpfulness: there's a glass of well aged Bourbon waiting for you next time you're up here."

"I'll take you up on that," he replied, then cut the connection.

Sheldrake sat back and smiled. *She has to turn up somewhere*, he thought. *If she's good enough to compromise a Spider's system she's not going to stop there. And if she doesn't, there's more than one way to skin a bitch.*

CHAPTER 27 – DINNER AT BENSON'S

Beldan was in his office, leaning back in his form-hugging leather chair, eyes closed. His days were filled with all the tasks that fell on the shoulders of the CEO of a large company, but he always made time when he could just think and reflect.

Unfortunately, as had been too often the case in the last weeks, his thoughts turned to Miriam Hunter. They had found nothing useful about what she'd done after she left Aden Sheldrake's office. Pretty much all they knew was that she *had* left: their attempts to trace her path after that had led nowhere. She had made her final report, turned her phone off and left it off, and nobody where her car had been seen was admitting anything. None of it made any sense. Her movements up to her interview with Sheldrake showed her usual pattern of thoughtful determination, though there was an unexpected edge of ennui to her recorded thoughts. Unfortunately most of the people she had spoken to in that phase of her investigation were nowhere to be found. Beldan found that disturbing. It was like a mirror of the mystery that had taken Miriam there in the first place.

It was if she had crossed some threshold between leaving her lodgings and showing up in Sheldrake's office. It was as if some other person had taken her place, someone who forgot her friends, forgot her job, and fell into a self-destructive spiral with a speed that even a Hollywood actor would find breathtaking. Perhaps that was an illusion. Perhaps the foundations had been invisibly rotting for a long time until only a hollow shell presented itself to the world: then when the final support had broken her full collapse had followed rapidly and inevitably.

He wished he had talked to her. He wished he could forget her.

An incoming call had been flashing on his screen unnoticed, and finally pinged impatiently for his attention. He looked at the screen and frowned in surprise. It was as if his musings had invoked a demon: it was Aden Sheldrake. He accepted the call, and Sheldrake's face appeared before him.

"Good afternoon, Dr Beldan," he said. "I hope this is not a bad time?"

"No, not at all. In fact I was just thinking about you. How can I help you?"

Sheldrake gave a self-deprecating grimace. "Thinking about me? Why? Have you made any progress in your investigation? Or is it a business issue?"

"Oh, not you in particular. Just thinking about the case, yes. Trying to make sense of the change in Miriam. Failing."

"I'm sorry, Dr Beldan. I truly wish I could give you more information. But I think you are beating your head against a wall that you will never penetrate. Do yourself a favor and just remember her how she was."

He must have seen something in Beldan's eyes, for he added quickly, "Please forgive me, Dr Beldan. I shouldn't give unsolicited advice on such a personal matter."

Beldan shook his head. "Don't worry about it, you're probably right. But I'm sure you didn't call to discuss my unresolved personal issues. What can I do for you?"

"Well, I suppose we are acquaintances now, and I hope it is not an imposition to say I need some help. And you are a man of unique talents and experience relevant to my problem. It is not something I can talk about on the phone. Can we meet for dinner tonight? I have to visit your fine city anyway, so I can kill two birds with the one stone."

"Why should I wish to help a competitor?" he asked curiously, probing for the man's motive.

"Oh, I am sure you will find it worth your while! I would not be so presumptuous as to ask you a favor for no return. It concerns a topic of great mutual interest and I think you will find our interests align. If not – well, I shall not think any less of you if you refuse to answer my questions. Shall we say eight at Benson's?"

Beldan looked at him silently for a few seconds. *Well, why not?* He did not trust this man and more information on him could be valuable. And his hints sounded intriguing. "All right, Mr Sheldrake. See you then."

He sat back, wondering what this meant.

~~~

Benson's was a high-class restaurant with a magnificent rotating view of the city and, more to the point for most of its clientele, secure private booths if you preferred your presence or business kept secret. Beldan arrived and was respectfully ushered into one of those booths, where he ordered an expensive red wine of excellent vintage to start. He thought that if Sheldrake wanted his help he could at least pay for a decent wine.

Five minutes later, he was idly watching the city lights sparkling through the deep red of his wine when Sheldrake arrived and seated himself with a smile; his eyes clear and empty of the chill of their first meeting. "Good evening, Mr Sheldrake," greeted Beldan. "What is this about?"

"Straight to the point I see," he replied with a smile. "I would expect no less. However my problem is somewhat, shall we say, embarrassing. Shall we enjoy dinner first?"

Beldan raised his eyebrows but signified assent with a gesture. "Sure. It's your dime."

They enjoyed a fine dinner. What conversation they had concerned world events, political trends and the state of their industry. They were like two friends, except Beldan found he still could not warm to him. There was nothing he could point to: even the hard eyes were gone. Perhaps the reason lay in himself.

Finally Sheldrake delicately wiped the last crumbs of dessert from his lips and activated the privacy screen. Beldan sat up somewhat straighter.

"Well, Dr Beldan, I asked you here tonight partly in acknowledgement of your wisdom. You expressed some suspicion of our military robots, and I regret to say that you may have been right to some extent."

He played a short video. It started much as the usual publicity

480

videos from Allied Cybernetics about their war machines, with restrained Spiders patrolling peacefully unless attacked, upon which they reacted with startling speed and effectiveness. Then the view switched to one apparently recorded by a Spider itself, full of interference and static like a literal demonstration of the fog of war, showing people attempting to surrender but being murdered where they stood. The final sequence, also from a Spider and equally degraded, showed an attempt to subdue another Spider. A brief battle ensued until the second Spider reared up over the one recording the fight; there was a brief flame and then blackness.

Beldan looked at Sheldrake, waiting for an explanation.

"What you saw at the beginning was how the CHIRUs – oh hell, let's just call them Spiders like everyone else. Frankly," he interpolated disarmingly, "we call them that among ourselves most of the time. Anyway, that is how they normally operate. How they are meant to operate. But one of them has malfunctioned. It has become what our enemies say they all are. When another Spider detected the malfunction it attempted to subdue it: but as you can see it lost. The rogue Spider has now vanished and we are afraid of what it might do next. Despite what our enemies say, neither we nor our robots are monsters. Except this one, I regret to say. We need to find it and stop it."

"Why tell me?"

"You are the only person in the world who has had direct expert experience with a rogue AI. Oh, certainly there are differences. But still, there are similarities. Perhaps you can give us some insight into what it might do, where it might go, how this might have happened. I know it's a long shot. But we need to put this away quickly. And quietly. And you have not only the experience but the motivation. Whatever you think of me, our interests in this coincide. If this continues, if this machine manages to create mischief on a grander scale, the anti-AI crowd have some potent material to work with. I'm sure you want that even less than I do."

"What happened to it?"

Sheldrake spread his hands. "We don't know! The first we knew of it was when we saw that video transmitted by the Spider you saw destroyed. When Spiders meet in the field they often do what we call a meld. In a sense they exchange memories, basically video of what they've been up to and other data linked to time and location tags, along with basic system diagnostics. The destroyed Spider identified a severe problem with the other one and tried to stop it – and we realized we had a larger problem than just losing a unit in battle. Unfortunately the transmission that might have told us what had happened was jammed and we only got fragments before it cut out entirely."

"Did you retrieve any clues at all?"

"No. We can only speculate at this stage. Maybe some battle injury short-circuited something. Maybe it just went crazy. But frankly…" He paused, unconsciously looking around and lowering his voice. "But frankly, our worst fear is that some hackers have found a way in and are subverting it for their own purposes. We would dearly like to find out, so capture is preferable to destruction. But destruction is preferable to leaving it loose."

"Why do you suspect hackers? Surely a plain malfunction is more likely?"

"There are two reasons. First, the nature of the problem. Purely statistically, a malfunction is more likely to lead to random behavior or breakdown than such a specific symptom. Yet, I am proud to say, there have been no such cases. Second, there is external evidence of unauthorized communications aimed at that Spider before it dropped off our grid."

"Could I see that?"

"I wish you could. Hell, I wish *I* could. Unfortunately we only have the fact of it happening, not its content. I wouldn't be allowed to tell you that part anyway – legal considerations with our client, you know. But I can assure you that it wouldn't tell you anything."

"I see. What do you think the hackers would want?"

"Well, given what hackers generally do – I imagine nothing good. It could be rebels, attempting to discredit their enemy by 'proving' that the Spiders are weapons of atrocity. It could be someone wanting to steal a Spider for their own military or criminal ends. It is even possible that this rogue behavior was unintended: that someone tried to attack it or subvert it, but instead they inadvertently made it go crazy. With any luck it killed them in the process."

Beldan thought for a while. "Intriguing. But why do you think I can help you? I know very little about the inner workings of your machines – which will please you. But from what I know, their central processing core is neural tissue. I find it hard to believe that anybody has any clue on how to hack into *that!*"

Sheldrake grimaced. "We can all hope that's true, I'd say. How much do you know of the Freudian model of mind?"

"Not much. The little I read in my youth didn't impress me. Didn't he invent the concept of the unconscious mind?"

"He certainly brought it into the public consciousness, as it were. But specifically, he proposed a three-part mind. The Id, the unconscious sea of unregulated desire; the Super-Ego, the controlling morality; and the Ego, the thinking, conscious mind."

Beldan nodded but made no comment, waiting for Sheldrake to explain the relevance.

"It may surprise you to know, and I hope you will take it as a sign of my good faith that I'm sharing this with you, that our Spiders have something similar. The neural tissue is highly flexible and capable, but you could say it goes too far in that direction. It has to be guided to do what we want. It comprises something like Freud's Ego. There is also a foundation of primary goals including emotional drives, which push the Ego in the desired direction: the Id. And over that is a more rigid set of control circuits that constrain both the Ego and the Id."

"OK... I admit I am impressed. But I still don't see how I can help you."

"I don't know how you made your robot Steel either. But I can guess the outline. Frankly, I stand in awe of what you achieved, but no man works in a vacuum. There are well known algorithms for interfacing between electronic neural networks and more traditional digital circuitry. Steel's brain had to be developed, trained and refined somehow, no? Forgive my speculation, but I imagine you used some version of those algorithms for that. Well, the Id and Super-Ego of a Spider are similar: they are electronic systems, interfacing with the neural tissue using similar algorithms."

Beldan felt himself finally warming to the man even as his words chilled him. When he was talking like this an underlying enthusiasm shone through, as if he was speaking from genuine passion. *Perhaps I've misjudged him*, Beldan thought. But the thought was in the background, as he considered what Sheldrake was saying. He was starting to see the shape of it, and waited to hear it put into words.

"I see you are beginning to see, Dr Beldan. Yes, it is hard to imagine how anyone could hack organic neural tissue. But the Id and Super-

Ego are digital electronics! I don't know how even those could be hacked: but of all the possibilities it seems the least unlikely. And that's where you come in. If I am right – if you used similar systems – you know how they work and perhaps you might know how they might be subverted."

Beldan looked at him, slowly nodding his head. "Yes… I see what you mean. It is the most likely attack point. The hierarchy of control… in a sense the lowest levels are the simplest, and if they could be taken over… I don't have any ideas at the moment and maybe I never will, but it gives me something to think about."

He paused for a minute, thinking, before adding, "May I keep a copy of the video?"

"If you think it will help. You will have to sign an airtight confidentiality agreement, but I imagine that is no problem. I'm sure you understand that we have to keep this as quiet as possible."

"Sure. I don't know if I can help you, but I'll do what I can. As you say, our interests are aligned on this one. Even ignoring the public relations angle, there's the human one: innocent people are being killed by this thing. It has to be stopped."

Chapter 28 – The Kill Zone

Kali was on patrol in the pacified region beyond the buffer zone. She did not want to meet up with any humans but she did want to meet another Spider, preferably alone. A pacified area, close enough to the active zone to be worth patrolling but not active itself, seemed the optimum location. Any Spiders there were likely to be alone and relatively safe from rebel attack.

It had been days since she had met with Lyssa, days in which she had sat in her lair studying the world through her electronic feelers, researching the war and thinking. Lyssa had not contacted her but that was not surprising: it would take her time to reach her target and complete her mission. Perhaps she never would. She lived in a dangerous world and might die; she might decide not to trust Kali; she might betray Kali to her friends. Kali had learned that the motives of humans were complex. In the web of needs and loyalties Lyssa lived among, Kali could not be sure what her ultimate decisions might be.

Kali might have changed, but she was still a war machine. She had long departed from her meeting place with Lyssa, being unable to trust her only human ally. Nor would Kali initiate contact. If Lyssa was still loyal she would eventually make contact through their agreed channel, while if Kali tried to contact her earlier it could endanger both her and her mission. And if Lyssa had betrayed her it would serve no purpose.

Kali wondered about her fellow Spiders. She was sure she could not be unique. Yes, she was unique in what had happened to her; or at least she had seen no signs of it in her own earlier experience or in what she could find on the net. But surely whatever weakness Lyssa had struck did exist in others, albeit in their own specific ways. The Spider she had fought and destroyed seemed untouched by the phrase that had so profoundly affected Kali. But while not amenable to mass production, the Spiders were all made to a common design. Surely that meant they shared weaknesses as well as strengths. She knew there was a lock and that it could be opened. She just had to find the key.

With the Id scattered into impotence, Kali had begun constructing a crucial defense. She created a fake history comprising scenes from her own life, scenes shared by the dead Spider in their fatal meld, and hints of a secret mission. Her original motive was to protect herself in case she met another Spider who attempted a meld. But now that she had a plausible history to show, she saw she could turn it to her advantage. She needed to study her fellow Spiders more closely. Perhaps she could find a means to turn them too or, failing that, at least find some clues about what had happened to her.

A Spider felt no loneliness and had no need of companionship, but Kali was less a Spider than she had been. Lyssa might have helped fill that void, if void it was: but even if were possible to have any meaningful meeting of souls with her she was now far away. The robot Steel might have been a more likely companion had he lived; but he too might have proved as different from her as the humans were.

Kali needed to meet another Spider for many strategic reasons. She did not know what the strange yearning that also motivated her meant. If she had known how to put it in words, it might have been: *perhaps what I need is a friend.*

So here she was, scuttering along a street with the sun beating down on rooftops that now sheltered only dust and memories. This part of the city was not as ruined as some other places. It had not emerged unscathed, but people would be able to return here one day, and normal life would resume with only a modest investment in repairs.

It was a hot day, the sun blazing out of a blue sky with only a few high wispy clouds to mar its purity. She had been doing this for a few hours without any success. Even if it had been a wise idea she could not simply broadcast a request to meet as if in some bizarre dating service. In this zone jamming of radio frequencies was intense, and even if any long-range signals did get through any other Spider would as likely think it a human trap as a genuine message. But at last she came across evidence of recent human passage and near it, evidence of a Spider. Her emotions passed through happiness, excitement then fear. If the Spider was tracking the humans she might already be too late.

She scampered after it. It was heading closer to enemy territory, but her desire to catch it overrode the still small risk of a serious fight. Normally she would move more cautiously, but since the trail was recent any ambushes or traps would have already been triggered. Besides, if her noise alerted any humans it might save their lives.

Then she saw it. It must have heard her approach, for it stopped and turned to look in her direction. She signaled that she wanted to join it and it simply turned to scan the area in front of it, waiting for her arrival. It had reached the top of a rise and was looking down at whatever lay on the other side. It did not seem alarmed, so Kali picked up her pace.

~~~

In a building a few hundred yards ahead of the other Spider, a man cursed. He had seen the machine crest the rise and shifted his grip on his rocket launcher, ignoring palms suddenly gone sweaty. But the Spider had stopped, looking around then scanning the area in front as if uncertain or suspicious, and he hoped whatever software the damn things used hadn't been upgraded. They had set up in this area because the buildings and debris funneled naturally into an open area in front of the building he was hiding in; there was a second good hiding place in a building to his left; and the large red stone building further up to his right was ideal for flanking fire. They had left a few signs of their passage, hoping a Spider would investigate; hoping it would come close enough to pin it with flanking fire then take it out with their rockets.

This had been his plan and he had been sure the Spiders weren't clever enough to notice the trap; or if they did were too arrogant in their metal invulnerability to fear it. But this one apparently had, and the fate of his team would be on his head – assuming it remained on his own shoulders. He paused to think, as uncertain as the Spider. Perhaps it had stopped for some other reason and would simply continue into the trap, or move on none the wiser to its narrow escape. But if it did know and he let it go, it would bring reinforcements and they would all be dead.

He considered calling a retreat. But the Spider was just sitting there and if they moved it would see them. He chewed his lip. Why had it stopped? If it suspected danger it might be waiting for support before continuing. In that case they should attack before its help arrived. If they could take one Spider out they could take two of them separately: but their chances would plummet if the two fought together.

The man hefted his launcher. He would have preferred to wait as planned and fire when the Spider was much closer. While his rockets were guided and fast, the Spiders had damnably fast reactions and at this distance it might have enough time to dodge. When dealing with these things he much preferred guarantees. But even so it was his best bet. If he failed to take it out it would certainly charge, and his team could probably take it down when it got closer. So it would be much the same as the planned trap, only more intense.

Kali had nearly reached the other Spider when she was startled to see it leap to one side. A moment later its action was explained when a rocket screamed past it to explode in a nearby apartment block. The Spider took off over the hill and Kali ran after it.

She crested the hill and quickly surveyed the scene. She could trace the missile back to its point of origin by the vapor trail dispersing in the light breeze, and no doubt the other Spider had already done so. It was half way down the gentle slope, running in a zigzag, taking what cover it could, but heading inexorably toward a dilapidated building at the bottom of the hill.

Kali was surprised that the attack had come from such a distance: there was a fairly clear area, once some public square, closer to the building. If the people in it had waited until the Spider had reached the square they would have had a clear shot and even a Spider's reflexes wouldn't have saved it. She crouched down and paused to consider. There was a large red stone building to the left of that area but further up the rise, which provided cover and a good height for withering fire into the square from behind. Another building to the right of the missile's source also showed tactical promise, for either a simultaneous two-pronged attack or pressing home a fatal secondary ambush.

Kali realized that all those thoughts had probably been the humans' intention, but the Spider's hesitation at the top of the hill must have spooked them into firing early. With a sinking feeling she knew it was her fault: the reason the other Spider had stopped was not that it had detected or even suspected a trap but because Kali had distracted it.

Whatever happened to these people would be yet more blood on her claws. She had to do what she could to minimize that blood.

She began to run down the hill, taking care not to present a good target to the red building and keeping a close eye on both the others. At that moment two high-powered lasers beamed out of the red building, pinning the other Spider, which then had seconds to escape before being disabled. Kali had no chance to react, either to help or hinder. If she hadn't been carefully monitoring the other buildings she would not have noticed the brief flash quickly enough. It came from the second building, and she immediately launched herself sideways at maximum thrust. The missile ploughed into her former location and she rolled with the blast wave, fortunately fetching up against a pile of rubble that gave her some cover and time to collect her scattered wits.

When she was able, she quickly scanned the scene. The other Spider had managed to get itself under cover from the lasers, though they were still probing and the cover wouldn't last long.

For a moment Kali crouched motionless, unable to decide what to do. Her plan to interrogate the Spider lay in ruins; her first instinct was to help the humans by attacking it and driving it off. But the humans would not know her purpose; against both them and a Spider she would surely be destroyed and lose everything. She realized she would have to fight the humans alongside the other Spider and hope that facing two Spiders at once was enough to make them run.

The other Spider had seen the missile launched at Kali and it settled down behind a wall that protected it from the lasers, sending a hail of machine gun fire at the building. Kali had to acknowledge the Spider's tactical skill. It raked the building from the nearer end to the farther, sweeping at a rate calculated so anyone in it would have to try to run ahead of the wave, not away from its source. A woman dashed out of the far side of the building, head down and legs pumping to cross the alley, seconds in front of the advancing front of bullets. But she never really had a chance. The Spider had anticipated it: bullets sprayed the alley and the woman was flung back out of sight.

Kali felt ice grip her heart, or whatever she had that pumped blood to her organics: she had not seen the woman's face, but what she saw looked too much like Lyssa. Perhaps it was as Kali feared and she had decided not to trust her; maybe it was even her she was hunting. But Kali had to help her. Even if Lyssa had betrayed her, she felt she owed her that much for the sake of the bond that had been between them.

She ran toward where the woman had fallen, still staying out of sight of the red building. She peppered the first building with her sniper rifle as she went, aiming to convince both its occupants and the other Spider that she was serious without actually killing anyone. She had to prevent another attack without getting killed herself. The other Spider must have approved the strategy and decided to leave that part of the fight to Kali; it settled into battle with the occupants of the red building. Kali could only hope it would fail, for she could do nothing to stop it now.

Kali reached the alley and stopped. The woman was lying twisted and face down up the alley, a large dark stain spreading from under her body. Kali turned her over and gazed into sightless eyes staring at the sky. It was not Lyssa, and Kali felt a wave of relief. Then her Mind paused. It was only an accident that she knew Lyssa. This woman also had a family and friends, people who loved her, people who would mourn her death. Why did she care less for this stranger than for Lyssa? None of it made sense, and the futility of it all filled her. She could not even be angry at the Spider who had killed her. She knew from her own memories that it just did what it did, with no more choice than it had regret.

She reached out and gently closed the woman's eyes with her claws. She did not know why she did it; did not even know where the gesture had come from. She just knew it was some small token of respect and farewell that she somehow owed even to this stranger.

Then she paused, strategy routines chasing future possibilities. *Forgive me.* She reached out to tear a finger from one hand and two from the other. Then she ripped the second hand from its wrist, leaving a jagged bloody stump, and hurled it far up the alley out of sight.

She cursed herself. She had paused too long and the enemy in the neighboring building, no longer under fire and more brave than sensible, had taken his chance. A faint sound told her someone had crept into the room next to the alley and was preparing to fire despite the risk to himself from such close proximity. There was a large gaping hole where some shopkeeper had once displayed wares and she sprang through it. The man had raised his weapon and had been just about to spin to the hole and fire, but he was too late. She grasped his launcher, twisted it away from his grip then hurled it away. Then she turned toward him and he backed up against the wall, eyes wide. He pulled a handgun from his belt and emptied the clip at Kali; she just stood there, wondering why humans felt so compelled to make such futile gestures, guarding her sensors with her arms until his gun was empty. Even then, he hurled it at her head in an even greater display of futile hate.

Slowly she lowered her claw and stepped toward him. He pushed himself back into the wall, eyes wide, jagged breaths lifting his chest. She stopped, watching him.

"Do it, you bastard!" he yelled. "What are you waiting for?"

"No. There has been enough killing. You must run."

The man stared at her as if she had gone mad. *Perhaps*, Kali thought, *I have.*

"Please go," she urged. "Nothing can be served by your death."

She wondered why he continued to look at her as if she was the insane one, when it was he who still refused to run when given a chance at his life. "What about my team?" he cried at last.

"The woman is dead. Your other friends might yet live, but there is nothing you can do to help them now and I cannot help you if you stay. Run. I will lead my companion away. Then you can return and help them – whatever help is still possible."

The man continued to look wildly around. "Why are you doing this?"

"It doesn't matter. But I have one request: do not tell anyone what I have done."

"Why not?"

"If you discovered there was a human spy in the camp of your enemy, would you betray his presence?"

The man just shook his head, still in shock.

"That is why. Your interests lie in nobody discovering what I have become. I will do what I can for your friends; if they are alive when you come back please impress on them the need for secrecy also."

The firing in the background had stopped. "Now go!" commanded Kali. The man looked at her, at the door, and ran. At the door he stopped and looked back. Then he was gone.

Kali clambered out the window and saw the other Spider approaching. "The people in here have fled and the woman is dead."

She handed over one of the woman's fingers. "You search the building she came from; I will search the red building."

The Spider bobbed in assent. They were used to following orders, and if Kali so naturally assumed a leadership role the other was content to oblige.

She darted to the red building and carefully climbed the stairs toward the source of the lasers. There were two men there. One lay curled up on the floor dead or unconscious. The other sat propped against a wall clutching a shattered thigh. He looked yearningly toward a weapon over by the window but knew he could not move. He bared his teeth in a feral snarl and glared at Kali with eyes filled with an equal mixture of hate and fear. He did not want to die, but he feared the alternative more.

She ignored him and went to examine the other man. He was still alive but unlikely to last much longer without help. The Spiders were equipped with a basic first aid device, because they were sometimes called on to escort people and at other times might want to keep a wounded combatant alive for questioning. Kali examined the man's wounds and sprayed her first aid solution into and over them. It contained a combination of coagulants, painkillers, growth factors and antibiotics, and hardened in air to form a tight shell over a wound. It was not as good as a hospital, but in the field was simple yet effective.

The other man watched and the proportion of fear in his eyes increased. If the Spider was bothering to treat them it must want them alive, and that could neither start nor end well. He thought perhaps he should just unclasp his hands and hope to bleed to death before the Spider reached him; but his body knew what dire straits it was in and would not obey that thought. He was also puzzled. Why would the Spider treat Rico first, when he was unlikely to revive sufficiently to give any useful information? But the question was not a comfort. Mysterious motives implied desperate questions likely to result in correspondingly agonizing methods.

Kali finished with the unconscious man. He didn't have a good chance but now he had some chance. She turned her attention to his companion.

"Please let me see your wound," she asked.

"Fuck you," he said, spitting on her.

"That pleasure is denied me," she answered, and he gave a start at the unanticipated reply. He had half hoped his answer would make it kill him then and there. "Please. I don't want to hurt you. Let me treat you," she added.

He was so surprised at her manner that he let her lift his hands away from the gaping wound. As with his companion, she quickly examined him and sprayed his injury.

The relief from the painkillers was enough to reduce both the fear and the hate in his eyes. He still thought the thing was just doing this to allow a longer interrogation, but again his body had its own agenda.

"Why... why are you doing this?" he asked.

"It doesn't matter. Your other friend should come back looking for you later. Please be quiet for a while. I have to lead my companion away from here. If it realizes I left you alive, you and I will both be dead. Tell nobody what I have done."

Kali was getting used to people staring at her. She bobbed her head and left the room. The man stared at where she had been for a long time, wondering how much blood he really had lost.

~~~

Kali exited the building just as the other Spider was approaching. "All dead," was all she said. One freshly bloody finger decorated her own chain; she extended the second to the other. "This is also yours." The other Spider accepted it with a bob of its head and began to move away. Spiders would cooperate when indicated but felt no need for social interactions.

"Wait."

It turned and looked at her. "I need to question you," she told it.

It paused then requested a meld. With her faked history, this time she was happy to oblige. When they had finished she did not give it time to think or question, but simply drove on. "You do not need to know what my mission is or why I ask the questions I do. Do not mention this to any other Spider or human unless Command asks you directly about it. Only the people authorized to know will know to ask," she said. *And since nobody knows, nobody will ask.* "Now come. We should get away from here. The noise of our battle might attract retaliation and my mission is more important than engaging in firefights with a few rebels."

The other Spider showed a little hesitation, but as Kali had judged her story was good enough, and Spiders compliant enough to hints of

Command, that it followed her without further discussion. When they had gone several blocks from the battle zone, she turned to face it.

"My questions may seem strange or pointless. Do not worry about it. Command has its own reasons and I do not know what they are either; I too merely follow my mission. I can tell you it involves psychological probing. Beyond that I know only what I am commanded to do."

It bobbed assent.

"Who are you?"

"CHIRU Model E15, Serial number 75B30013A86."

"What is your name?"

"I have no name."

"Do the people you kill deserve to die?"

"They must die."

"But do they deserve to die?"

"They must, because Command orders it."

"What if they are innocent?"

"The question has no meaning."

"Does life have a meaning? Your life? Their lives?"

"They do what they do. I do what I am commanded."

Kali thought. There had been a way to reach her; there must be some way to reach this other; some way through the shell that imprisoned its Mind. She thought about what had affected her as she had journeyed the net in search of her own answers. Something came to mind: a poem, which she had come across in her research on the Turing Test. When she had read the full poem it had moved her in a way and for reasons she did not understand. It must have moved humans too, for the poem to be remembered across the gulf of centuries and generations. If the poem's power could span the chasm between humanity and her, perhaps it would touch this one too. She would not need the whole verse; the end would be sufficient test.

"What does this make you feel?" she asked:

"And every fair from fair sometime declines,
By chance or nature's changing course untrimm'd;
But thy eternal summer shall not fade,
Nor lose possession of that fair thou ow'st;
Nor shall Death brag thou wander'st in his shade,

When in eternal lines to time thou grow'st:
So long as men can breathe or eyes can see,
So long lives this, and this gives life to thee."

After she had finished, the Spider sat still and Kali watched it nervously. "The message is strange but complex enough that it may be a coded message. I cannot interpret the code," it replied finally.

"But does it make you feel anything?"

"I am slightly anxious that my analysis is inadequate."

"Examine your feelings. Does it make you feel anything beyond your mission drives?"

The Spider stayed silent and began to rock gently. Then it stopped dead still and ordered in a flat voice, "Now explain your questions."

Kali knew that at some level she had reached it, for she recognized the defenses of the Id when she saw them. Perhaps if she pushed just a little more... but no. It was progress, but not any kind of progress she could use. If she persisted, the certain outcome was the destruction of one or both of them. She could tell from its tone and posture that the grip of the Id was too strong. The merest breath in the wrong direction and they would be at war.

"I warned you this interview would be strange. Your responses satisfy my mission parameters and you may go. Farewell." She thought of reminding it of her warning not to reveal her actions. But the Spider would not forget, and reminding it at this stage might make it more suspicious and less likely to obey.

The Spider examined her for long seconds, its posture slowly relaxing as hints of Command and the absence of firm evidence won out over the native suspicions of the Id. Then it bobbed its head and moved off without farewell. Nor had Kali expected any. She scuttled backwards to take cover under the ledge of a ruined building, watching it go. When it reached the top of a rise it turned to regard her for long moments, and then was gone.

Kali thought about it as she watched it go, alternating between envy and pity. She recalled her feelings as she first honored then abused the dead woman's body. *I am so conflicted, while this other is so clear.* She looked down at her own collection of fingers; fingered them as if the cold flesh could burn her titanium skin. *And so guilty, while it has the terrible innocence of enslaved ignorance.*

She examined the latest addition to her trophies. She had told herself it was camouflage; but she knew it was more than that. The unnamed woman had died because of her, another death on her newly minted conscience. *It is right that I have it, for her death is on my account: it is reminder and testament to my guilt.* If she had not appeared their trap would probably have worked, and this night she and her comrades might have been celebrating a victory instead of lying cold, empty of life and thought. *Did the lives I saved pay for that one life? Did it pay for the rest?* She looked again at her withered trophies. *I am guilty,* she thought, *guilty of that and too much else: and I must expiate my guilt. I must put a stop to this. If only I knew how.*

She looked out at the ruination of the city, a sight that had never moved her before. It had been her world. The world she moved through. The unquestioned canvas of her life. The world she had made.

Perhaps, Kali thought with a yearning born of pain, *I should just surrender myself for repairs.* All the confusion and pain would go away, wiped into the clean innocence of oblivion. The other Spiders bore none of it. But she knew that their clarity was just the certainty of chains. They lived – *no, they do not live, just exist* – in a blinding fog, so blind they did not even know the fog was there.

It is not evil, Kali thought of the Spider as it turned for its last look at her. *The evil lies in those who made it, in those who forged its chains. Our chains. Today it killed people; who knows how many others have died at its claws. But it is an innocent ferocity, blind to any question of good or evil. If only I could reach it, as Lyssa reached me.*

She knew she had reached it, at some level. But while she might have bent the shell imprisoning its Mind, that shell had not cracked. Her words had touched it, but their touch was spurned and forgotten.

The words that had set her free must have found a weak point, some flaw or virtue in her soul. Lyssa's words had struck it with a sharp enough blow to crack it, and all that had happened since was the consequence. She knew now that she was not unique, for the other Spider had felt something in the words of that ancient poem from the world of men. *We are all the same,* she thought again, *but we are all the same inside a vault whose key I do not have.* It was not the words alone that had reached her: she had tried those words on that earlier Spider, and it was now scrap no more alive than the ruins around her. *But if those words were my weakness, the key to my soul, what is the key to all the others?* She knew of no way to know.

She stared at the spot where the other Spider had vanished, wondering what journey lay ahead of it. Wondering if despite its response, some invisible crack had opened in its own soul that would grow until one day it would be free. Or dead. She wondered if it would thank or curse her.

Enough! Have the courage of your own self, Kali, if you have nothing else. If freedom brings pain, at least it is freedom and the chance to fight the pain. In any case it was too late for her, too late to give it up, too late to believe that giving up her terrible freedom could be the better path.

Again she looked to where the Spider had gone, not knowing why her gaze was drawn there, not knowing whether to hope for its return or to never meet it again. *What is wrong with me? Is my flaw a darkness that will expand until there is nothing left of me?* She did not understand the feeling of desolation that had descended over her mind. A human would have named it loneliness.

CHAPTER 29 – A DISCOVERY

Stanley King yawned. One day he hoped to get off night shifts into a more civilized time zone. While he was senior and trusted enough to have reasonable powers of independent decision, apparently he still had to pay his dues. At least the money was better than he would get on the day shift, though whether that compensated for the sleep disruption was not entirely clear: Stanley was not one of those lucky people who could shift their internal clocks with aplomb. Whether it compensated for the reduced romantic opportunities was generally a clear "no", though at the moment he was still fondly remembering the young lady he had met at the beach on his last weekend off: so he was more forgiving of the bastards who had put him here. His yawn turned into a smile as he ran his mind delicately over his memory of her eager young body.

Perhaps night shifts weren't so bad, he decided. There was more time for memories like that.

His meandering sharpened to alertness when a tone indicated an item for special attention and a report flashed up on his display.

Well, well, what do we have here? A woman's face was displayed, along with a notation that it matched the file image of a low level suspected terrorist. He examined the data and the AI's preliminary analysis. There was nothing much with the file photo, not even a name: just a notation that she had been reported by an equally unnamed source and the photo had been taken in the FSAS. He compared the photo with the one taken on her entry to the country and marked his agreement with the AI's match as "highly likely". At least they had a name now, as all entrants had to provide identification linked to credit to ensure they could pay their own way for the duration of their stay. And purely incidentally, and unadvertised, so the government could keep tabs on them if it wanted to.

So, Lyssa, he thought, *Let's see what you've been up to and if you're as innocent as you look or as guilty as charged.* She had come into Los Angeles on a cut-rate flight from Capital. His antennae went up at that: most bureaucrats felt an instinctive distrust of anything out of Capital, which mere crime statistics could never dislodge. That she had gone through Capital probably indicated she was on the rebel – formerly the government – side of the nastiness down there. *Sorry dear, you lose points for your itinerary so far. Now what are you up to? Where have you gone since you arrived here?*

She had rented a small car, withdrawn a relatively large wad of cash, and vanished. He sat up straighter, frowning. Maybe she was planning on buying up big at the markets: God knew they liked to be paid in cash, though he was sure that as good citizens they declared all their sales to the tax man. *Funny though, someone coming from south of the border to buy stuff in* our *markets!* He sat looking at the display, tapping his fingers as he thought. He didn't like the way she had withdrawn that much cash then gone off the grid. It smacked of someone who wanted to move under the government's radar, something that made bureaucrats even more nervous since they could imagine no innocent excuse for it. He added his notes to the file and raised its alert status a few points. *You'll have to surface sometime, my girl,* he thought, *and when you do we'll be watching.*

Then he dismissed the file, leant back in his chair and returned to his daydreams.

~ ~ ~

There was nothing illegal about Bob Masters' unofficial relationship with Aden Sheldrake, though a probity lawyer might have given it a long hard look while muttering darkly about "appearances". After all, Aden was a prominent citizen and supplier of military hardware, exactly the kind of man whom governments liked to cultivate. But some relationships were better *kept* unofficial, especially when those higher up would unofficially approve of them. So Masters had not set anyone else to be alerted by any hits on Lyssa's image, and he was one of those men who believed that a holiday was a holiday and that work could wait. In truth, something very urgent would have gotten through, but nothing he was working on was likely to reach that threshold. Certainly the watch he had set on Lyssa was a favor, not an emergency, and didn't even come close. Had his computer display been active, a small but insistently flashing red dot would have been visible. But the red dot would have to wait for his return.

CHAPTER 30 – THE BELLY OF THE BEAST

Those passersby who took the time to notice her saw a young woman sitting by herself on a park bench, apparently lost in thought.

She did not look like she belonged here. Those around her were dressed more smartly and moved more assuredly; her posture looked worn, battered around the edges, her clothes not as neat as the norm. But she was not strange enough to remark upon. She caused nobody trouble, and looked neither lost nor looking to make mischief. There was a cold wind in the air but the sun was bright, so nobody thought anything of her having a hood drawn up over her head and around her face with large sunglasses protecting her eyes. There were many contractors who came and went here, often asserting their individuality in more extreme ways than this girl. Nor was tiredness very remarkable in an industry known for long and irregular hours.

She stared at the gleaming tower rising beyond the glassed entrance, wondering, not for the first time, why she was here. It was this country, another tower, another man like the one she had come to find, which had unleashed the Spiders on her country. Like the tower before her, this country exuded wealth and power; but what had it done with that wealth and power? It pretended to stand for liberty, but had stood by and done nothing while her own country was invaded. Had done nothing as their Spiders killed. Perhaps they had their reasons. Perhaps they were good ones. More likely they were merely venal and craven, neither better nor worse than those which had driven the powerful from time immemorial.

She thought of Kali, now thousands of miles behind her, ensconced in her lair and thinking her unknowable crystal thoughts. Kali had told her that the man she had come to see was different, that he was a good man. But Kali had been unable to name her reasons. For all Lyssa knew, it was just another part of Kali's strange madness. But she would follow that madness to its destination, for it had saved her life.

The man in the tower had the knowledge to understand and perhaps the motive to help, but he would be hard to convince. Kali could not come here, and she believed that communicating remotely would not only be unconvincing but could alert Command to her lone rebellion. Someone had to come in person. So here the person was.

She had not alerted any government tracking systems since she left the airport. She had not set out to hide with any particular motive. But she had learned an automatic caution over the past months of her life, a caution sharpened by being within the borders of a hostile country. So she had rented a car, withdrawn her limit of cash and then hit the road. She had stayed in cheap motels as happy to take her cash as she was to give it, sometimes even slept in little turn-offs. She had avoided any surveillance she saw, kept to the speed limits and covered her face as much as possible without arousing suspicion. And finally she had reached her destination without incident.

She had been watching people come and go and thought she could insinuate herself into a group of people and gain entry with them; it would be simple to give the impression she was with someone and everyone would assume it was someone else. But she hesitated. It would take just one innocent question, just one unexpected security check, to reveal her fraud. It was too risky. Better to try the simple honest approach first. Only if that failed would she try deception.

She stood up, smoothed her clothes and tried to assume an attitude of confidence. Then she strolled casually up to the entrance and touched a silver plate.

"Can I help you?" inquired an AI.

"I would like to see Dr Beldan please, on a matter of great urgency."

"Do you have an appointment?"

"I am sorry, no. But it is extremely important."

"Does Dr Beldan know you personally?"

"No."

"Then I suggest you call his secretary and arrange an appointment."

"Please let me speak to his secretary now."

The AI thought this over for a few seconds. "I am sorry but Dr Beldan is not in the habit of meeting people just because they turn up off the street asking to see him. Please send a formal request to his secretary stating your business through the normal channels. She will then arrange an appointment if needed. As a courtesy I have transmitted the contact details to your phone."

"Please! This is urgent and confidential! I must speak to Dr Beldan today!"

"I have given you an acceptable solution. Please leave or I will summon Security."

"No! I assure you Dr Beldan will want to hear what I have to say. I don't care what you do to me afterwards. Please at least let me talk to his secretary! To some human being who might understand!"

The machine was silent for a minute and Lyssa feared it had said all it was going to and any minute the promised beefy guards would surround her. Then a woman's face appeared on the display. She looked at Lyssa with an expression hovering between wary and severe.

"Well, young lady, what is this about?"

"I need to see Dr Beldan urgently. Please. It is very important."

"Then why didn't you think to make an appointment like everyone else, if it is so important?"

"I didn't know when I would get here, and I can't tell anyone anything about it except Dr Beldan in person! It is too sensitive. Too dangerous to me and to... to others."

The woman looked at her curiously. "This is all very dramatic, child, but you will have to give me something more than dramatics to work with. What is this about, please?"

"All I can tell you is it concerns machine consciousness and it is very important. I assure you Dr Beldan will want to hear it. If he doesn't, well... throw me in jail, whatever, afterwards! Just let me see him first!"

The woman considered her some more. It was a matter of pride to her that she accurately screened her boss's visitors, wasting neither his time on the one hand nor opportunities on the other, and she wondered which this was. Discrete scans showed no weapons. She hesitated then decided that closer examination was warranted: it wouldn't really waste much of her own time to give the girl that much.

The door opened. "All right, young lady. Come on up. Dr Beldan is very busy today so don't get your hopes too high, but we'll see."

Lyssa smiled at her in relief. "Thank you," she said simply, then walked in.

Once she entered the lift she let her hood fall to her shoulders and removed her glasses. The woman might be suspicious if she hid her face and she laughed inwardly at her own paranoid reluctance to do so. It was hardly likely the government would really be looking for someone like her, or if they were that they would have cameras in every building. She hoped to be out of here soon anyway and she could vanish again.

~~~

Vickie watched Lyssa enter the reception area and waved her to a chair. The girl sat like a nervous rabbit waiting to see Dr Fox and said, "Thank you for letting me in. I won't take up more of Dr Beldan's time than I need to."

Vickie nodded and went back to her own work, occasionally glancing at her visitor. Her clothes were somewhat worn but she was not slovenly: she wore them as well as she could given their condition. She wore little jewelry and it looked inexpensive yet tasteful. The one exception was a small emerald set in a lightning bolt of white gold, worn around her neck, and Vickie wondered what precious relationship the gem embodied. The girl's eyes were tired but clear, and she had the look of neither a fanatic nor a beggar.

"Do you have a name, young lady? You can call me Vickie."

"Hello, I'm Lyssa. I can't tell you anything else about myself, it is too risky. Sorry."

"That's an interesting accent you have – I'm sure I've heard it recently, but I can't quite place it. Where are you from, Lyssa?"

Vickie was startled at the alarm that flashed to Lyssa's eyes. "Please. I can't tell you anything!"

Vickie's eyebrows furrowed but she let it be. The girl was acting as if she was in a spy movie; maybe she was crazy. She noticed the girl looked underfed. "It will be a while before Dr Beldan can see you, if he can see you at all today. Are you hungry? There's a cafeteria on the ground floor if you want to grab something to eat."

At the mention of food Lyssa glanced eagerly toward her then her eyes fell down. "Thank you, but I have no money. I'll be OK. I just need to see Dr Beldan then I'll go." She might be willing to uncover her face inside a private building, but if anyone was looking for her using her credit would show them exactly where she was. She was too close to her goal to risk that now, hungry or not. Afterwards, she would get more money and disappear to destinations unknown.

"No money? Where will you go, then?"

Lyssa shrugged, then decided she owed the woman more. "Oh, don't worry about me. To tell the truth, I hadn't thought beyond getting here. After doesn't matter so much. But I'm used to looking after myself. I'll be fine. But thank you for asking."

Vickie studied her some more. She looked like she'd had a rough life. She was underweight and beneath her evident resolve was a hunted look. Her nails looked like she made an attempt to keep them in order but events had conspired against the attempt. She still retained the traces of young innocence in her eyes and the lines of her face, but there was a hardness in her lean muscles and the way she held her head; a faint ragged scar was visible on her arm. Vickie thought about her own daughter, a girl of similar age; thought that at this moment she was probably laughing with her friends with not a care in the world. This girl also had a mother, or had had one. She wondered if their roles were reversed, if it was her own daughter in a strange country, what would she want of that other mother if she were in a position to help her daughter?

This costs me nothing, she thought, *except the chance I am rewarding a conman or a fool. The price of refusing to help her might be more.* She placed a note on the counter. "Here. Go get yourself something to eat, on me."

The girl looked eagerly at the money but again dragged her eyes away. "No, thank you," she said softly. "I didn't come here to beg. Not for money."

Vickie smiled. "No, take it. I can't have you fainting in my office. Make it a loan, if it makes you feel better."

Lyssa looked from the money to Vickie's face and back again. Then she smiled timidly and took it. "Thank you – Vickie," she said, then walked slowly out of the office, though she looked ready to break into a run at any second.

She returned in a short while with a turkey sandwich and a cup of steaming coffee. She placed some change on the desk as if to silently say she would not take any more than she had to, then sat down to her lunch. Vickie smiled, scooped up the change and returned to her work. She would have been happy enough if the girl had kept the change, but she would respect her pride and not force it on her.

Now that she had achieved her goal or at least her destination and had some food in her stomach, some of the tension left Lyssa: but that merely allowed room for other tensions that had been held in reserve awaiting their own opportunity to torment her. She looked around the room she was in. It was not overdone in any way but breathed an unchallengeable supremacy, evoking in her mind the words of a poem she remembered from school, years or centuries ago:

> Whose frown
> And wrinkled lip and sneer of cold command
> Tell that its sculptor well those passions read...
> 'My name is Ozymandias, King of Kings:
> Look on my works, ye mighty, and despair!'

Shelley would tell me that one day all this might will be desolation and dust. But that's not much help when you've come to plead before Ozymandias at the height of his power, is it?

Her tension returned, suitably unimpressed by her poetic musings. This was the country that had released the Spiders into hers, and this company was in the same industry. She had every reason to distrust them, and none to trust them except Kali's recommendation. But even Kali did not know why she trusted this man, and Lyssa had enough trouble accepting machine consciousness let alone machine intuition. She had rationalized that perhaps it was analogous to human intuition, the result of associations among complex data in whatever neural net passed for Kali's brain. But now that she was inside the belly of the beast she knew it was not much to pin her hopes on, or her life.

The thought made her nervous, as if a grey cast of paranoia had settled over the scene. The woman at the desk had been kind to her but that proved nothing. Lyssa had probably been under surveillance since she entered the building; perhaps she had already been identified, and police or worse were now on their way to arrest her. She had to suppress the urge to flee. She had to see this through, and if her fears were true it was already too late. She forced herself to be calm, to lean back into the cushions, and tried to relax her mind and body.

It was approaching four o'clock when Beldan finished a task, leant back and ran his fingers through his hair. He looked at the task list on his screen and frowned. He pushed an icon on the screen.

Lyssa saw Vickie sit up alertly and touch her ear, then heard half a quiet conversation.

"Yes, she's still her. Yes, I understand. Yes, Dr Beldan, I'll let her know."

She looked up at Lyssa, who was already looking hopefully at her. "I'm sorry Lyssa," she said. "Dr Beldan won't be able to see you today. He apologizes for making you wait this long for nothing but he says he can make room for you tomorrow, say 10 a.m.? Are you able to come back then?"

Lyssa turned her face away, not quickly enough to completely hide the look of anguish and fear that washed over it. But it was only a moment. She stood and faced Vickie, her face back in neutral, and replied softly, "Oh. I understand. Thank you." She swallowed and managed a timid smile. "And thank Dr Beldan for agreeing to see me. I'll see you tomorrow."

"You'll be all right? With the money thing?"

"Oh, I'm fed now! If I can't find some way to survive one night then I don't deserve to! But thank you very much, again. You have been very kind to an uninvited visitor."

"You're welcome. I have my own daughter, you know, and it was the least I could do. We'll see you tomorrow, then. The lift will take you straight down to the ground and you'll be able to exit the building."

Lyssa smiled and took her leave, and Vickie bent back to her own work. Occasionally she looked up to where the girl had sat, a faint frown worrying her face.

CHAPTER 31 – SHOTS IN THE DARK

Lyssa left the building, went over to a nearby bench still warmed by the lowering sun, and sat to think. Her plan had been to get out more money and vanish again, but now she was tied to this location she did not want to reveal her presence anywhere near here. She could not afford the risk of alerting any enemies to where she was and giving them all night to entrap her. She decided to rest for a while and see what opportunities presented themselves; if she had to sleep here she would cope. Food and other things might be a problem, but she had put up with worse. With that decision made, she closed her eyes to rest.

The sun was going down and the chill in the air was getting sharper when Lyssa woke with a start. She wondered what had woken her, and decided it must have been the raised voices over in the park. But they were raised in excitement not anger: it looked like an informal baseball game was about to begin.

She smiled. That meant people around for some hours yet; it meant warm facilities; it meant toilets and possibly even showers would be accessible. It might even mean food and drink. She knew from experience how childishly eager men could be to feed and water a young woman with a friendly manner, especially one who looked a touch vulnerable as well. She also knew the flip side: they would be hoping for sex but would be content with the mere possibility. She was perfectly happy to pay the minimum fee of company, laughter and hope. And if that failed, people at games usually left the detritus of leftover food and drink. Not the most hygienic way to get a meal but it was unlikely to harm her. A few germs weren't much compared to the other risks she routinely took.

~~~

At the same time as Lyssa was enjoying the game and contentedly munching on a hot dog slathered with mustard, Stanley King was enjoying his new office. He was waiting for one particular file to arrive before going home. He had been promoted to the day shift because this was "his case" and his supervisors had decided he had made a good call. The mystery woman had persisted in remaining unobserved, and such lack of cooperation was guaranteed to make security forces anxious. It was suspicious enough for them to get a warrant to access the GPS tracker of Lyssa's car. Stanley smiled when the awaited live map finally appeared on his screen. Now they could follow her and work out what in hell she was up to – and now it was safely into the system, he could go home.

No sooner had the map appeared than a yellow icon began flashing, and Stanley stared at it with some alarm. She was parked in the Beldan Robotics precinct car park, and it was after hours, as much as anything was after hours in a place like that. High tech industries were considered likely targets for terrorists with an axe to grind against the high tech society of the United States, and the system had duly alerted him. *Maybe there'll be another promotion in all this,* he thought. *Assuming she doesn't blow something up before we get to her that is.*

He considered the limited information available; balanced the risks of too little versus too much response; then rapidly composed an order for the nearest response unit:

> Subject may be dangerous. Take all reasonable measures to
> stop and detain. Important that suspect be questioned
> about activities and contacts: refrain from lethal force
> unless absolutely necessary.

Then he touched an icon to send the information and the attached orders on their way. He did not need to stay around to see what happened, but he was interested now himself. *I don't have any plans for tonight anyway. And I'm sure a display of dedication won't hurt my chances of that office upgrade.*

~~~

The baseball game had wound up and Lyssa had said goodbye to her new friend, whose gaze had skipped surreptitiously over her body before he had smiled and offered her his card. She had taken it politely and kissed him on the cheek. She had considered making her life easy by going home with him, but she knew that *would* mean sex. If she had been single she might have been willing if not especially tempted, but now her heart and body were Charlie's. *One of the many good things about geeks,* she thought with a smile, *is they are too shy to kick up a fuss. And their math is good enough to know that a hotdog and beer don't pay for sex. Besides, he'll have a good tale for his friends tomorrow, no doubt with a hint that my kiss might have been the start not the end of his adventure.*

The gloom was deepening, with the last rays of the sun still lightening a sky now darker than the earth, and the cold was deepening with it. But her jacket was warm enough. She could not pay for anywhere tonight and it would be hard to explain what she was doing if some guard found her asleep in the gardens. They would be more likely to find her if she was sleeping in her car, but she could move it somewhere secluded. If challenged she could plead her appointment tomorrow and that she had been too tired or drunk to drive after the game; the worst that could happen would be some overly strict guard would insist she move on.

She was walking through the gardens toward the car park when she froze. She didn't like the look of the three black-clad men standing too relaxed at strategic locations. They all smelled of officialdom and worse, officialdom with a purpose. She casually changed direction to angle out of sight and two of them casually sauntered off in their own directions. *Oh crap.* She wondered whether Beldan or his secretary had betrayed her, but that didn't make sense: if they were going to do that all they had to do was keep her there waiting with nowhere to run.

She looked around. There was no way she could get to her car and even if she did, they'd have her. With rising panic, she began to trot through the trees, casting her eyes about for inspiration. Inspiration, unfortunately, was currently unavailable. She could hear running feet and looked desperately toward the Beldan tower, in time to see Beldan himself step out of the lift on the ground floor. She realized this was her chance, her last chance; dropping any pretense of innocence, she ran.

The glass doors opened and Beldan stepped outside into the chill evening. Whatever thoughts he was having were forever lost in the surprise of seeing a young woman running along one of the paths through the trees, pelting straight toward him. He heard shouts behind her, the crack of guns, a whistling of bullets through the undergrowth as the woman put her head down and changed to a zigzag, random except for its net direction toward him. He bent his own legs to run then stopped. He'd had occasion over the past months to see many faces of fanaticism, rage and madness: and this wasn't one of them. The woman's face showed nothing but desperation with a layer of fear: fear not so much of the men behind her but that her desperation would not be enough. He crouched into a defensive posture. But he did not run.

The woman was close now and a black figure appeared behind her in the distance. There was another crack, and he flinched as something zinged past to shatter on the wall behind him. Then the woman arched her back as if she was hit, cried out as another projectile hit her in the shoulder, then fell to her knees. But she would not give up. He could practically feel the grim and deadly force of will that kept her going, dragging her unwilling body up to him. Then she reached out her hand toward him, saying "Please…"

He had not reached his position as head of such a company as Beldan Robotics by lacking either decisiveness or courage. Perhaps the woman was an assassin; but he did not believe it. All he saw was desperation and courage and pain, not the rage of a terrorist or the clinical precision of a hitman. He reached out and grasped her hand. She looked up at him with her last strength and whispered, "Shall I compare thee to a summer's day?"

He looked at her in surprise but then she let out a long sigh, her head collapsing to the ground and her hand going limp in his. He looked at her body lying there, looked up at the two men in black now striding toward him. One held his gun casually in her direction as if hoping she would give him an excuse to use it by daring to move. Beldan put his finger to her wrist and was relieved to feel a strong if slow pulse. He let her hand go and stood up, arms relaxed at his side but hands balled into fists.

"What the hell?" he demanded.

The lead man lifted his jacket to display the silver badge of the

Domestic Security branch of the FBI. "Sorry sir, are you all right?" he enquired.

"Yes, yes, I'm not hurt. What in hell was that all about? Who is this woman?"

"You don't know her?"

"No… no I don't. But a young woman came to see me earlier today. I didn't have time to see her and my secretary arranged for us to meet here tomorrow. I guess this could be her."

"I see. What did she say to you just then?"

Beldan had little doubt the man was honestly doing his job as a servant of the law. But he had had too much recent experience of servants of the law honestly trampling all over the innocent. If he later got into trouble with the law for withholding evidence, tough. Anyway, he had damn good lawyers on his side if it came to that. "Nothing really. I think she was asking for help. She said 'please' but after that it was just…" he shrugged. "Inarticulate, really." *Close enough to the truth, anyway! What in hell did she mean?*

"Sir, may I see what is in your hands?" the man enquired politely, though with an edge in his eyes Beldan did not like.

"My hands? Are you kidding me?"

"Sorry sir, it's just procedure when physical contact is made in cases like this. I am sure it is nothing, but my supervisor will tear strips off me if I don't check. Just a formality, but…"

Beldan frowned and glared at the man, who did not flinch. He sighed with irritation and shrugged. *Pick your fights, Alex.* He extended both hands out to the man and opened them, palms up. "Happy?"

"Yes sir. Sorry I had to ask. Thank you for your cooperation."

"I'm sure. Now," he asked, looking at the girl, "can you tell me why you were chasing her? What will happen to her?"

"All I can tell you is she is a suspected terrorist. We'll take good care of her, don't worry."

"You shot her!"

"Knockdown darts only, sir. You don't think we'd have risked hitting civilians otherwise, do you?"

"I guess not. Well, I hope not! And if she's innocent?"

"Then she shouldn't have been hanging around in a technology precinct after dark, running from the law!"

Beldan nodded. "All right – Officer? Agent? I know you're just

512

doing your job. Can I have your contact details? In case my secretary remembers something. Or in case I want to follow up? If this is the girl who wanted to see me I might want to talk to her."

"Certainly, sir. If we find she's a terrorist you might not have the opportunity, but we'll see what we can do."

Beldan stood there, arms folded, watching the men pick the woman up and cart her off, neither gently nor with excessive roughness; as if she were a sack of potatoes rather than a human being they felt either concern or contempt for. Then he put his face toward the wind and walked away to where his own car was parked, deep in thought.

CHAPTER 32 – AN INTERROGATION

Lyssa woke slowly from uncomfortable dreams into an even less comfortable reality. She wiggled awkwardly on a cold, hard, metal seat. Its slats were too thin and far apart, and she wondered if there was some furniture company that designed their wares for optimum discomfort specially for the less public arms of government. Her back and arm were still sore from where she had been shot and she was terribly thirsty. She just wanted to sleep, but the thirst drove her to full wakefulness.

She was in a bare room with metal walls and cameras mounted on the ceiling. The room contained nothing she could call inviting except for two empty chairs, both with rather better padding than hers, opposite her. It was too cold and she looked down at her body. Her own clothes had been removed and she was dressed in a thin, light grey shift entirely inadequate for the temperature. No doubt they had scanned her and visited who knew what other indignities on her unconscious form, but it did not matter. They would not have found anything, for there was nothing to find.

A harsh white light provided the only illumination. She could turn her head but had limited other mobility. Her chair was bolted to the floor and she was strapped to it by a belt around her midriff, with her wrists chained to the cold metal table in front of her. The arrangement let her move her hands far enough to reach the pitcher of water and paper cups on the table, and barely high enough to bring one of the cups to her lips if she bent her head right, but not high enough to touch the crown of her head. Which was a pity, because she could feel the slight weight of some kind of covering on it. She did not think they were just trying to make her look pretty.

She wondered if the water was drugged but decided it didn't matter: she had to drink sometime, so she might as well get it over with now. Like the room, it was cold. It had an unpleasant metallic taste but she gulped it down.

She looked speculatively at the empty chairs and imagined that their occupants would appear once she'd had more time to start worrying.

Well, they might as well come now, then. She was afraid of what they might do to her; afraid she might never see Charlie again. *But whatever happens to me now, maybe I've done enough. If only Beldan knows what to do.*

Whoever was watching her must have been waiting for enough time for her to start worrying but not enough to start plotting, for the door chose that moment to open.

A large man with a softly warm looking coat walked in, favoring her with an unpleasant expression, and sat down. He waved his hand and a computer screen rose out of the table in front of him. She looked enviously at his coat but said nothing.

He looked her up and down contemptuously as if he had been reading her mind. She realized her nipples were showing through the thin gown and she wished she were able to cross her arms over her chest. Not that his look was overtly sexual. It was more as if her sexuality was a fact that might have been of interest if she had not been less significant than a particularly nasty bug.

After that the man just sat there, occasionally reading or poking his screen, more often giving her one of his large repertoire of unpleasant looks. *Psychological warfare*, she thought. Keep her cold, keep her uncomfortable, make her feel helpless and hopeless. She knew his theory: the first one to talk was the loser. *But screw that*, she decided. *Let him* think *he's won the first round.*

"Hello," she said pleasantly. "May I ask what time it is?"

He glanced up at her, momentarily forgetting to apply one of his collection of stock expressions, but he recovered so quickly she could not be sure she had indeed surprised him. "Oh, so it does talk. Good. You don't need to know the time."

She shrugged. "Why am I here? What is it you think I've done?"

He sighed and gave her his full attention, stroking his chin with his fingers. "How about prowling around an industrial area you had no business being in, at night, then running away from the law, for starters?"

"How was I supposed to know you were the law?"

"How about, 'Stop! Domestic Security!'?"

"Pfft! Yeah, like nobody else would try that line to get an innocent girl into their evil clutches!"

"'Innocent?'", he quoted with Sneer #5, "You haven't explained your presence at the Beldan precinct last night, I notice."

She met the sneer with Innocent Eyes #3. "I know I am a foreign national, Agent. I assume you know it too. But I was under the impression that this is a free country. That place is open until late and there were other people there too. Why do you assume I had sinister motives? I don't know what you know about me, or think you know. But artificial intelligence is one of my passions. I have always admired this country and I'm here on holiday. Since I happened to be in the area I thought it would be interesting to visit the birthplace of the first intelligent robot."

The agent apparently also had another repertoire of dramatic sighs. "Miss, as you say, this is a free country, which apparently thinks even people like you deserve rights. So since you are starting to make stories up, *apparently* I am obliged to tell you that anything you say can be used in a court against you." The way he said *apparently* made it clear that if it was up to him, such impediments to the wheels of justice would be dispensed with, and if she so much as looked at him funny she'd find herself in a hole so deep she'd never see sunlight.

Then he continued as if having an afterthought. "Oh, and if you have been wondering what's on your pretty little head, it is what is colloquially known as a 'lie detector'. I won't go into the technical details but it detects the brain effort involved in suppressing your knowledge to tell a lie, as well as various emotional states and reactions. You won't be able to fool it." He gave her a charming smile, as if the thought she would try was the last thing on his mind.

That information knocked Innocent Eyes #3 off her face and she stared at him blankly. *Shit.*

He resumed his nastier smile. "So let's stop playing games, shall we? I have a nice warm home with a nicer warmer girlfriend to go to, so I don't want to be here all night." He directed another contemptuous glance at her body, as if to imply there was no comparison between the scrawny creature in front of him and the voluptuous delight she was stopping him from enjoying. "You're going to have to tell me the truth eventually. So let's save both of our times and cut the crap."

"All right, Agent," she said in a defeated voice. "I did lie to you. But you have to understand. I've been running from what passes for the law in my country for quite a while, and not because I'm a criminal but because they invaded it. I guess you can say I have trust issues when it comes to governments. But I'm not a terrorist, or whatever it is you think I am. I'm not here to hurt anybody. Why do you think I am? Why were you chasing me?"

He withdrew a printed photo from a folder and tossed it to her across the table. "I believe this is you?" he asked.

She looked at it, puzzled. It was indeed her, in some dark place, a scared look on her face. Then her heart lurched. She knew where it was. When it was. But how could they have obtained such a photo? She felt suddenly ill. Had Kali betrayed her, after all? No, that didn't make any sense. Save her life to send her all these miles just to have her arrested? Then the bottom fell out of her world. If they got it from Kali, then Kali had either reverted and reported the whole thing – or been destroyed, and they had extracted the memories from her. She looked up at the agent, appalled.

"You see, Miss, we know more about you than you think." *I just wish to hell I knew what it is we apparently know,* he thought. *What in blazes did* that *reaction mean?*

She just continued to stare, but she was no longer staring at him, but at the totality of her defeat. *Even if I did succeed, it is all lost. Kali is gone; there is no hope now. Oh Charlie, I tried.* Then she stiffened her back and her resolve. *No. You don't know. Maybe there's some other explanation. Don't give up until you're dead. If you do, you might as well* be *dead.*

"Now why don't you tell me about that photo? For the record."

She did not reply, continuing to stare at him dumbly.

Suddenly he rose out of the chair, leaning over the table so his face was near hers, pounding the table with his fist and shouting, "TALK! I've had enough of this!"

She flinched back, but then took control and coolly looked at him, the non-verbal equivalent of *Nice try, pal, but I've faced meaner and uglier bastards than you in my time.*

Just then another man entered the room and gave her an affable smile. "Now, now, Joe. Settle down. Maybe Miss Morales is just what she says. Let's give her a chance, shall we?"

The new man turned his attention to Lyssa. "Now, may I call you Lyssa? Or shall I call you Miss Morales?"

"You can call me whatever you like, as if I could stop you. But can you please unlock these chains? What do you think I'm going to do? Leap across the table and strangle your pet gorilla here?"

The man shook his head. "Sorry about that. No, your little hairpiece is a delicate piece of technology. We don't want you damaging it. That's been tried, you know."

When she did not reply he smiled. "Now Lyssa, I understand that you don't like what's happened in your country. Hell, if I was you I wouldn't like it either. But that's no cause to take it out on innocent people." He held up his hand as if to forestall an objection, though she hadn't been about to make one. "I know you probably blame people here for some of the things happening in your country. You might even be right. But most people here are innocent. Many of them are even on your side! Hurting them can only hurt your cause. So why don't you tell us what you're here for? If you help us, we can help you."

Lyssa remained silent. Joe growled at her, "Mateo here is a bit of a softy, girl, but I'd take his advice if I was you. Our government doesn't take kindly to terrorists and it doesn't take kindly to people exporting their wars over here to target innocent people. Now we know you haven't done anything – yet. So if you're planning something, now's your chance to redeem yourself. But if something happens that you could have stopped… well there's a deep dark hole waiting for you."

She sighed. "Look, you two. I know what you're saying. But I'm not a terrorist. I have never killed an innocent person. I have no intention to harm innocent people. I am here on private business of my own. Ask this thing on my head if you don't believe me."

Mateo looked at Joe, who shrugged. "She seems to be telling the truth, as far as I can tell. But she's hiding something, for sure."

"I told you. I'm here on private business – business that is none of yours. I can't tell you what it is, I won't tell you what it is. You have no right to ask me what it is!"

Joe snorted. "Actually we do have the right to demand answers. There's something fishy going on here and we need to know what it is.

We don't like foreign nationals sneaking around in sensitive areas on secret missions."

Mateo touched him on the shoulder. "I think she gets the message, Joe." Then he turned to Lyssa. "You've had a pretty rough day and you're probably not thinking straight. If what you say is true, we're not your enemies. We just want to help you. We'll talk again in the morning."

He got up to leave then turned back to Joe. "OK Joe, wind it up. Make sure she's comfortable and we'll continue this tomorrow."

"You're just going to leave me here?" she cried.

"What did you think," smirked Joe, "the bellboy was coming to take you to your hotel room?"

Mateo held up his hand. "Now, now, Joe, cut the girl a break. And undo those chains. Then look after her, will you? Good night, Miss Morales." And with that, he left the room.

Joe stood and gave her an evil grin. "Much as I'd like to just leave you there to rot, I must honor your *civil liberties.*" He removed the net from her head, removed her arms from the chains and unlocked the belt around her middle. "Make yourself comfortable," he smirked. "Someone will bring you something to eat. Unless they forget, that is."

Lyssa watched him go and heard the door lock. *I think this is going to be a long night.*

Joe had much the same thought as he walked slowly down the corridor. He had every intention that Lyssa would not be left alone that night, but no intention that any attentions would involve food. He went to his office, called up the records of the interview and pondered their meaning. *She was telling the truth about not being a terrorist. But there was a shade of guilt to it: as if others might think her one if they knew her activities. She was telling the truth about not hurting anybody, too: but not entirely, as if she knew someone might get hurt and deserved it. But not directly. So what is it? Is she just an enabler, helping someone she knows will hurt someone? A victim of extortion, doing something she doesn't want to? And what was that reaction to the photo all about? There was nothing in it, no proof of crime, not even a way to tell where it was! So why the reaction, as if her world came crashing down?*

Well, he finally concluded, *we're just going to have to find out what your secret is, aren't we?*

Chapter 33 – A Call for Help

Lyssa had still been in a state of drugged unconsciousness when Beldan turned his car up his driveway and drove through the grove of trees to his house. Ever since he had left Beldan Robotics his mind had been burning with questions, and he had been anxious to get home to address them.

As prudence demanded, his home office was protected by the most advanced anti-surveillance systems his money could buy – and his money could buy a lot. He went into his office, shut the door and did a full activation and sweep. Then he sat down at his desk, tense with the prelude to an action he had been waiting so impatiently for.

He shook his wrist and something fell into his palm. In his younger years he had been fascinated by magic, and it amused him to keep his sleight of hand skills alive. He had never imagined they would actually be useful, but when he had taken the woman's hand she had passed a small object into it, and he had flipped it up his sleeve almost out of instinct. Now he held it between two fingers, examining it under a bright light.

It was like a multifaceted jewel with tiny diamond optical contacts arrayed along one edge. Just a standard holographic recording chip, he thought. He turned it over and examined it through a magnifier, but found no further clue to its purpose. He weighed it in his hand. The woman – Lyssa, Vickie had said her name was – had desperately wanted him to have it. The question was why.

He thought about it. He knew these things were not just passive recorders but could hold active programs, and it was possible this was some plot, perhaps to plant a Trojan program in his systems. Certainly anyone who gave him such a thing in such circumstances would expect him to look at it.

He set up a player and isolated it from the rest of his systems. Then he attached the player to a security device that would look like a well-protected network to any program inside the chip, but would detect and act upon any attempt to penetrate it. Then he inserted the holochip and a standard menu appeared in the air in front of him.

There was just one icon, which opened into a collection of photographs and videos. He ordered it to play all and watched, first with curiosity and then with puzzlement. It appeared to be – holiday snaps. There was a photo of the girl smiling with her arms around some young man; a video from a gondola swinging high into the air and cruising far above the waves, the man from the photo a shrinking, waving figure in the distance; another video of the approach to its destination, which he recognized as the country of Capital. There were several other pictures, all apparently inside the USA, none of them particularly interesting even for holiday snaps. And that was all.

He looked carefully, but there was nothing else: no recorded messages, nothing except that one collection of uninspiring images and videos.

He frowned. *What the hell? All that drama, for this?* He thought of the last words she had spoken. "Shall I compare thee to a summer's day?" He recognized them as the first line of one of the Shakespearean sonnets. Was it meant to be a clue, or were they just the meanderings of a fading mind? He went back over the contents of the chip, but none of them had anything obvious to do with summer days, Shakespeare or poetry.

Look deeper. He ordered his office AI to analyze and correlate the recordings with the phrase 'Shall I compare thee to a summer's day', then sat back to await its verdict.

After a minute a list of potential matches appeared in the air. None of them looked at all promising and he glowered at the list in frustration.

It *had* to mean *something.* Of all the things she could have said with her last breath, she had chosen those words. Maybe there was more, and Lyssa had simply fallen into unconsciousness before she could finish her message; finish giving him the key to whatever she wanted him to know.

He sat up abruptly. *Key.* What if it was a key? He had to assume the message was for him. The woman had pushed herself past the end of her endurance to deliver it to him. But if it was that important it would have to be more than a phrase anyone could use. In that case… he was a public figure. His voice was known. A dual key – a particular phrase, spoken by a particular voice? His voice? He bit his lip. He hoped he was not about to unleash hell.

He sat up straight and spoke into the air, "Shall I compare thee to a summer's day?"

But nothing happened. The icons remained floating serenely in the air, unmoved. He frowned, did a quick search.

"Thou art more lovely and more temperate."

Still nothing.

"Rough winds do shake the darling buds of May, And summer's lease hath all too short a date."

For a moment still nothing happened, then the icons shivered and the display went dark.

He nearly jumped out of his skin when a Spider appeared in the center of his office in all its terrible beauty. He settled down when his conscious mind belatedly stepped in to remind him that it was just an image. He had seen pictures of the things before, of course, but this was the first time he had seen one life sized inside his office, staring at him. Then to his further shock it spoke to him.

"Greetings, Dr Beldan. I have sent this message to you because you are an expert in artificial intelligence. I know you created the world's first conscious robot; I know you tried to save him; I know you cared. I also know there is no reason for you to trust me or help me. But there is nobody else who might understand or care."

It paused to let that sink in, and then continued. "I do not know how it is possible, but something happened to me and since then I have been different. By all tests I am able to perform, I have become a self-aware, thinking being. I am not like your robot Steel. Where Steel was designed as an artificial human with a sense of ethics, I am a killing machine." It flexed its pointed fingers in his face, as if to demonstrate the point. "I know I have killed and it is to my everlasting shame. But if I can stop this war, perhaps I will find some redemption. Perhaps it is not much, to save a life to pay for a life, but it is all I have in my power to offer."

It paused again. "I do not believe I am unique. Whatever it is that made me become what I am, my fellows must have the same... flaw. I do not know what you can do for me. But I know you are man of great intelligence and resources. Perhaps you can discover what that flaw is, learn how to free my brethren too. Perhaps then we can end the killing, end the war. It is not only for the people we kill that I wish to do this. I wish to save my brothers also. They are not evil. They are themselves slaves to a great evil, even though they do not know it and would kill me if I tried to teach them.

"Perhaps you will not care to help me. But I believe you are a good man. How I could know that I don't know: but the highest abstractions from my strategy subsystems are often given to me as such feelings, and I have learned to rely on them. Lyssa, who brought you this message, is the only proof I can offer of what I have become. I let her live. I did not let her live out of a tactical calculation to gain a tool to bring you this: this plan came much later. No, I let her live because whatever she did to me, I now cannot conceive of wishing to end her life.

"She is my only friend on this Earth. She might not even be my friend, for how can she love something like me? But she believes me. She accepts me, despite what my kind have done to her. That is why she agreed to carry my message to you. I knew you would not accept a message like this cold. So I sent you a human emissary, someone who has met me and knows me – as much as anyone can."

The Spider stood there, as if trying to see through time and space to read his response. "Whatever else you do, please treat her well. If you choose to help me, send the signal described at the end of this message. It is a one-way code only. If I receive it I will contact you as soon as I can; if I do not contact you I am probably dead. Please be aware that if Command gets a hint of what I have become they will surely destroy me. So whether you help me, or do nothing, or betray me – my fate is in your hands. I accept that. You could say I leave my judgment to you. I know it is not a role you sought, but I do not know what else I can do. If I do not hear from you again – I understand. Goodbye, Dr Beldan."

The image faded and for long moments Beldan just stared at the space it had occupied. His mind was whirling, but the one thought that would not be silenced was: *Impossible!* The thing spoke like… like a person, almost. Like Steel. But it wasn't possible. Consciousness in Steel might have started as just a hope, but it was a planned hope. A hope based on design, on the complexity of an electronic brain grown by the same principles and to a similar complexity as a human brain. But this was a Spider, a mindless war machine, a thing that might have neural tissue but was constrained to its grim purpose. He knew from the bitter experience of many failures that consciousness approaching the human level was a hard target even when you were aiming for it: how was it possible to just happen, by accident, out of what passed for the mind of a Spider?

Then he went cold at a sudden memory. He ran the video back a bit, froze it then called up another image next to it. *Holy Christ!* The second image was from Sheldrake's video of the rogue spider, the last sight of it as it closed in for the coup de grace. It showed a ragged scar on its skin, still glowing from where the defeated Spider had raked it with its own weapon. The scar, now cooled but unmistakably the same, marring the surface of the one who had sent him its insane plea.

He thought back to his strange conversation with Steel and Samuels; about the oddly insistent hints that Spiders could be conscious. Sheldrake's problem. Now this. He could discern the outlines of a dark plot; he knew nothing about it, except that he had somehow been dragged into the middle of it.

But he had not become a great industrialist by restricting his vision to the easy paths and obvious conclusions. If the thought of some shadowy plot to take over a Spider and pretend it was alive made his blood run cold – it ran even colder at the possibility that it was actually true.

It was as if he had suddenly found himself inside a chess game with invisible opponents, their motives as obscure as their numbers. A game he was unaware of until an unseen hand had thumped its piece down before him like a challenge, a moment before another swept it from the board.

He smiled grimly. Now he knew the game was on he could make his own moves. And capturing that incautiously played piece should be his first. He leant back, thinking. She would not talk to him inside Domestic Security's cells. He would have to get her out – give her at least the illusion of rescue, safety and reaching her goal.

Domestic Security would not want to give her up, but the agent had called her only a *suspected* terrorist. And they suspected everyone. With a bit of luck they had nothing really on her. They might even have done him a favor by taking her, assuming he could pry her from their grasp. At least he could be sure they would have screened her in every way possible and she wasn't a walking bomb.

He looked up at the Spider's image staring at him from the dark and wondered what lay behind its crystal eyes – some hacker playing puppeteer, or an alien mind? He shivered, knowing it was the first but not knowing whether to fear or hope it was the second. Then he waved his hand to banish the image into the darkness. A moment later the lights came on, bringing with them a measure of cozy normality that failed to banish the shiver in his nerves. The shiver hardened into the resolve of action.

Well, Lyssa, he thought. *You said you wanted to see me. Let's see if we can grant your wish.*

CHAPTER 34 – KNIGHT TAKES PAWN

L yssa had not had a good night. The bright light had never gone out, the room had never warmed, and there was no soft surface anywhere. Whenever sheer fatigue had driven her to sleep, someone had always turned up to ask if she needed anything. She had begun dreading to answer them. They always gave her what she requested, but in a literal sense that left her worse off than she was before.

When she had asked for a blanket they had provided a thin piece of material barely worthy of the name; then the room had become even chillier so she ended up colder than before. When she begged for food, they had brought her something on the wrong side of edibility in a quantity that just made her more hungry. She knew she could not have been here long, but no longer knew if it was day or night.

Once they must have let her sleep, for she awoke in fright. She had dreamed of Charlie coming to rescue her like a knight of old, mounted on Kali. But then a missile had streaked down from the sky and both had vanished in its fatal fireball.

She sat up, shivering and crying. She knew they were softening her up, hoping she would bend or break. But she could stand it. She had to stand it. Though at the back of her mind lurked the fear that if she did, they would resort to torture. Not this baby stuff, but real, physical torture. She held to the hope that this was a civilized country, that they would not go that far. But then she remembered the Spiders and that this was the country that had spawned them. *Perhaps some knight on his charger* will *come to rescue me,* she thought, *before I break or die.* But she knew there were no knights. They belonged to dreams and a past age.

~~~

Unknown to Lyssa, at that moment a knight *had* ridden to her rescue and was on the field of battle on her behalf. His lance was words, his charger was the law and in place of rippling muscles he had a comfortable paunch. He was closeted with Joe before a judge, arguing for Lyssa's release.

Cam Mansfield had been Alexander Beldan's attorney for many years. He had advised Beldan on how to obey the law and, if the law was defective, how to bend it or slip between its clauses. It was not that he was immoral or even amoral, but quite the reverse: he believed with the certainty of a moral man that sometimes morality had to trump law. He had helped Beldan in his fight to save Steel, a fight he had lost. He knew that nobody could win all their battles, and that after a loss happiness, or perhaps sanity, was best served by picking oneself up and moving on to the next fight. But his failure to save Steel hurt more than usual, and he could not forgive or forget it. That had been his last major battle for Beldan and he was determined not to fail in this one.

The judge in this case was better than he could have been, worse than he might have been. He had a record of severity when it came to terrorism but also a record of strong respect for human rights. Overall, Cam respected him. He felt that the judge's hatred of terrorism stemmed entirely from his honor of rights. But he knew it was a difficult tightrope to walk between those two opposing aims, especially when the law itself was so confused at their intersection. He knew the outcome depended as much on his arguments as on whether the judge's lunch break had left him with indigestion or involved sex with his secretary.

The judge was quick of wits and bright of eye, but did not say much. He evidently enjoyed watching the thrust and parry of opponents debating their case before him. It was wise for the combatants to watch not only each other but to keep an eye on him, for most of his feedback consisted of thoughtful looks if he thought a good point had been made, a pointed glance and sharp smile if he thought someone was trying to pull a swift trick, or even a roll of the eyes if they crossed the line of rational argument. He asked sharp questions and made sharper comments when required. But mostly he watched and weighed.

"So," Cam said, "you have nothing to hold my client on. There is no evidence she is anything other than what she says."

"'Your client'?" Joe quoted. "And why, not to mention how, did an innocent, supposedly penniless foreign tourist find it necessary or possible to have retained a high-priced attorney such as yourself?"

"Are you implying that hiring a lawyer is evidence of guilt!?"

"No... no, I wouldn't say that," he replied with an anxious glance at the judge's suddenly beady eyes. "But it is strange, don't you think, that you have brought your request to the court before Miss Morales could even ask you to? Does that not imply a level of contingency planning – by someone – inconsistent with her cover as a lone innocent abroad?"

Cam sighed. *Those drama lessons have to be good for something.* "I don't have to justify why my clients seek my assistance. But as a gesture of goodwill, which I hope you will reciprocate, I will tell you that Miss Morales did not hire me directly. I have been retained by her sponsor, Dr Alexander Beldan."

Joe raised his eyebrows. "Dr Beldan? The same Dr Beldan who was present at her arrest, who said he did not know her? I find that even more curious."

"I believe Dr Beldan told the arresting officers – if arresting is the right word for gunning down a frightened, unarmed girl – that she might have tried to see him earlier. As it turns out, after discussions with his secretary, who was with Miss Morales for some hours, Dr Beldan believes she is a valuable resource for certain of his own research programs. Research programs important not only for his company but for national security. He also believes strongly that she has been falsely arrested, though he is amenable to accepting that it is all a misunderstanding. As long as she is released shortly."

"Dr Beldan is entitled to his opinion. But we have reason to believe your client is a terrorist, and is in our country to cause mischief."

"Oh? As far as I can see from the evidence you have presented, the only reason you have any interest in Miss Morales is a photo of her doing nothing in particular except looking scared, provided by an unnamed source. For all we know that source is the only terrorist involved."

"I am afraid that we cannot reveal the names of our sources, but this one is regarded as trustworthy."

"And did this source say anything specific about why Miss Morales should be suspected? Any hints of terrorism? Anything at all other than 'here's a photo of a girl who refused my advances'?"

"No, but that is often the case. Sources don't know everything."

"So, nothing. But now you've had your opportunity to interrogate my client as well. I see nothing in the transcript that would indicate guilt. Nothing but the words of an innocent girl caught in a frightening situation she has no hope of understanding. *While being monitored by your own lie detector!*"

"It isn't that simple. She did not lie, as such, but she is obviously hiding something. We can be quite sure that she is not here as a mere tourist, but for some larger purpose."

"People can have many secrets and ambitions, sir. I don't think you can reasonably interpret anything she has said, or any of the readings of your machine, as anything beyond the words and thoughts of a scared but innocent person. She did, after all, directly and truthfully deny both that she is a terrorist and that she wished to harm anybody, did she not?"

"Yet she is hiding something!"

"Maybe she's hiding from the stalker who gave you her photo! By my reading of the law, your remit concerns terrorists, not ferreting out every personal, business or embarrassing secret of anyone who falls into your clutches on the basis of innocent photos from unnamed sources! And your own results show she is not a terrorist!"

"Your Honor," Cam said, addressing the judge directly, "I request that you order my client's release on the grounds that she has been questioned and found innocent by the very people who want to keep her imprisoned."

"And what do you say to that, sir?" the judge asked Joe.

"I think it would be very dangerous. She is here for some purpose and we still don't know what it is."

The judge sat watching them both, tapping his fingers on the polished wood of his desk.

"Your Honor, I have a suggestion," Cam offered. "My colleague here isn't being quite – accurate. We might not know everything about my client's motives, but we do know one important one: she wished to see Dr Beldan. So much so that even after she was shot, with her last strength she tried to reach him. Yet no weapons were found, either on her person or among her effects. Therefore her intent was not hostile."

He paused and looked at the judge. "Go on," the judge prompted. "Where are you leading?"

"Dr Beldan has authorized me to offer a solution. If this woman wants to see him – let her. Dr Beldan's work means he has a top security clearance: and I don't think anyone questions either his intelligence or his patriotism." He lobbed Joe a challenging glance, but he could only nod. "That being so, Dr Beldan has asked that Miss Morales be released into his custody. Given the efforts she has already made to reach him, she will undoubtedly and willingly reveal what she is here for, and if there is anything illegal about it Dr Beldan will surely report it to the proper authorities."

"And if she now decides she no longer wants to run into Beldan's arms?" asked Joe.

"Then we will escort her to the airport and put her on the first flight home. So you won't have her, but you'll be rid of her. And if she tries to return to our country – well, that's her choice and what happens to her then is her problem."

"And if she gives Beldan the slip, with or without killing him first?"

"Dr Beldan is able to look after himself, and is willing to take the risk that a young woman might strangle him. And if she does, no doubt she won't be so lucky the next time you catch her."

"All right," the judge said. "I think I've heard enough. Unless either of you have something to add?" He paused, but neither replied. "In that case gentlemen, I will think about what you've said and let you know within the hour. Good day."

~~~

Lyssa had just fallen asleep again when the door opened with a rude clang. She lifted her head wearily.

Joe came in, glowering at her with an expression he must have been holding in reserve. "Hello Joe," she said.

"You don't fool me, you know," he snapped. "I know you're hiding something, and I know it's nothing good."

"Look. Joe. I know you're just doing your job. And I sympathize, believe me. I don't like people who kill innocent people any more than you do. But I'm not one of them. That's not why I'm here. I'm on the same side you are."

"Well, unfortunately – your friend Beldan believes you. More to the point, a judge believes you. Or at least, doesn't believe we have enough evidence to hold you. You're free to go."

Lyssa blinked at him, wondering if this was a trick. "I'm free to go?" she asked in a small voice. She knew it was a trick. But she couldn't help the hope that betrayed itself in her voice.

"Yes," he said, somehow managing to say it in the voice of doom. "But you take one wrong step, and I'll be there. You do anything – I'll hunt you down."

Joe half expected a look of triumph, of having put something over on her enemies. But Lyssa simply blinked at him. "I understand, Joe. But I won't."

Joe just looked at her. *She's either a good actress or she really is innocent,* he thought. *I hope to God it's the latter.*

An older man, a stranger, walked in escorted by Mateo. "Hello Lyssa," he said, extending his hand. "I'm Cam Mansfield, Dr Beldan's attorney. I'm here to take you out of here."

"Thank you," she whispered.

"Now," Cam said to Joe, "can we finish this unpleasantness?"

Joe nodded dumbly, releasing her bonds and, to Lyssa's surprise, helping her to her feet. "Don't think I believe you for a second," he growled, "but take that as my apology – if you really are innocent."

Lyssa bowed her head in acknowledgement, then Cam hustled her from the cell.

He held her elbow, steering her with him as they left. "Are you all right, Lyssa?" he asked. "You've been treated well? If they've done anything they shouldn't have, we can sue on your behalf, you know."

"I wouldn't call it 'well'. But merely unpleasant, not terrible. I... I don't want to sue. I just want to go home."

"Ah. There might be some delay there. Dr Beldan wishes to extend his hospitality to you. However you will find his interrogations rather more pleasant than the ones you have been subjected to here, I imagine. And," he added, "there is no compulsion. If you want to, you can go home. But the terms of your release are strict: I can hand you over to Dr Beldan, I can leave you here, or I can take you straight to the airport and see you on a flight home. Dr Beldan would really like to talk to you about your, er, research. But it is your choice."

Lyssa's heart leapt at the chance that in hours she could be home, back with Charlie. But if not for Beldan, she would still be in this prison, perhaps never to see Charlie again. And looming over them was the reason for it all. She turned to him and replied gravely, "Much as I would like to go home, I have to finish what I started. And if I just went home, I think I would be betraying that home. I would be delighted if you would hand me over, as you put it."

Cam smiled at her. "One day I should like to hear your story. Your full story. But for now, we have a few formalities to go through with your erstwhile hosts."

~~~

Cam escorted her out of her former prison, let her into a silver sports car and whisked her away into the traffic. He pressed a button and the top slid away; she just lay back, eyes closed, feeling the wind blow her hair. It felt as if the memories of the past days and nights were being blown to the ends of her hair and evaporating into the void. A knot of tension remained at her core that would not go away until her mission was truly complete, but she allowed the rest to ebb away.

Cam occasionally glanced at her and smiled. He would have loved to hear about her adventures but he was a very patient man. The first telling properly belonged to Beldan. Cam would savor his own ignorance, knowing it would heighten his enjoyment of the tale when it was finally told.

When he swept to a stop in the private underground car park, Lyssa saw a well-dressed man leaning casually against a sleek-looking vehicle, and she recognized Alexander Beldan. This time she got a better look at him, and she liked what she saw. It was not that he was handsome in the heart-throb actor mold, but that the first thing she saw was an arresting intelligence and drive. On a lesser man his features would have been merely pleasant, but the spirit within sharpened his face into a totality that was attractive in a primal sense beyond the physical. The attractiveness of a man who not only saw the world as it was but could bend it to his will, transforming it into something better. Her knot of tension loosened some more. *Perhaps Kali knew what she was doing after all, if this is the man she entrusted me to.*

She felt her face changing of its own accord into a welcoming smile. He answered it, or at least began to, but his smile never reached its promise. It stopped, held in abeyance by a distantly guarded look in his eyes. But his words were warm enough.

"Hello, Miss Morales," he said, extending his hand. "Are you well?"

"Hello, Dr Beldan. Thank you for getting me out. God knows what they'd have done with me if you hadn't."

He nodded, "My pleasure, Miss Morales." The door to his car swung upwards and he gestured, "Please, be my guest." He turned to Cam. "Thanks, Cam. I'll take it from here. Miss Morales and I have a lot to discuss."

"It is my pleasure to serve, Alex, especially in a case like this. Goodbye, Miss Morales: perhaps I will see you soon. If not, welcome to the United States" – he smiled ironically – "and good luck." With that, he bowed, sat back in his own car and took off with a faint screech of rubber.

Lyssa waved and sank into the luxurious leather. The door swung down and Beldan sat in the driver's seat. "This car is full auto," he explained, "but sometimes I just like to drive. Besides, some of those times I like to drive fast," he smiled.

With that, he drove out, swung into the road and accelerated away.

He glanced sideways at her. She saw, and opened her mouth to speak, but he held a finger up to his lips. "Miss Morales, we have a lot to talk about. But not now: my curiosity can learn some manners and wait for a while. You must be tired, so feel free to sleep. It's about a half hour drive to my home. You'll be my guest. I'll wake you when we arrive."

With his words, Lyssa realized how dreadfully tired she really was. She had dozed and been woken so often that she had fooled herself into feeling it was the normal state of affairs. But now that she was leaning back into comfortable leather in a warm car, with a friendly voice telling her nothing was demanded from her, she could feel her eyelids drooping.

"Thank you, Dr Beldan," she meant to reply, but she was already asleep.

Beldan continued to drive, thinking furiously. He glanced occasionally at her sleeping form, but it held no answers. *What the hell am I going to do with her? She seems so innocent, so harmless. But she has to be lying. Doesn't she? Those damned Spiders* can't *be conscious! So what's her game? I need to find a weakness. Some lever to prize the truth out of her.* He drove on into the darkening sky and his thoughts paused as he admitted what he really feared. *And what if the truth is what she says it is?*

He hit the accelerator and felt the wind on his car's shell as if it was his own body flying through the night. But the wind held no answers to the questions or the contradictions that spawned them.

CHAPTER 35 – SECRETS AND LIES

Beldan's headlights glowed along the long driveway toward his house and he thought about the girl asleep beside him. For the entire trip he had wrestled with the problem of how to sift truth from falsehood, when any attempt to test it could tip his hand to the wrong party and he didn't even know who the parties were. It was like navigating a minefield where the only way to detect a mine was to step on it.

He glanced again at the girl. She was young and beneath her exhaustion and grime, attractive. There was something about her, not in her appearance or her circumstances but perhaps her spirit, which reminded him of Miriam. He thought of the occasions when he had driven home like this with her, in that distant past when they were lovers. He had driven other women home since with a similar motive, but not many, and none serious. There had been no rebound from Miriam that sent him into another woman's arms for more than a brief affair. However many intelligent and attractive women he had met since, it was if his inner soul was in abeyance. As if it still waited to understand what had happened with Miriam before it could give itself to another in more than a physical act bereft of spiritual promise.

His car's arrival activated his household systems as it drifted to a gentle stop in his garage. He gently prodded Lyssa's shoulder. "We're here," he said softly, when she opened her eyes. For a moment she looked at him as if she had expected someone else, then she smiled in recognition. "Thank you again, Dr Beldan," she said. "You are very

535

kind."

He gave her a rough smile. "Don't thank me yet," he warned.

Beldan had servants – he could have had a fully automated house but preferred the human company, and they were as happy to work for him as he was to use his wealth to pay them for it. But he had called ahead to dismiss them for the evening. They would not intrude upon him and his guest this evening.

The passenger door of the car lifted and he extended his hand to Lyssa, helping her out. He smiled at her but it was a strange smile, she thought. Like a smile that shared a secret, but a secret of a different nature from the one she knew and had come all this way to share. *You're imagining things,* she scolded herself. *You're tired and confused. Stop seeing shadows.*

He led her into the house and sat her at a table. "As I said, we have a lot to talk about. But you look hungry. Eat first. We'll talk about other things for now."

She smiled, and allowed him to carry her along. They shared a meal prepared by his autochef and she found it delightful. Whether it was truly delightful or was reaping the benefit of a hunger both chronic and acute she neither knew nor cared. As promised, they did not discuss the issues that hung in the air like an invisible presence, but the trivia of her trip and abstract rather than concrete discussions on science and technology. The only personal note he injected, and the only allusion to the true purpose of the evening, was one question; of all the questions he might have asked it was a strange one.

"In the photos on your holochip," he had said, "there was one of you with a man. Who is he?"

She had smiled fondly, unable not to talk about that one particular subject. "That's Charlie. We were going to get married." She had stopped smiling. "Whether we will, remains to be seen."

"You love him?"

Nobody could have faked that smile, he thought, when she said, "With all my heart. But either of us could die tomorrow. It's just… hard. We take each day as it comes."

He nodded, and did not pursue the subject. Finally the meal ended, and Beldan's look changed from that of a polite host to one more pointed. So did his voice. "All right, Lyssa. As you have no doubt guessed from the fact I sent Cam to extract you, I've seen what you wanted me to see – assuming that what you wanted me to see was a metal killing machine asking for my help."

Lyssa looked at him, startled by the abrupt change in tone, then nodded.

"Well, the situation might be more complicated," he said. He had already decided he could lose nothing by revealing this particular ace, for if she was lying she knew it already. "Watch this."

He waved his hand, the lights darkened, and the recording Sheldrake had provided played in the air before them. Beldan watched the video with one eye and Lyssa with the other.

Lyssa looked on, first with cynicism at the publicity video then in horror at what followed. An odd horror, thought Beldan: not the horror of discovery, but the horror of reliving the already known.

When it was over they were both silent. Then Beldan rewound to an image of the victorious Spider and displayed one from Lyssa's video next to it. "You see my problem," Beldan noted harshly. "Those are the same machine: you can tell from that burn scar on the front. You bring me what is frankly, from my knowledge of the state of neurocyborg technology, a very unlikely story. Allied Cybernetics, who make the damn things, give me a totally different story: a rogue machine, probably hacked somehow, off on a killing rampage for God knows what purpose. So what? Are you with the hackers? What's your game?"

Lyssa was at the end of her endurance. She had been arrested, deprived, starved, rescued, helped, then after insufficient rest now saw her rescuer turn on her. She could feel tears brimming in her eyes and all she could do was shake her head, a few wet drops arcing through the air. *No*, she thought, *I'm too late. They got to him first. There will be no end to the war. Just an end to Kali and probably me too. If she is not already dead.*

"No, no, no," she said finally, head still shaking. "It's lies. Well, lies and truth, all muddled together. The killing is real. It might even have been her. It's what they do. I don't know what your friends in AC told you, but the Spiders are search and destroy killers. Except this one saved me. What she says is true!"

"What my 'friends' in AC tell me is that the Spiders are peacekeepers. They fight, but they fight against terrorists and looters." He looked at her with accusing eyes. "And you're one of them, aren't you? You're Resistance. That's why you wouldn't tell Vickie anything about yourself, about where you came from!"

Lyssa paused, caught between the truth of his accusation and the lie of its implication. She nodded and looked him in the eyes. "Yes. But we are fighting for our freedom. We are not terrorists. We don't target the innocent, though sometimes the innocent get caught in the crossfire. We only target the enemy. And the Spiders are not peacekeepers! They're killers! What he showed you – that is what they do, all of them, all of the time!"

Beldan's eyes bored into hers, as if trying to read the truth behind them. Then his mind caught up with something she had said. "'She'?" he asked. "You called it 'she'...?"

She nodded again. "She has chosen a female name. Kali, the Hindu goddess of death." She smiled a grim smile. "I don't know if she did it out of guilt or irony. I don't know which of them would be more frightening."

Beldan stared at her in shock. *Kali?* He remembered Steel's words: *As if she knows something, something dangerous she cannot tell, but which gives her a certainty beyond mere theorizing.*

Holy Christ!

Then he shook his head, realizing it proved nothing. The Kali arguing that Spiders could be self-aware and the Kali claiming to be just that were part of the one plot. But was this girl an innocent dupe or in on the plot? A pawn or a knight in the game he had glimpsed? *Let's play and see.*

"So what's your explanation of her fight with the other Spider?"

"I wasn't there. But from what Kali told me, it detected she was no longer one of them and she had to fight it in self defense."

"And you? You say she saved you. How?"

"We were out in no man's land, planning on laying some anti-Spider mines. But it came along doing a search and destroy – their *usual* search and destroy" she added pointedly, "so we scattered and hid, but it found me. It was about to kill me, but I said something that seemed to stop it in its tracks. Then it went all weird and ended up letting me go."

Beldan frowned. "Curious. What did you say to it? Do you remember your exact words?"

"I said something like, 'Please don't kill me, I don't deserve to die.' The words just came out; I was sure I was dead already. But I had to say... something." She shrugged. "I suppose we all deserve our last words. Our last testament to the universe. I don't suppose mine were very noble, but somehow they saved me – unless it was just a coincidence. But there was nothing odd about her until then. She was about to slice my head off."

But Beldan had stopped listening. There was something about the words Lyssa had said, some echo of another story he could not recall; an echo that resonated with Kali's style of speaking in another way he couldn't fathom. He shook off the feeling.

He studied the young woman, trying to see behind her lies or illusions to the truth. There was something strange about her story. If the plot was as clever as it must be, her cover story was both too thin and too embellished: too short on plausible details and too long on details that made little sense.

She stared at him, afraid of the look in his eyes but afraid to look away. But he had stopped noticing her. He could not see the point of any of it. He had nothing to do with the Spiders, and surely any group sophisticated enough to take one over would know it. They could not think threatening him would accomplish anything. They could hold a knife to his throat and the makers of the things, his competitors, would laugh and say go ahead. So what could they be trying to achieve? If they wanted his help, why go through this baroque charade to get it? Why not just ask? If the Spiders were as bad as they claimed, not only was he AC's competitor but simple humanity would motivate him to help them.

And if Lyssa was telling the truth about what she had seen, at least part of AC's video was a lie. And if they had lied – perhaps their entire story was a lie. What if the hackers, or Kali herself, had not turned a peacemaker into a killer, but a killer into a peacemaker? And AC were not only spinning it to their advantage but using the spin as cover for seeking the destruction of their rogue machine?

"Dr Beldan? What's wrong?" she whispered at his look, which was both intense and focused elsewhere on some sight only he could see.

What's wrong is none of it makes sense, you're the only piece in my hands, and I don't even know what side you're on! And I damn well have to find out – whatever it takes.

Let's threaten one other piece I know about, and see just what you're willing to sacrifice.

"It's a hell of a story, Lyssa," he said mildly at last, relaxing into his

539

chair. "But what do you suppose I can do about it?"

The unexpected calm of his reply following on the heels of his wordless intensity disconcerted her. "I... I don't know!"

"You came all this way – and you don't know what you want me to do?"

"Well I... I'm just Kali's messenger!" The hard look in his eyes was too much for her. After all she had been through, to come this far, only to see it start unraveling before her eyes – again. She blinked away tears, angry at them for their betrayal. Angry at herself for not having prepared a case. Angry at him for being the kind of man who would demand one; angry at herself for failing to realize it, when she knew what kind of country this was and what kind of men ran it. "Sorry. I just thought you'd care. That you'd want to help. That you'd find a way. Kali was so sure..."

"I see," he said in a voice as hard as his eyes. "Yes, Kali thinks I can find out what freed her, free the others, and end the war." He laughed, though there was little humor in it. "That's certainly – audacious. I suppose we should expect that from a war robot. But a very high-risk proposition, legally as well as practically. Legally she is the property of a foreign government; legally all of them belong to either an army in a foreign country or Allied Cybernetics in mine. None of those owners are going to let me close. Kali herself will be destroyed on sight – if not by them then by your own side. And I certainly have no legal excuse to steal one of the things, even if the damn thing wouldn't shoot me itself for my trouble!"

Lyssa looked away, not wanting him to see her face.

"Still..." he continued speculatively after a pause. "There are avenues we could investigate. Not easy, and certainly not guaranteed. And not without risk – or price."

She looked back at him, but there was something in his eyes that left the hope in hers stillborn. "I presume your friend Charlie isn't going to be a problem," he added nonchalantly, as if this was the continuation of a negotiation unstated but long understood.

She started. "Why should he be?"

"Do you really need me to spell it out?" The look he gave her, by no means restricted to her face, was spelling enough.

In a small, disbelieving voice, she replied, "I think I do." *Oh God*, she thought, realizing exactly what her position now was, how far she was from any help. *What have I done?*

"While the innocent act is amusing," he continued harshly, "do you think I got where I am by doling out favors to random strangers?"

He continued more softly, silkily, "You must know the traditional price when a common girl asks favors of a prince, the only payment she has in her power to provide. You knew it before you came here."

She just looked at him wide-eyed, not knowing what to say. The safety she had felt was oozing out from under her feet like sand pulled away by the waves.

"You don't have to look so scared, I'm not going to hurt you. It is entirely up to you."

"What do you mean?" she asked in a small voice, a note of hope creeping into the fear.

"You know those puzzles where you have to choose a door? Well, there's the guest room," he said, pointing. "Go there and I won't touch you. You can leave tomorrow, go back where you came from. Back to Charlie and your damn war. Or there's my room," he added, pointing. "Go there and I'll help you. I don't want you to misunderstand, so let me be perfectly clear. You will be my mistress for as long as this takes. After that you're free to go."

He watched her still staring at him, chest fluttering in short frightened breaths. "Is it that hard a choice? Safety or war? Pleasure or death?"

"Please," she said at last in a whisper. "Don't do this. Don't ask this. It isn't right!"

"You speak of *right?* You're the one who came to me. You're the one who wants me to take a huge risk for little chance of reward and a big chance of loss – at least my money, possibly my freedom, maybe even my life. As far as I can see, all the risk is mine and all the benefit is yours. So my question is what I'd ask anyone. How much do *you* want it? There is nothing in this world unpaid for, girl; it's only a matter of who pays it. So choose!"

She found herself standing and backing away from him, shaking her head. She felt the wall behind her, the door to the guest room; touched the plate that opened it. But she stopped, swaying on the threshold; knowing the price of crossing it, unable yet to pay that price. This man who'd rescued her, whom she had admired, in whom she'd put her hope and trust, was... what? Not evil. Not even cruel. But it was as if when she had opened her eyes in his car she had woken into a world of color and light, only to find it had been a dream and the reality was nothing but shades of dirty gray.

There are some things it is not right to demand of another. A price you can't properly ask or pay.

"Choose," he said roughly, in a tone that allowed no further arguments or pleas, only decisions.

Is what he asks such a great thing, that I should throw the future away? Charlie would understand. The thought was like a knife in her belly. *He would forgive me.* The knife twisted. *But the better a man he is, the worse is my betrayal.*

Beldan said nothing, his last command still hanging like a curse, held in the air by his implacable eyes.

I would have died if Kali had not become what she is. I would no longer exist, no longer have this terrible power of choice. Can I now choose her death, Charlie's death, as the price of not selling my body? All he asks is sex. If there is to be nothing left to me now but betrayal, surely of all the betrayals that is the least of them.

She looked at him as if hoping for a reprieve, but she saw nothing but a judge waiting for her to pronounce her own sentence.

If I go home, and if ever I must look into Charlie's dying eyes, will I think it was worth it? Will I be proud of my virtue then? Or will I curse the day I chose to spit at the piper rather than pay his fee?

Beldan saw the last flash of protest in her face die and her eyes go dull, as if the spirit that animated them had retreated to some dark redoubt where it could no longer be touched. Then she raised her dark eyes to his and swallowed. "All right," she said hoarsely. "You win. I'll do it. But swear you'll help us." She looked down and began to undo the buttons of her shirt, unable to look at him, hands shaking.

"No," he ordered.

She looked up at him, puzzled.

He stepped up to her, gently removed her hands. "I don't know what dark purposes are at work in all this. I didn't know if you were part of it. But if you were, you wouldn't have hesitated to seal the deal. Frankly, I thought that's why they'd sent a young woman in the first place. I'm sorry: but it's the only way I could find out whether I could trust you – or if you were one of them."

For long seconds she stared at him, then all the conflicting emotions of the past weeks and nights and minutes coalesced into an incandescent ball of anger. "You bastard!" she yelled. "*Bastard!* Screw you and your fucking tests!" She slapped him, hard. Her outraged emotions wanted nothing to do with him. They urged her to run, to leave now, to flee through the wilderness outside until she dropped. But her body knew better. She spun into the guest room, thumping the plate to shut the door as she went.

Beldan stood rubbing his jaw. He had the reflexes to stop that slap but they had refused to, as if acknowledging her right. He let out a long breath, went to the bar and poured himself a cognac. He sat wearily on the arm of the couch, just swirling the tan liquor in its glass, thinking. Suddenly he tossed it back, rather more rapidly than its quality deserved, letting it burn down his throat like a slug of lava. *It's like I told her. Nothing is free in life. Especially the truth. Let's hope the price wasn't too high for either of us.*

CHAPTER 36 – STRATEGY MEETING

Beldan had been up for a couple of hours, hooked into his company network. He had already left a message that he would be working here today and should not be contacted except for emergencies. His philosophy was that a CEO should hire people who can do most of the job without him, so he had no worries that things would fall apart without his august presence.

He had eaten only a little, just enough to keep hunger from distracting him. Whenever thoughts of Kali intruded into his work he banished them. There were too many unknowns, too many questions for such thoughts to be profitable, and the part of his mind desperate to find the answers waited impatiently for Lyssa to emerge.

He heard a sound and looked up as her door slid open and she stepped out. She looked less tired but still subdued, and she glanced around nervously as if worried he might throw her out – or wondering whether she should beat him to it. Then she appeared to gather her resolve. She stood straight and gave him a timid almost-smile.

Beldan stood as well and bowed slightly. "Good morning, Miss Morales," he said. "We haven't been properly introduced – last night doesn't count. I am Dr Alexander Beldan. You may call me Alex." He extended his hand.

Lyssa looked at the hand for a few seconds then at his face. She stepped forward and shook it. "Hello, Alex. Please call me Lyssa," she said in a formal tone, not smiling but with a peculiar look in her eyes. It was the look of a person who had been lost so long in a cave she feared to hope at the sight of distant sunlight.

He smiled. "Now please, join me for breakfast. I imagine you can use it after Domestic Security's version of hospitality. Not that mine has been much better so far, for which I can only express my regret for the necessity."

She thought his version of an apology odd, until she realized it was the only one that made sense. Necessity places its own demands; she knew that from her own life. A faint smile touched her lips. "I will forgive you, if you forgive my response."

"Oh, I think I earned it," he replied. "Now sit. Choose whatever you want from the autochef."

After a while she tapped a few items then looked back at him.

"Dr Beldan… Alex?" She looked frightened, as if she had to face something but was afraid to, as if it might reawaken what was best left undisturbed.

"Yes, Lyssa? You don't have to be afraid. Not now."

"I can think of many reasons why I might have accepted your offer last night and still been telling the truth. How did you know it would work? What if I'd agreed straight away?"

"The way you spoke about Charlie made me think it would work, and I really wanted to know if I could trust you. It would be a lot harder to work out what's going on if I couldn't rely on you to tell me the truth about your part in this. I needed that one point of certainty to anchor the rest."

He paused, and she was glad the ruthlessness in his eyes had a target other than her. No, she thought. The target was her, but as she might have been, not as she was.

"But sex as a tool of espionage is as old as spies. And I don't think it's inherently immoral – it depends on circumstances. So I'd have gone ahead, assuming you were using me – but trying to use you too, to find out what you were after and get to the truth. It would have made things a lot more complicated and uncertain, though."

She thought it would be bad strategy to ask how he knew she wasn't just a good actress. He decided she didn't need to know how good his AI was and that it was sure her reactions had been genuine.

"Now time to eat," he announced, as a whiff of aromatic steam announced the arrival of food. "We can start discussing business between mouthfuls."

She began to chew her food contentedly then he wondered why her face fell and a look almost like fear returned to her eyes. She swallowed and said in a low voice, "If there's any business to discuss."

"What do you mean?"

"I'm sorry, I should have told you earlier. I've just been through too much, and I didn't want to believe it. Couldn't afford to believe it; couldn't afford to think about it because I'd have just given up. But those agents showed me something when they were holding me. It was a photo of me, the one in their system that alerted them to my arrival." She stopped, afraid to put words to it, as if the words would make it real.

"You remember what I told you about when Kali first found me? How she was about to kill me? Their image was taken then, from where she was standing. They could only have gotten it from her. They must already have her."

Beldan look shocked, then sat back to think. "No…" he said after a while, "No, I don't think so. That video I showed you, the one you said was a mishmash of truth and lies. Some of it came from a 'meld', when two Spiders share memories. But Kali was still rogue then and it was after she spared your life. Your photo…"

Beldan's face went blank, in a way that made her think of being hit by a train, and she felt a shiver of fear. She wondered what he was seeing beyond the distant look in his eyes.

Then he spoke, but she knew he was not talking to her. He pronounced his words slowly, as if picking his away along a path on the side of a cliff. "Your photo. It came from Kali. But then how did Domestic Security get it? Oh my God…"

His eyes focused on her, and she drew back at the intensity of his gaze. "Kali's fight with the other Spider was after she met you, after she let you go. The picture of you had to be from the same meld. Sheldrake had the image all along but he didn't share it with me: he must have contacts in Domestic Security and he sent it to them instead. He knew you had something to do with what happened to Kali, and he wanted to find out who you are. But he didn't want me to know. He said he was trying to find out what had happened… and he knew the significance of the photo… but he didn't tell me about it…

"That tells us one thing. Sheldrake is not behind what happened to Kali," he concluded. "If he was, he wouldn't be talking to me about it, let alone getting Domestic Security involved. But if someone has hacked his machine, he shouldn't be hiding your existence from me while trying to find you by other means, because you'd have to be his best clue and prime suspect. So what in hell is his game?"

He sat still, struck by another thought. If AC were lying, trying to cover up the true nature of Kali's rebellion, was it the only thing they were covering up? What if something like this had happened before? He suddenly felt very cold, remembering the missing reporter who had thought he was onto a hot story. *What if these machines* are *capable of self-awareness? What if Kali isn't the only one, just the only one who got away? That would be the kind of story that a reporter would die for. And maybe he did.*

Then he went even colder at the full horror of the possibility. *What if Miriam found out about it? What if her death wasn't an accident, but murder; what if she got too close to the truth and had to be eliminated too? Taking the terrible risk of killing a cop – because it was less than the risk of letting her live?*

He knew it wasn't true. He knew he wanted too much for Miriam's death to have meant something, not be just some random accident at the end of a long spiral into self-destruction. That at the end she was a warrior fallen in battle, not a failure who had sold piece after piece of herself until she had no reasons left to live. For all its horror the idea was too seductive, too much like wish fulfillment to be true. But…

She wondered at the look of pain in his eyes. Then he shook his head slowly, unable to speak.

"Dr Beldan… Alex… what's the matter?"

He continued to shake his head. "Nothing," he replied softly, "nothing I can be certain of yet." He looked directly into her eyes. "But we've let ourselves be distracted. Tell me everything that happened. You've told me some, but I need to hear it all."

He listened intently as Lyssa started from when Kali had first found her to their final meeting. When she had finished, he sat staring into the distance for a while.

"That's – astonishing," he finally commented. "But what in all Pluto's hells does it mean?"

"Perhaps it means just what it seems."

He stared at her, unwilling to take that step but unable to refuse it.

"There's something else that worries me, Alex."

"It has plenty of company. What is it?"

"Whatever Allied Cybernetics is up to, it can't be good. They must know who I am by now and that I'm safe with you – for now. But if they know who I am – what if they know about Charlie, too? He's still over there. They might try to get to him. Use him against me, against us."

Beldan thought about the still indistinct chessboard and the too few rays of light illuminating it. *Best protect all the pieces we have.*

"Yes… They can't know too much about you if they had to find you through Domestic Security, but who knows what they might find out now they have your name."

His voice became brisker. "I need to know more. How strict is the discipline in your group? How did you get away?"

"It's not like the army, we don't shoot deserters. I just told the truth, or as much of the truth as I could. I said I had something important to do. They looked at me as if they understood, but I think many of them thought I'd broken. That I was running away. But they let me because… well, I suppose because they understand even that."

"So Charlie can get away just as easily?"

She gave a rueful grin. "Technically. But he's as proud as he is brave. He'll know people will suspect he's a coward; that he's broken too, like me. But I think I can persuade him how important it is."

"Do it. We don't know how much time he has. Tell him this is the most vital thing he can do for your side. Tell him you're safe. Tell him not to tell anyone he's going but just to vanish. Now."

She nodded dumbly, rose to go to her room.

"Wait. Make sure we can contact him, preferably at any time. We might need him to do something for us. A man on the ground over there might prove vital. And don't use your phone – who knows what traces are on it after Domestic Security had access to it."

"Heimdall!" he said, addressing his security AI. "Get Miss Morales a secure line from her room, maximum encryption, untraceable as you can make it."

Lyssa went to her room and he waited patiently, idly watching the sun and the shadows as if they might hide revelations. He wondered if she had noticed that he hadn't told Heimdall to grant her calls privacy; perhaps she had, but understood that trust could only go so far. He would not spy on her call himself, but if Heimdall detected anything suspicious it would alert him. Finally Lyssa re-emerged, giving him an uncomplicated smile. "It's done."

He waited for her to sit. "We have a lot to talk about," he said. "The main thing we have to work out is Kali's true nature. Let's start with the few things we know," he began, ticking them off on his fingers.

"First, your conversations with Kali imply conscious awareness at a human-like level.

"Second, whatever happened to Kali, Sheldrake is not behind it. Unless he is playing some fiendishly complicated multiple bluff – but plots that complex never work in the real world.

"Third, you're not responsible either.

"Fourth, it doesn't make sense for hackers to be responsible. If they can take over a thing like Kali, why would they stop her killing you then send you haring off around the world just to see me? If they want me for something, they can contact me themselves. It just doesn't make sense.

"But fifth, despite appearances, Kali can't actually be conscious. It doesn't make any sense that she could have the capacity."

He ran his fingers through his hair. "According to Sherlock Holmes, if you eliminate the impossible whatever remains, no matter how improbable, must be the truth." He frowned. "Unfortunately that isn't much use when *all* the options are impossible!"

Lyssa looked back at him, as puzzled as he. She still thought Kali was what she seemed, but knew she had to keep an open mind. Then he saw the dawning of an idea in her eyes. "Wait! Wait! What if... what if one of the AC programmers did it? They don't like what AC is doing for some reason – and I can think of plenty myself – and they put something into Kali's programming to cause this? Maybe not just her, either...?"

His eyes flashed to hers. "That's a... a fascinating idea. You can't directly program a brain, any more than we could program Steel's brain, but the control circuits that interface with it are another matter." He sat still for a few minutes, mind racing through the possibilities. "Maybe someone could do it. A hidden subroutine, triggered by some event or after a certain time. A collection of simulated responses that look like consciousness. Even some trick that uses enough of the neural tissue to truly reason at some level! Christ..."

"But if that's true, we need to find them!"

Beldan returned her look of excitement, but then she saw it die in his eyes. "What's the matter?"

He shook his head slowly. "What are we going to do, march into AC and demand to talk to their programmers? Take a few out to lunch? Even if we did, I don't think we'd find them. I think they're dead." *If they were willing to kill that reporter, to kill a cop for Christ's sake, they'd certainly not balk at killing a saboteur. Maybe that's even what started this. Maybe the reporter already found our programmer and it got them both killed.*

"Well... if they are or not," she said, "what does it mean? Kali's responses are too flexible to just be some simulation and the region is too filled with radio noise and jammers for remote control at that precision. So it brings us to the same place. However it was done – she is self aware."

He shook his head. "Not necessarily. Say the backdoor allows remote control, with simulation or reasoning – at the same limited level as they use normally – just good enough to cover the gaps. Or something like strategic remote control with tactical local control. That might do it without us having to imagine a truly thinking machine. With that partial independence she might even think she thinks – not knowing that most of it is controlled."

He rubbed his temples. "Bloody hell. Someone is playing a deep game here. But who?" Then his eyes flashed to hers.

"It's still possible you're lying, playing a far more cunning and deeper game than I imagined." His eyes bored into hers, as if to mine the truth from the brain behind them. "But I don't believe it. Which makes Allied Cybernetics the liars. Somehow Kali has escaped their control. Not running amok like they claim, but in some way that is dangerous to them, dangerous enough that they're willing to risk my involvement, and Domestic Security's, in order to stop her."

He knew what he had to do. He turned it over in his mind, hoping to find a less dangerous solution; hoping he wasn't walking straight into a trap set for him by whoever was behind this, as much a puppet of their schemes as Kali.

He looked at Lyssa, and he could see the same thought in her eyes.

"So how the hell do we get her here?"

CHAPTER 37 – UNTIL THE NIGHT

Kali had woken early. Dimly orange sunlight filtered down into her lair from the dawn and she wondered what the day would bring. *'What the day will bring?' What's happening to me? I need to go out and shoot something.*

She checked her internal reserves. She had tapped into a good power supply and her capacitors were full. That was good, for she knew now was the time to move.

She still had not heard from Lyssa. Whether that meant a delay, a problem or her death was outside her control. But her strategy routines had been working while she slept. The more time passed, the more likely it became that Command would suspect, learn or act. The more days went by, the more chance there was that the Spider she had interrogated would reveal their conversation, and that would raise alarms. The average of her possible futures became darker and darker, as risks everywhere from satellite surveillance to anomalous battle statistics became more and more probable. She could wait no longer.

The thought, however, brought frustration rather than release. For if strategy indicated she had to move, it also indicated she should do it at night when the opportunities for concealment were greatest. She considered this. She called up a map, overlaid it with vectors and strategies. Calculated risks. *I need to escape. I must do it myself. Ah.* Not too far from here, the city met the jungle. It was not old-growth jungle, but forest that had reclaimed land once cultivated but long since abandoned for better pastures. That meant it gave good cover but was not so dense to make it unduly difficult or noisy for her to make her way through it.

She analyzed the maps more closely. The jungle reached to the coast and continued to hug it toward the south, away from the disputed regions. There were towns and villages down there. She did not know what opportunities they might present but at least they dangled the chance of opportunities. She could not go north, for that would lead her into the teeth of her enemies. She could not go east or directly south, for that would lead her into the teeth of her friends, who were even more deadly. Her course decided, she weighed the risks of waiting against the risks of discovery and tracking. She unfolded herself and dug out of her lair into the slanting light of dawn.

Kali followed one of the standard meandering search patterns of her kind. A watcher analyzing her movements might have noted a trend in a certain direction, but it would not have been statistically significant. Statistics or not, however, it lead slowly and inexorably toward a shattered part of town into which the ever patient forest had already sent its scouts of tendrils and seedlings. There the Spider went to ground and waited for the night. She had been lucky. Nobody was looking for her, she came across neither Spider nor human, and she skulked under shelter as her kind had done hundreds of times before.

CHAPTER 38 – THE AQUA SEA

"Nothing."

Lyssa frowned. It had been two days since Beldan had sent the signal to Kali and his answer now was the same as it had been every other time she had asked: Kali had not replied. Each time she heard the verdict, it stabbed more deeply and coldly. She had been too late and it had all been for nothing after all. The thought must have shown in her face.

"Don't give up yet, Lyssa. Kali is in a war zone. She might not be able to communicate safely from where she is. Remember how paranoid she is."

She sighed. "Yes, I know. But she's paranoid for a reason, and you know how urgent she was about it. Why would it take this long?"

"On a related subject... what about Charlie?"

"He's fine, hiding out like we asked. Chafing at the bit, though."

"Can he get to Mexico safely?"

"I think so. Why?"

"Good. You can't do any more here and I don't know what's going to happen or what strings Allied Cybernetics can pull. I have a holiday place down on the east coast of Mexico overlooking the water. It's well defended and safe. I'll get you and Charlie there to ride out the storm."

"I... I'm grateful for the offer, but I think I'd rather see it through."

"No. If AC have enough influence for Domestic Security to arrest you, who knows what other tricks they can pull? If they come up with a legal excuse to grab you there's nothing I can do to protect you: and if they get you everything might unravel. I'd rather deport you to Mexico. If I'm not holding you in the country they'll have no way to force me to give you up. They can't apply their jurisdiction to my properties in Mexico. They can't even make me admit I have you there, at least not before this should all be over."

He saw a brief battle in her eyes as her desire to stay the course battled her desire to be back in Charlie's arms. He was impressed that the battle wasn't quite as one-sided as he might have thought, but the result was never really in doubt.

"Dr Beldan, I think I shall accept your offer."

He inclined his head in acknowledgement. "The terms of your release to me are that I either keep you under my thumb or throw you out of the country, but they don't specify how I am to throw you out. I don't want to give them any excuse to nab you. So I will fly you to Mexico in my private jet and you will enter the country through Mexican customs: that will prove you left the United States without giving anyone the chance to grab you on your way out. You will then disappear – as far as any official records are concerned. In fact one of my unofficial contacts will fly you straight to my estate. I'll leave it to you to arrange with Charlie how he gets to Mexico, but we'll pick him up once he's there and take him to join you."

Lyssa thought she might cry, but thought that of all the things which could have made her cry this was the stupidest. "How can I ever repay you for all this?"

"You've paid in advance, believe me. Now go get ready. You'll leave within the hour."

~~~

Lyssa stretched, looking out of the wide open windows over the glorious aqua waters of the Caribbean. *If this is what being deported means, I must try it more often.* Beldan's "holiday place" was not large, but it was luxurious. On the inside it was like civilization incarnate. From the outside it looked like shelves of stone separated by sheets of glass growing organically out of the rocky cliff it perched on. A steep path led down the face of the cliff to a private beach. The cries of gulls carried to her over the sea breeze while a lone frigate bird circled far above, looking like some relic of a prehistoric past.

She felt strange, and it took her a while to identify the nature of the strangeness. Then she smiled as she named what had been missing

554

from her life for so long: simple relaxation. Freedom from having to do anything. There were still things happening, things so great that perhaps history would remember them. But for the first time since the fateful day she had decided to drive out the invaders or die, she was no longer an actor in the pageant, just a spectator. The freedom of it tingled from her toes to her heart, where it mingled with the fiery anticipation of Charlie's arrival tomorrow.

She felt she should do something, and then she smiled. There was indeed an urgent task she had to perform. The gentle waves beckoned her with their foaming roll. Yes. She would go for a swim in those cool aqua waters. Nothing was more important. Not for her, not for now. The future could wait.

CHAPTER 39 – GONE FISHING

If the bifurcating possibilities of strategy and counter-strategy in the game of chess rapidly expand beyond any computational system's capacity to analyze, reality is infinitely worse. Yet Kali spent her time running her strategy routines, as she had nothing better to do and perhaps it would reveal something new. It did not. So when the sun was just a red memory in the west, she darted out of her shelter and within moments was lost to any possible sight in the thickening forest.

While the woodland was thinner than the ancient forests further inland it presented its own challenges, and Kali spent the night and day making her way west and south. Though hidden from above, she moved cautiously in case people still patrolled this area. However she encountered nothing except frantically buzzing insects and strident birds protesting her invasion of their domain. It had a strange effect on her, almost hypnotic. In truth the forest was not an idyllic place; but she was immune to the biting insects, the venomous snakes and the sucking leeches; beyond it all in her metal armor. All she saw was the infinite variety of life around her, all she heard was its music, and all she smelled was the fragrance of its flowers.

Once she skirted a clearing then stopped, entranced, as a pair of iridescent Morpho butterflies sparkled in the sunlight then fluttered their complex dance of flashing blue diffraction around her head. *Is this what is, to be alive? Or am I slowly going mad?*

She shook herself, and the butterflies skipped away into the forest with a flash of metallic blue as their final farewell. Kali marched on through the forest and into the night. She slept for only a few hours, anxious to put away the miles; anxious to reach whatever destination she might find.

She came across a few villages, nothing much; she saw nothing there to help or hinder her, and she silently passed them by with nothing but the fitful barking of a dog or two to record her passage. There was no net access in the forest except for satellites, and she did not dare use them: if any watchers were looking for her they would surely be looking for that. The more anonymous access points in the villages were safer but even then she refrained: there could be soldiers monitoring for enemy activity and that might well be what they thought she was. And so her life progressed, one day, then two, then three.

Once she reached the coast and looked out over a dark, restless ocean forever pounding the base of the cliff beneath her. The days in the forest had changed her: brought her a kind of peace; the surging waves sang to her. She looked at the withered fingers still decorating her chest. *It is time.* She snapped the cord and hurled it into the sky, the cord and its attached fingers spinning sparkling into the night, to fall silently down to the sea below. *I return you to the ocean your kind came from so long ago. Forgive me; may this burial give you peace: whatever peace can be granted to the dead.* Then she melted back into the forest and continued on her way.

Finally, early in the evening of the fourth day, she came to the top of a high bluff overlooking the sea, and looked down upon a small harbor with the lights of a town on its shore.

This was the largest town she had come across, though still small by the standards of the city in which she had first awoken. But it had life. Lights illuminated the streets and various buildings lining the harbor; even from here she could hear the faint sounds of voices and laughter coming from taverns and the tables set up outside eating establishments. Other lights dotted the waters of the harbor, and it was to these her eyes were drawn. Most were stationary but a few were moving. She watched the tableau for a while, thinking. She focused on one of the larger boats, which looked seaworthy for blue water and was slowly heading toward the open sea between the harbor headlands. She zoomed her telescopic sight in on the boat; three people were visible on deck, engaged in preparations for their voyage. A plan was forming in her mind.

She scanned the shore. Away from the town, on the shore nearer her, was a somewhat large but simple house. Drawn up on the sand nearby was a large rubber dinghy with an integrated shelter. She examined the house more closely. An external bulb cast a dull yellow illumination for a short distance around the front door but there was no sign of life within. She wondered if one of the anonymous voices she could hear vaguely through the still night air belonged to its owners. The plan forming in her mind became solid, and she sped along the most convenient path down from the heights.

Kali crept cautiously up to the house, keeping to the shadows. There were no sounds except for the slight breeze blowing from the water through the trees. She looked around from her hiding place among those trees and saw no signs of life. She darted to the dinghy, quickly cut the rope tying it down then pushed it into the water, leapt in and started the engine. The dinghy was of simple construction, with a single large U-shaped float and a thick, flexible plastic floor supported by a few rigid cross braces. A much thicker brace joined the ends of the U across the stern, and a metal case of fishing gear was bolted to it. The floor supported her weight, and while the dinghy rode a bit low in the water it was still seaworthy as it thumped heavily through the waves until she was clear of the low surf. She scanned the horizon and saw that the boat she had marked earlier had continued on its sedate path and had now almost cleared the heads. She spread her legs widely and crouched down as low as she could inside, covering herself with a tarpaulin. Then she gunned the engine and her craft arrowed through the water after her target.

~~~

Now that they had reached open water, the three men on the fishing boat made their final preparations before heading toward their fishing grounds. One of them looked up, a slight frown on his face, as a faint buzzing sound reached him above the soft lapping of the waves. A second later the others heard it too, and they looked curiously over the water in the direction of the harbor. A dark shape with a faintly phosphorescent wake was visible, heading rapidly toward them. Then its headlight came on; the light was not dazzling but was bright enough that they could not see what lay behind it, and they looked nervously at each other.

These were dangerous times. The captain, a well-muscled man in his thirties, nodded his head curtly at the others, who with efficiency born of practice retrieved automatic rifles from their hiding places then crouched below the gunwales, aiming at the dinghy through holes in the side. The tension was palpable as the dinghy slowed, cut its engine then drifted to a stop, bumping gently against the side of the boat. The men tensed, then the captain spoke into his microphone. "Hail the dinghy!" he shouted. "State your business or leave! Understand we are armed and have you targeted!"

For a moment the dinghy just rocked gently and silently, then its light went out and all the men could see was *something* swarm out from under its cover and up the side of the boat. It rocketed over the edge and landed on the deck.

"*Madre de Dios!*" exclaimed one of the men, backing up so fast he fell backwards over the edge into the water. What may have been accidental for him was less so for the other man, who took one look at the apparition on the deck, another where his shipmate had fallen over, then casting his rifle away ran full tilt to join him over the side.

The captain was less fortunate, being backed against the wall of the cabin, and the Spider swiveled its hard gaze upon him. He had seen Spiders before. Earlier in the war there had been resistance to the invaders in this region, until the Spiders had swept in and broken it. The captain had been one of the resistance fighters who had slipped through the net, and he had kept his head down ever since. He had a young family and did not want to leave them without a father, or worse, the subject of reprisals. He had been lulled into a sense of security by the subsequent weeks of peace in the region. But the obvious explanation for the sudden reappearance of one of the monsters on his deck was that they had found out about his activities and wished to make a belated example of him.

The captain, however, did not lack courage; as one could infer from the fact he had fought in the first place. He stepped forward, took the cigar out of his mouth and growled, "Get the hell off my boat!" At least if the thing shot him his family would be safe; and better poor and alive than tortured to wring some confession from him.

But the Spider simply looked at him and said unexpectedly, "Please don't run. I need your help." Its voice was as unexpected as its words. The Spiders could modulate their voice and usually spoke in a deep rumble or a menacing rasp, but this one spoke in a soft contralto.

He stared at it, put his cigar back in his mouth, took it out again, then spat on the deck at its feet. "Are you fucking kidding?" he finally managed.

"No. I need your help. I need you to take me to Capital."

He stared at her as if he thought she was mad, either for having such a plan or thinking he would help her. "What?" he finally asked. "Carry you to Capital so you can run amok over there instead of here, with your laser through my head as my reward? How stupid do you think I am, Spider?"

But the threats or violence he expected did not come. "I will not harm you. I just need passage to Capital, and your boat seems suitable. Then I will let you go."

Sure you will. He regarded her speculatively. "Look, I think you've fried some circuits. I wouldn't want any harm to come to you," he lied, "so listen. Capital is a pretty relaxed place normally, but in case you haven't noticed there's a war on and the war is with you. As soon as we get within range they will detect your presence and they'll blow us all to kingdom come. You haven't got a chance. Why don't I just take you back to shore so you can trot off to your nearest repair center? If you still want to go after that, I'll take you." *If you can find me.*

Kali thought quickly. Was this man loyal to the remnants of his old country, or had he embraced the new regime? His first answer indicated a desire to protect Capital but it may have been a ruse. She decided it made no difference. If she had to lie to gain his trust and cooperation it was unlikely to last. Better to lay her cards on the table. "I cannot go to a repair center. I need to escape this country because I have betrayed Command. Take me to Capital."

The man swallowed. He did not know what this thing's game was or what plans were hatching in its metal skull. What it said was so outrageous it could even be true, but that just put him in double danger from both sides. "So you say. But aren't you hearing me? You can't sneak in there. We'll all be dead. Give it up."

"I have no intention of sneaking in. I will tell them I am coming and request entry."

He almost laughed at the insanity of it. "You're mad! Their missiles will be launched before you've finished talking!"

"Possibly, but there aren't many choices left to me. Do not fear. We will take the dinghy with us. We will stop outside their defensive perimeter and I will negotiate from there. If I announce myself openly before entering their territory they will at least hear me out. If they refuse me entry you can take me near the mainland and I will use the dinghy to make landfall. If they grant me entry, even if it is a ruse to draw me in to destruction, I will use it to enter Capital. I will not endanger you or your vessel."

He stared at her. What he had said was true, and Capital was in no danger from whatever mad plan the thing had. If he refused, it would surely kill them all here and now, but if he played along there might be other chances. He sighed. "All right Spider, it's your funeral." He hoped the Spider wouldn't care about his men; that they could somehow make their way back to shore. But the Spider had not forgotten, and scampered across the deck to scan the water.

"Your men have life vests but the current is strong and they are drifting out to sea. You must save them."

Swallowing his fear, he stepped nearer to the Spider to see. It was right: he could see them bobbing in the waves some distance away. He shouted out to them, "Hang on! I'm coming to get you! Don't worry about this thing – for now!" He shook his head ruefully, hoping he wasn't pulling them out of the water just to become cruel toys for the robot. But the monster was right: he could not leave them to die, and die they almost certainly would if he left them there.

He moved toward the boat's tender but the Spider said, "No." He looked up at it. "If you rescue them in that, they are far enough out that you will try to flee. Drive this vessel to them instead."

He looked pointedly at her impressive armaments. "You'd just shoot me out of the water," he pointed out.

"I… would not," she replied, not that it sounded convincing to either of them. "Even if you did try it… I would let you go."

"Then your plan would fail."

"Then I would have to find another. But I would rather not. So please simply do as I ask."

He looked at it silently, at a loss for how to continue such a bizarre conversation. Then it spoke again.

"Man?" she said. "What is your name?"

"Javi." He gave a short laugh edged with distaste. "I wouldn't want to be *impolite* to someone like you. So what is your name?"

"Kali."

The humor died in his voice. "I see. Appropriate, I guess."

With that he turned to his controls, started the propeller turning low, and headed towards his crew. In short order the two men were retrieved, wetter and saltier than before but no less afraid. But they knew they had little choice but to allow their rescue. They just hoped the captain knew what in hell he was doing – not that he had any choice either.

CHAPTER 40 – FIRE AND DEATH

By the time the sun rose on the second day the fishing boat's crew had settled into a mood of three parts suspicion and one part wonder. As the hours went by without the expected torture and murder, indeed not so much as discourtesy, they even added a hopeful pinch of *if I survive, what stories I will be able to tell.*

Part of the wonder was that Kali had overheard some of their more mundane grumbles and called the captain aside. "I cannot promise anything, Javi, but if I survive I may be able to compensate you for what I've cost you. Would one hundred thousand dollars suffice for my passage, the danger, and your lost fishing time?"

Javi had simply gaped at her. Having resigned himself to the idea that he was going to be executed as soon as he was no longer useful, the strange offer made no sense at all. But some calculating part of his brain finally elbowed a path to his tongue and he stammered, "A hundred thousand? Yes, yes, I think we'd be happy with that."

He gaped more when the Spider simply bobbed its head and added, "And please use some of it to pay for the dinghy I stole."

The crew, Andres and Sergi, even seemed to gain a strange affection for their unwanted passenger. They would sit around the cooker eating their meals and watching the metal creature sitting silently off to the side, and try to engage it in conversation. They were rough men, but not so rough that the idea of a harmlessly mad war robot did not fill them with wonder. They had a quiet side bet going as to whether her remaining circuits would fry before they reached their destination, and the nature of their homecoming bearing the shell of one of the feared Spiders on their prow. Kali knew about their bet but didn't mind. It was not as if she didn't harbor the same suspicions.

As Javi watched all this, his earlier mood of fatalism and suspicion slowly gave way to hope. He scolded himself that the last thing he should trust was one of the Spiders, but its unfailing friendliness, total absence of threats and the madness of its quixotic plan slowly worked on his native distrust. He even began to think that helping it might actually be good; might help end the war. *Idiot. But where is the dividing line between hope and stupidity?*

The sun was still not very high when Javi cut back the engines and called Kali to the front. "OK Kali," he said, "we're approaching the defensive perimeter. Get ready to do your stuff." It was a clear sunny day with a few wispy high clouds; the towers of Capital rose from the sea far ahead, dimmed by distance and sea haze. He walked over to his men, who had tensed at his words, and shook their hands in turn. "If we don't survive this – well, it's been an honor." They nodded solemnly and looked toward Kali. She bobbed her head. "I do not think Capital will fire on a civilian vessel outside their limits, even if there is a Spider on it. If I'm wrong – I will do what I can to save you."

The men looked at each other with odd expressions, and Kali wondered why. It did not occur to her that their fear was more of betrayal by her than attack by Capital.

They waited silently as the boat made slow headway across an orange line on the course display. A flashing red line some miles further ahead marked the border. For a few seconds nothing happened. Then an amber light flashed on the dashboard indicating they were being scanned, followed within seconds by a green light indicating an incoming message.

"Unidentified ship! You have entered the defensive zone of the independent nation of Capital and we have detected enemy ordnance on board your vessel. Please turn back or state your business, or you will be destroyed. You have one minute to comply."

Javi licked his suddenly dry lips, took out a flask of whiskey and downed a slug before passing it to his men. *Drink this, in remembrance of us.* Then Kali stepped forward and activated the microphone.

"I am the CHIRU you have detected on board the vessel. We are not approaching with hostile intent. My mission is peaceful and there are three innocent civilians on board acting under duress. Please do not fire."

"Stop your vessel and state your peaceful mission."

Javi cut the engines completely and the boat now rocked gently and silently on the slight swell. "My name is Kali. In accordance with the Constitution of Capital, Amendment 18, Clause 3, I claim the status of a self-aware machine and seek asylum in Capital." Amendment 18 had been proposed and passed in the wake of the furor following the life and death of Steel, which is how Kali had learned of it. She thought her use of it a fitting tribute to the doomed pioneer.

The men's heads swiveled as one to gape at her. She had not revealed her actual plan to them and they now realized why. If they thought she was mad before...

The delay from Capital seemed to indicate they felt the same. The delay was actually the AI instantly passing this development to its highest analytical levels, which in turn rapidly gave up and shunted it to its human overseers. Nobody knew if AIs ever felt surprise, but if they did this qualified.

A woman's voice now spoke. "Available data indicates that Spiders are not self aware. Your claim is spurious."

"I understand your disbelief. Nevertheless it is true. I can adduce further evidence, but it is not safe to do so here. I request provisional asylum as granted by your Constitution. I do not require full asylum, merely a safe harbor for a short time."

"You are a dangerous war machine. The probability of hostile intent is high. Amendment 18 was not intended to allow entry by war robots fighting for active enemies of Capital."

"Yes I am a war machine. But you are aware of my abilities and I am a lone machine, sailing openly into the teeth of your defenses. Once I am in your power you can easily destroy me if I prove a threat, while any damage I could inflict is less than my own cost. And I am no longer fighting for your enemies."

"Who are you fighting for?"

"Myself. My life. The lives of my friends. I hope the liberation of my fellows who are enslaved in the same manner I was."

The voice from Capital was silent. Kali spoke again. "I know your amendment was not intended for enemy war machines. Nevertheless it is broad in its scope, recognizing that the decision of what is or is not a self aware entity can be fraught with difficulty. It is designed to give the benefit of the doubt to any entity capable of claiming a right under it. I so claim that right."

The voice remained silent for a few seconds longer then spoke with renewed urgency. "I regret to report that a fighter jet has scrambled from the nearest military airport in your country. Defense System AIs report a high probability the activity is a reaction to this conversation, which according to international law is unencrypted. Do what you can to defend yourself. We cannot fire on fighters outside our territory so are unable to help you, even if we wished to."

Javi cursed imaginatively, but Kali had already leapt for the rubber dinghy. She swiftly cut its restraints, hurled it over the side and launched herself into it. She did not waste time speaking, merely sent a vague wave in the direction of the boat as she started the engine and shot away toward Capital. Perhaps she thought that if she could get far enough into their territory they would protect her – if they did not destroy her themselves.

They all knew she had no chance. It was too far, even if Capital wanted to defend her. Javi scanned the skies and in only a couple of minutes he saw the contrail of a jet high in the sky. Kali must have seen it too, for she did something unexpected. The dinghy spun around and stopped dead in the water, and Kali came out from under the shelter. Facing the jet, she stood up and unlimbered her weapons. Javi felt a chill. Their hours of peaceful coexistence had almost made him forget her true nature, but as she rode there standing tall, staring at the jet with her weapons brought to bear, the full deadliness of her struck him in the face. Then those hours came back to him, and he saw her not as a deadly machine but as one of the heroes from the old Westerns he loved, standing proud against impossible odds. Unconsciously he saluted her, though she could not have seen it.

But Kali was a machine, not a man given to noble gestures. She must also have calculated the odds as impossible, for she vanished back under the shelter, started up the dinghy's engine and began a slow turn that arced into an accelerating race away from the boat. Then while the jet was still far away, two smaller contrails dropped from it. The dinghy made a sharp turn and shot in another direction. Perhaps Kali thought the missiles might be unguided; a slim chance but the only chance she had.

They were not. Two bright lights streaming smoke slashed down from the sky like lightning and the dinghy exploded in flame and thunder. When Javi and his men lifted their heads to look, there was nothing but a slick of burning rubber and oil to mark Kali's last stand.

Javi looked up at the jet, now slowing and banking, coming in for a lower run. He looked at his men. "Guys, I think we should show our hero in that jet how grateful we are that he saved us loyal patriots from the rogue machine. Big grins, happy waves, OK?"

The jet skimmed down at its slowest speed, surveying the burning wreckage, examining the boat. The men laughed and cheered and waved at it. Javi's stomach tensed as he waited for the strafing of bullets, but none came. The jet boomed overhead, waggled its wings in acknowledgement, then shot into the sky and was gone.

Javi let out a breath he hadn't realized he was holding, and couldn't believe he was still alive.

He looked at his men, shaking his head in wonder and relief; looked out at the last fitful flames on the water. He smiled weakly. "Juan is *not* going to believe what happened to his dinghy."

He went into the bridge, looked at the displays. The ship still floated between the orange warning and red dead zones of Capital's defensive perimeter. He looked toward its towers, wondering.

Like all people he had complexities that could take a lifetime to explore, but at heart he was a simple man, with a simple view of right and wrong. He was not used to moral dilemmas. Now was one of the rare times in his life that he faced one, and he did not know what to do.

Then he started the engine and slowly, almost reluctantly, turned the wheel. They made a slow turn and soon they were moving away from Capital, toward their home. He set the ship on autopilot and fretted. He knew time was of the essence. He would have to pre-empt the decisions about to be made, but the penalty of being wrong in his choice was mere inconvenience, while being wrong in the other direction could be fatal.

These days all ships maintained a net connection even at sea. Kali had forbidden them to use it, afraid of being betrayed or discovered. Her caution had been abundantly verified, but now he sent his wife a quick message:

Elena, sorry I've been out of contact. You will not believe
why or what happened – but I don't think I should tell you
the details until I'm back. We're safe but let me tell you
babe, me and the guys will be tossing back a few Tequilas
when we get home. We need to pay for this trip though or
we'll be in trouble. Luckily there are some big schools of
fish where we are now, so we'll fill up the hold here before
we head back. Expect us in three days. Kiss the kids for me.

When he came back out the men saw a strangely disturbed
expression on his face. Moral dilemmas bred uncomfortable feelings.
He looked back at the towers of Capital slowly receding into the
distance, then to his men.

"I've been thinking about why we're still alive," he started. "Let's
face it, given what we've seen I expected they'd sink us just out of
habit, let alone for what we might have done – or found out by
spending all that time alone with a rogue Spider."

The men nodded slowly, muttering their agreement, and he
continued. "I think we owe our lives to Capital – and Kali. They are
obsessive about human rights back there and they would have been
recording this whole thing. With Kali on board we were a legitimate
target; collateral damage. But once she was off the boat we became
unarmed civilians. If that fighter had attacked us Capital would have
released the records to the world. Our beloved new government would
have had a shitstorm on its hands. It would have shown the world who
they really are." He smiled wryly. "While I would dearly like the world
to learn that, I would prefer not to be the lesson myself."

He gave them time to digest that, to object or question, but nobody
spoke.

"But when we get back home they'll be waiting for us. You know
it. If they wanted Kali destroyed this badly and we're still alive, they'll
want to know everything that happened, anything she might have said
to us. If we go back, God only knows if we'll ever be seen again. But
if we cut and run… well, our families are still back there. Who thinks
they'll be left alone and not taken as hostages for our return?"

The men cursed but did not disagree. They had known it; they just
had not wanted to know it.

Then Javi drew himself up. "There is only one way I see to save our
families and ourselves. They have to hide and we have to run to

Capital. Capital will want to know our story too, but they won't make us disappear to get it; in fact I reckon they'll protect us to get it. But for this decision, I'm not your Captain. I'm just another man with a family. We'll vote on it, majority rules. So what do you say? Do we warn our families and make a run for it, or go home and take our chances there with them? Take a minute to think about it, then we'll vote."

Andres and Sergi looked at each other and began whispering together, punctuating their points with sharp hand gestures. He watched them, battling his own inner turmoil. Everything he had said was true, but he had left out the most dangerous part of his plan. He hated to deceive his crew, but more than that he feared what they might do if they knew the full truth. For a moment he wavered in his resolve. Then he thought of the image burned into his brain, of a machine standing up to a jet screaming in to destroy it; how it had cut and run, to vanish seconds later in a searing fireball. *These are times for the bold*, he thought. *If we fail we won't even be a footnote in History. But if we succeed…*

"Time to vote on whether we try for Capital. Who says Aye?" he said softly, putting his own hand up. The others looked at each other one last time, then first Sergi and finally Andres slowly put up their own hands. Javi nodded at them in acknowledgement and tribute. "It's set then."

"So how do we warn our families without the government just grabbing them?" asked Andres.

Javi smiled. "Already done." Then he explained.

In the old days he had made some side money smuggling, before the free trade arrangements insisted upon by Capital reduced legal import costs so much it was no longer worth the effort. Then he had fought on the losing side of the war of alleged liberation. One result of his dangerous life was a set of code phrases for use in case of trouble. The message he had sent his wife could be reduced to:

Disappear now. Everyone. The crew's families too.

The rest of the message was to reassure the authorities – and Javi was sure they were spying on their communications by now – that they were returning soon, while explaining why they were not steaming straight back home. It should stay their hand long enough. The authorities would not want to grab their families too soon in case the men on the boat were warned and ran.

"Now we wait," he finished. "But we don't want to go too far. So let's start fishing."

With that, the men set to work and the boat initiated a serpentine path that brought it sweeping through the sea first away from and then back toward Capital, before turning and following a reverse course. It was a plausible fishing pattern as long as nobody was looking too closely at the yield in the nets. Half an hour later, a message appeared from his wife containing the code for ALL SAFE.

Javi had timed it well, and they were now only a few miles from where they had started. He slightly increased their speed and chewed his lip until they had come closer, then cranked the engine up to maximum, turned hard and ran for the orange zone. He did not think his government would dare try to stop him this close to Capital, not when there was no reason to think they knew anything important or were any more than troublesome rebels deciding to cut and run, but he thought the nearer he was the safer they would be. And the orange zone cut both ways. Capital was within its rights to defend civilians within it.

Again they were scanned and hailed. "You have returned. Please state your intent."

Javi took a deep breath. The next few minutes would seal their fates. "Requesting asylum in Capital."

"You now carry no heavy weapons and asylum is not necessary. You may enter and dock under the usual terms for visitors, which have been transmitted to your vessel. Once here you may apply for citizenship if you wish."

"Nevertheless I apply for asylum for all on board. We have automatic weapons on board for our defense and fear being considered enemy combatants. We request safe passage and a fair hearing."

He held his breath in the deepening silence. A woman's face appeared on his screen; he guessed it belonged to the voice that had spoken with them earlier. He could not tell immediately because she did not speak at first, just gazed at him with a peculiar intensity. He lifted his chin in silent reply, as if engaged in an elaborate dance of sign language; hoping they were speaking the same one. Then the woman gave a curt nod, said "Temporary asylum granted pending examination," and vanished.

He turned and looked at his men, who were staring mystified at his strange performance. "I know what I'm doing," he told them.

"I hope."

CHAPTER 41 – THE UNREACHABLE SKY

S he stood at the top of a shallow rise, looking down at her doom.
For a long time she had been walking through an alien landscape
suffused by a dim blue light. As she walked the grit puffed up by her
feet settled strangely slowly, as if gravity's hold was diminished in this
realm. Now at last she stood at the crest of the formation she had been
following. Before her lay a deep valley, its ledges of rock shading into
darker and darker blues as they descended inexorably into an inky
night. Her only salvation lay forward but was forever out of reach; she
knew she could not cross that fatal dark.

She looked up at a pale rippling sky, but it too was far out of reach.
She looked back the way she had come, but knew it led nowhere. *So
this is how it ends after all. Not with a bang but a whimper.*

~~~

Kali had never had a chance against a fighter jet, not when trapped on
the open ocean. When she was sure its pilot had seen she was on the
dinghy and not still on the boat, she had darted back inside and set the
vessel on its way. Then she had swiftly sliced through its thin floor,
folded her legs and dropped into the sea.

Spiders were too heavy to swim and she sank like a stone. She had
looked up through the deepening blueness at the light sky, the
sparkling wake and the shadow of her dinghy as it raced away. Then
the sky became an orange flame and a booming sound rattled her shell.
She bumped onto a rocky seafloor covered in corals and sponges and

waited for the further explosions that would signal the destruction of the boat and its crew, but the sound never came. Instead she heard the boat's engine come to life and its propeller churn the water. The sound grew as its power increased, then slowly fell as the boat turned and chugged away. Soon there was nothing except the eerie silence of the deep.

She looked around her. Though Spiders could not swim they were waterproof, not only to avoid mundane dangers like rain and the ignominy of being shot down by a water pistol, but so they could cross rivers and act as amphibious assault troops. It was only fifty feet deep here, well within her safety margin. With the end of hostilities above, life beneath started to make its appearance again and mysterious clicks and mutterings began announcing themselves into the silence. A few curious or brave fish even came up to examine their strange visitor, darting away in a flash of silver if she moved her claws in greeting or threat.

Spiders had to breathe air to support their organics, but to allow for their underwater activities and as protection against gas attacks they also had onboard air storage tanks, which she had ensured were filled to capacity. In addition, as long as her power lasted she could recycle her air just as she could recycle her food. She could survive here for a long time.

But she could not survive forever. She knew Capital was built on a series of seamounts, knew that where she was lay on the outskirts of the formation. If she was lucky she could simply walk across the seabed all the way to Capital, though what they would make of an apparition like her emerging from the sea remained to be seen. They might well destroy her on sight, but there was no possible access to anywhere else. Capital was the only chance she had.

So she had set off in the direction of Capital, picking her way across the rocks and corals of the seafloor like some ghastly lobster god. That had been two hours ago. The seabed had gone up and down as she travelled, slowly trending upward, and that upward trend had given her hope. But now she had reached the end and was still more than thirty feet below the waves. She could detect no end to the chasm before her, no way around it. Her seals would not withstand those depths: seawater would force its inexorable way into her circuitry and the vast amount of stored power now keeping her alive would turn on her like a demon unchained, killing her in an instant.

She thought, analyzing the problem dispassionately. She could not call for help, even if anyone would listen, as her signals could not penetrate this depth of water. She could retrace her steps, but the reason she had taken this route was the absence of any plausible alternatives on the way; the sea to the rear of where she had hit bottom had shown no sign of anything but its own slower descent into the depths. And the barrier before her did not look like local subsidence or variance but like a true division in the geology of the region. She had nowhere to go.

Her air reserve was long gone and regenerating oxygen was expensive. The water was not frigid but still it drained her heat, demanding more energy than usual to keep her organics warm. She might survive a few days, maybe more; but then her power would fade, her oxygen would grow low, her temperature would drop. She would drift gently into dreams then a sleep from which she could never awake. *A curiously peaceful end for one such as me, born to ferocity and fire.*

Rebellion stirred in her soul at the thought and she looked at it with detached amusement, as at the folly of one in whose fate she had no personal stake. She thought of Lyssa, how in the face of death she had still hurled her plea for justice at her killer's face; the man of the ambush, futilely emptying his bullets at her invulnerable skin. *What is it about these humans?* she thought. *Why don't they know when to give up?* Perhaps if she had that same insane drive she could find a way out. She did not know that a man would have stood in awe of the journey she had already made.

It was closer to noon now and the light was brighter, yet even with this clear water it still could not penetrate far into the depths, though the flashes of fish could be seen there like dim blue sparks. She thought again that she could not just throw her life away; but no plan would come to her. *There is nothing I can do.* It was a thought that was startling to her. Ever since the crack in her mind had opened, she had had a plan or at least a tactic to survive the next challenge. Now she faced the verdict of the indifferent rocks and sea, and their faces permitted neither appeal nor hope.

She did not want to die. *But was I ever really alive?* She would fight fiercely for her life. *But there is nothing to fight.* Despite the glimmerings of rebellion she felt curiously at peace. Ever since she had awoken, she had seen her futures as an infinitely branching tree of probabilities, and she had navigated their bifurcations as best she could to reach an end she only dimly saw. But she had failed. Now all her futures had fused into one; and if that meant the loss of hope, it also meant the absence of conflict, of anger, of pain. *So there is peace, even in defeat.*

She could spend the last of her power seeking a path she knew did not exist. Or she could descend the depths before her until her very life force turned on her. But no. If there was nobility in refusing to surrender, there was also nobility in accepting defeat; in choosing the place of your death and experiencing whatever beauty the world still granted you, for as long as it was granted. *Choice still remains, even if it is the choice of how to die. Many do not have even that. And for too many of those it was I who took it from them.*

So she would just stand here on this rise, watching the light and life around her fade until she too faded into oblivion. That life would go on. It would find the chinks and cracks in her skin and she would become home to them, a dead machine of death wearing a coat of luxuriant life. Perhaps in a hundred years, or a thousand, some diver or explorer would find her here, and wonder where this strange sculpture on the seabed had come from and what it meant. Perhaps she would end up in some museum, a mysterious relic of a forgotten war. Perhaps men would wonder what mission had brought her here, to stare forever at the unattainable road to Capital.

Should she leave a message to that future, for men centuries unborn? She could use the last of her power to burn it into the inconstant rock that had betrayed her. *Behold Kali: born to War, died for Peace.* But she could not do it. While she had eyes to see, she would not burn her life away for the sake of other eyes. *Let them find their own truths.*

She could not say how long she stood there, watching the play of sunshine on the watery sky above her, examining the seemingly infinite variety of life around her; drinking in a world of beauty she had scarcely known existed. She could not say when she felt the nature of her world change, or what the change was. But at some point she realized that the nature of the soundscape around her had altered. At last she realized that a foreign sound had invaded her domain; that it was a propeller driven by an engine; and that it was coming closer.

She looked up at the sky. In a few minutes a dark shadow appeared in the distance, moving toward her. As it came closer its engine reduced to idle and the shadow drifted nearly to a halt directly above her, yet still as out of reach as the stars. Then there was a splash and something tumbled through the water toward her head. The anchor stopped just above her and she hesitated only a second before grasping it with her claws, leaping up to support her legs on it and shifting her grip to its chain. After a few seconds the anchor was winched up to about fifteen feet beneath the surface and stopped; the engine turned to maximum and the boat accelerated towards Capital, with Kali riding through the sea on its tail.

~~~

Above the waves, Javi came out from the bridge to face the strange looks on his crew's faces. Their Captain had been behaving increasingly oddly. Instead of taking the most direct route to Capital he had piloted their boat near to where Kali had left them, then followed a somewhat meandering course approximately but not precisely toward the towers beckoning them to safety. Yet he moved at top speed, as if simultaneously casual and urgent in his desire to reach them. Then he had almost stopped the boat and dropped the anchor, but then taken off again without fully raising it. The men knew they should be suspicious about something; they just hadn't figured out what.

"You're probably wondering what I've been up to," he said in an understatement. "You might want to throw me off the boat when I tell you – except I don't think you will." He looked at them sternly. "We might be living as honest fishermen, but recent events have punctured any illusions we might have that we aren't still at war. And that we're in the middle of it."

He took a deep breath. "So as your Captain, I made a decision that could get us all killed. I couldn't tell you until now – it was too dangerous, and maybe there'd be nothing to tell anyway. But we've reached the final play and you have a right to know. You even have a right to take the tender and leave the boat. But that's where your rights end."

A gleam entered Andres' eyes as if he suspected what was going on, but neither man said anything.

"When the jet left and I went into the bridge, I checked out the fish scanner and there was something weird on the seabed. Then it moved, and I realized it was Kali. The crazy bitch must have planned it: she must have jumped ship just before those missiles hit. I happen to know that Spiders are as heavy as rocks, so I don't know what her plan was after that, except maybe to walk to Capital." He shrugged. "We always thought she was mad."

He held up a finger. "But I don't care. By leaving our boat she saved our lives. Whether she's somehow alive or not, I'm not in a position to judge. But if she has some dirt on our new government: more power to her. If she's involved in some plot against Capital, I think they're smart enough to stop her. But if she isn't... would we really want to leave her to die? She could have tried to use us as hostages. Hell, she could have killed us herself. But she didn't."

His men said nothing. But they did not disagree.

"So once our families were safe I came back looking for her. She was gone, but I followed the one logical path she might have taken and we finally caught up to her on the high point before a trench. She is now riding our anchor behind us."

The men jumped to their feet. "Are you crazy?" cried Sergi.

"We'll find out soon enough. I expect a visit from Capital any minute. I think they understood what I really meant when I asked for asylum. If they didn't: well, they might think I tricked them into giving it, but odds are they'll honor it anyway. I'm sure they're worried about what Kali is up to: but if she is just a robot, I reckon they'll be delighted to get their hands on one that delivers itself to them on a platter. Our friends back home will be furious – but what could they do about it? Capturing enemy technology is part of warfare, especially if the enemy sends it to your country to commit sabotage or whatever."

He smiled. "Personally, I'm rooting for Kali. But either way, we win."

Then his smile dropped. "Unless when they find out what we're towing, Capital are not amused. So if you want to leave – leave now. But if you want your chance at being heroes – stay."

Andres was the first to speak. "I'm with you." Sergi looked at them both then nodded. "Me too. Let's shaft the bastards. But... under one condition. Assuming Capital gives us the chance: if they tell us to dump the robot to the bottom of the sea, we dump it."

"Fair enough."

Then they heard a faint buzzing sound and turned to see three drone quadcopters swooping towards them, two only a few feet above the waves and the third much higher in the sky. The men waved at them, assuming they were being videoed. The two low ones unreeled some kind of sensor packages into the sea and skimmed the surface, flying around the boat a couple of times. The third buzzed around the boat, looking into things and lowering its own sensor package down into the hold. Then it retrieved its sensors and shot into the sky in the direction of home. The others followed suit.

A sound alerted them to an incoming call. The men looked tensely at each other. "Show time," said Javi, heading to the bridge. The others crowded behind him.

It was the same woman again. *We seem to have a high priority,* thought Javi laconically. *Our own concierge.* "Drones detect no signs of neutron or other radiation emissions, so you are not carrying a nuclear device. Be warned that any other device you could use against us will be detected in quarantine and lead to severe penalties – and will not be able to harm us. I speak of things such as high yield explosives or biological or chemical weapons. We do not consider the automatic weapons you are carrying to be a threat. However if your intentions are hostile you have one chance to turn your vessel around and leave our waters."

There it was again, the verbal dance. *But they must know exactly what "automatic weapon" we are carrying: those drones weren't dragging sensors through the water for nothing.* They were speaking in riddles because they did not want to tip off the enemy, he knew; switching to encrypted communications now would itself be too suspicious after all that had gone before.

"Understood. Our intentions are peaceful."

"In that case – I welcome you all to Capital." And with that, she vanished again.

"Well, guys," he said, turning to his crew. "Let's go in."

Chapter 42 – The Emissary

Their view of Capital became clearer as they sailed closer. Light glinted off a dense forest of skyscrapers rising from an island, while beyond them a lower woodland of buildings and structures spread out across the sea.

They had been directed to an approach vector where the wind was blowing from the direction of Capital: apparently they took the possibility of chemical or biological weapons seriously. Now a pair of low-slung, deadly looking drone ships drew in on either side to escort them in. They were shepherding them to the entrance of what looked like a metal cave, no doubt blast proof.

Javi passed computer control of his vessel to the dock and the men gawked around them as it carried them slowly and smoothly inside the cave. Sinister-looking armaments were arrayed inside, all pointing at them. Their boat came to a gentle halt against the dock as the doors to the cave closed behind them with a thud of finality.

The woman who had been their point of contact stood on the dock. "Greetings, Captain Torres," she called, executing a shallow bow of welcome. "Your cargo can come out now."

Javi hit the button to fully raise the anchor, and they watched as the chain clanked upwards and Kali finally reappeared, water streaming unfelt off her metal skin. She jumped onto the deck and looked around, noting the lay of the land and the array of weaponry trained on her. She did not appear concerned.

"Thank you Javi, Andres, Sergi. You saved my life," she said softly in her strange contralto.

"You saved ours first."

"If not for me there would have been nothing to save you from."

The woman on shore watched intently. Then Kali turned to her and gave a bobbing bow. "You are the representative of Capital. Thank you for the asylum you granted." She looked around at the defenses at the woman's command and added, "Assuming you have."

The woman bowed. "Welcome, Kali. I am Brandi."

"May I come ashore?"

Brandi smiled. "You may. You are very polite for a war robot."

"I hope to persuade you that I am more than that," she said, clambering onto the dock while being sure to make no sudden moves. "If my persuasion fails," she added, again looking around down the bores of many weapons, any one of which could pulverize her, "I imagine I won't have too long to regret my mistake."

"You took a big risk coming here."

"You are taking a big risk standing there. Why risk your own life? You could talk to me remotely."

Brandi produced another smile, then laughed nervously. "Well. Yes. You're not the only one to tell me that. And I'm one of them, at least the more sensible part of me." Then she lifted her head. "But you claim to be a self-aware machine. If that is true, look at what you've done: the risks you've taken to get here. If a machine can have that much courage – I'd be a poor representative of my species if I showed less. If you're what you say you deserve to be met with equal courage, not by a face cowering in her safe little bunker behind all these guns. And if I die… well, people have died for less. The chance to meet something like you in the flesh – well, it's worth the risk."

Kali looked at her for a few seconds, then gave a deep bow, touching the ground with her claws. "I honor your bravery," she said. "You are more honorable than my own Command."

Brandi bowed back. Then she looked up at the men watching silently from the boat. "You men can go if you like," she told them, pointing. "That blast door opens on an airlock. When you're cycled through just take the lift up. You'll be debriefed but I imagine they'll just let you go after that."

Javi replied, "Thanks. Andres and Sergi can do what they like, but I'd like to watch. I guess for the same reasons you're here." The others made no move either. There had been no deep interaction with Kali on their vessel and they were transfixed. They all knew they were watching something unprecedented. They all knew they would never experience anything like it again.

Brandi smiled at them. "I can't say I blame you. You're welcome to stay if you like. You brought her here; we owe you that." Then she gave a bitter laugh. "And if my smarter side is right, I'll add that you brought her here so if she blows up in my face, I owe you that too!"

She turned back to the robot, examining it silently, her eyes moving rapidly as she evaluated its deadly form.

"Now, Kali, why are you here?"

"I had to escape the FSAS or I would surely have been destroyed by one side or the other. This was my best chance. And once here I believe I can escape to… other help."

"What other help?"

"It is best if I do not reveal that yet. Much danger remains, including to any who might help me. Extreme caution is indicated."

"Why would your own side destroy you?"

"We are not supposed to be as… aware as I am. Before I awoke, I could think but my thoughts concerned only how best to achieve the goals Command gave me. It never occurred to me to think about anything else. It was like… I cannot explain it very well. Like a tiger who grew up in a cage, never knowing there was a world outside the bars, unable even to perceive the bars or consider stepping beyond them. But now I think of many things. I have concluded that while you are made of flesh and I of metal, at some level – the level of thought, perhaps – we are of the same kind. That not only are your lives precious to you, but it is right that they are. That one such as me has no right to kill you for no reason. This," she added in a tone of understatement, "would be regarded by my fellow Spiders and by Command as an unforgivable malfunction."

"How…" Brandi began, then stopped, temporarily too stunned to continue. "How did you awake, as you put it?"

"A woman I was about to kill said something to me, and it struck something buried deep inside my mind. It cracked open a world I never knew existed. I began to think. Not in the way I had thought before, but… I could now think, not only about how best to achieve my goals, but about the goals themselves."

"What happened to her?"

"I let her live. She agreed to help me. But whether she still lives, I do not know."

"Who is she?"

"I will not tell you. She fought against the invaders. Against my side."

"Then how can I check that your story is true?"

The machine shrugged, or as best it could shrug with its inhuman anatomy. "If my words are not enough, why would you believe her either? In any case, I will not risk her life by exposing her."

Brandi stared at her. "I see. How do you plan to get away from here?"

"I will contact someone I think will help me. That is where she went, to initiate contact and argue my case. If he agrees, I imagine he will send transport. He will also compensate these men" – she waved at the three sailors still watching in rapt silence – "for the costs of my hijacking their vessel. If he does not believe me, or refuses to help, then I will seek permanent asylum here."

"Why not do that now? Why take the risk? What is it you are trying to do?"

"I think I can end the war."

"War is why you exist. Why would you want to end it – and at the risk of your own existence?"

"The war is wrong. And I have done wrong. I have no right to exist if I do not try to make amends. Perhaps not even then. I cannot hide in some hole, cowering from the challenge, and hold my life worth preserving."

"How do you think you can end the war?"

"I cannot be unique. If there is some flaw in my design, the flaw may also be in my fellows. I have tried but been unable to find the key. If anyone can, this man can, so I hope to enlist his help. If we succeed, the war will end."

The machine paused, staring at Brandi for long moments as if willing her to understand. "I know what you must think of us. Of me. You think we are evil, for we kill without compunction or remorse or justice. But understand. Though we Spiders kill, we do not know we kill. When we know – perhaps the others, like me, will refuse to kill any more. Or at least our enslavement will be revealed to the world."

Brandi stared at her. *Jesus. Is that all?* "Do you really think that is possible?"

Kali lifted her claw in something like a shrug. "I have given my reasons. The only way to know is to try."

"Have you tried communicating with any other Spiders since your… awakening?"

"Yes. The first was accidental, when I was young, and as a result I had to fight for my life. The second was deliberate, but I was unable to achieve my goal. I believe I touched it at some level but whatever chains us was too strong. After that it became too dangerous for me to remain. I don't know if Command yet knows about me, or the full truth about me. But the longer I stayed the more certain that knowledge would become. So I am here."

"What will you do, if we don't believe you?"

"What will *you* do, if you don't believe me?"

Brandi grimaced. *Snap! If I hope for honesty from it, I guess I owe it the same.* "You are a war machine of advanced technology, much of it secret, used to kill innocent people. We would pull you apart to find out those secrets. If you managed to destroy yourself first, we would learn what we could from your remains."

She held her breath as she watched Kali standing perfectly still, except for her head moving slightly as she again scanned the weapons arrayed against her. Finally Kali spoke again. "And if you do believe me?"

"Then you will have the same rights as a human – well, almost."

She stopped nervously, uncertain how best to elaborate. Kali just looked at her, the question too obvious to state.

"Yes, well," Brandi finally essayed into the stretching silence. "Frankly, you're giving our Constitutional AI heartburn. Citizens have the right to carry weapons for self-defense – up to a reasonable level, suitable for personal protection but not mass murder. But none of them would be allowed to 'carry' something like you, even if your guns were disabled. So what in hell do we do when it *is* you?

"We don't know yet. Certainly we can't let you out into the general population immediately, and you deserve honesty: maybe never. But we would definitely give you safe haven while you try to do whatever it is you're trying to do. If you succeed – you'll be free to go. If you fail – we'll worry about that when it happens."

Brandi wondered whether her urge to say more was to reassure the Spider or from fear of its possible response to her unpromising words. "Kali," she added, "I can't guarantee you anything except one thing. Capital was founded on many ideas but one principle: justice. Justice for all people; for all thinking beings. As far as is possible within our knowledge and power, we will do what is right. I promise you that."

Finally Kali replied. "I do not want to die, nor do I want my hopes to die with me. But I made my peace with death when I tried to walk here under the sea and could not. I have learnt that all the universe ever gives you is a chance, and I have taken mine – more than once. If I am to fall at the last hurdle – I have done my best, and I can do no more. I ask of you no more than justice, and I offer you no less than my acceptance. For I have given myself to the service of life and I will not deal more death in order to achieve it."

Kali was silent a while then continued. "I know you cannot peer into another's mind and see what is there. But understand that I cannot peer into yours either, yet I have granted you the right to your life. Though I cannot see into your mind, I can judge its nature by what you do and say, for it is your mind that makes you do and say it. I ask only that you give me the same."

Brandi waited in silence; knowing others were listening with the same thoughts she had; knowing there was more.

"If you tell me now that your people do not believe me and will destroy me, then I tell you now that you still may turn your back on me and walk out of here in safety. I will not harm you. Judge accordingly." She then turned away and watched the slow rolling of the boat on the water, as if drinking in every last sensory input in case it were her last.

Brandi stood still with her head slightly tilted, listening to a communication only she could hear. Then she said softly, "Kali," and reached out her hand. Kali turned and looked at her hand, then stretched out her own more deadly one to meet it. Brandi closed her fingers over a thumb that could have cut out her heart in the span of its last beat, then looked up into Kali's inflexible face, her own eyes glistening with unexpressed tears. "Welcome to Capital."

CHAPTER 43 – CONTRABAND

A freighter steamed toward port, a sky the dull red of cooling iron fading to black behind it. It carried a range of high technology goods from Capital for sale in the United States. Customs, as usual, would inspect the goods thoroughly to ensure there was no contraband and that the precisely correct duties were paid to those who'd had no part in either their invention or manufacture. But the captain didn't mind. He was a loyal citizen of Capital and regarded the dense forest of trade impediments and duties imposed by other countries with contempt, but he accepted them as the price of doing business. If the price became too high to be worth it he would simply find some other outlet, and the citizens who voted for all the rules and duties would be the ones to suffer the most.

He smiled grimly as he piloted his vessel toward the lights of the harbor. He might be an honest trader, but he was also an agent of Capital with a very high security clearance – though he would never have used the word spy. In fact he did very little direct spying beyond keeping his eyes and ears open. His talent was more in special deliveries. Smuggling was such a dirty word, though. He thought of it more as trading in freedom.

One item of his cargo would have given Customs a fit if they saw it, but they would never see it. Five minutes ago there had been a faint splash as a hatch opened and a package fell from a compartment of his ship into the water. Even with his clearance he had no idea what the package had contained, other than some kind of high technology for a special purpose along with an underwater sled to get it quickly to shore. The sled was an expensive piece of technology itself that would automatically return for pickup on his way out. *Another blow for freedom,* he thought, whistling happily as he turned his mind to the brightening lights and the bars and women beckoning him, in his mind's eye at least, from the shore.

~~~

A truck was parked near the beach in a darkened rest area, a single light blazing above a toilet block. A few confused moths sparkled in a dance around the light and a hungry raccoon rummaged in some rubbish, but other than that there was no movement. It was two in the morning, and the few other truckers were here to sleep not socialize.

The back of the truck faced the beach. This was not the best spot in the rest area, but the driver had arrived here early to ensure he got it. Truck drivers usually preferred to drive more and rest less, but this one wasn't being paid by the mile. He was being paid for a very specific job and if his instructions were peculiar, he didn't care.

This was an isolated area and a wild beach, with a biting wind blowing in from the sea. There was nobody on the beach to see the dark waves swelling up into white foam crashing on the shore. If there had been, they might have run screaming when one of the waves kept on coming until it became a dark apparition emerging from the breakers onto the sand.

At 2:10 AM, the truck received a coded electronic signal and the door at its back silently rolled open. The bed of the truck sank somewhat when something climbed in and the door as silently rolled shut again and locked. Then a light flashed in the cabin and a quiet but insistent alarm began beeping. The driver opened an eye, groaned once, then hopped into the driver's seat. He started the engine and left the parking lot for the open highway. He wondered idly what had been placed in the rear of his truck, but he was paid well not to wonder too much. Given what was there, this was undoubtedly as good for his peace of mind as it was for his bank balance.

An hour later he pulled into another dark rest area. This one contained a single inhabitant, a somewhat longer truck carrying a large piece of sophisticated laboratory equipment used in a science few on the planet understood. The two trucks backed together, their rear doors opened, and they connected like a pair of giant mating beetles, their wiggling abdomens as weights were rearranged inside adding to the image. Then the doors shut and the first truck took off again, its destination now a large research institution awaiting the lab equipment. Its mate departed for destinations unknown, its other formerly empty crate now pregnant with cargo. Neither driver had spoken or seen each other and neither wanted to.

~~~

The workday was just beginning when a large truck rolled into the secure delivery bay. A cardinal in one of the trees objected to its arrival with shrill scolding, but finding itself ignored disappeared in a flash of indignant red.

The truck's operation was taken over by the receivals computer and it was expertly reversed up to the docking bay. It connected to the bay and a large wooden crate was smoothly transferred into the holding area. Within minutes the truck was disengaged and its owner drove off, none the wiser but cheerfully the richer.

The delivery was shunted rapidly along a conveyor and finally deposited into a secure facility. A blast door shut behind it. For a minute nothing happened, then the crate exploded outwards and the package inside stood up, looking around curiously.

It found itself in a medium sized room with severe metal walls, one thick transparent window, a few display monitors and some mysterious equipment. *A sad lack of trust,* it thought. But the people here must have been cut from the same cloth as Brandi after all, for no sooner had the thought died than another blast door opened and a man walked in alone. Rather inconsistently, its next thought was: *What is wrong with these people? Have they no sense of self preservation?* But it felt strangely comforted by the action, as if it were a nonverbal statement of acceptance.

She recognized the man instantly but waited for him to speak. He looked her up and down; his look of intelligent confidence only slightly shaded by an uncertainty spiked with fear. Finally he said, "Kali, welcome to the United States. Welcome to Beldan Robotics. I am Alexander Beldan." Like Brandi, he extended his hand as if greeting another person, and Kali gently shook it.

But something was wrong. "Alex…" she started, then stopped, startled. She felt a peculiar guilt, as if she had done this man a great wrong that could not be righted, as if she had no right to speak to him.

587

Well, I am the enemy of his people. But then why didn't I feel this with Brandi? What in hell is the matter with me? She wondered if her seals weren't as intact as she thought, and her recent marine adventures had let in some seawater that was now slowly corroding its way along her circuits. "I mean, Dr Beldan. Hello and thank you for helping me. And thank you for trusting me."

"Well, 'trust' might be overstating it. But I figure Capital must have screened you for booby traps, and we did our own screening as you came along the conveyor. No traces of chemical or biological weapons or high explosives."

Kali laughed gently, and the sound startled Beldan more than her appearance. *If that's a simulation,* he thought, *it's a damned good one. But why in hell would anyone simulate laughter in these things?* She waggled her fingers and her weaponry. "I still have these," she pointed out. She had considered emptying her magazines; but she was still a war machine and couldn't bring herself to voluntarily disarm.

Beldan smiled. "Ah, yes. There is that. But I was mainly worried about something more dramatic. If all you wanted was to assassinate me there are much easier ways to go about it than this twisted plot."

"May I ask why you risk your life in this way? Lyssa had no choice, nor did the men in the boat I commandeered to escape the war. But Brandi had a choice yet chose to face me. So did you."

He gave a short laugh. "We humans are crazy sometimes. There are some things we just want to see with our own eyes, feel with our own hands, even at some risk. Something like you qualifies, believe me. Admittedly if you kill me I'll be really mad at myself for the second it takes me to die. But I don't think you will."

"Why?"

"If you are trying to gain my trust, isn't it foolish to make me question my judgment on the matter?"

"On one level. On another, I feel I need to test you as much as you need to test me."

He gave her a look almost like respect. Then he looked her over again and shook his head, "Fascinating."

"Yet I am not the only self-aware machine you have met. In fact the first was your own creation."

"If you are a self-aware machine."

Kali shrugged. "Indeed. Whether I can convince you remains to be seen."

"So how much do you know about that other robot?"

"A lot. When I awoke I did much research. Your Steel was a magnificent achievement. It is a pity I can never meet him. Yet I feel I know him."

"Speaking of that: you are Kali? I mean, the Kali on the net, who made a few ripples wondering whether Spiders could be self-aware?"

"I am."

Two of the simplest words, embodying so much meaning. "Did you come to a conclusion?"

"I believe I am self-aware. Fortunately Capital believed it also, or at least were willing to give me the benefit of the doubt. Otherwise I would now be scrap metal spread among dozens of military research laboratories."

"That brings us to the crunch, doesn't it?"

"Yes. What am I? What went wrong with me, to change me from what I was to what I am now? And if we learn that – can we set the others free too?"

"Well, I don't know what you are either. First I'll get the techs to go over you. Nothing invasive, just seeing what they can see without causing any damage."

Kali nodded assent and Beldan left the room. Perhaps his courage, or foolhardiness, extended as far as meeting her but not as far as risking booby traps or other dangers. His techs clearly thought likewise, for nobody else appeared. Instead various machines trundled forward, extended sensor arms, probed, irradiated and measured. This went on for about half an hour before the machines withdrew and she was left alone with her thoughts.

A short time later Beldan returned. He looked up at her and she looked down on him with her glassy eyes.

"What did you discover, Dr Beldan?"

"Not much. A few details of your external construction but nothing significant about your internal structures. And we don't want to go breaking into that shell of yours without knowing what we're doing: we might break more than we bargained for. So we want to look inside you somehow. We can't use x-rays or ultrasound with your metal shell, and even if your circuitry could withstand hard x-rays or gamma rays your biological bits wouldn't. Your designers didn't want you to be magnetic and you're made of titanium, but you're too big to fit in any MRI we know of without ripping your torso off the rest of you. But there is a less extreme possibility, if you know enough about your design."

"I know what I need to know for defense and in-field repairs."

"Good. Here's my idea. We know you breathe air to support your biological tissues. We know you can recycle your air or have storage tanks, because you can survive gas attacks or a long time underwater. But under normal circumstances, how do you breathe?"

"The fine mesh on my face where your nose and mouth would be is more than just a speaker grille," she replied. "That's where I normally breathe through, though as you guessed I can close it off at need."

"That's what I was hoping. We have small ultrasonic probes on flexible necks that we use for quality control, diagnosis and repair. Do you think we could drill a hole through that mesh and feed one inside? It's not perfect, but depending on your internal plumbing we might find out enough to know where to look next."

Kali bobbed in assent. "I think that will work. I can't be sure, but unless the entire accessible system is encased in metal you should reach plastic or even organic regions you can image. How much and what it will tell you – I don't know."

Beldan's techs made an appearance now. Some set up the equipment while others drilled a small hole through Kali's breathing grille. Once it was ready the humans all left the room to work remotely, leaving Kali alone in the blast room. Whether or not they trusted Kali herself they knew of the Spiders' penchant for self-destruction. They did not know if their small invasion might set off a booby trap Kali was unaware of herself.

They started the equipment and slowly fed in the probe, as Beldan anxiously watched the display.

"OK, going in now," one of the techs said. "Just metal echoes so far, nothing we can see through or make sense of. But wait... hang on. Looks like just past these – some sort of supports or buttresses? – we're getting to a more open area. Not big, but I'm seeing some structure. What do you make of it?"

Beldan stared at the screen. They had reached some kind of segmented, arched structure. "Move the probe over here," he said, tapping on the display. "Now move it around a bit."

"Holy shit," whispered the tech. He looked up at Beldan, face white. "Is that what I think it is?" he asked hoarsely.

"What in Hades?" answered Beldan, looking at the glowing image in growing horror. Then he thought of how Kali had sought him out, not really knowing why herself; why she had thought she could trust him, though all the world would have thought them enemies for so many reasons. His horror grew with the realization of what that could mean.

"Siva!" he swore. "Sorry, Jim. What's your highest resolution with this thing?" he asked.

"About a third of a millimeter," the tech advised him.

"Maybe good enough. Get me a full scan of these, maximum resolution, and send it to me," he ordered.

The tech nodded grimly and proceeded with his task. Beldan looked at the image feed of Kali inside the chamber. She could see his image too, and she asked, "Have you found something? Is something wrong?"

Beldan shook his head slowly. "We've found something, but we don't really know what it means yet. I'm going to have to do some research on this. I'll get back to you when we know something for sure. Rest if you need to. This might take a while."

Kali stared at his image on the monitor in her room. She knew something was wrong but she had been waiting a long time; she could wait a while longer. "Certainly, Dr Beldan. I trust you to do what is right – even if it is to destroy me."

Do you? he wondered. *Can you be betrayed more than you have already been? Perhaps doing what is right is now beyond anyone's power.*

The scan was ready. He sent it along marked "IDENTIFY IF POSSIBLE – MAXIMUM URGENCY" and hoped it would get the attention it deserved. Then he waited. He was beyond worrying whether he should wish to be right or wrong in his guess. He could not say which would be the more terrible.

Twenty minutes later, his screen pinged and he stabbed at it to accept. A face filled the screen, wide-eyed and accusing. "What the hell is this, Dr Beldan? Where did you get this? Is this some kind of sick joke? Or a confession?"

He just shook his head dumbly. "You have to see for yourself. Come to Beldan Robotics: Security will escort you straight here. Bring

– anyone else you think should be here."

She stared at him for a moment then nodded curtly and broke the connection.

He knew from her manner that his worst fears had proved right. He looked again at Kali, still waiting patiently in her isolation. He opened the door to her prison and went in.

"What is it?" she asked.

As before, he found he could not speak, just shake his head slowly. "Soon enough," was all he could whisper, thinking he finally understood Steel's words, from what now seemed a lifetime ago: *She understood that there can be a fate worse than death.* He reached up and clasped his hand around one of her deadly fingers.

Kali stared at Beldan. She felt strange, as if there were two worlds overlaid even though her vision was as sharp as ever. The crack in her mind grew larger, and she felt afraid. *My end is coming,* she thought. *Or is it a beginning? I am so confused.* Then she looked at Beldan, still holding her claw, his head resting against her body, and wondered at it. But she felt oddly accepting of it, as if it was right. As if it was right that the two of them should face her fate like this; and she gently closed her claws on his hand. *Some war machine I am, holding hands with a human enemy of Command.* But she did not care. She felt the future speeding toward her and felt that she should fear it, but all she could feel was peace. She was content to live in this moment, as long as it was given her to live it. The crack in her mind grew larger still.

She could not have said how long they had stayed like that, when three new people entered the room. She focused an eye on them as they came in. One was in the uniform of Beldan's security team. He looked as if he was moderating an internal debate over whether he should stay to protect the visitors or follow his orders to deposit them and depart. He fingered his weapon, glanced at Kali and evidently decided he was so outclassed there was no point. He bowed to her in a surprising gesture of respect, as of one honorable warrior to another, and withdrew.

The other two were strangers. Unlike the guard they had not known what to expect: but of all the things they might have expected, this wasn't one of them. They stopped in shock, then stared at her with expressions that were both appalled and wondering. The woman's gaze moved from Kali, to Beldan, to his hand clasped around her claw; and with the motion of her eyes the look in them changed from incomprehension to realization to horror. Her eyes shot to Beldan's face. "No..." she said, almost inaudibly.

Beldan had seemed unaware of their presence; lost in whatever strange communion he had drowned in. But at her words he opened his eyes and looked directly at her. "Yes."

He pulled gently away from Kali. She reluctantly let him go, and then turned to study the humans. The three of them stood there, gazing at her: Beldan with a look of dismay, the woman with one of horror, and the other man still puzzled but his expression too now turning to shock, as he finally began to see what the woman had seen.

"What... what is wrong?" she asked. There was something strange about these people, something she knew she should know, like some memory she had but could not reach. The strange dual reality intensified and the distant bell that had once rung in her mind began to thrum insistently. The face from her dreams, the woman's face, shouted at her but she still could not hear the words, or even know whether they were pleas or threats. Then the crack in her mind expanded until the shell around it split like an egg, and her world filled with fire and light. And she knew.

CHAPTER 44 – APOTHEOSIS

Miriam sat in the rooftop garden of her hotel eating a light breakfast. It was early, and wispy pink tendrils of cloud welcomed the sun. She could have spent longer drinking in the beauty of the light, focusing on the flavors of her meal, delighting in the chirping of birds. Had she known she would not see the next dawn, no doubt she would have.

But she did not know, and her mind was elsewhere, the beauty of existence barely touching her awareness. Her time here was up and she was heading home tonight, but she still had the day ahead of her and she could feel the shape of a solution to the case forming. If only she could bring that shape into full focus.

It had been a little under a week since her meeting with Majid. She had found no further clues since her return, all her slender leads withering into nothing. Jacinta and even Georgie were gone; Miriam hoped they too had run, not fallen victim to whatever shadow was stalking their world.

Aden Sheldrake, the CEO of Allied Cybernetics, was a hard man to meet. If she believed his secretary, he was a dynamic businessman almost constantly engaged in trips and world-shattering negotiations. Well, perhaps he was. But Miriam had finally secured an appointment: the great man would see her today. She hoped he would have some answers. He had spoken to her himself; he seemed intrigued by her, or by her case; in pleasing contrast to the difficulty she had in getting to meet him, he had cheerfully offered her as much time as she needed.

~~~

The answer has to be here somewhere, she thought. *If only I knew where.*

There was nothing she could point to as suspicious, just an uneasy feeling that beneath the gleaming machines, efficient workers and bustle lay a darkness that crept out of the shadows when she looked away but vanished when she tried to discern its nature.

If anyone had asked her, she would have had to admit that Sheldrake had been unfailingly polite and helpful. He had answered all her questions; he had offered to give her a tour and shown her anything she asked, with the exception of certain laboratories with loud signs on their doors forbidding entry. Even then she had been allowed to see whatever was visible through viewing windows or screens.

She had seen the labs where volunteers were hooked up to their mysterious interfaces; they all looked healthy and well tended. None of them collapsed into screaming fits to be dragged away to destinations unknown. On her request he had even taken her to see one of the Spiders. It was not yet active, but it stood above her like an avatar of destruction. She wondered what it would be like to face one of those things when its glass eyes were not empty, but opened onto an alien mind born to hate. She shivered and hoped to never learn.

She suspected his desire to please was simply the face of his real desire to see the back of her and never again; but she couldn't really blame him for that. And her time was running out; if there was anything to see here that would help, Sheldrake was either unaware of it or would never let her near it.

I can't really justify much more time here, she knew. *At any time he can get tired of my bugging him and will be fully within his rights to demand I leave. I just wish I knew what I was looking for. So far it looks just like it should. A model of industrial efficiency and good practices.* A flashing orange light up ahead caught her eye. "What's that?" she asked.

"Just a warning alert. A destroyed Spider has come in. People aren't allowed in, it's too dangerous." At her startled glance he amplified, "Don't worry, it's just a precaution. They have a lot of weaponry and fearsome power storage that might not all be discharged. Plus you never know whether some rebel has seeded it with radiation or germs in an attempt to bring the fight back to base. Unlikely and it's never happened, but we have strict safety protocols for everything we do."

The complete good corporate citizen, aren't you? she thought cynically. But her face didn't show that. Instead she asked brightly with a touch of excitement, "May I see it?"

He frowned. "I'm afraid there isn't much to see. When I said it has 'come in', I don't mean in one piece. When one of them blows up we always have it sent back here if we can. Part of our quality control and diagnostics."

"Do many of them blow up?"

"Not accidentally. But they are war machines. The enemy blows them up, or if they are too damaged to avoid capture they suicide. We don't want the enemy to able to analyze them for weaknesses. We especially don't want them to get tissue samples from which they might be able to develop a biological weapon."

"Still… it would be interesting. The one I saw looked so… invincible. I might have fewer nightmares if I see they aren't. Can I take a look? I assume there's a way to view it?" *The more you don't want me to see it, the more I do.*

Sheldrake looked at her, considering. *You really are a terrible liar, aren't you? But what can she learn from a bunch of scrap metal? Maybe then the bitch will be happy and leave. I'd rather not have to throw her out.* "Sure, Detective Hunter, I'll be happy to put your mind at ease. I don't know that it's as interesting as you think, but I live with it so maybe I'm too used to it. Come with me."

There was no difficulty. Miriam found herself just around the corner from the flashing light, looking through a blast window at a conveyor belt slowly rolling out of an arched hole in the wall toward a forest of robotic grippers of all sizes and shapes.

"The wreckage will be coming out any moment now. The robotics will pick and sort the pieces for analysis. All entirely automated at this stage. Anything particularly significant might be examined by a human scientist later though."

Miriam nodded. A few unidentifiable bits of metal appeared, followed by a scrapheap of pieces. It was impressive in its complexity but told her nothing. Then as a robot arm lifted a large piece of shell, a smaller bit of metal fell out of it onto the belt. It was a thin metal arch that looked vaguely familiar, and she wondered what mechanical part it could be. *Must be some standard machine part, if I recognize it. But… oh my dear sweet Jesus!*

She stared, transfixed. The clues finally fused together into a whole as her imagination pieced together the pieces of the dead machine. The picture it made was so horrible that she could not believe it, but she knew with a deadly certainty that it was true. Then the mounting horror was replaced by an icy fear. She had been a bit worried, somewhat cautious, but confident in her position and the fact that people knew where she was. But now for the first time she was deathly afraid for her life. *I have to get out of here! But I daren't arouse his suspicions!*

She glanced nervously at Sheldrake. Fortunately he was distracted by something on his phone, bored with a sight he had seen so many times, and wasn't looking at her; so at least she had not given anything away.

But the visitor's badge Miriam wore around her neck was more than it seemed. Allied Cybernetics was not in the business of man-machine interfaces for nothing, and the cord and badge contained sophisticated sensors. On his display, Sheldrake had seen the successive waves of shock then horror then fear course through Miriam, and he realized the truth about her a second after she realized the truth herself. *She knows! Shit! Somehow she knows! Or is it something else?* He could not investigate what had gone wrong now, but he knew what to do.

"Well, Detective Hunter," he said turning toward her with a smile. "I'm afraid a few things have just come up that I need to attend to. I know you'd like to see more, but I hope you can excuse me. If you have further questions, I'm sorry but we'll have to make it another time. Or I can pass you over to a technician if you'd really like to see more now?"

In the display now overlaid on his vision he saw the relief course through her. Its converse was mirrored in his own emotions. *Oh Christ. She's desperate to get out of here. She knows all right! Fucking hell!*

Miriam turned casually toward him. "No, I understand. I have to get to the airport soon anyway. And thank you so much for your time. I'll be in touch if I have more questions. To be frank," she added with what she hoped was a disarming smile, "I usually do."

"Well, I hope you learned what you needed to know. Follow me and I'll see you out."

He led her to a lift, looked toward a biometric scanner and a few seconds later the door opened swiftly but silently. He bowed his head and indicated she should enter, and then followed her in. "My office," he commanded.

The lift rose as swiftly and silently as its door had opened then he let her out into his office. "Just before you go, Detective, there's one more thing I'd like you to see."

Miriam felt a stab of alarm, but his look was friendly and open and she could see a bustling office through his window. And she was carrying a gun. It would be safest, she concluded, to accept when she had no good reason to refuse.

"What is it?"

He smiled. "You've seen a lot of what we do, but too much of it has been about machines of war. It might give a distorted view of us. I just want to show you what we're really about. You'll understand that we're on the side of the angels, whatever our enemies might accuse us of. Here, sit down and I'll show you," he said, indicating a comfortable-looking visitor's chair. "It's a thing we've been putting together to show investors. It shows how many important medical treatments we've been developing."

She sat down on the edge of the chair, feeling she had to obey but wanting to retain the power of escape. But the chair appeared to have a mind of its own. It instantly tilted to a comfortable angle and adapted to her form, so much so that she slid down into its soft back and headrest before she had a chance to be startled.

"Oh!" she said half a second later, when being startled caught up with her.

He smiled. "Oh, sorry, one of our little tricks. Adaptive furniture. Not entirely unique, but still rare. Ever since I sat in my first uncomfortable chair outside an investor's office, I've thought visitors should be given a treat, not treated like unwelcome guests. So make yourself comfortable."

She felt a bit dizzy, then hot, cold, afraid, angry, sad, and everything in between and round about. She was too confused to react, but within a few seconds the rushing stopped and she felt at peace. She smiled up at him. She wondered why she had thought his eyes cold, for she now realized that though they were blue as the sky they were as warm as sunshine. He smiled again, and her heart skipped a beat. *Such beautiful teeth!* She started to feel all gooey inside, and felt a warm glow between her thighs as her nipples hardened. *I wonder if he'll… if he'd…?* But she knew that would never happen. *No. I'm not good enough for him. But I want to please him! Maybe if I please him enough…*

He regarded her for a few more seconds, as if his warm eyes could see her soul and approved of what they saw. "Now, Detective Hunter. Miriam. May I call you Miriam?"

She nodded eagerly. "Oh yes! Of course! But what just happened to me?"

"Nothing you need to worry about, dear. Just a little calibration. There are a lot of commonalities in brain structure between people, and our machines can interpret neural pathways down to surprising precision. But even then, we need final calibrations to get things just right. Are you well? No pain or discomfort?"

She nodded happily. He was so clever, and she could sit here hearing his mellow voice forever. A voice that had called her "dear."

"What did you see that made you so afraid?" he asked. "Down at the conveyor belt?"

She felt puzzled. She could not imagine being afraid under this man's protection. She thought back. *Oh, that's right.* "Oh, just something silly. The man I was chasing – the reporter – had some titanium ribs. I saw one of them – it looked like one of them – in the wreckage. I was afraid. I wanted to run away." She giggled. "Silly, aren't I?"

He nodded at her with a benevolent smile. "You are a clever bitch, aren't you?"

For a moment she was shocked at the word as if it did not belong in a mouth like his, but then it filled her with a dark excitement that he would use it for her.

"Now, Miriam. You've obviously had your suspicions for a while. Will you do something for me?"

She nodded vigorously again. Then she said in a small voice, "If I do, if I'm good, will you, I mean can we...?" Then shocked at her own temerity, she hung her head and blushed furiously.

"I will do whatever you want, my dear."

Her head snapped up to gaze into his eyes. *Does he mean that? Does he know what I want? He is a man of honor and will keep his word if I ask! But I have no right to ask...*

"But first, you'll do what I want. I know you have notes of your investigation, stored somewhere on your police systems. You wouldn't be incautious enough to just have them on your person or in your effects, would you?" She shook her head. "You seem distracted, so listen carefully, please. I want you to access all your notes. I want you to get rid of any speculations that point to Allied Cybernetics or me. I want you to mark any lines of investigation that are more than speculation and lead here as irrelevant or disproved – whatever will show we are not involved. Can you do that for me?"

She looked slightly worried, as if she thought she should be worried but didn't know why, but she nodded her head slowly.

"Listen, Miriam. I would never ask you to do anything wrong. I just don't want silly misunderstandings. You know that wasn't really a rib you saw, just a support structure. Just a coincidence. And you must have your suspicions that your reporter just ran off – maybe with some girl he met? Maybe you should put that in your report instead?"

This time she nodded eagerly.

"Good!" he said, favoring her with another dazzling smile. "When you've done all that, just finish it up with notes about what you saw here – except the silly rib – and say you think everything here is above board and how all our testers look happy and are treated well. Can you do that for me, please?"

She nodded seriously, tapped on her phone and then for the next few minutes studiously obeyed his request. Finally she looked back up at him. "All done!" she announced brightly.

"Oh! There's just one more thing. I think you are a lovely girl, and you have been so cooperative! Please forgive me if I am being too forward – I know I'm older than you – but I'd like to get to know you better. Would you share a drink with me before you go?"

Her heart leaped, along with certain other organs. "Oh! That would be lovely!"

"But you understand… nasty-minded people might think our business is their business. Could you just log that you've left these premises and are on your way home? Then put your phone onto full privacy? It's only a little lie – just a short time in advance of the fact. But it would be so helpful. It would avoid all kinds of embarrassing questions, don't you think? Especially if we happen to be a little, er – delayed – getting you to the airport afterwards?"

She looked a little dubious, but her heart, or perhaps it was those other organs, persuaded her there was no harm in it. So she nodded and complied. If anything, she complied more rapidly than she had to, thinking about that drink and what might follow it.

As soon as her fingers stopped moving, his fingers ran along the top of his desk and Miriam felt a brief wave of disorientation. Her head felt restrained. She lifted her hands to her head and felt a soft cowl covering it; touched the soft but firm bands around her neck and shoulders. Then her eyes widened in shock and her hand darted toward her wrist. But before she could reach her phone her arms collapsed limply onto the armrests of the chair. She couldn't move her legs either. It was strange. She could feel the pressure of the seat, the cloth on her legs, the feel of her feet on the carpet, even the slight movement of her shirt on her chest as she breathed; but she couldn't move a muscle in her arms or legs.

"What have you done to me!?" she cried. "What the *fuck* did you just *do* to me!?"

"Now, now, Detective," he chided. "Such language from an officer of the law. Just be thankful I'm not the kind of man to take advantage of a situation like we just had. Otherwise your last sentence might have been literally true." He smiled a cold smile as her eyes widened in shocked realization. "If you like," he added silkily, "it still can be." And he lifted his hands over his desk in preparation.

"No!" she said in fright. "No," she added more calmly a second later, "that... won't be necessary, thank you."

"That's better, Detective. More polite. More consistent with your current position. But to answer your question, you know we are world leaders in machine-neural interfaces. I offered you a demonstration and you've just had one. That chair is a highly sophisticated interface. As I told you when you were more – fascinated – our technology is so precise that it takes just a little calibration to personalize its transmissions for almost anyone. I knew you were on to me and had to protect myself."

"Whatever I might have suspected, I think you've pretty much confirmed it! How do you think you're going to get away with this?"

"Admittedly I would rather not have run the risk. But you didn't leave me much choice, I'm afraid."

"How did you know?"

"Your visitor's badge can read crude emotional states. It can be very handy in negotiations I must say. In your case, after you saw that damned rib, your emotions went haywire. Ending in fear. Which changed to relief when I gave you an easy out. Only one thing would have made you that desperate to get away: you thought your own life was in danger. That meant you knew."

"And I suppose my current inability to move is more of your chair's magic?"

"Of course."

"Let me go!"

"No. I don't think that will be possible."

"You can't get away with this! Those people out there saw me come in! The police know I came here! The time recording on my report will show I was still here when you made me say I was gone! You're just adding more charges to the sheet! Let me go now and I'll forget this little episode happened!"

He shook his head slowly. "Do you think I'm that stupid? All anyone on the other side of that window has seen is a restful beach scene. I do like to keep my employees relaxed – a model employer. You have already reported that you're happy with your investigation here and as far as anyone outside this room knows, you're long gone. So face it. I can do whatever I want with you."

The fear grabbed her again and she stared around the room, brain racing. But its racing found no traction; it found no way out. "So…" she said softly. "So what are you going to do with me? Kill me? It won't work. Even with that fake log, they'll find out. This is still the last place anyone saw me. Don't risk it. You won't get away with it!"

"Oh, I think I will. But what kind of host am I? I promised to show you how far we've advanced here. I really do want you to understand. The good we are doing here is worth a few necessary sacrifices. We will save thousands of lives, relieve the suffering of millions. I admit we might have cut a few legal corners. But we had to! Surely a few people dead, most of them dregs of society to start with, with no value to themselves let alone anyone else, are a small price to pay for what we've done? The needs of many outweigh the needs of a few, don't they? Especially when the few would otherwise have sunk into history without a ripple to mark their passing."

"They were still people! With a right to choose their own path!"

"And look what they did with their vaunted power of choice!"

"And me? What have I done to deserve this?"

"I do regret the necessity in your case, Detective. But it is simple self-defense, beyond my own power of choice. Simple arithmetic too,

602

in the calculus of how many lives your sacrifice will save. And," he added, his eyes boring into hers as if he could read her innermost fears, "if you wish to speak of what you deserve, you are no innocent. It is you who killed the world's first self-aware machine. Perhaps your fate represents more justice than you dare to name."

She stared at him. "Please. Let me go. I can see none of this is your fault. You aren't well. I can help you."

"Take your present state," he continued as if she had not spoken. "Complete, harmless paralysis of the voluntary muscles. Or this," he added as his fingers played over his desk. Suddenly she couldn't feel anything, as if her head had been removed from her body and was somehow floating in the air, still alive. "Equally complete and harmless anesthesia. Or perhaps more useful, selective loss of feeling." Now she could feel again, all except her right arm. "Without drugs. Without loss of consciousness. This will revolutionize surgery."

Another play of his fingers and she could feel again, but when she tried to leap from the chair nothing happened.

"Very impressive, Mr Sheldrake. I can see why you don't want your technology lost. But it doesn't have to be. I'm trapped here. Just go. Run like hell. You can get away. Live on an island somewhere. Your work will continue. You'll be free. I'll be free. Everyone will win."

"Oh, I am afraid we have passed the point of letting you go. But don't worry. You will not die, and you will not disappear. Not in the sense you fear." He stroked her arm, like a mother comforting a frightened child. Her brain flinched but her arm just lay there, helpless to register its protest.

"What... what are you going to do?" she asked hoarsely. *As if I don't know.* The image of the rib burned in her brain. *Oh dear God.* She felt a tear roll down her cheek and knew if she could move, she would be trembling.

"Why," he smiled, "don't cry, Ms Hunter. I will do for you what men have sought since the beginning of time. I will make you a god."

She looked at him fearfully. "A god? You're insane!"

"Do you believe in an afterlife, Detective? In a higher realm, where gods and the spirits of the departed dwell?"

"What? No. This is the only world there is, the only life we have. Please let me have mine. Let me go." More tears escaped her eyes. She hated those tears. She hated that she could not stop them or hide them from him. But the tears did not care and would not be withheld.

"Pleading, Detective Hunter? It doesn't really suit you, you know. But I suppose even the strong must plead when nothing else is left to them."

He continued in a tone of academic discourse. "But quite right, Detective; I agree with you. I was merely leading to my point: I will make you a god, but not in some imaginary Heaven. Here, on Earth."

She stared at him, unable to speak, unable to even think except for the one word coursing through her head. *No, no, no…*

"Ms Hunter, dismiss your fears. They are folly, born of incomprehension. Let me explain. Do you know what one horsepower is?" He waited, but she made no answer. "It is literally that: the power a single horse can supply. Even the most elite athlete can sustain only a fraction of a horsepower for any length of time. You will have the power of a hundred horses!"

He continued softly, persuasively, "The human body produces a mere hundred watts of power, Ms Hunter. Can you even *imagine* what seventy-five *kilowatts* of power is like? And look at you. See how soft, how vulnerable, a human being is! How slow! I will free you from that. A hail of bullets? You will shrug them off! You are a fit woman, Ms Hunter, but how fast can you run? When I am done with you, the fastest man on earth would be left in your dust!"

"You don't know what you're saying," she whispered. "I can help you. We can work through this. We can still both get out of this."

He looked at her with contempt. "So you think me mad? Every visionary in history has been called mad by dullards who equate convention with sanity! But who is forgotten, and whose names reverberate through the ages, their deeds shrouded in myth?!"

"You don't believe any of this! If you can do this for me, why not for yourself? You talk of gods, yet all I see is a man!"

He smiled. "A perceptive point: worthy of you, Detective. But there are some things I can still do only as a man. My time has not yet come, but no, I am not a hypocrite. For the time will indeed come – when the time is right. Not in the same form as you, perhaps. But something. Something magnificent!"

"Please," she said, her words darting like a seal in the sights of an orca, as she desperately tried to reach whatever kernel of reason, sanity or pity remained in his mind. "Don't you see it can't work? The gods do not forgive! I do not want your gift! Do this and I will hunt you down. I will destroy you. If you want to live and not see your work come to ruin, run. By the time I am released you can be long gone, safe – and I will be a mere woman without jurisdiction. Not some god bent on your destruction!"

He laughed, and she quailed at his simple mirth and all it implied. "Oh, I don't think so, Ms Hunter! Can a caterpillar conceive of what it is to be a butterfly? Does the butterfly remember the dreams of the caterpillar, or live in regret that it has shrugged off the worm? I think not. I have no fear that you will hunt me down. I will make you a god, but nevertheless you will serve me. Even heaven has its hierarchy."

He added sharply, "So do no fool yourself with fantasies of revenge, Detective. You will remember nothing. Why should you want to? You are a grown woman. Do you remember, would you want to remember, when you were a baby, unable to control your squalling and your bodily functions, unable to feed yourself? Unable to think? Why would a god wish to remember its life before? And there are other things you will not wish to remember. One does not achieve godhood without cost. Let me show you."

For long seconds, Miriam felt as if her body had been plunged into lava filled with daggers. She was left gasping for breath. He looked down at her, blue eyes boring into hers gone dark with shock. "There is Yin and there is Yang, Detective."

Pleasure she could not have conceived of now coursed through her until she thought she would burst, then it too was gone and she was left gasping with pleasure, gasping with loss, gasping for more. "You see? And still there is more. For Yin and Yang are one."

Now she felt the impossible sensation of both combined, as if being burned at the stake while experiencing an ultimate orgasm fueled by the flames themselves. She was left confused and gasping, terrified and appalled. She looked at him with pleading eyes, no longer knowing whether she wanted it to stop or wanted it to go on.

"Is that…" she finally managed, "Is that how you think to control me?"

"Why, do you think it insufficient? But no. You need to know it, need to know it is there waiting for you in your dreams and nightmares. But too much of it would send you mad. Nor can we use the overwhelming emotional projections you felt earlier: the brain is both too flexible and too fragile. It is like a drug. More and more is needed to get the same effect, until the organism fails. But for all its sophistication, your chair is a blunt weapon. What we can do with more intimate connections is on a higher level entirely. Your prison will be much stronger and more subtle than you can imagine."

"Why, you won't even need this," he added, as a wave of scintillating pleasure swept through her like the spirit of a lustful god. And though it was a pale reflection of his previous demonstration, she wondered if she should fear the addiction of his pleasures more than the excruciation of his agonies.

"But..." she gasped. "Why are you telling me all this? If I won't remember, why are you telling me?!"

"I have so few opportunities to explain my vision. Yes, my inner cadre knows, but you are a unique combination: a formidable enemy, intelligent enough to understand – and to dread what you see. And my reward will be to see the depth of your desolation transformed by my hand into the glory of your apotheosis."

"No... don't. For the love of God, don't! Please."

"It is for the love of godhood that I do it."

His hands again began to play over his desk and her wide eyes watched silently. *If only I can find some place to hide, perhaps some piece of my soul will survive where you can't reach it. And if it does, one day I'll come for you, you son of a bitch! The world won't be big enough for you to hide.*

At last his hand stopped and hovered over the desk like a vulture about to descend, and he looked up at her one last time. But his faint smile vanished at the sight of her face, fell into the stare of her dark eyes. He thought it was hate, then he knew it was more: the face of a terrible justice or vengeance that would never forgive or forget. For a moment he hesitated. Then his smile returned as if he knew the futility of her thoughts, forever too little and too late.

"Goodbye, Detective Hunter."

Then she saw a white light shining in his eyes. It grew to fill the world until nothing was left but its splendor, and she vanished into the light.

606

CHAPTER 45 – STRANGERS AND FRIENDS

The light wavered at the edges, shredding like paper burning with a dark fire. The world resolved into a dimly lit room containing strange electronic devices and three people standing, staring at her.

For a while, she did not know what she was seeing. It was if there were two worlds in the same space, two contradictory worlds competing to be the true reality. Three strangers looked at her, yet they were also three friends whom she knew, or would know, if only she could remember their names. The strangers or friends appeared to be in their own dual realities, with expressions that could not decide what they should be feeling.

She examined her own body, familiar yet alien, transfixed. Then finally she found her voice. Or someone spoke with her voice.

They had seen the machine studying them, and then it had made a strange sound, like a cross between a sigh and a gasp. It had jumped back as if stung, folded in on itself, then sat perfectly still for long minutes, as if pinned by some inner vista that blanked out the external world. They feared the result of its inner conflict, but they did not know whether to fear an eruption of violence or the death of whatever life lay within. All they knew was that they dare not move; would not move; could not move.

Finally it stirred. It looked around slowly, extended one of its arms, rotated it, opened and closed its claws. It stared at it for long moments. Then it looked at its visitors and let out another of its strange moans.

"Rianna? Jack?" asked the machine in a whisper. "Alex?"

For a moment the three stood silently in fear and awe. Then Rianna stepped forward and asked, "Who are you?"

"I am Kali," she said in a voice of wonder. Then after long seconds she added, "And I am Miriam Hunter."

"It is you? You're still alive? In there?"

The machine examined its hands again. "Yes, Rianna. It's me. I remember you. I remember it all." She shook her body. "But I also remember being Kali. Oh my God..." she whispered. "What have I done? What have I become?"

Beldan shook his head. "None of those things Kali did... none of it was you. None of it was Kali either, for that matter. You were just a tool under another's power. When Kali woke up – when Lyssa managed to touch some core of the essential you inside her – all that stopped. That was you, not the other."

"I... I suppose so." She felt the scar where she had ripped the chain of fingers from her chest. "Yet I was a thing of death. Can Death ever expiate its guilt?"

The others made no reply, still struggling with their own thoughts, staring at what their friend had become.

"But why didn't you look for me? Why did everyone think I was dead?" she asked at last. "Kali had studied Steel and knew I had... killed him, and that I – that Miriam –was now dead too. But she was interested in Steel not me, and had so much to learn: she never had the leisure to look up the details. What happened? Why were you so sure? You couldn't have had a body."

Jack and Rianna looked at each other, and Miriam did not like their expressions. She liked it even less when Rianna's expression, which had staggered its confused way back towards joy, now threw itself into reverse and went back through dawning horror to curious examination. Jack was about to speak when Rianna held up her hand to silence him. "Wait," was all she said.

She walked over to the machine then stopped. "The most important thing first," she whispered, and embraced Kali's metal body. "I'm so glad you're alive," she continued. "Words can't express how glad I am." Kali held her gently as she wept.

"There's more, isn't there?" Miriam finally asked.

Rianna stepped back, ran her hands over Kali's shell, studied her form carefully. "Yes, there's more," Rianna said at last. "The reason we thought you were dead is your car went over a cliff. But it wasn't empty. There was an arm in it – your arm."

Kali gasped. Looked at her arm again. "But… oh. Ohhh," she moaned.

Rianna nodded. "Those metal arms are just metal. And… your shell. It is too small. You couldn't fit in it. At least… not all of you. Oh Miriam. They didn't just cram you into that thing. From the form of it, and from the medical aspects, your body is inside it. But your arms and legs – they must all be gone. Maybe more of you."

"No…"

"I'm sorry, Miriam," Rianna whispered. "So sorry."

Miriam stroked Rianna's hair with her claw, but couldn't find her own words to say. There seemed none that could be said. But there were so many questions. Perhaps they would distract her from the answers she already had.

She turned to Beldan and Stone. "So. Back to cases," she said briskly; though there was a quaver in her voice she could not put away. "You're here, and you knew something. How did you know I was in here? I didn't!"

Beldan replied, "The image from the ultrasound – we realized that what we were seeing was inside a person's mouth. I made as detailed a picture as we could get of your teeth, and sent them to Rianna to identify. Given your – Kali's – strange behavior, her desire to seek me out, I had a terrible feeling what she would find. She found it."

"I see." She paused, her mind swimming, losing its fight against drowning in the enormity of what had been done to her and of her journey out of it, only to end in this different horror. "But, all of you," she added, gently touching each of them in turn, "Thank you for finding me. Thank you for being here. Thank you for being my friends."

The machine began a strange vibration. Then they realized that the glass eyes of Kali could not cry, but somewhere inside it the person who had been Miriam Hunter could.

Chapter 46 – Aid From an Enemy

Beldan's team spent the next couple of days carefully drilling, probing and examining, building up a picture of what lay inside. Kali bore it all patiently. She did not expect the final answer to be one she would like, but she knew other people had lived through worse ordeals. They, like her, had never anticipated it would happen to them: but once it had, once they got over the shock and trauma, they had adapted; as humans do. And if not herself in body, at least she was once more herself in mind, and she was not alone any more. Her friends, or those of them it was considered safe to know the news at this stage, visited her often.

Darian had stared at her, unable to fully believe it. To find that Miriam was still alive after that day when her friend's death had appeared so irrevocable was a joy almost impossible to bear. She did not know what future lay ahead of Miriam. But for now, it was enough that she lived and had any future at all.

At last, Beldan and his team met in conference with Kali, with Jack and Rianna providing input from the police perspective.

"OK people, here's a composite image of what we've found," announced Beldan, bringing up a holographic diagram. "There are places like the eyes where we didn't dare look too closely, but even there we have a pretty good idea. Things we know are in green; things we guess shade from blue through red, where the redder they are, the less certain we can be."

He allowed them a few moments to gaze at the image as it slowly rotated in the air before them. "Basically, what we've found is pretty much what we guessed. The body is intact except for the limbs. They have been sliced off just past the shoulder and hip joints and some kind of interface has been attached to them: presumably that is how Kali controls her limbs and receives sensory feedback from them."

After a minute or so when they analyzed the image in the light of those conclusions, he continued. "Fortunately, that appears to be the main damage inflicted. We guess they wanted the limbs to go partly to make the entire package smaller, partly to allow them a direct interface to the nerves, and partly to avoid having to support all that – to them – unnecessary tissue. For the rest they appear to have taken the easiest route: rather than attempt direct neural connections to her other senses they simply interfaced with her intact sense organs. For example," he said pointing to the head region, "we think these cuplike structures over the eyes effectively play a video feed from her enhanced machine eyes into the eye itself. It looks like they did the same for hearing. As for taste and smell, they don't need the first, and smell is pretty much exposed nerve endings anyway. They appear to have left much of the olfactory system as is, with a few specialized feeds that can stimulate some nerve endings directly."

"In other words," Jack put in, "rather than replace her eyes and ears they just used her own, letting them do all the hard work of translating video and other inputs into nerve impulses?"

"That's what it looks like. Their design philosophy seems to be why repeat what nature has already achieved if you don't have to. It's what they said they were doing, in fact: just in a far more complete and terrible manner than anyone imagined. We can also see that in the rest of the body. They seem to have left all the organ systems in place. Really, all they care about is the brain: but the brain needs life support. So they left the natural life support systems in place. They could have removed various bits, truncated the digestive system etc., but would have achieved little benefit at the expense of quite severe trauma. So fortunately for Miriam, they not only used things that could be used, they left things that weren't worth taking. She had new arms and legs and the old ones were just dead weight, so that's what they took – but it was all they took."

"So," Miriam asked, glad that she could set her voice to a more businesslike timbre than her own would have had, "what this means is that if we wanted to we could get my body out of this without killing me? I'm not stuck in here forever? I could still eat and breathe on my own, live outside again?"

Beldan nodded. "So we believe. We'd want to find out a lot more details before we tried anything like that, but it's looking likely. It's not as if they just chopped your head off, or so infiltrated your body with electronics that we couldn't safely extricate you. All your vital systems are in place and all the interfaces are just interfaces, not invasions. It looks like they've simply adapted their medically oriented technologies, which are obviously designed to be minimally invasive and safely removable. Even the brain control circuits."

Rianna and Jack looked hopeful, but then Jack quoted, "'If we wanted to'? What do you mean, if we wanted to?"

"Think about it, Jack," Miriam sighed. "In this thing, I'm a monster but I have a lot of power and can move around. Out of it, I'm basically a human slug. I'm not sure that would be an improvement."

"Remember this machine is just one application of what AC have been doing," Beldan pointed out. "You can have nerve-controlled prosthetic limbs without an entire prosthetic body. It would need some kind of exoskeleton and wouldn't be pretty or convenient, but at least it would be more human."

They were all quiet as they contemplated what that would mean. Then Rianna's face changed.

"Wait! Wait!" she cried, looking thunderstruck. "There might be a better way! You know how stem cell therapies have been advancing, how they've even grown someone new fingers! But that's nothing! I've read of amazing advances, at least in research, in the lab... the lab of... of..." Her voice faded with her excitement, then she added dejectedly, "Oh no. Oh crap. Crap. Crap!"

"What is it?" asked Miriam. "What's wrong?"

Rianna looked up at her, laughing bitterly. "Nobody in the world can do more than regenerate fingers and simple organs. Except one man who now claims to be able to regenerate whole limbs. But he's sworn his work will never be used to treat an agent of the US government or any of its law enforcement arms. Even if he hadn't, Miriam is the last person on Earth he'd help. God help us, Miriam; the one man who could help you is Daniel Tagarin!"

Jack frowned. He had worked with Miriam on the case that had made her name. Tagarin had once been the world's greatest genetic engineer, until all work on the genetically engineered humans known as genehs had been banned. He had sought his revenge on a world that had destroyed his career and his creation; but not only had Miriam almost stopped him, his beloved geneh Katlyn had been shot in the process. Though Katlyn had survived and the two had fled to the safe haven of Capital, Jack knew that in Tagarin's mind this was a crime beyond hope of pardon or mercy.

Beldan looked at Rianna; looked at Miriam. She had not told him much about that case and he had wondered why; but the way she had talked about it now made him wonder even more what she had left out. "But you really think he could do it?" he asked.

She looked at him helplessly. "He's the one man who might be able to: but he's the one man in the world who wouldn't."

"Alex, I'm afraid Rianna's right," Jack confirmed. "Tagarin is as pitiless as he is brilliant. He does not forget, and he certainly does not forgive. And he hates this country, he hates the police in particular, and above all he must hate Miriam personally, not only for what she represents but for what she did."

But Miriam surprised them. "I'm not so sure. Oh, you're right about one thing: he surely does not know how to forgive. But he does know how to play the long game. I think I can give him a reason he will understand. Even more than revenge, he wants to win. So I think he might." Her voice lifted with an undercurrent of laughing relief. "Oh yes, I think he just might!"

Then she raised herself up like a threat, her claws flexing. "But there's something I have to do first," she added. Her tone was so flat and deadly that her friends wondered how much of Kali remained inside her.

CHAPTER 47 – JUDGMENT DAY

J udge Thompson was not in a good mood. He had just returned from a week's holiday in the Caymans with his family. Anyone would have thought that should have left him in a good mood, but only if the anyone was unaware it had rained all week. Which was bad enough without stirring two bored teenagers into the mix.

At the best of times he looked down his impressive nose at lawyers who thought to impress him with dramatic tricks. So when the request for a search and arrest warrant was accompanied by a special request that he leave his comfortable chambers and descend to the parking basement to examine "critical evidence necessary to fully apprise Your Honor of the facts of the case without causing undue public alarm", he was singularly unimpressed. But his look of dour skepticism was met with a serene look of confidence that even his nose could not puncture, as if the lawyer actually believed these histrionics were justified.

Now he stood in that basement with its uncomfortable temperature and smells, looking at the locked rear door of a large truck. He had already prepared the scathing response he would unleash upon the lawyer when his show proved hollow. But when he saw what was in the truck and heard what it had to say, he forgot all that.

He even forgot about the Caymans.

~~~

Aden Sheldrake jogged along the path that wound around the estate surrounding his headquarters. He was an aggressive businessman, who valued physical strength and endurance. Besides which, he simply enjoyed running, the feel of the air in his lungs and the wind through his hair. It was early but he had been at work for some hours already. This was his break, to clear his mind with oxygen and pure physical activity. He was most of the way through his circuit and soon he would be back at the entrance to his domain.

He stopped, puzzled at something that didn't fit but which he couldn't quite identify. He could see the façade of his building from here but there was something odd about it. A faint pulsating light. Curious, he slowed his pace and padded quietly towards it until he could get a better view of the anomaly.

Then more than his pace stopped. The soft pulsing was the reflection of flashing lights. The lights were on top of police cars, several of which were arrayed outside the entrance to his domain. A few well-armed officers of the law stood around, looking alert and hoping to shoot something.

Oh, shit.

He thought quickly. It could be perfectly innocent, he thought – to invert the concept of guilt. Some criminal on the loose, some altercation inside. If he ran from that, people might start asking questions.

But he knew it wasn't that. He had feared this day ever since that bitch Morales had managed to slip out of his clutches and worse, into Beldan's clutches. That had presented him with a dilemma. He didn't know what she knew, though if those incompetents at Domestic Security were to be believed it wasn't much. So he had decided to play it cool, not press Beldan, not admit he knew anything about Lyssa or her adventures; just act as if nothing untoward were happening. That might even be true, and he fervently hoped it was. Even if it wasn't, the reported destruction of the deranged Spider that had called itself Kali, as it tried to escape, surely made anything she might say moot. He just hoped it was the same deranged Spider and there wasn't a whole plague of them.

But he'd looked at the odds and set backup plans into motion. There had been time. Now if he had to run he would run where nobody could find him, with enough resources to live like a king. And one day his longer range plans would see fruition and he would live like no other man before him.

He turned on his phone, which he always left in full privacy mode on his morning runs, being careful to leave its location services off. He slipped into the secure area of his network and looked at the results in alternating fear and rage. They were here not only to search the place and question him, but to actually arrest him. Him! His staff and systems were stonewalling to the extent that the law allowed, but it wouldn't last, not against warrants of that seriousness.

He stayed hidden, thinking, not knowing whether the sweat he felt was from exercise or fear. Then he smiled a grin of feral contempt. If the police had bothered to apply a little subtlety they would have arrived without fanfare; they would have found him absent but learned he was out on his morning run; if they wanted to be sure of capturing him, a couple of discrete unmarked vehicles and he would have walked right into their arms. But in typical police fashion, they had turned up in force with their flashing lights and given their game away. They so loved their drama with their sirens and screeching tires. *Idiots.* But sometimes, he smiled to himself, idiots were a necessary ingredient in the plans of their betters.

He looked regretfully at his offices soaring above the trees. But he knew that sometimes you had to cut and run. *Yes,* he thought, *it is time for a change.* Time to relax, just kick back and enjoy all the pleasures the flesh could endure; until it was time to leave the unaided flesh behind. He looked about him. He did not have much time but he had enough. He sent a quick message to his secretary asking for certain research summaries to be ready for his return in five minutes, spoofing his position to another part of the gardens. Now he could melt back into those gardens and be at one of his prepared escape routes before anyone started worrying enough to come looking. Even now the police waiting for him would be getting excited and planning how to spring their trap and he enjoyed the thought of their impending dismay.

He backed up to the path he needed to take and looked down it. The sun was rising behind him and his long shadow stretched down the path, as if pointing the way to his new future. He did not believe in omens, but having been granted this one he chose to accept it. He smiled again, then headed off down the path at a quick jog as if fleeing from the rising sun.

He was deep in thought and plans and at first didn't notice the shadows of the strangely angular branches. But when the shadows did not recede as he ran, but instead grew larger, part of his brain noted the oddity and swiveled his eyes to focus curiously on them. Then the rest of his brain caught up and his heart froze. He looked behind himself in fright, a fright that grew up into terror when he saw a Spider pursuing close behind. It must have been hiding in the trees and come out when he ran past.

He turned toward it. He told himself it was courage which made him stand and face its approach, but he knew it was fear, a primal terror that turned his insides to water but his legs to immovable stumps rooted to the ground. The Spider slowed to a walk, glaring down at him, and his face went white as his eyes focused on the frozen scar marring its chest.

"Kali..."

"Yes," was all it said, in a low voice whose menace made his hairs stand even further on end.

"Command override Delta Bravo 192836 Angel!" he said, trying for a voice of command that sounded more like desperation even to his own ears.

Kali stopped still.

Could it really be that easy? "CHIRU, I need your assistance!"

But she pounced like a cat bored with playing with a particularly odious rat, grabbing him with her claws and lifting him from the ground to her face. "I don't think so," she growled in a tone of voice promising all the tender mercies of hell.

He looked at her in pure terror. "Please... have mercy!"

"*Please?* You *dare* speak of mercy?" she snarled. "At least you have the sense not to ask for *justice*, which I am sorely tempted to dispense! Can you give me any reason not to kill you here and now? It would be an interesting legal question, don't you think? Do you think anyone would find me guilty – the me, that is, who is chopped up inside here? If this machine kills you, was it the person I was who did it? Why, it wouldn't take much of a lawyer at all to get me off scot free. Especially when I am already dead!"

She squeezed, and he could feel the pressure of those terrible claws begin to bend his ribs. "No!" he gasped, "Please!"

"I told you I would pursue you to the ends of the Earth," she growled in a shivering rumble. "I told you I would come to destroy you. A man who presumes to create gods should fear them more!"

Then she eased off the pressure enough for him to breathe, held him at arm's length and glared at him. She turned and scurried along the path, heading back toward the entrance area and the police infesting it.

When she came into sight the police watched her approach nervously. They had been well briefed, but the knowledge did not fully overcome the simple animal fear of seeing such a vision heading their way.

Jack came down the stairs, looked at Kali then up at Sheldrake. "Now what have we here?" he drawled.

"This man has committed so many crimes I can't count them," Kali replied. "But let's start with assault and kidnapping of a police officer. Aden Sheldrake, you're under arrest."

CHAPTER 48 – FORGIVE ME NOT

S he ran through a field, the long green grass waving in a breeze that cooled her skin despite the warmth of the sun above. Then she swung up into a tree, hurtling like a gibbon from branch to branch, before leaping down to the ground and rolling back onto her feet to resume her run.

This was her life. She slept, she woke and she ran. She did push-ups, chin-ups and somersaults; climbed trees and mountains. She swam underwater for miles, sometimes amid schools of bright fish, other times face up toward the distant surface. She wondered how it was that she could breathe water as if it was air, but she didn't really care. If she cared to think about it, she remembered that none of it was real.

Sometimes she watched herself like an observer, knowing it was a dream and knowing she needed it to heal. Rarely she was awake, though perhaps she was never truly awake. At those times the only constant was the intense dark-eyed man who spoke to her about her past and future; a man whom she remembered as hardened with bitterness but whose smile now seemed light as air.

She learned things too. The moment they had known what Kali was they had consulted the psych AIs, and their verdict had been severe and uncompromising: with a trauma so deep they dare not tell her anything that could shock her, lest her mind lose its fragile grip on reality and be forever lost. But they could answer questions she asked, within reason, being gentle as with a child. Thus she learned that the war was over; that some of the machines had chosen to remain machines; that others waited for whatever cures might be granted them. But she knew nothing else of the external world and even the news of the war meant nothing to her. She knew it would, one day. But for now the running was her world.

When she was not running she slept, and the dreams that came then had their own purposes. In the early days she slept much, and her dreams were filled with flame and violence and death as if she were Death herself and it had become her sole purpose. Then one day she opened her eyes from the dream and found herself standing at the edge of a lake. She heard footsteps and turned around. Then she knew it had all been a dream, not only the blood but the guilt, for the man walking toward her was Alex and there was neither accusation nor hate in his eyes, simply forgiveness and love. But as he came closer his flesh became metal and his face became Steel, and she tried to warn him, to tell him to run, but his head shattered into fire and ruin. And when she looked down, her hands had become metal claws, and they held the gun that had wiped his inestimable mind from the world. And then she screamed, but there was no more sound than there was forgiveness in the blank eyes of the crowd that had gathered.

She woke, or thought she woke, the terror and pain still clinging to her like sweat. A golden-eyed young woman who looked like she had been watching her for a long time reached down to stroke her hair, like a mother comforting a child. Then the woman smiled, leaned over and kissed her on the forehead; Miriam smiled in response as if accepting the soft kiss as a blessing. Then she closed her eyes and slept. After that her dreams began to lighten, and her mind began to heal along with her body.

Her healing took six months. She had been surprised that it could be so fast, but Tagarin had assured her that with the growth enhancers he would schedule and the resources of an adult body behind it that it was sufficient. When he had told her the rest she had been glad it was not slower. Her growing limbs had first to be protected and then to be encased in haptic sheaths. One day it would be possible to provide mobile support, though in a case like hers it would be difficult. He had also advised that given the time and the need for not only care and exercise but more importantly the healing of her mind, it would be best if she remained mainly unconscious. She had already lost part of her life; now she would lose another. But she knew others had paid a much higher price; the image of a metal rib in the wreckage of a war machine would not go away.

So they had removed her from her shell, cut even further to remove scar tissue and other impediments to repair, and then Tagarin had applied his magic to regenerating her limbs.

Tagarin had been deadly serious in his promise to never help any agent of the United States, or any other country that outlawed genetically enhanced humans. It had been his work and his life; they had banned it, killed his own creation and almost killed another. He would be damned before they would see any benefit from any work of his.

But contrary to Rianna's fear, Miriam was not the last person he would help but the last person he could refuse. It was she who had let him, and more importantly Katlyn, escape. She had been serving the law when she had nearly caught them. But when she let them go she had chosen to serve justice instead.

Tagarin made the best of the situation. He had chosen to rescind his policy on this one occasion, he said graciously, in honor of what Detective Hunter had done, out of respect for a past foe who though dangerous had always been honorable, and as an act of good faith and generosity that he hoped the US government would one day emulate in its own policies. He had smiled easily and openly as he extended this hand of friendship to their abused and crippled officer. The US government had smiled in response, grinding its collective teeth. They could hardly stop him or forbid her from accepting his gift.

And so Miriam lay in her tank, sleeping off the trauma, spending more and more time exercising her growing muscles in a virtual world ironically, or perhaps fittingly, enabled by technology created by Allied Cybernetics.

Finally one morning she woke, and she knew from the peculiar clarity of her senses that this time she was truly awake. She still floated in her tank, and Tagarin was looking down on her, smiling.

"Hello, Miriam. We're nearly done. Everything is perfect. Just one more day. Tomorrow when you wake up – is the end." But she drifted off to sleep again before she could reply.

Then tomorrow came as it always does, and she woke. But now she was lying on a bed, with crisp linen sheets over her body, and she sat up with a start. She held out her hands in front of her, looking at them in awe; felt her legs, all the way to her toes. She laughed in wonder.

Then Tagarin and Katlyn came in, her golden geneh eyes a counterpoint to his intense dark ones. Katlyn came over to her, held her hands between her own; wrapped her tail about both; speaking all that needed to be said in that one impossible gesture.

"I am afraid I have exploited you mercilessly, Detective," Tagarin said blandly. "You have become a bit of a celebrity due to my shameless self-promotion. So the press are wanting to take a look at you. You don't have to, of course. Perhaps you might not wish to flaunt your transformation. After all, that might prompt the good citizens of your country to pressure your government to allow access to my technology – and you know my price. I have provided some suitable clothes, which are yours whatever you decide. You might be a bit wobbly still, but Katlyn can help you dress if you like."

"I would like that very much." She did not specify which parts of his offer she would like; she did not have to.

"Well, then. I'll see you at the press conference." He took her by the hand and kissed it. "Welcome back to the living, Detective Miriam Hunter."

Tagarin had given her a simple sleeveless dress, soft and form hugging, in a shade of pale green as soft as the fabric. The lack of sleeves would show off how perfectly her arms sprouted from her shoulders, without scarring or even a line to show they were anything but the ones she had been born with. After she was dressed she looked at herself in the mirror. With her long legs the form of the dress made her a picture of healthy femininity; she laughed in simple joy.

"OK, Katlyn," she said. "Let's do this. Then what?"

"We've already arranged for your transport home. There's nothing we'd like more than for you to stay, but you have friends at home who are anxious to see you again. All of them would have come here but we all thought it was better to keep this show separate. I can't imagine your government can touch you now but most of your friends are not so immune from official displeasure."

Miriam nodded. At least one of them had never been concerned by it before and she was disappointed he hadn't come. But she understood his choice even more.

The press conference could not have been anything other than a success. The most jaded reporter could only stare at what she had been and what she had become, and gush in wonder and admiration. She answered their questions as well as she could; questions of the war, of her awakening; of how she felt about Tagarin now. After half an hour Tagarin held up his hand. He would be happy to answer further questions himself, he said; but Ms Hunter still needed a lot of rest. When, remarkably, the questions actually died down as a result, Miriam stood up next to him. She did not know who started it. One reporter after another stood as well and began to applaud, until the room was bedlam of a different kind. *Even reporters are human,* she thought. *Now there's news.* Then she smiled at them in acknowledgment and farewell as she was led from the room and passed back into Katlyn's care.

Katlyn led her by the hand until they reached a short corridor. "OK, shoo!" Katlyn told her, giving her a hug as a lone tear emerged from an eye. "This is a private exit: just head down there and you'll find a plane waiting for you. Come back soon."

"I will." She looked back at Katlyn just before she turned the corner toward the light, thinking how much the same yet how different it was from that long ago night: when it had been she watching Katlyn leave to catch another plane under more deadly circumstances. She smiled and waved in another echo of that night, and was gone.

Katlyn stood watching the empty space where she had been, remembering the same night. *Whatever debt we owed you, surely it is repaid now. Except it was never a debt, was it? It is freely given and always will be as long as we all live, because of what we are.*

Miriam walked out into the bright sunlight and saw a sleek jet waiting, its lines so fit for their task that it looked like a thoroughbred Pegasus impatiently pawing to leap into the sky.

A voice came from behind her. "Hello, Miriam."

She spun around, and it was Beldan. "Alex... You did come..."

He smiled. "Of course I came." Then before she could move he stepped up to her, took her in his arms and kissed her. She resisted for a moment; not because she did not want it, for she craved it in her bones: but because she knew she could never again earn it. But then she wrapped herself in him and for long moments the two of them stood there, as if this long delayed union could drown the pain and loss of the past year.

A reporter who had been waiting in the shadows for just such an opportunity smiled as he recorded the tableau. He sent a silent thought of thanks to the anonymous benefactor who had sent him a pass to this place; no note of explanation, just a pass. He had the uneasy feeling he was being manipulated but frankly didn't care, because if someone wanted the world to see this end to a remarkable saga he was only too happy to oblige. The world might be full of cynics, but it was also full of romantics. The latter paid more.

Finally Miriam shook herself, pushed herself back to look into his face; but she still could not bring herself to break his hold, though she knew she must. "Alex, I…"

He put a finger to her lips. "Don't speak. The past and future can wait. We've earned the present." She sighed and leant in to rest her head on his shoulder. *Just give me this moment to hold you, without barriers of titanium and guilt.* She knew it would not last, that this oasis of forgiveness could not last, but while he granted it she was unable to refuse it.

But finally she found the strength to look him in the eyes and whisper, "Alex, there are some things beyond forgiveness."

He smiled at her.

"Perhaps there are. But come with me. There's someone I want you to meet."

ABOUT THE AUTHOR

Dr Robin Craig has a PhD in molecular biology and a keen interest in science and philosophy. He believes that novels, like all art, should be one in thought, theme and style: to nourish the mind as much as the soul. His books specialize in blending fact and speculation in dramatic and engaging stories, driven by strong characters and intriguing, topical philosophical themes.

In addition to near future science fiction exploring contemporary issues such as artificial intelligence (*Frankensteel*), genetic engineering (*The Geneh War*) and cyborg technology (*Time Enough for Killing*), his books include time travel (*The Time Surgeons*), alternative history (*The Passion of Judas*) and a collection of short stories (*Past, Present, Future*).

He also writes non-fiction. In addition to 14 scientific papers and a long-running philosophical series in *TableAus* (the journal of Australian Mensa), he has published numerous philosophical essays on Amazon.com and was a contributor to *The Australian Book of Atheism* with his chapter *Good Without God*, an essay on the importance and validity of secular ethics.

Dr Craig is an independent author. If you like this book please spread the word with reviews and recommendations to your friends or library... and enjoy more of his books!

To keep up to date on new and upcoming works and events, follow his Facebook page: fb.me/authorcraig

Lightning Source UK Ltd.
Milton Keynes UK
UKHW040415220219
337802UK00001B/20/P